BLACKSPIRE

Benjamin Sperduto

OWL HOLLOW PRESS

Owl Hollow Press, LLC, Springville, UT 84663

Library of Congress Cataloging-in-Publication Data
Blackspire / B. Sperduto. — First edition.

Summary:
When a lowly guild laborer chances upon a long forgotten relic, he unwittingly sets in motion a chain of events that puts five unsuspecting souls on a collision course with a criminal mastermind scheming to bend the city to his will.

ISBN 978-1-945654-68-8 (paperback)
ISBN 978-1-945654-69-5 (e-book)

Cover Design and Illustration: Donn Marlou Ramirez

For Mom and Dad.
Thanks for always believing in me.

PRELUDE
THE CITY

The sun sank below the horizon beyond the outer wall later than the day before, leaving the murky sky above the city blackened and bruised.

One by one, flickering specks of greasy light forced their way out of the gloom to push aside the shadows smothering the crooked streets and ogreish piles of stone and wood that passed for buildings.

A heavy, miasmic fog gathered in the close alleyways and jammed corners, its putrid tendrils slinking tentatively into the wider streets and clawing at the moist underbelly of the neighborhoods nearest the slow-moving river.

The stench that spent most of the day festering in the hot air above the city sank back down to ground level as the temperature dropped and smothered it; a heavy, moldering blanket thrown over a man already dying of plague.

Hungry dogs barked here and there, some running in packs in search of stray pigs and chickens wandering stupidly through the ill-lit streets and rooting through the day's refuse gathered along every thoroughfare. Drunkards bawled out to whores and beggars as they stumbled in and out of the seething taverns.

The peculiar chorus reverberated across the city, from the crumbling streets of Lowtown to waterlogged muck of Mire Shore to the secluded estates of High Ridge. It pulsed unevenly, a withering heart ready to give out and choke on the cold blood lurching thickly through its wrinkled veins.

Looming over it all, the spire kept watch over the sprawling city, a shard of purest night rising from the depths of the earth and stabbing into the vastness of space thousands of miles above.

Or was it reversed?

Had the spire instead plunged down from the blackest heavens to impale the earth, inflicting a mortal wound to bring about a slow, lingering death, a death many millennia in the unfolding?

A question best left to the wise, to the foolish, to the mad.

Weary from the labors of the long summer day, the city of Blackspire fell under the sway of its patchwork lullaby and slumbered.

But it still dreamed.

And where the spire's shadow fell, there stirred the nightmares.

Nightmares and death.

1

THE SPADER

Something soft and wet splattered against the window.

Grisel rolled over and fumbled for the tinderbox on the bedside table. His clumsy fingers knocked most of its contents to the wooden floor.

"Stupid…"

He flopped out of bed to gather the scattered pieces. After he finished, he struck one of the matchsticks and lit the candle on the bedside table.

Nicalene mumbled something from under the sheets, but she did not wake up.

Grumbling to himself and scratching at his shaved scalp, Grisel returned the tinderbox to the table.

Something splattered against the window again.

His tiny apartment was just big enough to accommodate the narrow bed, the table beside it, and the tall cabinet crammed awkwardly into the corner. The doorways at each end of the room opened into identical rooms that housed his neighbors. Mrs. Rickendole, a crotchety hag of an old lady, lived in the place to the right, and there was a young couple in the next room over who had two children, the younger of which rarely seemed to shut the hell up during the day. The husband's name was Purbin, but Grisel could never remember the wife's name and he did not give a toss about the kids. He also barely knew the guy living in the last room to the right. A foreigner with an unfamiliar accent, he kept to himself most of the time, and Grisel only saw him pass through once or twice.

There were three rooms through the left door, all of which he knew better since he walked through them every day to reach the stairwell leading down to the entrance of the crumbling tenement. Next door was Tupin, a quiet, wormish fellow who worked as a file clerk somewhere on Crookwing Street. Left of his room were the Tamercum brothers, Felski and Wurgim. Nobody knew how they paid their way, but Grisel was pretty sure it was not legal, whatever it was.

Sedina lived in the first room on the northeast wing, next to the stairwell, which allowed her to come and go as she pleased without disturbing anyone. She brought a sticker back with her from the street every now and again, but she usually did her business elsewhere, which suited her neighbors just fine.

Nicalene hated her, though. Still thought Grisel snuck over there whenever she was gone to get a quick fix.

Despite being squished in the middle of the row, Grisel's place was the second priciest one on the floor. Sedina may not have had to climb over anyone to get to the stairs, but Grisel had something that none of his neighbors had.

A window.

Of course, he could not see anything outside it now. A thick, grayish paste covered most of the glass surface. He stepped over to the window, undid the latch, and pushed it open. The muck running down the window reeked of manure, bile, and fish guts.

"Oi! Hold up!" someone outside shouted.

Two men stood in the muddy street below his second story apartment. One of them, broad shouldered and thick limbed, had his shovel cocked back like a catapult arm ready to sling another scoop of street gunk against the window. The other, slimmer man had a shovel of his own resting against his shoulder; he carried an unlit oil lantern in his other hand. Both of them wore knee-high boots and brown, canvas overalls.

"Get your skinny ass down here, Grisel!" the man with the lantern said. "Or I'll have Meaty here put rocks in the next scoop!"

Grisel knew that unless he cleaned the gunk off the window before he left, it would dry and harden up on the glass as firm as cement by morning. He also knew Meaty was accurate enough to hit him in the face with the sludgy mixture if he did anything other than close the window and go down to join them.

"Be right down."

He pulled the window shut.

"Pissants."

He stepped over to the closet and pulled out his overalls. They were heavy, fashioned from a coarse fabric that felt like fine sandpaper grit on the outside and rough burlap on the inside. They fit loosely over his pants and shirt but were far from comfortable. After wrestling them on, he shoved his feet into a pair of black leather boots that came up to his knees. He looped the straps affixed to the top of the boots through the metal ringlets dangling from the knees of the overalls and tied them them tight.

Once he secured the boots, he reached for the belt hanging from a hook on the side of the cabinet. It had a dozen pouches and pockets, many of them filled with a tool carved from hardened wood and tipped with a metal implement of some kind. Some were narrow and sharp, others broad and blunted. He pulled the belt around his waist and snapped the metal buckle into place.

Nicalene rolled over and pulled the covers away from her face. A clump of black hair covered her eyes, but not the white trail of dried saliva running down the side of her face.

Gods. What a mess.

"You get up today?" Grisel asked.

She groaned and shoved her face into her pillow.

Grisel grabbed the shovel leaning against the cabinet. He jabbed the handle into her side and she jerked back.

"Don't turn away when I'm talking to you! You drag your ass out bed today or not?"

Nicalene muttered something unintelligible. Whether she was groggy from too much sleep or high on whatever junk she was taking these days, he could not quite tell.

Grisel grunted.

Not much point yelling at you when you're like this, is there?

He reached back inside the closet to get his mask. The heavy, leather contraption consisted of bulging, fisheye goggles and adjustable straps that wrapped around his head to hold it tightly against his face. A second, smaller set of straps held the scent basket in place over his nose and mouth. He held the mask up to his ear and shook it.

Dried bits of flowers and herbs rattled inside the basket. They would need to be replaced soon.

Dammit. Always something...

He tromped out of the room, pushing aside the thin sheet that separated his apartment from Tupin's. The clerk was still awake, his room dimly lit by a single candle. Naked from the waist down and squatting over a chamber pot, Tupin waved at his guest.

"Evening, Grisel," he said. "Have a bit more work for you in a minute or two."

"Wouldn't want to throw out your breakfast."

Tupin laughed as Grisel moved into the next room. The Tamercums were nowhere to be seen, but that wasn't too odd. Their business, whatever it was, usually kept them out late. Grisel took a bit longer to pass through their empty apartment, wondering what they had hidden there. The brothers had their crooked, dirty fingers shoved into all sorts of dark nooks and crannies throughout the city.

Wonder if they know what Nicalene's into these days.

Sedina's room, always neat and orderly, was empty as well. The faint odor of stale perfume and oily lotion hung in the air, a sure sign that she had been there recently. Grisel took a deep breath, savoring the last good smell he would encounter for the next several hours. As he exhaled, he strode across the room to the heavy, wooden door on the far wall. The door was secured by a metal latch, making it the only firm barrier between the apartments and the outside world.

Grisel opened the door and stepped into the dim stairwell. A large opening on the streetside wall, partially covered by wooden slats, let in some light from outside. Although the window was sufficient to illuminate the stairwell during the day, it did little more than make a faint outline of the steps visible at night. Luckily, Grisel did not need much light. After living there for years, he knew the dimensions of the stairwell well enough that he could have negotiated it by muscle memory alone. The stairs groaned loudly as he made his way down to the ground floor.

Three vagrants, two women and an older man, lay curled up on the downstairs floor near the base of the steps, all of them dressed in mismatched tatters. A pair of small rats scurried over their bodies, nibbling at the insects nestled deep in the fabric of their clothes. The rodents perked up and sniffed the air as Grisel approached. They bolted away before he reached the bottom of the stairs.

Grisel slapped the old man on the back with the flat of his shovel. "Get up, you!"

The man squawked and rolled over against one of the women, both of whom shot up at the sound of Grisel's voice.

"This ain't your roof, you buggers! Best shove off before I put you all to pavement!"

One of the women protested, chattering in some foreign tongue that Grisel did not understand.

He shook his head and prodded at her with the shovel handle. "Don't care," he said. "Get out!"

The old man was already on his feet and hobbling towards the door. As soon as he pushed it open, a muddy projectile struck him in the face to knock him flat on his back.

Meaty stood in the street a few yards beyond the door with a muddy shovel in hand.

"Meaty, you shitsucker!" Grisel said. "That better not have been for me!"

Meaty shrugged and laughed as Grisel herded the derelict women outside. They huddled together, crying, and staggered down the street.

Grisel set his shovel aside and grabbed the old man by the leg.

"Meaty, make yourself useful, eh?"

Meaty stepped over and grasped the other leg to help Grisel haul the vagrant into the middle of the street. With his face still covered with a pasty mixture of mud and waste, the man did little more than mumble incoherently as they dragged him away from the building.

"That's good," Grisel said, dropping the man's leg. He landed a sharp kick to the vagrant's side. "Dumb gutterscum."

Meaty chuckled.

Grisel whirled towards him with a sneer and shoved him in the chest hard enough to make him stumble backward. "What are you laughing at, anyway? You ever try to sling that slop in my face again, and you won't even be able to lift a fucking shovel when I'm done with you!"

A firm hand clamped down on Grisel's shoulder. He turned around to find Meaty's companion glaring at him.

"That's enough, Grisel," he said. "You know Meaty here didn't mean nothing by it. Besides, it ain't like you're going to stay clean and pretty all night for that hog of yours upstairs."

Grisel jerked away from the man's grip.

"Piss off, Jaspen." He gestured up to his window. "I ought to make you scrub that stuff off my window with your tongue."

Meaty laughed, but a quick glare from Jaspen silenced him.

"Just get your spade, mate," he said. "We're late enough as it is."

Grisel growled under his breath as he stomped back to the building and retrieved his shovel. He tried to pull the door shut, but the latch would not slide into place no matter how hard he pulled.

"Door broken?" Jaspen asked.

"Since last week," Grisel said. "Word's getting round to the gutterscums now. Third time this week I've caught one sleeping by the steps."

"Nobody told the landlord?"

Grisel grunted. "Like he gives a toss."

The two men went on bickering as they walked down the street with Meaty trailing a few paces behind, laughing occasionally.

They left the mud sodden old vagrant sobbing in the middle of the street.

VINEWALL STREET SLITHERED through the heart of Lowtown like a crooked river, the densely packed buildings on either side forming high, unbroken banks that choked off the flow of what had once been a wide thoroughfare. The upper floors of the numerous houses, shops, and tenements extended out over the street, forming a partial canopy that shielded all but the middle of the roadway below from rain and sunlight. In some stretches, the foundations of the buildings pushed outward, causing the street to narrow so severely that a single wagon could scarcely squeeze through. The looming overhangs of the second, third, and fourth stories were especially close here, sometimes even touching to form an artificial ceiling that prevented the heavy, moist air from escaping from the ground level.

Despite being one of the city's oldest districts, Lowtown existed in a near constant state of urban renewal. Recently erected wooden shacks routinely propped up the walls of centuries-old stone structures, and imposing, multistoried monuments of ancient timber stood surrounded by more modest homes of cleanly hewn stone imported from foreign quarries. The district's building practices were driven by a ravenous architectural cannibalism that consumed all that was old and infirm. With nearly every available inch of ground long since claimed, aspiring builders were forced to either build atop existing structures or demolish and reconstitute them to suit their desires.

No one architectural style predominated along Vinewall. Although concessions to necessity and convention stood alongside more ambitious construction efforts, the reek of decay besmirched all structures regardless of their apparent quality. Stone crumbled away from homes and collected in little piles along the edges of the street. Wooden beams exposed to the wet air were either discolored with mildew or darkened with rot. Sheltered from the sunlight and nurtured by the humidity, a tangled network of vines sprawled across the surface of most of the exposed walls, lending the street its distinctive name. Flowers bloomed from some of the vines, lurid splashes of stark colors upon an otherwise drab canvas of weathered stone and waterlogged timber.

As the only major road connecting Lowtown's northern and southern boroughs, Vinewall was well traveled and densely populated. Thousands of citizens crammed into the decaying structures lining the length of the street, and thousands more from other districts of the city traversed the roadway every day alongside hundreds of foreign visitors. Although Vinewall was mostly paved with cobblestones, it was in a wretched state of repair. Aside from the steady deterioration following centuries of use, the road was steadily being scavenged by builders desperate for a cheap supply of stone. Broken patches of stone were filled in with nothing more than packed dirt that quickly turned to mud after a heavy rain. With so little sunlight filtering down to the ground, the mud holes became a permanent road hazard for travelers and a breeding ground for swarms of biting insects.

Although several houses had indoor privies, most of Lowtown's denizens regularly dumped their waste into the street without thought. Troughs of urine and waste gathered along the sides of the streets and sporadic puddles formed nearer the center whenever the inhabitants of the upper stories emptied buckets and chamber pots out their windows and balconies. If travelers below were fortunate, they would hear a warning first. During the day, livestock and pack animals roamed the length and breadth of the street, relieving themselves wherever and whenever they wished. Heavy wagon wheels and careless footsteps quickly scattered and mashed down the piles of manure.

Rotten vegetables and moldering fruits also found their way into the street, joined there by unwanted bits gutted away from various animals, mostly fish bones, scales, skin, and gizzards. A slimy, fetid sheet of moisture clung to everything near the ground and the overhangs above the street kept the fouled air from escaping. In the narrower sections of the road, the air was thick and still, sometimes even coalescing into a visible mist of putrid fog.

The street's wretched ingredients were continuously churned up during the day by boots, hooves, and wagon wheels into a thick, grayish paste that smelled like a heap of wet, bloated corpses. Scarves soaked in scented liquids were a common sight among visitors to Lowtown, the stench of the streets being vile enough in some places to cause stomach illness. Although the residents had become adept at ignoring the oppressive smell, no one ever truly grew accustomed to it. Among Lowtown's boroughs, conditions proved best in Coldwater and Carbuncle, where most of the streets were at least paved and wide enough to permit some breathing room. By contrast, the streets of Pigshire, Cadgerwalk, and Wallside were more likely to be muddy morasses, filled with the vile refuse of Lowtown's struggling tanneries, butcheries, and dyehouses. None of them, however, compared with the misery of Sinkhole, which collected the fetid runoff from its Lowtown neighbors and the northern district of Spiresreach.

After the residents retired to their beds, the men of the Spaders Guild descended upon Lowtown's mired streets. They waged an unceasing war against the city's filth, armed with little more than shovels and stubborn determination. Night after night they swarmed through the streets like maggots eating dead flesh away from an open wound. The sound of shovels scooping up heavy loads of reeking muck echoed through narrow alleys, sometimes rousing entire neighborhoods from their slumber. But there were few who dared begrudge the spaders for the disturbance lest they find their doors barricaded by piles of mud and dung in the morning. For most citizens, however, the occasional nighttime disruption was a fair price to pay for having the roadways cleared of gunge every week or so.

Grisel worked silently alongside Meaty and Jaspen as they shoveled scoop after scoop of slop into the wagon parked in the middle of the street. Another three-man crew worked on the opposite side of the wagon, slowly working their way down the lane as they cleared away the accumulated waste. All six men were clad in the distinctive clothing of their trade, the same heavy overalls, leather boots, and masks Grisel had pulled from his closet several hours ago. Their sweaty heads and arms were entirely shorn of hair, an unfortunate necessity given the nature of their work. Each spader worked with the kind of diligent precision that was only made possible by rigors of repetition.

Scoop. Turn. Fling.
Scoop. Turn. Fling.
Scoop. Turn. Fling.

Even Lowtown's wealthiest boroughs were not so well lit as other, more prosperous districts of Blackspire. Although most of the buildings sported iron hooks for hanging oil lanterns, most of them were empty. There were posts with built-in lanterns placed every few dozen yards along the sides of the street, but few of them were regularly refueled or lit by the local residents. Without dependable street lighting, spaders generally provided their own illumination by hanging oil lanterns from hooks on their wagons. They carried out their unpleasant work on the outskirts of a dull, sickly glow that could scarcely push back the heavy shroud of the night.

The contents of the small basket strapped over the mouth and nose of Grisel's mask were supposed to diffuse the appalling odor released into the air with every thrust of the shovel, but they had not been replaced for several days. As it was, they merely provided a hint of fragrance to the street's diverse array of pungent stenches.

Grisel reached up to adjust the basket. It rattled loudly when he moved it.

"We getting paid this week?" he asked.

"Nah," Jaspen said without breaking his shoveling motion. "Got paid last week, remember?"

"Need to buy some new smells. Old ones getting dried out."

Meaty chuckled.

"Laugh it up, bootlicker," Grisel said. "Surprised you even bother to wear a mask."

"Maybe you could afford some if that hog back at your place wasn't rolling around in all your earnings," Jaspen said.

"That right? Supposing I should follow your example and get Meaty here to hide it up my ass?"

Jaspen shook his head. "Don't get so pissy. Just saying that some of us have the sense to pay them to leave when we're done with them, not keep paying them to stick around."

"Maybe I like the company," Grisel said. "You think of that?"

"Would explain why you have to pay her. Can't think of who'd keep your company for free."

"Piss off."

Jaspen laughed. "Ever the charmer, ain't he, Meaty?"

"Charmer," Meaty said, nodding.

Grisel restrained the urge to bash the oaf over the head with his shovel and went back to scooping muck off the street.

They worked in silence while the night wore on, taking a few steps down the street after every half dozen or so scoops. Between the two three-man crews, it did not take long for the wagon to fill up. On a typical night, they would fill five or six wagons, their only respite coming as they waited for a new wagon to arrive from the works. The wagons ran on a strict schedule, constantly cycling in and out of the works district to the streets that were selected for cleaning that night. Sometimes an empty wagon arrived ahead of schedule and robbed the spaders of their much-deserved break. Experienced crews had long since learned to pace their labors to match the wagon timetables and thus get the most out of the empty time during changeovers.

The wagons were ugly, utilitarian contraptions of heavy lumber and crudely hammered metal. Iron plating sheathed the outside rim of the large wheels. Thick boards slotted into metal brackets along the sides to keep their vile payloads from spilling back into the street as they lurched towards the dumping grounds in the works district. Although scrubbed clean of filth every morning, the stench of the city's waste slowly seeped into the woodgrain the longer a wagon was in use. After several years of service, most wagons actually smelled worse empty than they did when filled with fresher sludge.

Too heavy to be pulled by a single draft animal, the wagon was hitched up to a mul, a hulking, six-legged fabricant fashioned by a combination of craftsmanship and sorcery. Despite its crude outward appearance, the mul was a sophisticated piece of arcane engineering far beyond the skill of any craftsman in Lowtown. Only experienced artificers from the wealthier districts north of the Saven River possessed such abilities. Due to its complexity and rarity, the mul probably cost the guild more money than the six spaders assigned to it made in a year. Unless it was moving, the massive brute was completely silent, incapable of enough conscious thought to drive it to distraction as the spaders busied themselves around it. Whenever the wagon needed moving, a few quick shovel taps on the cobblestones urged the mul forward.

Whenever the spader crew filled the wagon, Jaspen ordered them to stop shoveling. He then slapped the mul's flank with his spade, which prompted the dumb fabricant to return to the works. No one needed to accompany it. The mul had been navigating the streets of Lowtown for more than a century; it knew its way around by a combination of training, experience, and instinct. Before the wagon pulled away, Jaspen retrieved his lantern from the hook on the wagon's side to keep the darkness at bay once the mul departed. One of the spaders on the opposite side did the same; the lanterns' greasy globes of light extended just far enough into the street to brush against one another faintly.

Grisel and the rest of the spaders leaned against the vine-covered walls of the buildings lining the cleared sections of the street. They unfastened their heavy belts and placed them on the recently exposed cobblestones alongside their shovels. Meaty sat down and immediately passed out while Jaspen kept a close eye on the other crew. Two of them were younger journeymen, only recently promoted to their crew. As the most experienced spader among them, Jaspen had the responsibility of keeping an eye on the kids to make sure they met the standards expected of them.

Grisel unbuckled his mask and wiped the sweat from his chin and upper lip. Although the temperature had dropped after sunset, the close and nearly covered streets crisscrossing Lowtown had a way of trapping the heat that had been soaked up by the thick layer of waste smothering the ground. The hottest months of summer were still on the horizon, but the nights were already uncomfortably warm. Grisel's wet shirt clung to his skin, the coarse fabric scratching him every time he moved. He thought about taking it off, but he had nowhere to stash it for the rest of the night.

With his mask removed, there was nothing to hold the wretchedness of the street at bay. Grisel winced briefly as his olfactories adjusted to the reeking air. It was a common misconception that spaders could smell nothing, that part of their training included the scalding of their nasal passages until they were rendered useless. While Grisel and his kind were quite acclimated to all manner of unpleasant odors, their ability to tolerate them was more an act of will than of sensory mutilation.

Jaspen joined him after he finished staring down the other crew, unbuckling his mask and scratching at his stubbled chin. He was taller, heavier, and darker skinned than Grisel, but his head was similarly shorn.

"How the freshies look?" Grisel asked.

Jaspen grunted. "Sloppy and lazy. Ought to tell them not to follow your example anymore."

"Piss off."

"Pull your spade out of your ass, Grisel. Quit taking your misery with Nicalette out on us all night."

"Nicalene."

"What?"

"Her name's Nicalene."

Jaspen rolled his eyes. "That ain't the point, mate. None of us likes being out here, but you don't need to go making it worse with all your carping."

Grisel grunted. He was still pissed off about the muck Meaty slung against his window, no doubt at Jaspen's instruction. There was little chance that Nicalene would clean it off before he returned home.

Doubt she'll even be getting out of bed at all. Lazy bitch.

He was thinking about how to respond to Jaspen's remark when the clank of boot heels upon cobblestones echoed down the street. The spaders seldom encountered anyone at such a late hour.

"Who the hell is that?" Grisel asked.

Jaspen shrugged as he stepped forward and held his lantern aloft, his eyes squinting to cut through the darkness. A small, bouncing ball of light lilted down the street towards them. It grew larger as it approached and revealed the men walking inside it. There were four of them in all, each one dressed in a mail shirt covered with a leather cuirass. Sheathed swords dangled from their belts and three of them wore caps with rows of metal plates riveted into the leather. Although their equipment was somewhat shoddy, the blue strip of fabric wrapped around their left arm marked them as officers of the watch.

The lone bareheaded man also carried the lantern. Walking at the head of the group, his bearing was more erect than the others and his equipment seemed to be in better condition. He stopped a few feet short of Jaspen and bowed his head curtly, a gesture that Jaspen returned.

"Evening, spader," the man said. "You in charge of this lot?"

"Yeah, I am," Jaspen said.

"Captain Rheinmak, commander, Pigshire Watch. I need to borrow one of your men."

"What for?"

"We've got us a floater over on High Cross Street."

Grisel groaned along with the rest of the spaders.

If Jaspen shared their distaste for the news, he gave no indication of it, only sighing with a slight bit of annoyance as he turned towards Grisel.

"Get your gear and go with him."

Already angry with Jaspen on account of his ceaseless verbal barbs, he now had a better reason to be pissed off.

"No bloody way! It ain't my turn! I got the last one! Why don't you send this bucket of lard?"

He planted his boot against Meaty's shoulder, sending the slumbering spader face first into the freshly shoveled street. The big man woke with a start and glared up at Grisel.

"Shut up, Grisel!" Jaspen said. "Meaty gets too squeamish about them and you know it. I can't send any of the freshies out to do it, and I've got to stay here with the crew. You're all I've got. You ain't doing much more than making the rest of us miserable anyway. Now get your gear and do as I fucking say!"

Meaty clambered to his feet as Grisel retrieved his belt and strapped it into place, cursing under his breath.

"Here," Meaty said, extending a closed fist to his companion. When Grisel looked down, Meaty opened his hand to reveal a small pile of salt rock chunks. Grisel slapped Meaty on the arm and took them.

"Thanks, mate," he said, slipping the chunks into a pouch attached to his belt.

Grisel snatched his shovel and glared at Jaspen, who regarded him with a wry grin. He tried to imagine how satisfying it would be to slam the flat of the shovel against his face.

Jaspen tossed him a length of coiled rope. "Twenty feet," he said. "Outta be enough."

"Thanks for the vote of confidence, mate," Grisel said, his lip curled in a sneer.

"My pleasure," Jaspen said. "He's all yours, Captain. Don't be afraid to kick him around a bit if he bites."

But Rheinmak was already turning away as Jaspen spoke and did nothing to acknowledge him further. Grisel fell in with the other men behind the captain as he led them away from the crew.

"This way, spader," he said. "Got a nice fresh one for you tonight."

Rheinmak's men chuckled, but Grisel ignored them.

He was too busy thinking about wringing Jaspen's neck.

2
THE CUTTER

No official, civic demarcation existed to identify the boundaries of Lowtown's infamous Sinkhole borough. Although Blackspire's maps clearly indicated its presence in the northeast corner of the Lowtown district, the boundary separating it from neighboring boroughs shifted according to little more than the discretion of the mapmaker. There was no natural border to indicate the end of one and the beginning of the other, no agreed upon street and certainly nothing so indisputable as a wall or canal. The distinction largely remained one of context; a traveler simply "knew" when he had passed beyond the impoverished slums of Pigshire or Coldwater to enter the miserable, suffocating squalor of Sinkhole.

Although the buildings along Sootwalk Street were more or less maintained, a few steps down any branching alleyway or cross street revealed a crumbling ghetto populated by the most wretched of the city's poor. Winding, muddy streets were surrounded by crudely fashioned hovels built with the collapsed remains of once grander structures. Whereas Lowtown's buildings represented a riotous diversity of architectural styles and creative engineering, Sinktown edifices were monstrous testaments to necessity. Collapsing stone walls stood propped up with wooden braces and strips of rusted iron held together splintered beams buckling under the weight of waterlogged roofs. Wastewater from the surrounding areas flowed down the streets to saturate the borough's low-lying core, rendering it a breeding ground for pestilence and noxious, waterborne parasites.

And yet, the neighborhood teamed with life. During the day, Sinktown's residents scattered throughout the city, desperate for any work that might pay enough to keep their miserly landlords at bay for another week.

Too poor to afford the exquisite luxuries of Spiresreach's emporiums, the exotic wares peddled in Westgate's bazaars, or even the meager offerings of Lowtown's aspiring merchants, they bartered most of what they needed from their neighbors. For the rest, they turned to the brokers. Every borough in Lowtown had one or two—someone with the right connections to get whatever was needed, for a price. Their numbers were even greater in Sinkhole, where every common thug with connections beyond the borough fancied himself an aspiring crime lord.

Lowtown's brokers usually got their start running petty gangs, extorting coin from vulnerable citizens by demanding "protection" payments in the gang's territory. The real power, however, was in moneylending and security. In the absence of reputable bankers and strong government authority in Lowtown, powerful brokers were often the only source of money and protection for aspiring merchants looking to establish a market for their trade. Such relationships were generally reciprocal, allowing the brokers to lean heavily upon their borrowers to keep entire neighborhoods under their control. They kept the local watch authorities in line with a steady stream of bribes and packed Lowtown's sole political institution, the Assembly of Notables, with suitably pliable members. The brokers protected their power jealously, crushing any competitors who refused to be brought under their influence. Almost every criminal in Lowtown, then, fit somewhere in a complex food chain of obligations leading back to the district's most powerful brokers.

Fear followed closely behind the darkness when night fell in Sinkhole. The unlit streets and crooked alleys combined to form a torturous maze navigable only by those who had memorized its layout. Gangs of thugs and cutpurses prowled unseen within the black, pouncing on anyone foolish enough to be caught outdoors after nightfall. Some of them were bent on robbery or driven by the sheer, ecstatic joy of violence, but a few harbored more perverse, monstrous intentions. Fearful residents lucky enough to have a roof of their own locked and barricaded their doors; those without homes or shelter hid as well as they could and prayed for the dawn to come.

The little house on the corner of Tallowshire and Eelsbrook Streets was spacious by the standards of the neighborhood. A single story structure with a wooden floor, a fireplace, and a small loft tucked away in one corner, it contained few possessions beyond a table in the center of the room and a small bed pushed against one of the walls. Pots and baskets filled with dry foodstuffs were clustered around the fireplace. A single family had the house all to itself, a luxury that many of their neighbors did not enjoy.

The small candle on the table gave off just enough light to illuminate the center area of the room, leaving the walls and corners drenched in shadow. Sitting on the chair pulled up to the table, Lemrick could not see his wife lying on the bed. The end of the ladder that led up to the children's loft disappeared into the darkness hovering over him like a swollen stormcloud.

More than half of the candle had melted away, a puddle of hot grease pooling on the wood beneath its base.

Arden Belarius studied him from the shadows, watching his lips and nostrils twitching. A thin, steady stream of water and blood trickled from Lemrick's ruined eye.

"Do you know the tale of Ingvie's woe, Lemrick?"

He walked around the house as he spoke, always making sure that his voice originated from a different point in the darkness.

Lemrick closed his good eye and shook his head. "N…no."

"I thought not," Arden said. "Ingvie was a common man like yourself. A common man conscripted to fight against a mighty foe threatening to destroy his king and country. He feared for the wife and children he left behind, feared he wouldn't be able to protect them. And he was right to fear, Lemrick. Do you know why?"

Lemrick kept his eyes shut and said nothing. Arden slapped the side of his head. The blow was not forceful enough to hurt him, rather akin to the sharp, correcting rap of an instructive parent.

"Pay attention, Lemrick. Why was Ingvie right to fear?"

Lemrick's good eye snapped open. He shook his head again. "I don't know," he said, his voice nearly cracking.

"He was right to fear because he was weak. Because he knew nothing of war or how to survive it. But Ingvie was a man of faith. He prayed to the gods for aid, to help him defeat the enemies of his people. And the goddess Rashana heard his prayer. She didn't have to answer it, but she did. All she asked in return was that he honor her and no other with his prayers, that he credit his deeds to her name and not to others. Ingvie accepted her terms, and through Rashana's blessing he became a mighty warrior. It was his hand that slew the champion of the invaders, his sword that won victory for his people, for his king, and for his family.

"But victory brought him fame the likes of which he'd never dreamed. Ingvie, too drunk on success that was not his alone, forgot to honor his benefactor. He took what was given to him and used it for his own benefit. He became wealthy and renowned throughout the kingdom before he finally saw fit to return home to the humble abode he'd left so long ago."

He grasped Lemrick's hair and yanked his head backward. "Do you know what he found waiting there for him?"

"No," Lemrick said, quivering.

"His wife raped with a sword and hanged from the rafters to bleed out. His son jammed, twisted and broken, into the fireplace, his flesh seared from the bone. His daughter flayed alive, little bits of her scattered across the floor like so many stars in the sky. And in the middle of it all was Rashana, the goddess herself in human form.

"And she said to him, 'What was rightly owed me in pride, I take now in flesh and hold your debt fulfilled.'"

Arden released Lemrick's hair and struck him near the temple with the back of his fist. The blow sent him reeling, face first, to the floor.

"Is that the way you plan to pay your debts, Lemrick?"

Lemrick tried to get to his feet, but Arden pressed his boot heel against his neck and forced him back down against the floorboards.

"What's it to be, then?" Arden asked. "Shall I take the payment all at once or would you like me to return every night to claim a little bit at a time as installments?"

"Please," Lemrick said, stammering, "I'll do anything, just—"

Arden hoisted him off the floor. Broad shouldered and muscular, he had more than enough strength to keep a firm hold on Lemrick when he tried to squirm away.

"You're not hearing me, Lemrick. Men like Rensure don't send me to make deals. They send me to collect what's owed them. And if they don't get paid, then I don't get paid, so I really don't give fuck all about your promises."

"Just a few more days," Lemrick said, gasping. "Tell Rensure that I just need a few more days."

Stupid bastard.

Arden shook his head. "Not good enough."

He punched Lemrick squarely in the face, shattering his nose. Blood flowed freely over his lips and trickled down his nasal passages as he struggled to breathe. Arden let him drop to the floor in a sobbing heap.

You had to make this hard, didn't you?

Arden stalked over to the bed, where Lemrick's wife lay bound and gagged. She tried to squirm away when he grabbed her, but he was too strong to resist. He dragged her across the floor and forced her into the chair nearest her husband. Once he had her in place, he reached for the hand axe strapped to his belt near the small of his back.

"W…what are you doing?" Lemrick asked between choked gasps.

Arden shrugged as he placed the axe on the table. "That depends on you, now doesn't it?"

He grabbed Lemrick's wife's bound arms and stretched them over the table. "I'm going to ask you a question. You answer honestly, everyone stays happy and we move on to the next question."

Still holding the woman's arms in place with one hand, he picked up his axe with the other.

"If you lie to me or I think you're lying to me, then I take a bit of your debt out of the missus here. Keep lying to me and we'll move on to one of your boys tied up in the loft."

Lemrick shook his head, his entire body trembling. "Please, don't do this."

Don't make me, then.

"I'm just asking the questions, Lemrick. You're the one who decides what happens. Now, then: How much money do you still owe to Rensure?"

The sweat running down Lemrick's face mixed with the blood seeping from his many cuts. "Four hundred and fifty marks."

Arden nodded. "You're off to a good start. How many marks do you have here now?"

Lemrick wiped the thick layer of mucus, blood, and sweat from his lips. "None," he said. "I don't have anything."

You stupid, gutless little scrape.

"I find that very difficult to believe, Lemrick."

Arden raised the axe.

"Very difficult."

ASIDE FROM THE somewhat reputable areas around Sootwalk Street, most of Sinkhole went completely dark after sunset. A few neighborhoods took up collections to pay for a lamplighter to maintain a handful of lanterns during the night, but such efforts were usually a short-lived waste of precious coin. Delinquent youths made a game of stealing or smashing lanterns when the lighter's back was turned. Worse, the lighter was bound to be mugged or even killed once his routine became well known.

Any source of light that endured for more than a few evenings did so only with the tacit approval of the predators lurking in the darkness. Gangs, brokers, and smugglers could be paid to leave the odd lantern unbroken, especially if it suited their needs. Light formed the first line of defense against ambushes from rivals and helped to facilitate an array of criminal endeavors beyond base skullduggery. Viewed from above, the scattered, yellowish islands peeking through the darkness would have roughly indicated the topography of Sinkhole's villainy.

One such pocket of light contained a rather quaint shack on the west end of Cutsbreath Street. Its stone foundation supported walls of mismatched lumber held together with crumbling resin of unclear origin. The wood-shingled roof had been patched several times with thatch and bits of slate, leaving it more or less waterproof. A large oil lantern dangled from a chain affixed to the arm of a wooden post a few feet from the door.

Arden waited on the outskirts of the light for several minutes until the shack's door swung open. A thin man slipped outside and quietly closed the door behind him before disappearing into the darkness. Once he was gone, Arden moved towards the shack and rapped his knuckles against the door.

A piece of wood slid open to reveal a narrow viewing slot at eye level. Light poured through the opening, and a pair of eyes peered out at him.

"Yeah?"

"Name's Arden. I'm here to see Rensure."

"What's your business?"

"Tell him I've collected on Lemrick's debt."

The viewing slot closed. After a muffled exchange of voices inside, someone pulled the rusty, iron bolt from its latch. The door creaked open just wide enough for Arden to step inside.

It was a small living space, no bigger than any other house in the neighborhood, but the décor was certainly higher quality. The round table in the center of the room was carved from ashwood, which had to be imported to Blackspire at great expense. Some of the chairs pulled up to the table even had cushions. A rug covered the wooden floor and the walls displayed a mismatched array of tapestries and paintings. The only light came from the fireplace built into the far wall.

Stacks of loose paper and canvas pouches bulging with coins covered the table, nearly obscuring the small man sitting on the far side of it. An unremarkable looking man of middle age, his hair was already gray at the temples and receding quickly from the forehead. Neither skinny nor heavy set, he could have passed for a practitioner of any number of trades, legal or otherwise. Busily counting coins and scrawling the totals upon a sheet of paper, the man did not look up as Arden stepped inside.

How the hells did a shitheel like you ever get the run of this quarter?

A broad-chested oaf shut the door behind him and slid the iron latch back into place. The man was a bit taller than Arden and much heavier, though a good portion of his bulk consisted of fat rather than muscle. He had the build of someone who had always been larger and stronger than his peers by virtue of nature, his musculature looking rather lumpy and undefined. Arden watched his movements carefully as the man stepped past him and quickly surmised that he was every bit as clumsy as his appearance suggested. While his strength was no doubt substantial, his sheer size was probably his best asset as a bodyguard.

Probably never had a good beating. And too dumb to know it could happen.

"Mister Rensure will see you now," the guard said, his voice slow and deliberate.

Rensure still did not look up from his work. "So you're the cutter Moxie told me about. Harden, was it?"

"Arden."

"Right," Rensure said, though he might have said the same if Arden gave a completely different name. He gestured towards one of the empty chairs. "Have a seat, why don't you?"

Arden positioned himself carefully as he moved towards the table, making sure to keep Rensure's bodyguard within his peripheral vision. "I prefer to stand."

Rensure shrugged as he leaned back into his padded chair and looked up at Arden, his face slightly twisted with annoyance. "Suit yourself. Moxie tells me you've got a gift for collections, that so?"

Strange way of putting it. "I have a way with folks, sure."

"Well, then, I take it you have something for me?"

Arden pulled a purse from his coat pocket and tossed it onto the table. Rensure raised his eyebrows slightly.

"You work fast," he said, reaching out to open the purse. "How much, then?"

"One twenty."

Rensure pursed his lips and grumbled as the coins clattered onto the table. "Worthless scrape. Is that all?"

"Believe me," Arden said, "he'd have coughed it up if there was more."

"You tell him things ain't square between he and I?"

Arden nodded. "He knows as much."

Rensure frowned as he counted out the coins and spitefully recorded the amount on a sheet of paper. Arden watched him patiently for several seconds, but the broker gave no indication that he had anything more to say.

"You're forgetting something," he said.

"Yeah? What's that?" Rensure's attention didn't stray from his papers and coins.

"My cut."

"Of one twenty?" The broker snorted. "Piss off! My nephew could have beaten that much out of him and he's too simple to string five words together."

"Ten percent, Rensure," Arden said, keeping his tone level. "I told Moxie that's my rate."

Rensure slammed his palm down on the table. "Look, I don't give a toss what you're used to over in Cadgerwalk or wherever the hells you was last. You want your cut in my quarter, you bring me the fucking results just like everyone else."

Arden placed his hands on the table and leaned towards the broker. "If your people could get results then you wouldn't need someone like me in the first place. You send me out to collect, I get what's there to be had. If you want a better return, maybe you shouldn't be lending marks out to shiftless leeches who can't pay up when a cutter comes knocking."

Rensure gnawed on his lower lip as he set his pen down and pushed a pile of coins to the side. He glared at Arden with an expression that he had no doubt spent many years refining to the most venomous effect. Arden assumed it was enough to terrify most of his ignorant underlings.

"Talk out of turn again, old son, and I promise you you'll never speak again. It's a dark and lonely walk back to whatever hole you crawled out of, so you best think real hard about who you go pissing on whilst you're in my quarter."

Arden smiled. "I suppose I'd better. Be a shame for anyone here to get hurt."

Rensure's gaze darted from Arden to his bodyguard and back again, his body tense. Arden ignored the movements and instead scanned over the coins and money purses piled atop the table.

"Seems to me you've got more than enough here to cover my rate," he said. He waited for Rensure to make eye contact before he continued. "Not sure about Mister Dhrath's, though."

The bodyguard made his move as Arden finished speaking, but he was far too slow. Arden heard the first heavy footfall and spun around to land a sharp kick in the lumbering oaf's crotch. As he doubled over, coughing, Arden grabbed two fistfuls of hair and smashed his knee into the man's face, shattering his nose. With the guard still bent in half, Arden drove the point of his elbow against the back of his neck. The bones snapped under the impact and the thug went completely limp.

Rensure was out of his chair before the body hit the ground, knife in hand. Arden wheeled about, grabbing the broker's wrist to turn the blade aside and pull him off balance. As Rensure stumbled forward, Arden clamped his free arm around the broker's neck and wrestled him to the ground. The knife clattered harmlessly to the wooden floor as Rensure struggled against Arden's suffocating grip.

"You think this is how I spend my time, Rensure? Running errands for two-bit knobs like you? Let me tell you something about your little 'quarter.' You get to run it because Mister Dhrath says it's yours to run so long as you keep the marks flowing. But do you know what happens when they're not flowing like they used to? That tells him some miserable little scrape is skimming off the top, that somebody doesn't remember his place in the natural fucking order of things. And when somebody needs a reminder about where they belong, he sends me to sort out the mess. You follow me?"

Rensure tried to nod, or maybe he was fighting to take a breath.

I'll take that as a yes.

Arden forced the broker face down onto the wooden floor. Then he pressed his knee into the small of Rensure's back to hold him in place and slammed his foot down on the broker's outstretched arm.

"Now, then. I'm going to ask you a few simple questions," he said, reaching for his axe. "Tell me the truth like a good lad, and we move on to the next question. If you lie to me or I think you're lying to me…"

He slammed the axe into the wood floor scarcely an inch from Rensure's nose. "In that case, we start settling those debts of yours the old-fashioned way."

Rensure began to cry.

True colors coming through now, aren't they?

"Better buck up, old son," he said. "If I can't hear you, then I'll just have to assume you're lying to me. And you don't want me to do that, do you, Rensure?"

"No…"

"Good. Now then, how much money have you stolen from Mister Dhrath?"

"I ain't stolen nothing! Nothing! I swear!" Rensure said, sobbing.

Arden shook his head. "You testing my nerve, Rensure, or do you just think I'm as simple as that sodding nephew of yours?"

He pulled the axe free and raised it over his head, taking aim at Rensure's outstretched hand, still pinned to the floor by his foot.

"Can you write with both hands?"

The axe dropped with a heavy thud.

A split second passed between the impact and Rensure's realization that some part of him had been cleaved away.

Then he screamed.

ARDEN STEPPED OUT of the shack and closed the door behind him. The neighborhood appeared deserted, but he could feel the eyes watching him from the darkness. Some of them no doubt belonged to Rensure's thugs, others to the gutterscums too stupid to ignore the screams that had ceased some time ago.

He slung the heavy sack filled with marks over his shoulder and stepped into the street. The lantern hanging from the nearby post was dimming now, its fuel almost spent.

"Anyone who tries to follow me dies," Arden said, addressing the gallery regarding him from the darkness.

"Anyone touches me, I kill him and come back tomorrow to kill his family and his friends."

He waited for a moment, allowing doubt to sink into the minds of anyone foolish enough to test his sincerity.

"Now, piss off."

Arden turned eastward and set off down Cutsbreath Street. He knew its course well enough that he did not need any light to guide the way.

No one followed him.

3
THE STONE

Captain Rheinmak was a right bastard.

On their way to the tottering house on High Cross Street, Grisel watched him berate his men for showing signs of fatigue, order the beating of a vagrant near Goldwine Square, and threaten to arrest a little girl's parents for some unspecified crime after she dared to empty a chamber pot into the street after they passed by her window. The captain carried himself with the smug sort of authority that needed to be continually nurtured by crass belligerence.

Not that Grisel much cared about any of the people unfortunate enough to get in Rheinmak's way. A few of them might have deserved what they got, but even if not, they should have been smart enough to stay out of sight of an approaching watch patrol. Of course, Grisel also realized that had the captain not needed a spader at the moment, a fair portion of that choler would probably be aimed at him as well. When Rheinmak did deign to direct a remark his way, Grisel simply offered an affirming grunt. He kept whatever opinions he had to himself.

The house on High Cross Street was a crumbling hulk of a building propped up by shoddy brickwork and moss-covered wooden scaffolding. Patches of stone peeked out from behind the uneven layers of bricks, faint indicators that the building might have once served a more important function than housing a filthy collection of squatters. The original roof had either collapsed or been torn off, replaced by ugly shingles half-buried under a thick layer of soot and grime.

Two armed men leaned against the wall alongside the building's main entrance. Grisel had a hard time making out their faces in the dim lantern light, but one of them looked like he was asleep before a sharp elbow from his comrade spurred him to attention. If Rheinmak noticed, though, he gave no indication of it, instead looking over the building and then glancing around the area.

"Anyone come by?" he asked.

"No, sir," one of them said. "Not a soul."

Rheinmak nodded and turned to Grisel. "First floor," he said. "Second door on the left."

Grisel nodded as he retrieved the salts Meaty had given him and placed them inside his mask's basket.

"I'll need two of your men to hold the rope," he said.

Rheinmak grunted, then pointed to the two men standing by the door. "You heard him. Get moving."

The guards said nothing in protest, but their faces twisted painfully at the command. One of them scooped up the lantern at their feet and tilted his head towards the door.

"Come on, then."

Grisel followed them inside, shovel in one hand and the length of rope Jaspen had given him in the other.

The door opened into a spacious entry room with a small stove tucked into the stonework along the left wall. A group of bleary-eyed tenants huddled around a table near the stove, their faces faintly illuminated by the light of a few candles. There were five of them, a single family from the looks of it. Grisel did not need to see much of them to know what they were. They were dirty and poor, just like most everyone else in Pigshire borough, and undoubtedly shared the ground floor's common area with the rest of the building's wretched tenants.

The ceiling was low enough that Grisel could have placed his hand flat against it. A spiral staircase fashioned out of iron stood on the far end of the room, presumably leading up to the small rooms on the floors above them. From the outside, the building looked large enough to contain three floors, but if the rest of the ceilings were as low as the ground floor's, it could probably cram in an additional level.

To the right, there were three small rooms, only one of which, the middle room, still had a door affixed to the hinges; the others were covered with a strip of fabric. None of the rooms seemed very big, but Grisel guessed that the family at the table probably squeezed into one of them. Even in the slums of Pigshire, living space was expensive.

The moist air reeked of sweat and manure.

He followed the two guards to the door leading into the second room on the left. They stood a few steps away from it. "In there."

Grisel strapped his mask on, bringing the fish-eye goggles over his eyes and buckling the basket in place over his mouth and nose. The powerful fumes of the salts inside seared his nostrils, and he took a few breaths to adjust to the burning sensation. He handed the rope to one of the guards and nodded towards the door.

"Give me that lamp," he said, his voice slightly muffled by his mask. The guard handed it over with a grunt. Grisel considered warning them to breathe through their mouths when he opened the door, but he did not expect them to be showing him any courtesy as he worked. There was little reason to be considerate.

He pulled the door open and felt the warm, fetid air sweep over his exposed skin. One of the guards gagged and the other one turned away, his hand clamping over his mouth.

Grisel could not smell anything through the scorching fumes of the salts. He thrust the lantern into the room and immediately noticed the outline of the gaping hole in the center of the wooden floor. A few tentative prods of his foot convinced him that the remaining floorboards could hold his weight. He stepped into the room and inched toward the edge of the chasm.

The privy's cesspit beneath the floor was about two yards wide, its walls lined with stone. Careful to avoid leaning on any of the broken boards that partially extended over the hole, Grisel leaned over the edge and tried to peer down to the bottom. In the murky darkness below, he could see the faint outlines of the floorboards floating on the pasty surface. There was another, less regular shape heaped against the stone wall.

Poor bastard.

He turned back to the door and waved for the guards to come in. They moved into the room slowly, both of them covering their mouth and nose as they drew nearer to the hole. Grisel set the lantern down and snatched his rope back. As he tied one end of it around his spade, one of the men tentatively looked into the cesspit.

"You see this a lot, spader?"

Grisel shrugged. "Four, maybe five times a year."

It was no exaggeration. There were private privies like this one all over the city. The better ones were regularly maintained, and depending upon how many people used them, they needed to be dug out every year or two. Smarter tenants usually replaced the privy's floorboards around the same time. All the moisture rising up from the pit caused rot to set into the wood faster than usual. Once the floorboards rotted through, it was only a matter of time before they gave way.

Grisel had probably fished more than a dozen people out of privy cesspits over the years. The pits were usually deep enough that people could not climb out once they fell in. Some of the poor sods ended up going in headfirst and drowning, but most of them choked on the fumes. The noxious air festering at the bottom of a cesspit could become concentrated enough to poison a grown man in just a few short breaths.

In either case, it was a bad way to go.

Grisel pulled the guard looking into the hole over toward his companion, who was still lingering near the doorway. He shoved a section of rope into their hands.

"Keep it held steady and let me go down at my own speed, got it? I'll send him up first, so just start pulling when I tell you."

The men nodded and Grisel made his way back to the edge of the cesspit. He held his shovel over the hole and let it fall spade first. The length of rope unraveled quickly as the makeshift anchor plummeted into the darkness. It clanked against something and then clattered along the stone-lined wall before splashing down at the bottom.

He reached into one of his pocket pouches and pulled out a cord with two amber stones attached to it. When he touched the stones together, they gave off a faint glow almost as bright as the lantern.

"Those daystones?" one of the men asked.

Grisel nodded. "Not a good idea taking open flame into a pit. Fumes can catch fire."

He wrapped the cord around his wrist and tied off the loop to form a bracelet. Then, slowly and cautiously, he took hold of the rope and lowered himself into the cesspit.

The shaft was unusually deep, requiring almost the entire length of rope to reach the bottom. When he was about halfway to the bottom, he looked below and saw the half-submerged corpse slumped against the wall, a pile of broken boards floating around it. He slid down the last few feet of rope and splashed into the knee-deep pool of sludge. His boots sank several inches into the compacted muck covering the pit's floor. Even the smelling salts failed to completely mask the stench welling up around him as he disturbed the still, thick liquid lapping around his legs. The heavy moisture fogged up his goggles slightly, but not enough to obscure his vision.

Grisel worked quickly. He recovered his spade and removed the end of the rope from its handle. Setting the tool aside, he then pulled the corpse away from the wall and looped the rope around its chest. He made sure not to look at the body too closely and took special care to avoid seeing the face. In his experience, bodies proved easier to deal with when he thought of them as just another pile of refuse, a foul-smelling byproduct of urban life. There was no point in projecting any qualities upon a dead man's flesh, nothing to be gained from wondering if he was a good man or bad, if anyone would mourn his passing, or if casual acquaintances would even stop to wonder whatever happened to him when they no longer crossed his path.

Nothing special distinguished the dead man from the pool of waste it had fallen into. The corpse was simply waste of another sort, and equally unwanted at that.

Once he secured the body, Grisel looked up to the cesspit's opening and called out to the guards. "Pull him up!"

The rope remained still.

Dammit.

Grisel waited a moment before calling up again. "Hey, you fucking listening up there? Pull him up, I said!"

Nothing.

Probably can't hear me through this bloody mask.

He thought about climbing up the rope and then having them haul the body up after him, but then he would have to come back down to retrieve his shovel. Climbing the rope would also be difficult with the corpse pulling it tight against the cesspit wall.

There was no way around it. He had to take of his mask.

Dammit.

Grisel took a few measured breaths before breathing deeply and unbuckling the basket from his mask to expose his mouth and nose. The stench assaulted him, clawing at his lips and his scrunched nose.

"Hey! You hear me up there?"

A wisp of the foul air squirmed up his nose as he quickly pulled the basket back over his face.

"Aye, spader!"

About time.

He took another deep breath of the salts before removing the basket again.

"Pull this deader up, will you?"

Grisel tried to buckle the basket back into place, but his hands were slick with ordure and he fought to get a good grip on the strap. The guards hoisted on the rope as he struggled with the latch and the corpse lurched upward. One of the limbs struck Grisel's shovel as the body scraped against the stone. He reached out to catch it, but as he did, he lost his concentration and took in a gulp of air.

The fumes poured down his throat like spoiled milk, and a cold shock knifed through his lungs. He clamped his mouth shut and blew the rancid air out of his nostrils, the way he was trained to do, but it was too late to drive out the gases he had already sucked down. Grisel staggered, falling against the cesspit wall as his legs gave out beneath him and his head pounded. He grasped frantically for anything to break his fall, terrified that he might never get up again if he toppled into the soupy muck.

His fingers closed around something soft and he gripped it fiercely. Suddenly, he felt himself being hauled upward and found himself staring into the bulging eyes of a dead man.

To Grisel's horror, they were not vacant.

The bloated, grime-encrusted face glared at him with a ravening malevolence. Slack, putrescent lips curled back to reveal a jagged row of broken teeth. A gust of hot air reeking of sulfur spilled out of its blackened maw as the distended, clouded eyes regarded him with a mixture of hatred and revulsion. The execrable gaze held him fast, and for a moment, he thought he felt wet, tumid fingers clamped over his throat and arm.

His heart all but burst through his chest and only a frantic blaze of panic gave Grisel the strength to push away from the swollen corpse. As he threw himself back, his hand caught on a cord dangling from the dead man's neck and pulled it free. Grisel slammed against the opposite side of the cesspit and immediately yanked the basket back over his face. A deep draw of the smelling salts scorched all trace of the noxious miasma from his lungs. By the second breath, he felt his heart rate slowing. After the third, the stabbing pain in his skull gave way to a dull ache.

The corpse lurched slowly up the cesspit wall, each tug of the rope by the strong-armed men above pulling it farther away from him.

Grisel stared intently at the dead man's face.

The features were limp, the eyes vacuous. No trace of malignant awareness, or anything notable at all, really. Just another waste byproduct to be hauled out of sight and out of mind with the rest of the dung.

Grisel leaned his head against the cesspit wall and closed his eyes. He savored the burning sensation that accompanied each breath.

Must be seeing things. Hallucinating.

No other explanation made sense. Any spader knew one whiff of the air at the bottom of a cesspit could make a man painfully ill or even kill him. It was not too much a stretch to believe the same noxious air could play tricks on his mind. Grisel never heard of it happening to anyone, but he also seldom talked to anyone dumb enough to take his mask off at the bottom of a cesspit.

He tried to push the image of the dead man out of his mind by focusing on reattaching the basket's strap to his mask. By the time he finally fixed it, the guards above had hauled the corpse out of the cesspit and had tossed the rope back to him. The rope did not extend quite as far this time.

Come on, shitheels. Give me a bit more slack, will you?

When he reached up to grab the end of the rope, he noticed something resting atop one of the floating bits of wood that he missed before.

The object appeared to be a black chunk of stone, just a bit smaller than the palm of his hand. A leather cord had been wrapped around it several times and connected to a longer length to fashion a crude necklace. He bent over and picked up the stone to find that the cord had broken just below the knot.

Must be the necklace I tore off when I fell.

He held his luminous bracelet up to the black stone. Strangely, the surface did not seem to reflect the light at all despite being as smooth and polished as glass. When he looked closer, he saw nothing staring back at him. For all its apparent sheen, the stone might as well have been a chunk of black granite. He had never seen anything quite like it before, certainly not on anybody fool enough to drown in a cesspit.

Might be worth something. Maybe a lot, even.

Grisel looked up at the cesspit's opening. The guards were not peering over the edge at him.

None the wiser…

He slipped the stone into his pocket and tied the end of the rope to his shovel. When he was finished, he tugged once on the rope to make sure the guards were still holding it. The rope held firm, and he started climbing out of the wretched pit.

When he got to the top, he found the corpse lying near the edge of the hole in the floor. A strip of rope was still wrapped around his chest; the guards had opted to simply cut the rope instead of untying the knot. Neither man offered to help Grisel to clamber over the edge of the cesspit. Once he was out, they dropped the rope, leaving it to him to haul up his shovel and coil the rope. He glared up at them occasionally as he worked, wondering if either of them would take the initiative to drag the body out of the house.

Grisel unbuckled his mask, then removed his daystone bracelet and returned it to his belt pouch. He pointed to the dead body with his shovel.

"He's all yours."

The guards exchanged awkward, uncertain glances.

One of them let out a thin, hesitant laugh. "Still a little dirty, ain't he?"

Grisel mustered as much smugness as he could manage into a single smile.

"Not my problem, mate," he said. "You got a body in a shithole, I get it out because that's what I do. But once the body ain't in the pit anymore, then he's just another dead sod for you to haul off to the Deadhouse for the undertakers to mark in those little books they keep up, isn't he? Now, if your new friend here decides to take a shit in the street on the way there, then by all means, send a little birdy to let me know, and I'll drop everything I'm doing to come make it nice and tidy. Otherwise, piss off."

He pushed by the guards and stepped out of the room before they could pool enough wit between the two of them to offer a response. For all his bravado, Grisel was thankful to get away from that stinking corpse. Even if its slackened face had little in common with the hideous visage he imagined seeing in the cesspit, he did not want to be anywhere near the damned thing.

The family gathered around the table looked up at him as he strode into the common room. Someone sneered at him, which reminded Grisel that much of his body was covered in a slimy layer of human waste. The oils in the fabric of his overalls would keep the stench from seeping into the fibers, but he would smell horrible until he had a chance to wash the sewage away.

He paused near the table. "That your only privy?"

The oldest man nodded.

"Looks due to be scooped out. Tell your lessor that he'd best have us do it before he has the floor fixed."

The man muttered something that sounded like an acknowledgement. Grisel did not care enough to have him clarify.

Something banged against the wall behind him and Grisel turned to see the guards carelessly dragging the body out of the privy room. They had wrapped their hands in strips of cloth to avoid touching the vile corpse, but doing so had made it difficult for them to keep a firm grip on it. After managing to pull it clear of the doorway, they had a slightly easier time hauling it through the common area towards the exit. The body left a slick, wet trail of stinking ordure behind it like a giant, rancid slug.

Grisel looked back to the family. A few of them watched the guards hefting the corpse through the front door; the others stared down blankly at the table.

"He one of yours?" he asked.

The heavy-set woman, probably the mother to the children, shook her head. "No. Just moved into the next room a few days past. Fell in after we went to sleep."

The man next to her hung his head. "Hell of a way to die."

Grisel imagined the loud crack of the floorboards echoing through the house, the splash of the body plunging into the fetid pool at the bottom of the privy. He shrugged the thought away before it took him back into the cesspit.

His gaze drifted to the trail of waste smeared across the floor next to his dripping boots. "You can sop this up off the floor with water and rags, but you'll need to douse it with vinegar to get rid of the smell. Best do it quick before it sets into the wood."

The woman nodded but avoided looking at him again. The man next to her remained silent.

There was nothing left for anyone to say.

Grisel strode out of the common room and stepped into the street. After being in the tight confines of the cesspit, even the heavy air of Pigshire felt refreshing. He closed his eyes and let it filter through his beleaguered lungs.

The guards had already loaded the corpse into a wheelbarrow by the time he joined them. Captain Rheinmak walked over to him, careful to keep a reasonable distance.

"We'll take him from here, spader," Rheinmak said. "I'll see that the quartermaster back at the watchhouse has the fee delivered to the guild by sunset tomorrow."

Grisel nodded. According to the guild's contract with the district, he was within his rights to charge a personal fee on top of the guild's standard service rates, but he had a feeling Rheinmak would not be keen to entertain the request. It would be less of a headache to pester Jaspen later on to get him a percentage of the fee from the guild treasury. He would probably have to argue about it, but at least he avoided running the risk of losing any teeth, which was the likely outcome of any disagreement with a nasty sod like Rheinmak.

"Happy I could be of service," Grisel said, trying to sell the enthusiasm with a smile.

Rheinmak grunted. "Right. You can find your way back, I trust?"

Grisel could. He did not want to spend another minute with Rheinmak and his thugs anyway. "Yeah, sure."

The captain strode back to his men and barked at them to get underway. One watchman gathered up the wheelbarrow and set off down the street. The others followed close behind with Rheinmak hissing after them.

Shitsuckers.

Grisel swung his shovel across his shoulders and draped his arms over it as he started back toward Vinewall Street.

The sun would not rise for a few more hours, but he already felt exhausted. Every time he closed his eyes, he saw that vicious, dead face glowering back at him. He tried to think of something else, anything, to occupy his mind as he made his way down the dark, empty street.

Eventually, his thoughts turned to the strange, black stone in his pocket.

Maybe if he got lucky for a change, it would be worth something.

4

THE BODY

The man's pale skin sagged loosely over his flesh, already turning bluish-gray around the joints. A thin strip of wire held his broken jaw shut. The ruined stump of his left arm was sewn inside the sleeve of a heavy, woolen shirt that also covered the gaping hole some hooked implement had torn into his midsection. A blanket wrapped around his legs concealed the filed down shards of bone protruding from his skin. The small tin lantern sitting next to his head gave off a thick, flowery stench that smothered the fetor of decay. A much larger oil lamp hung from a wrought iron stand next to table, pushing the darkness back with a sphere of greasy light.

Calandra tapped her fingertips against the wooden table's pitted surface while she glared at the slender man standing on the opposite side. He looked up from the corpse resting between them, his jaundiced eyes gleaming in the lantern's light.

She met his gaze with disinterest, her fingers still tapping on the wood. "Well?"

The man sneered and leaned back over the corpse's face.

Calandra crossed her arms and sighed loudly. "Look, I haven't got all night," she said. "Now do you know him or not?"

The man shook his head. "No."

"You're sure?"

He glanced at what remained of the corpse's arm. The wound should have been covered well enough to prevent any fluid from seeping out, but there were a few dark stains around the sleeve's stitching.

Bandaging must have worked free when they moved him.

"Yeah," the man said, looking back to her. "I'm sure."

She was getting tired of dealing with this one. "Fine. Come on, then."

Calandra took the oil lantern from its hook and walked between the long rows of tables that ran down the middle of the mortuary's cavernous chamber. There were thirty tables in all, ugly wooden things scarred and stained by years of heavy use. One by one, they emerged from the darkness and then faded back into the black as Calandra filed past them. Most of the tables were empty, but corpses rested upon a few of them, each one dressed in the same rough, bland woolen fabric. Roughspun blankets covered a few of the bodies, but most simply lay exposed to the air.

The mortuary's central viewing chamber was naturally dark, even during the day when the sunlight pushed meekly through the thick, glass windows positioned high upon the walls. After sunset, however, the place turned completely black, illuminated only by whatever candles and lanterns the poor souls assigned to the night shift carried with them. There were a few small islands of light scattered throughout other parts of the room as mortuary workers went about tending to recently received bodies. They labored quietly, keeping their voices hushed and their movements careful and deliberate. Occasionally a louder noise, a dropped instrument or a surprised grunt, rose above the grim silence that smothered the room and echoed harshly off the cold, stone walls.

Although formally known as the Coldwater Mortuary, the locals knew the place better as the Deadhouse. The Undertakers Guild did not much care for the nickname, of course, but there was little it could do to stop people from using it.

Calandra veered through the rows of tables with a familiar ease; she could have found the way back to her desk even without the lantern. The jaundiced-eyed man scuttled along behind her, following a bit too closely for her liking. She glared over her shoulder at him, which was enough to drive the spindly-legged thing back a few paces, just on the outskirts of her lantern's light. By the time she reached the large desk near the chamber's entrance, he had fallen far enough behindthat she could no longer hear his labored breathing.

Keldun, a thick-necked man with a mace at his side stood between Calandra's desk and the chamber's entrance. He spent several years with the Coldwater Watch before Calandra hired him away to keep the gangs and street urchins run off from the Deadhouse. When she approached, he moved closer to her desk and set his lantern on the floor.

Calandra hung her lantern on the hook next to her desk and pulled out the chair to sit down. Keldun inched a bit closer to the jaundiced-eyed man while she produced a metal lockbox from one of the desk's drawers. She unlatched it and reached inside to pull out a small handful of tenthmarks.

One by one, she counted the coins and stacked them on the desk.

"...four, five, and six."

The man shuffled his feet as Calandra opened the thick ledger sitting on the desk and marked down the names he had provided for the unidentified corpses.

When she was finished, she pushed the marks across the desk. "There. Now be on your way."

"Only six?" He snatched up the coins and stared at them. "It was ten last time."

Calandra glared at him. "Last time you gave me five names. Today you gave me two. Next time I'll get some other gutterscum in here with a better set of eyes to sort out the stiffs."

The man nibbled at his lips. He glanced first at Keldun, who stood waiting to escort him out of the chamber, and then back to the marks in his hand. Calandra ignored him, pretending instead to review the ledger while he made up his mind about how important the extra marks were to him. Finally, he spoke up.

"I…I may know that last one you showed me."

Calandra raised an eyebrow. "You'll have to do better than that and you know it. Give me a name and a location or get out."

The man swallowed and lowered his head. "Drisden," he said. "Name's Drisden. Works on Nockwall Street."

"Now we're getting somewhere," Calandra said, picking up her pen and recording the information in her ledger. "You know where he lives?"

She looked up at the man as he shook his head.

"But you know who did that to him, don't you?"

A slight nod.

"And you're afraid he'll find out."

Another nod.

Calandra reached into the lockbox and took out a quartermark. She offered the coin to the trembling informant.

"I don't care how he got here," she said. "All I care about is putting names to the bodies before they start to rot out from under me. Got it?"

The man stepped forward, his hand outstretched. Calandra shoved the coin into his palm and looked to Keldun.

"Show him out and bring in another one," she said. "And I don't want to see him skulking around here before next week."

Keldun gripped the vagrant by the arm. "You heard her. Move."

Calandra went back to her ledger as the guard half escorted, half hauled the man out of the chamber.

The results on the page were not encouraging. Three viewings had only produced two positive identifications out of ten. She had a list of names to go with eight of the bodies, but the discrepancies were already mounting; several of the names were associated with the same corpse.

One body had even been identified as three different people by three different viewers.

She was still staring at the list of names when Keldun returned to the chamber. He was alone.

"Nobody?" she asked.

The guard shook his head.

"Dammit," she said, slapping her pen down on the desk. There were usually half a dozen vagrants loitering around the mortuary looking to identify bodies for a few extra marks.

Never there when you need them.

Calandra shoved the lockbox back into its drawer and closed her ledger. "Well, I guess we'll just have to sort out the ones we've got."

Keldun remained by the door as she retrieved the lantern from its hook and walked back over to the tables. Another mortuary worker stood there holding his lantern over one of the corpses. Calandra quickly identified Tarl's big, thickly-set frame even before he turned to face her. He wore a heavy, leather apron over his roughly stitched clothes; the dark splotches smeared across the apron betrayed the often grisly nature of his duties. Despite being an ugly brute of a man, he had a soft and friendly face.

Tarl smiled at her, but Calandra did not return the expression. She was too busy scanning the slack faces laid out on the tables. Of course, even in another situation, she would have found some reason to either ignore him or otherwise maintain a cold degree of emotional distance.

"You have the cart handy?" she asked.

"Yes, ma'am."

"Load up four and seven for the crypt. We'll send out notices for them in the morning."

Tarl rubbed his jowls and mumbled something.

"What's wrong?" Calandra asked.

"Not sure if we got the room," he said. "Lots of nobodies."

Out of the hundreds of corpses that came through the mortuary every week, perhaps only a third of them were ever identified. Of that portion, a few would be claimed by friends or relatives in the city, but most would be left to rot in lonely anonymity. They might have had names to identify them, but there was no one to mourn their passing or long for their presence.

Unknown, unwanted, unnoticed; it made no difference which term applied. To the mortuary workers, they were the nobodies.

"When was the last time anyone took a tally down there?"

Tarl shrugged.

Calandra fought the urge to kick one of the table legs. She was not supposed to have to worry about cycling unclaimed bodies out of the crypt. Lerris should have handled that duty during the day shift.

As if she needed another reason to hate the overbearing bitch.

"Let's have a look then," she said. "Load these two up and we'll head down there."

BEFORE COLDWATER'S ASSEMBLY of Notables turned it into a storehouse for Lowtown's dead, the mortuary had served as a place of worship. Expanded several times over the centuries, the complex sprawled over a large chunk of Coldwater borough. As the building itself grew above the streets, a network of tunnels and rooms lay hidden beneath it, likely dug out to provide shelter for some illicit cult that branched off from any one of the churches that occupied the temple at various times throughout history. The dry, subterranean air was well suited to the preservation of the dead, so the Undertakers Guild converted the largest chambers into crypts. Most of the underground rooms stored Lowtown's corpses until surviving family members could claim them.

Calandra hated going down into the crypt. The air was thick with fumes from the various oils and chemical solutions slathered over each corpse to slow the process of decay. Although they brought in a rat catcher to sweep through the rooms and eliminate vermin every few months, Calandra had seen rodents the size of cats nesting inside bodies on more than one occasion. Once a corpse was identified and transferred to the crypt, it was only supposed to remain there for a few days, a week at most. Occasionally, however, a nobody would be moved somewhere and forgotten, leaving it to fester and rot until some unfortunate worker stumbled upon it.

The lantern provided just enough light to illuminate the center of the storeroom as she stepped inside, leaving the walls sheathed in darkness. Corpses lay stretched out in rows along the walls, their feet facing outward. Standing in the entryway, the feet formed the edges of a grisly road extending into a black void.

Slowly, Calandra moved inside.

A small tag dangled from a bit of cord tied around every other ankle. She knelt to examine each one as she moved through the room. Most provided only a name and a date. Occasionally, a tag included a street name or even an address, but just as often the ink was smudged so badly that it was impossible make out the date indicating when the body arrived in the crypt. Whenever she found a tag that was either illegible or older than a week, she pulled it loose from the cord.

Tarl lumbered a few steps behind her with his cart, two fresh bodies loaded on top, one resting heavily on the other. He remained mostly quiet while Calandra went about her work, though he sometimes snorted harshly whenever an unpleasant odor drifted past his nostrils.

When Calandra reached the end of the room, she counted the tags in her hand.

"Damn."

There was more work to be done here than she anticipated.

She wondered if the other storerooms scattered throughout the crypt were similarly packed with bodies that should have been moved out weeks ago.

Lerris was supposed to keep track of how long corpses were being stored down in the crypts. As much as Calandra loathed being in her immediate superior's presence, she knew she had to confront her about her carelessness in the morning.

Dammit, Lerris. Suppose I have to clear this room out now, but I'll be damned if I'm going to check the others for you.

She turned to Tarl and gestured to the corpses. "We need to move seven of these nobodies out of here."

Tarl grunted, then glanced back at the cart. "Can't fit that many."

"Yes, I know that!"

Tarl winced at her sharp tone, and she immediately felt bad for snapping at him. Despite his size and strength, Tarl was quite sensitive and responded poorly to verbal outbursts.

"I'm sorry," she said. "I didn't mean to yell."

She forced herself to smile. The result seemed to be enough to reassure Tarl. He exhaled slowly and then nodded.

"I know it's a hassle," she said, "but you'll just have to make more than one trip, okay?"

Tarl grunted, resigned to his task. "Okay. Where do you want the freshies?"

It won't make much of a difference the way Lerris keeps this place.

The current occupants adhered to no established order, at least not an obvious one. Calandra pointed to the corpses nearest the back wall as she set her lantern down on the floor.

"Put them back there. They'll be the last ones we need to move out anyway."

Tarl hoisted the first of the two additions out of the cart while Calandra tugged one of the older corpses away from the wall. It slid easily across the dry floor, which made her quite thankful. On more than one occasion, she yanked on an ankle only to have shriveling ligaments tear free of the bone and leave the limb connected by nothing more than rancid flesh. As she pulled the body out of its space, Tarl moved around her and gently placed the fresh corpse on the exposed floor. They repeated the process to swap the second body into place, and Tarl then went about loading the old bodies into the now empty cart.

Once that was done, Calandra pointed out a third tagless corpse and the big worker stacked it atop the two he had already loaded.

"Go ahead and haul these three upstairs to the furnace," she said. "I'll pull the other four out of the room for you."

Tarl grunted as he gripped the cart's handles and pushed it out the door. He paused long enough to pick up the lantern outside the door and then trudged up the gently sloping tunnel that led out of the crypts.

Calandra looked down at the four corpses she still had to move. "Damn you, Lerris."

She grabbed the nearest set of tagless ankles and hauled the unclaimed body to the door. Each step took her farther from the lantern and deeper into the shadows. By the time she pulled the corpse clear of the room, she was in almost total darkness. As she pushed the body against the wall of the tunnel, she heard the scuffling of Tarl making his way back to her.

Except the sound came from the wrong direction.

Calandra nearly stumbled over the corpse at her feet as she pressed her back against the wall and peered down the long, black tunnel. She held her breath and listened, hoping that perhaps her imagination had merely run away from her.

The scuffling sound drifted up from the deeper chambers of the crypt once again.

Something's definitely down there.

Calandra crept back into the storeroom to retrieve her lantern. She considered running back up to the mortuary to fetch Keldun, but she knew he would ridicule her if the source of the noise turned out to be nothing more than a big rat. Cautiously, she stepped out of the room and inched down the tunnel, keeping close to the wall.

The scraping grew louder as she went further into the darkness, accompanied by something heavy moving across the ground.

What the hell is that? Is it big enough to drag a whole body?

The tunnel curved sharply to the left as it descended and Calandra stopped short when she saw the dim glow of a lantern far ahead.

A figure stepped from one of the rooms, its dark form little more than a ghostly silhouette in the lantern's light.

Calandra gasped and stood shock still for an instant before she had the presence of mind to extinguish her lantern's flame. The dark rushed in to fill the space around her as she stared dumbly at the figure standing astride the tunnel.

All of the mortuary's night workers were up in the main chamber. It was not unheard of for a day worker to stay later than usual to tend to the crypts, but she supervised the shift change herself when she arrived earlier in the evening. Everyone was accounted for, so the crypts should have been empty save for herself and Tarl.

That left only one possible explanation.

Bodysnatchers…

Everything had a price on the streets of Lowtown, even the dead. City laws banned the Undertakers Guild from trafficking in corpses centuries ago, but there was still a strong demand for intact bodies, especially from alchemists, aspiring surgeons, and sorcerers in neighboring districts. Although independent collectors still gathered the dead from residences and back alleys, they were prohibited from selling the bodies to anyone but the undertakers. Many corpses, of course, never made their way to the grave or the Deadhouse; family members instead sold their deceased loved ones to body smugglers for a handful of quartermarks in the poorest boroughs. Several mortuary supervisors had even been arrested for cutting backdoor deals with bodysnatcher gangs to make corpses vanish in the night.

Again, Calandra considered running to summon Keldun, but she doubted she could move through the dark tunnel quickly without drawing attention to herself. Even if she could alert him, there was no telling how many body snatchers were down there or if any of them were armed. Her warning could well lead him to his death.

But curiosity held her fast more than any concern for safety. She tried to work out how they got into the crypts without being seen. They could not have tunneled in from outside; the earth surrounding the crypts was far too rocky. The mortuary's outer and inner gates, not to mention the heavy door that led down to the crypts themselves, remained locked during the night.

Could they have slipped inside during the day?

She would not put it past Lerris to turn a blind eye to the intrusion, provided she got a few marks for her trouble. That might explain her poor attention to the bodies stashed in the crypts. She could easily make a body or two "disappear" from the records in exchange for a bit of coin.

As Calandra worked out possible scenarios, two more figures joined the one standing in the tunnel. Although the light was too dim for her to make out many details, the new arrivals were much bigger, their upper bodies bulging with enough musculature to pull their spines over into a permanent hunch.

Both of them carried a limp corpse under each arm.

The first figure whispered something and turned to follow the tunnel deeper into the crypts. Corpses in hand, the other two followed obediently, but slowly, moving at an almost plodding pace. The light gradually dimmed as they descended, fading away entirely as they moved around a bend in the tunnel.

Calandra gasped for a lungful of stale air. She had been holding her breath since she happened upon the lantern light. For a moment, she considered following them, but she would have to relight her lantern before venturing any farther. Worse, if the intruders backtracked for any reason, she probably would not be lucky enough to avoid notice a second time.

"Miss Calandra?"

She nearly dropped her lantern at the sound of Tarl's voice. The big man had rolled his cart down to the crypts and now stood outside the storeroom where he left her.

Her stomach seized up, expecting the intruders to double back toward the sound at any moment. If they did, they would find her stumbling through the black and Tarl meandering obliviously towards them. She thought of the massive, hunchbacked figures effortlessly carrying a body under each arm and what those brutish limbs could do to her slender, fragile body.

But no light appeared from the deepest reach of the tunnel. If the strange figures heard Tarl's calls, they remained indifferent.

Calandra moved back towards the glow of Tarl's lantern.

"I'm down here," she said.

She knew she should tell Tarl about her discovery, that they should inform Keldun and close off the crypts until the local watch patrol could be alerted, but instead she found herself formulating excuses for why she was wandering down the pitch-black tunnel with an extinguished lantern.

The intruders had gone deeper into the crypts despite already carrying as many corpses as seemed possible. Unless they meant to hide out in the darkness until they could slip out during the day, they must have had some way of getting inside from deep below. Could there be some ancient passageway connecting the crypts to the surface? A forgotten escape route for the heathen cults that once spilled sacrificial blood on the stone and soil floors?

If she let slip someone had infiltrated the storehouses, there would be dozens of mortuary workers and hired guards on patrol during the next several nights. And if someone within the mortuary were involved with the theft, which she strongly suspected, the thieves would be warned of the increased vigilance.

When she reached Tarl, she was ready to feed him a story about how she had chased a rat away from the room, that the wind had blown out her lantern as she ran. A flimsy excuse, perhaps, but Tarl was probably simple enough to believe it. She forced herself to breathe more quickly, hopefully convincing him that she had actually been running.

None of it was necessary.

"You ought to be more careful down here, Miss Calandra. Easy to get lost in the dark."

Tarl said no more about the situation. He helped her relight her lantern and went about setting the other corpses onto the cart.

KELDUN WAS WAITING for Calandra when she emerged from the crypts.

"Fresh meat for you."

Dammit. Not now.

She needed to check the crypt records against the actual body count in the storerooms. If there were no discrepancies, then somebody, probably that snake Lerris, had tampered with the records to help the bodysnatchers make off with corpses unnoticed. The process would take most of the night and she did not want to waste precious time preparing a new stiff for identification.

"Did they bring it in yet?"

"No," Keldun said. "Not sure where you'll want this one."

Calandra scowled as she stepped around him.

Another messy one, probably.

A small group of armed men, all of them clad in the well-worn gear of the Pigshire Watch, stood just inside the mortuary's front gate. They had pushed a wheelbarrow inside, but they made an obvious effort to keep some distance from it while they waited for her. The wheelbarrow was a bit small, so the arms and legs of the corpse inside had spilled over the top of the bucket. Even in the dim light of the gate's lanterns, the body's clothes and skin glistened with a slick coating of some viscous liquid.

When Calandra emerged from the mortuary, one of the guards stepped forward to intercept her. She recognized Rheinmak's contemptuous scowl immediately.

Not this gutterscum. Not tonight.

"Evening, Captain," she said, bowing her head slightly.

Rheinmak greeted her with a foul, snarling expression. She guessed it might have been his best attempt at a smile. He looked her in the eye for only a moment before his gaze drifted down to the base of her neck where a few wayward strands of brown hair brushed delicately against her dark skin.

Calandra cursed herself for not wrapping her shawl around her neck and shoulders before stepping outside to greet the visitors. Despite her attire's modesty, she felt exposed under Rheinmak's penetrating leer. She wanted to push away from him, to throw some kind of barrier between the two of them. Like a petulant child unable to get its way, she crossed her arms tightly against her chest, as if her flesh and bone limbs could somehow protect her from the hard, ravening eyes regarding her.

"How can I help you, Captain?" she said, scarcely able to force the words through her nearly clenched teeth.

Rheinmak flashed his awful grin again before snapping his fingers at his men.

"Got a nice one for you tonight," he said, his gaze still lingering on Calandra. "Didn't think you'd want this one dumped on your stoop, though."

One of the guards pushed the wheelbarrow towards the mortuary's inner door. As it came closer, the unmistakable stench of raw sewage hit Calandra hard. Years of working closely with dead bodies had toughened her stomach and taught her mind to ignore whatever foul odors they emitted, but she was unaccustomed to the fetor of highly concentrated human waste.

She covered her mouth as the guard brought the wheelbarrow alongside her.

"Dump it there," she said, indicating a patch of ground far from the door.

Rheinmak was still staring at her when she looked back to him, and she quickly crossed her arms again to deny him an uncontested examination of her body.

The wet stench clung to the air, pressing in on her skin and clothing.

"Where did you find it?" she asked, trying to keep her voice as cold and distant as possible.

Rheinmak snorted, but he finally stopped staring at her, instead turning to watch his man tip the wheelbarrow forward to dump the body onto the ground.

"Poor bastard fell into the privy in his place over on High Cross Street. Nobody there knew him by name."

Calandra glanced at the body. *How could they make anything of this mess?*

"Are you investigating the death?" she asked.

Rheinmak smiled and laughed. It was a cruel, harsh sound. "He fell into a cesspit. Case closed."

Asshole.

"Fine, then," she said. "Do you remember the house number where you found him?"

Rheinmak was looking at her neck again. "Twelve. Or maybe eleven."

Calandra had had enough. There was no point in prolonging their uncomfortable exchange. She turned sharply and strode back to the door. "Thank you, Captain. You and your men know the way out."

Rheinmak said something, but she ignored it.

If you have something worth hearing, you can leave a bloody message at the door.

Calandra left the ordure-coated body lying outside in a heap. She would send Tarl and a few others to fetch buckets of water and clean it off before they hauled it inside for examination. If the body had drowned in a privy, there would be sewage in the lungs to be pumped out.

That would be a messy and unpleasant task.

She wished the morning would come sooner.

5
THE HEIR

E mber Morangine's chair creaked as he leaned back and folded his slender arms against his chest. He sat at the far end of a semicircular table overlooking the mass of petitioners gathered in the hall, most of them waiting impatiently to bring their various claims, cases, and complaints before Coldwater borough's Assembly of Notables. As the highest political and legal authority in Lowtown, the Assembly managed finances, oversaw courts, and contracted services throughout the district. There had been a time when Coldwater's Assembly was one of several, each one representing a different borough, but centuries of institutional decay had eroded their power and legitimacy. Now the Crown and the city's Law and Commerce Diets recognized no other authority in Lowtown.

Several assemblymen watched Ember closely, some no doubt taking their lead from his actions. Although young for a member of the assembly, he held his seat by right of title, the same as his father and grandmother before him. A distant cousin of the Margrave, his status and blood elevated him above his baser colleagues, most of whom only held their position through bribery, patronage, or extortion.

Year after year, the Assembly of Notables's composition changed, but Ember was still there. Like his father and grandmother before him, he would hold his seat until death pried him away from it.

He glared at the man standing before the Assembly, already frustrated by the debate his presence would no doubt instigate.

"Must we hear this petition now?" he asked. "Surely there will be ample opportunity for this body to—"

The ambassador from the Spaders Guild stomped his boot against the hall's marble floor.

"Am I to understand that the Assembly of Notables now picks and chooses which petitions it will hear? By what right does—?"

A woman's voice, stern and sharp, interrupted him from the other end of the semi-circular table.

Trinn Harmyndri. Of course, it would be you, wouldn't it?

Unlike her peers, Trinn was one of only three Assembly members who owed her seat to the capricious will of the mob, elected every year by a plebiscite of citizens from throughout the district.

"Pay no mind to Lord Morangine's bellyaching, Ambassador," she said. "Enough of this body remains bound to its sacred trust to keep him from denying the good, working people of this city their rightful voice."

Scattered laughter rang out from the gallery of petitioners, and not a few Assembly members.

Ember scowled.

Lord *Morangine, is it? Self-righteous bitch.*

"Very well," he said. "Have your say, spader. I'm sure you bring news of such immeasurable significance that the Margrave himself will hear tell of its profundity before we adjourn for the day."

The ambassador glared at him before answering with a curt bow. He then launched into his well-rehearsed speech regarding the pending expiration of the guild's contract with the Assembly to keep the streets clear of waste and refuse.

Ember knew all the particulars. The harangue had changed little since the first time he heard it many years ago. A lengthy recounting of the long relationship between the guild and the Assembly, the poor state of the Lowtown streets before the first contract, the many generations of reliably skilled service, and so on.

It was all he could do to keep from rolling his eyes. Guilds were supposed to be associations of specialized tradesmen, after all. Ember failed to see what could possibly be so special about shoveling dung.

The only thing that ever seemed to change about the speech was the conclusion, the rather pivotal bit about the next contract's price.

Damned leeches, that's what you are.

This year, the ambassador announced that the guild's fees would increase by five percent, a full point higher than last year.

"Five percent?" Ember asked. "Do you intend to hand out gilded shovels to newly fashioned journeymen?"

The comment drew a few laughs, not as many as Trinn's barb, but enough to remind the attendees that Ember yet held some sympathetic ears in the Assembly. Long ago, the Spaders Guild negotiated an addendum to its contract with the Assembly that allowed the agreement to renew automatically at a higher rate. The deal had been struck to avoid work stoppages, which might threaten the public health. While the Assembly reserved the right to not renew the contract, it had never introduced a measure to do so. Ember was not the only Assembly member who believed the arrangement had tilted heavily in the guild's favor in recent years.

"Lowtown's boroughs are packed more tightly every year, Assemblyman," the ambassador said. "Every extra mouth leads to more waste clogging the streets. The guild is stretched thinly enough as it is. Unless we expand our ranks, we estimate that a quarter of Lowtown's streets will be unpassable by winter. The five percent increase will help finance several new teams of journeymen spaders."

Ember grunted. "At several times the wage of a common laborer, I expect."

"A spader is far more than a common laborer, Assemblyman."

But he's still shoveling shit, isn't he?

"The Assembly will consider your proposal most carefully, Ambassador," Trinn said. "I'm sure I speak for the entire Assembly when I tell you how much we appreciate the guild's steadfast service to the six boroughs."

The ambassador smiled and bowed.

"I look forward to our negotiations, my lady."

My lady, indeed.

Ember scowled through the rest of the morning's petitions. Contract disputes, housing complaints, petty acts of violence, and the like. Few, if any, were distinguishable from the ones he heard yesterday, or the days—the weeks, even—before that. When he first assumed his father's seat in the Assembly, a handful of petitions managed to capture his fascination each day. Now, after five dreary years of the mundanity of daily governance, it took something truly remarkable to rouse him from his bored indifference.

No petitions rose to such lofty heights today.

Ithlene Beniquorra presided over the Assembly this morning. Some petitioners she hurried along, occasionally even threatening to have them removed if they failed to state their business quickly enough for her tastes. To others, however, she showed great deference, allowing them to take up a great deal more time even when their petition seemed of lesser import compared to others. In a few instances, she all but advocated on their behalf to the rest of the Assembly. A gifted orator with an acerbic wit and a keen legal mind, her grandstanding provided a welcome respite from the otherwise dull proceedings.

To the casual observer, her outbursts and favor seemed random, but Ember knew better. Like several other members of the Assembly, Ithlene owed her seat to the influence of Lowtown's brokers, the real power on the district's streets. A craven mixture of moneylenders, vice peddlers, and legbreaking thugs, the brokers kept a grip on several Assembly seats and the district's pitiful excuse for civil administration with a steady stream of bribes and well-placed threats. If political pets like Ithlene refused to govern to patron's liking, they were easily replaced by someone more pliable.

Given her long tenure in the Assembly, Ithlene obviously knew how to appease her benefactors. Ember did not mind her compromised integrity, but he did wish she could be a bit more subtle about it. There was a crass banality to her corruption, blindingly obvious to any dimwitted, baseborn petitioner who cared to observe how she treated the cases brought before her.

Obviously, she never received the advice Ember's father gave him: *"Never let anyone see who benefits from your decisions. A disagreement between two men is a matter of course and easily stomached, but when a man believes the world is against him, he fosters a vengeful hatred that can only be quenched by violence."*

His grandmother, of course, made the same point in much simpler, if cruder, terms: *"Corruption's like shit, boy. Nobody much minds the smell so long as you don't shove their noses in it."*

So far, though, Ithlene had avoided any such retribution. That was just as well as far as Ember was concerned. He knew how to leverage her corruption against her when he needed her support on important Assembly rulings. For all her bluster and bravado, Ithlene was easily controlled. She had no beliefs worth clinging to, no moral integrity she feared to compromise.

Ember would happily replace one sanctimonious crusader like Trinn with a dozen Ithlenes.

The crowd gathered near the hall's entrance dwindled steadily after midday. More petitioners would be standing outside, of course, most having waited all day to come before the Assembly. Some would return home for the evening and try their luck tomorrow. The more determined among them would sit on the cold cobblestones along Vinewall Street all night, waiting for the hall's doors to open a few hours after sunrise. Since her election to the Assembly, Trinn had made a habit of visiting them on her way home, sometimes even hearing their petitions on the spot.

Ember recalled something his grandmother used to say about stray animals: *"Better off killing a stray cat than feeding it, otherwise a whole flock of them will wind up pissing and fucking outside your window."*

After hearing the final petitioner for the day, Ithlene called the Assembly to attention with a single strike of her gavel, which roused the two members who had dozed off during the proceedings.

"Now, then," she said, "is there any more business for the Assembly to attend to on this day or shall we adjourn to tend to personal affairs?"

Ember rose from his seat.

"This body has yet to debate the matter of the Spaders Guild contract," he said. "Three times now the guild's ambassador has come to fling its demands upon the borough and each time elicited little more than a shrug from my esteemed colleagues. I should like to know if my fellow Assembly members intend to hand the whole of the treasury, meager though it may be, over to a motley gang of simple laborers playing at being skilled tradesmen."

A few Assembly members groaned. They were well accustomed to Ember's tirades against Lowtown's various guilds. Others, however, leaned forward to give him their full attention. His position that the Spaders Guild and their like had grown too powerful for its own good was not without supporters.

Trinn stood, scowling. "As I'm sure you're well aware, the guild's contract will not renew for another three months. I hardly see the need to—"

"Three months might as well be three days," Ember said. "Are we to simply cross off the date from last year's contract and add another digit to the payment total without so much as a discussion? Surely it's in the borough's interest to negotiate the best deal it can obtain?"

"This body's relationship with the Spaders Guild has proven mutually beneficial for far longer than either of us have served as members, Assemblyman."

Mutually beneficial! Hardly a way to describe a parasite's relation to its unwitting host.

"With all due respect, Assemblywoman Trinn, given your ongoing associations with the leading members of several guilds, I don't think—"

Trinn slammed her fist down on the table. "I will not apologize for consulting with the very citizens who have entrusted me to represent them in this Assembly! Perhaps you would better understand the responsibilities of your position had you not inherited it thanks to the happenstance of an archaic tradition."

Several Assembly members gasped, and a few drew back from the table, obviously fearful that a shouting match might break out. Ithlene struck the gavel again and stabbed her finger in Trinn's direction.

"That's quite enough, Trinn! You've been warned to keep that sort of talk in check on many occasions. When I'm chairing this body, you will address your fellow Assembly members with respect or I'll call for a vote of censure. Do I make myself clear?"

Trinn refused to even look at Ithlene, instead glaring at Ember as he eased into his chair with a thinly concealed smirk.

Go on, then, girl; speak your mind. Let's see where those fancy ideals of yours get you.

Much to Ember's disappointment, Trinn took her seat with a scowl.

"My apologies," she said.

"I take no offense, of course," Ember said, knowing full well that the words were not directed at him, "but I appreciate your humility all the same."

Trinn shot him a hateful look, but she kept her mouth shut this time.

Pity...

"Now then," Ithlene said, "I believe Assemblyman Ember wished to make a point about the pending negotiations with the Spaders Guild?"

THE MORANGINE ESTATE hardly qualified as servants' housing by the standards of Blackspire's wealthier northern districts, but it easily ranked among the most impressive residences in Lowtown. Situated within walking distance of the Coldwater Assembly Hall, the manse was large enough to house a dozen people comfortably. A high stone wall tipped with curved, wrought iron bars discouraged unwelcome visitors and shut the estate grounds off from the bustling activity on the surrounding streets.

What did it matter that dry, shriveled vines covered much of the once resplendent yard, or that all but one of the great manse's wings remained shuttered off, left unused for decades? Passersby still gazed and gawked at the lofty parapets behind the estate's imposing wall, dreaming of what it must be like to live in such luxury. Some of them even remembered that the Morangine family once ruled over Coldwater borough as a personal fiefdom, a reward for assisting the Margrave in some civil war or another many centuries ago.

For Ember Morangine, however, those days were little more than a bitter dream. Each successive generation saw his family's fortunes diminish, the gradual decay of the Morangine estate providing a potent symbol of that decline. Occasionally the lineage chanced to produce an exceptional scion who managed to arrest the deterioration, a clarion echo of far more potent ancestors. Ember's grandmother had been such an exemplar. At the height of her influence, even the Margrave took council with her on all matters concerning Lowtown and its boroughs. But age and blood eventually betrayed her, leaving the family's revived fortunes in the profligate hands of Ember's father, who spoke wisely, yet seemed incapable of following that counsel. By the time he took his own life, he left his only child an inheritance of debt and humiliation. After selling off what little property holdings the family yet retained to pay off his father's creditors, Ember had nothing left to his name but the crumbling Morangine estate and the meager salary from his family's ancestral Assembly seat.

He pulled the tarred stopper from the bottle and poured two fingers worth of black spirits into a glass. After returning the bottle to the cabinet, he swirled the liquid around and around, watching it slosh up a hairsbreadth short of the brim.

Trinn's sanctimonious voice still echoed in his head.

That bitch will be the death of me yet...

"A trying day, was it, sir?"

Ember had not heard Yimina enter the room before she deigned to speak. The manse's cavernous chambers and moldering timbers swallowed up all but the loudest noises. Sometimes it took hours for his steward to notice his return from his daily business.

"No more than most," he said.

Yimina chuckled behind him. Ember could picture the wry grin on her face without bothering to turn around.

"A lie," she said. "You wouldn't be at your grandmother's brine sap otherwise."

Ember looked at the black liquid swirling at the bottom of the glass. He had forgotten the exact vintage long ago, but it was old, far older than his grandmother, even. A single sip dried out his mouth, like swallowing a mouthful of salt. The burning sensation followed, leaving his tongue tingling and numb.

"She would understand," he said.

"Of course."

He set the glass down and removed his coat. Yimina stepped around him to take the garment before he could toss it over a nearby chair. She wore her blonde hair up today, which highlighted the gray strands nearest her scalp. Her faded black dress looked dangerously close to being tattered, much like Ember's own garments.

His father would disapprove of that, he knew. The man always put such a premium on appearances. Then again, his father's desperate need to project an image of wealth drove the family into debt and to the very brink of ruin.

"Something wrong, sir?"

Yimina's concern only served to highlight her many wrinkles, the worry lines along her forehead, the crows' feet at the corner of her eyes. She wore her years well for being some fifteen years older than Ember, but certain expressions exposed her age more than others. He knew every one of those lines, had watched most of them grow out of nothing. Yimina was the first face he could remember seeing, only one of many firsts she embodied.

First caregiver. First friend. First teacher. First protector. First advisor. First lover.

"It's nothing," he said. "Nothing out of the ordinary, at least."

"I see," she said, folding his coat over her arm. "A...gentleman delivered a message for you after your departure this morning. I left it there." She gestured to the table along the back wall of the study.

He took another sip of the brine sap. The first drink was already tickling at the back of his skull.

"What sort of 'gentleman'?"

"The sort I'd prefer to keep on the other side of a locked door. Stank of swine and piss and looked like he'd spent the night in a cesspit trench."

Could describe most of Lowtown.

Ember walked to the table and retrieved the letter, which was still sealed with a glob of wax. The seal bore no signet mark that might have identified its origins. He broke the wax and unfolded the letter.

> *Returned and waiting.*
> *You know where to find me.*
> *Three days or I'm gone.*
> *—K*

"About damn time," Ember said, almost to himself.

"What was that?"

He scrunched the letter up and looked at Yimina. Her dress hung loosely from her shoulders, looking more like something a lowly housemaid might wear. Of course, she was probably been cleaning before Ember returned home that afternoon. If she was not tending to him in some capacity, she spent most of her time waging a hopeless, one-woman war against the manse's steady deterioration.

"Change into something more presentable," he said. "We're going out."

"Is this a social visit, sir, or business?"

"I think you can guess, can't you?"

Yimina nodded. "I'll bring a blade, then."

Ember drank the last of the brine sap, wincing as the searing stuff trickled down his throat.

"Best bring the knives as well."

"THERE ARE TWO rules that have never steered me wrong, boy: never trust a man who doesn't drink, and never do business with a man who won't swear."

Somehow, Ember doubted his grandmother had the patrons of *The Broken Boot* in mind when she shared that parcel of wisdom.

Situated on the eastern side of Cadgerwalk borough, the winesink got its name from the pile of ruined shoes stacked up as high as a man next to the door. The proprietor had a brother or a cousin (Ember could not recall which) in with one of the tanneries in neighboring Pigshire. He gave out a cup of ale or wine to anyone who handed over their old shoes. Word was that he sold the leather to be reused as scrap, which probably brought him a good deal more coin than a tenthmark for some sour wine.

Naturally, the place stank of sweaty feet, and fights inevitably broke out after some drunkard mashed a boot on another fool's exposed toe. On Ember's last visit, some braggart groped at Yimina's breasts when she walked by him.

Her blade nicked an artery in his arm when she lashed out, which sent the man screaming into the streets. They never bothered to find out if he lived or bled out in some filth-encrusted alley.

Neither of them cared, really.

Ember had dressed down for the visit as best he could, but even his most threadbare coat probably cost more than some of the *Boot's* patrons made in a year. Yimina's attire stood out quite a bit less, or at least it would have if she were a man. Although new fashions steadily trickled down to the slums of Lowtown from Blackspire's more cosmopolitan districts, a woman in pants and a buff coat was still unusual enough to attract attention anywhere in the city, especially one wearing a sword at her side.

"What's this brute's name again?" he asked Yimina as they approached the entrance. The pile of boots stood almost as high as the doorframe today.

"The foreign one? Raugov."

Ember paused outside the door and took a deep breath. The air reeked of stale sweat and spoiled meat.

Gods, I hate this place.

"Let's get this over with."

The interior smelled twice as bad as the outside. Heavy curtains covered the windows, so even during the daylight hours, the place remained as gloomy as a mine shaft. More than twenty men milled about inside, most of them clustered in groups around the high tables scattered about the common room, none of which had chairs or stools lest the patrons grow too comfortable and overstay their welcome. A few women drifted among the drunkards, some carrying jugs of wine while others traipsed before the men to draw their attention and affections. Like most of Lowtown's winesinks, *The Broken Boot* tolerated the presence of common street whores provided they did not start any trouble.

Ember made his way to the main serving bar with Yimina following close behind. A bearded man handed out ale in exchange for coin and worn out footwear, pausing occasionally to exchange pleasantries, or trade insults, with men he obviously knew. It took Ember a few tries to wave the man down, but he finally ambled over.

"Help you, friend?"

"I'm here to see Raugov."

The bearded man looked him over, then glanced at Yimina.

"Aye. He said a fine-looking fellow might come calling on him. Up the stairs with the rest of his boys. Can't miss him."

He pointed to the staircase at the opposite end of the room, but Ember already knew the way.

"Come on," he said to Yimina. "And don't take your eyes off him when we get up there."

"I could use an extra set in this place."

Ember did not disagree.

A burly man stood at the bottom of the stairs, his arms crossed and his cleft lip sneering. He wore a wide leather belt with a hatchet slipped prominently through a loop near the buckle. His fingers twiddled against the metal blade as Ember and Yimina approached.

Ember could tell from the thug's posture that he did not consider them a threat. He was flatfooted, his considerable weight shifted back on his heels. If things turned ugly, the spring-loaded knives hidden up Yimina's sleeves could slit his throat before his fat fingers managed to pull the hatchet in his belt free.

He would hardly be the first fool to underestimate her.

"I'm here to see—"

"I know why you're here, rich man," the guard said. "Seen you get pointed this way. Mr. Raugov's expecting you." He pointed at the sword dangling from Yimina's side. "Your lady friend there, she's going to have to leave that blade with me if she wants to go with you."

Ember expected as much, so he nodded and signaled for Yimina to comply.

He also expected that the half-witted thug would never think to search her for hidden weapons.

"Go on up, then," the man said, tucking the sheathed blade under his arm as he stepped aside.

Idiot.

The stairs led up to a single room lit by an iron candelabrum suspended from the ceiling by a single length of chain. A round table stood in the center, around which sat six men playing some sort of dice game Ember did not recognize.

One of the men stood out from the others, a hardened cutter with olive-tinged skin and a tangle of wiry, copper hair. He wore a sleeveless coat covered with fishscales, a fashion rarely seen in Blackspire. Ember guessed he was from somewhere to the south, probably the Sarathane Islands, but verifying the man's origins was not among his priorities.

"Morangine," he said, his accent as coarse as the sands of whatever godsforsaken shore he had sailed from. "Expected to see you sooner."

"Raugov," Ember said as he circled the table, regarding the other men engaged in the game. None of them looked nasty enough to be Raugov's men. Probably unlucky sods from below hoping to swindle a few marks with a lucky run of dice.

Judging by the size of their winnings, luck was not with them today.

"Care to join us for a few throws?" Raugov asked.

"Oh, no. I do my best to avoid games of chance where coin is involved. It's a vice that runs too deeply in the blood to risk indulging, I'm afraid."

Raugov sniggered. "Pity. Some of this lot would benefit from another fool at the table."

Three of the players laughed uneasily, but the other two remained sullen faced.

They're already in the hole. Stupid bastards, don't you know who this cutter works for?

Ember reached into his coat pocket and withdrew a sealed letter. "I have something for your boss."

"Let's have a look, then." Raugov snatched the letter from his hand, cracked the seal, and unfolded the paper. He stared at it for several seconds, his eyes scarcely moving over the script. Ember doubted Raugov could actually read, but guessed that, like most illiterate Lowtowners, he could recognize street names when he saw them.

"You can tell him that he has three days to collect his prize, but I'd get around to it sooner if I were him."

Raugov grunted and placed the letter on the table. He pushed a small stack of marks into the center of the table. "Next roll," he said, reaching for the bone dice. "Breaking low."

Ember hated being ignored. He slammed his hand down over the dice before Raugov could snatch them up. "I've kept my end of the bargain, Raugov. Do I have your boss's assurance that he'll keep his?"

Raugov glared at him and sneered, his lips pulling back to reveal teeth filed down to sharp points. "Mister Dhrath always keeps his word, Morangine. If you've done as you've said, he'll stand by it. If not...well, I don't need to tell you what'll happen then, do I?"

"I don't much appreciate threats," Ember said, "especially when I've shown nothing but good faith in all our dealings and have naught to show for it."

Raugov clamped his hand over Ember's and squeezed. "Who's making threats, Assemblyman?"

Pain shot up Ember's forearm. He clenched his teeth to keep from crying out.

Raugov smiled again. "You'd better think long and hard before you go making an accusation like that."

EMBER WAS STILL cradling his hand when they reached the outskirts of Coldwater borough.

"You really should let me look at that, sir," Yimina said.

"I'm fine, dammit!"

The skin around his wrist had already bruised up, but he was pretty sure nothing was broken. His pride hurt far worse than his hand, anyway.

That bastard. Who does he think he is?

"If you'd told me you were going to provoke him like that, I would have—"

"Would have what? Put a knife in his chest? Where would we be then? Throwing a year's worth of planning into a cesspit for the sake of teaching some foreign mongrel a lesson, that's where we'd be."

Yimina hung her head while Ember ranted. "I'm sorry, sir. I just—"

"Forget it," Ember said, his mood darkening with every step. "It was my fault. I should know better than to expect any measure of courtesy from scum like that."

Damn you, Dhrath. Damn you and all your legbreaking brutes.

"I don't see why you keep debasing yourself to stay in this broker's good graces."

"Because I need him," Ember said, his temper slipping away. "He's got the watch under his slimy tentacles, and without the watch on my side, all of this will be for nothing. And I don't need to be reminded of that fact again, thank you."

Yimina took the hint and remained silent for the rest of the walk back to the manse while Ember sulked and glowered.

Once they were back inside, Ember went to his desk and hurriedly penned another letter. His hand ached as he scribbled the message.

"Don't bother changing," he said. "I need you to deliver this message."

"Where?"

"Our friend over in Sinkhole. She'd best know that we'll be getting underway soon."

"Is she ready?"

Ember shrugged as he folded the letter and sealed it with a glob of hot wax.

Whether she was ready or not hardly mattered to him. He was tired of dealing with Raugov and his broker boss, tired of watching his family estate crumble to bits around him, and most of all, he was tired of listening to the demands of the damned Spaders Guild every day.

One way or another, he was ready to put all of that behind him.

6

THE DEALERS

Crammed between the eastern boundary of Coldwater and the sludgy waters of the Saven River, the Spaders Guild's work yard almost took up enough space to be considered a borough unto itself. The guildhall stood near the center of the area, an ugly, squat building of wood and stone rebuilt nearly a century ago using the materials from the previous hall. That reconstruction project was not undertaken out of some desire to aggrandize the guild, but rather out of vulgar necessity since portions of the old building were collapsing after years of neglect. Many spaders, noting the current structure's sagging walls and uneven roof, grumbled that it was already nearing time for another such renovation.

Although the large hall housed the guild's administrative heart, the barns and storehouses located in the yard area behind the hall saw the most frequent activity during both day and night. The old wagons that transported waste from all parts of the city to be dumped in the outflowing waters of the Saven were stored there, along with the gigantic muls responsible for pulling them. On the training grounds, young initiates learned to withstand the more unpleasant aspects of their occupation by having their heads dunked in barrels of piss and their clothes filled with waste. Work crews assembled in all parts of the yard throughout the day, receiving orders to clean up streets all across the city. Work details flowed continually out to the yard from the guild secretaries inside the deteriorating hall.

Several rows of hand-operated water pumps stood at the far end of the yard near the river. Connected to the Saven by a series of pipes and meandering channels, the pumps stayed busiest during shift changes. Spaders returning from their odious duties clustered around them, waiting for the chance to douse themselves and their equipment with water drawn from the river. Although the Saven's slow moving waters were hardly pure, they were sufficient to wash away the filth of a spader's day. In most cases, a spader only needed a few minutes to clean his gear with water and rags, but anyone unlucky enough to clean out privies or cesspits could be stuck by the pumps for much longer, often resorting to coarse soaps and heavy brushes to scour away the more pungent effluents they encountered during their shift.

The sun was already up by the time Grisel finished sluicing the gunk from his clothes and skin. Meaty and Jaspen laughed when they walked by him, still scrubbing the privy's stench out of his leathers.

"Missed a spot," Meaty said.

Jaspen, as usual, was not so good-natured. "Why all the fuss, mate? That sow back at your place is used to rolling in mud anyway!"

Grisel snarled something back at them, some crass assemblage of non-sense tossed together in a pitiful attempt at wit. He barely even remember what he said by the time they were gone.

It probably sounded stupid, though. He was pretty sure of that.

After he cleaned his gear, he grabbed his shovel and made his way to the quartermaster's desk, located on the ground floor of the guildhall. The building's interior was as shoddily constructed as the outside. Every piece of wood and stone looked a little crooked; if the builders responsible for the hall possessed a plumb-bob level of any kind, apparently none of them knew how to use it. Poorly reinforced walls sagged under the weight of the heavy ceiling and the uneven floorboards could be a serious tripping hazard in poor light.

Nobody in the guild really cared whether or not the building was an embarrassment. Much like the spaders themselves, it served a utilitarian function that did not call for lavish aggrandizement. When the hall finally deteriorated to the point of uselessness, it would be rebuilt again, probably badly. Until then, the guild would continue to conduct its unending business within those slowly crumbling walls without complaint.

The quartermaster's desk was the hall's main hub of activity during shift changes. He had the responsibility of tracking the many services spader crews provided throughout the city. If a crew did anything more than cleaning the streets, such as unclogging an overburdened sewage channel or emptying waste from the gutters after residents decided to use them as a makeshift privy, the work had to be reported to the quartermaster so the guild could assess and collect the appropriate fees.

Like most spaders, Grisel was only slightly literate. He knew enough script to sign his name and recognize important words like street names, but he could only express a few rudimentary ideas in writing. Unable to deliver a written report to the quartermaster, he had to relay the information orally.

Unfortunately, that meant waiting in line.

The line moved quickly, but Grisel still resented the lost time. On most days, he was simply eager to join Meaty and Jaspen at the tavern, but today he had other plans. His hand slipped into his pocket several times to hold the small chunk of black stone he recovered from the corpse.

Got to be worth something.

The quartermaster was a fat slob of a man, his sweaty girth oozing over the table as he scribbled line after line into his ledgers. He rarely looked up at the spaders dutifully filing past his table. Every report received the same mindless attention, his fleshswollen jowls quivering in time with the staccato movements of his pen.

"Name...? Crew...? Service...? Client...? Address...? Time...?"

Despite his disorderly physical appearance, the quartermaster worked with a peerless, and ruthless, efficiency. He never followed up on his basic questions, just moved down to the next heading on the page after every response. Sometimes the spader failed to provide the necessary information, but the quartermaster was not so much irked as disappointed by such omissions. He handed out no reprimands, but a scolding probably would have been preferable to his silent, condescending judgment.

The spader in front of Grisel gave his report quickly. Like the men before him, he stood dutifully by the desk until the quartermaster dismissed him with a limp wave of his fat hand.

Grisel ran his information through his head while he waited to be called forward. He gave a wrong address to the quartermaster once during his second apprentice year and lost his pay for a week as punishment. The penalty was supposed to teach him to be more attentive to details, but all it really did was make him even more paranoid about making mistakes.

Then again, maybe there was little difference between attentiveness and paranoia.

"Next."

He stepped forward and responded to the quartermaster's prompts with a practiced mindlessness. The information was recorded into the guild ledgers so it could be referenced when the Lowtown watch rendered payment for Grisel's services. If the payment failed to arrive within a month or so, the bookkeepers reviewing the guild's exhaustive records on the guildhall's second floor would make note of the discrepancy and send a collection bill to the watch. It was a tediously complicated system that Grisel did not understand very well, but he recognized the importance of rending an accurate report.

The quartermaster gave no reaction beyond scribbling the information into his ledger with sharp, concise pen strokes that seemed to record far more than Grisel's simplistic responses. He drew a firm, almost violent line under the entry to separate it from the next report and sent Grisel on his way.

"Next."

LOWTOWN'S FILTHY STREETS already teemed with activity by the time sunlight spilled over the city's towering outer wall. The district may have lacked the prosperous craft guilds, factory houses, and trade emporiums of neighboring Spiresreach, but the signs of a vibrant, if lower order, economy could be found everywhere. People and livestock crowded through the narrow, winding course of Vinewall Street as it snaked through Coldwater borough, a great mass of stink and sweat every bit as sluggish as the choked waters of the Saven.

Rival street venders struggled jealously to secure the best locations for their carts, most of them stuffed with aging foodstuffs no longer fit to be consumed by the city's more prosperous denizens. Unable to afford fresh shipments from beyond the city, Lowtown's merchants purchased whatever went unsold in nearby districts and hauled it back by the bucketful to replenish their carts. They called out to passersby, each one declaring his pile of moldering produce the finest available south of the river.

Few Lowtowners were deceived, however, and drove a hard bargain after the best pieces were picked over soon after they arrived. The venders were quick to cut such deals to avoid having to dump most of their rotting stock in the back alleys to be consumed by rats and other scavengers. Stray dogs lingered near most of the carts, drawn by the strong odor of squishy, overripe fruits. Vendors kept them at bay with long sticks, poking at the mongrels' thin ribcages and hissing at them to be on their way.

The ground floors of several tenements had been converted into makeshift storefronts, the occupants peddling whatever meager selection of goods they managed to fabricate in the rooms above. Families mobilized their households like tiny factories, churning out low quality clothing, poorly dyed fabrics, and crude tools. Aside from a few couriers and destitute orphans, few children scurried along the streets. Most of them were locked inside the windowless rooms of cramped tenements, working under the slightly more skilled direction of their elders. Children too small for such labor lurked along the edges of the street, waiting to waylay anyone who looked like they had enough coin to purchase whatever wares their families had for sale. When an unwary mark strayed too close, the children shrieked loudly and rushed out to redirect him toward some hovel of a shop. They scuffled with one another for attention, and a good many were simply knocked aside by their annoyed targets. Flocks of black carrion birds circled low overhead and watched the seething crowd intently from their rooftop perches. They squawked excitedly at any disturbance, their shrill cries indistinguishable from those of the children below.

Rickety scaffolds covered many of the district's buildings and laborers swarmed over them like insects, sometimes tearing down crumbling walls and in other places erecting new edifices with reclaimed stone and lumber. Runners carried buckets of water and stone through the streets to impatient masons and salvaged bits of wood from forgotten alleyways. Some of the work sites were deemed important enough to warrant protection from off-duty watchmen, usually because the building's owner had some pull with a local watch officer. Armed mercenaries in the employ of local brokers supervised other construction sites, a constant reminder of who held the real power in the streets.

Watch patrols drifted through the streets at irregular intervals, travelling in groups of three or four men armed with maces and short swords. They broke up altercations and hauled any thieves they stumbled upon back to the nearest watchhouse for questioning. The beggars gathering near Vinewall's many intersections scanned constantly for signs of patrols, fearful of being arrested or beaten for vagrancy by one of the more cruelly arbitrary watch captains. Most of the district's homeless preferred to avoid the danger altogether, keeping out of sight in the back alleys where they waged a ceaseless war with stray animals for the right to sift through the borough's refuse.

The spire loomed over it all, a grim, black sentinel stabbing into the gray veil above the city. Situated north of Lowtown in the center of the city, the spire was the one common experience shared by Blackspire's residents both noble and small. Thrusting up from the earth to reach so high that the peak faded from sight, the spire remained visible in every district. Even visitors approaching Blackspire from many miles away could not see the very top of the ominous pillar. Although learned scholars from around the world had many theories about the spire's origins, no one knew how high it reached.

Grisel noticed none of this as he sifted through crowded streets. He might as well have stared at the sky, flummoxed by its unmoving vastness. The urban landscape was a natural environment to his senses, as mundane and predictable as a grassy hilltop. Unless some raucous disturbance caught his attention, he moved along as if he were the only living creature in the city, wholly unaware of the strangers brushing against him every few steps. Even the spire was a familiar sight to him, having lived under its shadow his entire life.

He veered off the stone surface of Vinewall Street and onto the uneven cobblestones of Rattlebone Way. The old, poorly maintained road got its name from the way it brutalized travellers while their carriage wheels rolled over the bulging cobblestones, most of them badly chipped and cracked. Unwary pedestrians could easily twist an ankle or stub a toe if they took a careless step.

Grisel, of course, had his own reason for hating the street: it was maddeningly difficult to shovel those damned cobblestones clean.

Rattlebone Way was not so busy as Vinewall, with fewer vender carts and more modest storefronts. Although quite a few more beggars gathered along the sides of the road, fewer people traversed it overall.

Several intersections came and went as he walked. Some of the streets proved more hospitable than others, but the overall quality of the road surfaces deteriorated as he moved farther from Vinewall.

He eventually reached a circular intersection that joined Rattlebone Way with seven other streets, each one stretching only a short distance before bending and disappearing behind a forest of decaying structures. A large, stone cistern in the center of the street had once collected rainwater for the surrounding residents, but now stood cracked and covered with black moss and ugly, thorn-laden vines. Rumors insisted that it had been a well once and was only converted to a cistern once it ran dry. The surrounding borough, Coldwater, was supposedly even named after it.

Maybe the ugly thing had been a point of pride once, but nobody had bothered tending to it for decades.

Grisel made for the squat building standing a short distance down the second muddy street to the left. No sign indicated the street's name, and for all he knew, it did not even have one. A crooked shingle, much too faded to read, stood above the building's entrance.

A small bell sounded when he pushed the door open and stepped inside.

The interior was completely black, the windows covered by heavy drapes. When the door closed behind him, Grisel could see nothing.

"Just a moment," a chiming, childish voice said.

A match sparked to life on the far side of the room to light an oil lantern. Dull, yellowish light filled the space, revealing the vast assortment of trinkets hanging from the walls and piled atop several tables.

The figure holding the lantern was slender and small, no more than half Grisel's height. Wrapped in a heavy, grayish-brown coat with green trim and an upturned collar, he looked like he was dressed for a snowstorm. His round little face was pale, almost corpselike, and his narrow mouth not much more than a faint line cut through the skin. A set of bulky goggles with shiny, black lenses covered his eyes and much of the face around them. Wispy strands of dark hair dangled over the leather straps.

"Good morning, friend Grisel," he said. The voice still sounded like a child's, but with a sort of shimmer to it, an accent he found all but impossible to place.

Grisel had only met a few ghulans in his lifetime, but the damned halfmen always sounded the same. He heard somewhere that it had to do with the way their tongues were shaped, but he had not plans to kiss one to find out.

He stepped into the middle of the room, carefully probing his dark surroundings to avoid crashing into any of the myriad items scattered across the floor.

"Sun ain't out today, Uthan," he said. "You could use some bloody light in this hole of yours."

"The sun is a cunning serpent, friend Grisel."

Grisel jumped at the voice lilting out of the darkness to his right. Carta, Uthan's wife, or pair or twin or whatever the hell the ghulans called it, slid from the shadows soundlessly. She was almost physically identical to Uthan, but her face was a bit narrower and her soft hair a queer shade falling somewhere between white and green. An identical set of heavy goggles covered her eyes; her coat was similar in style to his, but trimmed with blue rather than green.

"It slips under rocks and lurks in the moss," she said, drifting across the room toward Uthan.

"And waits for fools to misstep," Uthan said.

"Until it blinds with venom and kills with fang."

They spoke the last line of their little saying with one voice, as if they had rehearsed it before Grisel walked in on them.

He knew that was not the case, though. One of them always seemed to be finishing the other's thoughts. He asked them about it once, but they only smiled like a pair of bratty children who knew they had just gotten away with something.

The ghulans stood there staring at him. At least, it seemed like they were staring at him. He could not quite tell with those damned goggles strapped over their eyes. The halfmen spent most of their lives in the miles and miles of pitch-black caves beneath the Draakvale Mountains, far to the north of Blackspire. Many a talespinner claimed that even a glimpse of direct sunlight was enough to blind a ghulan forever, but Grisel was pretty sure that was a bunch of nonsense. Whatever the truth, though, Uthan and Carta certainly did their best to avoid the sun.

Grisel realized then that he was the one doing most of the staring, that they were politely waiting for him to explain what he was doing in their shop.

"Listen," he said, "I've got something I want you to have a look at."

He reached into his pocket and grasped the stone.

Carta took a step forward. "A mystery, we hope!"

"We see so few of them here," Uthan said.

"Trinkets and trifles and broken heirlooms," Carta said, sighing.

Grisel pulled out the black stone and showed it to ghulans. "I hope this don't get counted among them."

Carta leaned closer, her small tongue rubbing along her narrow upper lip.

Uthan reached for it, but hesitated. "May we?"

Grisel nodded and placed the chunk in his hand. The ghulan held it close to his goggles for a moment, then let Carta have a closer look.

"Very fine," she said.

Uthan nodded. "Yes. And old."

Grisel felt a few pounds lighter. *"Very fine"* sounded good enough on its own, but *"very fine"* and *"old"* sounded like a far more valuable combination.

"Where did you get it?" Carta asked.

Grisel felt heavy again. The ghulans never asked him where he got anything.

"I didn't steal it, if that's what you mean."

Carta giggled. "Of course not, friend Grisel."

"But the question stands all the same," Uthan said. "We've not seen its like here in Lowtown's quarries."

"Quarries?" Grisel asked, scratching his head. "There's no quarries around here."

Uthan smiled. "Gold and jewels and silver are mined from men as surely as the earth, friend Grisel."

"And Lowtown has such miners in abundance, yes?"

Grisel hated keeping up with their rambling metaphors, but he certainly saw some truth in Carta's observation. The Lowtown watch would struggle to keep all the cutpurses and muggers in line even if it was not on the take from the brokers and their gangs.

"Do you think it'll move for a good price?"

The ghulans looked up at him in unison.

"No."

Grisel tried to process their response, but he was much too tired to exhibit patience. "The fuck you mean, 'no?' You just said it was fine and old!"

Carta smiled, her cheeks quivering like she was trying to hold back laughter. Grisel wanted to smash his fist against that thin-lipped mouth of hers.

"You misunderstand us, friend Grisel," Uthan said.

"No one in this borough could afford such a treasure," Carta added.

Uthan grunted. "Probably no one in all of Lowtown."

"Or even Spiresreach."

Grisel was not sure if he should be excited or frustrated.

"So, what are you saying?" he asked. "Are you telling me nobody south of the river can afford what it's worth?"

The thought made him uneasy. He still had a hunch that the chunk of stone might have been lifted from an estate in one of the wealthier districts. Just showing it to some stiff-backed noblemen or north bank well-to-do could be enough to send his hand to a chopping block if news of such a theft became widely known.

The ghulans exchanged a glance.

"Difficult to say," Carta said.

"Not without a few inquries," Uthan added.

Inquiries were their specialty. The ghulans seemed to know everyone in the surrounding boroughs by name. Rumor on the streets claimed they were well-connected to a few of Lowtown's more powerful brokers, that their quaint little shop was something of a clearing house for the district's smugglers, moneylenders, and thieves.

Not that Grisel cared what went on there one bit. All he knew was the pair would pay good money for anything they considered valuable. Now that he had their interest, the only trick would be negotiating the price.

"Say you ask around? Think you'll find anyone that's interested?"

Uthan scratched his hairless chin. "There's always interest in such things."

"It's the willingness to make good on that interest that's in question," Carta said.

Will you get to the damned point?

"Right, I get it," he said. "But say you do find someone with both. How much do you think you can get for it?"

Uthan shrugged. "A thousand marks, perhaps?"

Grisel's jaw dropped. "A thousand marks? Full marks?"

Carta nodded. "Oh, certainly! Maybe even twice that."

Twice that…

He would have settled for a few dozen marks, but two thousand? That was far more than he made in a year, maybe even two years. Two thousand marks would pay off his apprenticeship debt to the Spaders Guild and perhaps leave enough to purchase a master's title. As a master, he would no longer be restricted to working out of the Lowtown guildhall.

He could sell his services independently north of the river, hiring his own journeymen and even taking on apprentices, for a fee, of course.

"You think you can find a buyer, then?" he asked, still in shock.

"Give us a few days," Uthan said.

Carta smiled that faint smile of hers again. "We know a few people with a taste for such things."

"We will show it to—"

"The hells you will!" Grisel snatched the black rock out of the ghulan's hand. "I'll be keeping it right here with me!"

He had no real reason to distrust them, but he was damned if he was going to leave his chance of crawling out of the Lowtown gutters in any hands but his own.

Uthan pulled his hand away and Carta let out a little gasp. Grisel could not tell if it was the sound of shock or outrage. He wished they would take their damned goggles off once in a while so he could at least read something, anything, from their eyes.

The ghulans looked at each other, their eyes hidden behind those black lenses, but they said nothing. Grisel wondered if they had some way of communicating silently. It seemed unlikely; ghulans could not mindspeak like cephalins, at least as far as he knew. Still, the pair always seemed to be able to convey a great deal without a single word or expression passing between them.

Carta finally shrugged slightly and Uthan nodded.

"As you wish," he said.

"But it could take us a bit longer."

Uthan retrieved a sheet of parchment from his desk and Carta took up a stylus.

"May we at least have a sketch to share?"

"Words are rarely enough to part a buyer from his coin."

Grisel consented to their practicality and handed the thing over. The ghulans passed it back and forth as they took turns scribbling across the parchment. They worked quickly and precisely, occasionally hissing little breaths through their narrow lips. Grisel disliked the sound of the native ghulani tongue; its faint, whispering rasps made the speakers sound especially devious and secretive.

After they finished, Carta passed the stone back to Grisel. He turned it over in his hand a few times, admiring the hard, irregular cuts that had hewn it down to its current size. The dark surface seemed to swallow the light surrounding it. He considered asking the ghulans about the stone's peculiarities, but he did not want to stick around in the dingy shop any longer than he had to.

"Right," he said. "Guess I should I check back with you in a few days?"

"Give us a week," Carta said.

"Yes, time to spread the word. More buyers means a better price, no?"

You mean a better cut for yourself.

He knew the ghulans would take some percentage of the sale as a fee for brokering a deal. If he thought he could find a buyer himself, he would have cut them out altogether. But the ghulans had the connections. They knew merchants and high-born nobles throughout Blackspire, whereas he rarely set foot outside of Lowtown and had never even been to the districts north of the Saven despite having lived in the city for his whole life.

Like it or not, he needed them.

BY THE TIME he finished with the ghulans, Grisel was much too tired to join his mates for a drink at the tavern. He took the fastest route back to his tenement, wading through the deep mud of Blackdirt Alley and braving the stench of Redfoot Street, where the butchers had already dumped the unused bits of the morning's first slaughter outside their doors.

But Grisel was willing to put up with some discomfort if it meant getting home faster. Whenever he sank ankle deep into the muck or tasted spoiled meat in the heavy, wet air, he imagined walking the clean, wide streets of Crowngate, or perhaps the open grounds of a small estate somewhere in High Ridge. He could not decide which one was more appealing.

The fiction was always short lived, rudely interrupted whenever a foul-smelling pedestrian bumped into him. Sometimes he gave them a shove in return, though he always made sure to keep a hand close to his pocket. He refused to take the chance that some gutterscum pickpocket might deprive him of his precious discovery.

Daylight did nothing to improve his tenement's appearance. The building looked even closer to collapsing than it did at nighttime. He glanced up at his window and cursed at the sight of the hardened muck covering the glass. It would take hours to scrape it off without damaging the window.

Meaty and Jaspen would probably come by just to laugh at him while he chiseled away at it.

Stupid shitheels.

Wurgim Tamercum loitered outside the door with a hammer and a spool of thick wire. He looked up as Grisel approached and flashed a grin to expose his blackened teeth. The older of the Tamercums, Wurgim was a big man with a powerful taste for nightroot, a vice that left him with little more than dull wits and rotting gums. Most of his hair had fallen out, his skin pockmarked and scabbed from gods knew what. His clothes were of decent quality, though, and the steel-headed axe in his belt probably cost more than Grisel made in a month.

Whatever the Tamercums did to pay their way, it obviously paid well.

"Morning, shitboot," Wurgim said before going back to chewing the wad of nightroot tucked inside his cheek.

Grisel did not bother responding. Wurgim was too dumb to know when he was being insulted anyway. "What you doing down here?"

"Felski says fix door," Wurgim said, the words occasionally interrupted by the sound of his lips smacking together between chews.

Several years younger and several inches shorter than his brother, Felski had enough brains for the two of them. Grisel was pretty sure Felski would sic Wurgim and his axe on him if he knew what he carried in his pocket.

Until he stashed it somewhere safe, he needed to avoid arousing any suspicion.

He strode past Wurgim without another word. The elder Tamercum was a simpleton, but Grisel was not about to let their encounter stick out in his mind. The longer he stood there talking to Wurgim, the greater the chance of him mentioning the conversation to Felski, who would rightly wonder where Grisel was coming back from at that hour.

Most of the tenants on his floor were gone during the day. Sedina's room was cold and sterile. The sweet scent of her perfume and oils had long since faded. She was probably still in whatever bed she visited the previous night.

Grisel took a deep breath before stepping into Felski's room. He wanted to give the little snake no indication that his night had been different from any other. The worry was unnecessary, though, as his room was as empty as Sedina's on one side and Tupin's on the other.

Nicalene was still asleep in bed when he reached his room. Lying face down, her tangled, black hair covered her face and upper back. Her sleep had been restless again. Most of the sheets had pulled away and her shift was bunched up near her waist, exposing her pale thighs and the lower curve of her behind.

He should have been angry with her. She had slept through most of the last two days and seemed content to do nothing more than live under his roof and occasionally slink out during the day for wine or whatever junk she was getting from people like Felski Tamercum. He caught her with a pouch of nightroot once and threatened to kick her out on the street if he ever saw a speck of black in her mouth.

Gods only know what she's into now.

But the anger did not come as he looked at her slumbering form. He focused instead on the way her shift clung to her body's curves, the way her black hair spilled across her soft, pale skin. Her legs were parted slightly, exposing the soft skin of her inner thigh. She shifted slightly and let out a low groan, her movements pulling the shift up to reveal more of her backside.

Wonder who she's dreaming about.

He stared at her as he stripped off his spader gear, his cock hardening swiftly. The clothes dropped in a pile next to the bed and he climbed into bed alongside her, one hand running down her leg and the other cupping one of her breasts. She groaned again as he pressed against her and kissed her ear.

"Hey, come on, how about a nice welcome home?"

She turned over, one of her hands pushing against his waist to hold him at bay. "Piss off," she said, still half asleep. "Not now…"

Gods damn it, woman!

Grisel rolled onto his back and stared at the ceiling.

Pity I can't pay Sedina a visit. It's what you think I do anyway.

Pulling the bedsheets over his naked body, he turned to face the wall, his back to Nicalene. He tried to jerk off, but he failed to muster the necessary enthusiasm for it to amount to much and he went limp again before he finished.

His breathing slowed gradually, keeping time with his heartbeat. Fatigue seeped first into his muscles and then down to his bones. A serene calm settled over him, shielding him from the sounds outside his window, the shrieks of children, the braying of animals, the pounding of Wurgim's hammer.

Should put that stone somewhere safe, somewhere even Nicalene won't know about…

He could do that after he rested for just a bit longer.

So tired…

Grisel's eyelids grew too heavy to hold open and he let them fall.

Just a bit longer…

7
THE BROKER

The rickety staircase leading up to the second story flat creaked loudly under Arden's weight. Some of the steps sagged more than usual, and twice he heard a rippling crackle as dried-out wood splintered and cracked. When he reached the door, he let out the deep breath he did not realize he held in his chest.

He slotted the heavy, iron key into the lock and pushed the door open. The half-rusted hinges creaked loudly to announce his arrival; it was a pitiful alarm, but he was glad for it should any uninvited guests decide to come calling.

Heavy curtains covered the windows, making the single room hovel quite dark. Arden left the door open long enough to pull the curtains back and allow the dull light to press through the thick glass. A short time after dawn, the sun had yet to peer out from behind the clouds. Even on a clear day, the smoky haze hanging perpetually over the city had a way of diffusing the sunlight before it could filter down to the streets.

The boy slumbered on the little bed tucked into the far corner of the room. Arden pulled one of the chairs away from the nearby table and sat down beside the bed.

He watched the boy for the better part of an hour—watched his little chest rise and fall with every breath, the occasional twitch of his eyelids, and the wordless mumbling of his lips. Buried under so many heavy blankets, the boy seemed small, though he was small enough already in fact.

When the boy finally opened his eyes, Arden had nearly fallen asleep himself. His senses revived quickly, and he smiled, careful not to show any of his cracked teeth.

"Good morning."

The boy did not answer. He only groaned and turned his head to stare up at the ceiling.

Not like him to be so quiet.

"Are you well?" He placed his hand on the boy's forehead.

A little warm. Maybe from the blankets?

Arden hoped to keep the boy from catching a chill during the night, but he may have been excessive. He pulled the heavy fur blanket away, allowing the warmth trapped beneath to escape.

He'll be fine. Just needs some air is all.

Arden stood and opened one of the windows. The stench of the streets below drifted in, but the room felt a bit less claustrophobic.

The boy groaned again. A sharper, more reactionary sound this time.

Arden returned to his side.

"Does something hurt?"

The boy nodded, his face twisting. "Belly…"

He brushed a lock of sandy hair from the boy's face and took his hand.

"A sharp pain or an ache?"

"Sharp." The boy clenched his teeth.

Arden traced his fingers down the boy's cheek and felt under his chin, just below the jawbone.

No signs of swelling. Not yet, at least.

He leaned over the bed. "Open up. Let me see your tongue."

The boy obeyed. A bit of clear film covered his tongue, hardly unusual. Arden looked closer, trying to peer into the back of his throat, but he saw no cause for concern.

"Are you still tired?"

The boy nodded. Arden got up and poured him a bit of sweetwine from the clay jug sitting on the table.

"Drink," he said.

The boy took the cup and pressed it against his lips weakly. As he drank, Arden realized how pale he looked.

"Go back to sleep," he said when the boy finished. "I have a few matters that need attending. I won't be gone long."

He rubbed the boy's fair hair. "You stay right here, understand?"

The boy nodded. "Yes, sir."

Arden made it to the door before the boy called out.

"Will I be sick again, Father?"

He took a moment to collect his thoughts before he turned and answered.

Can't let him see that I'm worried about it.

"Get some rest, lad. We'll talk when I return."

HALVID HAD ALWAYS been a sick boy.

When he was three, he nearly died from an awful, retching cough that lasted for nearly four months. There was the time he was bitten by some accursed insect in Gulhn that made his arm swell up until it was as thick as his thigh, and the dry flu he caught when they were travelling through the scrub plains near Kormur. No matter where Arden took him, there was always some peculiar, local affliction that managed to find him.

But always, there was the fever.

It came on fast and strong, with little warning. His skin burned, his stomach roiled with knives, and his throat all but swelled shut. Tiny lesions sprang up on his tongue and mouth, sometimes red, sometimes black, and sometimes white. Blisters formed all over his skin as his body tried to force the sickness out. When they burst, the pain became unbearable, and Halvid would cry until his body was little more than a withered, dried out husk.

The fever first took him when he was no more than a toddler. A short-lived affliction then, it lasted less than a week. But it returned many times after that, sometimes fading away as suddenly as it came and other times enduring for weeks or more. There was no predicting when it might strike, no discernable cause that might be avoided.

Arden took the boy to dozens of healers, priests, witches, and sorcerers. None of them knew the cause of the illness. None of them knew how to cure it.

The fever had last taken him more than a year ago, a short bout that burned fiercely but briefly, running its course in a matter of days.

The time before that, however, lasted for two months and very nearly killed him.

Before the fever finally broke, Arden had considered ending the boy's misery the only way he knew how.

The gods are wicked and cruel, he had thought, sitting next to Halvid's bed with a pillow in his lap. It would have been so easy to smother the boy, so easy to make good on the promise that he would soon feel better, that the fever would pass as it had always done before.

But he could never bring himself to do it. He buried his own face in the pillow instead and sobbed, sobbed until he felt Halvid's shriveled, bony hand stroking his hair and heard a weak, pitiful voice telling him that everything would be well again soon.

Can't worry about that now. Not where I'm going...

Arden brushed his concern aside as he approached the main gate of Dhrath's Keep. The tallest building in Carbuncle borough, the old stone tower was an ugly, squat thing that seemed ready to come tumbling down in the face of a stiff wind. Thin tendrils of rust ran down its walls, each one leading back up to the corroded, iron bars covering the second and third story windows or the sheets of metal riveted over the crown of the parapet far above. The first dozen feet or so of stone blocks were charred black in uneven streaks, a grim reminder that the keep was hardly immune to siege, even from the poor wretches that lived beneath its shadow. A stone wall about ten feet high surrounded the tower itself, with an open yard area between the two.

The keep stood roughly in the center of the borough atop a low mound of earth with a gentle, but steady, incline. Swelling up as it did like an infected boil on the face of the district, the mound and the surrounding neighborhood that made up the borough had been known as Carbuncle as long as anyone could remember. Despite being the highest point in Lowtown, it was hardly fit to be called a hill.

One of the guards standing watch outside the gate recognized Arden and went inside to announce his arrival. The other guard was unfamiliar and young, probably freshly recruited from some street gang if the ugly, exaggerated scars up and down his arms were any indication. Dhrath disliked competition, but he tolerated a few of the borough's gangs because they gave him a steady stream of fresh thugs who knew a thing or two about hurting people.

This one looked ideal for guard duty; nasty enough to scare off any unwanted guests and dumb enough to enjoy standing around looking mean all day long.

After a few minutes, the first guard returned and sent Arden through the outer gate. He did not need to be shown the way, but a young man met him at the tower's entrance to guide him through the anteroom. Two more armed men stood before the wooden door that led to the reception hall, each one clad in chainmail and armed with an axe. They eyed Arden closely, but moved aside at his escort's command.

When he stepped into the keep's reception hall, the thick scent of brine washed over him as thoroughly as if he had been dunked into the sea. The back portion of the hall's floor had been dug up to form a pool filled with black seawater. Filmy puddles gathered in the depressions of what remained of the floor and the cold, clammy air clung stubbornly to every surface. Water dripped intermittently from the ceiling, each drop splashing against the stone floor or plunking into the pool. The sounds echoed around the circular room, never allowing the comfort of silence to settle over the hall fully.

A simple, unadorned chair stood at the edge of the dark pool. It was a crude piece of decor, hewn from black, pitted rock and covered with moldy patches of moss. A simple, wooden bucket sat on the floor at the foot of the chair.

Arden waited while his guide closed the door behind them and crossed the floor to retrieve the bucket.

About damn time you showed up.

The voice took shape in Arden's mind as if it were his own thought. It sounded like him, yet upon further reflection it could have sounded like any other voice he ever heard.

He felt colder, his skin prickling up with gooseflesh.

"I had to tend to something before I came by."

Bullshit. You think I got nothing better to do than wait around for you?

The voice sounded like the knight he squired for when he was a boy. Ser Tarthen Dovala, a miserable sod that liked to punctuate every command with a slap of his gauntleted hand. He died a halfwit, unable to do so much as take a piss on his own after a mace caved in the most of his skull.

"Well, I'm here now," he said. "Do you want your money or not?"

Laughter filled his head, seeming to originate from at least a dozen mouths.

The water to the right of the chair stirred.

No need to get so testy. You know how much I value my time.

A pair of long, thick tentacles covered with round suckers slithered out of the water and slid across the stone floor. Another one followed them to haul the rest of the cephalin's slimy, bulbous body into the open air. Several more tentacles sprawled across the floor, each one as long as Arden was tall. The pair of beady, black eyes perched just in front of a bag of soft flesh nearly the size of a wine barrel had no pupils, but they seemed to hone in on him all the same.

Dhrath's muscular arms pulled his boneless form across the floor and dragged it up into the chair easily. Once in place, the tips of his tentacles continued to writhe slowly, some of them draped over the seat and others coiled up beneath him.

So, what do you have for me, old man?

Dhrath called just about everyone "old man." Cephalins reached adulthood early, but they rarely lived long enough to enjoy their accomplishments. Arden guessed that Dhrath was half his age, which meant the broker had maybe another five to ten years to live. It was a fiendish jest for a being with so much power and cunning to be forced to cram a lifetime of ambition into a few short decades.

The gods are wicked and cruel.

"I looked in on Rensure, like you asked," Arden said.

And?

The voice turned playful, almost childish. Arden could not quite place it. Maybe his brother's voice from when he was young?

"Like you thought. He's been shorting you at least twenty percent a month for a while now."

Dhrath's fleshy body quivered. Arden's heartbeat quickened and he felt the urge to hit something, but the feeling disappeared a moment later.

I trust you explained things to him?

"He was a slow learner."

One of Dhrath's tentacles lashed out to slap his servant on the back of the head. The boy dipped the bucket into the water and then dumped it over Dhrath's body, which swelled slightly at the water's cold touch.

Moxie was always smarter anyway. We'll see what she can do with his quarter. You get back what he owes?

Arden held out the sack of marks he retrieved from Rensure.

"I took what he had, but it looks like he loaned a good share of it out. Moxie's trying to track them all down, but most are probably like the scrape Rensure sent me to collect from. I'll be surprised if half of them can pay up."

The boy set the bucket down and stepped over to take the sack of marks. Arden handed it over slowly. He could not hear whatever instructions Dhrath had given his servant, just as the servant had only heard Arden's half of the conversation. Even though the cephalin probably wanted him to hand the money over, Arden hated assuming anything where Dhrath was concerned. Of course, the slimy bastard could have projected his thoughts for both of them to hear, but he seemed to enjoy keeping everyone in the dark.

Cost of doing business, old man.

Arden caught the boy by the arm before he returned to Dhrath's side.

"We've all got costs," he said. "Seems to me you've been skimping on some of yours of late."

Dhrath's tentacles went very still and Arden found it impossible to pull his gaze away from those beady, black eyes. The room darkened and fell out of focus, but the boneless pile of flesh on the chair remained painfully sharp. Arden shivered, his skin tingling as if those slimy tentacles were coiling around him.

Do we have some problem I'm not aware of, Arden?

The sound in his head was harsh, but indistinct. It searched for a voice, but Arden fought to wall off his memories to keep one from pushing to the fore. His skin felt clammy, and a weight pressed against his chest.

Careful, you old fool. He can kill you with a thought.

"No problem, no," he said, pushing the words through his tightening throat. "Just want the coin I'm owed is all."

The pressure vanished as suddenly as it appeared, but Arden struggled to avoid gasping for air. He was not about to let the damn cephalin see him squirm.

The pay you're owed, eh? Seems to me I'm not getting my coin's worth out of you lately. May be that it's time to find your sort of help elsewhere. You keen on scrounging out a life out there with the rest of the gutterscums?

He knew then that Dhrath was toying with him. The slimy bastard had invested too much in Arden to cut him loose now. Killing him was one thing, but Dhrath would never permit anyone else profit on his investment.

Still, the cephalin wanted to make a point, and Arden knew he had to play along if he wanted to get what he was owed.

"Forgive me," he said. "I forgot my place."

As if you'd ever let me.

Blackspire was not known for being friendly to outsiders. Immigrants without a trade were kept outside the city gates, most of them clustering in the hovels and lean-tos that clung to the outer wall like barnacles. It was even harder to bring children into the city; they were extra mouths to feed at best and vulnerable disease carriers at worst.

Arden had a trade, of course, but not exactly the easiest sort to regulate. Blackspire was already fit to bursting with mercenaries and conscripted soldiers from the quarrelsome lands of Delinor and Karthea. Only a few of them found work in the city watch or in the employ of some nobleman's personal guard, so the last thing the civic authorities needed was more unemployed men with a knack for violence.

Between his red-handed trade and his sickly son, Arden never would have been allowed inside the city's formidable walls had it not been for a few well-placed bribes. Powerful brokers like Dhrath were always on the lookout for desperate men peering hopefully through Blackspire's iron gates.

Desperate men were easily bought, easily used, and easily controlled.

The servant scooped up another bucket of saltwater and dumped it over Dhrath's soft flesh. Arden thought he heard a curt laugh echo faintly around the hall.

See that you don't go making it a habit. You want to cry about your coin, I've got another shiftless scrape that needs sorting out.

Arden sighed. Dhrath always had some poor lackwit who needed one kind of sorting or another. He wondered if there was anyone in Lowtown that did not owe the slick-skinned fiend something.

"I'm listening."

ARDEN WAS TIRED and thirsty by the time he left the great hall. He could have wandered to some other part of the keep to demand a drink from one of the servants, but his thirst was nothing compared his desire to get away from the close, damp air stuffed between those walls of blackened stone. Dhrath's goons paid him no mind as he hurried through the anteroom and strode out onto Shale Street, the poorly paved road meandering through the heart of Carbuncle borough.

Unlike the keep itself, the buildings there remained in decent condition. Dhrath owned most everything within sight of the crumbling stone tower, though, and he kept the rates high enough to drive away all but the most prosperous of Lowtown's otherwise destitute citizenry. Many of the residents there were skilled laborers fortunate enough to find work in Spiresreach, but not so fortunate that they could afford to live there.

The air in Carbuncle tasted a bit clearer compared to the neighboring Lowtown boroughs. It lacked the butcheries and the wagons filled with rotting produce, and many of the buildings even had working privies that did not empty into the street. At the top of the hill, a system of storm drains emptied into an ancient cistern beneath the ground, which channeled rain water down the hill to a series of collection basins. Still, nobody with any sense would describe the air as pleasant. Scraggly haired goats and underfed pigs still had the run of the streets along with the occasional flock of chickens. They left piles of manure wherever they went, and the ripe stench only served to mask the stink of the borough's human residents.

As far as Arden cared, anything smelled better than that brine-encrusted pit Dhrath wallowed inside. The first few breaths of the wet, salty air may have scoured his lungs clean, but the ones that followed seared the lining of his throat and seemed to suck every ounce of moisture from his skin. For all the dampness, he always left there feeling like he had wandered for days across a barren, sun-battered desert of a salt flat.

Arden's building was on the south side of Carbuncle borough, near the intersection of Needlehead and Holdfast Streets. Although fairly close to Dhrath's keep, the place seemed much farther during the day when the streets were full of laborers, vagrants, and travellers. Traffic always proved busier along the major streets, especially where Shale and Vinewall crossed paths, but even Carbuncle's alleyways remained well trod thanks to the numerous little workshops and storefronts tucked away in many of the smaller, cheaper buildings. The names seemed to change almost weekly, with many of the meager businesses being used to pay off outstanding debts or swapping owners after a night of ill-advised wagering.

Dhrath had his slimy tentacles in just about every transaction, of course. Word had it that as many as five brokers used to carve up Carbuncle between them, but they had all been squeezed out after the cephalin arrived nearly ten years back. He was content to allow a few of the small time gangs have a corner or two to themselves, but only to save him the trouble of cracking down on the local competition himself. The Carbuncle Watch was wrapped up tight in his grip and, if the rumors were to be believed, he had enough pull over every watch captain in Lowtown to do whatever he wanted in the district.

The sky looked every bit as flat and gray as it had yesterday and the several days before that, but the clouds were less effective at blocking out the sun's heat than its light. After the chill of Dhrath's Keep, Arden found the outside air uncomfortably warm. He had already sweat out what little moisture he had not lost to the salty air inside the keep by the time he reached the bottom of the hill.

Going to be hot again. And summer's still a good month away.

Needlehead Street swung sharply westward before it veered south again to cross over Holdfast. The spire loomed over the cityscape to his right as Arden turned to follow the road. Small puffs of smoke swirled around its massive base, climbing steadily to melt into the haze several hundred feet above the city's core. The spire's black stone faded there only to reemerge from the fog hundreds of feet higher before it punctured the gray sheet of clouds and disappeared entirely.

Arden had lived in the city long enough to not be awestruck by the sight of its namesake structure every time he saw it, but only residents born beneath the spire's shadow were ever truly accustomed to it. Visible for dozens of miles beyond the walls and from everywhere within them, the spire was an eternal landmark, towering over the city and its sur- roundings like some terrible, chthonic god. His gaze drifted to it whenever its coal black stone entered his field of vision. Sometimes he could catch himself being drawn in and looked away, but once it seized his attention there was nothing to do but stare.

The street eventually curved to the left, pulling Arden, and his gaze, southward once more. He rubbed his eyes, feeling the weight of too many sleepless nights pressing down on them. Days had passed since he got more than an hour or two of rest.

He doubted he would get more today. Halvid would be waking soon, and the fever might already be setting in. If the boy got sick again, it would mean another visit to the apothecaries to replenish their supply of the creams and oils that helped keep his skin from burning and swelling. The last bout of the fever had all but exhausted Arden's meager savings. He could afford enough medicines to keep the worst of the fever at bay for perhaps a few days.

After that, the boy would be at its mercy.

There never seemed to be enough coin to go around. Dhrath had paid him for sorting out the business with Rensure, but it was less than half of what he expected. The cephalin had grown miserly in recent months, complaining that half the city was indebted to him yet refused to make good on obligations. Arden thought it more likely that he was getting squeezed by Mire Shore's brokers. Although Dhrath had a sizable share in just about every illicit transaction in Lowtown, the district's black market would quickly vanish without access to the tottering docks nestled along the Saven River's swampy southern shore. Whenever the river bosses hiked their rates, Dhrath simply shunted the cost down to his underlings to keep his own coffers level.

Arden was only a few blocks from his flat when he turned off Needlehead and headed eastward. Coldwater borough was close, and he wanted to get a look at the place Dhrath had described to him. The owner was well behind on his payments and would need a pointed reminder of his debt obligations very soon. If Arden could collect all or even most of the balance, there would be another payment waiting for him. He hoped it would be enough to see Halvid through his fever.

First, however, he needed to learn what sort of person he was dealing with.

Before he could really lean on somebody, Arden had to get to know him. A snake like Rensure was easy to understand; he preyed on the weak and ruthlessly sacrificed others to protect himself. Once Arden saw how he preferred to do both, there was nothing more worth knowing about him. The same held true for small-time brokers and gang leaders. Although the more successful ones possessed a certain cunning intelligence, they tended to be uncomplicated people. Violence was their principle weapon, and it was one that could easily be turned against them to great effect.

Poor sods like Lemrick were a bit harder to sort out. Most of them had not repaid their debts because they simply lacked the coin. Maybe a deal they were counting on fell through or some unforeseen expense came up; Arden was always hearing new excuses. Very few of them thought that they could pull one over on a broker and actually get away with it. Some failed to fully grasp the terms of the deals they made.

None of that mattered, of course. Once a broker sent someone like Arden to collect, the debt was going to be repaid one way or another.

He thought of poor Lemrick's wife crumpled on the ground, her sobbing husband cradling the ruin that had once been her hand. Had it been courage, stubbornness, or stupidity that made him hold his tongue as Arden hacked off the woman's fingers one by one? It hardly mattered now. Without any coin, Lemrick would be unable to afford proper treatment for the wound. If the flesh turned rancid, she would probably die of fever.

She may be dead already.

Did that make Arden a murderer? He supposed it did, although he hardly needed knowledge of one more death to make that determination.

Even so, he regretted what happened in that Sinkhole shack. Had Lemrick been one of Dhrath's borrowers, Arden would have observed him for a few days before approaching him. He would have learned what the man valued, what he feared. Then, when the time came, he would know the best way to squeeze him. Had he known more about Lemrick, he might have been able to coax the coin out of him with a single threat. As it was, he had to resort to more general intimidation and crude violence to get what he needed.

Sometimes that was enough.

Sometimes it ended badly.

But he had not really been there for Lemrick in the first place; he was after Rensure. Poor Lemrick and his wife were just a means to an end, tools to get him closer to his real target. It was simple, dumb luck that Lemrick happened to seek a loan from a man foolish enough to steal money from Dhrath. Had he lived in another borough, his late payment may have only earned him a broken nose from a broker's thugs.

But Dhrath cast a long shadow, and both Lemrick and his poor wife paid the price for Rensure's greed.

The gods are wicked and cruel.

But so are you, Arden Belarius.

8

THE LEECH

The *Bleating Goat* kept its doors locked until midday, but a small crowd of sweaty workers from the nearby butcheries usually gathered outside before then. Rumor had it that the winesink used to open earlier in the day, but too many workers kept wandering off for a morning drink and forgot to come back after the second. The proprietor eventually agreed to shutter the place until most of the day's work in the borough's shophouses was finished.

Like most buildings on Redfoot Street, *The Bleating Goat* had clearly not been built to serve its present function. It resembled the sort of old, two story tenement houses common throughout Pigshire borough, only if someone gutted the walls of the first floor to create a common room. The place stank of piss and spoiled pork, but the wine was as cheap as it was strong and the mood always more boisterous than the cleaner taverns of neighboring Cadgerwalk. By nightfall, the common room filled up with workers, beggars, and rogues looking to fritter away their coin on good drink and pleasurable company. The whores followed them in from the streets, hoping to take a bit of that coin for themselves. Drunken braggarts came to blows over spilled cups and drew blades to lay claim to disheveled streetwalkers.

Most of the winesink's regulars considered it a dull evening if the Pigshire Watch hauled less than five men off to the stocks for the night.

But it was more than just drink and disreputable company that made *The Bleating Goat* so popular. The private rooms on the second floor catered to patrons in search of stronger vices. Nightroot, firedust, dreamleeches, and even stranger tastes awaited anyone who managed to weasel their way upstairs. Four armed thugs took turns guarding the steps leading up to the private rooms. Each one maintained a different set of rules governing whom they allowed to pass, rules that often changed from day to day. Sometimes all it took was a friendly word, but other days only a select few were permitted to go upstairs.

Most often, however, admission simply came down to a matter of coin. Even then the villains took great pleasure in confounding expectations. A sufficient bribe one day might be considered so low as to be insulting the next. Similarly, a generous amount last week might be too presumptuous for another. The maddening system drove away the undetermined and the ignorant, leaving only the dedicated, well-connected customers who dared not endanger their special status with loose talk or rabble rousing.

There was a time when Nicalene knew the temperament of every guard. She could tell when old Brack had lost most of his rent to the dice again or when Salis had been at it with his insufferable brother. She knew Esran was a greasy-lipped lecher who could be talked into anything so long as she slipped a hand down his pants while she asked him. Of course, that would never work with Givey; he was too uptight about his job and preferred men to women anyway.

But none of them were there today. Nicalene had not been to the *Goat* in more than a year and most of the old, familiar faces had moved on since then. The man guarding the staircase hardly looked like a man at all. While big enough for the job, to be sure, the soft fuzz framing his pudgy face betrayed his youth. Something about his eyes and the bridge of his nose was familiar, but Nicalene was pretty sure she had never seen him before.

More importantly, he probably did not know her.

She recognized the old hag serving brackish slop out of the kitchen, but all of the serving girls were new. Most of the patrons clustered around the tables and booths were strangers to her as well.

Doesn't take long, does it?

The changes should not have surprised her. Most of the regulars had a way of moving on after a few months or years, their faces replaced by an influx of new ones as time crept along. She never noticed the turnover when she spent so much time there before but coming back now after so long reminded her how quickly people could pass through each other's lives.

Nicalene slithered through the crowd of workers and hooked her elbow onto the bar counter at the back of the common room. She gave the barkeep a chance to notice her before she pulled a quartermark from her satchel and slapped it down on the wood. The barkeep nodded in her direction, more a gesture of annoyance than acknowledgment.

Come on, shitheel. You ain't got nothing better to do.

Slowly, deliberately, he made his way over to her, pausing to banter with each customer between them. She tugged clumsily at her shawl, wishing she had worn something with a higher neckline.

He snatched the coin off the counter and bit it. Much to her disappointment, he did not break a tooth in the process.

"What you want?" he asked, rubbing the coin between his grime-encrusted fingers.

"Looking for Tawny. He still come around?"

He scrunched up his lips at the name.

"Not seen him for six months, maybe more. Heard he got knifed over in Carbuncle."

Well, there goes my in...

She nodded toward the stairs, tilting her head enough make her meaning obvious.

"Who's running things these days then?"

The barkeep looked her over, his tongue pushing against the inside of his cheek. He held up the coin again.

"There more where this come from?"

Stupid question.

They always came back with stupid questions.

"Enough for what I need," she said.

And you're not getting any more.

When she made no move to fetch another coin from her satchel, he snorted and slipped the coin into his pocket.

"Go on up," he said, stabbing his thumb toward the stairs. "Tell him you're here to see Muskrat."

Nicalene pushed away from the counter and rolled her eyes as soon as she turned her back on the barkeep.

Asshole.

She wondered how many idiots wasted half their coin trying to pry something useful out of his thick skull.

The man-boy guarding the steps stood a little straighter when Nicalene approached him. His chubby face was cute in a babyish sort of way, but his body looked more lumpy than brawny. She wondered if he had every actually been in a fight; as a kid, he probably managed to avoid fights being so much bigger than everyone else his age.

That would not last long in a place like the *Goat*. Half the patrons were too stupid to be afraid of anyone, no matter their size. And that was to say nothing about the experienced cutters with no reason to fear anybody.

He looked young enough that he might not have had a woman yet. Maybe he tossed about in a straw pile with a newly-bled serving girl at some point, but even that seemed like more than he could handle.

Nicalene pulled her shawl back over her shoulders, exposing the pale skin of her chest underneath. She had chosen the blue dress she used to wear whenever she made a trip to the *Goat*. An undershirt should have gone beneath the garment, but the man who gave it to her (*Breton? Bronet? What the hell was his name?*) always insisted that she wear nothing underneath. The low neckline plunged down almost to mid-chest where strips of wire woven into the fabric pushed her breasts together. When she pulled the dress out that morning, she remembered the way men would gawk at her in it, how they shoved each other aside just to position themselves to brush up against her in the crowded, boisterous winesinks from Coldwater to Wallside.

It was tighter than before though, her body having filled out a bit with age in the years since then. She brought the shawl along out of habit but was glad to have it with her after the first man she passed on the street sniggered at her. At first, she thought he was reacting to something else, to someone else. But when the next few men ignored her and the women glared at her reproachfully, she pulled the fabric over her exposed cleavage and stared at the ground ahead of her feet.

She could have run back home to change, but she did not want to take the chance of waking Grisel up and having to explain what she was up to. He was already pissed off that she stayed in bed yesterday, though he still made a point of pawing at her like a clumsy dog when he got home. The bastard ruined a perfectly good dream, but at least he had the decency to take the hint when she told him to leave her be. She could not imagine any conversation with him going well.

Of course, avoiding Grisel was just one of the reasons to stay away. She was stupid enough to buy a bundle of cheap nightroot from the Tamercum brothers shortly after she moved into the place. Now the little one harassed her every time she saw him, always asking if she needed something to improve her mood even though she had not bought anything from him for well over a year. He made sure to avoid badgering her while Grisel was around, probably pleased with the thought that he shared some big secret with her. Their root tasted awful anyway; even if she did want to chew a bit, she would have found something better than the junk they were dealing.

Then there was that bitch Sedina…

Nicalene scowled at the very thought of her.

I'll be damned before I let that smug whore see me like this.

The pudgy-faced guard cleared his throat as Nicalene took the first step and stopped. She cocked her hips slightly and arched her back just enough to push her breasts against the dress's tight, wire binding.

He looked her over once, a little too quickly for her liking.

Stupid, stupid, stupid.

She fought the urge to yank the shawl back over her chest.

"Help you, lady?"

Lady? How old do you think I am, you little shitboot?

"Here to see Muskrat," she said, trying not to scowl.

The man-boy glanced at the bar, where the barkeep gave an annoyed nod.

"All right, then," he said. "Go on up. Third door on the left."

He stepped aside and Nicalene strode up the stairs. As soon as she walked past him, she pulled the shawl down again.

The room looked like a cross between a kitchen and an alchemist's workshop. Chopped bits of various plants and piles of crushed powder covered one table, all of which probably came from the canvas sacks and wooden crates stacked up wherever there was enough space on the floor. Glass carafes and clay bowls lay scattered across the table on the far end of the room. A few of them were suspended by metal stands over an open flame, mostly large candles or oil wicks. The room smelled of burning leather and boiled vinegar.

Muskrat lived up to the expectations of his name. Short, wiry, and unkempt, he looked like he bathed in a cesspit. He scuttled around the room excitedly, grabbing handfuls of ingredients from one table and dropping them into one of the many mixtures he concocted at the other.

Nicalene did not announce herself when she crept through the door. She was still debating whether or not to keep herself covered up by the time Muskrat noticed her.

He looked her over, his face twisting into a sneer. "Don't think I know you."

"I haven't been around for a while," she said. "What happened to Tawny?"

Muskrat's eyes narrowed briefly before he laughed.

"Old friend of his, eh? Wouldn't go speaking his name in these parts if I was you."

Friend.

That was certainly a stretch.

Nicalene shrugged. "Nothing to me. You running things here?"

"That's right." He looked her over again. Nicalene almost pulled the shawl back but thought better of it.

Stop being so bloody desperate, will you?

"What you looking for, anyway?" he asked.

"Something strong. How fresh are your dreamleeches?"

Muskrat smiled. He was missing a few of his back teeth, which only lent him a stronger resemblance to his namesake.

"Real fresh," he said, his gaze falling to her chest. "Big and juicy."

Nicalene had played through this scenario with Tawny more than once. He always had a thing for her too. When she was broke, he eagerly took payment in kind. The exchange never bothered her too much; he tended to be quick about it and fixed her up with better junk than she could usually afford.

Of course, she stumbled through most of those transactions in a dull haze, her mind and body either riding the last waves of some high or reeling from withdrawal symptoms. Although she could still taste yesterday's wine in the back of her mouth, the pleasant numbness that accompanied it had worn off.

In her current state of mind, the idea of Muskrat's greasy hands on her skin made her want to retch. She wondered if she would feel differently after she got what she was after.

The thought proved discomforting.

"Let me see one," she said.

Muskrat chuckled as he retrieved a big, black, ceramic jar from one of the nearby boxes. Thin ropes kept the lid tied down, and he took his time removing them. After prying off the lid, he picked up a pair of long, iron tongs and dipped them inside.

The pulsating, purple and crimson thing he pulled out was a foot long and about three fingers thick.

Nicalene barely managed to suppress a gasp, but she could not stop her eyes from widening at the sight of the thing.

"Beauty, ain't she?" Muskrat said, beaming.

"H...how much?"

"Fifty marks."

Nicalene nearly choked.

Fifty whole *marks?*

Even with the money she took from Grisel's stash, it was far more than she had.

The dreamleech quivered, its slimy secretions oozing from the glistening skin. A heavy drop of the stuff fell back into the jar, thudding loudly against the writhing mass of flesh inside.

Something cold clawed at her stomach, a familiar, half-forgotten pain. She felt parched and famished all at once, her skin tingling and shivering.

She reached into her satchel and closed her fingers around the black chunk of polished stone she found in Grisel's pocket.

Surely the thing was worth fifty marks.

Probably a lot more.

Muskrat would be all too happy to take it in trade, she was certain. But that was the problem. The stone could be worth enough to buy the whole jar of dreamleeches, maybe enough to buy everything in the room or the winesink itself. If she handed it over now, she would never know how much she was giving away.

Don't be so hasty for a simple fix, girl.

She watched the dreamleech squirm between the tongs, its purple and crimson skin shimmering under the light.

But you're more than a simple fix, aren't you, pretty thing?

Nicalene withdrew her hand and pulled back her shawl. Muskrat licked at his cracked lips as she took a step toward him.

"A bit short of that, I'm afraid," she said, her voice low and breathy. "Maybe we can work something out?"

She fell into the old routine easily, almost thoughtlessly. Her conscious mind retreated into its dark, silent hiding place while her body's baser instincts took over. Muskrat tried to put up a fight, but men like him were weak and lonely. She saw that from the moment she entered the room: the way he avoided looking her in the eye, the way he kept shifting his weight from one leg to the other, the way his hands kept fidgeting. Some people might have thought it was from whatever he was taking, but Nicalene knew the difference.

He looked at her the same way they all used to look at her. Not like the half-wit boy guarding the steps who could hardly get it up yet or the barkeep who probably forced himself on the witless serving girls every night. Not like the men sniggering at her when she walked by or the tavern louts who moved aside to avoid touching her.

When she pressed her body against his and breathed into his pockmarked face, whatever will Muskrat had to resist withered. The dreamleech slipped from the tongs and splashed back inside the jar as her hand slid over his hardening cock.

She still had to choke the bile back down her throat when he finally put his hands on her, but it was easier after that. Sometimes they made her look at them, but Muskrat had no interest in her face. He bent her over one of the tables as he groped at her breasts with one hand and pulled up her dress with the other.

Nicalene grit her teeth and groaned as he took her, but her mind stayed far from that foul-smelling room. For a moment, she was a child again, standing in the crowd that had gathered to watch a troop of street performers. It was a pleasant memory, one that she often returned to. She was older in the next reminiscence, sitting in the crowd of some ramshackle theater and cheering for the beautiful voice echoing through the air.

Then she was on the stage, a thousand strange faces glaring down at her from the darkness. Someone laughed at her and the others joined in. She tried to duck away, to escape their scorn, but her naked body would not respond. Her skin began to sag, wrinkles and limp flesh pulling away from her bones until she was a withered old hag. The laughter thundered in her ears and she wanted to scream back at it, but her jaw had clenched shut so tightly that her teeth ground away to nothing.

Muskrat finished quickly, just as she expected. His ragged breaths quick and heavy, he staggered away from her, nearly tripping on the breeches around his ankles. Nicalene pushed one of her breasts back inside her blue dress and scrubbed at her eyes before she turned around to face him.

She pointed at the black jar.

"Give me the biggest one you've got."

MUSKRAT SHOWED HER to one of the second floor's unoccupied rooms, empty save for a straw-filled mat in one corner and a crusty chamber pot in another. Thin razors of light shone through the gaps of the boarded windows. The heavy, wet odor of piss and sweat hung in the air.

Nicalene stepped inside and closed the door, very nearly hitting Muskrat in the face as he explained how he would let no one disturb her. She leaned against the wall and sank down to the floor, cradling the jar against her chest.

What the hell am I doing here?

Grisel had threatened to kick her out onto the street last year, shortly after she moved in with him. He found her half-naked and passed out on the floor with her teeth stained black from chewing the wretched night-root she bought from the Tamercums. One of them might have touched her before she passed out, but she was not certain and she sure as hell never mentioned it to Grisel. He tied her up in bed for a week and paid somebody he trusted to keep an eye on her during his shift until all the junk worked through her system.

She still resented Grisel over that week, one of the worst of her life. Maybe she would have felt differently if he stayed with her the whole time as she suffered through painful withdrawal symptoms. He said he could not afford to miss work, but Nicalene thought that was just an excuse to avoid her.

She could see the real reason in those judgmental eyes of his. He always judged her for something or other, as if shoveling shit all night lent him some kind of moral authority.

After she got clean, things were better for a while, but before long Grisel started badgering her about finding work. She scrubbed dishes somewhere in Coldwater for a while and spent a few months in a Wallside dyeshop, but all of it made her miserable. The days felt endless and the nights empty. She found herself marking time by the slow, steady deterioration of the people she passed on the street each day. The old women looked a little more bent every time she saw them, the sick a little sicker. She noticed that children sometimes simply vanished. Maybe they ran away, died of a fever, or got shipped off to be "servants" in some other borough but she never found out.

She forgot when she started drinking heavily again or why, but at some point, she stopped working entirely. Grisel did not notice at first since he worked during the night and slept through the day, but he pieced it together pretty quickly.

Although he sometimes yelled at her about finding more work, he no longer dragged her out of bed during the day to send her looking like he used to do. Somehow, the indifference felt worse than the scolding.

She spent the last two months in various stages of drunkenness. Grisel barely spoke to her anymore, although that never stopped him from sleeping with her whenever she was willing. But even that happened less and less of late. Nicalene had a suspicion that he was sneaking off to Sedina's bed a few times a week, but she had no proof of it. She wondered why she should care anyway.

The dreamleech quivered inside the jar, sending a shudder up Nicalene's spine.

Not yet, pretty thing.

She placed the jar down on the floor and reached into her satchel to withdraw the black stone. It felt warm in her hand, as if some part of it sought to melt into her skin and become a part of her.

Grisel would be angry when he realized what she had done. She could not say what drove her to go through his pockets when she woke up; it was almost as if something called out to her, begging for her gentle, delicate touch. Once she found the stone, the compulsion to escape from everything and everyone crept back. To seek refuge in a warm place where nothing could hurt her, and where everything about her life, about her, could be beautiful again.

She had tied Grisel's prize to a leather cord from one of her old necklaces before she left for the *Goat*. Wearing it in the open would be foolish, of course, so she stuffed it deep inside her satchel. She still had no idea what she planned to do with it. Maybe she could sell it and move to a better part of the city, or even out of the city entirely.

And then what?

Whatever she did, she realized now that she could never go back to Grisel. Surely, he had big plans for the thing, otherwise, he would have already hawked it somewhere.

It was still early in the afternoon. He would be asleep for at least a few more hours.

She still had time to go back, to slip it back into his pocket and climb back into bed with him, maybe even go look for work to distract him.

And then what?

The jar trembled, rocking ever so slightly as the thing inside squirmed in a pool of thick slime.

Something wet ran down the inside of her thigh.

Fuck it.

She slipped the leather cord around her neck, the black stone nestling between her breasts. A faint swell of heat rushed over her skin, like basking beneath a noonday sun. She squirmed out of her blue dress until she was naked save for the stone resting heavily upon her chest.

Picking up the jar, she made her way over to the straw mat and sat down.

She removed the lid as she lay down on her back.

After taking a deep breath, she upended the jar over her chest.

The dreamleech plopped onto her skin with a wet thump, its cold, slimy secretion pouring out of the jar with it and splashing over her. It squirmed briefly, adjusting to the light and open air before it righted itself and began to probe at her stomach with its circular, sucker mouth.

She felt a sudden, knifing pain when it bit into her flesh, and Nicalene clenched her teeth tightly to keep from screaming.

But the pain proved mercifully brief. Moments after attaching itself, the dreamleech pumped its numbing saliva into the wound, sending tremors of electricity through Nicalene's body.

She gasped as she set the pot aside and looked down at the fat, slimy thing sucking at her flesh. Its purple skin glistened, and the crimson streaks running down its long body glowed as it fed.

The tingling sensation reached the base of her skull and Nicalene moaned as if the most delicate fingers of the most skilled massager were kneading out the tangled kinks of her brain.

She smiled in anticipation, knowing the best part was yet to come.

The dreamleech's hallucinogenic slime took only a handful of heartbeats to soak into her pores and interact with the saliva already coursing through her body. When it did, her senses erupted with pleasure. Her body spasmed, her eyes and limbs jerking uncontrollably as she slipped into an induced coma. The world bled away, every trace of sadness and misery washed away by a tide of pure, ecstatic joy.

Nicalene stood on the stage again, only this time not naked, but draped in a magnificent gown of fur, silk, and feathers. More light filtered down, and she could see the audience in full, a scruffy assortment of foul-tempered burghers. They tried to laugh at her, but something caught in their throats and they coughed up gouts of black smoke before bursting into flames.

The fire seemed to cheer for her, and Nicalene bowed gracefully.

She laughed.

Time folded in on itself, helping her to be in all places at once, and yet remaining in none of them. She would never know how long the dream-leech sucked at her when its slime seeped into the core of the porous chunk of black stone lying against her chest.

The change came slowly while her consciousness remained adrift in a blissful womb of ignorance and satiation. Something cold nipped at her fingertips and toes. A prickling, probing pain in her chest.

Then her blood turned to burning ice and a spike of cold, unworked iron forced its way into her ribcage.

Nicalene screamed, but the voice she heard did not belong to her.

She snapped back to the stage, her flesh searing as she frantically tore away her ostentatious costuming. The skin beneath turned to ash, bits of it flaking away like dust crumbling off old stonework. She looked around a stormcloud of gray faces glaring down at her, their flickering, yellow eyes slicing her soul away piece by piece.

Awareness poured back into her naked body and Nicalene jerked up from the mat. The dreamleech squirmed, frantically trying to keep its hold on her stomach. She seized the thing with both hands and tore it away from her flesh, leaving a nasty, bloody wound. The dreamleech's slimy skin made it slippery, but she held the creature firmly enough to smash it against the wooden floor. It exploded like an overripe melon, drenching her in her own blood.

Nicalene staggered to her feet, blood still pumping from the wound on her stomach. She snatched her dress and satchel from the floor just as Muskrat burst through the door.

He said something in a language Nicalene thought she should have understood but could not quite comprehend. When he saw what remained of the dreamleech, he howled angrily and brought his fist back to strike her.

The blow never landed.

Nicalene moved as if still in a dream, flowing under the dealer's clumsy swing and seizing him by the throat with her bloody hand. She squeezed, her fingernails digging into his skin and injecting crackling streaks of black energy through his flesh. He gagged on his burning lungs as blood filled the whites of his eyes. Black blisters welled up and hardened on his skin before his body finally went limp.

She dropped him and staggered away from the corpse. When she looked down, she noticed the leather cord dangling loosely from her neck. Grisel's stone had torn free.

No! Where did...

Something else caught her eye, something smooth and black nestled between her breasts.

The stone was embedded in her chest, buried amidst the flesh and bone.

Nicalene fell to her knees and screamed, frantically clawing at the thing, her nails cutting into her skin as she sobbed.

The next few moments compressed into a flurry of disjointed images and sounds.

A cautious, inquisitive voice reining in her panic.

Someone pulling her bloodied fingers away from her chest and telling her she would be all right.

The hands helping her into her blue dress, covering her with a coat or a blanket, guiding her out of the room.

"W... who?" she asked.

"Quiet now," whispered a young man's voice. "Come with me."

Nicalene obeyed, her body following the stranger out the door while her conscious mind retreated once more into its darkest hiding place.

9

THE MESSENGER

The dining hall had been designed to accommodate a much larger table, one that stretched from one end of the room to the other and seated more than twenty guests. Ember had never seen that table, unfortunately. One of his ancestors sold it off, no doubt to pay some gambling debt or recoup the losses from an ill-advised investment. The modest, rectangular table now occuping the hall could seat no more than six comfortably. Floating in the heart of that great open space, it felt even smaller, a little island of pitted wood resting like a shriveled leaf upon the still surface of a vast lake.

Yimina refilled his goblet with wine, then proceeded to offer the same to Ember's guests. Ithlene accepted, of course. She was never too far from a drink at any point in the day. Armille Trendar eagerly thrust his goblet out before Yimina even finished refilling Ithlene's. Cambin Domoch refused, naturally, teetotaler that he was. Ember doubted he had taken more than a sip since he arrived.

"Never trust a man who doesn't drink, boy."

Ember downed a gulp of wine and leaned back in his chair. "Five votes, then. That's where we are after six months?"

Cambin grunted. Although older than the rest, age had yet to dull his wits.

Or his tongue.

"Four votes by my count," he said. "And that's if I can rely on everyone in this room."

Armille set his goblet down forcefully enough get their attention. Disheveled and crude at the best of times, he looked particularly combative after multiple servings of wine. "Are you suggesting something, old man?"

102 · BENJAMIN SPERDUTO

"Suggesting?" Cambin asked. "Not at all. I'm stating a fact."

Armille rose from his seat, scowling. "I'm not going to sit here and—"

"Yes, you are, Armille," Ember said, glaring at his fellow Assemblyman. "You're going to sit down and shut your fool mouth while we figure this out."

The two men glared at each other for a tense moment before Ithlene placed her hand on Armille's arm.

"Oh, be still," she said. "Don't act as if you have any integrity left to besmirch. Your honorable word is bought and paid for the same as ours, just like our seats."

Speak for yourself.

Armille slumped into his chair with a scowl. "All the same, I don't appreciate being treated with such disrespect."

Cambin scoffed. "Perhaps if you did more to secure the votes we need, you might actually earn that respect for a change."

"Enough bickering," Ember said, waving his arms as if he could clear such idle chatter away like so much smoke. "We can count on Tinderhov's vote in addition to ours. That gets us to five."

"You're sure Lorvie will be with us?" Ithlene asked.

"If she thinks it will get her in my good graces, yes. I might have to fawn over her a bit before that, but she'll come around when its time."

Like Ember, Lorvie Tinderhov held her Assembly seat by right of title. Her family used to be among the most powerful in Lowtown, but a prolonged stretch of inept heirs had left the Tinderhovs in even worse circumstances than Morangines. Rumors claimed that at some point, the family took to incest to stanch the loss of wealth to other families. Inbreeding or no, the family had a long history of churning out half-wits. Poor Lorvie was a few years older than Ember, but she still had the mind of a child.

The fact that she had adored Ember from the time they were young made it that much easier for him to manipulate her.

"What about Mendin?" Armille asked. "I thought you aristocratic cunts always stuck together?"

Ember glared at him again. "He's a stubborn old man. Still holds a grudge against me for something my grandmother did to him before I was even born. If he knows I'm in favor of a measure, he'll vote against it out of pure spite."

"In any case," Cambin said, "he's too busy cozying up to Trinn thinking he can weasel into the mob's good graces."

"Tarsa and Rendulcar seem to be lining up behind her as well," Ithlene said. "Most of their backing comes from small time brokers in

Cadgerwalk and Wallside. They think they're going to build up a faction that can push back against Dhrath."

She refrained from pointing out that all three of Ember's guests owed their seats on the Assembly of Notables to Dhrath's support and machinations.

You've got a tentacle down everyone's pants, don't you, you slimy bastard?

"Then five against four is where we stand," Armille said. "We need to scrape up two more votes somehow."

"What about Norvel?" Ithlene asked. "He's in up to his neck with Coldwater's moneylenders. Surely they have an interest in how much money the borough taxes and spends?"

Cambin shook his head. "They have an interest in making sure it does just that. The more debts the district authorities run up, the more people come crawling to them for loans. That alone will make Norvel a hard sell."

"Murga," Ember said. "That fat sod would sell his children off for a slab of good meat. We just need to find what he's got an appetite for these days."

"That leaves Harik and Selinis," Armille said. "Hardly the best choices for pinning down the deciding vote."

Ember rarely agreed with Armille, but he had to admit the observation was accurate. Selinis Omescha and Harik Gondulin were, along with Trinn, the only members of the Assembly of Notables who held their seats thanks to a popular election rather than heredity or nepotism. That made them a little trickier to deal with than their colleagues.

"No point wasting time with Selinis. If a measure doesn't do anything to address immorality or add another religious holiday to the calendar, she could care less about it."

"Could work to our advantage," Ithlene said. "Maybe we can convince her to abstain when it's time for a vote."

Cambin scoffed. "She's too stubborn for that. That one never misses a chance to make sure those wailing voters of hers have a say in any matter of consequence."

"Harik, then?" Ithlene asked.

"Just as stubborn, if you ask me," Armille said.

Ember nodded. "Maybe, but he's also a barely literate mule. I'd be shocked if he understood a tenth of what's said during most Assembly debates."

"And he doesn't much care for guilds of any stripe," Ithlene said.

That notable detail had not slipped Ember's mind. An untrained laborer before his election to the assembly, Harik became a central figure in the workers riots targeting Lowtown's craft guilds several years ago. The mobs turned out in force to elect him to office after his predecessor perished under suspicious circumstances. Despite not accomplishing anything more than delivering insulting speeches from the Assembly Hall steps decrying guild intimidation tactics, he remained popular among the district's impoverished laborers.

Maybe...

"Hardly an ironclad alliance," Cambin said, shaking his head.

Armille drained the rest of his goblet and sighed. "How long until the spader contract expires again?"

"A little less than three months," Ithlene said. "The guildmasters are probably getting anxious after Ember's spat with the ambassador. They don't often face opposition to renewing their contract." She looked across the table at Ember. "Maybe it would have been better to hold your tongue rather than—"

Ember slapped his hand down on the table. "Damn the Spaders and their ambassador. If I'd let him go on any longer there was a good chance of him or that bitch Trinn asking for a vote to renew the contract right then and there. They do that before we get our support together, we could be stuck with the bastards bleeding our coffers dry for another year. Is that what you'd prefer?"

"Of course not," Ithlene said, crossing her arms and scowling. "But I'd rather they went right on thinking a good portion of the Assembly wasn't trying to upend the negotiations before they've even started."

Ember rolled his eyes. "Let them think whatever they want. It won't make any difference so long as we have the votes to force their hand."

"It will take more than votes to get the better of the spaders in these negotiations," Cambin said. "You still haven't told us how you plan to do that."

And I won't. Not yet.

"You let me worry about that," Ember said.

Armille laughed. "So you keep telling us, yet I'm beginning to wonder if our blind trust is misplaced."

"Wonder away, then. I don't give a damn if you think you should trust me or not. So long as Dhrath has confidence in me to see this through, I know I'll find each of you lining up to give your support when the time comes. I'm sure I don't have to remind you how your beloved benefactor feels about faithless surrogates in the Assembly?"

Armille slumped his shoulders and sank into his seat. Cambin and Ithlene averted their eyes, neither of them willing to suggest they might dare to defy the most feared broker in Lowtown. Dhrath's sponsorship helped to elevate each of them to their Assembly seats and kept them there so long as they promoted his interests. When he told them to cast their vote behind a measure, he expected them to obey.

And if they did not, the broker would find someone who would. After, of course, he "created" an opening in the Assembly.

Ember let all of that sink in for a moment before he reached for his goblet.

"Now, then," he said, "there is one other matter we need to take into consideration. Our self-styled champion of Lowtown's seething masses isn't likely to back down even if we carry a measure with seven votes. Assemblywoman Trinn is many things, but she's no foolish neophyte. She'll seize on any chance to block us with some tangled point of procedure that hasn't been invoked for centuries."

Ithlene groaned. "No shortage of those precedents if she's willing to dig through the records long enough to find them."

Ember knew of several tactics to delay votes from taking place and at least one or two ways to invalidate voting results, but that only covered things he recalled from his own lifetime. Surely the Assembly's history was replete with far more obtuse methods of achieving gridlock.

"Difficult," Cambin said. "And quite impossible with a commanding majority. I know of no measure capable of overturning a result supported by nine members."

Armille chuckled, although his former humor had not yet returned. "A moment ago we were scratching to get to seven votes. Now you're suggesting nine?"

Ember shared his concern. Securing four additional votes to get to nine would be difficult, probably impossible under the circumstances.

If we had another three months, maybe…

"What about the quorum rules?" Ithlene asked. "The Assembly can convene and hear petitions with only seven, but how many have to be present to call for a vote on a measure?"

They all looked to Cambin, who had spent more years in the Assembly than the rest of them put together.

"Nine," he said, "but seven votes are still needed for approval."

Ithlene nodded. "Difficult to arrange, but we know Trinn and Mendin will never side with us. Same as Tarsa and Rendulcar. Take them away and we're left with our quorum."

"Risky," Armille said. "The aftermath could get complicated."

Maybe more complicated than failing.

Ember rose from his chair. "Everything about this is a risk. We need to consider every option, desirable or otherwise. But none of them will matter if we can't even sort out how we're going to get to seven votes."

The others nodded.

"Where do you want to start, then?" Ithlene asked.

Ember thought for a moment, considering each Assembly member in turn before he spoke. He finally settled on a sweaty, swollen face that looked like the offspring of a hog and a toad.

"Murga," he said. "Tell me what we know for sure about Murga. Is it true the fat sod has a litter of bastards scattered around Pigshire?"

EMBER'S GUESTS DEPARTED well past midnight, leaving him in peace at last after hours of fitful debate over how to best persuade two recalcitrant Assembly members to join their coalition. Orchestrating their plans down to the finest detail had grown tiresome. Sometimes he questioned whether his allies could do anything for themselves. Years of bribes and petty corruption had made them averse to risks, rendered them incapable of taking so much as a piss without first securing a go ahead from their benefactors.

With leadership like that, could anyone be surprised that Lowtown's boroughs were so dysfunctional?

While Ember hardly considered himself a paragon of civic righteousness, at least his assembly seat was not held in the grip of some bloodless broker. Odds were good that at least one of his guests was already scurrying off to relay news of the meeting to one of Dhrath's men.

Bootlicking cunts.

He left his dinner coat slung over the table and extinguished the candles in the dining room before he climbed the main staircase to the manse's second floor. Most of the bedchambers there were shut up behind locked doors, some of them sealed long before Ember was born. Aside from Ember's room, only one chamber remained open and furnished, mostly for the purpose of accommodating guests. Yimina slept there sometimes, usually when Ember wanted his bed all to himself for one reason or another.

Ember heard Yimina hurrying up the stairs before he could reach the safety of his chamber door. She had not shown her face for some time, leading him to assume she was already asleep.

Moving awfully fast at this hour. Must be something important.

Ember groaned. He was tired after talking in circles with his supposed allies for most of the night, and all he could think about was collapsing in bed.

"Whatever it is, it can wait until morning," he said.

Yimina reached the top of the stairs quickly and hurried down the hall to catch up to him. Before he could push by her, she planted herself outside his door and delivered the same scowl she had given him from the time he could walk.

She grabbed his arm and leaned in close to him. "No, sir, it really can't. I would have told you earlier, but I didn't think you'd want your guests to know."

"To know what?"

Yimina leaned even closer to whisper into his ear. "She's sent...someone for you. A messenger, I think. I found him skulking around the back entrance when I went outside to empty a wash basin. Said she insisted that he speak directly to you and only to you."

"Why didn't you tell me this earlier?"

"I'm sorry, sir, but I didn't want to distract you from your guests. Besides, it's probably for the best that they didn't see...him."

Ember trusted Yimina's instincts. She generally had a good read on people, and it took a great deal to put her off balance. If she found the messenger discomforting, Ember could only imagine how poorly his fellow assembly members would have reacted.

He sighed. "Yes, that was probably for the best. Where's this charming fellow at the moment?"

"I shut him up in old library. Told him you'd be with him as soon as you were free. I checked in on him a few times, but he hasn't budged."

Ember rubbed at his eyes.

Of all the times...

"I guess there's no hope of putting him off any longer, then. Come on. Let's go see what's so damned important."

Carrying a candle to light their way, Yimina led him down the steps and through the manse's first floor to the east wing's library. The room was not completely shuttered, but it had gone unused for anything other than storage for many years. When they reached the door, she passed the candle holder to Ember.

"You'll need this," she said as she slipped a key into the lock. The hinges groaned when the door opened. Stale air wafted into the hallway, carrying the scent of mold and rotting wood upon it. The candlelight scarcely illuminated anything beyond the door's threshold, creating little more than a faint, yellow bubble pushing back against the indeterminate blackness.

"Wait here," Ember said. "I'll call out if I need you."

Yimina gave him the scowl again, but she said nothing as Ember stepped inside the library.

Old furniture and stacks of unmarked crates covered with heavy, moth eaten sheets crowded the otherwise expansive room. Nothing there had been disturbed for many years, as was evident from the thick layers of dust and cobwebs clumped atop every surface. The place felt like the tomb of some ancient lord, its contents doomed to decay alongside their owner's shriveling husk.

"Hello?"

Ember's voice did not echo through the room, but rather thudded wetly against the old blankets and moldering wood.

Something stirred beyond the candlelight's reach.

"Lord Morangine?"

A man about Ember's size stepped forward, his movements slow and deliberate. Dressed like a common street beggar, he wore a burlap sheet over his shoulders as if it were a traveler's cloak. Dark veins, vericose and swollen, stood out on the exposed flesh around his wrists and hands. His eyes were completely white, shimmering faintly when the light struck them. The skin around the eyes was bruised black and blue, with tiny, purplish lines streaking down his sunken cheeks.

Most troubling, however, was the fact that he did not appear to be breathing.

"Yes, I'm Ember Morangine." He did his best to keep his voice steady. "My steward tells me you've brought me a message?"

The stranger finally drew breath, though he seemed to do so only to force the dry, rattling voice from his throat.

"The Twiceborn sends you her regards," he said. "This one brings her words for you to hear."

Hearing that voice put Ember's teeth on edge. The sooner he could be rid of this thing, the better. "Go on, then."

The messenger continued to stare blindly ahead, its white eyes incapable of focusing on anything. It took another rasping breath and went on speaking.

"My work is proceeding more swiftly after relocation. I have arranged for a steady supply of materials and expect to have the first batch available for you by the end of the month."

The end of the month? That's far sooner than we expected.

The messenger continued: "Understand that it will become very difficult to keep my work hidden after that point. Discovery by the watch or one of the guilds is almost certain. I trust that you will be able to deliver on your promises of protection in that event."

One month. Ember had not dared to hope that she would move so quickly.

We need to get those votes now.

"Of course," he said. "You needn't—"

"Given my progress," the messenger said, completely ignoring Ember's reply, "it may become necessary to replenish the raw materials necessary for my work. Should the need arise, I will send another messenger to facilitate procurement."

Procurement. That sounded a bit too much like payment for Ember's liking.

"Now just a moment, your master made no mention of—"

"In the meantime, Lord Morangine," the messenger said, again ignoring him, "I give you my most sincere regards and look forward to our next meeting. Please see that this messenger returns to me unharmed. Its discovery could create undue suspicion surrounding our activities. Should you need to contact me for any reason, pass your message along to one of my children on Merrowshead Street."

Ember crossed his arms and scowled, waiting for the bizarre emissary to continue, but it remained silent, staring blankly ahead.

"Is that all?" he asked.

"This one brings the Twiceborn's words and nothing more. It will repeat her words if you wish."

"No, no," Ember said, waving his hands. "I don't need to hear it again. Does she expect you to bring a reply?"

The messenger's slack expression betrayed nothing, neither a thought nor a single stray motivation. "No. But this one can carry your words if you wish."

"Then tell her that everything is in order. I will contact her should any problems arise. Is that simple enough for you to understand?"

"This one carries words, Lord Morangine. It need not understand them."

"Fine. You'll tell her what I said?"

"This one will carry your words to the Twiceborn."

Ember turned and walked back to the doorway, where Yimina stood waiting for him.

"Is everything—?"

"Get that damned thing out of my home," he said, shoving the candle holder into her hands. "Take it out the back way and be quick about it. Make sure no one sees you, understand?"

Yimina nodded. "Of course, sir."

"Lock the doors when you return," he said. "And don't disturb my chambers. I need time alone to think."

"As you wish."

Ember strode past her and navigated through the dark manse, carefully feeling his way along the walls to avoid stumbling. When he reached the staircase, muscle memory guided him up the steps and to his bedchamber. He did not bother lighting the candle on his bedside table, instead flinging his tired body down upon the feather-stuffed mattress.

Dhrath. Twiceborn. Trinn. The Spaders.

Any one of them was difficult to manage on their own. Somehow, he had to deal with all of them at once.

"You think any damn fool can run this borough, boy? That's what the mob thinks. And that's why it'll burn if they ever get their way."

While he always understood his grandmother's observation about governance on an emotional level, he realized now that he failed to appreciate the point she was trying to make. Anyone could identify and deal with a single problem for the benefit of a single interest. The mob seldom thought beyond its own stomach, while letches like his father were driven by similarly base desires with no regard for what such urges might wrought. What set the politically capable apart from the politically incompetent was the ability to balance multiple problems and interests against one another while still being able to anticipate the consequences.

That was how the Morangines once dominated Coldwater borough, and the greater part of Lowtown before that. If even a hint of those days were to return, Ember would have to see his way through his current predicament.

Two votes, he thought as he drifted off to sleep. *It either begins or ends with two votes.*

10
THE WOMAN

The day was half gone by the time Calandra finally staggered out of the mortuary and headed home.

She and Tarl had gone straight to work on the fresh arrival, scrubbing the skin clean and feeding tubes down its throat to pump the liquefied waste from the stomach and lungs. A typical body took only an hour or two to prep if there was no physical trauma to repair, but this one took more than the remainder of her shift. After she finished cleaning and dressing the corpse, she had Tarl carry it over to a table in the back of the viewing chamber before sending the poor, hardworking devil home.

That had been around noon. If she had any sense, she would have followed him out the door.

But she had a hard time forgetting what she saw roaming the crypts during the night, nor could she shake the idea that Lerris might be involved with the bodysnatchers somehow. Unfortunately, the arrival of the latest corpse prevented her from checking the records for any discrepancies. Once Lerris arrived, it would be impossible to review the ledger without arousing suspicion. Although the overdue bodies themselves had already been hauled off to the furnace for cremation, she still had their identification tags stuffed inside her pockets.

Her investigation would have to wait another day.

Lerris was supposed to relieve her shortly after dawn, but she usually arrived at least an hour late. Today proved no different. Calandra said as little to her as possible, scarcely acknowledging the hateful woman's arrival as she and Tarl went about their work.

"Looks like a nasty one you've got there, girl," Lerris said while making her initial rounds.

She laughed sharply.

"Best scrub those dainty little fingers of yours when you're done with him unless you want every pigsticker in the borough following you home."

Calandra kept her teeth together and went on working.

Although only a few years older, Lerris looked like she had worked in the dry, toxic air of the Deadhouse for much longer. When Calandra served her apprenticeship for the Undertakers Guild, her master advised her to always set a portion of her pay aside for the lotions and salves that could remoisturize the skin and protect her flesh and hair from the harsh chemicals used to clean the corpses.

Lerris, as she was fond of pointing out, had not received such helpful advice.

Her skin was as dry and rough as stale bread. Thin scabs covered most of her joints, even at the knuckles. Occasionally they cracked and seeped a thin, reddish yellow substance that dripped onto the papers at her desk. Her eyes had absorbed so many fumes over the years that they now possessed a faintly green tint, and her thin lips were always slit and chapped. Much of her straw-colored hair had fallen out, but she kept her sleeveless robe's hood pulled over her head most of the time.

Even at this early hour, her breath already stank of sour wine.

Lerris stood at the foot of the table for several minutes, watching Calandra and Tarl as they finished syphoning the vile liquid from the corpse's deflated lungs with a throat pump. Only when Calandra withdrew the long, brass tube from the dead man's windpipe did she snarl some curse under her breath and move along to scowl at someone else.

After she finished with the corpse, Calandra doused her arms with scouring powder and scraped them clean with a bit of water and a stiff-bristled brush. The powder made her skin tingle and probably took off as much flesh as it did dirt. Although it left her arms pink and tender, she at least felt clean after spending the last several hours covered in a slick layer of bile and excrement. When she got home, she would coat herself with murkseed oil for an hour to keep her scorched skin from scaling and flaking.

Lerris had settled down at her desk by the time Calandra got around to cleaning herself. The vile woman made a big show of sifting through the paperwork from the previous evening. Every now and again, Lerris looked up at her, but she never said anything.

More importantly, she never mentioned the corpse Calandra had been working on during morning, not even to ask why no ledger entry documented its arrival.

Calandra had not intended to omit the record, at least not at first. When the corpse arrived, she was too preoccupied with questioning how the bodysnatchers gained access to the crypts to remember to record the details. When she did think of it, she was already helping Tarl drain the body's sewage-laden lungs and could not step away to tend to menial paperwork. Once Lerris arrived, however, she simply had no opportunity to make the entry without being noticed.

The circumstances of the oversight were quite irrelevant; Lerris was not the sort of woman to let such mistakes go unpunished. The last time Calandra made an error in the records, the bitch made her forfeit three days' pay. The Undertakers Guild staked its reputation on its records, Lerris told her. Should the guild fail to produce viable information to the local watch or Crown authorities, that reputation, to say nothing of the lucrative contracts and tax exemptions that went with it, could be jeopardized.

Not that Calandra believed a word of that. The error had been relatively minor, a simple transposition of a few street names. With Lerris, the reasons were usually far more personal. She seldom missed an opportunity to lord anything over Calandra's head.

Maybe she's already noticed. She could be biding her time, waiting until she thinks I'm not expecting anything.

The concern was warranted, especially since she saw Calandra and Tarl cleaning the corpse when she came in that morning.

Or perhaps Calandra gave Lerris more credit that she deserved. Maybe she simply missed the fact that there was no log entry to document the corpse's arrival. And if she missed something so blindingly obvious, maybe the surplus bodies in the crypts were the plain and simple result of negligence.

She couldn't be that *incompetent...could she?*

But there were too many mislabeled bodies for the situation to be a mere oversight. And who other than Lerris could be responsible for such blatant meddling? Calandra wondered what the guildmasters would think about her abetting the bodysnatchers in the crypts. The guild's punishments for mishandling corpses tended to be swift and decisive, both to set an example for other members and to demonstrate to civic authorities how seriously the guild regarded its responsibilities.

If Lerris was involved with the bodysnatchers, then, she certainly had good reason to avoid any questions about the records.

Maybe she thinks I know something. Maybe she's afraid I heard them in the crypts last night and hopes I'll just keep my mouth shut.

Calandra had no proof of any malfeasance, of course, only suspicions.

For now.

Lerris barely looked up when Calandra approached the desk to gather her hat, shawl, and satchel.

"On your way, then?" she asked.

ACT

"Been a long night."

Lerris gnawed at one of her fingernails. Some of her teeth were going gray in spots. "Anything I need to know about last night?"

Calandra rubbed her cheek, pretending to think about any number of dull evenings from previous weeks.

"Nothing," she said. "Got a few more names, but that's about it. Had them moved down below."

She watched Lerris's eyes closely, hoping to catch a glimpse of something, some indication that she had something to hide. Aside from the persistent twitching at the corner of her mouth, her wrinkled face betrayed nothing.

"You take them down yourself?"

Calandra shook her head. "Of course not. Tarl saw to it."

Lerris snorted. "Good. Wouldn't want you to catch a chill down there."

Calandra let the insinuation go unanswered. Hard experience told her it was usually easier to let the crusty bitch have the last word.

Lerris leaned back in her chair as Calandra donned her hat and pulled her satchel over her shoulder.

"In a hurry, are you? Got some rake waiting to pounce on you someplace?"

Lerris's green-tinged eyes clawed at the collar of her shirt. Calandra hurriedly wrapped the shawl around her neck and crossed her arms against her chest.

"My shift's done," she said, meeting Lerris's leer with a stern glare. "What I do on my time is none of your business."

For a moment, Lerris just stared at her, her sickly eyes fit to bursting with venom. She bit off a piece of a fingernail and spat at Calandra's feet.

"Don't waste time here on my account, then."

CALANDRA HAD WORKED at the Deadhouse for less than a week the first time Lerris tried to touch her.

It started innocently enough, of course. Lerris made a big fuss about her skin and her hair, loudly bemoaning that no one saw fit to tell her how to protect her young body from the hazards of their occupation. At first, Calandra was glad to be working with another woman, as precious few of them completed their apprenticeship to become journeymen undertakers. Lerris had also attained her rank at a young age and possessed a wealth of experience that she promised to impart.

But Calandra got a better idea of her real intentions the first time she asked for "help" down in the crypts.

She broke her wrist in the ensuing scuffle and left Lerris with a blackened eye. The bone took weeks to heal, but the emotional scars from the encounter ran far deeper. Calandra never told anyone what went on in the darkness, and they both provided all sorts of excuses for their respective injuries. Lerris never forgave her for it, and she was not the sort of woman to take rejection lightly.

Calandra petitioned for months to transfer to the night shift after that, and she spent each day waiting for some "accident" to befall her. When the guildmasters finally agreed to reassign her, she felt like she had wriggled free from a hangman's noose. The schedule proved difficult to endure, but it was preferable to spending her days under Lerris's baleful stare.

SITUATED AT THE intersection of Dustwalk and Caravel Street, the Moonvale Theater remained a prominent Coldwater landmark even though no troubadours had performed upon its stage for decades. In addition to being much taller than the neighboring buildings, the theater stood out because of the intricate woodwork framing its doors and windows. The uniformly old wood had darkened after more than a century of absorbing soot and dust from the city's foul air.

Calandra traversed the short distance between the theater and the Deadhouse every day. The walk took longer when her shift ended late, forcing her to contend with the heavier, midday traffic for merchants and workers packing the streets. When she finally reached the theater, she walked down the narrow alley behind it, which led to the private, back entrance. A small courtyard behind the building served as a practice area and storage space back when the theater was still in use, but it stood mostly empty now. The space might have been covered by a roof in those day, but little remained beyond an uneven layer of clay bricks, half of which were either cracked or missing.

The back door was as old as the rest of the building, and Calandra had to jiggle her key in the lock to force it open. She entered the building through what used to be a backstage area. Various props, most of them broken, lay strewn haphazardly about the room. Several dozen rolls of moth-eaten canvas backdrops leaned against the back wall, stacked up behind bits of wooden scenery cutouts. The whole place smelled of mildew and rotting wood.

During the theater's prime years, a large, heavy curtain separated the backstage area from the main auditorium, but nothing remained of it but the heavy support chains hanging from the ceiling. The stage extended in a semicircle out into the center of the room, surrounded by three tiers of bench seating. Only a few of the benches remained, but the stage itself was in decent condition. The playing surface rose a foot above the floor, supported by a skillfully constructed latticework of support beams beneath it. The large windows positioned high along the three walls looking down on the stage would have manipulated the stage's lighting when the theater was still in use, but now they were covered by soot-encrusted sheets of cheap canvas. Sunlight stabbed through the numerous holes worn open by harsh weather, decay, and insects.

As decrepit as the place looked now, Calandra had to admit that it must have been quite a sight in its heyday. That admission allowed her brother, Beyland, to convince her to help buy the place nearly two years ago. He "knew someone," he claimed, who could "get them a fair price." Her brother was running a successful stage troupe at the time, but most of their meager earnings went to the brokers that owned most of Lowtown's theaters. Owning a theater, he insisted, was where the real money could be had. And since the Moonvale Theater had living quarters on its second floor, they would be investing in a home as well as a business. When he took her to the aging building, he showed her not what it was, but what it could be. He envisioned a beautifully restored auditorium that would outshine every other venue in Lowtown. Not only would his own troupe perform there, but every stage company in the city, even those north of the Saven, would give up a percentage of their profits for the privilege of performing there.

Ever the performer, Beyland made an inspired case.

And ever the fool, Calandra had believed him.

What he did not tell her, or maybe what he did not know, was that purchasing the theater was only the first step in a much longer and extremely expensive process. First they had to repair the roof and walls just to make the building livable again. By the time they finally moved into the place, Beyland had lost half of his troupe to competitors offering more regular work. Further renovations, at least on the scale Beyland envisioned, were simply out of the question.

They also neglected to consider the hefty tax obligations of owning such a large property until a "representative" from Coldwater's Assembly of Notables came to collect their annual duties, which wiped out the rest of Calandra's meager savings. The rest of the troupe left shortly afterwards, taking advantage of their ability to simply walk away from Beyland's endeavor.

Calandra, of course, did not have the same luxury.

A young man sat near the edge of the stage with several stacks of papers arranged around him. He ignored Calandra as she walked toward him, even when her footfalls echoed through the cavernous auditorium. She stopped a few feet short of him and waited for him to notice her, but he went on furiously scribbling something upon a long sheet of parchment. The papers on the floor sported various images of the theater's walls, seating area, and stage. A few even featured drawings of elaborate systems of pulleys and gears for controlling window shutters.

Calandra coughed loudly.

Kardi nearly fell over, flinging the papers high into the air as he scrambled to catch himself. Some of the pages flew up into the second row of seating. Even as tired as she was, Calandra had to laugh.

"Gods, Cal, don't sneak up on me like that!"

Calandra offered her hand to pull him up. Kardi was a little younger than her brother, who was himself a few years younger than her. Like Beyland, he spent most of his time daydreaming. Her brother pestered him relentlessly for plans to renovate the theater, but his artistic ambitions generally outstripped their ability to finance them.

According to Beyland, Kardi used to work for some renowned theater owner north of the Saven. The circumstances that brought him to Lowtown remained a bit unclear, however, as was the nature of his employment. Judging from the sketches he made, Kardi plainly had some talent, but his stories about working at the theater were vague enough that Calandra wondered if he ever did anything more than scrub the floors there.

Beyland never told her where he met Kardi, but she suspected they spent a night passed out together at a local winesink. At some point during the last few months, he apparently moved into one of the empty rooms upstairs. Calandra planned on renting that room out at some point, but Beyland insisted that he needed Kardi's help to get the theater up and running. Since he could not afford to pay him, providing him a roof was an equitable exchange.

At least, that was how Beyland saw it. Calandra was more realistic. She knew damn well how much coin they could be collecting by renting that room out.

Kardi took her hand and stood up. Although slight of build already, he seemed a bit thinner than usual. When Calandra got a better look at his face, she saw the dark circles around his sunken, unfocused eyes. He smiled at her with his crooked teeth and she saw the bits of black gunk clinging to his gumlines.

Nightroot.

She wondered if Beyland had been sharing in the habit again.

"What are you doing down here, Kardi?"

The sharpness of the question seemed to catch him off guard. He fidgeted, rubbing his hands together and chewing on spit.

"Just sketching out some ideas before Beyland gets back. "

Calandra sighed. "He's not here now? He said he wanted to get back to writing today."

It was far from the first time Beyland failed to keep to that promise. Although the theater needed more work, it was certainly serviceable if he could only manage to pull a production together. But he needed a troupe in order to do that, and to recruit a troupe, he first needed a play to perform. He had supposedly been writing for more than a year, but Calandra had yet to see anything more than a few incomplete soliloquies and monologues, none of them very good.

Kardi shrugged. "I don't think he's written much of anything lately. Said something this morning about needing more inspiration."

The nervous tone of his response made her want to shove him off the stage. Beyland's idea of inspiration usually involved something more than staring wistfully into the sky.

If he was curled up in some back alley shithole with a pouch of firedust again...

I'll give you some inspiration, little brother.

"He say where he was going?" she asked, though she doubted she actually wanted to know the answer.

"No. You know how he is when he's got his mind set on something."

Calandra did.

Shame he can't set it on something productive once in a while.

When she did not respond, Kardi knelt to gather up his scattered papers. He shuffled them loudly, arranging them in some specific order only he understood. Calandra rubbed her eyes, wishing she went to sleep hours ago.

"How's the planning coming?" she asked.

Kardi's face brightened again.

"Oh, good! Good! I've been trying to figure how to get the most out of these windows..."

He went on talking, but Calandra tuned him out. None of his elaborate planning mattered anyway. Beyland could not afford to have the work done, and even if he could, he had no show to put on the stage.

His troupe had him figured long before Calandra realized his dream had turned into a nightmare.

SHE SLEPT FOR only an hour or two before the screams from Beyland's room woke her up.

Groggy at first, she needed a few moments to realize the voice did not belong to her brother. Calandra rolled out of bed, pulled her shawl over her undershirt, and stumbled to the door.

Kardi rolled on the floor of the narrow hallway, clutching at his arm and sobbing. Blood seeped from between his fingers.

She knelt beside him to get a better look at the wound. The cut was shallow, but it looked nasty, likely inflicted by something too dull to slice through the skin cleanly. Despite all the blood, no arteries had been severed. For as much as the gash probably hurt, he was in no danger of bleeding out.

"What happened?" she asked.

Too caught up in his sobbing to respond coherently, Kardi managed only to nod in the direction of Beyland's room. Another scream ripped down the hallway, this one loud enough to make Calandra shiver. She pushed by Kardi and threw open the door to her brother's room.

Beyland stood over his bed trying to restrain a writhing, naked woman. He had a firm grip on her arms, but her legs kicked out wildly, throwing her body up and down on the mattress. Her back jerked so fiercely she seemed ready to dislocate both of her shoulders if Beyland kept hold of her.

The sounds she made were unlike anything Calandra had heard before, half-choked screams buried within guttural snarls and bits of some obtuse language.

"Beyland, what—?"

"Help me!" he said. "Get her legs!"

Calandra rushed over to the bed and caught one of the woman's ankles. The other foot slammed into her shoulder, but she managed to grab it before it could hit her again. There was blood everywhere, most of it streaming from a badly tied bandage wrapped around her midsection. Calandra tried to get a glimpse of the woman's face, but she did not get beyond the shimmering chunk of black stone embedded in her chest.

Almost the size of her fist, the stone's glistening surface seemed to drain the rest of her senses away, pulling her attention to it completely. She almost lost her grip on the woman's thrashing legs before she heard a distant voice screaming at her.

"Get her legs down, dammit!"

Calandra blinked, snapping away from the stone's hypnotic pull. She glanced at the woman's face to see her eyes glazed over with a black, inky film. Her features twisted and contorted like an animal caught in some trap, her curled lips continuously spewing a profane litany of snarls and queer phrasings.

The woman grew stronger as she struggled, occasionally pulling an arm away from Beyland's grasp and blindly beating at him with her fist. Calandra felt a steady wave of heat coming off her body. The women's skin grew almost painfully hot the longer Calandra held onto her.

And then, abruptly, she lost consciousness and her naked body fell still.

They stood there in dumbstruck surprise for a few moments before Beyland gently set her arms down and gestured for Calandra to do the same with her legs.

"What the hell was that about?" she asked.

"I don't know," Beyland said, wiping the sweat from his brow. "Some kind of fit. We were barely inside the theater when it took her."

Calandra noticed Beyland staring at the unconscious woman's chest. She grit her teeth.

"Don't just leave her like this," she said, her tone every bit as reproachful as their mother's had once been. "Get these sheets off the floor while I clean her up."

Beyland nodded and went about gathering the sheets that had fallen from the bed during the struggle. Calandra fetched the washbasin from a nearby table and gently dabbed a wet rag over the woman's body to sop up the blood. Most of it was still wet and came off the skin easily. Numerous scratches stood out on her chest, all of them clustered around the black stone embedded between her breasts.

The scratches were not the source of all the blood, however.

Beneath a stained bandage wrapped loosely around the woman's midsection, Calandra found a large, circular cut about the width of a walnut just below the left breast. Blood still trickled slowly from the wound.

She had seen identical marks on quite a few corpses back at the Deadhouse. Only one thing she knew of that left an incision like that.

Gods... The thing must have been huge. She's lucky to be alive.

Beyland hissed over her shoulder. "I tried to wrap that up earlier. Is it bad?"

She shook her head. "I don't think so. It's not deep, so it should start to scab over if she doesn't move around too much. We should staunch it, though, just to be sure. Get me a clean rag."

Beyland helped her fashion a new bandage and secure it tightly against the wound. After they finished, they draped the sheets over the strange woman's body. Her pale skin all but blended in with the sheet, but her hair shone as black as the foreboding spire at the heart of the city.

"Are you going to tell me what's going on here," Calandra asked, "or do I have to beat it out of you?"

Beyland blew the air from his lungs and placed his hands on top of his head. He kept staring at the woman.

Calandra wondered if it would be more effective to yank on his ear or kick him in the shin.

The loud moans coming from the hallway robbed her of the opportunity to make a decision.

"Kardi!" Beyland said as he hurried to the door. "Are you okay?"

Calandra took the bloodied rag from the washbasin and followed him into the hallway. Kardi's sweat-slicked skin had lost its color and he was breathing heavily now, still clutching at his wounded arm. She shouldered past Beyland and yanked the bloody arm out of his grasp.

"Ouch!"

Kardi shuddered and sobbed as she picked at his wound.

She much preferred patching up a dead man's wounds rather than hassle with a living man's.

At least a corpse has the decency to keep quiet.

Calandra slapped him across the cheek before his whimpering went any further.

"Shut up and sit still," she said. "It barely broke the skin, whatever it was."

Kardi bit his lip and squeezed his eyelids together. A slow trickle of water leaked from the corners of his eyes.

"Teeth," Beyland said. "Her teeth."

Calandra dabbed the blood away from the small gash torn into his flesh. The bleeding had already slowed.

"Hell of a bite," she said. "Was that before or after the fit started?"

"After. Kardi helped me get her up the steps before she turned on him."

She pressed the rag tightly against the wound and placed Kardi's free hand over it.

"Hold that tight until I come back."

She lifted his chin so that their gazes met.

"If it doesn't stop bleeding by then," she said, "we'll have a surgeon cut it off at the elbow."

Kardi's jaw dropped as Calandra rose and went back to the bedroom. Beyland followed closely after her.

"Why did you tell him that?" he asked. "His arm doesn't look that—"

"It'll shut him up for a while," she said, looking the slumbering woman over. "Who the hell is she, anyway?"

"I...I don't know."

She glared at him. "You're going to have to do better than that, little brother."

Beyland sighed.

And then he told her where the woman came from. Told her how he tromped over to Pigshire just after midday to visit some dump of a winesink called *The Bleating Goat*. He never got around to explaining why he went there, but it hardly mattered. After seeing the wound on the woman's skin, Calandra knew exactly what sort of place he planned on visiting.

It took everything she had to conceal her anger as he went on with his story.

He told her how he went upstairs to see an old friend, which was such a flimsy lie that Calandra doubted even Kardi would believe it. After that, he heard someone screaming and then found the naked woman, covered in blood and standing over a dead body while she tore at the stone in her chest with her fingernails.

"I didn't know what to do," he said. "I...I just tried to calm her down, you know? She was terrified. Looked about half crazy, too, but there was something about her that made me want to help her."

I'm sure the fact she was naked had nothing to do with it.

"So you brought her here?" she asked.

Beyland crossed his arms, the same as he used to do when their father caught him in some mischief.

"Well, what was I supposed to do, Cal? Leave her there? She was obviously in trouble. I helped her get her clothes, wrapped my cloak around her, and led her out of the place before anyone was the wiser. The common room was pretty full by then. I doubt anybody even heard her scream."

Calandra rubbed her eyes. She was tired enough after getting back late and this situation made her head hurt.

"How many people there know you?"

"Nobody," Beyland said. "I've never—"

"Don't you lie to me, Beyland! You dragged this junkie away from a murder! How many people there know you?"

He looked at his feet, his crossed arms tightening.

"A few," he said, "maybe. I don't know."

Calandra grabbed him by the jaw and jerked his head up to look at his eyes. She studied them closely, searching for the telltale signs of orange glitter in the whites, but found nothing. If he was using firedust again, he had been clean for a few days.

"Gods, you're an idiot," she said, releasing him. She looked down at the woman, who looked almost serene now.

Her gaze lingered on the lump between her breasts.

"What the hell is that thing in her chest?"

Beyland shook his head. "It was like that when I found her. Thought it was a necklace or something at first, but it looks like part of her skin. I've never seen anything like it before."

Calandra wished she were still asleep and that this whole mess was just a bad dream.

"She can't stay here, Beyland," she said. "The watch might be looking for her already. If they find her here—"

"You can't throw her out on the street now, Cal!" he said, uncrossing his arms.

Calandra turned and shoved him with one hand. Beyland stumbled back a few steps before catching his balance on the bedpost.

"Don't make this about me, you little scamp! You're the one that should have left her in that place!"

They glared at each other for a moment before Beyland looked down and rubbed his hand across his face.

"I...I'm sorry, Cal," he said, his voice almost too quiet to hear. "I couldn't help myself. I just saw her and I knew I had to, I don't know, do something. I know I should have turned around, just walked away, but I couldn't."

He looked up at her, tears clinging to his eyelids.

"She needed me, Cal. Nobody's ever needed me before, at least not like that."

Calandra sighed. There was something slightly pathetic about her brother's confession, but when she looked at him, she noticed he stood differently than normal. He did not fidget or shift his weight from foot to foot, nor did he wring his hands or cross his arms like a petulant child. She had a hard time identifying what had changed, but there *was* something peculiar about his demeanor.

Dammit. Who's the idiot now?

"Three days," she said. "She can stay for three days, but once she's healed up enough to get on her way, I want her out."

Beyland said something in response, but Calandra had already turned away by the time he spoke up.

She was too tired to listen anymore.

11
THE DEBT

A rden was sure he got the address wrong.

He walked by the crumbling lean-to on Mothweed Street three times before he finally decided to try the door. Most of the buildings in Sinkhole lacked any street numbers and the rest refused to follow the seemingly logical order that residents of more organized boroughs like Coldwater took for granted. People in Sinkhole also tended to move around a good bit, squatting in one place only for a few months before getting booted out by someone tougher or more desperate. Arden knew the street layout well enough, but even he had trouble finding places without some direction from the locals.

Without the cover of darkness, Sinkhole's poverty proved impossible to ignore. Heaps of refuse piled outside the buildings, and the sick and itinerant sat alongside every street, gazing dumbly at stray animals and the people walking past. Sinkhole's residents slinked to their mud-drenched holes well before dark. They knew better than to get caught away from home when night settled over the borough. Most of them were on their way there already, pointedly avoiding eye contact with Arden as they went. Puddles of standing water turned every street into a hazard, and the damp air had soaked into every piece of fabric, wood, and even stonework. The place smelled like a puss-filled wound.

This has to be the place.

Arden would not have guessed anyone lived in the Mothweed house. Most of the roof had collapsed, demolishing whatever remained of the second floor in the process. From the condition of the wreckage, the damage probably occurred some time ago; moss and a few flowering, grayish-brown patches of mothweed covered much of the exposed wood. Rot had further weakened the foundation, causing the whole place to keel over against the house next to it.

No signs or writing marked the hovel as anything noteworthy. No windows looked out on the street and the narrow, flimsy-looking door dangled precariously from rusted hinges.

Arden sighed and rubbed his forehead. As expected, he got little more than a few hours of sleep that afternoon. Gathering information on Dhrath's debtor took up most of the morning, and by the time he returned to his flat, he found Halvid exhibiting the early signs of fever. He dozed off while sitting in the chair beside the boy's bed, but the sleep was disjointed, broken up every few minutes by a groan or some delirious murmur.

When Arden did manage to slumber, his dreams tormented him with half-remembered battlefields and the vacant stares of men long dead.

The gods are wicked and cruel.

He finally woke up for good around dusk. Halvid had passed out by then, his skin warm to the touch. Arden hated leaving him alone, but he had little choice. Taking what little money remained to him, he sought out the same apothecary who treated the boy's previous bout of illness.

Business, it seemed, had been good. So good that the prices had doubled since the last time he visited. Even if he had enough money to buy what he was after, it would not have mattered. Out of season, the old man explained. Seems the stuff rarely kept long enough to make it worth keeping on hand anymore. On his way out the door, one of the old man's assistants, a girl by the name of Linsene, took him aside. She told him the apothecary sometimes sent her out for ingredients he found "difficult" to come by. Arden took her meaning and promised to keep his mouth shut. That was how he got pointed towards Sinkhole and the crumbling house on Mothweed Street.

Best get this over with before it gets dark.

Arden wanted no part Sinkhole's nighttime dangers. A few of the vagrants lingering near Mothweed's ditches sized him up on the way there. Most of them were smart enough to recognize he was more than they could handle, at least on their own. After the sun went down, though, they would come for him in force.

He banged his fist against the door, the decaying wood rattling loudly under his knuckles.

Several moments went by with no response. The wait stretched to a minute as Sinkhole's pitiable residents shuffled by him without saying a word.

Arden knocked again, harder this time.

A muffled voice grumbled behind the door. Someone drew a wooden latch back and pushed the door open just enough to peer outside. A pair of mismatched eyes stared through the gap.

"Who're you, then?"

Arden inched closer to the door, close enough that he could force his way inside if he needed to.

"No one important," he said. "I'm here to see Twiceborn."

The eyes flitted to Arden's boots, belt, and cloak. While modest for other boroughs, they marked him for an outsider here. Strolling into Sinkhole wearing anything that was not worn through or tattered was a sure way to stand out from the locals.

"I'm looking for medicine," Arden said. "Heard she's got stuff for pain."

No answer.

"Linsene sent me. I can pay."

What am I supposed to do? Beg?

The door swung open so quickly it nearly hit him.

A short, ugly man with sloped shoulders and a twisted back stood in the doorway. His discolored skin gave way to rough patches, possibly scarring from a plague of some kind. Much of his hair had fallen out in sporadic patches, which left his head looking oddly crooked. The mismatched eyes, one green, one blue, were difficult to ignore. Arden found himself coming back to them no matter how much he tried to avoid the man's unsettling gaze.

As he waved Arden inside, his forearm pulled clear of his shirt's roughspun sleeve. A line of stitching, probably horsegut from the look of it, ran along the underside of his arm.

Arden stepped through the door and into a drab, unfurnished room. A few hooks on the nearby wall provided space for hanging cloaks. Most of the wood inside looked gray and pitted, like the exterior. A strong, chemical odor Arden could not quite place hung in the air. When he inhaled, it stung the insides of his nostrils.

"This way."

The strange man led him to another room in the back of the building. Like the main room, it lacked furniture, with no trappings other than a burlap rug covering the dusty floor. Arden's guide pulled the rug back to reveal a large trapdoor in the center of the floor. He pulled the door open, revealing earthen steps descending into the blackness below.

The queer odor was stronger here, strong enough to make his throat burn when he took a breath.

What the hells are they doing in this place?

The man with the mismatched eyes picked up a lantern sitting on the first step, lit it, and started downward.

"Watch your step."

He descended slowly, his stiff joints preventing him from moving too quickly. Arden followed after him, never more than an armslength behind. The dozen or so steps leading into the cellar varied considerably in height and width. Arden steadied himself against the earthen wall, thankful the man was not moving any faster.

The room at the bottom of the stairs was about a third the size of the building above. It probably served as a storage space for wine or salted meats back when the place was built, but time had shown that to be a foolish decision. Old, crumbling mudbricks lined the walls, most of them so soaked through with water seeping down from the streets that they were almost indistinguishable from an ordinary, earthen wall. Bundles of straw lay strewn across the floor to sop up the water dripping steadily from the low ceiling's moldering beams. Most of the straw was speckled black with rot.

Arden found the damp, chemical-laden air hard to breathe. Even a shallow breath made him want to cough.

The man with the mismatched eyes made nothing of his discomfort, instead moving to the narrow tunnel chiseled through one of the nearby walls. He grunted something and Arden followed.

After a short distance, they entered another small cellar and Arden realized they now stood beneath a different building. A stack of wooden crates in the corner looked like they had gone untouched for years. His guide turned then to the right and led him through another tunnel cut into the wall.

How many of these cellars have they connected?

He had never heard anything about people digging tunnels to such an extent. Could Dhrath or any of his people in Sinkhole know about them? Arden supposed he could ask, but the prospect of knowing something that slippery bastard did not was simply too satisfying to risk learning otherwise.

Then again, how secret could it be if they allowed him, a complete stranger, to see it?

They passed through two more cellars, both stuffed full with crates, barrels, and clay jars, before they came across another person.

Or at least what passed for one.

The wretched thing looked like a woman, or maybe a boy; Arden could not quite tell from the stature since its heavy clothes reduced it to a sexless mass of wool. Horsegut stitching and strips of leather held the mangled face together. A little flap of fabric covering what remained of its mouth fluttered with every breath. Stooped over some sort of grinding device set up in the cellar's corner, the thing worked a large crank around and around, pulverizing something soft and squishy inside a wooden drum with every turn.

At first, Arden thought it was staring at him, but as he walked past, he saw that the white and black eyes were painted stones.

Fleshcrafter's work. No doubting that.

Given Dhrath's distaste for sorcery of any kind, Arden wondered how much the broker might value knowing a fleshcrafter might be operating out of Sinkhole.

The next few tunnel dwellers they encountered more closely resembled the man with the mismatched eyes than the thing turning the grinder crank. Arden saw a pair of broad-shouldered men reinforcing a collapsing wall in one cellar, one with a leather patch over his missing nose and the other with a metal brace strapped to his forearm. A young woman with mottled skin occupied the next room. She worked on a complicated leather harness of some sort, but she kept her gaze upon them until they left the room, whispering under her breath all the while.

They travelled deeper into the subterranean labyrinth until they reached a larger, more carefully constructed cellar. The floor was covered with flat stones, and the walls shorn up with chiseled blocks likely exhumed from half a hundred crumbling buildings in Sinkhole. There were a few tables pushed against the walls and a small fire pit dug into the floor in the center of the room. The smoke escaped the room through several metal grates in the wooden ceiling. A ladder affixed to a wall near the back corner led up to a closed trap door.

Arden wondered which of the borough's tottering wrecks stood above them.

The air was so thick with fumes he could barely keep his eyes open for more than a few seconds. Even the slightest breath burned his lungs and his exposed skin tingled like insects scurried over it.

A tall, thin woman stood next to a table covered with dozens of glass cylinders and stacks of weathered paper. No part of her skin was exposed to the harsh air. She wore a set of heavy overalls that resembled those favored by the Spaders Guild; the tan, long sleeved shirt beneath it looked too flexible to be leather but lacked the familiar weave of any fabric Arden had seen. Probably some foreign material or something made by the more skilled artisans north of Lowtown. The shirt's sleeves fastened to her gloves, its high collar pulled tight around her neck by a few strips of thin fabric. Her black hair, streaked through with bits of white and gray, was cut short enough for several strands to stand on end.

She wore a spader mask over her face. Considering the quality of the air, the precaution was probably well founded.

The mask's glass goggles made it impossible to see her eyes. She might have looked up when they came in, but Arden was uncertain. Her hands went right on working, transferring liquids from one container to another, sifting through her many sheaves of paper, and reaching for any number of odd ingredients strewn across the table.

"Someone to see you, Twiceborn," the man with the mismatched eyes said. "Said he needs some medicine."

The masked face turned, seeming to stare directly at Arden.

"Don't know him."

She sounded younger than he expected, her voice slightly muffled by the mask.

Arden's guide shrugged. "Says Linsene sent him."

Twiceborn muttered something that did not penetrate the mask intact.

"I can pay," Arden said. "Linsene wouldn't have sent me otherwise."

She unbuckled the mask's mouthpiece, revealing a pair of thin, colorless lips and a narrow chin.

"I'm more concerned about your tongue," she said. The voice sounded even younger with the mask removed. "You're one of Dhrath's, aren't you?"

Don't know me, do you?

Arden nodded.

"I'm paid up with his people through summer, just so you know. Best to keep ahead of such things in my experience."

Payments were hardly the only thing she liked keeping ahead of. Arden was not above using his association with Dhrath as a negotiating tool. Prices had a way of dropping precipitously whenever he insinuated someone might be falling behind on protection payments.

Her casual remark, however, had deftly deprived him of that bit of leverage.

Smart, this one.

"Seems wise," Arden said.

"Linsene's a good judge of people, but she's got a soft heart." Twiceborn cocked her head sideways and crossed her arms. "So, she either trusts you or pities you. Which would you say is more likely?"

Arden hated this kind of banter. At least the old apothecary never made him dance to get what he was after.

"You'll have to ask her. I can't speak for anyone but myself."

"A little self-reflection might do you some good," she said, her thin lips forming the words with emotionless precision.

Arden forced a smile.

Bitch.

"I'll take it under advisement."

Twiceborn sighed. "Of course, you will. Now then, what are you looking for?"

Arden listed the medicines he needed from memory. Twiceborn listened closely, nodding after each item. When he finished, she sent the man with the mismatched eyes to gather up everything he requested. She then raised the issue of price, which was significantly higher than Arden expected. He thought about protesting or trying to bargain her down a bit, but he doubted she would budge. Twiceborn was no fool; she knew he would not be there if he could have found what he needed anywhere else.

That meant paying a premium.

"So, who's dying?" she asked as she handed over the medicine.

The question caught him off guard. When he did not answer immediately, she replied for him.

"You're obviously healthy and there are better and cheaper ways to get high. Must be someone close. Parent? Wife? Child?"

Arden scowled. "Are we done here?"

Twiceborn smiled, her lips pulling back far enough to reveal her yellowing teeth. Coupled with the dark goggles covering her eyes, it made her resemble one of the pallid snakes that slithered in the muddy trenches of Sinkhole's alleyways.

Arden had no doubt she was every bit as venomous.

UNDER THE RIGHT conditions, sections of Coldwater borough could be serene, almost pretty at night. After a particularly hot day, thin wisps of fog rolled in from the river, blanketing the streets like a fallen, wet cloud. Lanterns glowed like swollen fireflies in the misty gloom, some hanging from streetside posts while others swung lazily at the sides of armed watch patrols. At just the right hour, the place took on a dreamlike quality, offering a glimpse into a world far from the grimy, crumbling environs of the decrepit city.

On most nights, however, the streets more closely resembled the bleak corridors of some labyrinthine dungeon. Local watch patrols appeared frequently enough to keep the main streets relatively safe, but they only occasionally forayed into the multitude of branching alleyways that criss-crossed the borough like the strands of a misshapen spiderweb. The lighting there was intermittent at best, leaving some side streets in darkness for several blocks. For someone not familiar with Coldwater's streets, a few wrong turns could take them from relative safety to an abrupt, and usually violent, encounter with the borough's less reputable elements.

Arden generally did not concern himself with taking a wrong turn. For one thing, he knew just about every shortcut, hideaway, and choke point in Coldwater; knowledge that proved handy when he tracked down some poor sod dumb enough to think he could outrun his bad choices. Some of them knew better than to run. Once Arden came for them, the smart ones recognized that it was already too late for that.

This Calandra girl seemed like a smart one.

She took a circuitous route from the Moonvale Theater to the mortuary. Sometimes she stopped beneath the light of a lantern, waiting until she caught a glimpse of a watch patrol before continuing on her way. There were a few taverns and winesinks along Dustwalk that closed well after midnight and catered to a rather disreputable crowd. She avoided all of them, turning down the narrower side streets and veering back once she was well clear of the establishments. Twice she cut over to Sylvaneye Street, which ran roughly parallel to Dustwalk, and followed it for several blocks before crossing over again. She always kept to the light and stayed away from the occasional vagrant slumbering in the ditches and any fellow nightwalkers that passed her.

Every so often, she glanced over her shoulder, a quick look to make sure that no one was close enough to reach her in a few strides. She never noticed Arden trailing farther behind her. Even if she did happen to see him, he knew how to move just the right way to divert any passing suspicions. He could be a drunk staggering home one moment, a homeless beggar the next, or even a lone watchman checking if doors were good and locked.

In any case, she never noticed him slowly close the distance between them. He got a sense of how often she checked behind her and drifted to the far side of the street whenever she seemed ready to do so.

They were almost within sight of the Deadhouse when he took her.

Arden struck quickly, swooping across the street to clamp one hand over her mouth and wrap his arm around her slender body. By the time she squirmed, he had already hoisted her up and hauled her into a dark, narrow alleyway.

"Stop fighting, girl," he said. "We need to have a talk about your little brother."

Her body froze for a moment, every muscle tightening. Holding her firmly against his broad chest, a tinge of warmth rippled across his skin. She tried to crane her neck around to get a look at him, but he turned her face away from his.

"Listen to me good, now," he said. "I'm going to let you go and we're going to have a nice, civilized conversation. Once we're done, you can be on your way and I'll be on mine. You call out for help, I hurt you. You try to run, I hurt you. Give me a nod if you understand."

She nodded once, curtly.

Smart as you look, aren't you?

Arden removed his hand from her mouth and relaxed his grip on her arms. She took a small step forward and his skin went cold as her body pulled away from his.

The shadows of the alley made it hard to see her dark skin and features clearly, but Arden's memory filled in the blanks easily enough. He tried to imagine how he appeared to her, a looming, thuggish thing lurking in the night.

"I've got a message for your brother, girl."

He rarely had an aversion to using names, but he felt strange about calling her by her name for some reason.

You're getting soft, old man.

"Mister Dhrath is getting impatient," he said. "He's starting to wonder if he made a bad investment."

He could not quite make out Calandra's expression, but he saw her shake her head clearly enough.

"I don't know what you're talking about," she said, her voice trembling, but strangely calm considering the circumstances. "Who the hell is Dhrath and what does he have to do with my brother?"

Ignorance, even genuine ignorance, made a poor excuse for anything as far as Arden was concerned. He clenched his fist out of habit but saw no sense in breaking that delicate nose of hers.

Maybe she doesn't know, he thought.

"Your brother owes quite a bit of money to Mister Dhrath," he said. "Two years back, he came asking for money to restore that theater you've been living in. Mister Dhrath's been wondering why he hasn't had any payments come in yet."

"No," she said. "There has to be some mistake. I gave him the rest of the money he needed to buy the place. He added it to what he'd saved from…"

Her voice trailed off as the realization hit her. For a long while, she just stood there in silence. Then she put her head in her hands and shuddered.

"Oh, gods…"

He could have said more, explained the obligations Beyland agreed to when he made the bargain. But there was no need. The time for negotiations had long since passed.

One way or another, Dhrath would collect. The only real question was over the medium of exchange.

"How… how much?" she asked, recovering a bit of her composure.

"Two thousand marks."

He let the number hang in the air.

"Mister Dhrath isn't known for his patience, girl," he said. "When it's past time to collect, he sends me to get what's there to be had."

Arden knew they did not have much. He had slipped into the Moonvale Theater when Beyland and his friend were still fast asleep, hours before Calandra returned home. He would be surprised if they had more than a hundred marks worth of coin and goods in the whole place.

The discovery proved disappointing. If they failed to muster up enough coin, Arden stood to lose as much as Dhrath if not more. At least Dhrath could count on other sources of income. Arden's meager pay came from a percentage of what he collected. If Dhrath was not satisfied with the delivered sum, he would receive very little in return.

If Halvid's condition continued to worsen, that would be a problem. Arden's visit to Twiceborn cost him far more than he anticipated. Once their stock of medicine ran dry, he would have trouble affording more.

"Why come to me?" she asked. "Why don't you take it up with Beyland?"

"Because we both know he's not good for it."

"And what do you expect me to do, exactly?" she said. There was an edge to her voice, but Arden could not tell if she intended it for him or her brother.

"I expect you to do whatever you can to help your brother."

Easy, now. Give her just enough to work with...

"I'll give you two days to start coming up with the money," he said. "I don't get something to reassure Mister Dhrath by then, I take him your brother so he can pay off his debt a piece at a time."

If the threat frightened her, she did a good job of hiding it.

"How long can you give us after that?"

Arden shrugged.

"Depends on what you bring me in two days."

Careful. Don't put it too far out of reach.

"The first hundred marks would be a start," he said. "Mister Dhrath's quite particular, but it might buy you some time if I convince him you're good for the rest."

Calandra glanced at the nearby street. No one had walked by in the time since Arden snatched her away. The nearest watch patrol, he knew, was several streets away. If she was hoping that someone might stumble upon them, maybe she was less clever than he thought.

"You'll be finding me, I expect?" she asked. The question took him by surprise. Usually they tried to bargain for more time, desperate to stave off the inevitable. A waste of time, but it never stopped the fools from trying. That was why he went to Calandra and not her brother. He knew Beyland would grovel, beg for time, and blurt out half a dozen contradictory excuses for why he deserved another chance to make good on his debt.

His sister, though, was not the sort who went to pieces when some-body leaned on her. That much became obvious as he watched her coming back home from the mortuary earlier in the day. What he had yet to learn was how quickly she would accept her circumstances, how she would deal with a situation wholly beyond her control.

Now he knew.

"Two days," he said. "I'll be waiting outside the theater. You or your brother try to sneak off before then, I'll take it as a personal slight. But I don't think you're the sort to run out on me, now are you?"

"Two days." Calandra looked back at him. The darkness still hid much of her face, but the light from the street lanterns glimmered faintly in her eyes.

Arden thought about her slender body pressed against him, her hard, tensed muscles rubbing against his skin.

"Can I go now?" she asked.

Her hollow tone betrayed nothing. She might as well have been speak-ing to one of the corpses she handled inside the Deadhouse.

He disliked the way she kept surprising him. While Arden did not necessarily enjoy frightening people, he did like the sense of control that came with it. Fear made people predictable, which made it easy to antici-pate what they might do next.

Right now, though, he had no idea what Calandra was thinking or what she might do before he saw her again.

"Go on, then," he said.

She moved quickly and decisively, stepping out of the alley without even glancing back to see if he followed her.

Arden made no effort to stop her. Once she was gone, he walked down the alley in the opposite direction, turning to follow its course as it wound like a slithering eel between Coldwater's old, stone buildings.

He wondered if Calandra had some idea in her head for scraping to-gether the kind of coin Dhrath was expecting. She clearly had plenty of guts and might be clever enough to come up with some scheme, but even so, he doubted their next meeting would be a pleasant one.

Dhrath would not like the idea of having the payment dragged out, but Arden thought he could convince the slimy bastard to give him at least another few weeks if he had a steady trickle of coin to show for it. Even so, he wondered how Calandra could keep up the payments at that rate. Maybe she had something stashed away somewhere or thought she could find more work during the day after her shift at the mortuary ended.

Whatever she did, it was not likely to amount to much. And a percent-age of "nothing much" was practically nothing. If he had any sense, he would have mugged her brother when he left the theater that morning and hauled him back to Dhrath's keep in a sack. Dhrath always paid a few marks to anybody that brought him a shirker.

But he needed more coin than that.

If he was lucky, he could squeeze a few payments from Calandra before she ran out of ideas. After that, he could still take Beyland to Dhrath and collect the fee. His sister would put up a fight, of course. She might even go and do something rash like try to bargain for her brother's life. If it came to that, he would have to move on Beyland while she was out of the way.

As Arden ran the possible scenarios through his mind, he found himself worrying about Calandra's reaction. In his line of work, being hated was nothing out of the ordinary. It should not have troubled him that she would probably wind up hating him no matter how the situation played out.

Somehow, though, it did.

Need a woman is all. Been too long without one.

A flimsy excuse, maybe, but it *had* been a long time. There were plenty of them after Halvid's mother died, especially early on. Things became more difficult as he got older, though. The boy never knew his mother, so Arden wanted to avoid having some winesink whore give him any ideas of what a proper woman should be like. He used to visit a few of the cheaper brothels over in Pigshire, but even that became an expensive luxury whenever the boy's fever flared up.

Take the coin where you can get it, fool. They'll get what's coming to them either way.

That applied to Calandra as much as anyone. She let her brother use her, after all, and allowed herself to be drawn into his problems. If she were as clever as she made herself out to be, she clearly lacked the good sense to walk out of that theater long ago.

She had a choice, same as everyone in that cesspit of a city.

Same as you.

The gods are wicked and cruel.

Arden had a hard time shaking off memories of the amber light reflecting off Calandra's eyes.

12
THE DRAMATIST

The gown's fabric was cool to the touch and each movement sent it sliding gently across her naked flesh. It conformed to every curve of her body, every angle of her limbs, caressing her as delicately as a springtime breeze. Beams of moonlight refracted off the tens of thousands of tiny stones embroidered into the fabric, each one no bigger than a grain of sand, to send a dazzling cascade of color in every direction. Gasps, screams, and sighs followed her every movement, a chorus of pleasure altering its pitch and intensity in time with her breath.

She spoke and the world went still, like the air just before a lightning strike.

The voice was unfamiliar, but she knew it belonged to her as surely as the sensuous form encased within the shimmering gown. It lilted and compelled, resonating within the ears of anyone lucky enough to experience it. Their muscles tensed with each inflection, the cadence of her words massaging them with the utmost precision. They held their breaths when she took hers, none daring to break the serenity of the carefully placed silence.

Her bare feet carried her gracefully across the warm stone. The gown cast a swirling, prismatic barrage of stars before her, blinding and overwhelming everything in its path. Her hot and molten voice bared an edge, a blade fresh from the forge. It sliced through the cool night, carving into the sternest of hearts and sundering the bleakest souls. Tears fell freely and teeth set to gnashing, but she stood apart from the dolor, her careful movements and measured words directing the spectacle with the utmost mastery.

The crescendo proved unstoppable until a word slipped her mind. She stuttered, her lips trying to grasp the missing sound from the air. Her next step landed awkwardly and she nearly fell. The stones within the gown went dark, hungrily soaking up the moonlight to bury her inside a growing sphere of cold darkness. She struggled, tried to cry out, but her limbs were fat and heavy now, her lips too bloated and clumsy to form the words properly. The sounds she made were repulsive, like the ugly, primal grunting of some dysmorphic beast. Shadow and ice took her, dragging her through the stone floor and smothering her in the freezing, black depths of the most wretched of hells.

THE FAT, HALF-MELTED candle on the nearby table provided the only light inside the strange room. It gave off a thick, greasy odor that reeked of overcooked swine, but it burned brightly enough to drive the shadows back to the corners, which seemed a fair tradeoff. When she first woke, Nicalene kept still for quite some time, waiting for someone to come back to tend to the candle or extinguish it.

But no one ever came, so she eventually sat up in the unfamiliar bed. She was warm, a bit nauseated, and tasted something close to ash in her mouth, but those were minor complaints next to the dull ache on her left side and the burning pain in her chest. Slowly, hopeful that her memory might be playing tricks on her, Nicalene ran her hand down from the top of her neck towards the bottom rungs of her rib cage.

She stopped when her fingers brushed across a hardened lump nestled between the upper portions of her breasts.

Oh, gods…

A little more than half of the black stone was embedded directly into her breastbone. Her skin did not so much touch its surface as become one with it, seeming to form a single, unbroken surface rather than simply running against it like the skin around her nails. There was no blood, no sign of trauma. Even the burning sensation in her chest emanated from somewhere inside rather than the flesh around the stone.

The pain below her left breast was at once obvious and more familiar. She recalled ripping the dreamleech away from her skin before it retracted its serrated proboscis. Someone had taken the time to bandage the wound and stop the bleeding. Considering the size of the thing, she was lucky the leech missed any organs.

Nicalene sat up slowly, careful not to disturb her bandaging or pull at the skin surrounding the thing in her chest. Her concern proved unfounded. The flesh around the stone stretched to accommodate her movements without causing any pain or even discomfort.

Hesitantly, she reached up to touch it.

Although hard as a piece of marble, it was every bit as warm as her skin.

After staring at the stone for a long while, she pulled the sheets back and swung her legs over the side of the bed. Still naked, she rubbed her arms to warm herself as she looked for her clothes. She spotted her blue dress lying in a heap at the foot of the bed, but she could make out the bloodstains on the fabric even in the dim candlelight.

A dead man's face flashed through her mind, his cracked lips pulled back over crooked, rotting teeth.

She would never wear that rag ever again.

A wardrobe stood on the far end of the room, so she eased herself off the bed and slowly made her way to it. She pulled the doors open to reveal an assortment of clothing suited for both men and women. Every piece seemed a bit showy, but of good quality, most of them accented by a bright strip of color in a pronounced hemline or collar. The garments smelled musty, and the styling looked decidedly old fashioned. She found dresses, shirts, and pants in various sizes, as if the wardrobe had once stored the clothing for an entire family of modest means.

Or an acting troupe.

A long mirror hung from the inside of the wardrobe's right-hand door. Nicalene ignored it as long as she could, but vanity or curiosity (she could not decide which) eventually got the better of her.

Something's not right.

Her hair repulsed her, a too long, too tangled black mass of vile seaweed. She tried to brush it away, but there was so much of it. The coarse, wiry strands only fell back against her skin, lashing at her with a vindictive fury. The more she swiped at it, the more sensitive she became to its touch. Soon it was scraping at her, raking over her flesh as if a million tiny thorns had sprouted along every strand.

Nicalene staggered away from the mirror as she grabbed a handful of hair to pull it clear of her back and shoulders. It bit into her fingers, but she clenched her teeth and endured the pain as she frantically stumbled around the room in search of something to relieve her growing agony.

She found it next to the washbasin.

A curved barber's knife.

The blade was duller than it should have been, but still sharp enough for what she had in mind. Nicalene hacked and sawed at her hair wildly, trimming back every strand slicing against her face or ripping into her neck until she felt nothing but cool air against her skin. She left a good inch or two atop her head, with little clumps sticking out awkwardly here and there.

Even after she finished, her heart went on pounding.

There. Must be better now.

She went back to the mirror to stare at her frantic cut, knife still in hand. As she stared at her image in the mirror, her gaze drifted to her shoulders, her breasts, her hips, and her thighs.

That's not right either.

She straightened her back and squared her shoulders, but that only helped things a little. Her breasts were sacks of wet dough strapped around her chest, her legs mounds of unshaped clay. Every movement was labored, like wading through some viscous fluid. The weight of so much flesh suffocated her.

A bit of candlelight reflected off the black chunk of rock in her chest, causing the surface to glimmer faintly.

Nicalene tightened her grip on the knife.

Not right...

She pressed the blade against her right thigh.

A loud crash outside the room snapped Nicalene's attention away from the mirror. She felt the cold touch of the blade against her skin and dropped the knife with a gasp.

What the hell am I doing?

She rubbed her eyes and looked back to the mirror. The remaining hair sprouting atop her head looked like a misshapen clump of grass.

It looked utterly ridiculous.

If she did not recall the intense panic that drove her to take up the knife, she might have laughed.

Somebody outside shouted, and Nicalene became acutely aware of her surroundings once more. The place was unfamiliar, so she knew it was somewhere other than the *Goat*. Muskrat's dead body blinked into her mind again. She nearly gagged at the memory of her fingernails digging into his boiling skin.

Stop it. Don't think about that now...

She took several deep breaths to calm her stomach.

After the sickness passed, she snatched a faded, green dress from the wardrobe, something more modest than her discarded blue dress. Although still bit snug, the garment featured a high neckline that concealed most of the black stone and a hem that nearly reached her ankles. Once she smoothed out the wrinkles, she pulled the dress's white sash tightly around her waist and tied off the ends.

She took the fat, foul smelling candle from the bedside table and then checked the door handle, which turned without protest.

Unlocked.

Holding her breath, Nicalene opened the door. The narrow hallway outside led to another series of doors to her right and a spiraling stairwell descending to her left. Aside from the candle's light, the hall was completely dark.

A single voice echoed up the stairwell, but she could not make out any intelligible words. She tiptoed closer to the steps. A constant stream, the voice rarely paused for breath or waited for a response. The tone shifted regularly, occasionally sounding like more than one voice, but subtle consistencies made it clear there was only one speaker.

Like someone telling a story, or reciting dialogue from a play.

Still barefoot, she started down the stairs, gently probing the wooden steps as she went in case one of them creaked or groaned.

The staircase opened into a large room, much too large for the available light. Most of it remained cast in darkness since the candles burning near its center proved incapable of lighting such a vast space fully. Nicalene barely discerned a vague layout of the room, but she had enough light to make out the rows of rickety, old benches and the elevated floor in the center.

Her stomach fluttered when she recognized those telltale features.

A theater? Am I still dreaming?

The room was nothing like the cavernous auditorium from her dream. For all its faded grandeur, too much of it felt familiar, too similar to any number of decrepit buildings she passed by whenever she walked the streets of Lowtown.

A young man stood on the stage next to the rack of candles, too far away for Nicalene to make out his face. He sifted through a handful of papers, occasionally removing a sheet from the stack or crumpling one and tossing it aside angrily. All the while he went on talking, shifting back and forth from one leg to the other.

Whatever he was doing, he seemed fully absorbed by the task.

Nicalene started across the room.

She made it about halfway to the stage when the man glanced at her and jerked to attention.

"You're up!" he said. "You should still be in bed!"

Nicalene stopped as he set his papers aside and stepped down from the stage. She could not place his youthful features, but his face was dimly familiar. She recalled a tender arm wrapped around her, a reassuring voice.

"Quiet now. Come with me."

Had that been real? What about the gown? The theater? Muskrat's corpse with the black welts all over the skin?

Muskrat. That was *his name...wasn't it?*

She must have jumped or drawn back when he approached because he stopped after taking a few steps.

"It's okay," he said. "I'm not going to hurt you."

Nicalene nibbled at her lower lip, searching for the proper reply. The stranger just looked at her. His eyes were friendly enough, but she had known plenty of kind-eyed bastards in her day.

Shouldn't have left that knife upstairs.

"What happened to your hair?"

For some reason, men always started with stupid questions.

What the hells do you think happened?

"I cut it," she said.

He watched at her for a moment, perhaps waiting for her to elaborate.

Nicalene let him stare.

"Oh...well, it looks...good."

She took a few steps toward him, gauging his reactions. He flinched when she moved, his eyelids blinking a bit too rapidly. If he was a kidnapper with foul intentions, he certainly lacked the nerves she expected from one.

"How do you feel?" he asked.

"Better, I think."

A half-truth. She still felt a bit disoriented but thought it best not to mention that detail.

"That's good," he said. "You were in a bad way."

Was I now?

She was ready to have some answers.

"What happened?"

BEYLAND LAID IT all out for her: stumbling upon her at *The Bleating Goat*, helping her escape, bringing her back to his place in Coldwater, and her screaming fit after they arrived. Nicalene listened carefully, asking a pointed question here and there to clarify his occasionally rambling descriptions. He got evasive about a few things, such as what happened to Muskrat (he said there was a body, but he did not get a good look at it) and the extent of her "fit" (probably just lingering effects from the dream-leech, he surmised), but she decided not to press him too hard when he seemed uncomfortable.

Probably thought he was "protecting" her or something noble like that. He seemed rather proud of having "rescued" her from the *Goat*, though in all fairness, Nicalene knew she probably would have been held accountable for Muskrat's death, so maybe Beyland was not exaggerating as much as it seemed.

Men. Always looking for a way to call themselves a hero.

After Beyland finished, Nicalene eased herself onto one of the benches nearest the stage. Beyland made to sit beside her, but hesitated when she glared at him. His gaze occasionally drifted down to her chest, reminding her of the stone pushing against the dress's fabric.

He conveniently avoided mentioning that part of the story.

"You found some clothes that fit, I see," he said, smiling a bit.

She shrugged. "My old dress was stained. Found this in the wardrobe." She looked up and tried to smile. "One of yours, I take it?"

Beyland laughed a little more than he needed to.

When was the last time she made a man nervous? Five years? Seven? It seemed so long ago. Grisel had certainly never been nervous around her.

Grisel...

She pressed her hand over the stone.

How am I supposed to explain this?

Beyland was too busy trying to make a good impression to take notice of the gesture.

"Of a sort," he said. "I used to be part of an acting troupe. When the other actors left, I ended up with a few extra costumes." He smiled that funny way men did when they were pleased with themselves. "I'm glad you found one that fits so well."

Charming.

Nicalene imagined Grisel smashing his spade against poor Beyland's face.

Grisel...

He would be looking for her once he realized she had taken the stone.

Beyland fell silent while she was thinking. From the look on his face, he was about to ask her another stupid question.

"I wanted to join a troupe when I was a little girl," she said, looking for anything to deflect his attention. But the admission was true, at least. When she was younger, she spent hours reenacting scenes from bedtime stories on the street outside her family's tenement. That ended quickly, since her mother and aunts needed her nimble little fingers for spinning wool, especially once more of her sisters and cousins were married off.

By the time she was on her own, she was too old for any respectable troupe, but that did not stop her from trying. She even learned to read and fell in with a few actors, hoping they might give her a chance to take part in one of their performances. They made a lot of promises, but something always got in the way of making good on them. Meanwhile, Nicalene was expected to do more and more to stay in their good graces. When her humiliation finally overcome her ambitions, she walked away from her dreams of the stage.

"Probably wise that you didn't take up the stage trade," Beyland said. "Can't say it always keeps a roof over your head."

She looked around the dark room. "You seem to be doing well enough."

He laughed. "My sister lives here too. She's a journeyman with the Undertakers Guild."

Must pay a lot better than the damned spaders.

"What is this place, anyway?" she asked, her interest only half feigned.

Beyland hopped back onto the stage. "Where are my manners?" He threw his arms out grandly. "Welcome, my lady, to Coldwater borough's legendary Moonvale Theater!"

He bowed so deeply that Nicalene thought he would bounce his nose off his knee.

Quite to her surprise, she even chuckled at the sight.

Beyland rose and put his hands to his chest.

"My dear lady," he said, still speaking with an exaggerated, actor's voice. "You wound my delicate pride! What is the name of this merciless creature that so injures me with her every jest?"

Nicalene wondered how many foolish young girls fell for Beyland's routine.

Had she been that gullible once?

Did she want to be now?

"Why don't you tell me the real reason you brought me here," she said, "and if I believe it, I'll tell you my name."

Beyland seemed to shrink before her eyes, as if he suddenly realized he was playing to an empty theater. He sat down on the edge of the stage and tried to look her in the eyes before his gaze fell to his clasped hands.

"You...you needed help," he said.

Nicalene waited for more, but he did not elaborate. She refused to let him off that easily.

"Lots of girls in that place need help," she said. "You make a habit of helping them, too?"

His face tightened a bit and she wondered if she would have to put the question more directly. But then he shook his head, a short, curt denial.

"No," he said. "I'd never do something like that! I mean, even if I wanted to, why would I? The women in that place are all so dir—"

Even in the dim light, Nicalene saw the color run off his face when his brain caught up to his mouth.

"I mean, well, not *all* of them, obviously," he said. His legs bounced rapidly, which only made the rest of his body shudder as he spoke. "There's always a few, um, a lot actually, that, well, you know, they're not like the others that...um, well, what I mean is—"

"Nicalene."

Beyland blundered on for a few more words before he stopped and stared at her.

"What?"

"My name's Nicalene."

"Oh. That's...nice. Listen, I...I didn't mean to—"

"It's okay, Beyland," she said. "Forget it."

His gaze went back to his clasped hands.

Nicalene felt Muskrat's sweaty hands groping clumsily over her breasts, felt his hot breath clinging to the skin on the back of her neck. She heard the dreamleech splashing heavily in a jar of its own secretions, smelled something like piss mixed with charcoal.

"You're right about that place," she said. "Nobody really comes out clean, do they?"

Beyland looked up at her and shook his head.

"So what were you there for?" she asked.

This time, he seemed to choose his words more carefully.

"I don't know. I mean, I was there because I heard you could get fire-dust. The good stuff, not that piss-colored sand they sell over in Sinkhole. So that's why I went there, but why did I have to have it? That's...that's harder to explain."

Isn't it always?

He sighed and nibbled on his tongue. Nicalene knew the need was a hard thing to talk about. She tried to explain it to Grisel a few times, but he never wanted to hear any of it; just told her to clean up or get out. Maybe that was what she needed. If that was true, though, why had she ended up back there again?

She reached over and touched Beyland's clasped hands. He stopped fidgeting.

"Then don't explain."

He looked at her for a moment, then gave her a single nod.

"I thought I heard something crashing down here when I woke up," she said. "What happened?"

Beyland's smile returned quickly.

Eager as me to change the subject, aren't you?

"Sorry about that," he said. "I threw a stool off the stage."

Nicalene laughed.

It felt good to laugh.

"And what prompted that little tantrum?"

"Just frustrated," he said, picking up his stack of papers. "I've been trying to finish this play for two years now, but the damn thing doesn't want to cooperate."

"A play? What's it about?"

Beyland shrugged. "Oh, you know, the usual. Life, love, death, sorting out why we're here."

As if finding out would help.

"Sounds ambitious," she said. "How much have you finished?"

He shuffled through the pages. Nicalene saw a few lines scribbled upon each page, but none of them were anywhere close to full.

"Well," he said, "not much, really. It's a lot to take in, you know?"

Nicalene did not doubt that, but Beyland seemed a bit too wide-eyed for such a hefty subject.

"What do you have so far?"

"It starts out with a war hero coming home to find his wife has left him for another man. And then—"

"Wait, who is she?"

"What? The wife?"

"Yeah, why did she leave him?"

"She…well, she didn't want to wait for him to get back."

"Because she felt abandoned?"

Beyland squinted at her. "No, nothing like that. She told him that she'd wait for him. She wasn't true to her promise."

"What did he promise?"

He looked down at his pages, his eyes darting across the uneven scrawl. "Well, nothing, I guess. Look, the point is that he comes back and—"

Nicalene rolled her eyes. "And expects everything to be like it was before he left, sure. But who cares about that? He's the one that went and screwed everything up."

Beyland scratched his head. "How's that?"

She should have expected the stupid question, but it frustrated her all the same.

Now I see why you haven't gotten very far.

"What do you suppose she was doing every day he was gone?" she asked. "Sitting around waiting for him to come back? Why are you making her out to be the harlot? You don't think he's got a steady stream of camp whores coming in and out of his bed while he's at war?"

Nicalene wondered why the notion upset her so much. What did she care what Beyland wanted to say in a play he seemed unlikely to finish?

"No, of course not!" Beyland said. "He's an honorable man. He's true to his cause and—"

"Oh, so he only gets hard around his sword and armor, then? That's even worse. It's a wonder she didn't leave him sooner. Might as well have married his horse."

Nicalene realized went too far when Beyland tossed his papers aside. They scattered across the stage, some of them fluttering in the air.

He lowered his head and sighed, much louder this time. Nicalene was not sure how to react. She was used to men getting angry when she pushed them. Grisel never hit her, but he fought back like a cornered dog whenever she went at him over something. Even when she knew she had hurt him, the stubborn bastard never let her see the wound. Instead, he let it fester, paying her back in kind at every opportunity.

But Beyland was different, more vulnerable. A few hours ago, he wanted nothing more than to lose himself in a handful of firedust and now Nicalene was tearing down one of the few things that still mattered to him.

Hell of a way of showing gratitude, you petty bitch.

"I'm sorry, Beyland," she said, uncertainty creeping into her voice. "I didn't mean to be so harsh."

"No," he said, "you're right. I guess this is why I've never gotten past the first scene. The whole thing's built on a lie."

As Nicalene tried to think of what to say, one of the sheets of paper came to rest near her feet. She leaned over to retrieve it and held it up to the light to see the writing better. The ink had smeared a bit, still wet in places.

She read the passage aloud:

"Act 1, Scene 1: She stands alone in the darkness, her skin drinking deeply from the shadows. Whispers swirl around her, but she remains deaf to their pleas. When she moves, the night parts before her, guiding her back to a grand balcony overlooking a city of glass stretching toward the gray horizon. A single, silver tear trickles down her ashen cheek as the sallow sun rises."

A single dialogue marker stood out below the scene description.

"The Ashen Woman."

No dialogue followed the name.

Nicalene looked up and found Beyland staring at her.

"What is this?"

He shrugged. "Something I wrote this morning. The scene just…came to me."

"Who is she?"

"I…I don't know. Why do you think I threw the stool?"

Nicalene read the passage again. The description stood out vividly in her mind, as her imagination filled in the gaps to complete the bizarre, foreign vista.

But it was the name that really fascinated her.

The Ashen Woman.

She handed the page to Beyland.

"Keep writing."

13

THE FALL

Another scoop of muck splattered into the wagon, sending a shower of wet droplets through the air.

"Oi! Watch what you're doing there!"

The voice belonged to one of the younger spaders. Grisel might have tried to recall the boy's name if he wasn't so pissed off.

"Learn to duck, shitboot!"

Jaspen stewed a few feet away from the scene. For the better part of an hour, he looked ready to intervene, but he also seemed intent on letting things play out at this point. Meaty, as usual, said nothing; just went on working with that dumb grin on his fat face.

Assholes.

Grisel stabbed his shovel into the sloppy gunk piled along the streetside and hauled out another overflowing dollop. He heaved it into the wagon with an exaggerated grunt.

The splash was bigger this time, but the apprentice had moved a few steps away from the wagon after his scolding and avoided being struck.

Wising up. Too bad.

A good scuffle might have helped him feel better.

Nicalene was long gone by the time he woke up for his shift. Gone with what remained of their money. Gone with his precious black stone, the one bit of good luck that should have been his way out of that wretched neighborhood.

Remembering the situation pissed him off all over again.

Stupid, stupid, stupid.

He could not believe he forgot to hide the damned thing when he got back to his roof. Like an idiot, he was so eager to get into bed with Nicalene that he left the most valuable thing he ever touched out in the open for anyone to take after he passed out. Nicalene was not exactly trustworthy even when she was cold sober. He knew she was drinking heavily again, which meant it was only a matter of time until she slipped back into her older, nastier habits.

If she traded that stone for a pouch of firedust…

"Grisel!"

Jaspen grabbed his shovel and shook it. The wagon had moved down the street, the rest of the crew following close behind.

"Wake up and keep up!"

Grisel yanked his shovel free and glared at Jaspen. "Yeah, fine. I'm on it."

He started after the rest of the crew. Jaspen trailed a step behind him, scowling.

"What's up your ass tonight, mate?"

"Piss off, Jaspen."

Jaspen seized him by the arm and jerked him back so hard he though his shoulder might slip the socket.

"Stow it, Grisel! I don't need to be out here putting up with this all night. Ain't nobody here done you wrong, so why don't you tell me what your problem is now so Meaty and I don't have to beat it out of your skinny ass?"

Grisel grit his teeth and tried to tug his arm free, but Jaspen held him fast. After a brief attempt to squirm away, he slumped and glared down at his grime-encrusted boots.

"Nicalene ran off yesterday. Bitch cleaned me out on the way, too."

Jaspen turned him loose. "You pissing about?"

Grisel shook his head.

"Damn, mate, no wonder you're acting such a shitheel. How much she get?"

"Everything. Didn't leave a bloody quartermark."

Jaspen shook his head. He could have gone and mentioned the dozens of times he warned Grisel about not trusting her in his roof when he was gone and that taking her in was a dumb idea to begin with.

But he said nothing. Grisel was grateful to be spared the lecture.

"You got enough coin for your roof?"

"I should, long as we get paid on time."

"Look, mate," Jaspen said, keeping his voice low. "You need some help, you let me know, all right? You, me, and Meaty go back. Been out here a long time, we have. We ain't about to be scooping your miserable ass out of one of these dung piles, got me?"

Grisel nodded, but he scarcely heard the words. He was too busy imagining the look on Nicalene's face when she pulled the black stone from his pocket.

"Yeah, I got you," he said. "Thanks, mate."

"You know where she went?" Jaspen asked.

"Not for sure, no. Got a couple ideas of some places she used to hang out. Imagine she hit them first."

"Might be she's still there."

Grisel sighed. "Might be."

"Figure you could drop in; have nice friendly chat."

At first, he thought the same. But he also worried things might be more complicated.

"Could be she ain't alone, either," he said.

"You think she's been stepping out?"

Grisel shrugged. It would have been easy for her. He worked at night and slept through most of the day. Maybe somebody even put her up to it. Could someone have known what he had?

The Tamercums? Those bastards have always got an eye on her.

"You give her reason to?" Jaspen asked. "What about that trull a few rooms down from you? What was her name?"

"Sedina."

Nicalene hated Sedina; she made that quite clear at every opportunity. If Grisel so much as looked at her, Nicalene would badger him about it for days. And gods forbid if he actually *spoke* to her. A while back she accused him of thinking about Sedina whenever they were in bed together. He had no clue where she got that idea, but no amount of talking could get it out of her head.

He and Jaspen caught up with the rest of the crew; they were already heaving fresh scoops into the wagon. Meaty looked up from his shoveling as they approached.

"Yeah, Sedina," Jaspen said. "Meaty, you remember Sedina right? The one over at Grisel's with the curls and the legs?"

Meaty grinned like an idiot as he straddled his shovel and pretended to make love to it. The rest of the crew laughed along with Jaspen.

Grisel rolled his eyes.

Laugh it up, you sodding idiots.

"I ain't touched her since a while before Nicalene," he said to Jaspen once the spectacle died down.

"Pity," Jaspen said. "She was worth some broken feelings, eh, Meaty?"

"Pity," Meaty said.

"Piss off, the both of you. Ain't like either of you lived with a woman other than your mum."

Jaspen laughed. "Come on, mate, we're just talking. I'm feeling for you, but you can't let this stuff eat you up."

Grisel wanted to tell him where to shove his feelings, but deep down he knew Jaspen was trying to raise his spirits. Far as they saw it, a bit of coin was a small price to pay for getting rid of what they considered a headache. They knew nothing about the stone that was supposed to pay his way out of the ass end of Blackspire. If he got a good enough price, he might even have considered bringing them along with him.

He bet they would feel differently if they knew about that.

But it was more than just the stone and the money that galled him. Much to his own surprise, he was angry that Nicalene had just up and left him without so much as a word. He had taken her under his roof when she was too messed up to do much of anything. Maybe he could have treated her better from time to time, but he never hit her or stepped out on her, which was more than she could say for the ogres she was with before him.

What reason did he ever give her to do what she had done to him? Making her cut loose all that junk she was strung out on? Telling her to get her ass out of bed and start paying her way?

The more he thought about what she did, the more he wanted an answer.

"Look," he said, "I don't need you pissheads trying to cheer me up, all right? You're hard enough to be around when I'm in a good mood."

Jaspen smiled. Meaty chuckled and went back to shoveling.

"Listen, mate," Jaspen said, "why don't you get out of here. You ain't doing us any good bitching like this and we've got enough guys to cover for you anyway."

Grisel shook his head. "No bloody way! I can't go missing time now! You damn well know I need—"

Jaspen cut him off with a wave. "Don't worry about that. I'll put you down for the whole night. None of these boys have got the pull to say anything about it and Meaty here's too dumb to know you're gone."

Meaty looked up and smiled. "Who's gone?"

Grisel sighed. He was tired after getting to sleep so late in the day. A few extra hours of sleep would probably help.

"All right," he said. "Thanks, mate. Guess I owe you one."

Jaspen shrugged. "Don't worry about it. Figure it all evens out in the end."

He reached into one of the pouches tied to his belt and produced a pair of coins.

"Here," he said, shoving them into Grisel's hand.

Two whole marks!

"Jaspen, you don't have to—"

"Yeah, you're damn right I don't, so take them and go put them to good use before I change my mind, eh?"

Grisel nodded and, for the first time that night, managed a smile. "Figure I'll do that."

HE STOPPED BY the public cistern in Cur's Mark Square to wash the gunk off his boots before it could dry. The place was mostly deserted after midnight. A few vagrants sat tucked away in the alleys, the luckier ones rolled up in mud-soaked blankets. Oil lanterns hung from posts on the corner of each intersection, keeping the square well lit. A watch patrol meandered by before he finished, but they left him to his business. Even the most belligerent thugs from the watch knew better than to mess with a spader. The Assembly paid the guild far too much coin to keep the streets from overflowing with filth for it to allow the watch to harass them like it did everyone else.

Grisel glared at them as they strutted by with their third-hand shortswords and dented mauls dangling from their belts.

Nicalene told him how she avoided the stocks on a few occasions by letting the arresting watchman lead her off into some alley for a few messy minutes.

He wondered if she had been with any of this lot.

When he finished cleaning his gear, he went back to his tenement. Tired as he was, he knew he would have trouble falling asleep. The heavy coins clinked together in his pocket as he walked up the stairs. Two marks were more than enough coin to get him plenty drunk, which was probably what Jaspen had in mind. But Grisel knew no amount of drinking would change how he felt.

The only thing that would make him feel better was finding Nicalene and taking back what she stole from him. That was assuming she had not gone and done something stupid with it, which was a distinct possibility.

The sweet taste of blooming flowers hit him when he opened the door next to the stairs.

Sedina.

She sat on the edge of her bed, little more than a silhouette against the dim candlelight. Her plain dress was one of the simple, cheap outfits she wore when she was not on the prowl for a sticker. Although it fit her loosely, the hemline only came down to the knee, leaving a portion of her firmly toned leg visible. The sight could catch any man's attention, and usually made him imagine running his hand up the dress to caress her thigh.

"Well, well," she said, "look who's back early tonight. How've you been, Grisel?"

Her voice was a bit shriller than it ought to have been for a woman her age. Along with the crooked tooth on her lower jaw, it was one of her few noticeable flaws. Grisel never heard any men complain about either, but he doubted many of them had plans on settling her down to house and home.

"I been better," he said. "You seen Nicalene earlier?"

It was hard to tell in the poor light, but Grisel thought she sneered.

"Not a sign. Course I ain't been down to your room for a long while. Not since she came around, leastways."

Grisel nodded. Before he met Nicalene, Sedina had seen quite a bit of his room.

"Yeah, I know," he said. "Been a while, eh?"

"Long while. What happened? You loose track of her or something? She go crawling back to whatever hole you dragged her out of?"

"Don't start with that. I seen you go trotting into worse places to find a sticker."

Sedina chuckled. "That's different. I get my feet dirty for a bit of coin, sure, but she's the one paying for the privilege of being in that filth."

Grisel had a hard time disagreeing. Sedina was hardly a model of respectable behavior, but at least she knew how to pay her way and keep herself out of trouble.

"She ran off, didn't she?" Sedina asked.

Grisel looked at her for a long while before nodding. She had let her hair down, leaving it to tumble over her shoulders and cover the sides of her chest. Nicalene hated that hair. Any time Grisel ran his hand through Nicalene's hair, she asked him if he was thinking about Sedina.

"Yeah, sometime before I woke up for my shift."

"She take anything?"

The only thing that mattered.

"Yeah," he said. "Cleaned me out. Knew where I kept it all."

"Didn't think you were that dumb."

Neither did I.

Grisel wondered what Nicalene would say if she knew he was commiserating with Sedina. She would probably claim he was doing it all along, sneaking over to the whore's room at every opportunity. Maybe she would realize instead that she drove him to it, that she did something to make her own worst fear come true.

In the hours since he found her gone, Grisel thought about what he could say to her when he found her, what he could do to hurt enough to make up for what she had taken from him. Standing there before Sedina, her supple body leaning back on the bed, he finally had an answer.

He reached into his pocket and grabbed one of the marks.

"I ain't got much coin left," he said, "but I got a lot I need to get off my mind. Think you can help me with that?"

Sedina slid off the bed and pressed her body against his. She grabbed his wrist before he could withdraw the coin.

"Tell you what," she said, her breath hot against his face, "we go back, you and me. May be that I owe you one, anyway. You just promise to do something for me, okay?"

"What's that?" he asked as she undid his belt.

"I want you to tell that lazy bitch how good I was."

THE BLEATING GOAT proved every bit as wretched as he remembered it. Not that the rest of the winesinks scattered around Pigshire were much better, but there was a nasty taste to the air around the place that left a stink on anyone who wandered too close. The *Goat* usually kept its doors open through the night provided the owners kept up to date on bribes to the local watch patrols. Come sunrise, the bouncers dumped a handful of people outside in a heap, most of them too high to know they were lying facedown in street muck.

Of course, that was how they met. Jaspen used to joke that Nicalene was the sweetest smelling piece of trash Grisel ever scooped off the street.

She was wearing that blue dress she liked so much, the one some lecherous nightroot seller gave her years back. When he pulled her out of the mud, she clung to him fiercely and sobbed like a child; whether she was scared or still caught up in hysteria from the firedust, he never knew. Not that it really mattered. Helping her made him feel good, and when she finally came out of her haze a few days later, he could not recall ever being happier.

That day felt like such a long time ago now.

Grisel watched an assortment of drunkards, thugs, and trollops drift in and out of the *Goat* for nearly an hour. None of them looked familiar, but that hardly surprised him. Places like the *Goat* had a way of gnawing people down to the bone and heaving the leftovers into the gutter. If Nicalene really was hells bent on falling back on her old ways, she would wind up there eventually.

There was no sign of her at the first three places he checked. One of the girls at *The Brazen Butcher* said she's seen her around once or twice, but not in the last week. He hoped to avoid paying a visit to the *Goat*, but it was the only other winesink open so late. Tomorrow morning, he could start canvasing the rest of Pigshire and move into the neighboring boroughs. Somehow, he needed to fit sleep into that schedule; Jaspen could not afford to cover for him for two nights.

Whatever he did, though, he knew he had to find her soon. Every moment that went by made it even less likely she would still have his treasured find when he finally caught up with her. If she was smart, she might realize it was worth more than anybody in Lowtown could pay. That being the case, she would be stuck going to Carta and Uthan, same as him. Depending on how desperate she felt, she might just take whatever they could afford to offer her. If she was shortsighted enough to fall for that, the little bastards could turn a fine profit from the trick.

But that was if she made a smart decision, which would depend on what frame of mind she was in at any given moment. Grisel knew she was capable of anything once she got it in her head that she needed a fresh fix of something. There was a good chance his prize might end up around the neck of some ignorant, junk-dealing ganger who never realized it was worth more than everything he had ever owned or stolen.

Should have just left the damn thing with the ghulans like they wanted.

After all, what were Carta and Uthan going to do? Sell it out from under him? Surely that would do little for their reputation. Not that second-guessing himself helped his current predicament. Just add the decision to what seemed to be an ever-growing list of dumb choices he made lately.

He wondered if his tryst with Sedina belonged in that category as well. She had been good at distracting him, but the experience left a cold knot in his stomach. At first, he just wanted to get back at Nicalene by doing the very thing she seemed to fear most. He tried to imagine her being made to watch, sitting in the corner of the room while he climbed into bed with the woman she hated.

But it was a hollow vengeance. She just sat there, staring at them blankly. No matter how intensely he made love to Sedina, he never drove that air of callous indifference from Nicalene's face. Even worse, when his mind wandered, he imagined he was inside her again, her smooth, naked skin sliding against his own. Eventually he had to force his eyes open to focus on Sedina's face and keep Nicalene's at bay. Judging from the way she writhed beneath him, Sedina seemed to appreciate the extra attention, but it all felt forced for him. Only after he closed his eyes and thought of Nicalene's long, black hair matted against her sweating breasts was he able to finish.

He eventually worked up the nerve to go inside the *Goat*, trailing just a few steps behind a pair of drunkards ambling in off the street. The common room was not big, but it was busy and noisy, much as Grisel remembered it. Boisterous laborers filled most of the tables while men and women crowded around the serving counter, leaving hardly a section free. The smoke-stained, low hanging ceiling and the stink of cheap candles kept the air thick and stale, especially with so many patrons making their own odorous contributions.

Grisel made for the bar counter in the back, while looking over the faces clustered around the tables. A few dark-haired women stood out, but they were all too young, too old, too thin, or too fat.

He quickly spotted the staircase leading to the second floor.

If Nicalene was there, she would be upstairs.

A big, pock-faced man occupied the bottom step, his massive frame filling the width of the staircase. He scanned the common room continuously, only occasionally moving to push someone away whenever they settled too closely to the stairs.

Grisel used to know some of the *Goat*'s hired thugs back when Nicalene frequented the place, but that had been more than two years ago. Someone had probably sent them along to the Deadhouse long ago.

Someone behind him tapped his shoulder and he turned to find a girl with tangled, mousey hair staring back at him, her eyebrows raised.

"I said, 'Can I help you, mister?'"

She smiled. Her teeth were crooked, stained black along the gumline.

Might as well start somewhere.

"Yeah," he said, "I'm looking for somebody. A woman that might of come by last night. Used to be a regular a while back but hasn't been here for about a year."

The girl shook her head.

"We get lots of those types in here. What she look like?"

"About this tall," he said, holding his hand level with his eyes. "Black hair, probably wearing a blue dress. Would've come by before sundown, most like." He indicated the staircase. "Probably went upstairs before too long."

The girl's smile vanished. She glanced over at the bar and then back to him before it came back, a bit less cheerful this time.

"Let me ask someone for you, okay?"

"Yeah," he said. "Sure."

He watched the girl traipse around the tables and wedge herself between two men at the bar. She leaned over the counter to speak with the barkeep, but Grisel had a hard time getting a good look at either of them while they talked. Something about her reaction when he described Nicalene worried him, and the longer the conversation went on, the more he wondered if they were up to something.

Maybe Nicalene had passed out upstairs and they needed somebody to haul her out of there.

Then again, she could be *dead* upstairs and they needed somebody to claim the body.

Grisel was still sorting out the possibilities when the girl came back.

The smile had returned, but she seemed to have a hard time keeping eye contact. Had she seemed that skittish earlier? Perhaps she was and he just missed it. Judging from her teeth, she was a heavy nightroot chewer. Maybe her nerves were shot from too much of the stuff.

"Might be a girl like that went upstairs earlier. I'll take you up there, okay?"

The cold knot in Grisel's stomach tightened. He had hoped to find her here, but if she really was upstairs, their confrontation promised to be ugly.

"Let's go, then," he said.

She led him over to the stairs. The pock-faced sentinel blocking the way eyed them strangely as they approached, but he nodded and stepped aside after the girl whispered something into his ear. Grisel followed her up the steps, the big guard close behind. Once she reached the door, she undid the latch and pushed it open. The hallway beyond was dark, but she stepped through the door without hesitating.

Grisel squinted to make out anything in the darkness. Greasy light spilled through a doorway farther down the hall, but otherwise everything was pitch black.

A big hand pushed Grisel up the last step.

"Go on," the guard said.

He stumbled and nearly tripped over his own feet. The thug quickly seized his arms from behind and held them tight against his body. The door slammed shut behind them and something cold, hard, and sharp pressed against his throat.

He took the hint and stopped struggling.

"Not a sound outta that mouth, got it?" the girl said, her voice a low hiss.

Grisel nodded as much as he could without getting cut. The dagger withdrew and the big guard shoved him forward.

"Move."

His eyes adjusted to the dark as the girl led them down the hall toward the light. They passed a room on the left that smelled like a tannery and a dye house crammed into the same space. Something had been burning in there recently, probably cooking up whatever nasty street shit in demand these days. Mercifully, they kept moving.

The girl led them into a mostly empty room lit by a few fat candles on the floor opposite a straw-filled mattress. Two men waited for them in the center of the room. One was short, pudgy, and balding, dressed in a shoddy-looking shirt and doublet that he probably paid too much for in a neighboring borough. The other man was the hardest looking cutter that Grisel had ever seen. He seemed closer to a golem molded out of pinkish clay than a man with anything resembling feeling or emotion. His floor length coat looked battered enough to have survived half a dozen wars. Even though he did not appear to be armed, Grisel suspected he could kill the lot of them with his bare hands.

Only after they were inside the room did he notice the smell.

Something die in here?

He looked down and noticed the body lying next to the mattress. Black lesions covered its skin from head to toe. As far as Grisel could tell, the man was stone dead.

The floor beneath his feet was sticky with blood.

Don't be here, Nicalene. Please don't be here.

The shorter man eyed them strangely when they entered the room.

"Dammit, girl," he said. "Didn't I tell you nobody else tonight until—"

"Owin said to bring this one up," she said, betraying none of the skittishness she displayed downstairs. "Came in looking for a girl with black hair and a blue dress."

"That so?" the taller man said. His voice made Grisel want to shrink.

The man gestured for the guard to release him.

"What's your name, friend?"

"Grisel," he said. His voice sounded a bit more strident than he wanted, but he at least kept it from trembling.

"This girl you're looking for. What's her name?"

"Now hold on a minute," Grisel said, hoping he sounded more confident than he felt. "What's going on here, anyway? I walk into this place asking a simple question and I get dragged up here to get shaken down by you lot? How about you give me something and maybe then I'll feel like talking, eh?"

The short man shook his head and grumbled. "We ain't got time for this, Arden. You done wasted—"

Arden's hand shot out to snare the short man by his chubby neck. For a moment, Grisel thought he might actually try to tear the man's head from his shoulders.

"You've already done plenty of wasting near as I can tell. Now you want me to tell Dhrath what kind of house you're running here, or you want to keep your stupid mouth shut so I can sort your problem for you?"

Considering how tightly he squeezed the man's throat, he probably did not expect a genuine answer. Arden pushed him aside and turned back to Grisel.

Dhrath.

The name stuck in Grisel's head, like something half forgotten. He knew he had heard it before. Was it someone Nicalene knew? Maybe one of the other spaders mentioned it?

Regardless of how he heard the name, he did not feel good about the context in this instance.

"Let me tell you how this works, Grisel," Arden said. "You tell me everything you know about this girl of yours and you can turn around and walk right out that door. Or, you can play stupid or forgetful and make me get the same information out of you another way, the one that leaves you crawling or carried out of here."

The shorter man coughed next to Arden and rubbed his throat. He did not seem like the sort of man used to being pushed around, but he clearly had no interest in crossing his companion again. Grisel knew it was probably wise to follow his example.

He glanced down at the body next to the mattress. Could she have been involved in his death? As far as he knew, Nicalene had never killed anyone. Besides, if those big, black welts all over his body were any indication, it looked like died of some kind of plague rather than foul play.

But then why was Arden so keen to track her down? There must have been more to it, something they were keeping to themselves. Whatever had gone down in that room, they thought she was responsible. Arden's reasonable demeanor was well-practiced, but Grisel could read between his words to see the man behind them.

What the hell did you get into here, Nicalene?

"Well, Grisel?" Arden said. "What'll it be?"

He owed Nicalene nothing, not anymore. He brought her into his home when he barely knew her and helped her straighten herself out. Maybe he could have treated her better along the way, but she had no cause to hate him for it, especially compared to the abuse she suffered before they met. He made her a part of his life, trusted her. And she decided to repay him by running out and stealing from him, as if taking care of her the last two years was not good enough for her. If she wanted to crawl back to the piss-filled trench where he found her, Grisel saw no reason why he should stop her.

And if she wanted to get involved with dangerous people who lacked any qualms about taking what they wanted out of her skin, that was her choice, not his. There was no reason he should even think about getting involved.

He was the one with something to lose, after all. He was the one with a roof, with a good trade, and with a plan to raise himself out of the gutter.

If he had any sense, he should have told them everything, right down to the flavor of wine she preferred.

But something gnawed at his good sense, made him hesitate. Told him to do something truly daft.

Nicalene getting herself in trouble was one thing. Truth be told, Grisel even relished the idea. He wished he could be there when she realized how stupid she was to run out on him. But people like Arden, and probably this Dhrath fellow, were not the sort to deal in warnings and mild reproaches. If they found Nicalene, they were going to hurt her, maybe even kill her. Grisel did not want that on his conscience.

Mainly, though, he kept thinking about what she had taken from him. If any one of these villains found that chunk of stone on her, they sure as the spire were not going to ask her where she got it. Arden looked like the stubborn type, the sort that was either honorable or thick enough to pass everything he found along to his bosses, but Grisel doubted that even he would be able to resist pocketing the thing for himself.

If they found Nicalene before him, whatever slim chance he had of getting his rightful property back would be gone.

"Piss off."

Arden sighed. "Well, then, if that's how you want it."

Perhaps following some secret signal, the pock-faced thug behind him started moving. Grisel spun around on one foot, grabbed the guard by his jerkin, and smashed his knee into his groin as hard as he could.

Arden lunged for him, but Grisel managed to yank the guard's doubled-over body into his path, knocking both of them to the ground.

Before the short man could react to the scrum, Grisel ran into the hallway and headed for the stairs.

His fingers closed around the door handle when someone slammed into him.

The girl, you idiot!

She tried to get the knife to his throat, but had a much harder time of it without someone to hold his arms. Grisel threw an elbow blindly and felt something sharp rip into his skin as her body snapped backward. The knife clattered to the floor and she fell back choking on blood and broken teeth.

He heard the others crashing into the hallway and shouting as he yanked the door open.

The light from downstairs almost blinded him, but he staggered forward, his foot probing for the first step.

Whether the girl was trying to grab him or trip him, he never knew, but she managed to snag one of his ankles before he could find his footing. Already disoriented from adjusting to the sudden light, Grisel lost his balance and careened headlong down the stairs.

He landed awkwardly, his head bouncing off a step so hard that the impact reverberated throughout his entire body. The pain hit him quickly, knifing into him from so many places that he felt like he was engulfed in flame. He tumbled, limbs smacking limply against the rest of the steps along the way.

When he finally hit the bottom, the nausea and disorientation hit him. He tried to get up, to keep running before Arden and the others caught up to him, but his body would not respond.

The cold knot in his stomach seemed to have come untied somewhere during the fall. Now it spread over his body. The chill settled first in his fingers and toes, but it moved quickly. He tried to shake it off and failed, his deadened limbs growing much too heavy.

Panicked, he attempted to cry out for help, but the only sound that came out was a wet gurgle of blood and bile.

He blinked and found Arden looming over him. Grisel's vision had become fuzzy, but he was sure it was Arden.

"Damn it," he said. "Get him up."

Grisel blinked and Arden vanished, replaced by an ugly, pockmarked face.

A thick glob of spit splashed into his eyes.

"Ought to cut you up for that, shitheel."

"No," Arden said. "Bring him out back. I've got just the place for him."

Grisel's vision swirled as the ice crept up his neck.

Is this what dying feels like?

Cold needles stabbed into his eyes and everything smeared into a dull wash of muted color.

He thought of Nicalene, of what she had taken from him. But as hard as he tried, he could not bring himself to hate her for it. He thought instead of her gentle hands, her smooth skin, and her soft, black hair falling over her shoulders.

She looked sad.

She always looked so sad.

Then she was gone, leaving Grisel to sink down into the cold, black depths of the unknown.

Alone.

I'm sorry, Nicalene. I'm so sor...

14

THE BARGAIN

E mber walked past Danglethorn Alley twice before he finally asked a street merchant for directions. Scarcely wider than a footpath, the alley snaked between rows of tenement housing before finally terminating in a cul de sac ringed with three and four story buildings. *Belloch's Bower* stood nestled between two shorter tenements and would have been indistinguishable from its neighbors were it not for the men and women calling out from the upper floor balconies and the bawdry gathering outside the main entrance. A group of musicians played there while drunken patrons sang along tunelessly in a misguided effort to impress the young women, and not a few men, competing for their affections and the coin that would follow.

For many years, *Belloch's Bower* had been just another dilapidated Coldwater tenement. It was not until around the time Ember was born that it transformed into the largest and most successful brothel in Lowtown. The place still bore the name of its ambitious founder and landlord, Belloch Rajovunn, who scoured the whole of Blackspire to recruit a stable of prostitutes, sin peddlers, and all manner of eccentrics to bring "character" to his aspiring business venture. A genuine curiosity, it was the one place in Lowtown where a patron could enjoy a meal in one room, discuss the latest foreign philosophies with accomplished poets in another, and spend the rest of the evening in bed with a black eyed Selarnan girl or a hairless boy from Gulhn.

Although Ember rarely visited the place, he knew a great deal about it because his grandmother had been one of the principle investors in Belloch's ambitions. She took in a hefty cut of profits until Ember's father traded that privilege in exchange for the right to help himself to whatever the *Bower* had to offer. Ember tried not to think about how much coin his grandmother's arrangement might be providing him now.

One more inheritance squandered away.

Ember avoided making eye contact with the drunken louts teaming outside the main entrance. A young man with long, silken hair slid alongside him and touched his arm, but backed away after Ember shook his head. He scarcely took another step before a dark skinned Karthean woman approached. After Ember waved her off, the rest of the aspiring companions took the hint and left him alone.

The *Bower's* first floor had been converted into a huge common area, with tables, chairs, and benches scattered all over. Unlike a typical Lowtown winesink, the place looked more like an aristocrat's sitting room than a tavern hall. Pieces of art and sculpture hung from the walls, which were already decorated with a riotous array of colored tiles, woodwork, and stonework. To anyone who had visited the sprawling manses of High Ridge, or even Crowngate, the décor was a garish mess born of misguided lowborn tastes. For the denizens of Lowtown, however, *Belloch's Bower* offered a measure of luxury few of them ever had chance to glimpse.

Ember scanned the room several times before he spotted the man he was looking for holding court at a table near the back of the common area. An array of prostitutes and sycophants swirled around him, chatting and laughing as if the rest of the patrons lay far beneath their attention. The barrel chested man drank heartily from a tankard so large Ember doubted he could lift it with a single hand. He wore the drab, brown garments of a common laborer, but he looked much too clean for such an occupation.

Harik Gondulin liked to present himself as a friend of the people, a man of simple, earthy tastes and modest ambitions. It never seemed to matter how many times he made an embarrassment of himself in public; the common dregs of Lowtown either did not believe the stories of his drunken indiscretions or saw something of themselves in the retellings.

"Simpler folk love a good fool standing over them, even a vile one," his father once said. *"It gives them hope for their own prospects."*

After witnessing the capricious nature of the populace during his time in the Assembly, Ember was more inclined to defer to his grandmother's wisdom: *"The people are idiots, boy. Don't expect them to make any sense."*

When Harik spotted him, he lifted his tankard in Ember's direction and called out over the din.

"Lord Morangine! Come! Join us!"

So much for a quiet word.

Ember tried not to scowl as he walked over to the table. Harik snapped his fingers at one of his companions, a dense-looking man with a soot-stained beard.

"Best make way for His Lordship, friend! We're lucky he doesn't make us bow in his presence!"

The crowd gathered around the table erupted with laughter at the jest. They cackled again when the soot-bearded man hopped up from his chair and made a grandiose show of pulling it out for Ember to be seated.

Ember clenched his teeth and smiled at Harik.

Gods, you're an insufferable bastard.

"You're too kind, Assemblyman," he said, lowering himself into the offered seat.

Harik laughed. "Oh, quit your glowering, Morangine. There are worst fates than brushing alongside the hard-working men of this borough for an evening. Someone fetch this aristocratic cunt an ale!"

Another round of laughter rang out around the table before one of the women shoved a small tankard into Ember's hands.

"My thanks," he said, scarcely making eye contact with her.

"Now, then," Harik said, scratching at his chest, "what's this matter you wanted to discuss so desperately that it couldn't wait another day?"

Ember resisted the urge to glance around the table. He knew some of Harik's companions would be listening, but there was no sense in trying to discern which ones simply feigned interest and which would be peddling bits of the conversation in exchange for coin later that night.

"I'd hoped we might speak in private."

Harik scoffed. "I'm sure you did, Morangine. That's the trouble with you rich men, always trying to keep secrets from the people you're trying to screw over. The hardworking citizens of this borough have entrusted me to represent their interests. What kind of man would I be if I conducted business behind closed doors?"

A wise one.

Ember often wondered if Harik believed his own bluster, or if his throng of admirers were taken in by such sweeping pronouncements of integrity. He also questioned just how many of those "hardworking citizens" could afford an evening of drinks and whoring at the *Bower*. For all his claims of speaking for the people, Harik seemed to have few reservations about using his Assembly salary to support a lifestyle far beyond the means of his supposed constituents.

"As you wish, then," Ember said. "I thought we might have a word about the upcoming negotiations for the Spaders Guild contract."

Harik groaned. "That again? What more is there to say at this point? The city shits, someone needs to scoop it up, and the guild is willing to do it."

"For a price, of course. An increasingly steep price."

"Unsavory work commands an unsavory price. You'd know that if you ever had to work to put food on your table."

"And if you'd ever paid a man to do a job, you'd know that he'll take you for everything you've got if he's the only man available."

Harik raised an eyebrow. "You saying a man doesn't have a right to fair pay, rich boy?"

Thick as a rock, this one.

"Not at all," Ember said. "You know better than anyone what happens to a trade once a guild gets involved. They close ranks and shut out anybody who isn't lucky enough to be a member. Next thing you know, all those good working folk you talk about so much are stuck begging for scraps because the guild's convinced everyone that they're not fit to do the job."

A few of the men at the table grunted in agreement and looked expectantly at Harik, who had a reputation for publically railing against the guilds' monopolization of certain trades.

"That may be so," Harik said, "but what's it got to do with the spader contract?"

Idiot. Do I have to put it in pictures for you?

"Shoveling shit isn't exactly skilled labor, is it? Who's to say we couldn't pay any man here at this table to do the same work for half of what the district pays a bloody spader?"

Harik pursed his lips, then took a long drink from his tankard. Whispers spread around the table, the men no doubt considering the implications of Ember's question.

"What do you suggest, then?"

"Without a contract with the Assembly, the Spaders Guild has no exclusive right to street cleaning. The Assembly could contract individual laborers, or even leave it to the local boroughs to organize their own cleaning efforts. That means more opportunities for work and less need for the Assembly to levy the taxes to keep the spaders fat and comfortable. You keep telling everyone who'll listen that the guilds are keeping the common laborer under their boot heels. Here's your opportunity to finally do something about it."

Harik squinted and nibbled on his upper lip the way he did whenever someone asked him to render an original thought. His drinking companions watched him expectantly. Most of them looked like laborers themselves, the sort of men Harik often brought with him to places like the *Bower* to preserve his reputation with the mob. He would barely remember most of their names tomorrow, but they would all remember how he received Ember's proposal. If he passed up an opportunity to strike a blow against one of the guilds, word might spread among the masses that Harik Gondulin was no longer a "friend" of the people.

This is why a wise man conducts business behind closed doors, you fool.

"What say you, Assemblyman?" one of the men asked, breaking the heavy silence.

"Aye," another said, "I ain't fond of shoveling shit, but I got friends and cousins been out of work for months that'd be happy to scoop it up with their bare hands for regular coin."

A few others concurred, and one of the prostitutes muttered something about her brother needing steady work to pay off a gambling debt. Ember felt the mood at the table shifting, felt the pressure tilting toward Harik's side as most of his companions expressed enthusiasm for the proposal. Two men remained silent, however, and one of the prostitutes hardly seemed to care one way or the other. Maybe they were truly disinterested; maybe they were informants for a local broker or even one of the guilds. Ember could not quite judge which was more likely.

Harik finally raised his hand and everyone at the table fell silent. He glared at Ember, then nodded slowly.

"I see your point," he said. "But what is it that you want from me? You didn't ask for this meeting to help you plan this strategy of yours, now did you?"

Ember almost laughed at the suggestion. As if Harik could formulate any strategy beyond getting to the nearest winesink.

"Nothing so complicated, I assure you. To be perfectly honest, there's only one thing I need from you."

"And what's that?"

"Your vote."

EMBER RETURNED HOME in an uncharacteristically good mood.

Securing Harik's vote proved a far easier task than he expected. His commitment pushed Ember's coalition of Assembly votes to six, only one short of the seven they needed to bury the damned Spaders Guild for good. The seventh vote, however, was all but a foregone conclusion. If what Ithlene told him earlier that day was true, Murga Lochmas's vote could be bought without much difficulty.

They merely needed to determine his price. Much like Harik, Murga was a simple man of simple tastes. Whatever price he demanded would likely be petty and easily provided.

Ember's good mood faded when he found the manse's front door standing ajar.

It was unlike Yimina to forget something so simple.

Nor was it like her to extinguish every light inside before Ember bedded down for the night, but every window stood dark all the same.

Something's not right here.

He pushed the door open slowly and stepped into the dark foyer. Fumbling through the black, he found a small table just inside the entrance where he kept a candle and tinderbox. He struck a match and lit the candle.

"Yimina?"

For a moment, there was only silence. Then, before he could take another step inside, a strained voice called back.

"Here. In the study."

Ember moved quickly, fearing that perhaps Yimina had fallen ill or been injured somehow during the day. When he reached the study, however, he nearly dropped the candle in shock.

Yimina stood in the middle of the room, her toes balancing on a wobbly stool. Her hands were bound behind her back and she stood rigid, her neck straining at the end of a noose hanging down from one of the ceiling rafters. Another length of rope ran from one of the stool legs to a chair off to his right. A large figure sat there, immersed in shadow.

"Who the hells—?"

The figure struck a match and lit one of the candles on the table next to him.

"Good evening, Lord Morangine," the man said as the light washed over his cruel face.

Raugov.

"What's the meaning of this?" Ember asked, mustering enough anger to hide his fear. He alternated between glaring at Raugov and glancing worriedly at Yimina, who looked ready to lose her balance and fall from the stool at any moment.

Gods, how long has she been there?

"That's funny," Raugov said. "I might have asked you the same question."

He tossed a crumpled ball of paper at Ember's feet. Perplexed, Ember retrieved the paper and unfolded it to read the message scrawled upon it.

Even in the poor light, he immediately recognized his own handwriting.

"I don't understand," he said. "This is the message I brought to you at the *Boot* telling you where to meet Kaurgen."

"I know what it is, shitheel! What I want to know is why your man didn't show up there."

Oh no...

"What do you mean he didn't show?"

Raugov pulled the rope taut, causing the stool to quiver just enough to make Yimina gasp.

"I mean your man wasn't there! Now maybe he skipped out on his own or maybe the two of you have some kind of deal worked out, but either way, Mister Dhrath hasn't got what he was promised. And Mister Dhrath don't like not getting what he's promised."

Ember raised his hands, his heart racing. "Raugov, I swear to you, I have no idea what's going on. I didn't even see Kaurgen when he returned to Blackspire. He sent me a letter telling me he was ready to meet and I passed the information along to you. How do you expect me to know what kind of angle he's playing? He's a bloody thief, it's not my fault if he decided to double cross the both of us!"

Raugov stared at him without a trace of emotion, not even anger. He glanced at Yimina, still balancing perilously on the tips of her toes. One good tug on the rope would either pull the stool out from under her or cause her to lose her balance. The noose had too little slack in it for a drop that could break her neck, instead promising to slowly choke her to death.

Hold on, Yimina. Hold on...

"You got one chance to keep your sorry ass right with Mister Dhrath," Raugov said. "I don't like what I hear, your house bitch hangs. Now talk. I want to know everything about this Kaurgen: his roof, his friends, his history, everything."

Ember plumbed the depths of his memory for every scrap of information about Kaurgen. He told Raugov about how he first met the thief, three years back when he helped put Kaurgen in touch with a buyer in High Ridge for some trinket swindled from a retired general in Rickenwick. They never met in person, of course, but word got around pretty quickly that Ember knew how to put people in touch with the rogue. Kaurgen took on clients but rarely dealt directly with anyone. That was why Dhrath wanted to contract the thief's services as part of his deal with Ember in the first place. Ember sprinkled in a few details about Kaurgen's suspicious nature and his unpredictable temperament, about why he chose certain meeting places and how he delivered messages, but none of it seemed to impress Raugov. After every digression, the brutish thug flexed his fingers around the rope.

Clearly, only one piece of information would appease him.

"There's another thing he has me do for him," Ember said. "He doesn't keep a steady roof. Says he doesn't spend enough time in the city to make it worth his while, so he rents out a place each time he comes back. Whenever he arrives, he sends word to me and I put him in touch with a landlord who won't ask too many questions. After the deal's done,

I slip them a few marks and they tell me where he's staying, just in case I need to track him down."

Raugov chuckled. "You mean turn him in if the reward's high enough."

"The man's a thief by trade. I don't want his sort hiding in every shadow without me knowing about it."

Another laugh. "You've got balls, Morangine, I'll give you that. Where's he staying now?"

Ember knew if he gave up the address, Kaurgen was a dead man unless he had a damned good reason for not showing up for the meeting. As far as Dhrath was concerned, death was probably the only acceptable reason for not holding up his end of their deal.

Sorry, Kaurgen. You should have thought about who you were dealing with before you tried to pull one over on them.

"Over in Pigshire. A two-story shanty house on High Cross Street."

For the first time, Raugov relaxed his grip on the rope. "You got a street number?"

"Twelve."

"That so? And who's to say we'll find anything there when we come calling for him?"

"He couldn't have left the city," Ember said. "If he wanted to find another buyer, there's no better place. He knows he can't come to me if he wants another deal, so he'd have to ask around. That takes time. It could be that something happened to him. Maybe he bedded down with some whore and told her too much. Maybe he was sloppy, and some bounty killer tracked him down. In any case, he can't have just up and vanished, not without leaving a trail of some kind."

Raugov nodded slowly. "For your sake, you better hope so."

The two men stared at each other. When Raugov finally set the rope aside, Ember felt like a knife had been removed from his throat.

"Are we squared away, then?" he asked.

"For now," Raugov said. "We'll see how much what you've said is worth."

Ember did not doubt his information, but he worried how Dhrath might react to what he found at twelve High Cross.

Or rather, how he might react if he found nothing there at all.

"And what if he does turn up dead? What if he doesn't have what he promised to bring?"

Raugov smiled again, revealing the sharpened points of his teeth. "That all depends on Mister Dhrath, now doesn't it? Could be he'll write it off to bad luck. Or might be he holds you responsible. Maybe if you're lucky, he'll just take a bigger fee for his troubles. Or maybe he'll crack your skull open and suck out your brain."

Given how much he was cutting Dhrath in already, Ember almost preferred the latter option. "Hopefully, it won't come to that, then," he said.

Raugov rose from the chair and gestured to Yimina. "Best be careful cutting her down. Be a shame if she split that pretty head of hers on the floor."

The brute laughed again as he pushed by Ember.

"You have a pleasant evening, Lord Morangine," he said. "Be seeing you soon. Real soon, I hope."

As soon as Raugov left the room, Ember retrieved a knife from a nearby desk and pulled a chair over alongside Yimina. He carefully cut the rope dangling from the rafters before helping her down from the stool and onto the floor. She hacked and coughed when he pulled the noose away from her neck.

"Did he hurt you anywhere else?" Ember asked as he sawed through the rope binding her wrists.

Yimina shook her head. "I'm so sorry," she said, her voice hoarse.

"Stop that," Ember said, tearing the rope away from her hands. He wrapped his arms around her and pulled her close to his chest. "I'm just glad you're safe."

"Bastard was already inside when I came home. Blindsided me when I came through the door. Should have seen him. I put you in danger…"

Ember pulled away and lifted Yimina's chin to look into her eyes. "I said to stop that talk, dammit. You're safe now and here with me, understand?"

Yimina nodded and grasped his hand. "Yes, sir."

They embraced and laid back on the floor, both of them breathing heavily, her to catch her breath, and him to calm his nerves.

"What do we do now?" Yimina asked.

"Now? For right now, we hope they find Kaurgen exactly where I said he'd be."

But Ember's thoughts had already moved beyond that. Finding Kaurgen would be simple enough given what he knew about the thief's habits, especially if Dhrath's hounds were on his trail. Unless he had fled the city entirely, he would not be able to keep out of sight for long.

The bigger question pertained to Dhrath. Ember had grown tired of the broker's excessive demands and boundless arrogance. For the time being, he needed Dhrath's support if he hoped to take on the spaders. What happened after that, however, remained unclear to him.

Ember hated uncertainty.

"Come on," he said. "Let's get you upstairs."

MERROWSHEAD STREET BARELY stretched wide enough to qualify as a proper street. Located perilously close to Sinkhole, the crooked roadway ran behind a row of sturdy, three story brick flats to separate them from a tangled warren of old wooden tenements in various states of collapse. A fire had torn through the wooden buildings several decades ago, gutting most of their interiors and leaving hundreds dead in the inferno's wake. No one made a concerted effort to rebuild the damaged structures, close as they were to the diseased slums of Sinkhole.

Of course, that never stopped the tightfisted landlords from renting out space in the ruined tenements. For many unfortunate souls, it was their last desperate attempt to keep a roof in Coldwater borough. If they were lucky, they might find decent accommodations in neighboring Pigshire or Carbuncle. The less fortunate found themselves evicted, forced into the lawless muck and ruin of Sinkhole.

Merrowshead Street ran for less than a quarter of a mile before terminating in dead ends in both directions. Intersected by several alleyways cutting between the brick buildings on the southern side, the street flooded after the slightest rain and sometimes took weeks to dry out. Mosquitos bred rampantly in the still puddles and great packs of rats scurried out from the crumbling tenements to drink from the fetid water after sunset.

Despite the dire conditions, Merrowshead proved a popular destination for Coldwater's vagrants because the watch rarely ventured there. The tenement landlords knew better than to waste their time lodging formal complaints against the watch, instead hiring gangs from Sinkhole to clear the street of indigents every few months. Between those violent sweeps, however, Merrowshead filled up with makeshift lean-tos and tangled nests of trash that sprouted like islands in a blight-choked river.

Ember knew better than to visit the vile street after dark, especially without Yimina at his side, but he could not afford to wait until daybreak. Dhrath would be sure to have someone watching for him during the day now. Even if Raugov was occupied tracking down Kaurgen, the broker had eyes and ears throughout Lowtown. If Ember did anything out of the ordinary, Dhrath would probably know about it by the end of the day. A side trip to Merrowshead Street would certainly be considered unusual enough to arouse suspicion.

Tonight, then, was his best chance, maybe his only chance.

He smelled Merrowshead Street before he reached it, a powerful mixture of stale piss, rotten wood, and rat shit. The stench burned his nostrils as soon as he turned down an intersecting alleyway. Breathing through his mouth, Ember gripped his small lantern tightly and staggered toward the waterlogged street. He did his best to dress accordingly, wrapping his body with tattered garments and a moth-eaten cloak pulled from a cobwebbed closet in one of the manse's shuttered bedrooms. The disguise was a poor one; old and ragged as they were, the garments were still woven from quality, expensive fabric. Although Ember had smeared dirt across his face, it was difficult to hide his good physical health. He bore no scars from skin disease, nor did he exhibit any signs of physical trauma, such as improperly healed broken bones or mangled extremities. While a wealthy Coldwater resident might have crossed the street to avoid him, the truly destitute would see through his flimsy artifice without much difficulty.

Ember emerged from the alley and stepped into Merrowshead Street, doing his best to avoid stepping in ankle deep puddles. The occasional cluster of exposed cobblestones provided passably sure footing, but most of the time he had to hope that the wet earth would prove firm beneath his steps. He did not get very far before the mosquitoes found him. A buzzing cloud settled over him to nip at every exposed piece of flesh.

Small campfires bloomed up and down the street like wildflowers forcing their way up along the course of a dried-out riverbed. Bent figures huddled around the meager flames, most of them shriveled and scarred. Roaming packs of black rats, some of them as long as Ember's feet, skirted the outskirts of the light before disappearing into the darkness or scurrying into the brackish water.

Two older men glanced at Ember when they noticed the lantern's light, but they looked away quickly and shuffled to the opposite side of their fire. They pulled rags over their mouths when he passed them by, their eyes wide and darting.

Probably think I'm with the watch.

The watch may have been good at ignoring Merrowshead, but ambitious captains sometimes tried to gather information about dangerous areas to pass up the chain of command in hopes of impressing their superiors. Ember imagined that those amateur spies' disguises were rarely any more convincing than his own.

Fortunately, he did not have to go far to find what he was looking for.

The girl sat on a pile of broken bricks well clear of the campfires and the rest of the street's vagrants. Roughly ten years old, she wore a torn dress that no longer stretched down far enough to cover her scabbed, bruised knees. Some of her matted, brownish hair had fallen out, and she looked like she had not eaten in weeks.

When the lantern's light passed over the girl, her totally white eyes failed to blink or twitch. Her little shoulders and chest remained perfectly still, betraying the fact that she was not breathing.

She dangled a rather large rat from its tail, watching it writhe and snap its nasty little teeth at her. Every time her prisoner seemed to calm down, she flicked her fingers at its head, which set it to squirming and gnashing once more. Her slack face, pale, dirty, and bruised, regarded the display without a single expression to suggest what she thought about it.

How many of these "people" does she have, anyway?

Ember sidled up to the girl, careful to stay well clear of the rat's frantic escape attempts. She did not look up at him and gave no indication that she even noticed his presence.

"I have a message for you," he said, careful to keep his voice down. "A message for Twiceborn."

The girl's free hand slowly reached out to grasp the rat around the neck and squeezed.

"State your name and speak your words," she said, watching the rat squirm as she slowly choked the life out of it.

Ember glanced around to make sure no one nearby was listening to their exchange before he continued. "It's Ember," he said. "There's been a complication. The situation is shifting out of our favor now. We have to talk. Face to face. No more messengers. We can't waste time passing these…things of yours back and forth."

No reaction. The girl continued to squeeze the rat. It moved slower now, the will to fight slowly deteriorating under intense pressure. When the creature finally fell still, the girl turned her white-eyed gaze up to look at Ember.

"Do you have more words?"

"Yes, plenty of them," he said. "But you can tell Twiceborn that she's not going to get another one out of me unless we meet in-person."

The girl looked back to the rat. She released her grip on its neck and held the vermin close to watch it draw tiny, wheezing breaths.

"Do you understand what I'm telling you?" he asked.

The rat's legs twitched, and the girl clamped her fingers around its neck again. Ember heard a wet, snapping sound when she squeezed. She pulled her hand away, then shook the limp rodent by its tail.

Although the girl's expression remained unchanged, she cocked her head slightly to one side as she stared at the dead rat.

"I said—"

"Yes," she said. "This one hears your words and will deliver them."

She poked at the rat with her free hand, watching it dangle lifelessly in front of her.

"I think it's dead now."

The girl looked at him. Something about her numbed features made his stomach quiver. He noticed the flesh around her neck was dark and bruised.

"Your little pet there," he said. "It's dead."

She glanced at the rodent one last time before dropping it in the mud at her feet.

"Dead…" she said, her voice a scarcely intelligible mumble.

Ember stepped back from the girl, his boots squishing into the wet muck covering the street.

"I…I have to go," he said, turning away from her and retreating to the more familiar confines of the alleyway leading away from Merrowshead.

He looked back only once.

The girl had vanished.

15

THE APOSTATE

Calandra stopped the wheelbarrow just past the fourth bell, which marked the entrance to the deeper portions of the Deadhouse crypts. Almost a foot wide, it was the biggest of the main tunnel's signal bells and loud enough to be heard in the main Mortuary chamber more than one hundred feet above. A rope ran from the well-oiled hinge at the top of the bell to a series of piton hooks hammered into the tunnel wall at about chest height. The hooks formed a line that guided the rope deeper into the crypts, making it possible for any worker in distress to call to the surface for help.

Few workers ventured much deeper than the fourth bell anymore. The deep tunnels had been used for special burials back when the Law Diet tightened Blackspire's inhumation laws, and most of the space had been filled up for centuries. There were a few storage chambers that housed the more volatile chemicals needed to purify the dead and a curious citizen would occasionally ask to view an ancestor's remains, but most undertakers stayed clear of the deeper cryptways.

Calandra dimmed her lantern, pulled the cover into place, and returned it to the metal hook at the front of the wheelbarrow. The light was faint enough now that she could barely see her hand held out before her. Unless they walked along the tunnel in complete darkness, no one approaching would see her until they came within a few feet of her.

All she had to do now was wait.

She had made sure to tell Tarl she would be gone for some time, maybe even a few hours. Although she had some pretext ready to explain why she had to take a body down to the crypts and stay down there for so long, she did not need it. Part of her felt like she betrayed the simpleton's trust, but the sensible part insisted it would be better for both of them if he knew as little as possible about what she was doing.

The corpse in the wheelbarrow had not shown signs of decay yet. When they scrubbed it clean and pumped the waste out of it yesterday, they had poked a few holes in it to drain its fluids and allow the bad air to escape. Although Calandra knew the rot had already taken hold inside, it would not become evident for a few more days. Under the right conditions, the decomposition could be put off even longer.

In any case, she imagined it would be far more attractive to a bodysnatcher than the stiff, week-old corpses stashed in the rooms farther up the tunnel.

Calandra tried not to think too much about her reasons for being there. She found it better to focus on the present, listening for any sign of movement in the darkness. When her attention strayed, she corralled it by reminding herself of what she had found in the ledger. She double-checked the entries to be sure, but she no longer had any doubt that Lerris had altered the records to make bodies conveniently disappear.

Less than a day earlier, the discovery might have been cause for celebration. Armed with that piece of evidence, she could finally get back at the wretched hag for all the torment she suffered over the years. Now, however, it left her feeling relieved, hopeful, and disgusted all at the same time.

On top of all that, Calandra still wanted to strangle Beyland. He had always been irresponsible and shortsighted, but she did not fully appreciate how stupid he could be until now. When Dhrath's thug ambushed her and laid the truth of it on her, she considered leaving her brother to his fate. It would serve him right after everything he put her through over that damned theater of his. While Calandra was thankful to have a decent roof of their own, she'd dumped years worth of earnings into the place on little more than Beyland's promise that they would make it back once he got his new troupe underway. As far as she saw it, she had already sacrificed enough; if he failed to make good on a debt, that was his problem.

The situation was not that simple, of course. Arden left little doubt as to what his master did with people who skimped on their obligations. Idiot or not, Beyland was still her brother, and if he was senselss for cutting a deal with someone like Dhrath, she was as much a fool for enabling him. Thinking back on it, she should have questioned where he acquired so much coin when it came time to buy the theater. She knew him well enough to be suspicious of the notion that he had actually saved anything from his troupe days. Still, he radiated enthusiasm, so sure of himself, that she wanted to believe he had finally found his way.

In the end, though, it proved to be a dream.

And all dreams eventually end.

As much as she wanted to dump this at his feet, she knew telling him about her run-in with Arden was a bad idea. Beyland never met a problem he was not willing to run from and she had no intention of being left at the mercy of some bloodless broker when her brother's debts came due. Dhrath's people would probably just track him down anyway, and once that happened, there would be no hope of reasoning with them. Their only chance was to maintain the thug's good graces. If she strung him along with frequent payments, she hoped it would give her time to figure out a way to pay the debt off in full or get out of the city.

Even if they could find some means of leaving Blackspire, she had no idea where they might go. The city had a way of fostering an intense dependency in its denizens. It tugged at them like a whirlpool, sucking countless souls inside its circular walls and holding them there until they drowned.

She must have waited almost two hours before she heard something shambling up from the deep cryptways. Leaving her lantern hanging from the wheelbarrow's hook, she stepped into the mouth of the tunnel and peered into the darkness. A small, yellowish ball of light bobbed slowly toward her. She recognized it as the smeared, steady glow of a lantern, its wick choked down to keep the flame as dim as possible.

The figure holding the lantern aloft remained mostly in shadow, but its eyes glimmered brightly as if they contained tiny fires of their own. Two hulking lumps plodded along just behind the figure, lingering on the edge of the lantern's meager light.

What the hells are these things?

Calandra eased back from the edge of the tunnel. Her chest tightened, and her stomach quivered so badly she feared she might retch all over her shoes. Doubt gnawed at her as she struggled to keep her breathing slow and steady.

All the while, the shuffling footsteps grew louder.

You can do this, damn you. You have *to do this.*

She retrieved her lantern from the wheelbarrow and stepped into the tunnel.

The bodysnatchers stopped as soon as she moved into view. They stood only about a dozen feet from where Calandra waited. At that distance, she could see that the lead figure's glowing eyes were not eyes at all, but merely goggles reflecting the lantern's light. The goggles were part of a leather mask covering the figure's face. She still could not make out the shapes behind the lead figure, but they stood at least a head taller.

After staring at Calandra for a few seconds, the figure reached up and unbuckled one of the mask's straps to pull the lower portion away from its mouth.

"Well, well, well. Look's like someone's gone a bit astray."

A woman's voice, strong, precise, and cold.

"I know what you're doing down here," Calandra said, doing her best to keep her voice from trembling. She glanced at the rope on the nearby wall. One hard yank would sound the signal bell, but it would take a long time for anyone upstairs to reach her.

Too long to help me.

"I saw you last night," she said, a little less confidently. "All of you."

The woman smiled. "Did you now?"

She handed the lantern to one of the brutish figures behind her. Calandra's throat tightened when she saw the thing's mangled face. Although vaguely human, many of its features were enlarged or twisted. One eyebrow was so swollen it nearly covered up the eye beneath it. Some of the thing's teeth were twice as large as the others and a bony protrusion about the size of Calandra's nose jutted out through the skin at the top of its cheek. The weight of the creature's bulging muscles caused it to slump forward. Black, wiry hair grew in sporadic clumps all over its body.

While Calandra gawked at the creature, the woman rubbed her hands together and whispered something unintelligible. When she pulled her hands apart again, her outline in the dim light became indistinct.

What the hells is she doing?

Parts of the woman flickered like a dying flame, her face and fingers crumbling away as if they burned away into ash. Then she took a step forward and dissolved into the darkness.

Gods! She's a sorcerer!

Calandra staggered back as the stench of burning sulfur swept through the tunnel. The air around her grew warmer and she inhaled a mouthful of burning smoke. Coughing, she turned and reached blindly for the rope connected to the signal bell.

A hand closed around her wrist and wrenched her away from the rope. She dropped her lantern as something slammed into her back to pin her body against the tunnel wall. The lantern clattered to the ground and rolled a short distance down the tunnel before stopping abruptly.

"I'm curious," the woman said, her voice no more than a whisper in Calandra's ear, "just what did you think to do with this precious knowledge of yours?"

The woman's knee stabbed into the small of her back to keep her trapped against the wall. Calandra's throat felt seared from the smoke she had gulped down, but she managed to draw enough breath to croak out an answer.

"Bodies," she said, "get you...fresh bodies..."

The woman relaxed her grip slightly, just enough to let Calandra breathe.

"You think I need you for that? Seems to me I've got my pick of the crypts already."

Calandra nodded her head toward the wheelbarrow. "Look there. Brought you a sample."

The woman might have turned to look, but Calandra could not tell for sure considering her face was pressed into the dirt wall. Nothing happened for several moments, and she began to fear she misplayed her hand. After all, they could easily decide to kill her and drag her body down to the deep cryptways. Someone would come looking for her eventually, but it was not unheard of for a careless undertaker to fall down one of the sloped tunnels and become hopelessly lost in the utter blackness. Her body could go missing for months before they found her rotting carcass somewhere below.

Or maybe they'll just find me here with a broken neck and figure I slipped.

Her heart pounded quickly enough to send painful tremors through her whole body.

Finally, the woman broke the thick silence. "Hold her."

One of the hulking brutes lumbered closer. It pinned her against the wall with its forearm as the woman withdrew. The thing smelled as foul as it looked, and its sweat quickly soaked through the back of her shirt. Every ragged breath from its misshapen mouth stank of rotting meat.

"When did this one come in?" the woman asked.

She knows it's fresh. Good.

"Last night; drowned in a privy."

The woman let out a single, pitiless laugh. "Bad way to go. You cleaned him up?"

"Yes."

Another long pause. "Bring her to me."

The beast yanked Calandra away from the wall and spun her around to face the woman. It kept a firm grip on her arms, holding her so tightly that she thought her bones might crack under the pressure.

"This is good work," the woman said, inspecting the inside of the corpse's mouth. She had pulled the rest of her mask off at some point, the big goggles rested just above her forehead. The woman looked younger than Calandra expected, probably no more than a year or two older than her. Even so, there was no mistaking the gray streaks running through her short, black hair.

Sorcery, after all, had a price.

The woman turned to look at her. Even in the dim lantern light, Calandra could see that her eyes had no pupils. They were solid, grayish-black orbs that seemed to take in everything before her all at once.

Oh, gods, what am I doing down here?

"Why?"

The abruptness of the question took Calandra by surprise, but she gathered her wits quickly.

Don't panic. One thing at a time.

"You're paying Lerris for week-old corpses," she said. "I can get them to you fresh."

The woman stared at her with those dark, unblinking eyes for what felt like months.

Now.

"It'll cost you, though."

The woman raised one of her eyebrows. "What's your name, undertaker?"

"Calandra. Journeyman, grade four. I run the night shift."

The woman smiled again. Calandra was not sure if she should be afraid or not, but she felt the fright creeping into her bones all the same.

LERRIS ARRIVED AT her usual time, shuffling through the front gate a little past dawn. She looked especially haggard this morning. It was no great secret that she spent most of her time away from the Deadhouse drinking. On her worst mornings, she even kept a bucket next to her desk in case she got sick. Not that the drinking ever improved her mood. Lerris could be twice as nasty hung over, and everyone knew not to bother her until she had a chance to sober up somewhat.

Calandra did not move from her chair as Lerris approached the desk. She went on pretending to reference various names and dates in the mortuary's master ledger even when Lerris dropped her sack on the floor and plopped her withered, scabbed hands on the desk.

"You're late again," Calandra said.

Lerris snorted. "You the boss of me now, that it?"

That's about right.

Calandra scooped the ledger up and pushed the chair back.

"Come with me," she said. "There's something you need to see down in the crypt."

Lerris's puffy eyelids squinted over her greenish pupils. She licked her chapped lips.

"See what?" she asked. "There ain't nothing down there I don't already know about. More than I can say for you."

Calandra stifled a laugh and wished she could tell her how wrong she was about that. The less Lerris knew about her involvement with the bodysnatchers, the better. She had put herself in enough danger without giving the wretch any more reason to suspect she was up to something.

"That's good," she said. "You should be able to sort this out for me right quick, then."

Lerris grumbled at the response but followed a few steps behind her as they crossed the preparation chamber and approached the crypt gate. Tarl waited for them there. Once he saw Calandra, he handed her a lantern and opened the door.

They barely ventured in to the first group of storage rooms, where the unidentified corpses prior to cremation were stored. Calandra led Lerris into the first room and opened the ledger.

"I've been looking at the figures from the last few days," she said. "Says here that you marked a bunch of bodies for the furnace last week."

She set the lantern down and held the book out for Lerris to review.

"That's your mark here, here, and here, isn't it?"

Lerris folded her arms and scowled as she glanced over the page.

"Of course, it is," she said. "You expect me to leave them all down here to rot?"

"I don't," Calandra said. "Which is why I'm wondering why I had to have them hauled up to the furnace yesterday."

Lerris sneered, her withered skin pulling tight against her sharp cheekbones.

"The boys missed a few, then. So what? They're always trying to slack their way out of work. You ought to take it up with them, not waste my time down here."

"Maybe they missed one or two," Calandra said. "But *all* the ones you marked?"

She reached into her pocket and produced a handful of tags.

"Heard it was a bit crowded down here, so I came down to sort it out. Seems I'm not the only one creeping around down here after dark, am I?"

Lerris picked at a scab on one of her fingers as she clenched her teeth.

Calandra glanced down at the ledger again.

"I see here that you marked a few more for the furnace in the next room," she said. "Should we have a look over there, too?"

Lerris closed her eyes and hissed. "Enough!"

Now we're getting somewhere.

"How long has this been going on?"

Lerris seemed to shrink before her as she shrugged. "Three, four months?"

"How much?"

"Twenty marks a head."

Not a bad price, but still less than she expected. Of course, the bodies were all at least a week old. Gods knew what anyone wanted with them, but after what she had seen down in the crypts last night, Calandra did not want to know any more about the bizarre bodysnatchers than was necessary for doing business.

"I suppose you're going to enjoy this, aren't you?" Lerris asked. "You've been looking to get rid of me ever since you got here." She scowled again, her sickly, greenish eyes glimmering malevolently in the lantern light.

She thinks I mean to turn her in!

Calandra smiled. "You're right. I am enjoying this. I'm enjoying that you were stupid enough to think that you could keep getting away with it, all the while looking down that rotting nose of yours at the rest of us. All that talk about rules and keeping a house in order when there you were breaking your oaths just to scrap together enough coin for your next bottle."

Baring her gray-speckled teeth, Lerris lurched forward and grabbed Calandra by the arm.

"You don't know a thing about my life, you little bitch! You ain't got the right to judge me!"

Calandra yanked her arm free and shoved Lerris as hard as she could. The hag stumbled back and fell, landing hard on the earthen floor. As she tried to get up, Calandra stepped forward and kicked her in the stomach.

"Don't you EVER touch me again, you hear me?"

Lerris rolled on the ground, clutching at her midsection and groaning. She said nothing, but she managed to nod.

Calandra took several deep breaths to calm herself. She had never struck anyone like that before, never channeled years worth of malice into a physical attack. Hitting her should have felt more satisfying, but now she felt angrier than before.

Lerris was still choking on bile when Calandra pulled her up and leaned her against the nearest wall.

"This is how it's going to work from now on," she said. "You give me three-quarters of every payment you get from your friends and this little secret of yours stays between us. You try to end the deal, I turn you in to the guild. You screw me or if I so much as think you're trying to screw me, I turn you in. You say a word of this to anyone else, I go to the guild with an armload of proof while you stand there with nothing but your worthless word. You understand me?"

Lerris sobbed now, thick tears streaming down her cracked face. Stripped of all sense of foul dignity, she now seemed a broken, pathetic creature. But there was a queer ease behind her misery, something almost practiced. Calandra had often wondered if another woman lived somewhere behind all that hatred, someone who might explain the one that seemed to relish in tormenting her.

Was this what she looked like?

What has this woman been through?

Calandra squelched her pity before it had a chance to shake her resolve. She had come too far to let sentiment get in her way. Lerris' problems did not concern her; Calandra had to focus on her personal dilemmas.

She pushed Lerris against the wall again, just hard enough to get her attention.

"I said do you understand me?"

"Y…yes. I got you."

Calandra stepped back and let Lerris fall to her knees, coughing.

"Good." Lerris collected herself, getting her breathing under control and wiping her tears away. When she seemed better, Calandra reached out to help her up, but Lerris recoiled, scuttling away from her hand.

"No!" she said. "Please, don't touch me."

The words were mumbled in a different voice, not the raspy, acidic bite she usually heard from Lerris.

She's…afraid of me.

Nausea hit her suddenly, a slight quivering in her stomach that gave way to a roiling storm. Calandra backed out of the room and hurried upstairs before it swept over her.

She barely made it out one of the mortuary's side doors before she threw up.

16

THE FEVER

Halvid stirred his eggs around the plate with his fork, occasionally flicking a wayward piece over the side.

"You should eat some more," Arden said. "Keep your strength up."

The boy frowned. "I don't like the burnt pieces. They taste funny."

Grumbling, Arden reached across the table and picked a few bits of egg off the plate.

"There's nothing wrong with them," he said, tossing the pieces into his mouth. "See? Not choking to death, am I?"

Halvid gave him the courteous smile, the empty one that he used to avoid talking. Arden leaned back in his chair and sighed.

"How's your stomach?"

"Still a little sore."

The boy spent most of the previous night retching. Arden came home a few hours before dawn to find him wrapped in sheets soaked through with sweat and vomit. He was so exhausted that he fell asleep while Arden scrubbed him clean. When he woke, the boy could not stand up until he drank a large cup of vakenroot tonic to settle his stomach. Although the fever lingered, he seemed to be holding his food down now.

"You were out late again last night," Halvid said.

Arden nodded, shifting uneasily in his chair. He avoided talking to his son about how he paid their way.

"Some things came up," he said. "Took a while to sort it out."

Those "things" took most of the night, truth be told. He had only stopped by the *Goat* to collect the coin owed to Dhrath for the month. That included a cut of the street junk the brothers running the place sold out of the second floor. It was a lucrative business the fiend was willing to overlook so long as they made it worth his while. Arden had sorted a few problems for them in the past for a few extra marks. Usually nothing too serious, maybe a drunkard that liked roughing up the serving girls or a firedust junkie who thought he could get away without paying his debts.

There was nothing usual about what he found there last night, though.

"What kind of things?" The boy stared at him now, eyebrows raised.

Arden thought about the pusher's corpse, the black blisters covering its skin, each one hard as granite.

Bad things.

"Nothing you need worry about." He forced a courteous smile of his own, but it was not as effective as his son's.

Halvid shrugged and went back to stirring his eggs. His eyelids were heavy and the glands on the sides of his neck had already begun to swell.

Another day, maybe less.

The medicine procured from Twiceborn was potent, much better than the stuff he got from the apothecary. It held the worst of the fever in check, and there was no hint of blisters so far.

But Arden knew the signs. Once the swelling set in, there was no use hoping for a hasty remission. The medicine could provide the boy with some comfort and relief, but the fever's course was set now. He already experienced the stomach pains. Next would come the mouth sores and the tremors. And then, worst of all, the blisters.

Arden imagined the black welts he had seen on the corpse forming all over Halvid's skin, each one bulging as large as a plum before they hardened like scabs. Would the blisters turn a similar shade if the boy died before they burst? Would the skin begin to decay before his sweltering heart gave out, blackening over like rotten fruit?

He shook the thought away. Although he was no closer to understanding the cause of the fever, Arden remained convinced it was a natural affliction.

There was nothing natural about the corpse he saw last night. Even a fool could see it had been touched by something arcane.

If he had any sense, he would have gone straight to Dhrath with the news. The slimy bastard would want to know if some new player had moved into Lowtown, especially if they had a sorcerer at their disposal. Such power rarely found its way south of the Saven. Although not strictly regulated by law, the arcane arts were as subject to demand as any other trade. Wealthy merchants and nobles north of the river often paid exorbitant sums to secure the services, and loyalty, of a sorcerer, even an unskilled one. If the arcanist somehow displeased his employer, competition for him was fierce and he was rarely without a patron for long.

Once in a great while, though, a sorcerer burned one bridge too many and fled south of the river to avoid the retribution of vengeful masters.

Most of these renegades went into hiding, but if they were desperate enough, or nasty enough, they might offer their services to a broker in exchange for a sizable cut of profits. Considering that a single sorcerer might well alter the balance of power in Lowtown's underworld, they could afford to be greedy in their negotiations.

Dhrath maintained a consistent stance regarding any rogue arcanists looking to settle in Lowtown.

Kill them.

It made sense from the cephalin's perspective. Dhrath's formidable psychic abilities gave him an advantage over his rivals, an advantage he had no intention of losing by allowing a sorcerer to ply his trade freely in Lowtown's boroughs. He made it known that he would pay handsomely for the head of any known arcanist.

Naturally, the *Goat*'s owners wanted to keep the incident quiet. Already in deep enough with Dhrath, they did not need him taking a more active interest in their day-to-day dealings. Arden would have been happy to oblige them even if they had not paid him for his silence. Once word got out that a sorcerer might be running amok, Dhrath would have every one of his lackeys canvasing the boroughs to find them.

No one would get a reward for simply sounding the alarm, only for bringing in the wolf's head. Arden could not risk someone beating him to it.

When Halvid finally set his fork aside, Arden rose and took his plate. The boy slumped in the chair, gazing at the shuttered window.

"I don't like this place," he said.

Nobody likes this city.

"And why's that?"

"It's stuffy. Too many people."

"Blackspire's a big place, maybe the biggest." Arden set the plate aside to be cleaned and returned to the table. Halvid kept staring at the window, his blank expression unchanged.

"Why do we have to stay here? Why can't we just go someplace else?"

He placed a hand on the boy's shoulder. Even through the shirt, his skin felt hot. The fever was getting worse.

"We've been through this, Halvid. It's not just a matter of picking up and leaving. We have a roof of our own and there's steady work for me right here in the city. You don't want to go back to living in some dust-filled wagon, do you? Never stopping anywhere for more than a few weeks?"

Before they came to Blackspire, they made a life clinging to assorted merchant caravans travelling from city to city. By the time Halvid was five, he had crossed the continent no less than four times. The lifestyle had its own set of difficulties. Traders were always eager to bring Arden on for added protection, but there was not much recourse when the payments dried up after a few weeks. They knew he was unlikely to walk away when they were hundreds of miles from the nearest settlement.

Then there was the mercenary work. Plenty of towns and lords beyond Blackspire found reasons to quarrel with their neighbors every spring, making it easy enough to hire on with a company of sellswords. The pay could be good, but a lot of men did not live long enough to collect. Those who survived still had to endure the rigors of campaigning for months at a time, often through bad weather. It was no life to share with a family.

Halvid looked up at him, his eyes already a little bloodshot.

"You're not allowed to leave, are you?"

Arden almost winced at the directness of the question. After taking a deep breath, he sat down across the table from Halvid.

"It's not that simple," he said. "I owe Mister Dhrath a debt. You understand why that's important?"

"Haven't you paid him back by now?"

As if he'd let me.

"Getting us into the city was no small favor. There are thousands of people living outside the walls that aren't even allowed through the gates. Without Mister Dhrath's help, we'd still be out there, waiting and hoping for a chance to come inside. We have a life here because of him. That's not a debt you can simply repay with a few years of work; it takes something more than that."

Halvid sighed and lowered his head slightly as he nodded.

"I know," he said. "I'm sorry. I just...I wish..."

The boy swayed slightly as his voice trailed off. When he looked up, his swollen eyelids fluttered clumsily before his entire upper body went limp and pitched forward. Arden jumped up from his chair and caught him before his face smacked against the table.

"Halvid?"

He was warmer than only moments before, almost burning hot.

Dammit! Already?

Arden scooped the boy out of the chair and carried him over to his bed. Once he set Halvid down, he stripped off his clothes, careful not to disturb the skin. Beads of sweat formed on the boy's face and his breathing quickened. Arden fetched one of the nearby jars and scooped out a handful of lotion to slather across his skin.

The concoction did its work quickly, seeping through the pores and cooling the flesh. After a few minutes, the boy's breathing slowed to normal and his temperature backed down a bit. With a racing heart, Arden inspected the boy's skin, checking carefully around the armpits, neck, and groin. The swelling had not subsided, but there was no sign of blistering yet.

If the fever planned on running its expected course, the worst was yet to come.

Arden took stock of the remaining medicines. He had used up most of the lotion and had perhaps just enough vakenroot for a small dose of tonic. A few other salves were getting dangerously low. When the fever set upon the boy fully, he would not have enough of anything to ease him through it.

He did not bother checking his stash of coin again. Counting it one more time would not change the result. Even after taking the bribe to keep his mouth shut about what he saw at the *Goat*, he barely had enough to keep them in food for the rest of the month, much less replenish their supply of medicine.

There was a bit of sweetwine left in the clay jug on the table, so he poured the rest of it into his cup and slumped into one of the chairs. He had not slept much over the past few weeks and he was starting to wear around the edges. Short temper, spotty memory, a hitch in his reactions: all symptoms liable to get him killed in some dark ally if he let them get much worse.

But he was not going to get paid for sleeping. He needed to be out on the streets trying to track down whoever had made such a mess at the *Goat*. Without much to go on except a vague description of some woman and the stubborn sod who barged in looking for her, he tried to form a plan.

Grisel. Dumb bastard.

Maybe the fool was connected with what went down at the *Goat* and maybe he knew nothing, but he was the only real lead so far. One way or another, Arden would find out what Grisel knew soon enough. He always got answers out of people, even if the results were not always pretty.

If Grisel turned out to be a dead end, Arden would have to find his mysterious sorceress the hard way. That meant tracking down leads, asking questions, calling in favors. Lowtown might be a big place, but it was hard for a woman to keep to herself when she had so many neighbors. Somebody in one of those wretched boroughs would know her name, her roof, and how she paid her way.

He needed to get started before the trail went cold, but he worried about leaving Halvid alone for too long under the circumstances. The fainting spells could last for several hours, and the boy usually felt quite disoriented when he came out of them. Arden did not want him to wake up to an empty room, so he moved his chair beside the bed and drained the last of the sweetwine from his cup.

Halvid looked small, almost frail, lying on his father's bed. Arden reached down and took the child's hand. Almost without thinking, he started to sing.

It was a quiet, tuneless song. Arden knew the basic melody but had to mumble his way through most of the words and notes. The boy's mother used to sing it when he was an infant. Arden always refused to do the same whenever he was asked, joking that his braying would wake up half the borough before it put Halvid to sleep.

That was only half-true, of course. The song brought back too many memories he preferred to keep buried.

By the time he reached the end, Arden was quite drowsy. His voice, already quiet, trailed off to a whisper and it became a chore to keep his eyelids open.

When sleep finally took him, he dreamed he was back in Dhrath's Keep. One of the fiend's slimy tentacles wrapped around his neck, its suckers digging into his flesh. Dhrath's cold, hypnotic gaze crushed his spirit as surely as the tentacle crushed his windpipe. The cephalin held other people in his grasp, people Arden knew from another lifetime, from the years before he came to Blackspire.

All of them were dead, their eyes as black as seawater at midnight, their skin encrusted with a thin layer of salt.

Halvid was there, but the boy still lived. One of the tentacles coiled around his head to control his field of vision. The cephalin made the boy watch while he cracked his mother's skull open with his vicious beak and sucked out her brain.

Her vacant eyes looked straight through Arden. When she spoke, his voice passed between her slackened lips.

"A better place… A better life… I promise…"

Arden woke with such a start that he nearly tipped the chair over.

He did not dare fall asleep again.

THE SUN HAD not quite slunk below the horizon when he arrived at the Moonvale Theater, so Arden fell in with the steady flow of workers, street merchants, and travellers passing through the intersection of Dustwalk and Caravel Streets. In another borough, he might have simply turned his cloak inside out and passed himself off as a beggar clinging to the mouth of some alleyway. That would not work in Coldwater. While a bit more forgiving come nightfall, the borough's watch did not tolerate vagrants loitering along the main streets during the day. Coldwater fancied itself a cut above the rest of Lowtown; the shops were cleaner, the residents dressed better, and fewer animals ran loose. Too many homeless urchins gathering in the streets provided an inconvenient reminder that the borough was no better than neighboring Pigshire.

Calandra would not leave for her shift at the Mortuary for at least another two hours, but Arden liked to prepare for any eventuality. Casing her roof for a few days was not nearly long enough to have a fully detailed outline of her habits. Maybe she left early every fifth day to tend to some business he knew nothing about yet. Perhaps she went to a temple to pray to one god or another. Everything he had learned about her so far suggested a predictable personality and a reliable spirit to the core, but she already demonstrated an unsettling knack for confounding his expectations and he did not plan on giving her a chance to do so again.

There was the usual concern about keeping his query within easy reach. He doubted she would be stupid enough to run, but if she did, he positioned himself to ensure she would not get very far. In any case, she was unlikely to go anywhere without her brother, even though he was the one who got them into trouble in the first place. He found such loyalty admirable, if a little naïve. On the other hand, her brother was dumb enough to think running was an option. Calandra probably knew that as well. Arden doubted she had shared with her brother that Dhrath had called in his debt.

He circled the theater several times before it became dark enough for him to settle in the shadows of an alleyway without drawing attention. The lightboys came by a bit later with their tinderboxes, torches, and oilskins to replenish and light the street lanterns on every corner of Coldwater.

Not much older than Halvid.

Despite the similarity, he had a hard time imagining his son working alongside them.

Calandra exited soon after the lightboys set torches to the lanterns outside the theater.

She's early tonight.

He watched the way she twisted her slender neck to glance up and down the street, the way her shoulders tensed when a dog barked a few streets over. Draped in her usual undertaker garments, she wore the long leather apron draped over oil-treated fabrics that revealed little of her dark skin. Her dress hung loosely from her shoulders and scarcely cinched around her waist by the apron.

Arden remembered the feel of her body pressed against his in the darkness two nights ago.

He shivered.

After scanning the area, Calandra set off in the direction of the mortuary. She moved swifter than usual, even cutting through darker alleyways on a few occasions to take a more direct route. While she usually seemed intently aware of her surroundings, tonight she never so much as glanced over her shoulder.

What's on your mind tonight, girl?

Arden trailed her halfway to the Deadhouse before he closed the distance and clamped his hand on her shoulder to guide her into the nearest alleyway.

She gasped, but Arden's grip held firm.

"Don't make a scene, now," he said. "This way."

Calandra obeyed, following his lead into the shadows. After a few steps into the alley, he spun her around to face him. He expected her to take a step back, but she held her ground and glared at him. Her skin smelled of warm, sweetened milk. Arden relaxed his grip and his hand drifted down from her shoulder to her upper arm. The muscles beneath the fabric felt like strained lengths of rope.

Stronger than she looks.

"Well?" she asked.

Arden blinked at the question. How long had he been staring at her? He released her arm and stepped back.

"Time's up," he said, harsher than he would have liked. Anything less might have betrayed his unease. "What have you got for me?"

Calandra reached into her satchel and produced a small, cloth sack. She pressed it into his outstretched hand.

Heavy.

"Two hundred," she said.

Arden shook the bag slightly, just enough to make coins inside shift around. The weight felt about right.

"I told you to come up with one hundred."

Calandra scowled. "You want me to take half of it back?"

"I want to know where you got it and why you're paying more than I told you to pay."

"Beyland's in deep," she said. "Seemed like a good idea to get ahead. And what do you care how I came by it?"

Arden supposed it mattered little, not so long as Dhrath got what he was owed. He tucked the pouch into his coat pocket.

"I'll be counting this. If I find out it's less than what—"

"It's what I said. Not a mark less."

Arden disliked the touch of defiance in her voice. She sounded almost comfortable talking to him.

He lunged at her, one hand closing around her thin neck and the other pinning her arm behind her back as he forced her against the nearby wall. She tried to fight him off with her free arm but stopped struggling when he tightened his grip enough to close off her windpipe. Her eyes widened as she gasped for breath.

"You done mouthing off now, girl?"

Arden felt her pulse throbbing beneath his fingers, each beat following more closely after the last.

She held out for a few seconds before surrendering a frantic nod.

He released her and stepped back, giving her enough room to double over and gasp for breath.

"Don't go thinking that a bit of extra coin's going to square things away. Time will tell whether or not you're good for the rest of Beyland's debt, understand?"

Calandra remained bent over, both hands rubbing at her neck. For a moment, Arden wondered if he had injured her. He recalled other times he pushed someone too far, whether they deserved it or not. Something about this seemed different, though, and he felt relieved when Calandra managed a weak nod.

"One week," Arden said. "Two hundred marks. Ought to be simple enough at the rate you're working."

Another slow nod. She had recovered her breath but seemed determined to avoid looking at him. Normally, Arden demanded people look him in the eye when he leaned on them, just to make sure they understood who was in control of the situation.

But he did not feel like he was in control of anything at the moment. If she looked up at him, there was a good chance he would not be able to meet her gaze. His hands trembled and his skin tingled all over his body.

He mustered as much disdain as he could manage into his final command. "Get on your way, then."

Arden did not wait for her to respond or depart on her own accord. Whether he feared her reproach or how he would react to seeing her face was not clear. He only knew he could not bear to remain with her in that alleyway for another second. Without another word, he stepped into the street and left her cowering in the shadows.

His hands did not stop trembling for a long time.

HALVID COMPLAINED ABOUT a nasty itch just below his right armpit moments after Arden walked through the door.

The small cluster of white lumps Arden found there did not look serious yet, but the sight of them put him in a black mood. Sometime over the next day or two, the little bumps would swell up to form white blisters the size of a man's thumbnail. When Halvid moved, they would tear the skin and release a milky puss that stank of rotten fruit. Insects found the odor irresistible, driving some of them to lay eggs in the open wounds and enticing others to suck the boy's blood. Between the fever, vomiting, blood loss, and constant pain, Halvid would slip into catatonic slumber, the occasional twitching of his skinny limbs providing the only indication that he still lived.

Arden had seen the sickness play out many times before, but he could not remember it ever progressing so quickly. The blisters usually did not show up for at least a week after the first symptoms appeared. He wondered if the rapid onset would cause the fever to burn out early, perhaps running its course in as little as a week or two.

Whether the boy could survive a shorter, more intense episode or not…that he dared not consider.

None of the lotions or salves would be of much use against the blisters. Tasel Leaf powder mixed with salt residue could ease the itching and keep Halvid from scratching or accidentally rupturing the blisters, but the damned stuff did not come cheap and it spoiled quickly. He usually waited as long as possible to buy a pouch, just in case the fever tapered off prematurely. Even if he had thought to get some yesterday, he would still have trouble affording more than a pinch or two.

Without it, though, he had nothing to relieve the itching. If some of the torn blisters became infected, the fever might worsen, driving the boy's temperature too high for any medicine to contain.

Arden felt the bag of coins in his coat pocket pressing against his chest.

A hundred marks could probably buy a weeks' worth of the stuff.

Dhrath would be mollified with half of what Calandra gave him, at least for a while. By the time the broker started expecting larger payments, Arden figured he could track down the sorceress who made such a mess over at the *Goat*. The bounty on her head would probably be more than enough to cover the difference. Dhrath would still get his money, but in the meantime, Halvid would have a fighting chance of pulling through the fever.

Arden dumped the bag's contents onto the table and counted the marks out into two equal piles. When he finished, he returned one pile to the bag and put the other in his own coin purse. Tomorrow, he would track down Twiceborn in the Sinkhole slums. If she did not have what he needed, no one would.

Halvid drifted off to fitful sleep again. Arden sat on the edge of the boy's bed and stroked the soft hair atop his head.

"It'll be alright," he said. "I promise. I'm going to take care of everything."

The boy's skin felt hot again.

He moaned.

The gods are wicked and cruel.

17
THE CONFIDANTES

Nicalene took a deep breath and began to read.

"Blood and ash hold it all together, the mortar supporting this empire of bone, this kingdom of metal. We sheathe it all in colored glass and shimmering stone, but the bones hide just beneath the splendor, slumbering alongside the twisted steel that cleaved them, the bent iron that broke them. The rivers of blood flow across the fields of burned flesh, the ash of a million souls, some wicked, some pure. There they mix together and thicken, holding fast the foundations of our redoubts, the walls of our temples, the ramparts of our citadels. Would that the sun's light could fall upon it, the edifice might all turn to dust."

She stopped and reread the last sentence to herself.

"Would that the sun?" Ugh.

"What's wrong?"

Beyland teetered back and forth on a stool near the edge of the stage. He had already added a new row of teeth marks to his stylus since she started reading.

Nicalene shook her head. "That last line. It doesn't seem quite right."

"Well, it's supposed to suggest that if the light of truth could shine upon—"

"No, no, I get the idea. It's just the phrasing that's off. I don't like the way it sounds. Could you say it another way, maybe?"

Beyland nibbled on his stylus a bit more. "Yeah, I think so. Give it here."

She handed the sheet of paper back to him and watched him scratch out the offending line. He hesitated a moment before hurriedly adding something to replace it.

"Here," he said, thrusting the paper into her hands. "How's this?"

"Eternal dusk holds back the mordant sun, protects our grim monuments against its searing light. Should the long night end, the gruesome mortar would surely turn to dust and bring our glory crashing down to be swallowed by the hateful earth."

"Better?"

A bit melodramatic, maybe, but it makes an impression.

She nodded. "Better. How much more do you have?"

"A few pages. I still haven't quite worked out where it's going, but the words just keep flowing."

Nicalene smiled. She could not explain why, but she felt a bit of pride at hearing that.

"Do you know who she is yet?"

"Someone important, I think, or at least she used to be."

Weren't we all?

Nicaline rubbed the hard stone embedded in her chest. The black dress from the closet upstairs had a high neckline that covered the stone completely, but she struggled to keep her hand from touching it every time her mind wandered.

"Does it...does it hurt?" Beyland asked.

"No, not really."

Her answer was mostly true. The burning sensation persisted, but she no longer found it painful. Almost soothing now, the stone warmed her like a fire on a cold winter's night. Even the dreamleech bite had stopped hurting, the wound itself healing faster than anyone expected.

Beyland mostly avoided asking her questions about the stone; a good thing considering she had no answers for him. His sister proved far more curious, but Nicalene did not see much of her. She kept the same schedule that left Grisel in a perpetually bad mood. While Calandra treated Beyland well enough, she made little effort to hide her feelings about his guest.

Nicalene stepped off the stage and sat on one of the audience benches. She fiddled with her hair a bit, wondering again why she had felt an irrepressible urge to cut it. Beyland scrounged up a pair of shears yesterday, so at least she managed to make it look presentable. The short cut still served to remind her that she had no idea how the strange stone became embedded in her chest. Her dreams remained as vivid as yesterday's memories and had not intruded upon her waking mind again.

Although she would not admit it, the whole situation terrified her. Somewhere behind the burning sensation in her chest, she could sense something else whispering just quietly enough to remain beneath notice under most circumstances. When the world around her fell silent, Nicalene became certain of one thing: she was not alone.

"Beyland," she said, "I know I haven't given you many answers the last few days. You've been really good to me, better than anyone's been in a long time. I wish I could tell you more about what's going on. You deserve that much at least, but there's just a lot that I don't know for myself. I'm sorry."

Beyland set his papers aside and smiled. "You don't have to apologize. I know this is hard for you. Maybe it'll all come back to you at some point or maybe it won't, but you don't owe me an explanation in either case. I'm just glad you're feeling better."

Gods, is it really that simple for you?

Nicalene smiled. "And that I'm here to provide such exquisite critical feedback for your masterpiece."

They both laughed.

It felt good to laugh again.

When Beyland finished, he yawned and rubbed his eyes.

"Did you get any sleep last night?" Nicalene asked.

Beyland shook his head. "I was writing most of the night. Didn't want to lose track of my muse."

She's right here, you young fool.

The thought surprised her. She did not know quite what to make of it. Was it one of amused affection or something more genuine? Over the last few days, her emotions had moved faster and stronger than she was used to managing. After years of burying her feelings, she had almost forgotten how to interpret them.

She needed time alone, time to think.

"You should go get some sleep," she said. "I don't need you tending to my every need at all hours of the day, you know?"

Beyland yawned again as he nodded. "Okay, you win. But you have to promise to come wake me up if you need anything, okay?"

Do I really seem that helpless?

"I'm sure I can get by on my own for a few hours, Beyland."

"There's some bread and a jug of water in the kitchen if you want it," he said, gathering up his papers. "Help yourself. I can run out for more later."

She rose from the bench and accompanied Beyland to the stairs.

"I'll be fine," she said. "Get some rest."

After Beyland left, Nicalene went back to the stage and paced beneath the light filtering down through the theater's high windows. Not venturing outside since she arrived at the theater a few nights ago, the place felt a bit more confining every time she woke up. Beyland and Calandra agreed she should stay inside until she made a full recovery, but Nicalene doubted she would ever feel right as long as that chunk of black stone remained fused to her chest.

While she appreciated the hospitality and concern, the theater offered her nothing in the way of answers. Beyland offered to make a few inquiries about her condition, but Nicalene doubted he knew anyone who could provide any meaningful information. She needed more specialized advice, preferably from someone who had seen the strangest sights Blackspire had to offer.

Of course, her list of contacts was scarcely much better than Beyland's. Returning to the *Goat* was out of the question. Chances were that they had people out looking for her after the mess she made of Muskrat.

Served you right, shitheel.

While she did not feel much guilt about the dealer's death, she worried about whether the same thing might happen again. Killing a self-serving scrape like Muskrat was one thing, but she doubted she could forgive herself if a similar accident caused Beyland, or even Calandra, any harm.

One way or another, she needed answers.

The idea came suddenly, almost by accident. Not the ideal solution, perhaps, but probably the best option before her.

The ghulans.

She had a rough idea of the Moonvale Theater's location, so finding her way to the shop and back would be simple enough. As tired as Beyland looked, he would be asleep until nightfall at least, and Calandra reliably woke just before dusk. Barring some unforeseen problem, she could make it back long before either of them stirred.

Nicalene gave Beyland time to get settled in bed, then crept up the stairs to look in on him. His snores met her halfway down the hall, so she went back down to the stage to fetch the knee-high boots she left tucked beneath one of the benches. The directions to her destination floated through her head as she tightened the straps.

Duskwalk to Vinewall, Vinewall to Rattlebone, Rattlebone to Seven Points, then down...down...? Damn. What's that other street called?

The name did not matter. She could find her way well enough once she reached Seven Points.

See you soon, Beyland.

Taking another deep breath, Nicalene went to the theater's back door and strode outside into the daylight haze.

THE SHOP LOOKED a bit more cluttered than she remembered. Even in the dim light, she could make out the piles of trinkets and effects stacked atop every available inch of shelf and table space. Some of the items looked mundane; a mahogany jewelry box, a porcelain urn, a bejeweled dagger, and the like. Other objects confounded both reason and imagination; a glass box filled with fur, a wreath fashioned from antlers and knotted wood, a bronze plant that whistled and let off a tiny puff of steam whenever she looked at it, and so on.

"Hello?"

The door's unlocked. They must be here somewhere.

She ventured deeper into the shop, careful not to disturb any of the more unusual wares. A thick layer of soot covered the windows, blocking out most of the already meager afternoon light and condemning the far side of the storeroom to perpetual shadow. By the time she reached the rows of tall shelves, she could hardly make out her feet in the gloom.

The clinking of a metal latch being drawn into place cut through the silence. Standing between the shelves, Nicalene was unable to see what made the noise. When she moved to the end of the aisle and peeked around the corner, she nearly stumbled over the small figure standing there gazing up at her through dark goggles.

"Good day, friend Nicalene," Carta said, her little mouth smiling.

Before Nicalene could reply, light welled up from behind her, pushing back the shadows to reveal the ghulan woman fully. She wore the same grayish brown coat she had on every other time Nicalene had visited the store. Dull and unflattering, the garment revealed nothing of the figure beneath it.

"A fine surprise," a childish voice behind her said.

Turning around, Nicalene found Uthan, the other ghulan, holding a small lantern. He wore a nearly identical coat with green trim rather than blue. Nicalene still had not worked out the nature of Uthan and Carta's relationship. Once, she asked them once if they were married, to which they exchanged a rather mischievous giggle. After that embarrassing misstep, Nicalene never asked another question about it. Sadly, she had no opportunities for comparisons: they were the only ghulans in Lowtown, maybe in all of Blackspire for all she knew. After talking to a few people who came across other ghulans in their travels, she learned that the halfmen always came in pairs, that if one of them died, the other would lose the will to live.

Nicalene had not confirmed if that was true, but she hoped it was. Something about the story sounded pitiful and romantic all at once.

How are you getting along without me, Grisel? Did you curl up in bed and die?

She clenched her fists, remembering her promise not to waste any time thinking about Grisel.

"How can we help you, friend Nicalene?" Carta asked.

"Are you here with your own requests?" Uthan asked.

They spoke their next question as one, their glimmering voices perfectly harmonized.

"Or on behalf of another?"

Another?

Grisel.

Had he been there looking for her? If he thought she might try to sell the stone off to somebody, Uthan and Carta would be the logical place to start asking questions. But why, then, would she be coming on his behalf? Maybe he had contacted them about something else?

"I'm here of my own accord," she said, calling forth the same confident air she used on Beyland's stage. "Were you expecting otherwise?"

The ghulans exchanged a glance but said nothing.

Damn you both. You know something, don't you?

"Why then have you come, friend Nicalene?" Uthan asked.

"Yes," Carta said, "to what do we owe this rare pleasure of your visit?"

Nicalene considered turning around and leaving. The ghulans clearly expected Grisel to show up at some point in the near future, and when he did, they would almost certainly mention that she had visited. There was no reason for them to withhold that information.

Not unless I make it worth their while...

"I need some information." She reached into her satchel and grabbed a handful of marks, just enough to make them clink loudly against one another. "Information that stays between us."

Uthan's little head nodded, and Carta scurried across the room to lock the door and draw the heavy shutters over the windows. While his partner secured the shop, Uthan directed Nicalene toward a large desk near the center of the room. He hung his little lantern, now the only source of light, from an iron stand beside the desk. Carta stepped out of the shadows a moment later and took a seat beside Uthan.

"Please, friend Nicalene," Uthan said, "sit and share."

"And let us listen," Carta said, "so we might share in turn."

Nicalene eased herself into the chair opposite the ghulans. They leaned forward, resting their elbows on the desk, and staring at her from behind their black goggles.

"How much do you know about the side effects of dreamleech slime?"

Carta leaned over and whispered into Uthan's ear. He listened for a moment, then nodded.

"Blindness, coma, brain damage, loss of sensation in the limbs," he said. "Madness, in some cases."

"But this is known to all, friend Nicalene," Carta said.

"Especially to those with experience."

Uthan's comment would have stung more if Nicalene thought he meant to shame her, but she knew better. The ghulans never seemed to pass judgment on anyone.

Judgment, after all, was bad for business.

"What about its magical qualities?"

This time Uthan whispered into Carta's ear.

"Very slight in most cases," she said.

"But more potent in mature leeches," Uthan said.

"Distilled by apothecaries for sedatives. Very expensive."

Uthan nodded. "And still illegal, of course."

"Of course," Carta said.

Nicalene chose her next words carefully.

"If it came into contact with something else, something that had its own magical qualities or maybe an enchantment of some kind, would it be enough to cause a...reaction?"

The ghulans looked at each other for a moment, then took turns whispering back and forth. They carried on for a long while before looking back to Nicalene.

"Difficult to say," Carta said.

"And impossible to predict," Uthan said.

"So many variables."

"Too many outcomes."

The black stone in her chest felt warm. She fought the temptation to touch it.

"Friend Nicalene," Carta said, "we don't wish to be rude."

"Or cause you distress."

"But our time is of value."

"And we have gardens that need weeding."

In other words, get to the damn point. Right.

Nicalene nodded. "I'm sorry. It...it would be easier if I just showed you."

She undid the top buttons of her dress and pulled the fabric away to reveal the glistening stone nestled between her breasts.

If the sight shocked the ghulans, they hid it well. Their expressions were vague in the dim light and the clunky goggles concealed their eyes in any case. They stared at the stone in silence for some time before Uthan whispered something to Carta, who nodded as he spoke.

"When did this happen?" she asked.

"Two nights ago."

"How much dreamleech secretion touched it?" Uthan asked.

"The leech was in a jar of the stuff," Nicalene said. "I dumped all of it onto my chest, so I guess it was covered."

More murmuring back and forth.

"Does it hurt?" Carta asked.

"Not really. But it feels warm."

"Do you dream?" Uthan asked.

Nicalene thought of the audience, the one shrouded in darkness waiting to pounce upon her every misstep if she failed to hold them enraptured.

"Yes."

"Are your thoughts your own?" Carta asked.

As she pondered her answer, one of her hands drifted up to her hair. She thought of the barber's knife in her trembling hand as she pressed the blade against her thigh.

"Most of the time, but...sometimes I get strange ideas."

"Have you hurt anyone?"

The image of Muskrat's ruined corpse flashed through her mind.

She nodded, her lips trembling. "I...I don't know what happened. I just touched him and...and..."

Carta's little hand reached across the desk and touched hers. "It's okay, friend Nicalene."

"But we must know if we are to help you," Uthan said.

"Was it someone close to you?"

"No," Nicalene said. "He was a dealer. When I touched him, his skin bubbled into black blisters, like he was boiling inside."

Uthan leaned forward to take a closer look at the stone while Carta rummaged through one of the desk drawers.

"This happened only once?" he asked.

"Yes," Nicalene said, "right after I woke up and found it like this."

Carta produced a handheld looking glass with multiple different lenses affixed to a series of hinges. She flipped through several of them before settling on one and locking it into place.

"If I may?"

Nicalene nodded, and Carta climbed onto the desktop. She held the looking glass just a few inches from the stone.

"Have you ever seen anything like this before?" Nicalene asked.

"There are many strange sights in this world, friend Nicalene," Uthan said.

"And our humble eyes have seen but a few of them," Carta said.

"But knowledge stretches far beyond direct experience."

"And we may yet uncover what we have not seen."

When Carta finished her examination, she backed away from Nicalene and climbed down to her chair. She whispered to Uthan. After a few pensive moments, he nodded.

"Does friend Grisel know you've taken his prize?" Carta asked.

Now Nicalene understood why they were expecting Grisel. She felt stupid for not realizing it earlier. Where else would he have taken it if he was trying to sell it?

"He's probably sorted it out by now," she said. "Has he been looking for me?"

Uthan shook his head. "Not here. No sign of him for days now."

"Not since he brought it to us in search of a buyer."

"Did he tell you where he got it?" Nicalene asked.

"He would not say," Carta said.

"And we did not press."

Nicalene pressed her hands over her face, rubbing at her eyelids and cheekbones.

Dammit. This nightmare just doesn't end.

"What *can* you tell me?" she asked. "You must have some idea of what this thing might be."

"We have theories," Carta said.

Uthan nodded. "Theories without form."

"We must find the knowledge needed to shape them."

"Yes," Uthan said. "Questions and queries are in order."

"Give us time to ask them."

"A few days, no more."

"And we might set your mind at ease," the ghulans said together.

Nicalene was not sure she had a few days to spare. Beyland's sister might force him to boot her onto the street any day now. If that happened, she did not know where she would go.

Not that she had much choice. For all the ghulans' quirks, Nicalene knew she could trust them to keep her secret. Anyone else she might visit in Lowtown was as likely to sell her out to the watch on accusations of witchcraft as provide helpful information.

"A few days' time, then," Nicalene said.

"Do you have somewhere to stay?" Uthan asked.

"Somewhere safe?"

Nicalene shrugged. "Safe enough, I think. Nobody I know would look for me there, anyway."

"Good," Carta said. "Keep to yourself."

"And avoid stimulation."

Nicalene reached into her satchel and grabbed a few marks.

"No, no, friend Nicalene," Carta said.

"Wait and see what our search uncovers."

"It may yet turn to your advantage."

"And your profit."

The ghulans smiled at her with their thin-lipped mouths. They looked so similar in the dim light, like a pair of unusually mature children watching the oblivious adults a bit too closely. Nicalene had never seen them without their goggles on. She wondered if seeing their eyes would make it any easier to read their reactions or if that would only make her more uncomfortable.

A few more days. Might as well be a few years.

Nicalene stood up and tried to smile.

"Thank you," she said. "I'll be seeing you soon, I guess."

"Very soon, friend Nicalene," Uthan said.

"We look forward to it," Carta smiled wider than Nicalene ever recalled seeing.

THE WALK BACK to the Moonvale Theater felt much longer than the walk to the ghulans' shop. Nicalene nearly got herself lost at times, walking past streets she needed to turn down and taking detours when something unusual caught her attention. A tickle of panic ran through her muscles whenever she spotted a familiar face in the crowd, or even a face that merely looked familiar. When she came across a group of spaders on the way to their evening assembly point, she thought she saw Grisel among them. She quickly realized her mistake, but she still ducked into the nearest alley to hide for several minutes until they passed out of sight.

Bald headed bastards all look the same.

She finally made it back to the theater shortly before dusk. Although she distinctly remembered closing the back entrance when she left, she found the old wooden door standing slightly ajar. The discovery stopped her cold. Had Grisel somehow tracked her down? Was he waiting for her inside? Maybe one of the thugs from the *Goat* found out about Beyland and dragged him off to be interrogated and murdered. The terrible scenarios raced through her mind quickly enough to leave her lightheaded. For a moment, she considered walking away.

And go where?

The answer struck the sense back into her. She had nowhere else to go. Grisel certainly would not take her back, and she lacked the coin to afford a room for more than a week or two. The only alternative was to cling onto some lonely sod at the nearest winesink. Nicalene knew only too well how that story ended and refused to relive it again. Besides, throwing herself at somebody was a terrible way of hiding the fact that she had a piece of black rock sticking out of her chest.

Then there was that niggling sliver of self-loathing that kept on picking at her pride.

What makes you think they'd want you anyway?

Nicalene shook the thought aside before it could take root, but it angered her all the same. When she closed her eyes, she found herself back on the stage from her dream. A gust of hot air washed over her as the spiteful crowd burned. Their screams excited her, fulfilled her as she danced in time to their agony. She threw her head back and sang in the key of their suffering.

Never had she felt more alive, more powerful, more pure.

When she opened her eyes, she seemed to fall from a great height into a puddle of thick, black mud. Her limbs felt heavy, her senses dull and confused. Weak knees gave out, and she nearly fell down. Only after regaining her balance and taking a few deep breaths did she notice that the stone in her chest felt warmer than before, almost hot. Her skin tingled as if slowly catching fire.

What the hell was that about?

Avoiding stimulation sounded like simple advice. Following that advice suddenly seemed much harder than she anticipated.

Nicalene focused on the door handle, pushing every other thought from her mind. It no longer mattered who might be waiting inside. Such fears seemed inconsequential next to the power roiling inside her.

She pulled the door open and stepped into the theater. The backstage area looked deserted as usual, so Nicalene pressed through to the main stage. A young man sat there atop a stool with a rectangular board in hand. He busied himself drawing sketches on a sheet of paper affixed to the board.

The stage floorboards creaked beneath Nicalene's feet as she approached him, the sound echoing through the spacious theater. When the artist glanced up from his work, his eyes widened, and his drawing hand went to his bandaged arm.

"Hello, there," Nicalene said, stopping a few yards short of him. "Are you a friend of Beyland's?"

"Um, yeah," he said, his voice trembling like a frightened child's. "Name's Kardi."

"Oh, the artist, right? He told me all about you."

Kardi forced a smile, but it did not come across as very friendly.

"I'm Nicalene. It's nice to finally meet you."

"We've, um, met before."

Nicalene raised an eyebrow. "Really? I think I would remem—"

Kardi raised his bandaged arm and nodded to the wound.

"I was here when he brought you in," he said. "You freaked out over something and bit me."

The way he glared left Nicalene a bit confused. His expression fell somewhere between indignation and pride.

"I'm really sorry," she said, blushing a little. "I don't remember any-thing about that night. I hope it's not too bad."

He shrugged. "Calandra says it'll leave a scar. Beyland thinks I should tell people I got bit by a wolf or something."

A wolf? Could it really be that bad? Gods, he must think I'm crazy.

"I'm sure that will impress an eager girl or two," she said.

That got a smile out of him. Even from a distance, Nicalene could make out the black stains along the base of his teeth.

Nightroot.

"You think so?" he asked.

"Sure. Some girls are always eager to hear a story."

The dimwitted ones, anyway. Dimwitted and loose. Probably just what you're after. They might not even mind the nightroot.

Nicalene moved closer to get a better look at his sketch. The stench of cheap wine seeped from Kardi's pores.

"What are you working on?" she asked.

"Oh, this? Just something Beyland mentioned."

He tilted the sketchboard forward to show her the array of images scrawled upon the paper. A long, flowing dress dominated the page, but it lacked any detail beyond a simple outline.

"A dress?"

"Yeah, it's for something he's working on. I'm having a hard time getting an idea of what to do with it, though."

He looked up at Nicalene, his gaze sliding over her body.

"Hey," he said, "maybe you can help me model it?"

Don't get any ideas, you little shitheel.

"I guess. What do you need me to do?"

Kardi pointed to the center of the stage with his stylus.

"Just stand over there and pose. I need a reference to work with."

Nicalene wondered how that could possibly help, but she did as he asked.

"What should I do?" she asked.

"Just act like you're performing or something."

Brilliant direction. Thanks.

Nicalene closed her eyes and imagined what the theater would look like when it was full. She squared her shoulders and arched her back slightly.

"Good," Kardi said.

The vision came slowly this time, in glimpses. Her imaginary crowd shifted from a raucous gallery of Lowtown regulars to a far more sophis-ticated audience. The latter group remained distant and alien, their faces obscured by shadow. At first, she thought them aloof, but in truth they were entranced by her performance. Her still, powerful figure held their attention as surely as an oncoming storm. They loved her, but more out of fear than affection, as if the consequences of not loving her were too terrible for them to imagine.

"That's it!"

Kardi's high-pitched voice brought her back to the theater's dilapidated confines. She took in the pitiful rows of empty benches and felt her heart sag a little.

This place deserves more.

"Come have a look," Kardi said.

"You're done already?"

Kardi laughed.

"I should hope so. I've been drawing for quite a while!"

How long was I standing there?

Nicalene walked over and glanced at his sketch.

She gasped at the results. The detail was superb, from the sculpted neckline to the countless stones woven into the fabric.

"It's...it's beautiful."

And so familiar...

"This doesn't really do it justice," Kardi said. "The real thing would have little glass beads all over it that will make it shimmer in the moonlight."

Recognition hit Nicalene hard. She had no difficulty envisioning the finished product, no question of how it would feel against her skin.

Without a doubt, the dress matched the garment from her dream perfectly.

"How did you think of this?" she asked.

Kardi shrugged.

"I don't know. I saw you standing over there and it just came to me. Didn't even have an image in mind, really. I just started drawing and this is what came out."

Only after she stared at the dress long enough to take in every excruciating detail did she look at the rest of the sketch. Kardi had also portrayed the woman wearing it.

Oh, gods...

She was tall and slender, her features sharp as a dagger's edge. A short tangle of hair, much of it sticking up at odd angles, topped her exquisite scalp. The deeply sunken eyes and firmly set lips suggested an intensity bordering upon inhuman. Although the sketch lacked color, Kardi had filled in her skin so that it matched the tone of newly burned ash.

The ashen woman.

"That...doesn't look like me."

Kardi gave her a strange look, then inspected the sketch again.

"Huh," he said. "I guess she doesn't. That's strange. I was trying hard to make her look like you. Guess I was more focused on the dress."

Nicalene's skin felt hot again. She went on staring at the image even as the warmth spread throughout her body. The dull thump of her heartbeat echoed inside her skull.

"Are you okay?"

"I'm fine," she said, finally breaking away from the drawing. "I...I need to get some sleep. Excuse me."

Kardi said something as she strode by, but she tuned out everything save for the throbbing pulse of her heart pumping blood through her body. She climbed the stairs without thinking and shut herself in her room, sweat pouring down her skin by the time she locked the door behind her.

Gripped by an intense panic, she inched over to the mirror.

The woman waiting there for her was at once intimately familiar and utterly alien. From one angle, she saw herself, her rounded shoulders and broadening hips, her foolish, hackneyed haircut. But if she turned her head ever so slightly, enough to glimpse through the sliver of a cracked piece of glass, she saw another face glaring back at her.

The ashen woman's yellow eyes cut through Nicalene's flesh and sliced into her bones, riveting her in place. There was no turning away from that deathly aspect.

What do you want with me?

The ashen woman smiled, her lips curling back to reveal a glistening set of perfect, ivory teeth.

Nicalene tried to scream, but no sound came from her parched throat. Frantic, she threw herself backwards, finally breaking away from whatever force held her in place before the mirror. She stumbled across the room and collapsed upon the bed.

Too terrified to fall asleep, Nicalene buried her face in the pillow and sobbed.

18

THE ROOM

The room stank of mildew and rotting wood. A few slivers of light managed to slip between the boards nailed over the window, not enough to illuminate the entire space. Rats squabbled in the dark corners during the day and roamed freely after nightfall. Sometimes they scurried onto the cot to tear bits of fabric from the blankets. They made it quite clear the crumbling shack was their domain, and that its present occupant was merely passing through.

Grisel was unsure of how long he had been in the room. The first few days went by in a blurred haze. How much of it he was awake or asleep for was difficult to know, for there had been little to distinguish the conditions. Eventually he decided that if he felt pain, he must be awake.

The days lost any semblance of form. There was little light to mark the passage of time with any regularity, especially since a typical Blackspire day scarcely differed from dusk elsewhere. He quickly learned to mark the time by the rats' activity. If he could not spot more than three of the little black devils, then it was probably daytime.

Food and drink came irregularly. Some days the door inched open enough for an outstretched hand to deposit a fistful of leftover food on the floor. Grisel had to move quickly to beat the rats to the food, especially at night when they roamed about in small packs. Once the little bastards took hold of a scrap, they would defend it ferociously. The bite marks and scratches covering his forearms attested to their determination.

Grisel had yet to meet his captors. They occasionally looked in on him, peering through a small hole in the door that they covered on the outside with a heavy piece of leather. When they brought food, they told him to lie down on the other side of the room and only unlocked the door when he complied. Otherwise, they let him have the run of the little shack. One of the walls contained a privy closet. Judging by the closet's depth, Grisel guessed that the room was on the second floor of the building. He pressed his ear to the floor a few times, hoping to hear someone below, but he never heard anything more than the sound of his own ragged breath.

His head finally stopped hurting about two days after he began marking time. Although he still felt weak and the headaches came back when he moved around too much, at least he could think straight for a change.

On the evening of the third day, someone knocked on the door.

His captors never knocked.

"Yeah?" Grisel asked. He crossed to the door, kicking a rat away from his bare feet as he went.

The leather flap over the door slid aside. Lantern light poured through the small hole.

Grisel recognized the stern eyes staring back at him.

You.

"Thought you might be ready to talk," Arden said.

Grisel scratched at his stubbled jaw. "Well it ain't as if I've got the key to my own cell, have I?"

Arden glanced to his left. "Open it."

He stepped back while someone slotted a key into the lock. The door creaked open to reveal a broad-shouldered thug with a nasty scar along his forehead. He held a short length of knotted wood in his right hand.

"Back up, then," the man said, jabbing the end of his club at Grisel's chest.

Grisel obeyed, stepping back slowly as his captors entered the room. Arden set the lantern down on the floor and gestured to the cot.

"Sit down."

Grisel took a seat on the corner of the cot. As he sat, his jailor stepped outside briefly and returned with a high stool. He placed it next to the lantern for Arden.

"Leave us," Arden said.

Grisel glared at him while the thug stepped outside and pushed the door shut.

"How's your head?" Arden asked.

"The hells you care?"

Arden sat down on the stool. "I care about what you've got inside it, Grisel. About all the things you're going to share with me."

"That so, is it?"

Arden nodded. "Yeah, that's right. You know, after you fell down those stairs, I could have dumped you into the river or dragged you into some alleyway to die. Couple of the lads with me wanted to bleed you then and there. Would have if I'd let them."

"You saying I should be grateful, then?"

"I'm not asking you to be anything. Just thought you should know you're only alive by my say so."

A rat scampered along the outskirts of the lantern light behind Arden's stool.

Some life.

"Am I supposed to take that as a threat?"

Arden chuckled. "I think you're smart enough to know exactly how to take it."

Arden hardly struck Grisel as the sentimental sort. If he decided his prisoner was no longer worth the trouble, he probably had a variety of ways to ensure nobody found or identified the body.

Grisel lowered his head and sighed. He felt his headache returning. "So, what happens now?"

"Simple," Arden said. "I ask you questions, you give me answers. You tell me the truth, then we can talk about what happens next. You lie to me or I think you lie to me, then I give you a chance to correct yourself."

Grisel had a few ideas on how Arden might define "correction." None of them seemed promising.

"But we're not going to have to worry about that, are we?" Arden said. "I know you want to tell me the truth. Especially since you've had all this time up here to yourself, thinking about what the truth is worth to you. What would you say it's worth, Grisel?"

You still haven't found her, have you, shitsucker?

He nearly smiled at the realization but managed to hold his expression steady. If Arden was reduced to pressing him for information several days after the fact, his leads likely amounted to very little. It also meant that Nicalene had done a good job of laying low. Of course, that would be easy to do if she had sold off the stone and fled the city. Grisel doubted she was that clever, though. More likely she was loaded up in a hovel somewhere, all her coin wasted on overpriced street junk.

Strangely, Grisel could not decide which outcome would trouble him more.

"I already told you everything I know."

Arden sighed. He leaned forward, resting his elbows upon his knees. "Grisel, do you know the story of Naryn the Weasel?"

"Afraid my mum wasn't much the type for stories."

"He was a con man. Ran card and dice games on the streets to part wealthy travellers from their coin. One day he saw a man get stabbed outside a shop. When the watch came to investigate, nobody could say who it was did the killing. He was the only one to get a good look at the killer's face, good enough to recognize him. Could have turned him in then and there, but when the watch asked Naryn what he saw, he lied. Said he didn't know the guy, but that he'd keep a sharp eye out for him.

"After they went on their way, Naryn slipped off and tracked down the killer. He threatened to turn him in unless he paid him off good. So, the killer paid up and Naryn went on his way, feeling pretty good about himself. He ran a few more cons, made a bit more coin. When Naryn went home that night, though, he found the killer waiting for him. He'd already gutted Naryn's wife and smothered his kids. Before he cut Naryn's throat, he thanked him for helping him tie up all his loose ends. You see, after paying Naryn off, the killer spent the day following him, keeping tabs on everywhere he spent a bit of coin, finding out which people mattered to him and which ones he might have shared his secret with. And then he killed them. Every last one.

"You see, all Naryn had to do was tell the truth when he had the chance. But he got greedy, thought he had a handle on things. He didn't know the trouble he'd put himself in until it was too late. And then everyone he knew paid for it.

"Now, I'm going to ask you what you know about this woman of yours one more time, Grisel. But before you answer, I want you to think long and hard about what the truth's worth to you. I want you to think about your friends, your neighbors, your family. Everybody's got someone that matters to them, even a worthless shitheel like you. Think about what the truth's worth to them while you're at it, because if you don't tell me what I want to know, I promise you I'll find each and every one of them. Sooner or later, I'll find someone who knows something. How many of them I have to go through is up to you."

Grisel wondered how much Arden knew about him already. Nobody at the *Goat* knew him, but if Arden had his spader tags, which provided his name and work number, it was only a matter of time before he tracked down somebody who knew where he lived. Worse, a well-placed bribe at the guild would give him access to everything: his address, his work history, his friends. Grisel could give a toss about most of the people Arden might turn to down the line. Most of his neighbors probably had something bad coming to them anyway, especially the Tamercum brothers. Sedina deserved better, but Grisel had no illusions about her. She would sing whatever tune Arden asked to save her skin. She was a survivor; no point in blaming her for that.

But Jaspen and Meaty would be stubborn. The two were intolerably pigheaded under the best of circumstances. Arden would have to hurt them to make them talk. After all they had done for each other coming up through the guild, Grisel could not stomach the thought of condemning them to torture and maybe even death.

"So, Grisel," Arden said, "what can you tell me about this woman you were looking for the other night?"

Nicalene.

Grisel still had no idea what she had gotten herself into. She went and did stupid things before and saw her fair share of trouble before they met, but this was something worse. Men like Arden seldom took an interest in people for minor offenses. Grisel had seen the sort of thugs that Low-town's dealers and debt collectors sent out to deal with problems. Usually skilled at roughing people up or breaking furniture, most of them were barely smart enough to track down an address.

Arden was something altogether different, probably the right-hand cutter of a well-connected broker. Whatever Nicalene had done, she was less likely to charm or pity her way out of it like she did in the past. He imagined Nicalene in his place; withering under Arden's glare and terrified of whatever punishment he had in store for her.

Nobody would notice if she went missing since she had no family and most of her friends were dead, moved on, or strung out in some Sinkhole back alley. Even if Grisel sold her out now, nobody he knew would blame him for it. As far as they were concerned, he had done all he could for her. If she wanted to piss all over her last chance at a decent life, that was her choice, not his problem.

Nobody would care if Arden hurt her.

Nobody would care if her body turned up in the Saven's sludgy waters.

Nobody, Grisel realized, but him.

Damn you, Nicalene.

He met Arden's gaze, doing his best not to tremble under that unbending scrutiny.

"Well?"

Grisel leaned forward and spat on Arden's boot. "Go fuck yourself."

Arden glanced at his boot, watched the glob of spittle ooze off the leather and pool upon the floor.

He shrugged. "Your choice."

Arden stood up, opened the door, and motioned to the muscular thug outside to join him.

"Hold him down."

Grisel tried to scramble away, but he was too weak after being shuttered up in that cramped room for so long. A massive hand closed around his leg and yanked him off the bed. He landed on his tailbone, which caused his lower back to go numb before he could put up much of a struggle. The big man pressed on him, ramming his knees against Grisel's midsection and pinning his arms against the floor.

Arden calmly strode around the scuffle and pressed his boot on Grisel's left wrist. He reached under his coat.

"Maybe I didn't make myself clear…"

Grisel's eyes widened when Arden pulled an axe out from behind his back.

"Wait a minute, you—"

The thug's free hand clamped over Grisel's mouth and forced his head down.

"You think someone's going to come for you?" Arden asked. "That all your guild brothers are out canvassing the streets to find where you've gone? Nobody's looking for you, Grisel. Do you know why? Because you're a worthless gutterscum who'll never be missed by anybody in this borough who's worth a damn. What does it matter if you disappear? Things will go on the same as always, with hardly anyone the wiser."

Arden knelt beside him, his boot still holding Grisel's wrist against the floor.

"I decide whether or not you ever leave this room, no one else. You tell me what I want to know, and you get to go back to your pathetic little life."

He raised the axe.

"But you're the one that has to decide how many bits you want to take back with you."

Arden swung the axe downward. The blade struck the wooden floor with a wet thud. A shiver spiraled up Grisel's forearm, as if he stubbed his fingers against a stone wall.

Then the pain hit, a thousand searing needles jabbing into his hand. Grisel screamed, but the rough hand covering his mouth stifled the sound. The pain chilled as it slithered up his arm, setting his entire body to shivering.

Arden stood up. He pulled a strip of cloth from one of his coat pockets and wiped the blood off the axe.

"Let him up."

The heavy weight lifted away from Grisel's body and he rolled over to clutch his bleeding hand close. He tried hard to avoid looking to see how many fingers remained.

Arden dropped the bloody cloth beside him.

"You'd best wrap that up before you pass out."

Grisel tried to hold his chattering teeth together as his bloody stubs throbbed back and forth between excruciating pain and numbness.

"I'll be back soon," Arden said. "Think about how you want the conversation to go."

He fetched the lantern from the floor and stepped out of the room. The big thug followed close behind, grabbing the stool on his way out.

Grisel heard him chuckle as he closed the door. "Rats'll eat good tonight."

Darkness poured back into the room after the door banged shut. Without the lantern light to keep them at bay, the rats scampered from their hiding places, squeaking excitedly. Grisel forced himself to sit up and groped around to find the strip of cloth Arden had left behind. Carefully, he placed it over his wet hand.

A few feet to his left, the rats squealed and hissed as they squabbled with one another in the blackness.

GRISEL SPENT THE rest of the night pacing around the room, struggling to fend off exhaustion and the ceaseless pain until the dawn arrived. He managed to stanch the blood flow from his severed fingers before losing too much blood, but he still felt lightheaded. Keeping on his feet and moving helped him to stay awake, even if he felt delirious for most of the night. More importantly, walking kept the rats away. He felt them scurrying around his feet with every step. They tried to climb up his pant legs whenever he stopped, forcing him to kick the little bastards loose before they could nibble at the bloodstained fabric. Most of the rats finally retreated shortly after sunrise, leaving only a few of the bolder, hungrier vermin to skulk along the walls. Grisel sat on the edge of the cot, but he refused to lie down.

He inspected the blood-soaked cloth wrapped around his mangled hand. Most of the blood had dried, fusing the fabric to the raw, exposed flesh. Every movement broke a portion of the developing scabs, sending a sharp, biting pain up his arm. If he held his hand perfectly still, the pain eased to a throbbing, burning sensation. The crude bandaging smelled awful, a mixture of sweat, sour meat, and overripe fruit.

That had him worried. If rot set in, he might wind up losing the entire hand.

Two gone…

He avoided looking at the groove Arden's axe left in the floorboard. The rats had picked his severed fingers clean and lapped up most of the blood during the night, leaving nothing behind but little bits of white bone.

Every time he closed his eyes, he heard the sickening thud of Arden's hatchet cleaving through his fingers.

He'll be back soon.

The thought filled him with a dread so potent he momentarily forgot about the pain. He wondered what Arden would take next if he angered him again. Another finger or two? A hand? A foot?

Simply giving him what he wanted would be so easy. He could tell Arden everything, tell him about living with Nicalene, about her sordid past, about the way she betrayed his trust. He could provide enough leads to keep Arden occupied for weeks.

But he barely entertained the thought. If Arden was willing to resort to such extreme measures to find Nicalene, Grisel did not want to imagine what he might do once he actually found her. Every night of questioning he survived gave Nicalene a better chance of escaping.

All he had to do was keep spitting at Arden's feet.

Of course, defiance came easy when he sat alone in the locked room. It came easy last night, before he understood what a man like Arden was capable of. Would he be so defiant again now that he experienced the consequences of such resistance? Grisel did not know.

Waiting around helplessly to find out seemed like a very bad idea.

For the first time during his captivity, Grisel turned his mind to escape.

He quickly eliminated the door as a possibility, knowing it was locked and very likely guarded. The window seemed the most likely escape route, but the boards had been firmly nailed onto the frame. His fingers were too big to slip into the gaps between them. Without a prybar of some sort, the window was a dead end.

Any attempt to overpower his captors seemed hopeless and foolish. Even in perfect health, he probably stood no chance against either of them. He considered subterfuge of some kind, feigning sickness or death, to lure one of them into the room, but even if he got past them and through the door, he doubted he could outrun them in his current condition. Moreover, he had no idea where his makeshift prison was located. Without knowing the neighborhood, one wrong turn could lead into a dead end and land him right back in his rat-infested cell.

Pressing his ear against the boarded window told him little about the surrounding area. He heard none of the sounds that might indicate bustling activity: no criers, no animals, no dull murmur of a dozen conversations. Any number of rarely travelled alleys tucked into Lowtown's creases and corners might fit that description. Calling out for help was a fruitless endeavor. At best, nobody would be around to hear him. At worst, nobody would care, and the racket would only anger his captors.

After running through the obvious options, Grisel tried to imagine more unusual plans without much success. Creativity had never been one of his strong qualities. He found it harder and harder to concentrate as the day progressed. Fatigue tugged at his eyelids, and he took to peeling back a bit of his bandaging every so often in the hope that the stabbing pain might keep him awake. By dusk, his skin felt warm to the touch, a sure sign that fever had taken hold.

If he was going to do something, it had to be soon. He dreaded to think about what he might give up to Arden while delirious.

Nausea followed on the fever's heels, sending him scrambling to the privy closet to empty the paltry contents of his stomach. After he finished, he sank to his knees next to the wooden bench and tried to choke down the rest of his bile.

At least the place has a privy.

The word stuck in his mind.

Privy. The place has a privy. On the second floor.

Grisel hauled himself up to peer through the hole in the privy bench. The smell was not very strong, which suggested that the pit below saw little regular use.

How deep?

He staggered out to the main room and scanned the floor until he spotted a small piece of bone. The sense of revulsion from earlier at the thought of his severed digits vanished before his excitement. He scooped the bone up, went back to the privy, and dropped it through the hole.

One...two...

A tiny splash echoed up to his ears.

Twenty-five, thirty feet, maybe?

Grisel tried to calculate the privy's dimensions, estimating about fifteen feet to the ground floor, which left another ten to fifteen feet to the surface of the waste pool below ground. What was beyond his calculations was the depth of the cesspit itself. The pit he fished a body from a few nights earlier was over twenty feet deep, but most pits were rarely much deeper than ten or fifteen feet.

That meant the wastewater at the bottom could be anywhere from a few inches to ten or more feet deep.

No telling how wide, either.

Judging by how far the privy closet extended from the room, Grisel felt confident that the second-floor privy connected to the same cesspit used by the first floor. If the cesspit's stonework was poor, which was often the case in Lowtown privies, it might be possible for a determined soul to climb out.

Grisel backed away from the privy and took a deep breath.

Must be out of my sodding mind.

He pried off his shirt, pants, and shoes before stepping back inside the privy closet. The bench tore away from the floor easily, its soft, rotting wood disintegrating under pressure. He found the waste chute underneath, a roughly circular hole about two feet wide plunging straight down into total darkness.

The rats squealed excitedly out in the main room as they tore at the bloodied bits of clothing. Worried that the fabric might catch on something, Grisel carefully peeled the bandaging away from his hand. The pain pushed back the fever's delirium, but he also felt blood seeping from the wound again. He avoided looking at stubby remnants of his fingers. Once the bandage pulled free, he tossed it out for the rats.

Enjoy it while you can, you little bastards.

Grisel sat down next to the hole and dangled his legs inside. The chute's stone wall felt rough, promising to scrape him bloody on the way down.

Of course, a few cuts and bruises seemed trivial compared to the broken bones that might await him at the cesspit's bottom. If he broke a limb, Grisel knew he would be unable to climb out and would either drown or choke to death on fumes from concentrated waste. Even if he made it to the bottom intact, there was still the matter of climbing up the chute to the first-floor privy before the poisonous air suffocated him.

This is a terrible idea.

Darkness already reclaimed the room, but if he focused intently, Grisel could still see a few feet in front of him. He finally looked down at his mangled hand. The last two fingers were mostly gone, severed just below the first knuckle. Stubs of white bone peeked through the remaining flesh, which was bloated and blackened. Dried blood coated much of the skin down to the wrist. No matter how hard he tried to hold it steady, his hand continued to shake.

You're not getting another piece of me, you bastard.

Grisel took a deep breath and slid forward to plummet down the privy.

The drop itself proved mercifully short. He banged against the wall twice, ripping away large patches of skin in the process, but he cleared the waste chute quickly. The rest of the fall took him into the cesspit itself. He splashed into the water and sank down until his feet squished into the soft muck.

Too deep!

He pushed off from the ground and flailed his limbs to carry him upward until he broke the surface.

Don't breathe, don't breathe, don't breathe.

Fighting the instinct to take another deep breath, Grisel thrashed around until he found the cesspit wall. The rough stonework allowed him to get a purchase, but his hands proved too wet to grip the wall firmly enough to hoist his weary body out of the water. Each time he thought he had a firm grasp, his hand slipped.

Dammit!

His lungs burned as he scratched and clawed at the stone just to keep his head above water. He followed the cesspit wall as he flailed, hoping to find a better handhold. The wall eventually curved, and his free hand struck another section of stonework. The oblong shaped cesspit was narrower there, narrow enough for him to reach from one side to the other.

Frantic, Grisel extended his arms, found a slick handhold on both sides, and hoisted himself upwards.

Pain tore at his bloody hand, but Grisel clenched his teeth and ignored the sensation. He wedged his feet into gaps in the stone and pushed. Slowly, inch by agonizing inch, he hauled his body out of the water, each limb working in concert to climb the cesspit.

His legs had not quite cleared the water when he finally had to chance a breath.

The little gasp took in the slightest taste of the foul air, exhaling just enough to make room for it in the process. Every spader learned such breathing techniques, a survival measure for the direst circumstances. The mincing little breaths would only carry him so far, though. They were supposed to keep a spader alive until help could arrive.

No help would be coming for him.

Grisel continued climbing up the cesspit, carefully bracing his limbs and balancing his weight before shifting to grip a higher portion of the wall. Water dripped from his naked, bruised flesh, each drop splashing into the pool below. He moved slowly, knowing full well that one misstep would send him plunging into the fetid liquid.

If that happened, he probably would not have the strength to climb again.

His ascent proved so gradual that it was hard to judge how far he had actually progressed. The splashing water sounded farther away than before, but that could have been some trick of the echo. He fought the urge to open his eyes and look up, knowing that the pungent fumes might well blind him. All sense of time vanished, pushed aside by the urgency of trembling muscles and sore joints.

Only when his tiny breaths finally took in air that tasted like something other than searing acid did he chance opening his eyes. For a moment, he wondered if his eyelids responded because everything seemed just as black as before.

Of course you can't see anything, you idiot. You're down a cesspit.

The realization did not stop him from looking up anyway. Nothing interrupted the darkness. If not for the open air below him tugging at his increasingly heavy body, he would not have been able to discern up from down.

Gritting his teeth, Grisel resumed his climb.

He worked his way steadily upward, carefully testing each hand and foothold before tugging his weary body a few inches higher up the cesspit.

When his good hand finally touched smoother stone, he knew he had found the chute for the first-floor privy. A bit more probing in the dark located the wooden floorboards just above the stone.

Now comes the hard part...

Grisel struggled to position himself in such a way that he could reach up to the privy bench. After a few moments of groping, he found the open space where the bench covered the floor. Pushing with his legs, he stretched upward until his fingers bumped against the privy's lid. The wood felt sturdy, much sturdier than the bench on the second floor. He grasped the lip of the hole has firmly as he could manage and took a deep breath.

One...two...THREE!

Every muscle in Grisel's body screamed as he kicked away from his footholds and thrust his crippled hand upward. For a moment, he seemed to float in the darkness, neither rising nor falling, suspended by nothing but sheer force of will.

Then his left hand caught the lip of the privy hole and the void below seized him by the ankles, tugging at him like some vile serpent from the depths of the blackest sea.

Grisel dangled there for a moment, his body swinging back and forth while his muscles caught fire. His fingers strained to support his weight, but they held steady.

Reason and fear fled from his mind, driven out by a singular, over-bearing thought.

Pull!

Contracting his weary muscles, Grisel slowly hauled himself up toward the privy hole. His body trembled at the effort, shaking so badly that he nearly lost his grip. The bloody stumps on his left hand had long since gone numb, but they sent throbbing shivers through his forearm, threatening to deaden the whole limb at any moment.

Almost there...

When his head pushed the privy lid aside, he quickly shoved his left arm up through the hole and braced it against bench's surface. After a quick adjustment to his right-hand grip, he pulled his shoulder and head clear of the privy.

Grisel took a deep breath. The air in the privy closet felt clean and fresh compared to the reeking cesspit. A bit of light crept under the closet door. After the darkness of the cesspit, the otherwise faint glow burned like a thousand fires.

Once he got his right arm free, he had an easier time wriggling the rest of his body through the hole. His wet skin slipped over the wood without too much difficulty, and he collapsed onto the floor once he pulled his feet clear.

Keep moving, you idiot!

Trembling, Grisel got to his feet and leaned against the wall for support. Every muscle in his body felt like it had torn free from the bone. He had never felt so much pain; even his headlong tumble down the *Goat*'s stairs seemed a mere inconvenience by comparison.

He took a few more deep breaths to flush the rank air from his lungs before pushing the privy closet's door open just enough to peek out. The room's light originated from a small fireplace tucked into the corner opposite the privy. A black kettle hung over the flames, wisps of steam rising from within it. The room smelled of garlic and swine.

A large figure stepped into view to stir the contents of the kettle. Even from behind, Grisel recognized the man's broad shoulders and stooped posture.

Great...

He froze, unsure about what to do next. Sooner or later, his captor would need to use the privy. Exhausted, feverish, and naked, Grisel knew he would be quickly overpowered in a fight. Then he would wind up right back where he started, right back in the dark room with the rats.

Just as Grisel wondered what he had ever done to deserve such cruel misfortune, somebody knocked at the room's door out of sight.

The big thug strode over to the door and Grisel heard him greet his visitor.

Although no words were clear, he recognized the visitor's voice clearly enough.

Arden.

The door closed a few moments later, leaving the room silent save for the crackling fire.

Grisel wasted no time, pushing out of the closet and staggering toward the door as soon as they were gone. He knew he had only a few minutes before they entered the room upstairs and found him missing.

Then they would come looking for him.

He opened the door and peeked outside to make sure they could not see him from upstairs, but he saw no steps anywhere. Once he was certain they were gone, he slipped outside and closed the door as quietly as he could.

And then he ran.

When Grisel was a boy, he and his friends made a game of agitating stray dogs to get the mongrels to chase them through the streets. Every so often, somebody got caught, and the rest of the group would double back to beat the dog off the poor sod. Grisel remembered how it felt to be the one trailing the group, what it felt like to hear the hound snarling just behind him, nipping at his bare feet. He remembered the terror of knowing one misstep could mean having his throat torn out if nobody came back to help him quickly enough.

No one would be coming to help him now if Arden ran him down.

Grisel paid no heed to his surroundings, charging across the street and turning down the first alleyway he came upon. He stumbled every few steps, barely managing to keep his feet as he ran. Darkness gave way to light when he hurried past streetlamps, only to return when he ducked into another trash cluttered alley.

Keep moving!

His leg muscles started to give out, failing intermittently at first to send him careening into walls and slumbering vagrants. A few angered shouts followed him, but he kept running, heedless of direction. He knew if he allowed himself to let up, he was as good as dead.

I'm not going back, damn you!

He rounded a corner and slipped on a wet mixture of mud and ordure gathered along the edge of the street. His legs flung out from beneath him, and he tumbled to the hard ground.

Get up! Keep moving!

Grisel's stubborn limbs refused to cooperate, flapping and flailing uselessly in the muck.

Keep moving...

He managed to raise his head enough to look down the street. A group of men stood there watching him. Between the darkness and his dizziness, Grisel barely made them out.

"H...help..."

The men might have looked at each other. A few of them might have spoken. Grisel could not tell. The fever had oozed into his blood again, blurring his vision and sending an icy spasm down his spine. He tried one last time to get up, but his battered body finally surrendered to exhaustion.

Grisel swore he heard a dog barking somewhere.

Somewhere close.

19

THE VOTE

The *Broken Boot's* common room proved every bit as boisterous as Ember's previous visit. He even recognized some of the faces, which made him wonder how often the truly degenerate left the place. The stack of boots outside the door stood a little higher than before, but little else had changed. A palpable sense of misery hung over the room. Of course, he noticed the feeling before but recent events had rendered him more attuned to the clientele's despair.

Most of the men there would live short lives, their best years probably already behind them. Ember had always taken for granted that he would outlive them, spared as he was from the punishment of daily manual labor and the corrosive touch of the city's filth.

That was before he saw Yimina come so close to hanging to death in his own home. Death, he realized now, could strike from anywhere, at any time. Ignoring that fact was the surest way to wind up dead at a premature age.

Once again, his grandmother's crude advice rang true: *"Better to be a paranoid old fool than a dead young fool."*

He wondered what she would think about his answering Raugov's summons to the *Boot* alone.

Yimina all but begged to come along, but Ember insisted she remain at the manse. He worried that some assassin might slip inside while they were gone, or that thieves could make off with some evidence Dhrath might use to blackmail him.

Without Yimina at his side, the *Boot's* whores were on him almost from the moment he walked through the door. Most were younger than him, but a few looked to be about his age. Given that their usual stickers were rough men with rough tastes, a well-dressed guest like Ember always attracted their attention, and their affections. He ignored most of them, waving them away before they came within an arm's length. A few slipped in from his blindside, their arms slithering around his neck and over his shoulders like suckered tentacles. Those he brushed off more forcefully. If Ember found their appearance distasteful, he found their touch repulsive.

They promised pleasure and comfort, but he knew they would fail to provide the intense physical and emotional connection that he craved. There was only one person who could provide that level of intimacy, one person who understood him better than any common whore.

After he rebuffed the first wave of women, the rest took the hint and left him alone. Unlike his last visit, he avoided the bar and went straight toward the staircase at the back of the common room. A thick-necked guard met him there with a curt nod. Ember refrained from stating his business.

After all, he was expected.

The guard recognized him and waved him up the stairs without a word. Raugov sat waiting for him there, flanked by a pair of armed men. The table was prepped for another dice game, but no players occupied the stools. When Ember arrived, Raugov snapped his fingers at his thugs.

"Leave us," he said. "Go see if you can round up a few sods eager to part with their coin."

The men obeyed, sneering at Ember as they strode past him and made their way downstairs to the common room.

Ember did not bother waiting for Raugov to begin. "You sent for me?"

"I did. Bit surprised you came alone. I was looking forward to seeing that servant woman of yours again. What was her name? Yvina? Yonara?"

Bastard.

"Yimina," Ember said. "Her name's Yimina."

"Yimina... I hear she's handy with a blade. That so?"

"Pretty good. My father had her trained as a bodyguard when I was a boy."

Raugov laughed. "A killer wet nurse, eh? Clever man, your father. Must have been a looker when she was younger. Bet your father had other jobs for her too, didn't he?"

Ember stifled the urge to punch Raugov by imagining what it would be like to watch someone cut his tongue out.

"You didn't call me out here to talk about Yimina or my father," Ember said, scowling. "What do you want? I assume it has something to do with Kaurgen, yes?"

"Might be it does. Might be you won't like what I found."

"Spare me the veiled threats, Raugov. If you thought I was lying, you'd have come after me already. But I wasn't lying about where to find him, was I?"

Raugov sneered. "No. I guess you weren't lying on that count."

"I take it you found him then."

"We found his roof, but no sign of him or his goods. Looks like the watch gave his place a good tossing over. Could be they know more."

Ember disliked the sound of that. "The watch? I thought Dhrath had them under—"

"Don't you worry about that now, Morangine," Raugov said. "All you need to know is that Mister Dhrath's satisfied you're on the level. He ain't happy about this business with Kaurgen, but he seems to think that's got nothing to do with you."

"Sounds like you don't agree."

"Don't matter what I think. If Mister Dhrath says something's so, that's how it's going to be. Could be he changes his mind later, but for now you're back in his graces."

The idea that nothing but a flimsy whim could determine his standing with the most powerful broker in Lowtown made Ember uncomfortable.

"But we ain't here to talk about that now," Raugov said. "We've got other business to discuss, you and me."

We do?

"I'm listening," Ember said.

"Mister Dhrath hears that you've got an important measure coming up in the Assembly tomorrow."

Ember's throat tightened since he had no plans for a special vote, and certainly no plans he informed anyone, especially Dhrath, about. While he and his allies had secured the seven votes they needed to derail the spader negotiations, they needed more time to prepare for any procedural tactics that Trinn's coalition might pull on them.

Had Ilthene or one of the others told him something? Were they making their own plans behind his back or had they simply given him the wrong impression of their plans?

"Do I?" he asked. "Don't suppose you'd care to enlighten me?"

Raugov glared at him. "Mister Dhrath ain't happy with how slowly things are moving on your end so he's decided to give the Assembly a little push. One of your colleagues will call for a vote to reject the new spader contract. You've got enough votes to carry the day, and Mister Dhrath is getting tired of waiting to set this plan of yours in motion."

Ember choked back his anger, both over the poor timing of the measure and the feeling that the coalition he forged was about to get wrenched away from him.

"With all due respect to Mister Dhrath," Ember said, "I don't think he understands how fragile this situation is. We may have the votes to pass a general measure, but Assemblywoman Trinn will be violently opposed to this idea. There are procedural rules that she can use to stymie us, exceptions and revote provisions, that sort of thing. We're still working on ways to—"

"Don't you worry yourself about Trinn and her like," Raugov said, waving his hand dismissively. "We'll take care of them."

"We'll take care of them."

The potential meanings of that pronouncement raced through Ember's mind. He desperately wanted clarification, but it occurred to him that it would be better if he remained ignorant.

"You just make sure to support the measure and cast your vote when the time comes, Morangine. Is that clear?"

The only thing clear to him was that someone had betrayed him. Someone had conspired with Dhrath to push him aside and take the credit for a year's worth of careful planning.

Ember clenched his teeth and nodded. Standing there before Raugov, he had little choice but to agree with what he feared would be a hasty, ill-conceived plan.

"Good. I'll let Mister Dhrath know that you're still with him. He's eager to get this business finished."

This isn't finished...

"ARMILLE!" EMBER KNOCKED his half-full cup off the desk, sending it crashing against the nearby wall. "I bet you anything it's that simpering snake Armille!"

He raged all night over who seemed most likely to have cut a deal with Dhrath behind his back. His suspicions turned from Ithlene to Armille to Ithlene to Cambin and now back to Armille. Yimina listened dutifully, never offering more than a nod or a shrug whenever he directed a heated rhetorical question her way.

"Fuck!"

He slumped into the chair and rubbed at his temples. All that screaming had given him a headache. Or maybe it was from the wine. He was not used to drinking so much so quickly.

"That slimy bastard, Dhrath, thinks he can make the Assembly dance to whatever song he wants to play. This isn't some gang of ignorant street urchins peddling firedust in an alleyway. Word of this gets out the wrong way and the mob will be out to lynch the lot of us. And who could blame them?"

Maybe that's what he wants. As if he doesn't have enough influence over the Assembly already.

He laughed mirthlessly. "Listen to me, carrying on like I'm some guardian of civic virtue. If I keep this up, I'll start sounding like Trinn."

Yimina walked around behind him and placed her hands on his shoulders. "Would that be such a tragedy?"

"My family bled for the 'civic virtue' of this borough for generations and what do we have to show for it? A crumbling estate, a beggar's pension, and the undying enmity of the mob. That's what defending 'civic virtue' gives you to hand down to your heirs."

Ember knew his point might carry more weight if he had heirs of any kind. When he was younger, his grandmother advised him to put off marriage for as long as possible until his political or financial position was strong enough to command a beneficial match. Over the last few years, he turned down a number of proposals, always convincing himself that a more advantageous pairing might still present itself in the future.

Of course, that was not the only reason he rejected each offer.

"You need to get some rest," Yimina said. "You're going to hurt yourself if you keep carrying on like this."

She slid her hands up his neck and rubbed the muscles near the base of his skull. A tingling sensation radiated out from where her fingertips touched his skin. The pain in his head receded slightly as Yimina continued with her massage.

Ember sighed, expelling some of his seething anger along with his breath.

"That's better," she said.

"My grandmother wouldn't have let this happen," Ember said. "She wouldn't let some half-wit Assemblyman go behind her back like this."

"Your grandmother wasn't perfect, you know? She just made sure you never knew it when someone got the better of her. You were too young to remember, but she used to throw terrible fits when someone on the Assembly outmaneuvered her on some issue."

Ember was only ten years old when his grandmother died. She seemed larger than life when he was a child, and her memory only burned brighter when compared to his father's legacy of failure.

Still, maybe Yimina was right.

Maybe he had idealized her too much.

"I still should have seen this coming," he said. "Ithlene, Cambin, Armille; any one of those sycophants could have sold me out. They're already in Dhrath's slimy pockets anyway. One of them must have thought they could cut me out of the loop and win a bit more favor with him."

The thought was enough to drive him mad. None of them had ever taken a chance in their lives, always siding with popular opinion or with their benefactors in every Assembly decision. They lived in fear of losing their seats and rightly so. Too many missteps and they were liable to end up forced to pay their way like anyone else. As far as Ember could tell, none of them had any discernable skills beyond groveling at the feet of anyone powerful enough to keep them in office.

"I thought I had them under control," he said. "I should have taken more precautions, found some way to make sure they'd be loyal. Everybody has secrets that can tear them down, even in Lowtown."

Yimina moved around the chair and swung her leg over him to straddle his lap, her hands still massaging his neck. She smiled when Ember met her gaze.

"You're being too hard on yourself," she said. "You always are."

He reached up to brush some of her blonde locks from her face. There were more gray strands there than he remembered.

"That's why I have you to look out for me," he said.

Yimina leaned forward to kiss his cheek, then slid her mouth over to his ear. "Well, if you can calm down long enough to hear it, I have some news that should help your mood."

Ember ran one hand through her hair and caressed her thigh with the other. Her skin smelled of warm milk sweetened with honey. "I doubt that."

"A message from Twiceborn arrived while you were out," she said, her lips grazing against his earlobe. "Said she can meet you tomorrow, after nightfall."

That was good news. Good enough to drive away the last vestiges of his headache. He brushed his fingers along the length of Yimina's neck and then down to cradle one of her breasts.

"Did she say where?"

"*Belloch's Bower.* Said she'd find you there."

He never expected her to meet him in a public place. What would he do if Dhrath had someone following him? Did she have a plan to avoid them?

"What else did she—"

"Hush now," Yimina said. She pulled away from his ear and pressed her lips against his, her fingertips digging into his shoulders.

Ember shuddered as they kissed. A comforting, familiar warmth flooded through his body, embracing him, and pushing every anxiety and fear from his mind. He wrapped his arms around her and pulled her closer. Her soft breasts pressed against his chest as she slowly rocked her hips back and forth.

"That's it," she said, pulling her lips away from his just enough to whisper. "That's what you need..."

Ember tugged at her shirt, and Yimina placed her hands over his to help him remove it. Her breasts were not as firm as they once were, but the sight and touch of them still set his heart racing as intensely as when he was an ignorant, confused boy.

He bent down and pressed his lips against one of her hard nipples.

Yimina moaned softly as he sucked at her. "That's what my Ember needs, isn't it?"

She cradled his head against her breast and gently stroked his hair.

THE WALK TO the Assembly Hall the next morning seemed to take twice as long as a typical day. Ember spent most of the restless night trying to decide whether he should show up earlier or later than usual. In the end, he took Yimina's advice and followed his usual routine. When he arrived, he found two of his alleged allies, Ithlene and Armille already in their seats. Cambin occupied the center chair, an indication that he would be leading the Assembly's business today. They acknowledged him with the typical pleasantries, none of them giving an indication of which one had gone behind his back.

Five other Assembly members occupied their seats as well. He waved to Lorvie, the lovestruck simpleton who always smiled when he entered the room. To the others, Norvel, Murga, Harik, and Selinis, he merely nodded.

"Lord Morangine," Harik said, his voice booming through the hall as Ember took his seat. "So good of you to finally join us!"

"Yes, good indeed," Cambin said. "Now that we finally have a quorum, we can get down to business."

Quorum.

The word rattled around in Ember's brain as he scanned the faces assembled in the hall.

Trinn was missing. So too were Tarsa, Rendulcar, and Mendin, her closest allies.

You idiots! Could you possibly be more obvious?

"It seems a few of our colleagues are running behind today," Cambin said. "Let's begin with some budgetary matters, then, shall we? Perhaps they'll be along soon, and we can get down to more pressing business."

Cambin summoned a taxation clerk before the Assembly and proceeded to badger him about inconsistent collections. Ember tuned out the exchange, wondering instead what Dhrath might have done with the four missing Assembly members. His own experience with Raugov made him fear for their safety. Not that he particularly cared about their well-being, but he worried about the consequences that could follow if they were harmed, especially Trinn.

After Cambin dismissed the tax clerk, Armille rose from his seat.

"While we're discussing financial matters," he said, "I think now is as good a time as any to discuss the current state of the district's guild contracts."

Oh no...

Cambin nodded. "Very well, Assemblyman. Have your say."

"As I'm sure we're all aware, this Assembly contracts with the Spaders Guild to provide waste and sewage removal throughout the whole of the Lowtown district. Coldwater's citizens take on a great deal of this financial burden and some have suggested that it might well be in the Assembly's interest to pursue alternatives to the guild's increasing rates. In light of this fact, I propose that the Spaders Guild contract be permitted to expire and not be renewed. This will permit the Assembly to entertain other, more affordable labor sources."

Assemblywoman Selinis stood up to speak.

"But who other than the guild has the experience and manpower for this work? It seems foolish to simply—"

"There are plenty of hardworking men willing to shovel these streets for a bit of honest coin," Harik said, his voice drowning out his colleague's. "They've as much a right to that work as the guild, haven't they?"

"I'm not calling for the Spaders Guild to disband," Armille said. "If the guild wishes to contract for services at a more competitive rate, then the Assembly will certainly consider it."

That's a damned lie.

Ember should have known, considering he had been the one who crafted it.

The entire purpose of the proposal was to break the political and economic power of the Spaders Guild. Instead of depositing a huge sum of money into the guild's coffers, the same money could be freed up to pay a variety of workers at much lower rates. Anyone with a cheap labor force at their disposal stood ready to make a huge profit. More importantly, the scheme also created innumerable opportunities for money to disappear in a complicated sea of individual contracts.

The guild would protest, naturally, perhaps even riot. But that was the sort of thing the Lowtown Watch was created to deal with, and the watch's senior officers were firmly embedded in Dhrath's pocket.

Everything depended, however, on the guise of legality and legitimacy. If Lowtown's rabble came to believe that the Assembly had taken action to enrich itself at the public's expense, there would be rioting in every borough. Crafting a narrative to the contrary was delicate and time-consuming work. Ember had been laying the foundations of an anti-guild argument for months and still had much more to do.

Holding a vote on the measure when the guild's most prominent supporters were conspicuously absent from the Assembly meeting, however, threatened to undermine everything.

The debate carried on for several minutes while Ember stewed in silence. His allies presented laughably facile arguments to support their position, most of which might have sounded more convincing had he been able to coach them beforehand.

They have the votes and Trinn's not here to cut their words to ribbons. They don't care how any of it sounds so long as they carry the vote.

"Very well, then," Cambin said. "I think we've heard enough for the Assembly to make an informed decision on supporting or opposing the measure. Voting will now commence by seat."

Cambin started to his left, calling first on Murga.

"I support the measure."

A bribe well spent.

Next came Selinis, who predictably opposed the idea. Armille voted in favor and Norvel voted against. Cambin then turned to Ember.

"Assemblyman Ember?"

He desperately wanted to oppose the measure. The timing was all wrong and he did not want to get caught up in the firestorm of controversy he knew would likely follow once the decision became public. His elegantly constructed plan was being unraveled before his eyes by the impatience of his supposed allies. If he threw in with them now, it would be a dangerous fight to get what they ultimately wanted, far more dangerous than previously expected.

But for all that, the plan was not a complete ruin. There was still time to turn popular opinion against the guild, still time to deflect or silence accusations of corrupt bargaining. If he was lucky, he still might even be able to get through the impending struggle without any blood on his hands. And if not, he still had Twiceborn on his side. That gave him some leverage in his dealings with Dhrath, maybe enough to force the slimy bastard out of the picture eventually.

Of course, there was the more immediate problem of Raugov's threat. If he voted against the measure, retribution would be swift and fatal. And once Raugov finished with Ember, he was sure to go after Yimina.

Bastard.

"I support the measure," Ember said.

Cambin continued down the line, collecting more votes in favor. The tally stood at six to two when he reached the final present Assembly member, Lorvie Tinderhov.

"Support or oppose?" Cambin asked.

Lorvie had been rubbing her hands together throughout the voting process, making them slick with sweat by the time Cambin called upon her. Her lips trembled and she abstained from making eye contact with anyone. Ember knew conflict and complicated issues made her nervous, especially when they took her by surprise. Although he had talked to her to secure her support, he never would have called for a vote on something so important without telling her immediately beforehand.

"Lorvie?" Cambin asked.

When she finally raised her head, she looked directly at Ember.

Gods, she's terrified.

Ember showed the warm smile he used with her since the time they were young, the smile that always convinced her that whatever mischief they were up to was okay. Although he had never treated her especially well, she always trusted him.

Just nod your head. Remember what we talked about. Just nod your head and don't think about it.

She broke his gaze and scanned the Assembly seating area, her attention lingering on the empty seats.

"I…I don't think…I mean…shouldn't everyone be here for this?"

Ember felt a cold knot forming in his stomach.

Oh no.

"I'm sorry?" Cambin asked. Lorvie rarely spoke during Assembly meetings, even when forced to chair them.

"We're missing too many people," she said, seeming to gather confidence as she spoke. "I want to know what they think. I…I want to hear what Trinn thinks."

The knot tightened. Ember clenched his teeth.

"We have a quorum, Assemblywoman," Cambin said. "If they felt strongly enough about matters such as this, they would have been here."

"I don't know," she said. "It doesn't seem right. I don't know if I can vote without hearing what they think about it."

If Lorvie voted against the measure or abstained, no one would be able to reintroduce it until the full Assembly was in session. The Assembly's rules of order prevented a minimum quorum from holding a revote on a failed measure. But Ember realized the knot in his stomach had nothing to do with his concern that the measure might fail.

He was afraid for Lorvie's life if she failed to vote the way he claimed she would.

Like Ember, she held her seat on the Assembly by right of title. While other Assembly members had to appease powerful patrons or demanding constituents to retain their seats, Lorvie was free to vote as she wished without fear of consequence. This vote, however, was different. If she defied Dhrath, even out of ignorance, the broker might well have her killed as an example to the others that no Assembly member was beyond his reach.

Lorvie knew nothing about the machinations swirling around her. She probably had no idea who Dhrath even was, or that most of her Assembly colleagues were deeply indebted to various brokers and other factions for their positions. As the last living heir of the Tinderhov family, her death might well leave her seat up for sale to the highest bidder, following the same practice that led to the Assembly's current composition.

One more seat for Dhrath to wrap his tentacles around.

Look at me, Lorvie! Look at me!

Ember leaned forward in an obvious attempt to get her attention, raising his eyebrows again and again to signal that she should vote in favor of the measure.

Wrapped up in her own childish thoughts, she failed to notice him.

"Assemblywoman," Cambin said, "your vote please?"

Don't push her, damn you!

Tears formed at the corners of her eyes and her breath quickened. Ember knew her well enough to recognize that she was panicked. Unless someone calmed her down fast, she would retreat into her own head and refuse to interact with anyone.

But Ember could do nothing to stop it. Now that voting was underway, it was forbidden for anyone to make further appeals. If he spoke up now, he would be censured, which would render his own vote invalid.

"Lorvie! Your vote!" Cambin all but shouted at her now, impatient for the matter to be settled.

"No!" Lorvie said, shaking her head. "No, no, no, no. I vote no."

Oh, gods...

Several hushed curses sounded out. Cambin stared at her slack-jawed.

"You...you oppose the measure?"

Lorvie crossed her arms and lowered her head. She was done speaking. They would be lucky to get another word out of her for the rest of the day.

Selinis slapped her hand down on the table. "You heard her. A simple 'no' is still sufficient to voice opposition, is it not?"

"Of...of course," Cambin said, stumbling to find his voice. "The proposed measure fails then, by a vote of six in favor and three in opposition."

Ember stared down at the table. He could feel the others glaring at him, felt the angered recriminations of Armille and Ithlene. They would want to know why Lorvie had not voted the way he promised them. On the far end of the chamber, a trio of scribes hurriedly scribbled down the results of the voting and handed the sheets to clerks who carried them to the archives. Another set of clerks would post the proposed measure and the voting results outside the Assembly Hall within the hour.

By midday, the Spaders Guild would know that a sizable faction within the Assembly had tried to screw them.

For the moment, Ember did not care about that. He was more concerned with Lorvie's safety. By claiming to control her, he had unwittingly placed her life in danger. If anything happened to her, he would be to blame.

Sweet, simple Lorvie, who would never dream of harming anyone. Stupid, half-witted Lorvie, who Ember mocked and teased relentlessly as a child without a care for her feelings.

The realization hit Ember in waves, first in the gut, then the chest, and then the head. He felt dizzy, sick, and out of breath all at once. When he closed his eyes, he saw the brutish Raugov strangling Lorvie with his bare hands.

What have I done?

"The Assembly will adjourn for a short recess," Cambin said, now sweating profusely and looking more anxious than ever. "We will reconvene shortly after noon to hear the day's petitions."

Ember jumped up from his seat before any of his co-conspirators could approach him and rushed over to Lorvie. He seized her by the arm to hoist her out of her seat, then hurried out of the hall with her in tow.

She was sobbing by the time they reached the door.

"I'm sorry, Ember, I'm sorry. I know you said to—"

"Hush," he said. "Don't worry about that now."

Ember glanced over his shoulder to see if any of the others followed after them. Seeing no one, he guided Lorvie out one of the hall's side entrances and stepped into a narrow street, deserted save for a few cats prowling the shadows.

"It didn't feel right," Lorvie said. "Not without the others. That's why I said no. That's what Papa always told me. If I don't know how to vote, just vote no. I'm sorry, Ember. That's what Papa told me to do."

Ember placed his hands on her cheeks and made her look into his eyes. "It's okay, Lorvie. I understand. Now pull yourself together and listen to me. I need you to leave here right now and go to my house as fast as you can. Yimina is there now. Do you remember Yimina?"

Lorvie nodded.

"Good. I want you to tell her that I sent you, that you're going to stay with us for a few days. Do you remember the castle underneath the house? The place we used to play in when we were little?"

Another nod.

"Tell her that you're going to wait down there for me until I get back, do you understand?"

"O...okay," she said. "I need some things from——"

"No!" His tone startled her, and her lips trembled again. "This is very important, Lorvie. You go straight to my house. Don't go anywhere else, don't stop anywhere, don't talk to anyone, understand?"

"No. What's wrong, Ember? You're scaring me."

Ember leaned in to kiss her forehead. "I don't have time to explain, Lorvie. Just please do as I say for right now, okay?"

She blinked back tears as she nodded.

"There's a good girl," he said. "Now go. We'll talk tonight when I get home."

Lorvie moved slowly at first, but then turned and hurried down the street. Ember watched her round the corner at the nearest intersection and disappear.

After only a moment, Cambin burst through the door with Armille and Ithlene close behind him.

"Damn you, Ember!" Cambin said. "You told us we had her vote."

Ember wheeled on the old man, seizing him by his tunic and slamming him against the wall.

"And we would have if you idiots had given me a chance to warn her about the damn vote! What the hells were you thinking, stacking the Assembly like that? Where are Trinn and the others?"

Armille grabbed Ember's arm to pull him away from Cambin. "Absent. Just like we agreed. Now unhand him and let's sort out how we're going to salvage this."

Ember let Cambin go, and the old man bent over to cough. "Agreed? We didn't agree to this!"

"What are you talking about, Ember?" Ithlene asked. "We all knew this was the easiest way to get around the opposition."

"Stacking the vote in our favor was supposed to be a last resort," Ember said. "Even if we passed the measure, Trinn will have the mob battering down the doors after she tells them how the vote went down."

"Ember, calm down!" Ithlene said. "We can still salvage——"

"Salvage what? I had everything moving just the way we wanted before Dhrath decided to tug on all your strings. This was supposed to be clean. We only needed that slimy bastard to deal with the spaders, not with the Assembly. I told him and the lot of you that I had it in hand."

"Dhrath thought otherwise," Armille said. "Said you botched his payment, so he told us to take the lead."

Kaurgen...

"I held up my end of that bargain, dammit!" Ember said.

"That's not the way he saw it," Armille said.

Ember sighed. "What do we do now? The spaders will know how badly we're trying to screw them before sunset, and we can't hold another vote without the entire Assembly in session. That means we're going to need Trinn and the others. Only this time, they'll know what's coming and will whip the whole of Lowtown into a fever over the measure."

Armille and Ithlene exchanged a knowing glance, but Ember ignored it.

"You don't think we know that?" Cambin asked, his voice hoarse after all the coughing. "Don't think Dhrath would have a plan to deal with her?"

Ember hated the sound of that. Given his experience with Raugov, he had a good idea of how Dhrath dealt with problems.

"What are you talking about? Where is she? Where are the others?"

Ithlene shrugged. "Mendin was…detained at his estate. Rendulcar and Tarsa drew a sudden interest from the watch. They're probably still answering questions about some of their associations as we speak."

"And Trinn?"

Another glance between Armille and Ithlene.

"Tell him," Cambin said.

"There was no other way, Ember," Ithlene said. "She had too many connections, especially with the guilds. Would have asked too many questions."

The words *"had"* and *"would have"* rang out louder than the others.

Ember felt sick to his stomach.

It was supposed to be clean…

"You should have told me," he said.

"Would you have gone along with it if we had?" Cambin asked.

The question took Ember by surprise. He hated Trinn, had dearly wished for some misfortune to befall her on numerous occasions. But, somehow he found that wishing someone dead and being a party to their death were two entirely different matters.

"What does it matter now?" Armille asked. "If we can't find some way to scuttle the contract renewal, we'll be stuck with the damned spaders for another year."

"We'll need another vote," Ithlene said. "Can we reintroduce the measure with Trinn's seat vacant?"

Cambin thought for a moment, then nodded. "Yes, but only if her seat is officially vacant."

No one needed him to clarify his meaning.

Armille nodded. "I'll pass the word along. Could take a day or two."

Ember shook his head. "What a sodding mess."

"Don't start casting out judgments, Morangine," Cambin said, snarling. "You're the one who didn't deliver the key vote when it mattered. Where'd that idiot woman get to, anyway? We all saw you drag her out here."

"I tried to talk some sense into her, but she was hysterical," Ember said, delivering the lie as casually as he could manage. "Ran off before I could get more than a few words in. Probably best to let her calm down for a day or two."

"You sure you can bring her around, Ember?" Ithlene asked.

Ember glared at her. "She'll be fine if she knows what's coming. What twists things up is when the three of you decide to change every plan we had in place without telling me."

"It's the way Dhrath wanted it," Armille said.

The hells with Dhrath.

"Is there anything else you're not telling me?"

The three Assembly members glanced at one another with varying degrees of uncertainty.

None of you bastards trust each other, do you?

Dhrath had them all jumping at shadows now, which was probably just what the broker wanted.

Ember shook his head and marched back into the Assembly Hall without another word.

This was supposed to be clean. Clean and simple...

He should have known better. His grandmother used to tell a crude tavern story about a stones player who could outplay anybody he met. The story came to an abrupt end when an angry opponent upended the table and beat the man to death with his own tankard.

A bit direct for a morality tale, but Ember finally understood what she was trying to tell him. Politics had all the characteristics of a game, a game one could master with enough knowledge, practice, and foresight.

But for all the similarities, it was nothing like a game.

It was a war.

And like every war that tried to dress itself up in rules of engagement and codes of honor, none of those high-minded ideals meant a damn thing in the muddy, blood-soaked trenches of the front lines. Ember recognized that fact on an intellectual level, but Dhrath was the one who truly understood it, the one who lived with that reality every day.

Unless he adapted quickly, Ember would end up on a slab in the Deadhouse alongside Trinn.

THE ASSEMBLY RECONVENED in the afternoon only long enough to adjourn for the day. Lorvie's absence left the Assembly below its quorum, leaving Cambin no choice but to send the petitioners gathered outside the hall away with promises that they would be heard first thing tomorrow morning. Ember knew from experience that some of them would not bother to return. Unlike the Assembly members, most residents of Low-town could barely afford to lose more than a day of working time while they waited to present their petition.

He departed from the hall quickly to avoid any further arguments with his supposed allies. If he knew them as well as he thought he did, they would be scurrying back to Dhrath with a litany of excuses to justify their spectacular failure. They were sure to place most of the blame at his feet, of course, but Dhrath was probably astute enough to see through their childish finger pointing.

If all else failed, he could pry their brains open and find the truth of the matter for himself.

The notion made him shudder.

Bloody cephalins.

If not for their short lifespans and physical limitations, the wretched creatures would surely control every city and kingdom on the continent.

Ember went directly to *Belloch's Bower* after leaving the Assembly Hall. Nightfall was still several hours away, but he refrained from return-ing to the manse just yet. Dhrath's thugs were sure to be watching for him now, and if he went home right away, they would likely find out that Lorvie had gone there to hide. After the morning's proceedings, no one would be surprised he wanted to drink the rest of the day away.

The *Bower* was less busy than during his previous visit, but the place still throbbed with activity even in the daylight hours. Once again, he brushed away several prostitutes eager to part him from coin on his way inside. Most of them took the hint after a few rejections, and by the time he settled down at a small table and purchased a jug of wine, they no longer approached him. Left alone with his darkening thoughts, Ember stewed and drank the rest of the afternoon away. When he finally emptied the jug, he called for another and a loaf of sourbread to help soak up the wine. His mood blackened steadily, and he gradually lost track of time as he drank and brooded over the situation with Dhrath.

Ember was halfway into the second jug of wine when one of the Bow-er's whores slithered into the seat beside him and ran her hands across his shoulders and chest. She leaned over to whisper into his ear.

"I've been waiting for you, Ember."

"Piss off," he said, his wits too dulled by wine to question how she knew his name. "I don't want—"

She pressed a finger over his lips. "Don't put up a fight, now. It's all been arranged. All you need to do is come with me and I'll take care of the rest."

Ember glared at her, but she gave him a wry smile in return. She tugged at his sleeve while her other hand slid to rub his inner thigh.

"Come on, then," she said. "I know what you've been waiting for. Let me help you find it."

He reached up to push her away, but something about her plea make him pause.

Twiceborn said she'd find me here...

"All right," he said, taking the woman's hand. "Let's see about that."

She led him across the common area and up the staircase to the third floor. They walked by several rooms before she pushed one of the doors open and pulled Ember inside. The dark interior smelled of candlewax and sex. A heavy curtain covered the window on the far wall, and the only light came from a small candle burning next to the bed.

The whore's demeanor changed completely after she closed the door behind them. Ignoring Ember, she stalked into the darkness on the opposite side of the room. She whispered something before Ember heard lips pressing wetly against each other. Another voice, also female, breathed a reply after the kiss. Before Ember could interject, the whore stepped into the light again.

"I'll be outside," she said. "I'll take you back down when you've finished."

With that, she opened the door and left the room.

Ember stared into the darkness in the room's far corner. The candle provided a small flash of light that should have been sufficient to illuminate most of the room.

"I trust you'll forgive that little deception," a woman's voice said. "If anyone's following you, it's best for them to think you're seeing to your baser needs."

"Twiceborn?"

The darkness lost much of its substance, thinning out like a fading mist until it became ordinary shadow. A young woman, thin as a reed and ghostly pale with short, black hair, sat in a chair on the opposite side of the bed. She wore a tan shirt and what looked to be spader overalls. Her eyes were like solid orbs of black marble, bottomless and without pupils.

Paired with her short black hair streaked through with white and gray strands, Twiceborn struck a slightly unsettling image.

"You wanted to see me, yes?"

Ember nodded. "We've got problems. Dhrath's tightening his grip over the other Assembly members and has one of his brutes all but holding an axe over my head. He's already talking about getting a bigger cut of the profits once this is over and done. Today he tried to manipulate an Assembly vote by keeping four members from their seats, even killed one of them if what I heard is true. The bastard's trying to make a bigger place at the table for himself; he keeps it up, there won't be room for anyone else, not even us."

Twiceborn listened without emotion or any apparent interest. Ember might as well have been reciting taxation records for all the attention she paid him.

"Am I compromised?" she asked.

"What?"

"Does Dhrath know about our arrangement?"

Ember shook his head. "No, I don't think so. Not yet anyway. He just knows that I've promised to deliver a labor force capable of replacing the spaders."

"Then there's no reason for not proceeding as planned."

Except it might get me killed!

"Didn't you hear what I just said? Dhrath had an Assembly member killed! And not just any Assembly member. Trinn Harmyndri. Do you have any idea what will happen when people find out one of their elected representatives was murdered?"

Twiceborn shrugged. "Riots, I expect. Suppose we're overdue."

"Huge riots. Hell, half of Pigshire rioted just to celebrate her election. Those damned agitators will tear all of Lowtown apart when they hear what happened to her today. But that didn't stop Dhrath from taking her out. If she's not safe, what's to stop the bastard from coming after me?"

"Probably nothing. Which is all the more reason to do whatever you can to stay in his confidence, at least for now."

Ember sighed. He had hoped Twiceborn would be more concerned given the circumstances. After all, if Dhrath knew the half of what she was up to beneath her apothecary shop over in Sinkhole, he would probably burn the whole slum to ashes.

"Not as easy as it sounds," he said. "He already thinks I cut a deal with Kaurgen to screw him out of his payment."

For the first time, Twiceborn perked up, leaning forward in her chair, and looking directly at him with her black eyes. "Wait, what was that about Kaurgen?"

Ember hesitated. Kaurgen never mentioned Twiceborn before. The thief did have a reputation, however. Perhaps she merely recognized the name. Or maybe they crossed paths before she came to Lowtown. Rumor had it she used to be a court conjurer for some High Ridge nobleman before she did something to get herself exiled south of the Saven.

"I arranged a contract between the two of them," he said. "Dhrath wanted him to steal something for him, some family heirloom from a Nosgarrian baron. Kaurgen sent word to me when he got back and I set up the meeting for Dhrath, but the damned thief never showed. Probably halfway to Kormur by now, the feckless bastard."

Twiceborn shook her head. "That's not possible."

"Why not?"

"Because he's lying on a slab in my cellar."

Ember's jaw dropped. "You're sure it's him?"

"There's a brand on his left arm; the script's Karthean, but it gives his name and marks him as a thief. He must have gotten pinched in Gulhn at some point; they like to brand people for petty crimes to help keep tabs on them."

"How did—?"

"I have a new supplier in the Deadhouse," she said. "He was the first body she sent me. Came in a few days back. I didn't think anything of it until I got to work on him. There was a trace of...something in the corpse. Something that shouldn't have been there."

Ember shook his head. "I don't understand."

Twiceborn gestured for him to come closer, indicating a stool at the foot of the bed. "You'd better tell me everything. If Dhrath's looking for him, the situation might be even worse than you think."

While he was glad to see Twiceborn finally sharing his concern, her pronouncement only tugged harder at Ember's fraying nerves.

20

THE DAMNED

Calandra looked up from the ledger when Lerris finally stumbled through the door for her shift. Daylight had long since peeked through the windows positioned near the top of the mortuary's high walls.

Late again. Third time this week.

Lerris avoided making eye contact with anyone as she staggered toward the main desk, but workers still scurried away from her all the same, trained to avoid her wrath by years of unwarranted scolding. Although she had not snapped at anyone for days, few of the laborers took her recent melancholic mood for granted. They still busied themselves when she passed by, fearful that the mere sight of idle hands might rouse the vile hag from her torpor.

No one spoke to her as she limped across the mortuary floor, and she made no effort to acknowledge anyone's existence.

Calandra closed the ledger and crossed her arms when Lerris finally approached. The wretched woman looked like she had gone a month without washing herself. Even across the desk, Calandra could smell the stale drink on her breath.

"Where have you been?"

Lerris lowered her head. "Slept too long again," she said, her voice thin and brittle. "Been sick with something."

"Sick or falling down drunk?"

"The hells do you care?" Lerris asked, her voice barely rising above a petulant whisper.

"Because I don't need to be covering for you once my shift is over and done. You think I don't have better things to do with my time?"

"Yeah? Like what?"

Unable to come up with a satisfactory response, Calandra scowled. "Never mind," she said, rising from her chair and taking up the ledger. "Let's go have a look at things, shall we?"

Lerris fell in behind Calandra as she headed for the entrance to the crypts.

They passed a number of mortuary workers along the way. Most of them busied themselves scrubbing down the many tables in the preparation chamber, as there were relatively few bodies that needed attention from the night before. A few workers acknowledged Calandra but turned away before Lerris reached them.

She grabbed one of the lanterns sitting near the crypt entrance and lit it before unlatching the gate and going down the tunnel. Lerris struggled to keep up with her, wheezing and grumbling as she followed. When Calandra reached the first storage chamber, she stepped inside and set the lantern on the ground. She opened the ledger and compared the entries to the row of bodies pushed against one of the walls, taking note of any discrepancies. Lerris staggered into the room a few moments later, bending over to catch her breath.

"You got something for me today?" Calandra asked.

Lerris reached into one of her pockets and pulled out a small sack. Calandra took it from her and peeked at the marks inside.

"A little short, isn't it?"

Lerris shrugged. "Slow week."

That, at least, they could agree upon. Calandra could not remember the last time she saw so few bodies arrive at the Mortuary. Only half a dozen showed up last night. If the pace remained that slow, she would have a much harder time making the odd body disappear.

Just my luck.

She slipped the sack into her pocket and went back to the ledger. Lerris coughed behind her, a wet, rattling sound that made Calandra shiver.

"You ought to lay off the drink for a while. Maybe then you could finally get a decent night's sleep."

"Piss off."

Stubborn troll.

Calandra scowled while she finished reviewing the records. "How many are you slotting for the furnace today?"

Lerris glanced at the ledger before stepping over to the corpses. She bent over and poked a few of them.

"These two," she said, pointing to the corpses at her feet. "And that one there."

Calandra nodded. "Should be fine. They're overdue anyway."

She closed the ledger. Lerris would handle the bookkeeping, consigning several bodies to the furnace in the official records but only arranging for some of them to be burned. The others would disappear over the next few days, long before anyone noticed the "error."

Calandra thought about the black-eyed sorceress and her hulking companions hauling the corpses deeper into the depths of the earth.

"You know what she wants them for?" she asked.

Lerris shrugged. "Never asked. Don't care to know."

Their macabre partner had not been seen since Calandra struck the deal with her a few days earlier. In that time, she left another fresh body unattended in one of the deeper chambers. When she returned to look in on it before leaving for the day, she found the promised coin tucked into a nook in the wall.

"Probably a good idea. She didn't strike me as the talkative type. How'd you ever get mixed up with her, anyway?"

Lerris coughed again. "She came skulking about the place about a year back. Followed me to the tavern one night and bought me a drink. Then she said I was going to help her get what she needed."

"And you agreed? Just like that?"

"She weren't exactly asking. She was telling."

Lerris trembled a bit as she spoke. Until a few days ago, Calandra never thought she would be able to imagine that venomous woman being afraid of anyone. Now the sight seemed almost normal.

Maybe it's just the chill in the air. Or the hangover.

"We done here?" Lerris asked. "Can't take much more of this dead air."

"Yeah, just make sure you mark the right ones."

Calandra grabbed the lantern and turned to face Lerris.

"Oh, and one more thing. I've had enough of you showing up late smelling like you just stumbled out of a winesink. From now on, you get here for your shift on time or I send somebody out to drag your shriveled ass in here. Got it?"

Lerris's shoulders sagged, but she said nothing.

Calandra stepped toward her. "Is that clear?"

Lerris shrunk back, her gaze downcast. She nodded, but it seemed a feeble, resigned gesture.

"Good," Calandra said.

But the situation still felt wrong. Lerris's sudden transformation from tormentor to cowed accomplice troubled her for some strange reason. While she appreciated the lack of daily verbal abuse, she did worry that Lerris's increasingly despondent attitude might wind up getting one or both of them caught. Calandra seemed to have control of the situation at the moment, but she wondered if she was putting too much pressure on someone who could not handle any more strain.

Tarl stood waiting for them at the crypt entrance, his big arms folded over his bloody apron.

"Everything okay, Miss Calandra?"

She wondered how much he suspected. Tarl was dense, but he recalled everyone's work habits as well as his own routine. He knew how much Calandra hated going down to the crypts, especially in Lerris's company. Sooner or later, he might start wondering why she made such visits a part of her shift change routine.

"Fine, Tarl," she said. "Everything's fine. Just going over the records before heading home."

The smile slipped onto her face before she could restrain it.

Dammit.

She never smiled at the Deadhouse workers. Although she always treated them well, she never wanted any of them getting too comfortable around her.

Tarl grinned as he stepped aside to let her pass, but his good cheer faded when Lerris emerged from the crypts.

"Ma'am," he said, bowing slightly.

Halfway back to the desk, Lerris drew alongside her and whispered into her ear. "That dolt's too curious."

"Tarl? He's harmless."

"Don't be a fool, girl. You think any of these sods give a damn about us? They'd rat us out in a second if they thought they could get a few marks out of it."

Calandra was sure that several workers would do just that. Most made enough to scrape by, but they had debts and obligations like everyone else. The promise of a little extra coin could be a powerful incentive.

Not that I've got any right to judge. Not anymore.

"Let me worry about Tarl," Calandra said. "You just keep being your miserable self."

Lerris snorted. "Ought to lead him down there one of these nights. Let her have a *really* fresh one for a change."

Calandra fought the urge to shove Lerris into one of the preparation chamber's tables. She had betrayed one of the Undertakers Guild's most solemn vows by bartering the dead off to a sorceress of undoubtedly ill repute; she refused to consider even the faintest suggestion that murder might be necessary to keep that betrayal secret.

A few quick strides put Calandra ahead of her snickering accomplice. When she reached the desk, she tossed the ledger down and removed her leather apron. Lerris caught up to her moments later, still chuckling under her breath.

Calandra grabbed her shawl from the nearby hanger and glared at Lerris as she pulled it over her shoulders.

"Make sure this place is sorted when I get back. I had to get somebody to scrub down a bucket of knives and clippers after you left last night. We've got enough going down after dark to bother keeping up with your crew's job."

Lerris shrugged as she slumped into the chair and opened the ledger. "Yeah."

Calandra wanted to shout at her, to remind her that she still had obligations to fulfill whether she felt like working or not, but any outburst seemed like a waste of energy. Something about the way Lerris slouched in the chair told her that the woman was well beyond caring what anyone thought about her.

She wondered how long it would take her to reach the same point.

FOR THE FIRST time since she had begun working at the mortuary, Calandra did not go directly home after her shift ended. Instead, she went to a small tavern called *Nightwalkers Den*, located roughly halfway back to the theater. The place occupied the bottom floor of an old, two story building that once served as a flophouse for foreign travellers too cheap to seek accommodations at one of Coldwater's nicer inns. Now it catered to the poor sods unlucky enough to work night shifts throughout the borough, opening its doors just before sunrise and shuttering by mid-afternoon.

Calandra took a seat at one of the tables near the back and ordered a cup of mead. It cost her a whole quartermark, but the warm, sweet drink went down smooth and settled her quarrelsome stomach. Before she knew it, she finished half the cup and her head felt a bit lighter.

Easy now. You're liable to end up like Lerris at this rate.

A steady stream of patrons filtered into the tavern while she sipped at the rest of her drink. Most of them looked like members of the local watch, but a few spader crews, always easily identified by their shaved heads and leather overalls, drifted in to occupy the tables as well. She even recognized a few mortuary workers, though she knew none of them by name and they did not notice her watching them from the back of the room. The rest of the patrons appeared to have no profession beyond drinking themselves into a stupor before noon.

Calandra wondered how many of them had sent a friend or relative to the Deadhouse. Even if they lacked the coin for a proper funeral ceremony, at least they could be certain that the corpse would either be cremated or laid to rest deep beneath the earth.

Provided, of course, she had not designated that body to be passed along to the bodysnatchers lurking in the crypts. Gods only knew what might become of the remains in the hands of that black-eyed sorceress. Maybe she dissected them to satisfy her morbid curiosity, or perhaps she extracted the organs for some grisly experiment. If the hulking things accompanying her were any indication, perhaps she found even more creative uses for the slackened, malleable flesh of the freshly deceased.

Damn.

Calandra took another drink.

How did I get myself into this?

She wondered why she bothered asking. The answer was never far from her mind.

Beyland. Why did you have to be so bloody stupid?

Again, the answer came easily. Beyland always found some way of getting himself into more trouble than he could handle. Sometimes his mouth was the source of the problem, but more often it was just bad judgment. For all his charisma, Beyland had a hard time sorting his good friends from the bad. Too many of the artist and performer types filled his head with hopeless dreams before getting him strung out on firedust or nightroot again. Then there were the manipulators, the ones who latched onto Beyland's caring nature and bled him dry before abandoning him to a heap of unpleasant consequences. After being taken advantage of so many times, Calandra finally had to intervene and handle what little money he had left.

She took another drink and wondered which category best described Nicalene.

Seven days had gone by since Beyland dragged the strange woman home to the theater. Calandra wanted her out four days ago, but Beyland somehow kept managing to extend the eviction deadline. First, he claimed she was still too weak to head out on her own. Then it was because she had nowhere else to go. He even suggested that some unpleasant men might be looking for her, and he would not be able to live with himself if they cast her out to be scooped up by her pursuers.

Calandra relented, but not because of any reason her brother provided. While she lacked a good sense of Nicalene as a person, she would be a fool to miss the effect she had upon Beyland. Something about the woman seemed to inspire him, filling him with a confidence that Calandra had never seen in him before. He stopped moping around the theater, and he wrote more pages in a week's time than she had seen him produce in an entire year. Even when Nicalene was out of the room, Beyland seemed capable of discussing little else.

Damn fool acts like he's in love.

The notion troubled her.

Beyland had claimed to be in love on several occasions, but the fever usually passed quickly, replaced by some betrayal or another. Calandra also remembered the women who desperately wished that her brother would return their affections. In both cases, the passion burned away quickly, and some combination of disinterest or immaturity brushed the fledging emotions aside until the next relationship came along.

Nicalene was different, though. For one thing, she was a lot older than the sort of women Beyland tended to encounter. The weight of experience lent her a certain presence that clearly fascinated him. While she rarely shared much about her past, it nevertheless affected her every word and action. Anyone who watched them interact for a few seconds could see that Beyland desperately wanted to know everything about her.

Naturally, Calandra assumed Nicalene had something to hide. The strange stone embedded in her chest and the bizarre circumstances of her arrival seemed to be enough to validate the concern. Aside from the raving outburst during her first night, Nicalene had done nothing to arouse further suspicion. In fact, without Beyland carrying on about her all the time, Calandra might not have noticed she was even there. She doubted she said more than a dozen words to their guest over the past week.

I think it's time we had a little chat, Nicalene.

Calandra swirled the last of her mead around the bottom of the cup. She wondered if Lerris had started down the path to heavy drinking by stopping off for a drink on the way home every few days. How long before every few days turned into every day? One drink into several? A drink on the way home *from* work into a drink on the way *to* work?

One drink was certainly not enough to put Calandra's mind at ease. Was it any surprise that a wretch like Lerris needed more than one?

"You ain't got the right to judge me."

Lerris was right about that, at least. She had no right to judge anyone.

Not anymore.

Truth be told, Lerris probably had more justification for breaking her oaths than Calandra. At least the bodysnatching sorceress had threatened Lerris into compliance. Calandra had deliberately arranged to violate the guild's most hallowed edict for her own benefit. If her crime became known, no one would care that she did it to save her irresponsible little brother from a ruthless broker. The guildmasters could not afford to forgive or tolerate such a transgression. At best, she would be expelled from the guild and handed over to the watch for further punishment as a bodysnatcher. At worst, the guild would handle the matter internally to make an example of her. For its most serious oathbreakers, the Undertakers Guild reserved two punishments: live burial or incineration in the crematorium furnace.

Calandra shivered and emptied the rest of her cup.

With the coin she collected from Lerris, she now had enough to make the next debt payment to Arden. Sometime soon he would stop her on the way to the Mortuary and demand the money for his broker boss. She hoped that offering him a bit more on the first payment would convince him to give her more time to repay the total, but now she worried that it might establish false expectations for the future. Arranging to deliver fresh bodies to the crypts on a regular basis would prove difficult, especially if any of the mortuary workers became suspicious for any reason. If she failed to keep up the pace, the money she collected from Lerris would not be enough to cover the payments.

She thought about the way Arden had looked at her, the way his body tensed when he seized her in the alley. If she came up short when he came to collect, perhaps there were other ways she might barter for extra time.

The thought set her stomach to quivering again.

What the hell is wrong with me?

She tried to take another drink before realizing that she had already drained her cup.

Cursing, she fished another quartermark from the small sack of coins collected from Lerris.

USUALLY BEYLAND SAT on the stage when he wrote, either perched upon a stool or hunched down on his knees with pages and pages of scribbled notes surrounding him. The arrangement looked rather uncomfortable. Calandra asked him about it one time, but he muttered a very unsatisfactory answer. Something about having to imagine himself before the crowd, taking in the theater's angles from the stage, or some similarly artistic-sounding reason that explained little.

When Calandra finally made it back to the theater, she found her brother seated on the last row of benches, the farthest spot from the stage without exiting the building. As usual, Beyland failed to acknowledge her arrival.

She considered leaving him to his work and simply going upstairs to bed. Working such long shifts over the last few days had worn on her, and the two cups of mead she gulped down earlier hardly helped matters. More importantly, he accomplished so little most of the time that any disruption might compromise his recent gush of inspiration. Calandra still doubted that Beyland's writing would ever amount to anything useful, such as securing an influential patron who might subsidize his efforts, but he was far easier to live with when he felt like he was making progress of some kind.

The mead must have heightened her curiosity, however. No matter how much she tried to think about collapsing in bed, she kept wondering why Beyland sat in the back of the theater. Not only had she never seen him sit there before, but she also recalled him making several jests about the back rows being the refuge of ignorant, uncultured drunks willing to pay a few marks just to have a seat somewhere away from the stinking streets for a few hours.

She crossed the stage, stopping just short of the first row of benches.

"Good morning to you too, brother."

Beyland glanced up and managed a quick smile before returning to his scribbling.

"Hardly morning anymore, Cal. What took you so long? Trouble at the Deadhouse?"

Calandra was unsure what surprised her more, Beyland's curiosity or the fact that he actually had a sense of the time of day. She stepped down from the stage and walked along the aisle until she reached the last row of benches.

"Lerris was late again, the bitch. It made for a long night, so I stopped off for a drink on my way home."

Her brother stopped writing and he looked up at her, his mouth agape.

"*You* stopped for a drink?"

What's that supposed to mean, you little scamp?

"Hey, just because I can't find my way to a winesink blindfolded doesn't mean I'm a teetotaler."

Beyland laughed and went back to writing. "Sorry, Cal. I'm just having a hard time picturing it."

"Probably because you're too used to watching me keep you in line. Somebody around here has to take responsibility for things."

"It was a joke. You don't have to go making a lecture out of it."

"What are you doing way back here, anyway?" she asked, walking through the gallery and sitting on the bench across from him. "I thought you liked to see things from the stage."

Beyland shrugged. "So did I. Got to thinking about it, though, and I realized that it's a lot easier to picture the whole scene from back here. I can get a sense of where she's at in relation to everything else."

She?

Nicalene. It has to be.

Calandra had seen her peeking over Beyland's shoulder as he wrote and going through his completed pages while he worked. She had never seen anyone show so much interest in her brother's work. At the time, she dismissed it as calculated gratitude, but now she wondered if she misread Nicalene.

Or Beyland, for that matter.

"So, you're writing things with our guest in mind now?"

"Not on purpose," he said. "It's just that everything I write seems to make sense to her, like she's already lived it, you know?"

"Not really, no," Calandra said. "How do you know she's not just telling you what you want to hear?"

"It's not like that, Cal. Sometimes after one look at what I've done, she rips up the paper, and tells me to start over."

"What is that supposed to prove?"

"The weird thing is that she's always right. No matter how well I think the scene works, when she tells me to change something, it turns out better. She doesn't always know what needs to be changed or why, but she has this sense that it needs to be different."

"Maybe she's got some semblance of taste. You could get Kardi to tell you whether or not a scene works."

Beyland shook his head. "Not like this, Cal. She almost knows what I'm trying to write before I write it. Every time I describe a scene, it feels like she's right there guiding my hand. Even when I add in details from my dreams, she always seems to know what's going on or what I'm trying to say, like she'd been there with me the whole time."

The notion that Nicalene might somehow be influencing her brother's dreams troubled her. With any other woman, she probably would dismiss it as a coincidence. But she kept coming back to the night Beyland dragged Nicalene into the theater. Aside from Nicalene's thrashing and screaming, Calandra best recalled the black stone embedded in the woman's chest.

Not once had she asked Nicalene about it. In fact, she never asked the strange woman much of anything.

The stone troubled her all the same.

"What do we really know about her, anyway? What makes you think she's not dangerous? You remember what she did to Kardi the night you brought her here, don't you?"

"That was an accident and you know it," Beyland said. "Don't try to turn this into an interrogation. She hasn't done anything to harm any of us or given us a reason not to trust her."

Maybe. Not yet, anyway.

"Well, in any case, she can't stay here forever. Have you thought—?"

"You can't send her away, Cal."

Oh, can't I?

Beyland's body had gone completely still, and he stared at her with wide, unblinking eyes.

He's serious. What the hell is going on between them?

"For her sake," Calandra asked, "or yours?"

He thought for a moment before answering, the edge bleeding away from his panicked expression. "Both, I think. But I know for sure that I need her to finish this play."

Calandra pointed at the neatly stacked papers beside Beyland. "Is that what you've done so far?"

"Yeah. It's about halfway finished."

"Can I read it?"

"No."

"What? Why not?"

Beyland glanced down at the stack. He placed his hand over it. "I...I'm not ready to let anyone see it. Not till it's done."

"What about Nicalene? You let her read it, don't you?"

"That's different."

Like hell it is.

"What do you mean 'it's different'? I've read everything you've ever written, Beyland. What makes this so special?"

Beyland shrugged. "I'm sorry, Cal. It's just too personal. For her, I mean."

Calandra was unsure why his refusal made her so angry. It might have been true that she read all of Beyland's previous work, but she would be lying if she said she enjoyed much of it. She dreaded those days when he shoved some gods awful scene into her hands and grinned like a drunken fool while she tried to get through it without groaning. If anything, hearing that he tasked someone else with reading duties should have made her happy.

Why, then, did she feel like he had stuck a knife in her back? The idea that he put more trust in a strange woman he barely knew than in his own flesh and blood made her want to bash his addled skull.

"What, is she turning this into her confession? I don't suppose it tells how she wound up with a dreamleech stuck to her side and a chunk of stone in her chest?"

Beyland sprang off the bench to grab a fistful of Calandra's shawl. She jerked backward as he lunged and would have tumbled to the floor he before he gave the shawl a hard yank. The fabric tightened around Calandra's neck as he pulled her closer to his snarling face.

"You shut up about that! You don't know a thing about her!"

She swatted at Beyland's hands, but his grip held firm. His eyes glared through her, as if they stared at something, or someone, deep inside her.

"You hate her, don't you? That's why you want to get rid of her. You're just like all the others, all the other lying sycophants with their silken words and hidden knives."

The shawl squeezed the last bit of air from her throat. She fought to take a breath, but every frantic gasp died in her lungs.

Beyland...can't...breathe...

"What are you planning to do to her, damn you? You and your scheming nest of backstabbing harpies."

Dizziness hit her fast, sapping the strength from her limbs while her brother continued to throttle her. She struggled to focus and to remain conscious, but the weight of the void pressed down on her like an avalanche of cold, black snow.

Then a voice sliced through the haze, shocking her back to full awareness.

"Beyland! What are you doing? Stop it!"

Another set of hands came between them to clamp over Beyland's arms.

"Let her go!"

Beyland blinked and shook his head as if a bucketful of water doused him. He released his sister and backed away, his hands trembling. Calandra clawed at her shawl as she slumped onto the bench, but she barely managed more than mincing little breaths in the process.

"Easy, easy. Let me help you."

Nimble fingers loosened the shawl and pulled it free from her neck. She gasped for air, her chest heaving. After a few deep breaths, her head stopped spinning and the feeling inched back into her limbs. When she looked up, she found Nicalene hovering over her.

She could not decide if she wanted to punch her or hug her.

"Are you all right?"

Calandra gave her a curt nod, then peered around her to glare at Beyland, who had retreated to lean against the theater's back wall. He stared at the floor, his shoulders rising and falling with each breath. When he noticed her looking at him, he tried to say something, but the words came out in a garbled, stuttering mess.

Whatever he failed to say mattered little. Calandra could see it all on his face.

Nicalene reached out for him, but he brushed her hand aside and strode toward the staircase.

"Beyland, wait!"

Nicalene tried to follow, but Calandra grabbed her arm to stop her.

"No," she said, her voice little more than a croak. "Let him go."

Beyland quickened his pace until he all but ran up the stairs. Nicalene watched him leave before she sank onto the bench opposite Calandra. Tears formed at the corners of her eyes and her lower lip began to tremble.

She really does care about him, then.

Dammit.

Calandra reached over and placed her hand on Nicalene's knee. The strange woman looked up, her eyes full of confusion and misery.

"Has…has he ever…?"

Calandra shook her head. "No. I've never seen him lay a hand on anyone. Not even when we were little."

Nicalene had picked out a dress with a modest neckline, but Calandra could still spot the outline of the stone beneath it.

"Has he done this while I've been gone?"

"No," Nicalene said. "He's been nothing but kind to me. I heard him yelling and I thought someone might have come here looking for me."

"Who are you expecting?"

Nicalene shook her head. "Nobody important. Just someone… someone I used to live with. We didn't exactly part on good terms."

Calandra glanced down at the stone, wondering again how it might fit into Nicalene's past.

"Anyway, there's no way he would know where to find me," she said. "What was Beyland shouting about? It looked like he was really trying to kill you."

"We were talking about you, actually."

"Oh?"

"I said something he didn't like and he just…it was almost like he turned into someone else. That look in his eyes, it wasn't like my brother at all. I don't think he even knew who I was anymore."

Nicalene straightened her back. The dress's fabric pressed tightly against the stone, and Calandra no longer bothered to hide her interest.

"You know something about this, don't you?" Calandra asked. "It has to do with that thing in your chest."

Nicalene rubbed the stone.

Enough with the secrets, damn you.

"Listen, I've been a generous host. If I had a bit of sense, I'd have thrown your ass out on the street days ago. The only reason I've let you stay this long is because it seemed like you made my brother happier than I've seen him in years. But now he's trying to kill me for saying something about you he doesn't like, so something needs to change right now.

"I don't owe you a thing, Nicalene. Maybe you're a good person who's had a run of bad luck or maybe you've deserved every bad thing that's ever happened to you. I really don't care. What I do care about is my brother. He's the only family I've got left, and if you're in some kind of trouble that's putting him in danger, I want to know about it right now. You want to stay under our roof, then you'd better come clean about yourself, starting with that chunk of rock that's sticking out of your chest."

Nicalene stared at her in silence. For a moment, Calandra thought about how she would break the news to Beyland after she threw the woman out.

He would be angry, she knew. He might even hate her for it.

Would it be enough to make him try to kill her again?

Finally, Nicalene sighed. "I'm afraid I don't know very much about it myself."

Not good enough.

"But I'll tell you what I can."

Better.

21
THE HUNTER

Despite its age, the Pigshire Watch guardhouse still dwarfed every other building on Goblincraw Street. Most of the outer wall remained intact, patched up over the centuries with stonework from the interior and reinforced with wooden bracers. The main keep inside rose just high enough to peek over the wall. Several of the slate roof tiles had crumbled or broken free, exposing dozens of holes to the weather. The watchtowers that once stood at the keep's corners had collapsed long ago, leaving only pitiful stumps of stone to mark their location. A snarled pile of wood scaffolding rose from the north tower's ruins to form a makeshift lookout post high enough to provide a commanding view over the wall. The haphazard structure groaned and tottered in the face of a stiff wind but had stubbornly refused to fall for several years.

Arden knew little about the guardhouse. It had the look of a military fortification, maybe a barracks for a garrison force, but the place was centuries older than Blackspire's oldest citizens, even the ones unlucky enough to live many times the life of ordinary men. He supposed records existed somewhere that might reveal something of the place's origins. Gods knew the city had enough records buried in its subterranean archive vaults to stop up the Saven's flow with paper.

Not that knowing anything about the guardhouse would do him any good. The place was still a dump. Knowing its origin would just make it a dump with a fancy history. In that respect, it was not much different than anything else in Lowtown.

Or anyone.

The gods are wicked and cruel.

The rain started early in the morning and showed no sign of letting up. Arden's oil-treated coat kept most of him dry, but since it lacked a hood, his head felt like it had been dunked in a bucket of water for hours on end.

A member of the watch usually stood guard at the outer wall's wrought iron gate, but Arden had not seen anyone in the vicinity since his arrival. He guessed that the rain had driven the sentry inside, which suggested some lacking in the man's dedication to his duties. Not that Arden expected much more from a member of the watch. Most of them were little better than the thugs and cutpurses they were supposed to keep in line.

Oftentimes the only difference was whether or not they were on duty.

Arden picked up a chunk of stone that had fallen from the wall and banged it against the gate. The racket carried over the droning rainfall and across the small courtyard to the keep's wooden door. After the tenth or eleventh clang, the door cracked open and a man in a leather cap poked his head outside.

"Piss off!"

He ducked back inside and closed the door.

Asshole.

Arden went on hammering the rock against the iron bars.

He wished he could bash in Grisel's face instead.

Three days of hunting for the spader had turned up nothing. Between Halvid's worsening fever and Dhrath sending him out on petty errand after petty errand, he had precious little time to devote to the search. The only lead he had left to go on was Grisel's spader tags, which provided his identification number with the guild. Arden had a favor or two he could cash in with some spaders he leaned on in the past. If he got lucky, maybe they could look up Grisel's records at the guildhall and find his roof, but it would take a few days for the information to come through.

Despite his frustration, he found it hard not to admire the spader's determination. It took a special kind of resolve for someone to escape by crawling through the privy, especially with a maimed hand. Arden figured Grisel lacked the nerve to risk death for the slim chance of escape.

He misjudged him. Badly.

Arden hating misjudging people.

He banged the stone against the iron bars until the guard opened the door again.

"Oi! I told you to piss off!"

Did you now?

Arden stared at him blankly and went on hitting the gate.

The guard shoved past the door and stomped across the courtyard. "That's enough!"

Arden kept banging.

As the guard drew nearer, he unsheathed his short blade.

"I said that's enough, you!"

When he reached the gate, the guard thrust the sword between the bars. Arden twisted away from the blade and caught the man's wrist. He yanked hard, pulling the guard's arm through the gate, and leveraging it between the iron bars. The watch sentry screeched and dropped his blade as Arden applied pressure to the trapped limb.

"Another word out of you and I break your arm in half, got it?"

The squirming guard bit his lip and nodded.

"Now, if you'd been out here doing your job instead of keeping yourself nice and dry, maybe none of this would have been necessary. You be a good little lad now and go tell Captain Rheinmak that Mister Dhrath wants a word with him. You know who *he* is, don't you?"

Another nod.

"Good. Now be quick about it. You've already wasted enough of his time."

Still holding the guard's arm, Arden reached down to retrieve the fallen sword. The blade was dull and speckled with rust, but probably cost more than the guard made in a week.

"I'm going to hold onto this for right now. Bring Rheinmak out here and you can have it back."

Arden turned the guard loose and watched him scurry back to the keep while cradling his arm.

Worthless scrape.

The guard returned a few minutes later with a tall man wearing a mail hauberk of modest quality. When he saw Arden across the courtyard, he sneered.

"Well, well," he said. "If it isn't the tired old soldier himself."

Arden scowled. He forgot how much he hated Rheinmak.

The watch captain drew his cloak's hood over his head and strode across the courtyard, the sniveling guard hanging back by the door. When Rheinmak reached the gate, he gestured to the sword in Arden's hand.

"That looks like one of ours."

Arden tossed the weapon through the bars. It landed in the middle of the muddy courtyard, and the guard hurried to retrieve it before disappearing through the door again.

"Didn't want that half-wit running with it. Liable to hurt himself."

Rheinmak glared at him. "Kind of you."

"Call it a parental habit."

"Squidface sent you along to fetch me, then?"

Arden hoped Rheinmak would be stupid enough to think of that nickname when he went before Dhrath. The last person who did left the meeting with part of his brain running out his ears.

"That's right."

"Nice to see he's got such a fine hound in his kennels. What's he want this time?"

Arden shrugged. "Haven't a clue. A hound doesn't ask why he's made to run down rats, does he?"

Rheinmak sneered and looked up, letting the raindrops strike his face. "Can't this wait until tomorrow? I don't need to be out in this weather. Old scars and all."

Scars. Who do you think you're kidding?

Arden had never known Rheinmak to put himself in danger when he could send a few ignorant recruits to go in his stead. The captain owed his position to bribery, blackmail, and outright deceit rather than any virtuous qualities usually associated with a leader of men. His loyalties shifted so quickly that Dhrath never bothered to buy him off anymore. Instead, he simply watched to see who paid him off most recently.

Dhrath always made two things clear to scoundrels like Rheinmak: he would always pay more when he needed them, and none would escape his wrath if they crossed him. The captain knew that as well as anyone, which was why Arden found his bravado so hollow.

"Come off it, Rheinmak," Arden said. "You know he wouldn't have sent me if he didn't want to see you right bloody now."

Like most cephalins, Dhrath never quite got his tentacles around the concept of patience. Cursed with a lifespan less than half that of humans, cephalins lived for the present, constantly maximizing the moment to squeeze every last drop of opportunity from the brief stretch of time allotted to them by fate. Waiting cost Dhrath not only time but precious life.

"Right," Rheinmak said. "I suppose if I went back inside, you'd just find some way of climbing the wall and dragging me all the way to Carbuncle, wouldn't you?"

Maybe not in one piece.

"Something like that," Arden said. "So why don't you open the gate and let's get on with it."

Rheinmak sighed, but he unlocked the gate and stepped outside. "Fine company for such pleasant weather."

Arden grunted. "Oh, the pleasure is mine, ser captain. Now move."

The two men walked side-by-side down Goblincraw, veering around puddles and mounds of wet muck piled up along the street's edge. Rain kept some of Pigshire's residents indoors, but most of the criers and couriers employed by the borough's butchers remained undaunted by the weather. Horse and ox-drawn wagons still carried crates and fresh animals along the street's length, forcing travellers to step aside and clogging the narrower stretches of roadway when they tried to squeeze past one another.

At least the rain kept the stench out of the air for a while. Once the weather let up, the humidity would soak up most of the odor and drape it over the borough like a wet rag. Summer would not arrive for another two months, but the sticky heat had reached the city well ahead of the season proper.

Most of Pigshire's denizens recognized Rheinmak, or at least marked him as a member of the watch by the blue fabric wrapped around his left arm. Arden guessed that the ones stepping aside more quickly and avoiding eye contact knew the captain personally.

"I see you're as beloved as ever."

Rheinmak snorted. "Jest all you like. This borough would slit its throat and burn to the ground in a fortnight without my men keeping these wretches in line."

Arden doubted that. Brokers and gangs paid the watch to stay out of their way most of the time. The only order the watch seemed interested in keeping was the orderly collection of monthly duties from the citizenry. While they could be counted on to rough up vagrants, petty pickpockets, and debtors, few watch members had the courage to stand their ground against rioting workers or violent gangs.

Although the Lowtown watch was supposed to be a singular organization, in practice each borough's guardhouse operated independently, usually at the beck and call of the brokers or other powerful citizens. The Margrave sometimes appointed a Viscount to coordinate Lowtown's watch forces and bring the district under tighter administrative control, but in every case, power eventually devolved back to the boroughs and the Assembly of Notables after a decade or two. Arden had no idea how long it had been since a Viscount held sway over the watch, but judging by its current fractured and disreputable state, he guessed it had been many decades, if not a century or more.

Rheinmak kept his mouth shut as they walked, which suited Arden just fine. He had enough to think about without the watch captain pestering him. Halvid's fever remained his most pressing concern. The blisters arrived in force two days ago, and several of them had already ruptured. He kept them cleaned and covered as much as possible to prevent the insects from finding them, but every time he returned home, it seemed like a dozen more had either formed or broken. The fever kept the boy unconscious for long stretches, but he occasionally woke in the middle of the night, delirious from the pain. Arden used what little medicine he had left, but the fever's sudden onset had reduced his supply faster than he anticipated. Without the coin to finance another visit to Twiceborn, he had to hope his next collection from Calandra would be large enough for him to skim a bit more off the top.

Making up that lost money, however, no longer seemed quite so simple. Halvid's condition forced him to remain at the boy's side more than usual, leaving few opportunities for investigation. Questioning the regular *Goat* patrons about the suspected sorceress yielded little information, but he had yet to expand the search far beyond the immediate neighborhood. He was no closer to finding her now than when he first learned of her.

Then there was Grisel.

Fucking Grisel.

The spader was the link he needed to find her, and the bastard had walked away without a trace. He never thought to tie Grisel up because there was nowhere for him to go while he was locked inside the second story flat. When he arrived to question him and found the room empty save for the clothing and a broken privy bench, he thought the spader had committed suicide in the most gruesome way imaginable. Only after he found the ordure-smeared footprints on the first floor did he realize that the spader escaped.

Grisel was out there somewhere, hiding. Arden just had to find him. He was supposed to be good at finding people, but tracking a man down took time. If Dhrath continued to inundate him with petty requests like fetching a worthless shitboot like Rheinmak to the keep, he might never have the chance to hunt Grisel down. Without the spader back in hand soon, his problems were sure to multiply.

No Grisel, no sorceress.

No sorceress, no bounty.

No bounty, no medicine.

No medicine…

Arden walked a bit faster, pulling ahead of Rheinmak, who seemed content to get to Dhrath's Keep as slowly as possible.

"Keep up," Arden said. "I don't need to spend all day in this bloody weather."

Goblinscraw Street meandered through the sweaty heart of Pigshire to cross paths with Redfoot Street, which connected the borough to Coldwater to the east and Cadgerwalk to the west. A huge marketplace sprawled across the intersection, with covered stalls and wagons competing for space along the streets. The rain made little difference here, with hundreds of men, women, and children jostling for a place in line to claim the freshest cuts of meat from Pigshire's butcheries. Well-dressed servants from Coldwater found themselves pressed up against impatient merchants from Cadgerwalk and grim-faced laborers from Wallside. People occasionally shouted at one another over prices and quantities, but the dour weather kept the worst of their tempers in check today.

Arden and Rheinmak pushed their way through the crowd and continued along Goblinscraw until it reached the boundary of Carbuncle borough. An earthwork wall about waist high marked the borough's outskirts, no doubt the pitiful remains of some ancient fortification. About half a mile ahead of them, the low, broad hill that gave the borough its name welled up from the muddy earth. Dhrath's Keep, the fire-scorched tower atop the hill, overlooked the whole of Carbuncle. While impressive by Lowtown standards, the tower was a pitiful imitation of the spire, which rose thousands of feet toward the grim heavens from the center of Blackspire.

The foot traffic thinned out as they moved deeper into Carbuncle. Most of the borough's craftsmen made goods to the special requests of individual buyers, which kept the streets free of the criers that fought for the attention of each passersby in so many other boroughs. Rainwater gushed through the crooked grooves between the street's cobblestones like a bubbling brook snaking down a hillside. The water ate away at the mounds of mud and waste packed hard against the stone, occasionally dislodging chunks that half floated, half tumbled down to the base of the hill.

Arden glanced back at Rheinmak, who had fallen several paces behind him. The watch captain looked to be breathing a bit heavy.

"You planning to crawl the rest of the way?"

Rheinmak glared at him. "I'm trying to watch my footing, damn you. These cobblestones are like ice when they're wet."

Arden snickered, but he did not disagree. He hoped Rheinmak might slip and fall at some point.

Would serve you right, you bastard.

"Try to keep up. We're late enough as it is."

Rheinmak muttered something, but Arden missed it on account of the rain. He doubted it was worth his attention anyway. Rheinmak was a man known for his cruelty and corruption, not his wit or intelligence.

They continued up the gentle slope for another quarter mile before Goblinscraw merged with Shale Street, which veered toward the tower at the apex of the hill. Dhrath's Keep looked even more sinister than usual on a rainy day. The crumbling stones at its peak were pitted and scored by years of harsh weather. When Arden squinted, the upper third of the tower blended in with the slate gray clouds above, leaving only the blackened, rust-streaked foundation behind. Every time a powerful storm swept over the city, Arden held out a faint hope that the tower might have caved in on itself, crushing everyone inside.

It never happened, of course. The damned place had endured storms, riots, revolutions, and sieges for centuries. Arden had a feeling it would stand forever out of sheer spite.

The stone wall surrounding the keep had deteriorated significantly, standing only about ten feet high at the most preserved points, but it still formed an effective defense against the seething masses of Lowtown. Two men stood guard outside the main gate, but they stepped aside when they saw Arden approach.

"Go on in," one of them said. "Mister Dhrath's been asking for you all morning."

Slimy bastard. He should try crawling to the Pigshire guardhouse on all those arms of his. See how long it takes him.

Arden shook the thought aside. He had to focus his mind as narrowly as possible before stepping into Dhrath's audience chamber. The cephalin could pick up careless surface thoughts with alarming ease. Digging out the deeper or carefully guarded thoughts took more effort and usually had some nasty consequences, so Dhrath usually refrained from looking for what someone *really* thought unless he had good reason. Arden knew better than to give him one.

They stepped through the gate and crossed the open yard between the wall and the tower itself. A garden of sorts might have been there once, but now there was nothing but broken, cobblestone walkways and hard-packed dirt. A series of iron drainage grates prevented the rainfall from waterlogging the area, syphoning the water down to the ancient cistern beneath the hilltop's streets.

Arden ignored the man standing watch outside the tower's entrance, instead striding past him and through the open doorway. Two more men awaited them in the keep's antechamber. One of them stepped forward, axe in hand.

"That's far enough," he said.

Arden scowled. "Step aside, son. Mister Dhrath's expecting us."

The guard hefted the axe blade higher so that it rested against his chest.

"Right now, he's busy, so you can wait your turn just like the rest of the punters."

Rheinmak pulled his hood back and chuckled. The guard said nothing more, but his dismissive sneer spoke clearly enough.

Arden had to tolerate a degree of humiliation from Dhrath. He was not about to take the same from a dimwitted thug too stupid to handle anything more complicated than guarding a door, especially in front of an arrogant shitboot like Rheinmak.

Think you're that tough, do you?

He grabbed the guard's axe handle and jerked him close enough to headbutt him on the bridge of his nose. The soft bones snapped against Arden's forehead, and the guard dropped without a fight. Arden pried the axe loose before it hit the ground and rushed toward the other thug. He slammed the blunt side of the single-bladed axe into guard's mailed mid-section as he raised his own weapon, knocking the air from his lungs. The man collapsed, gasping for breath as his axe clattered to the ground. Arden kicked the weapon away and then smashed his boot heel down on the guard's hand to break a few of his fingers.

"There," he said. "Now you've both got something to think about the next time I tell you to step aside."

He tossed the axe across the room and glared at Rheinmak, who no longer looked at all amused by the situation.

"Let's go."

Arden pushed open the heavy door to Dhrath's chamber and stepped inside. The cephalin had already crawled up to his chair, his servant boy standing nearby with the bucket of brine at the ready. A muscular, hard looking cutter stood before him, clad in a sleeveless, fishskin coat that came down to his ankles. His olive skin and wiry, copper hair marked him as a Sarathane Islander, from the archipelago several hundred miles south of Blackspire.

A single glimpse was all it took for Arden to see that the man knew how to handle himself. Unlike the overconfident sods standing guard outside, the Sarathanean was harder, sharper, and colder.

Arden also recognized the fiendish spark in his eyes.

He saw it every time he looked into a mirror.

The gods are wicked and cruel.

A chilling chorus of voices swept through his mind as Dhrath's slimy body quivered on the stone chair.

Arden! What part of wait your turn are you too thick to understand?

Arden shrugged. "You wanted a word with Rheinmak. Here he is."

Dhrath's black eyes stared at him unblinking. Faint whispers tickled his ears and the water gathered on his skin felt like ice. Glimpses of his walk from the Pigshire guardhouse fluttered through his mind. Then he saw the battered guards rolling on the floor in pain.

I don't keep you around to kick in the help's teeth, old man. If I tell the boys outside to make you wait, then you bloody hells better wait. I've got business with Raugov right now. You two know each other?

The voice had a mocking, dismissive tone. It might have belonged to one of his former commanders from his mercenary days.

Arden glanced at the Sarathanean, wondering if Dhrath had spoken to both of their minds, or just to him. Not knowing who was privy to the conversation was the most maddening aspect of talking to the cephalin. If Dhrath spoke to both of them, did they hear the same thing? Arden had no way of knowing for sure.

He wondered what voice the slimy bastard plucked out of Raugov's past to get his point across.

The Sarathanean looked him up and down with a harsh and unyielding glare. Arden found no curiosity in his grey eyes, only a determined, unquestioning certainty. Although Raugov was only a bit bigger in stature, he was younger and almost certainly faster. Arden doubted he could best the man in a fight, at least not in a fair fight.

"Don't believe I've had the pleasure," he said, as much for Raugov's benefit as Dhrath's.

"Raugov. You must be Arden. Heard a lot about you."

I'm sure you have.

Dhrath slapped his water boy across the cheek with one of his tentacles, and the boy emptied his bucket on the cephalin. The water splashed off the chair and onto the floor, where little inclined grooves carried most of it back to the pool behind the stone chair.

Raugov's looking in on some double-crossing scamps for me, letting them know what happens when they don't hold up their end of a bargain. He's got a talent for it. Reminds me of you when you started out. Maybe you should tag along with him, give him a few pointers, eh?

A blend of voices this time. He thought he heard a bit of his father's disappointment.

Pointers. Right.

Arden kept staring at Raugov when he turned back to Dhrath. The slimy bastard must have been telling him something because Raugov took to nodding in silence. When he finally turned away from the cephalin, he gave Arden a broad grin, revealing his sharpened teeth.

"Pleasure to finally meet you, Arden," he said. "I'll see you around."

"I'm sure."

After the Sarathanean left the chamber, Dhrath slipped two of his tentacles off the chair and draped them across the stone floor.

Rheinmak, get over here.

Arden heard the voice clearly, but it sounded like several dozen voices from his memory speaking at once, far too many to interpret. Whatever Dhrath had to say to Rheinmak, he must have thought it was important enough for Arden to hear it too.

The watch captain obeyed, though he approached the throne rather slowly by way of mincing little steps. Arden took a small bit of pleasure from the humiliating sight. Rheinmak stopped a few feet short of Dhrath's outstretched arms.

You're in charge of patrolling High Cross Street, isn't that right?

Rheinmak nodded.

One of my boys was supposed to meet someone there to do a deal a week back, some foreigner by the name of Kaurgen. The guy didn't show, so they went to check out his roof over on High Cross. Story they brought back to me was that you sods had turned the place over, but nobody would say why. I was hoping you could tell me more.

"High Cross is a long street," Rheinmak said. "Got a house number?"

Twelve.

"Yeah, there was some poor scamp that fell into his privy. We had a spader fish him out and then hauled him to the Deadhouse. Next day the landlord paid us to send some men to clean his room out."

The corpse have a name?

"Not that I knew."

Your men find anything when they looked around? Something out of the ordinary?

Rheinmak shook his head. "Nothing I recall."

Several of Dhrath's tentacles twitched. The water boy filled the bucket again and dumped another helping of water over his master.

Bring him closer.

The Duke of Karthea's headsman. No mistaking that voice.

Arden stepped forward and grabbed Rheinmak by the arms. The watch captain stiffened, but Arden pinned one of his arms behind his back before he could squirm free. Dhrath's two outstretched tentacles rose from the floor as Arden shoved Rheinmak forward. One suckered limb coiled around the captain's neck and the other probed around his face and head. Once Dhrath had a firm grip, Arden released him and stepped back

It's not that I think you're lying to me, Rheinmak. Memories are a funny thing. You'd be amazed at how much men don't think they remember. I'd just like to see for myself.

The room fell silent save for the water splashing gently against the stone pool. Rheinmak's face was hidden from view from where Arden stood. He pictured the man's slackened face with eyes opened wide but vacant. As Dhrath dug deeper into his mind, the muscles would begin to tremble, steadily intensifying until his entire body convulsed. If the cephalin maintained contact for too long, he could cause permanent damage. The consequences were difficult to predict. Arden had seen Dhrath leave some men with paralyzed limbs and others with broken minds.

Whatever Dhrath was looking for must not have been buried too deeply because he released Rheinmak after only a few moments. The watch captain dropped to his knees gasping when the cephalin retracted his slithering tentacles.

Lucky bastard.

He felt a sliver of disappointment.

Get him out of here.

"Find what you're after?" Arden asked as he helped Rheinmak to his feet. Dhrath's answer came in the voice of a hardened sergeant Arden served under during the siege of Merth. He never knew the man's real name, but a glare from his good eye made the most quarrelsome men tremble.

Rheinmak took the body to the Deadhouse himself. Went through his pockets and took all the coin first. He didn't find what I'm after, though. After you get him out of here, I need you to track somebody down.

Another errand?

Arden struggled to keep his frustration in check. Any emotional reaction might arouse the cephalin's suspicions. The last thing he needed was Dhrath prodding around in his mind and finding out what he had been up to over the last few days.

"Who do you need me to find?"

A spader by the name of Grisel. He's the one Rheinmak called in to fish Kaurgen's body out of the shit.

The name caught Arden off guard and an image of the spader rolling on the floor cradling his mangled hand flashed through his mind. He reached for a thought to drive the image away, something strong enough to overpower every other concern.

What was that?

His mother's voice.

Arden tensed as he glanced up at Dhrath. He pictured Halvid's little body lying on the bed, his sweat-soaked sheets sticking to his hot, blistered skin.

The boy's sick again, is he?

Arden nodded. "The fever started a few days ago."

I trust this isn't going to interfere with anything?

"Of course not. I'll start looking for this Grisel straight away."

The water boy dumped another bucket of brine onto the cephalin. Dhrath's bulbous flesh quivered at the water's touch.

Good. Bring him to me when you find him, but don't make a scene about it. I don't need the guild making trouble for me if I can help it.

Arden grunted and grabbed Rheinmak by the arm. "Come on, shitheel. Let's leave Mister Dhrath in peace."

He pulled the bewildered watch captain alongside him and walked toward the exit. Dhrath let him go without prying at his thoughts any further, but Arden kept his defenses up all the same, still focusing on his son's condition. When he opened the heavy doors leading into the antechamber, he found the two wounded guards huddled against the far wall. They glared in his direction, but neither one dared to meet his gaze as he strode past them.

Only when they were clear of the keep's outer gate did Arden dare to think about Grisel again. He cursed himself for allowing the spader to get away from him. Losing his best lead on the sorceress proved bad enough, but the situation was far more dangerous now. If Dhrath got his tentacles on the spader, he would know just how much Arden had kept from him.

Dhrath hated secrets. Arden had seen the cephalin make that quite clear on numerous occasions, usually with fatal results.

Grisel. Where the hells have you gotten to?

Arden wondered just what he should do if he managed to find the spader. He would not be able to hide him away again, not without Dhrath finding out. Killing Grisel once he got the information he needed seemed the safest option, but he doubted he could hide that from Dhrath for very long either.

What does that slimy bastard want with him, anyway?

He wished he knew more about the deal Dhrath mentioned to Rheinmak. Grisel certainly had nothing of value when Arden captured him. If the man had taken something, maybe he hid it at his flat or given it to someone he trusted. Arden had planned to look in on the place again anyway. Maybe if he could find what Dhrath *really* wanted, he could get away with keeping Grisel safely away of the cephalin's tentacles.

A lot of "ifs" in that plan...

The rain fell harder as Arden led Rheinmak off Shale Street and onto the slick cobblestones of Goblinscraw. Thunder growled somewhere to the north, in the direction of the spire. The massive structure was scarcely visible through the rain, but Arden still felt like he walked beneath its heavy shadow.

22
THE STAGE

The slender man with thinning hair managed to cross the stage without stumbling. More impressively, he did it without looking at his feet. When he hit his mark at center stage, he threw his shoulders back and scanned the theater as if taking in some newly discovered land.

He had a presence about him, a dour menace that radiated across the stage.

Then he opened his mouth and ruined everything.

His thin, nasally voice cracked like brittle wax when he tried to project his lines to the back of the theater. Every word left him looking a bit smaller, a bit more pathetic. A fragile little man fearful of shattering under the force of a stern wind.

Nicalene rolled her eyes and whispered in Beyland's ear. "Shouldn't we put this poor sod out of his misery?"

Beyland waved her away. "Give him a chance. He can still recover."

Hard to recover something you never had.

She crossed her arms and clenched her teeth as the actor squawked his way through the rest of the scene. Each line felt like a razor scraping across rusty metal. His accent defied identification, but it was pronounced enough to mangle much of what he said. Nicalene peeked at Beyland a few times, but he remained just as impassive as he appeared for the others. No matter how bad the performance, Beyland remained determined to give each one a fair hearing.

Nicalene might have found such consideration admirable if she had not been forced to sit through each performance with him.

"Where did you find this one?" she asked.

"Kardi's worked with him before."

"You mean he's actually performed in public?"

Beyland shrugged. "Well, Kardi didn't say what he did. Might have just posed as a body reference for the artists."

Nicalene leaned forward on the bench to rest her elbows on her knees. The man went on speaking, stumbling here and there over any word longer than two syllables. Much of what he recited came from a lengthy monologue about betrayal. After a long afternoon of watching auditions, Nicalene could have delivered the lines from memory.

She wished Beyland had selected a shorter passage.

Gods take me...

"He looks the part though, right?"

Beyland's question caused her to sit up and take another look at the man. She saw the traces of the scornful, imposing aura he projected earlier, but his sniveling voice had cracked that mask beyond repair. But more importantly, the skin tone was all wrong, the eyes too placid and weak. Maybe Beyland saw something he found noteworthy, but Nicalene could find no qualities to render him worthy of further consideration.

"I don't see it," she said. "Maybe we're looking for different things."

When the man finished, he bowed to his audience and smiled. Beyland clapped, but Nicalene avoided making eye contact. She looked at the floor and leaned down to scratch at her ankles.

"Thank you," Beyland said. "You did a wonderful job. We're not quite finished looking at people yet, but we should have some decisions made in the next few days. Kardi will be in touch."

After giving his thanks, the man gathered up his things and left through the back-stage entrance. Beyland set his pile of notes aside and stood up to stretch his back.

"Well, what did you think?"

Nicalene shook her head. "Miserable. The whole lot of them."

Beyland's shoulders sagged. "Well, I'm afraid this is the best we can hope for. There aren't many actors out there who aren't already associated with a troupe."

"What about your old friends? The ones you used to perform with?"

"Most of them work in Spiresreach now. They haven't shown their faces here in Lowtown for months. Even if they did, it's hard to get someone to sign on without the promise of steady pay. We don't even know if the show will be successful."

Nicalene stood up and placed a hand on Beyland's shoulder. His muscles tensed at her touch. The reaction made her smile.

"Of course, it will be," she said. "You've said yourself that it's your best work. We just need to find the right people for it."

Beyland laughed. "Finishing it might help, too."

"You're almost done now. At the rate you've been going, you should be done in a few days."

"Maybe," Beyland said. "Sometimes the ending is the hardest thing. Especially when it's a tragic ending."

"I would think that's the easy part. Everybody dies, right?"

"No, no, no. Death's the easy way out. In a real tragedy, they're doomed to go on living when they'd rather be dead. The audience needs to see the characters fall farther than they ever thought possible, so far that they want everyone to die, just to spare them the pain of seeing all that suffering. That's what makes real tragedy."

Nicalene thought about how she felt morning she left Grisel's roof for the last time. Did she want to die then? She felt no conscious desire to end her life, just a callous indifference to her eventual fate. Something about that struck her as more tragic than simply longing for death.

Suffering, after all, required feeling.

What did it mean to not care about living or dying?

Something brushed across Nicalene's chest. She looked down to find her free hand rubbing the stone embedded between her breasts.

What do you know about tragedy?

A sharp, tingling sensation rippled along her bones. Feeling lightheaded, she reached out to steady herself against Beyland.

"Are you okay?" he asked.

"Fine. Just tired is all."

"Why don't I help you to your room? You could use some extra rest."

Nicalene wanted to protest, but she had to admit that Beyland was right. She barely slept after glimpsing the ashen woman in the mirror. When she did manage to get any sleep, it proved fitful at best. Dark figures watched her slumbering from the outer fringes of her consciousness. She found dreaming impossible so long as they skulked about in the dense shadows of memory and fear.

"Yeah," she said. "That's probably a good idea."

The day had not quite given way to dusk yet. If she retired to her room now, Nicalene could also avoid talking to Calandra again. Things had been tense since the incident with Beyland two days ago. Calandra decided against throwing her out on the street like she threatened, but she made it perfectly clear that she might change her mind at any time. She had hardly spoken to Nicalene since forcing her to come clean about her bizarre situation.

For his part, Beyland seemed happy to pretend nothing had happened. Nicalene wondered if he somehow forced himself to forget about assaulting his sister. Men, in her experience, had a way of burying their terrible deeds so deep that they forgot where to find them. Beyland did not strike her as that sort of man, though. Considering his sensitive nature, Nicalene imagined him dwelling constantly on his actions or doing everything he could think of to make amends with Calandra.

She found herself tracing the line where the stone fused into her skin.

Maybe she's right. Maybe it's not just affecting me.

Beyland helped her up the stairs and into her room. Nicalene eased herself onto the bed while he went to fetch a nightgown from the wardrobe. The sheet draped over the mirror remained in place.

She neglected to tell Calandra about what she saw there.

That detail would have gotten her kicked out for certain.

"Can I get anything for you?" Beyland asked. He placed the nightgown on the bed beside her. Nicalene nearly smiled when she looked up at him, but the thought of his gentle hands wrapping around his sister's neck drove it away. Not for the first time since that morning, she wondered if some careless word might set him upon her.

"No," she said. "You've done more than enough. Thank you."

Beyland smiled and gave a little bow. "As you wish. I'm going to try to wrap up the last scene tonight. Hopefully when you wake up, we'll have a finished play to peddle."

Hopefully, that will bring in better talent.

"I'm looking forward to it," she said.

Beyland paused at the door long enough to bid her 'good night' before leaving her in peace.

Nicalene locked the door behind him.

ONCE MORE, SHE found restful slumber elusive.

Between the bouts of tossing and turning, she managed only a few hours of light sleep, waking at the slightest noise or change in the air. Twice she sat up, convinced that someone was in the room with her. The first time, she tried to ignore the feeling, pulling the blanket over her head like she had done when she was a little girl afraid of the night. After the second time, she lit a candle and inspected every part of the room for an intruder of some kind.

What she would have done if she found one, she had no idea.

Sleep eluded her after that fruitless, candlelit search. She spent a long while staring into the darkness, occasionally convincing herself she had actually fallen asleep until she realized she was holding her breath. Every gasp brought her back to that room, reminding her there would be no dreams to provide her solace.

For one more night, at least.

Forget this.

Nicalene got out of bed and relit the candle. The shadows danced along the edge of the flickering light like insects scurrying over spilled honey. She still found it hard to believe she was alone.

She opened the wardrobe and inspected the dresses pushed over to one side that she knew fit. Her hand settled upon the ivory-colored dress with the plunging neckline. Instinct told her to put it back, but the fabric was cool to the touch and much lighter than the rest of the clothes she had worn over the last few days. Setting the candle aside, she wriggled out of her nightgown and pulled the ivory dress over her head.

The neckline proved lower than expected, plunging to nearly expose her nipples.

Not much left to the imagination.

The low cut left the black stone in her chest totally exposed. She tried to cover the stone as much as possible but set against the ivory fabric and her pale skin, it seemed to give off a dark glow unlike anything she had seen before. The stone felt warm, raising her body temperature just enough to make her feel a bit uncomfortable in the stuffy, windowless room.

Nicalene smoothed out the wrinkles where the dress bunched up around her hips. The fabric was unfamiliar, but it stretched and contracted slightly to accommodate her figure.

Some foreign style, maybe? Something imported for a special costume?

Whatever it was, it felt good against her skin. The fabric clung to her like water from a fresh spring rain, the sort of rain that never fell from Blackspire's soot-encrusted skies. When she moved, it gave way, breathing along with her.

She glanced at the covered mirror almost by accident at first, an involuntary gesture of curiosity. Good sense and fear forced her to look away for a time, but her gaze slowly drifted back. She ran her hands down her sides, sliding them over her hips and down her thighs.

I wonder how it looks...

The thought of the ashen woman staring back at her with those gleaming teeth and yellow eyes made Nicalene shudder. She stayed away from the mirror after she saw that dark face, and she refused to tell anyone else about it. Part of her held out hope that she imagined the whole thing, that fatigue or paranoia had played tricks on her mind.

Nicalene's hand reached out before she realized what she was doing, pulling the sheet away from the mirror's frame to reveal the polished glass beneath.

She gasped when she saw the figure reflected back at her.

The dress seemed to have been specially woven just for her at precisely this moment. It conformed to every inch of her figure like it was a part of her body. No imperfections reared up to mar the beautiful sight, not even her uneven, frayed haircut. The stone in her chest looked more like an accessory than an affliction, the centerpiece of an exotic ensemble that served only to augment her grace and beauty. Even in the meager candle-light, the color and texture of the fabric made her skin exude a pale, ghostly glow.

"Beautiful..."

She reached up to adjust her hair. It felt strange to her touch, coarser and wirier than she remembered. She leaned closer to the glass, holding the candle close to inspect the top of her head. Nothing about her hair looked unusual, but it still felt unpleasant. As she backed away from the mirror, her gaze focused on the eyes reflected back at her.

At first, she thought the flicker of the candlelight refracting off the glass was playing a trick on her. Moving the candle changed the texture of the image, but not the yellowish gleam in the center of her pupils. She blinked and shook her head, hoping she imagined what she saw.

No matter what she did, the same eyes always stared back at her.

The stone in her chest felt hot, sending rivulets of fire through her veins. She looked at her chest in the mirror and gasped at the sight of spindly, gray tendrils snaking out from the shimmering stone across her skin. They grew quickly to cover her breasts and to reach toward her neck, until they came together to form a solid patch of ashen skin.

When she glanced at her reflected eyes, they were totally yellow now.

Panting, she looked down at her actual body. Aside from the thing embedded in her chest, everything appeared normal. No second layer of skin spread over her flesh, and the black stone seemed totally inert despite the heat building inside her chest.

Slowly, her gaze drifted back to the mirror.

While her reflection completed its bizarre transformation, her body slimmed in places and elongated in others to take on a lithe, almost spin-dled shape. The ash spread all over her skin, covering everything but the stone in her chest and her burning, yellow eyes. Although the reflection moved like it still belonged to her, Nicalene knew better.

Who are you?

The reflection smiled, baring those gleaming teeth again.

What do you want from me?

The woman in the mirror placed a hand over her chest. Nicalene froze, not wanting to look down to see if she copied the gesture.

Strange thoughts came to her, echoes of distant pain and anger. Un-recognizable faces merged with voices from her past, swirling across a landscape of fractured dreams. Even attempting to make sense of it all made her dizzy. Somewhere deep within the torrent, she heard a voice.

Though indistinct and foreign, it called to her, steadying her before the tide sucked her under.

She wanted to reach for it, but fear made her recoil.

And then it all stopped.

The heat dissipated so quickly that she felt like someone dumped a bucket of cold water over her body. Shivering, she pulled her gaze away from the mirror for an instant. When she looked back, the ashen face with the yellow eyes had vanished, replaced by her familiar features and figure.

The stunning ivory gown she marveled at only seconds before was gone, replaced by a ridiculously gaudy white dress. It looked like the mockery of a wedding gown, perhaps intended for some besotted bar wench in a cruel comedy of mistaken identities.

How did I get into this thing?

She ripped the dress off and threw it across the room. Before fetching another garment from the wardrobe, she draped the bed sheet over the mirror again, careful not to look at the glass in the process. She placed her hand over the black stone. It felt cooler to the touch, almost cold.

Did that mean something? Maybe it was cursed. Or maybe she was losing her mind.

What she did know, however, was that she was never taking the sheet off that mirror again.

She donned a brown dress with white and yellow trim. The high collar covered the stone completely, and the garment fit loosely enough to slip over it without any problem.

After getting dressed, Nicalene sat down on the bed, shivering. Every time she blinked, she saw those yellow eyes staring back at her from inside the mirror.

After considering telling Beyland about what she saw, she decided against it. While he would almost certainly believe her, there was a chance that he would do something foolish in a misguided attempt to help her.

And what could he do about it, anyway? Beyland was no scholar, and certainly no sorcerer. At best, he would wind up revealing her existence to everyone living and working in Coldwater. Once that happened, it was only a matter of time before someone took an interest in tracking her down. She already knew Grisel was out there looking for her, but there was a good chance that the watch knew about what did at the *Goat*, not to mention whichever broker supplied the *Goat*'s dealers with their dream-leeches and firedust.

She had to talk to the ghulans again. Maybe they had managed to dredge up some helpful information since her last meeting.

In the meantime, she had no interest in struggling to fall asleep again. Taking up the candle, she rose from the bed and went to unlock the door. Whether she told Beyland about the strange woman in the mirror, she hoped that a bit of human company would do her some good.

BEYLAND SELDOM GOT as much sleep as he needed, that much Nicalene could tell from the moment she met him. When she found him passed out on the stage floor with sheets of paper strewn all around him, she finally understood why.

She tip-toed across the main theater, still dimly lit by a large candle resting beside Beyland. The many sheets of paper strewn across floor were covered with scribbled out passages and the meandering circles Beyland always drew when he was unsure of what to write.

Guess that ending was harder than he thought.

She sat down next to him and looked over a few of the sheets. Much of the scratched bits were rubbish, but she found a few interesting lines and phrases amidst the literary wreckage. He seemed to be having trouble developing his idea of tragedy. Every passage marched inexorably toward death, and each variation of the scenario failed to carry an emotional impact. In two versions of the ending, the mysterious ashen woman committed suicide as her enemies closed in. Another rendition left her captured and put to death. Sometimes Beyland gave up before he even reached the climax, scribbling out what he had written when it became evident that death was the narrative's logical consequence.

As Nicalene compared the multiple failures, she noticed that she found different aspects of them appealing. Each section showed promise that was distinctive, never in contradiction to the others. Taking up Beyland's stylus, she spread the sheets out before her and circled the noteworthy bits. When she finished, she moved the sheets around to see if the highlighted selections would fit together in some logical fashion. She had to tear a few of the pages in half, but a definite pattern emerged as she worked.

The narrative flowed roughly, sometimes jumbling characters and locations in unexpected ways. Yet something held them together, even when she joined seemingly contradictory passages. The haphazard story lurched along in many directions at once, but the undercurrent of a new theme ran beneath them all, an idea that defied the banal tragedy of death. Cloaked in bizarre metaphors and convoluted symbolism, it seemed unbound by logic and defiant of expectation. Nicalene never fancied herself much of a literary mind, but she had little trouble identifying the emerging theme.

Death was but a mundane, comforting tragedy. The prospect of a life unending, unhinged from the comfortable confines of mortal flesh, held much greater potential for sorrow. To exist forever, unbound from morality, from reason, from emotion, seemed a particularly tragic fate.

But Nicalene was no writer. Although she had a strong sense of where the story should progress, she lacked the first idea of how to connect the disjointed passages of her stitched together narrative. Grumbling, she numbered the circled sections. At least when Beyland woke up, he would have some idea of what she managed to pull from his scattered thoughts. After she finished, she stacked the papers in a neat pile beside him with a short note on top telling him what she had done.

The candle burned through most of its length, but not so much that the light had dimmed. Nicalene walked around the stage, gazing over the many rows of benches stretching into the darkness beyond the candlelight. She imagined the eyes watching her from the shadow, captivated by her every movement, her every breath. When she closed her eyes, she could see a faceless mass of onlookers, cold, gray, and distant.

They loved her.

They hated her.

They feared her.

The stone buried in her chest felt hot again, pulsating like a molten heartbeat. She might have imagined what it felt like to stand upon the stage before those adulating, frightened eyes, but it knew, calling forth the potent sensations of an ancient memory to heighten her impression of the moment.

Words came to her lips, but they took the shape of a language unrecognizable to her. They sounded at once harsh and mellifluous to her ear, each syllable urging her body into a corresponding motion.

A loud crash echoed through the theater, snapping Nicalene out of her performance daze. The sound originated behind her, near the backstage area. She saw Kardi stumble out from behind an overturned stack of old crates and into the light. He wobbled for a moment, but once he steadied himself, he reached down to fumble with his pants.

Were you watching me, you little shitsucker?

"Sorry," Kardi said, a little too loudly. "Awfully dark back here. Couldn't see where I was going."

"What are you doing back there?" Nicalene asked.

Kardi started toward her, his head bobbing in time with his uneven steps. "Just got back a bit ago. Had to meet somebody."

At this hour?

Nicalene had a pretty good idea what sort of "somebody" Kardi might meet in the middle of the night.

He smiled as he drew closer to her, his gaze sweeping over her body.

"Heard you talking out here," he said. "Didn't make much sense. Sure sounded nice, though."

You were *watching, then.*

"Just trying out a few things Beyland wrote. Sometimes you need to fill in the gaps. You know how his early drafts tend to jump around."

"Yeah, he doesn't make much sense most of the time. Even less since you came around."

Kardi stopped a few feet short of her. His eyes were wider than normal, the pupils practically floating in a murky, bloodshot sea.

Nicalene recognized the symptom immediately.

"Firedust again?" she asked. "I thought you were taking a break from that junk."

Kardi smiled. The humor in his expression hardened around the edges.

"Gods," he said, spittle flying from his lips as he hissed, "you sound like his bitch sister. She's always nagging at me about something or other."

"Could be you're giving her good reasons for it."

The smile vanished. "The hells you know about me, anyway?"

Nicalene fought the temptation to snap back. Anticipating how a man's temper would change when firedust burned a hole in his lungs was a difficult game.

Might have pushed him too far already.

"Never mind," she said. "You're a grown man. Do what you want."

Kardi's gaze drifted down to her chest. Her dress covered her breasts completely, but it revealed the stone beneath the fabric.

"That thing hurt?"

Nicalene stepped back and placed a hand over her chest.

"No," she said. "I don't really notice it that much."

Kardi moved forward, maintaining the short distance between them.

"I drew more pictures of you," he said, his gaze now slithering all over her body. "Good ones, not like those from the other day. I tried to match every curve, but I might have missed a few."

The smile returned, this time hungry and eager.

"You should model for me again. Let me have a good long look to make sure I get everything right."

Like hell...

"That sounds great, Kardi, but—"

He reached out and grabbed her by the arm.

"Why not right now?"

Nicalene tried to pull away gently, but Kardi tightened his grip. The heat in her chest grew more intense, almost painful.

"Let go," she said, still cautious about making any sudden movements.

Kardi ignored her. "This light is perfect for your skin. That smooth, gray skin."

What...?

He grabbed her other arm and pulled her closer, pressing her body tightly against his. Nicalene squirmed free and shoved him away. The fire in her chest spread to her shoulders and stomach now.

"That's enough!"

Kardi's features hardened, his cheeks and jawbone sharpening beneath the skin as his already bloodshot eyes clouded over with a crimson film. Nicalene tried to back away, but he lunged forward and caught her by the forearm. He wrenched her off balance as his body slammed into her, sending them both tumbling to the stage floor.

No!

Somehow, her free hand found its way to Kardi's throat before he could pin her down. Her nails dug into his skin as a torrent of searing heat raced down the length of her arm.

"No!"

Tiny streams of black fire coursed through Nicalene's fingertips and ripped into Kardi's soft flesh. The flames charred the skin around his neck and spread out in all directions from there, leaving streaks of black ash in their wake. Blisters welled up everywhere the fire touched, some growing as large as a child's fist before hardening and turning black as pitch. Kardi opened his mouth to scream, but the heat dried his mouth out before he could muster a single sound. Seconds later, blisters formed on his tongue and throat to strangle him even as the blood boiled inside his veins and heart. His bloodshot eyes went black, then turned to ooze and leaked from the sockets down his blistering cheeks.

Nicalene watched every moment of Kardi's agonizing death, felt his life burn out like a pile of leaves tossed into a raging inferno. For an instant, Kardi's face vanished and she saw someone else, a cruel, ashen face bent on her destruction.

She did not know the strange man's identity, but she knew she hated him and that he deserved to die a thousand deaths. A smile pushed its way through her lips, followed by deep, cruel laughter in a voice that did not belong to her.

The image faded quickly, replaced by Kardi's quivering, scarred features as their last traces of life burned away. Intense heat gave way to bitter cold, beginning in her chest and then writhing along her skin all the way down to her fingertips and toes.

Only then did Nicalene stop laughing.

She pushed Kardi's blistered corpse away and sat up. Her entire body shivered, even though her dress was soaked through with sweat. Faint wisps of steam rose from the blackened ruin beside her. The stench of burned flesh nearly made her sick, and she refused to look at the body again.

What have I done?

Time bent around her, freezing her in that moment as she stared down at her hands.

What's happening to me?

One of her hands moved to the stone in her chest. Even through the dress's fabric, it felt warm.

"Nicalene?"

The voice should have startled her, but in her state of shock, she scarcely registered the sound. Only when she felt Beyland's hand touch her shoulder did she realize that he had been talking to her for some time.

Nicalene looked up at him. Although his expression betrayed more concern than fear, the balance seemed ready to tip at a moment's notice.

"Are...are you okay?" he asked.

She turned away from him and looked at the smoldering corpse next to her.

"I...I killed him," she said. "Just like the other one."

"What happened?" Beyland asked. "I woke up when you shouted, and then...well, I saw..."

Nothing he said mattered.

From his stunned expression, Nicalene knew he had seen everything.

"He was high on firedust," she said. "We fell down when he grabbed me."

"Was he trying to hurt you?"

Nicalene glared at him.

As if that makes a difference.

"I was scared," she said. "I told him to stop, but he wouldn't listen. And then..."

She looked at the corpse again. The black blisters looked hard, like chunks of polished onyx.

"Beyland, I'm sorry," she said. "I know he was your friend, but—"

"We have to get rid of this."

What?

Nicalene stared at him, not quite believing what she heard.

"Get rid of it?"

"Yes," he said. "We can't have my sister come home to find this! She'll throw you out of here for sure, probably with the help of the watch."

A hundred questions flashed through Nicalene's mind. She wanted to ask them all at once.

"How? Won't somebody come looking for him?"

Beyland shook his head. "Kardi's been running short of friends for a while now. Nobody would be surprised to find him face down in a gutter choked out on nightroot. Calandra might ask where he's gone, but she certainly won't miss him."

Nicalene looked at the corpse again. Maybe Beyland had a point. After all, nobody would have missed her had she died with a dreamleech in her side at the *Goat*.

Nobody except Grisel.

Maybe.

Does he miss me now?

"Come on," Beyland said. "Help me get him wrapped up in one of the curtains. There's a trash heap a few streets away from here. We can dump him there and let somebody else sort him out."

He helped Nicalene off the floor and guided her toward the backstage area. As they walked, she inspected her hands for any trace of burn marks. They looked perfectly normal.

"What is it?" Beyland asked.

Nicalene shook her head.

"I don't know what's happening to me. What if this happens again? Aren't you afraid that I might hurt you?"

Beyland laughed. "No, not really."

"Why not?"

"Because it looks like you've only hurt people that try to hurt you."

He smiled at her, then took her hand and kissed it.

"And I swear to you that I will *never* do anything to hurt you."

You really mean it, don't you?

Nicalene found herself wondering if she found his promise reassuring or frightening.

23

THE RELIC

Grisel woke up to a painful kink in his neck and lower back. His blurry vision cleared a bit after he rubbed his eyes. Coarse strips of cloth covered much of his left hand, rendering it little more than a clumsy stump. Every muscle in his body felt sore and threatened to cramp at the slightest movement. His skin felt wet, clinging to the thin bedsheets drawn over his chest.

He groaned as clouded memories drifted through his mind. Splashing face down into soft muck, strong hands lifting him onto something, and roughspun rags scraping away as much skin as grime. Then the heat, the wretched, feverish heat boiling just beneath his skin. Faces hovered over him and voices echoed in the distance, but all of it seemed so far away.

The older memories came back to him much more clearly. He remembered the dark room with the rats, the barrage of questions, the torturous climb up the privy cesspit.

And there was Arden.

Arden and his axe.

He held his mangled hand over his face and scowled. The wounded fingers were still sore, but the pain was more a nagging reminder of the injury than something that demanded immediate attention. No blood had seeped into the bandaging, which he took as a good sign.

He wondered how long he had been lying on that uncomfortable bed.

Slowly, he tried to prop his upper body up on his elbows.

A strong hand pressed against his chest and pinned him against the bed.

"Down."

That voice...

Grisel looked up and found a familiar, ugly face staring back at him.

"Meaty?"

The big spader smiled. "Morning."

Grisel never felt so happy to see his old friend. If he had the strength, he would have leapt out of bed and hugged the big man.

"Where am I? The guildhall?"

"Naw," Meaty said, shaking his head. "Me and Jaspen's roof."

"How long have I been here?"

Meaty glanced up at the ceiling, his fat fingers ticking off the days. "'Bout a week."

A week? Too much time...

Before Grisel could muster another question, Meaty scooped a ladleful of water from a nearby bucket and held it to his friend's lips.

"Drink."

Grisel gulped the water down. It tasted cooler and sweeter than wine, soothing his parched throat as it slid down to his grumbling stomach.

"Hungry?" Meaty asked.

When Grisel nodded, Meaty set the ladle aside and stood up. "Wait here."

Where do you expect me to go like this?

The big spader lumbered across the room to the small fireplace set into one of the walls. A pot hung on a hook over a pile of red embers. Meaty fetched a bowl and filled it with a few spoonfuls of soup from the pot. Taking the opportunity to ease into a semi-upright posture, Grisel repositioned the pillows under his head. When Meaty returned with the soup bowl, he scowled but did not make a fuss about the new position.

Grisel held his hands out to receive the bowl, but he had difficulty keeping them from trembling. Despite raising an eyebrow at the gesture, Meaty handed the bowl over.

"Careful," he said.

His wounded hand made holding the bowl difficult, but Grisel eventually cradled it against his chest, which freed his right hand to manage the spoon. Meaty snickered as he struggled to get everything into just the right position. On any other occasion, Grisel would have snapped at him, but he was still too happy to see a friendly face again to care.

The soup tasted like stale fish guts. Jaspen never was much of a cook, and Meaty was even worse. Despite the taste, Grisel quickly gulped down several spoonfuls of the stuff. He was too hungry to be picky.

He handed the bowl back to Meaty when he finished.

"More?"

Grisel shook his head. The soup felt like it was gathering in a thick lump in the center of his gut. He hoped he would be able to keep it down.

Meaty set the bowl aside and placed one of his big hands against Grisel's forehead.

"Fever's gone," he said, nodding.

A weeklong fever. Must have been in bad shape.

The door opened before Grisel could ask another question, and he looked past Meaty to see Jaspen step inside.

"Oi! Look who's back among the living." Jaspen joined Meaty at the bedside. "How long's he been up?"

Meaty shrugged. "Just a bit."

Jaspen looked Grisel over. "You look like shit, mate. How you feel?"

"Like shit."

"That's better than the last few days, at least. Fever come back at all, Meaty?"

Meaty shook his head. "Naw."

"Good. We were worried about you for a while there, Grisel. Thought we'd have to haul your ass down to the Deadhouse."

Grisel grunted. "You should be so lucky."

His friends laughed at the quip, but Grisel could see they were relieved.

"How you feeling otherwise?" Jaspen asked. "Still tired?"

"No. Feel like I've done enough sleeping for this lifetime."

"Well that's good, because Meaty and me been dying to know what the hell happened since you ran off to find that backstabbing girl of yours. First you don't show up for your shift for days, then we get word from another crew that you up and stumbled out of the dark buck-ass naked, slicked end to end with shit and missing two fingers. You're lucky Meaty and me are generous sorts to take you in for a spell without any explanation. Ain't that so, Meaty?"

"Generous."

"But now that you're on the mend and back to your cheerful self, I think it's time we had a few answers."

Meaty nodded. "Answers."

Grisel sighed as he tried to gather his scattered thoughts.

"Right," he said. "I'll tell you what I can remember, leastways."

HE DID HIS best to lay out the whole story, starting with the night he left Jaspen's crew to look for Nicalene and wrapping up with the flight through the streets that ended with him passing out in the muck. Jaspen stopped a few times to ask questions or clarify a point, but for the most part, he and Meaty listened in silence. By the time Grisel finished, he felt hungry again. Meaty went to get him another bowl of soup while Jaspen filled him in on what happened after the spader crew picked him up on the night of his escape.

The crew foreman recognized him and knew he had been missing for a few days. Rather than sending Grisel back to the guildhall, he sent word to Jaspen, who had a crew working nearby. After talking it over with Meaty, Jaspen decided that their friend would be better off under their care than the guild's, especially since the guildmasters would ask them plenty of questions they could not answer about what Grisel had been up to for the last few days. His fever had already set in by the time they got him back to the house, but they managed to ride it out with some advice from a local apothecary.

By the time Grisel finished his second helping of soup, his thoughts turned to Nicalene once more.

"Do you know anything else about this Arden?" Jaspen asked.

"He mentioned somebody named Dhrath," Grisel said. "Like it was somebody he worked for."

Jaspen shook his head. "Don't ring a bell. You, Meaty?"

To Grisel's surprise, Meaty nodded. "Broker. Nasty."

"Where's his turf?" Grisel asked.

"Everywhere."

Jaspen scoffed. "You're chewing root, mate. Ain't nobody got that kind of pull in Lowtown."

Meaty shrugged. "What I hear."

"You don't hear shit," Jaspen said. "Who do you even talk to apart from us?"

As much as Grisel liked to give him a hard time, he had to admit that Meaty was not prone to exaggeration. He never shared anything unless he believed it himself.

"You can hear an awful lot when you keep your sodding mouth shut, Jaspen. You ought to give it a try sometime."

Meaty smiled. "Give it a try."

Jaspen glowered, but he choked down whatever insult he had ready.

"If Meaty's right," Grisel said, "then we'll have to be even more careful about what we do next."

"We?" Jaspen asked. "Hold on now, what's this 'we' stuff?"

"What, you think you ain't wrapped up in this already?"

"I think we ought to take this straight to the guild. Tell them that you got caught up in something that wasn't no fault of your own and make sure they keep this Arden guy off your back. Even if his boss has the kind of pull Meaty says, nobody in Lowtown's dumb enough to take on the Spaders."

"And where does that leave Nicalene?" Grisel asked.

"Nicalene? Who gives a damn about her? Maybe you've forgotten, but all this got started when she pinched everything you had stashed away so she could score a bucketful of street junk."

Jaspen was right. Grisel had been so concerned about Arden tracking Nicalene down that he had lost sight of the very reason he went to the *Goat* looking for her in the first place.

The stone.

Did she still have it?

As much as he worried about what Arden might do to Nicalene if he found her, the idea of the stone falling into someone else's hands was equally troubling. If she was smart enough to know what it was worth, there was only one place she could try to sell it.

The ghulans. They've probably got a buyer lined up by now, too.

"Maybe she's done me wrong," he said, "but that doesn't mean she deserves to get chopped into bits by some broker's legbreaker. Besides, if Arden gets his hands on her, then I'll never get anything back."

Jaspen put his hands on his head and groaned. "I can't believe I'm hearing this out of you. There's no way she hasn't spent all your coin by now and you know it."

He had to tell them about the stone. Leaving it out of the story had been easy enough earlier, but now he realized it was the only way to explain why he could not give up on the idea of finding her so easily.

Was it the only explanation, though? What if he just told them he wanted to find Nicalene because he cared about her? Was that reason enough? It seemed like it should be, but he saying so out loud proved too difficult.

"She didn't just take the coin I had stashed," Grisel said.

"What are you talking about?"

"There was something else, something worth a lot more. She probably doesn't even know what it's worth."

"What is it?"

The answer caught in Grisel's throat.

Maybe they didn't need to know *everything*.

"It's hard to explain, but trust me, it's not the sort of thing you want slipping through your fingers. If we can get it back, I'll give you a cut of what it's worth."

Jaspen crossed his arms. "How much are we talking?"

"A lot. Enough to pay off all our guild debts."

That caught their interest.

"And then some."

Jaspen and Meaty exchanged a quick glance. When Meaty nodded, Jaspen looked back to Grisel.

"What do you have in mind?"

Grisel pulled his bedsheets away and swung his legs over the side of the bed. He still felt weak, but he was done with resting.

"First, I need to pay someone another visit. You got a set of clothes I can borrow?"

JASPEN'S CLOTHES FIT poorly. They were obviously made for a man larger than Grisel, and he would have stood out from the rest of the citygoers if not for the long cloak he wrapped around his body. The cloak was heavy and hot, causing him to break into a sweat before he made it to the first intersection beyond Jaspen's door.

Grisel wished he could simply go back to his place to grab his own clothing, but he worried that Arden might have tracked down his roof somehow. There was a chance somebody had his place under watch . For all he knew, the Tammercum brothers might be on Dhrath's take, or maybe even one of his less objectionable neighbors. He hoped Sedina would not go out of her way to sell him out, but expecting her to take any risks on his behalf was too much.

Best to just steer clear for now.

The short walk from Jaspen and Meaty's place in Pigshire to the ghulans' shop in Coldwater usually didn't take long, but Grisel's attempts to avoid notice made the journey much longer. He kept his head down and tried not to walk too quickly. The two watch patrols he passed barely gave him a second look, and most of the other people milling through the busy streets ignored him so long as he stayed out of their path.

He peeked behind him every so often, each time half-expecting to spot Arden tailing after him. After going a week without shaving his face or head, Grisel hoped that he looked different enough that Arden might not recognize him at first glance. His chin and scalp itched horribly, bad enough that he seriously considered shearing his stubbled hair away before he left. Meaty talked him out of it. The cloak was the big spader's idea too. Grisel wondered how Meaty knew so much about brokers and staying out of sight. Nobody expected a spader to know the first thing about that sort of business.

Maybe that's why you don't talk so much. Too many secrets.

Grisel walked past the ghulans' shop a few times before he felt confident nobody else was there. Heavy curtains blocked each window, making it impossible to see inside, but the doors never budged. Unless someone had gone in to conduct lengthy negotiations before Grisel arrived, the place seemed likely to be empty.

He opened the door and stepped into the cluttered shop. Once the door closed, the darkness swept in around him. The ghulans usually kept a candle or lantern burning near the back of the shop to keep customers from knocking anything over when they came in, but the far wall remained completely drenched in thick shadow.

"Carta? Uthan? Anybody here?"

Something shuffled across the floor on the opposite side of the shop. "Friend Grisel?"

A spark ignited the oiled wick inside a lantern to illuminate the center of the room. Uthan stared at him, holding the lantern aloft. The ghulan wore the same heavy goggles and grayish-brown coat with green trim from every other time Grisel had seen him.

"Not very inviting in here," Grisel said. "You trying to scare people off?"

A tittering giggle bounced from the darkness as Carta stepped forward to join Uthan.

"There's much work to be done, friend Grisel," she said.

"And work is best done in the shadow."

"But we welcome the light when it brings long-missing friends."

"Yeah," Grisel said. "I know it's been a while."

He waited for the ghulans to ask him where he had been for so long, but they just went on staring at him.

"Um, I don't suppose you've found a buyer, have you?"

The ghulans looked at each other. Uthan whispered something into Carta's ear. She listened and nodded.

"Buyers we have at the ready," she said.

"But there is no treasure to sell," Uthan said.

"A pity you could not trust us, friend Grisel."

Damn. They know I've lost it.

"Nicalene. She brought it to you, didn't she?"

"She came to us, yes," Carta said.

"Though not to sell what she had taken."

"Why then?" Grisel asked.

"Come and sit with us, friend Grisel," Uthan said.

"We have learned much."

"And you must know as we do."

Carta stepped forward and took his wounded hand. "You are...less than whole."

Uthan leaned closer to inspect the bandaging, then gestured to one of the nearby shelves.

"We have much to ease your pain," he said.

"Should you have need."

Grisel shook his head. "No, it's fine. Just a little sore is all."

"A peculiar injury for a spader," Carta said.

"Perhaps earned through some other trade?"

Grisel considered telling them about Arden, but then he remembered that despite their innocent appearance, the ghulans were well connected to Lowtown's many brokers. For all he knew, they were in deep with Dhrath or someone like him.

He pulled his hand away from Carta's grasp.

"Rat bites," he said. "Nasty ones. Stuck my hand down a hole without burning it out first. Little bastards got me down to the bone. Had to chop them off to keep the rot from spreading to the rest of the hand."

The ghulans exchanged a long glance. Finally, Carta smiled at him. Something about the expression made Grisel uncomfortable. Was it a show of support? Amusement? He had a hard time sorting out the intent, especially since her eyes remained obscured by those damnable goggles.

"Terrible," she said

"Unfortunate."

Yeah, yeah, it's a real tragedy. Let's get on with it.

"Well, I'm trying not to think about it too much, so can we get back to what you needed to tell me?"

The ghulans nodded and then responded in unison. "As you wish."

"Your treasure is a rare one indeed, friend Grisel," Carta said.

"And ancient," Uthan said. "Older than the city itself."

"But still a part of it."

What the hells does that mean?

The ghulans exchanged another of their long glances, after which Uthan nodded.

"Come, friend Grisel," Carta said, extending her little hand.

"It will be easier to show you," Uthan said.

Grisel shrugged and took the ghulan's hand. She led him over to the shop's door, but she paused before opening it to pull her coat's hood over her head and wrap a scarf around her face. Uthan, trailing behind them, did the same.

After she and her partner covered up every bit of exposed skin, Carta turned the door handle and stepped outside, pulling Grisel along as she went. They walked around to the southernmost point of the circular inter-section down the street from the ghulans' shop and turned to face northward.

Uthan joined them and pointed to the sky, just above the roofline op-posite the stone cistern standing at the heart of the intersection.

"I don't get it," Grisel said. "What are—?"

Then he saw it.

It had always been there, of course, but it was so much a part of the cityscape that he took it for granted when Uthan pointed it out.

Briny clouds obscured its higher reaches and a haze of smoke clung to its foundations, but the main portion of the spire stood out clearly on the horizon, looming over the city like a black gravestone.

No bloody way...

"You think it has something to do with the spire?"

The ghulans tittered at the question.

"No, friend Grisel," Carta said, her childish voice taking on an amused, mocking tone. "Not 'something' to do with it."

"Everything, you might say," Uthan said.

Grisel thought back to the stone's characteristics, its rough-hewn shape, the smooth surfaces casting no reflections, the way it absorbed the light, the disquieting sense of "otherness" when he touched it.

"What, you think it's a piece of the spire?" he asked, raising an eyebrow. "That's impossible. Nothing living can get within a hundred yards of the damned thing. Everybody knows that."

"There are many things lost to this world, friend Grisel," Uthan said.

"Many practices forgotten," Carta said. "Much knowledge forsaken."

"But the city still dreams. And it remembers."

"If you know how to listen."

Grisel fought to keep from laughing. The ghulans' story sounded little better than the ridiculous tales of travelling charlatans who posed as alchemists to sell vials of lakewater to gullible farmers.

"Okay," he said, "let's say for a moment that I actually believe this crazy theory. What does any of it have to do with Nicalene coming to see you?"

Carta and Uthan looked at each other for a moment before they continued.

"Any portion of a greater whole retains some portion of the whole's power," Uthan said.

"Friend Nicalene has done something to awaken that power," Carta said.

"Given time, that power will consumer her."

"Unchecked, it could threaten all of Blackspire."

Grisel shook his head. "This is crazy. You actually expect me to believe this?"

Uthan shrugged. "We saw it with our own eyes, friend Grisel."

Carta nodded. "It has already joined with her, channeled its power through her."

"And taken at least one life already."

That got Grisel's attention.

He thought back to his first meeting with Arden and the blackened, blistered body he had seen that night at the *Goat*. Nicalene had been there, that much he knew for certain.

Could this be why Arden's after her?

Grisel looked down at the ghulans, but he could read nothing behind their dark goggles and scarves.

"Okay," he said, "tell me more."

"THAT'S THE DUMBEST heap of dung I've ever heard."

Meaty nodded. "Dumb."

"Look," Grisel said, "I don't know about all the ancient history and magic nonsense, but I know for damn sure that Arden thinks Nicalene was responsible for that corpse I saw at the *Goat*."

Jaspen groaned. "Grisel, mate, we've been over this. You said the guy looked like he had some kind of plague."

"But why would Arden be after Nicalene, then? She's got to be involved with it somehow. Besides, if what the ghulans said about the stone bonding with her is true, then—"

"What, that it's embedded inside her chest? Do you have any idea how stupid that sounds?"

Grisel shook his head. He had been arguing with Jaspen since he returned from the ghulans' shop and relayed the whole bizarre story. While he had his own doubts about many of the details, the ghulans seemed convinced by what they saw and researched. They were a strange pair, but as far as Grisel knew, their reputation for accuracy was well deserved. There was a reason, after all, everybody went to them to find out what things were worth.

"I ain't asking you to believe it, Jaspen, just that you cut me some bloody slack until I can find out what's really going on here."

Jaspen glared at him for a long while, then glanced over at Meaty. "What do you think about all this?"

The big spader shrugged but said nothing.

"Big help, you are," Jaspen said.

Grisel grabbed the cloak off the bed and wrapped it around his shoulders.

"Where you off to, then?"

"I've got to meet with this contact the ghulans have been talking to," Grisel said. "They say she's got the knowing of this sort of thing, that she might be able to do something about it."

"She got a name?"

"They called her Twiceborn, said she used to be the pet sorcerer for some High Ridge wank till he got tired of her and ran her across the river."

Jaspen grunted. "Sounds like a prize."

"Prize," Meaty said, chuckling.

"Where you meeting her?"

"Some winesink she likes on the north side of the borough, just on the lip of Sinkhole off Hogsgut."

"*Sapper's Belfry?*" Jaspen asked.

"Yeah, that's the one. You know it?"

"Heard of it. Never been there, though. You, Meaty?"

Meaty nodded. "Rough."

"There you have it," Jaspen said. "All the more reason to forget about all this and take your problems to the guild."

"What, you don't want a cut of the take once I get this thing back?"

Jaspen scoffed. "You don't even know if she's still in Lowtown. When was the last time the ghulans saw her, anyway?"

Grisel hated admitting it, but he shared Jaspen's concern. Nicalene had not returned to the ghulans after her initial visit, even though they had spent a lot of time gathering information for her. They figured she was just lying low, but Grisel worried that her absence might have more to do with Arden.

"About a week back."

Jaspen slapped Meaty on the arm. "You hear that? A week. She could be halfway to Marlorg by now."

That might have made sense to Jaspen and Meaty, but Grisel knew Nicalene better than that. She had grown up in the city, lived her entire life beneath the shadow of the spire. Where would she go if she left? Rickenwick? Kormur? They were mudroofed hovels next to sprawling Blackspire. She might be able to fall in with a landed Marlorgian nobleman for a time or win the admiration of some upstart shopkeeper in Selarna, but they would never be able to hold her interest for long. Sooner or later, she would yearn for the sounds of her birthplace, for the noxious scents and grisly sights that kept her senses on edge whenever she walked its snarled streets.

"No," Grisel said, "she may try to get out of Lowtown, maybe find a way to cross the river, but she won't leave the city."

Jaspen glared at him for several seconds before throwing his hands up.

"Fine, you stubborn shitheel. Do whatever you want. But if you don't come up with something worthwhile in the next two days, Meaty and me are dragging your skinny ass back to the guild to sort out this Arden business."

"Wait now, that ain't enough time to—"

"Two days, Grisel! You're in enough trouble as it is and I ain't about to get Meaty and me dragged into it. You don't like it, you can walk out that door and never come back. Now what's it going to be?"

Jaspen was right, of course. Grisel knew that. Every time he stepped outside, he put his friends at risk. He rubbed the bandaged nubs on his left hand. Arden was unlikely to waste time with fingers if he got the chance to interrogate him again.

And there was no telling what he might do to Jaspen or Meaty if he got his hands on them.

Grisel sighed. He had enough on his conscience already.

"Fine," he said. "Two days."

SAPPER'S BELFRY DID more than just sit on the edge of Sinkhole.

A good portion of the place literally dangled over it.

Nobody quite knew what caused the tower to fall over, but it had rested on its side for as long as anyone living could remember. Popular legend had it that some nefarious landlord had sapped the ground beneath its foundation to send it toppling down before swooping in to buy the place for a song. A competing tale maintained that it crumbled in the same quake that gave birth to Sinkhole, and the landlord simply rebuilt the interior sideways when he failed to sell the ruined property.

Whatever the truth, *Sapper's Belfry* remained one of Lowtown's more unique locales.

The tower lay entirely on its side, the uppermost peak now reaching over the slope leading to Sinktown. Wooden beams driven into the muddy hillside propped the hanging section up, but given their poor condition, only the winesink's bravest patrons requested one of the private booths tucked into the extreme end of the fallen tower.

Inside, the place looked much like any other cheap winesink in Pigshire. Whatever decorative arrangement the tower once featured had been stripped and replaced to accommodate its current horizontal orientation. An uneven wooden floor ran the length of the interior, forming the only flat surface in the otherwise circular structure. The walls and ceiling formed an unbroken arch that stretched about twenty feet at its widest point just above the floor. Wine and ale barrels were stowed beneath the floor, accessible by trap doors located behind the main serving counter. The only light came from the rusty candelabrums hanging from the ceiling, which were low enough to make some of the taller patrons duck their heads.

Sapper's Belfry did not serve food, catering mainly to Pigshire's poorest workers and the few Sinkhole wretches lucky or nasty enough to scrape together a few marks. Fights were common, especially when the place filled and space became tight. There were a few tables scattered along the length of the old tower, but many regulars simply sat on the floor when all the seats were taken.

Grisel found the place easily enough. Dusk had settled over the city by the time he got there, and the tables were already filling up. He followed a small group of butcher's boys through the front door. Nobody gave him a second glance as he made his way to the serving counter.

The keeper looked too young to be the owner. Maybe a son or a trusted relative? Grisel hoped he at least spent enough time there that he could remember everyone.

He paid a tenthmark for a cup of wine and downed it in three gulps. The drink proved sour and drier than he would have liked, but it went down easy enough. After he finished, he paid for another. He leaned over the counter as the keeper filled his cup.

"I'm looking to find one of your regulars," he said. "Woman by the name of Twiceborn?"

The young man finished pouring the drink and looked Grisel over slowly.

"You don't look like a watch man. Or a broker's cutter."

Grisel shook his head. "Just an honest working man."

"Wasting your time, mate. Don't think that one's got much use for honest men."

"I'd rather let her sort that, if you don't mind?"

The keeper shrugged and pointed to the far end of the building, the old tower peak.

"Suit yourself," he said. "She came in about an hour ago. Always takes the last booth. We used to charge for it, but nobody else ever wants to sit out there."

That because they're afraid of it falling or afraid of her?

"Thanks."

Grisel took his cup and walked the length of the building, stepping over drunks and avoiding overexcited patrons as he went. A series of wooden booths, complete with benches and tables, lined each wall at the far end of the winesink. Before he reached the first one, Grisel felt the floor shift slightly beneath his feet. The movement was not severe enough to make him lose balance, but it reminded him that nothing held the room aloft beyond rotting wood braces and crumbling masonry.

One by one, he made his way past the private booths. None of them were occupied, and nobody had even bothered to light the candles sitting at each table. However, a faint glow emanated from the last booth on the left, and when he reached it, he found a surprisingly young woman sitting alone with a large cup of wine.

Thin as a twig, the woman's short hair was as black as the Saven's waters at midnight, save for a few scattered streaks of white and gray. Her narrow face had a predatory, almost reptilian quality, and her skin looked frightfully pale. She wore a tan shirt with long sleeves that Grisel mistook for leather at first, but it hung too loosely from her shoulders to be animal hide. Immediately, he recognized the leather overalls and the mask sitting on the table next to her cup.

She's a spader?

No, he decided quickly. Not with hair like that. It would wind up encrusted with filth after even the easiest shift, same as the long-sleeved shirt.

She looked up at him, her unsettling black eyes solid and without pupils.

"You lost or something?" she asked.

Her voice left a chill in the air. Grisel tried his best not to shiver.

"No," he said. "I'm looking for someone named Twiceborn. Uthen and Carta sent me."

The woman smiled, her yellow teeth gleaming in the candlelight. "You must be Grisel."

He nodded. "Yeah."

She stood and extended her hand.

"Pleased to meet you, Grisel. Your friends are fond of formality, but Twiceborn is a bit of a mouthful in conversation. You can call me Tameris."

Grisel shook her hand. The grip was stronger than he expected.

"Tameris, then," he said. "Is Twiceborn some kind of nickname? A title or something?"

She flashed her yellow teeth again. Grisel half-expected a forked tongue to dart between them.

"You could say that."

More useless answers. She's as bad as the ghulans.

"Listen, Uthan and Carta said you might know a thing or two about this...um...problem with...um..."

"They told me what you want to know. You're here about the stone."

"Yeah, that."

Tameris gestured to the bench across the table.

"Sit with me and share a drink," she said. "We have a lot to discuss, you and I."

"That so?" Grisel asked as he slid into the booth.

"Let's start with you telling me about the body you pulled out of the privy over on High Cross."

Grisel nearly jumped out of his seat.

"How the hells do you know about that?"

Tameris smiled. "Let's just say I heard it from a mutual acquaintance."

He supposed she could have talked to Rheinmak or one of his men, or maybe one of the building's other tenants. But that did not quite add up. How could she possibly know that poor dead bastard in the privy had any connection to the stone?

"Not much to tell, really. The floor gave out while the poor sod was taking a shit, and he drowned when he fell to the bottom of the cesspit."

"What about the stone? Did he have it on him when you found him?"

Still dumbfounded by her apparent insight, he stared at her.

How could you possibly know that? Nobody saw what happened down in that cesspit. Nobody but me and the sodding corpse.

A cold lump formed in Grisel's stomach as he processed that last thought. The ghulans told him that Tameris was a sorceress of some sort, but they avoided elaborating on what manner of sorcery she practiced.

Her curious sobriquet, *Twiceborn*, suddenly seemed far more sinister than he imagined earlier.

"No," he said, shaking his head slowly. "It was on a cord, but I tore it loose by accident. Found it sitting on a bit of floorboard in the water."

"How fortunate."

Yeah, real lucky...

"There was something weird about it," he said. "I had to take my mask off at one point to call out for the watchmen to pull the body up. When I looked at his face, he seemed to come alive for a second. I thought I was just hallucinating from the fumes, but it sure seemed real in the moment."

Tameris nodded slowly. "No, you probably saw him true. Prolonged contact with the stone might well have imparted him with some spark of life. Not enough to reanimate him fully, of course, but enough to snap him back from the dark for an instant."

"How do you know so much about this?"

She smiled, flashing her yellowed teeth once again. "Did you know anything about him? How did you end up there in the first place?"

"No idea who he was. The watch showed up asking for a spader to fish out a floater. Rest of the crew said it was my turn."

"Not so fortunate."

"It didn't seem like that at first," he said. "Not after I found that stone. What is it, anyway? Is it really a piece of the spire like the ghulans say?"

Tameris took a drink of wine. The red liquid left a faint stain around her pale lips.

"Have you ever seen the spire, Grisel? Up close, I mean."

Grisel shook his head. He disliked admitting that he had rarely set foot beyond the boundaries of Lowtown.

"I don't remember much about my childhood, but I remember the spire. When I first came here it was all I could think about, all I wanted to talk about. I begged my mother to take me to the wall, to look out over The Break and see the true heart of the city. But she was just a servant girl in Crowngate. Couldn't afford to pay the passage tolls over the Saven even if she somehow got permission to stand atop the wall."

She took another drink before continuing.

"When I just couldn't stand it any longer, I ran away. Figured I could be there and back within a day or two if I was careful. Stowed aboard a ferry ship and slipped past the patrol sentries at the base of the wall in Spiresreach. A guard spotted me halfway up one of the stairways and chased me the rest of the way. I managed to get a good look from the top for a few moments before he caught up and gave me this."

Tameris turned her head to the right and traced a nasty scar running from an inch above her temple down to the base of her jawbone.

"But being so close...seeing all that shattered ground surrounding it... I've never felt so small and meaningless. It was like...standing at the feet of a god...a god that might step on you because he just doesn't care whether you exist or not."

She sipped at her wine and licked her reddened lips.

"Why are you telling me this?" Grisel asked.

"Because you need to understand what we're dealing with. The spire contains more power than you can possibly comprehend. Even a small fragment of its substance might be dangerous enough to destroy thousands of lives, and that's if the person using it doesn't know the first thing about using that power."

"And what if they do?"

"If you dig deep enough into the city's history, you can find stories about self-styled sorcerer kings who used shards of the spire to amplify their magic. They laid entire kingdoms to waste. Most of those stories are legends, but there are few with better claims to truth, especially the ones involving the Nosgarrians."

The mention of the infamous island kingdom on the far side of the world made Grisel's mouth dry. As far as he knew, there were few stories about the Nosgarrians which did not involve some combination of blood, fire, and death. Every few years, a Nosgarrian ship sailed up the Saven to conduct some trade or political negotiation and set the entire city on edge.

"What does that mean for Nicalene?" he asked.

Tameris leaned back against her seat and took another drink of wine. "I don't know yet. The ghulans tell me the stone has physically joined with her and she's already channeling its powers, if unknowingly. She also told them she has strange thoughts sometimes, thoughts that aren't her own."

"What could that mean?"

"Many of the records and stories detailing spire fragments mention that they absorb not just light, but also intangible things like memories, emotions, and souls. A skilled sorcerer might be able to draw those contents forth, but without guidance, they can well up to the surface unbidden. The longer she's in direct contact with the fragment, the more difficult it will be for her to distinguish between her own thoughts and memories and the echoes trapped inside the stone."

Grisel rubbed his forehead. He hoped this meeting would give him solutions, not complicate things even further.

"Are you saying Nicalene might not even be Nicalene anymore by the time we find her?"

Tameris shrugged. "It's possible, but it depends upon a lot of factors. Her force of will, her empathy, her fears, her dreams. That's why I need to know more about her. There could be things about her that make her particularly susceptible or resistant to the forces within the stone."

"Like what?"

"Anything that could make a personal connection with a memory or a soul trapped inside, something held in common. Like a shared ambition or personal tragedy."

Nicalene had no shortage of misfortune, broken dreams, and trauma. Grisel had seen her descend into a self-destructive spiral on many occasions. Adding a potentially devastating magical force to that reaction could prove deadly for anyone coming into contact with her.

"What happens if those forces overwhelm her?" he asked. "What if all of her memories and emotions get sucked into the stone with the…other things that are already trapped there? What happens to Nicalene then?"

Tameris shook her head. "Gone."

The finality of the answer hit Grisel hard. He gulped down more of his wine.

"Let's say we manage to find her," he said. "Could you remove the fragment from her chest?"

Tameris thought for a moment before answering. "I believe so. Theoretically, it should be a simple matter of fleshcraft."

"Theoretically," she says…

The qualification made Grisel uneasy, but he doubted she would give him a straightforward answer if he pressed her.

"So where do we start?" he asked.

"First, we'll need to find her, naturally. That shouldn't be too difficult. I presume you still have access to some things of hers? Clothing? Personal effects? The like?"

Grisel nodded. He would have to risk returning to his flat. Arden might well be watching for him there, but there was no alternative.

"In the meantime, I want to hear everything you know about Nica-lene," Tameris said. "But before we start, I need you to tell me something else."

"What's that?"

"Do you love her?"

Grisel stared at Tameris, unsure of how to answer.

Did he even have an answer?

"I...I don't know."

"Well, you'd better figure it out soon, because if we do this, you may be forced to make some difficult choices."

The question echoed through Grisel's head.

Do you love her?

It stayed with him even as he described Nicalene to Tameris.

Do you love her?

By the time he finished, the question was deafening, driving all thought from his mind.

Do you love her?

He was no closer to an answer.

24

THE SUCCESSOR

L orvie Tinderhov never reached the Morangine estate.

When Ember returned home after his meeting with Twiceborn, Yimina told him no one came knocking at the gate that day. The next morning, he left the manse early to visit the Tinderhov estate over on Flatbottom Street before going to the Assembly Hall. He hoped that perhaps she had panicked and returned home instead of going to his place, that he might find her there curled up beneath her blankets like she used to do whenever a great storm swept over the city.

But his slim hopes faded as soon as he arrived. The household servants had not seen her since she left for the Assembly Hall the previous morning. Even as he asked them if she ever failed to return home, he already knew what the answer would be. After offering some assurances that she would most likely turn up soon, Ember left the servants to their consternation and headed for the Assembly Hall.

He ducked into the first alleyway he came upon and threw up.

Ember spent the next few days glancing over his shoulder and squinting at shadows everywhere he went. Except for Assembly meetings, he refused to leave the house, and even then, he made sure to keep to high traffic streets in the daylight hours. Travelling anywhere at night was out of the question, even when Yimina offered to accompany him. Every morning he woke fearing he would find Raugov waiting for him in his sitting room. Or outside his front door. Or a hundred paces down the street. Or in his bed chambers when he retired for the night.

Dhrath lurked in the dark corners of his dreams, always out of sight. He could hear the cephalin's slimy skin sliding across the floor and his razor-sharp beak gnashing at the air. Sometimes, he saw Lorvie. Poor, stupid Lorvie, who never hurt a living soul in her short life. Her face was black now, the air choked out of her by the suckered tentacle wrapped around her neck. When he blinked, Lorvie's bloated face vanished, replaced by Trinn Harmyndri and her bulging, vacant eyes. The tentacle squeezed her throat, forcing a thick gulp of wet air upward.

His father's drunken voice gurgled through her lips.

"Another throw, lad, just one more throw and I'll win it all back. You'll see."

After two days, Lorvie's steward took to visiting the Deadhouse to find his mistress. Her corpse turned up a day later, battered, bloated, and torn. After an extensive examination, the undertakers concluded that she had been strangled and beaten to death.

"A mugging, they think," the steward told Ember. "Her necklace and rings were gone. Must have tried to put up a fight when they confronted her."

Lorvie putting up a fight over jewelry. The very idea nearly made him laugh. When Lorvie was a girl, her mother made her stop wearing jewelry altogether because she kept giving it away to beggars. Ember had not seen any indications of that generosity fading after she reached adulthood.

In any case, her death garnered little attention in Lowtown. Despite her family's illustrious history, Lorvie lived a very private life, rarely stepping outside her estate's outer wall. As an Assembly member, she was neither loved nor hated, and so no one felt compelled to lament or celebrate her passing.

With no heirs or next of kin to pass her seat along to, however, Lorvie's death threatened to spark a heated debate over how to replace her. Ember expected her seat to be opened up for purchase, a practice well-founded in precedent, but only after a challenge from the Assembly's popularly elected members, who would no doubt push for the seat to be filled by way of a plebiscite.

That debate, however, never had a chance to play out. On the day the Assembly announced news of Lorvie's death, a stable boy found Trinn Harmyndri's body hidden in a wagon beneath a pile of straw.

Then all hell broke loose.

Word of Trinn's death spread quickly. The next morning, an angry crowd gathered outside the Assembly hall, replacing the usual line of petitioners. Ember slipped through a side entrance when he arrived, but by midday, the crowd encircled the building, blocking off every exit and demanding to be heard. The Assembly responded by barring the gates and refusing to hear any petitions until the crowd dispersed. A lowly scribe announced the decision from a second story balcony.

He almost got to the end of the statement before someone in the crowd below heaved a stone at him.

The riot escalated quickly after that first act of violence. Rocks and chunks of brick pelted the Assembly hall, most of them bouncing harmlessly off the stone walls, but some smashing through windows and denting wooden doors. The Coldwater Watch sent a detachment of men to scatter the crowd before sunset, but their efforts amounted to little. There were simply too many protesters for a small group of armed men to handle. After fighting through the crowd, the watch did manage to secure the entrances to the hall, but they proved unable to clear a path for the Assembly members to leave.

Until the crowd dispersed, the Assembly was trapped inside.

Night arrived, but the standoff went on without change. Forced to spend the night barricaded within the Assembly hall, Ember snuck up to the second story windows to peek outside. The crowd seemed to grow by the hour. He tried to get some rest, but the incessant shouting and occasional barrage of rocks made sleep all but impossible.

His colleagues fared no better. Most of them could barely keep their eyes open the next morning.

Ithlene, Armille, and Cambin avoided making eye contact with him. He was not surprised by that. They had hardly even spoken to him since the failed voting incident a few days earlier.

This is all your fault, you idiots.

Ember waited for the remaining Assembly members, eleven of them now in all, to arrive before he spoke out. "So...do we know what they want beyond some poor sod's head on a pike for Trinn's murder?"

Murga Lochmas shifted his considerable bulk to point at Selinis and Harik. "Ask those two! They're the ones who answer to that rabid mob!"

"The people have a right to be angry after what happened to Trinn," Selinis said. "We owe them an answer, at the very least."

Ember glanced at Mendin, Tarsa, and Rendulcar. Whatever threats Dhrath and Raugov's thugs used to frighten them into submission must have been quite convincing. They had said very little in the days following their "missed" vote. Not that they had much choice, of course. With most of the watch's officers on the take from Dhrath, there was no one for them to turn to for help.

This was what you had in mind from the beginning, wasn't it, you bastard? Get your hooks into a few of us, and then lean on the others to control the entire Assembly.

Ember would have admired the cephalin's scheme if not for one of those hooks being embedded in his own skin.

"Who gives a damn what they want?" Cambin asked. "They're in a state of open rebellion as far as I'm concerned. When the watch gathers in strength, they'll haul every last one of them off to the gallows."

Ember chuckled. "You haven't looked out a window lately, have you? The entire Coldwater Watch doesn't have the manpower it would take to scatter the crowd, much less arrest everyone."

"Then we call on the other boroughs," Armille said. "Surely there's enough men between Coldwater, Pigshire, and Carbuncle to drive off this rabble."

"And how long do you think that will take?" Mendin Urbrike asked. "By the time they get here, those animals will have torn us to pieces."

Harik Gondulin bolted up from his seat. "Animals? What gives you the right to—"

"Oh, sit down, Harik," Ithlene said. "Everyone knows how much you care for supporters. What we don't know is if they still feel the same about you."

Harik stammered. "Are you implying that—"

"Don't think your beloved people haven't noticed you lining up to sample every perfumed whore in Coldwater." Ithlene sneered and jabbed her finger at him. "Maybe if you'd spent more time tending to their needs, they wouldn't feel the need to tear down the whole damn Assembly when their precious Trinn turned up dead!"

"How dare you suggest—?"

Ember stood up and slammed both hands down on his desk. "That's enough! Both of you! If we keep going at each other like this there won't be anything left for the crowd to string up when they batter the front gate down."

The long silence followed his outburst. Ember regarded each of the Assembly members in turn, his mood darkening a bit after every face.

Gods help us. None of you have any idea what to do next, do you?

In all honesty, Ember never held his colleagues in high regard. Part of that attitude stemmed from an aristocratic arrogance ingrained in him by his privileged upbringing, but he also had enough of his grandmother's political acumen to recognize when he was the smartest person in the room. As much as he had hated Trinn, at least he could respect her ability to form a coherent argument, determination to get results, and courage to speak her mind against opposition.

Ember laughed.

"What's so funny, Morangine?" Cambin asked.

"Nothing. Just a bit of gallows humor." He sat down and rang the small bell on his desk to summon an Assembly scribe.

"What are you doing?" Ithlene asked.

Ember shrugged. "Well, unless anyone here has a better idea, I suggest we listen to their demands before they lose any interest in talking."

Armille snorted. "Consider the demands of that mob? Are you mad?"

"As citizens of Lowtown, they have a right to be heard." Ember took up a stylus and scribbled instructions down on a sheet of parchment. "And as the lawfully selected members of the Assembly of Notables, we have an obligation to listen. Isn't that right, Selinis? Harik?"

As the two remaining Assembly members chosen by popular vote, they should have understood that better than the others. While they did not leap to Ember's defense, they straightened a bit in their seats.

That makes three.

Murga folded his fat arms over his chest. "What do you propose, Morangine?"

"We need to give them a chance to be reasonable. Right now, they're driven by ignorance and anger." Ember looked up from writing to scan the seated Assembly again. "Some of them might even have the misguided notion that we had something to do with Trinn Harmyndri's murder. We'll ask them to nominate representatives to present a lawful petition before the Assembly. Once they know we're willing to listen, they'll be forced to figure out what they really want to say."

Murga's face scrunched up as he glanced in turn to Rendulcar and Norvel, who sat on either side of him. They exchanged a few hushed words before nodding.

Six.

"And what makes you think they want to talk?" Mendin asked. "Most of those animals are baying for our blood."

Ember nodded. "Some, maybe. But most of them have been out there all night, or even since yesterday morning, demanding to be heard. Right now, they know there's still a chance they can wear us down and make us listen to them. Let's take the bargaining table to them. If we wait too long, even the reasonable ones may lose their patience. Then all of them *will* be baying for blood."

"And what if you're wrong?" Ithlene asked. "What if they're not interested in talking?"

Ember folded the parchment and set it aside as a scribe approached his desk. "Then it won't much matter what we do, now will it?"

Mendin exchanged scowls with Tarsa before both men shrugged and sighed.

Eight.

Cambin shook his head. "This is fool's play, Morangine. There's no reasoning with beasts like this. We need to hold firm. The Assembly will not be cowed into action by a lawless mob."

"That's not for you alone to decide," Ember said. "I propose to the Assembly that we proceed with my plan to open negotiations with the citizens gathered outside. All in favor?"

The hands went up slowly, some waiting to follow another's lead, but still raising all the same. Cambin slumped into his seat when he saw the final tally.

Eight hands out of eleven raised in favor, a clear majority.

Ember handed the folded parchment to the scribe. "Go to one of the balconies and announce this to the crowd. Read every word as it's written, understand?"

The scribe nodded and hurried off to carry out the task.

Ithlene glared at Ember. "You'd better be right about this."

THE CROWD ACCEPTED Ember's negotiation terms, just as he expected, but it took all morning for the citizens to select representatives to stand before the Assembly. While they bickered and debated outside over who might serve their interests best, another set of arguments played out inside the hall. According to convention, a different Assembly member presided over the body each day, and by that rule, the responsibility should have fallen to Cambin for the day. Ember invoked a rarely used bylaw in the Assembly's rules of order to select the head of the Assembly by vote. Armille and Ithlene protested, arguing that there was no compelling reason to break with precedent, but Ember countered by calling Cambin's willingness and ability to lead the delicate negotiations into question. When the time finally came to put the matter to a vote, Ember's newfound coalition mostly held, with only Mendin defecting to back Cambin.

Petty bastard. Don't go thinking I'll forget that.

A scribe hurried down from the second-floor balcony shortly after noon to inform them that the crowd's representatives were ready to present their petition. The group consisted of ten people, most of them cleaner and better dressed than much of the mob. Merchants, craftspeople, and guildsmen, from the look of them, probably the most respectable among the rabble outside. Ember had expected as much. By requesting the crowd to present formal petitions, he hoped to divert power away from the more impulsive, violent members with little to lose and into the hands of the shop owners, traders, and organized laborers who had an interest in the preservation of order.

The plan seemed to have worked, save for one representative who stood out from the rest. A woman with short blonde hair and a simple, brown dress stood near the back of the group. The dark stains on her dress marked her as a butchery worker of some sort. She carried a tattered, gray shawl, clutching it close to her chest as she approached the Assembly.

Ember recognized the garment.

304 · BENJAMIN SPERDUTO

It belonged to Trinn Harmyndri.

"Please," Ember said, "step forward and speak. The Assembly is most eager to—"

The butcher woman pushed past her companions and threw the gray shawl to the floor.

"Justice," she said. "We demand justice for Assemblywoman Trinn's murder."

Ember nodded. "I understand your sorrow over her loss. Her passing came as a shock to us all. I think I speak for the entire Assembly when I say that—"

The woman scoffed. "Spare us your false sympathies, Lord Morangine. It's no great secret that you despised Trinn. In fact, I wouldn't be surprised if you had something to do with her murder."

One of her companions stepped forward and grabbed her by the arm. "That's enough, Olynia! We didn't come here to level accusations, remember? That's not what Trinn would have wanted."

Olynia jerked her arm free and glared at Ember.

He knew that expression well. It was the same look he gave Raugov when the bastard nearly killed Yimina. "What is your name?"

"I am Olynia Bothenvael, third year journeyman of the Carvers Guild."

Not a relative, at least. Still, she must have been close to Trinn. The way she looked at him with such hatred suggested a familiarity that went beyond common knowledge of his reputation. More importantly, there had to be several dozen higher ranking guild members in the crowd outside who would have made more logical representatives than a third year journeyman.

She must have been *very* close.

"My apologies, Assemblyman," the man beside her said. "Assemblywoman Trinn's death has affected some more profoundly than others."

Ember shook his head. "No apology necessary. You all have a right to your grief. I assure you that the Assembly will do everything in its power to see that the people have their justice."

The man bowed his head. "I don't doubt that, Assemblyman."

"Unfortunately," Ember said, "it will be difficult to pursue that justice while the Assembly Hall remains under siege by the very citizenry it wishes to serve. Perhaps it would be best if you present your grievances on behalf of the crowd gathered outside?"

The man nodded. "Of course, Assemblyman." He signaled to one of his companions, who produced a sheet of parchment covered with hastily scrawled writing. "First, in addition to devoting substantial watch resources to investigating Assemblywoman Trinn's death, there's the matter of negligence among the Coldwater and Pigshire Watches, which might well have contributed to her tragic death…"

He went on for what seemed like days, detailing concerns over public safety, deteriorated housing, hazardous streets, corrupt officials, dishonest street peddlers, and even preposterous rumors of supernatural activity during the darkest nights of each month. Ember gave every grievance his full attention, no matter how ridiculous it might have sounded. Occasionally, a request drew a snicker or a groan from another Assembly member, usually Armille, Cambin, or Mendin, but a sharp glare silenced them quickly.

Much as Ember suspected, Trinn's death had provided an opportunity for every murmur of discontent over life in Lowtown to coalesce into a furious shout. Few of the demands seemed to have anything to do with the Assemblywoman's murder, but the longer the representatives went on, the better Ember felt about their chances of dealing with the problem. The Assembly lacked the resources to address every issue, but a few targeted efforts would go a long way toward creating the impression that it could. After the crowd dispersed and took note of those efforts in the coming days, the citizens would congratulate themselves for forcing change. Then they would go back to the drudgery of their daily lives and fail to notice when things went right back to the way they had been before.

"Of course," Ember said after a complaint about street butchers selling rotten meat after sunset. "I believe there are several ordinances already prohibiting such practices, but I assure you that the Assembly will see to it that the watch redoubles its enforcement. Are there any additional matters you wish to bring to our attention?"

The representative glanced at Olynia, the journeyman carver. She had gathered up Trinn's shawl and stood quietly off to the side of the group. "Just one, Assemblyman."

"Yes?"

"With Assemblywoman's Trinn's death, the people have been deprived of one of their trusted representatives. We should like to see her seat filled as soon as possible."

"Of course," Ember said. "I'm sure you understand it could take some time to organize a proper plebiscite for—"

"That won't be necessary, Assemblyman," Olynia said, stepping forward. "The people have already appointed me to take her place on the Assembly."

So, that's *what you're doing here.*

"Outrageous!" Cambin stood up, shaking his head. "You expect us to simply agree with the capricious will of that mob outside?"

"Quite irregular, indeed!" Mendin said. "The legitimacy of these elected seats is questionable enough already. To select a replacement in this fashion calls the entire principle into question."

Other Assembly members voiced concerns, arguing back and forth with each other and with the citizen representatives. Ember tuned the debate out, instead focusing his attention on Olynia. She still stood apart from the others, her face full of scorn and contempt.

This isn't about power for her. It's personal.

Maybe he could use that to his advantage.

Ember rose from his seat and called for silence. "While I am in agreement with my colleagues that the circumstances of this selection are highly irregular, so too were the circumstances of Assemblywoman Trinn's passing. The law requires that the citizens of Lowtown select a replacement by way of plebiscite, but the procedure for doing so has always been at the discretion of the citizenry." He looked to Cambin. "Assemblyman, your knowledge of history might exceed mine, but was there not a time when only citizens from Coldwater borough were permitted to stand for office, or even to vote?"

Cambin scowled, but he nodded. "True enough, yes. But I fail to see the relevance here."

"The relevance is that the citizen plebiscite belongs to the people to organize and deploy at their discretion. If the Assembly were to dictate such terms, why, the very legitimacy of the practice would be undermined. Surely, Assemblymen, you don't mean to call this tradition into question?"

Gods, if Trinn was here to hear me spouting this nonsense...

Cambin exchanged a confused glance with Mendin, then with Ithlene and Armille. Ember could hardly blame them. They probably thought he had lost his mind.

"I...I merely want to ensure that the people are confident in their decision, of course," Cambin said.

Ember nodded. "Good. Then unless there are any further objections, I recommend that we formally welcome Olynia Bothenvael to the Coldwater Assembly of Notables." He waited for someone to speak out, but even Mendin remained silent.

With that final issue out of the way, the Assembly and the group of representatives set about negotiating the dispersal of the crowd outside the hall. Once he secured assurances that the crowd would disband, Ember summoned three scribes and instructed them to write out the results of the talks. The process took almost as long as the talks themselves, and the sun had long since set by the time the representatives finally gathered to leave.

Breaking with custom, Ember stepped down from his seat to shake the hand of each representative. He characterized the unusual gesture as a show of good faith, but in truth, he needed an excuse to get closer to Olynia. When he took her hand, he leaned in close enough to whisper into her ear.

"We need to meet alone," he said. "I know who's behind Trinn's murder."

She withdrew her hand, but not before closing her fingers around the small scrap of parchment he pressed into it.

"I look forward to working with you, Assemblywoman."

WHEN OLYNIA AND the other representatives returned to announce the results of their negotiations, the crowd cheered loudly enough to shake the Assembly Hall's floors. Selinis and Harik accompanied them, but most of the Assembly members cowered inside, fearful that the crowd might decide at the last moment to seal the compact in their blood. Ithlene, Cambin, and Armille retreated to a meeting room on the second floor, no doubt to blame each other for the situation and hammer out how they would present this new development to Dhrath.

Ember took advantage of the confusion to slide out a side exit and get well clear of the excited gathering. Even the men of the watch tasked with defending the door were too distracted by the crowd to notice him slip out into the night. After traversing a few streets to put distance between him and the Assembly Hall, he veered northward and walked until he reached Redfoot Street. The light boys had already passed through to light the post mounted lanterns running along the streetside, so he had no trouble finding his way. When he crossed Shale Street, every second or third lantern remained dark, probably because the locals had not bothered to refill the oil during the day. Whatever the reasons, the intermittent light provided a good indication that he had crossed the boundary into Pigshire.

The Bleating Goat was already overflowing with its usual crude clientele. Day laborers, drunkards, and firedust snorters elbowed against one another in the wretched common room, all of them foul smelling and foul tempered. Ember did his best to avoid touching anyone as his squeezed into the place, pushing a few steps at a time toward the serving bar. When he reached it, he paid a fifthmark for a cup of rancid wine, then pushed into the crowd again, this time angling for one of the booths along the winesink's back wall. All the booths were taken, but he paid a group of tanners a quartermark each to clear out. They shuffled off to buy another round while Ember eased into the booth and sipped at his stale drink.

He had about three gulps left when Olynia walked through the door.

She grabbed a drink of her own before she sat down in the booth opposite him.

"Half expected you wouldn't show," he said.

She produced a scrap of paper and pushed it across the table. Ember recognized his handwriting: *Tonight. Bleating Goat.*

"And I didn't expect you'd actually be here," Olynia said.

Ember raised his cup. "Then here's to defying expectations."

She abstained from following his lead. "Is it true, Morangine? What you said earlier about Trinn?"

"Every word."

"And how do I know this isn't one more trick to save your own hide?"

Ember laughed. "Oh, believe me, I'm trying to save my hide. But that doesn't mean it's a trick. The truth is I'm one wrong move away from joining Trinn in a ditch."

Olynia scowled, her hand reaching down to her side. "You talk about her like that again, Morangine, and I'll split you open like a pig."

Journeyman carver, remember? Probably wouldn't even flinch when I started screaming.

"She meant a lot to you, didn't she?"

Her lip trembled a bit. "Everything."

More than just a friendship, then. Interesting.

He had heard rumors about Trinn's personal life, but Ember always had a hard time believing that her dedication to the Assembly left much time for a meaningful relationship.

"For what it's worth," he said, "she believed in what she was doing. And she was a fighter who didn't back down from anything."

Olynia grunted. "I know who she was, Morangine. What she stood for. What she believed was right. And it's no secret that you hated her for it."

Fair enough...

Ember smiled. "No more than she hated me. And not without reason, I expect."

She leaned back and folded her arms against her chest. "What's your stake in all of this? Word has it that you were the one who pressed the Assembly to ask for terms. And it was you, Lord Ember Morangine, who never made his contempt for the common citizen a secret, who actually convinced the rest of the Assembly into accepting me as Trinn's successor when you had every reason to oppose it. I scarcely believed what I was hearing when it happened, but then you press this note into my hand and whisper a secret into my ear and it all starts to make sense. You want something from me. What is it?"

Right to the heart of things. No wonder Trinn liked you.

"This is a delicate time for the Assembly," he said. "I need someone I can trust."

"And you think I'm just one more piece on the board to be played? I'm not doing this to get revenge, you know. I want whoever killed Trinn to pay, yes, but I intend to carry on the work she started. If you think you can buy me off by giving up a few names, you'd best walk away right now because there's nothing you can do that will make me betray everything she fought and died for."

Ember shook his head. "I'm not trying to buy anything from you. If you're anything like Trinn, you're not the sort who can be bought off anyway."

"Then what do you want? Why did you ask me to come here?"

He took a deep breath before answering. "Because I was wrong. I thought I had everything under control, that I could play the game better than anyone. But I was wrong, and someone who trusted me died for it."

Olynia leaned over the table. "I don't know what you think you're talking about, but Trinn never—"

"I'm not talking about Trinn."

She stared at him, trying to read his stern expression. "Lorvie. You're talking about Lorvie Tinderhov, aren't you?"

Ember nodded.

"I heard she'd turned up in the Deadhouse. Mugged by cutpurses, word had it."

"You believe that?" he asked. "You believe that after what happened to Trinn?"

Olynia sighed, then shook her head slowly. "No. I guess not. Do you know who's responsible?"

"There's a broker in Carbuncle, a cephilin. Runs most of Lowtown's gangs and has a good chunk of the watch under his control. Now he's trying to muscle in on the Assembly. Seems to think he'll be better off making the laws than breaking them."

"Dhrath," she said. "Trinn talked about him all the time. Said the bastard already had half the Assembly on the take."

"More than that now. The rest, he has under the knife. They don't do as he says, they turn up dead."

She took a long drink from her cup and slumped in her seat, scowling. "And I suppose you have a plan to deal with him, is that it?"

"I don't want to deal with him. I want to drag the slimy sod out of his hole and stake him out under the hot sun until he shrivels up and turns to dust. I want to cut off those suckered arms of his and feed them to a pack of starving dogs. I want to bury him in a cesspit so the whole bloody city pisses in his face and shits in his mouth every day. I don't want him dealt with; I want him dead."

Olynia stared at him, her mouth agape.

Ember tried to imagine what Trinn would think about the two of them in that moment, on the verge of forming an alliance that would have been unthinkable only a week ago.

Her now-familiar scowl returned.

That's the spirit.

"Okay," Olynia said. "Where do we start?"

25

THE BROKEN

The dead woman had rough skin for her age. Although she could not have been much older than thirty, her wrinkled face added at least another decade to her appearance. Her tanned, leathered flesh marked her as an immigrant, most likely from Karthea. Certainly, no one from Blackspire ever saw so much sun in a lifetime.

The body came in shortly after Calandra's shift started. It fit most of the criteria she was looking for: foreign, poor, and forgettable. The sort nobody ever bothered to claim. She had it moved several times during the night, just to make sure it became familiar enough to not be missed by the mortuary workers. When she hoisted the body into a cart and pushed it toward the crypt entrance, nobody bothered to look twice.

Calandra kept glancing at the corpse as she made her way down the black tunnel. Someone dumped the poor woman outside the Deadhouse gate without any explanation for her death. If disease had taken her, it was something without obvious symptoms, perhaps a respiratory malady or a blood fever. Organ failure or some other internal injury remained a strong possibility as well.

Under normal circumstances, Calandra would cut her open to determine the true cause of death. Part of her duty as an undertaker was to identify possible threats to the public health and dispose of potentially diseased bodies safely. But dissected corpses far less valuable than intact ones, at least in the eyes of her bodysnatching partner, so she left the body alone.

As Calandra pushed the corpse deeper into the crypts, she played out the same discomforting thoughts that accompanied every journey she made to drop off her grisly contraband. What was there to stop someone from doing the same to her? After all, Calandra had few contacts remaining in the city. Aside from her brother and a few associates from the mortuary and the guild, no one would notice her absence if she simply disappeared one day.

"What about you?" she said, her voice barely a whisper. "Anyone going to miss you?"

The corpse, thankfully, did not answer.

She stopped the cart just past a branching tunnel that led deeper into the crypt. The bodysnatchers often ventured nearer to the entrance to carry off the old bodies that Lerris set aside for them, but Calandra refused to leave fresh corpses so close to the mortuary where an astute worker would certainly notice them out of place. She wished she could simply toss the bodies into the tunnel and let them roll down to the bottom. That would minimize her risk, certainly, but the sorceress wanted the bodies as fresh and intact as possible, so she could not take the chance that a bone might break on the way down the slope.

Although few workers ventured so deeply into the crypts, Calandra never stopped worrying that someone might stumble upon one of the bodies she left for collection. A few anonymous reports to higher-ups in the guild could easily bring an investigator down from the dreary halls north of the Saven.

Calandra and Lerris's scheme was not likely to survive that level of scrutiny.

She lifted the corpse out of the cart and lowered it gently to the ground. With any luck, the bodysnatchers would find it before dawn. They always seemed to know when she left something for them. Maybe they sent scouts to inspect the passageway or maybe the sorceress had some scrying enchantment in place. How they managed it mattered little to Calandra. All she cared was that they carried the body away before anyone else stumbled upon it and that they left her payment behind.

The dead woman's eyelids opened as her head rolled back into the dirt. Blood had already drained from her eyes. Sunk deep within her skull, they looked like pickled balls of old cheese. Calandra stared at her slackened face, wondering how she spent her last hours of life. Death came as a relief nearly as often as a tragedy, but Calandra's occupation never required her to determine whether or not the dead welcomed their fate. The guild discouraged such questions on the grounds that they might lead undertakers to treat some bodies differently than others. Death was the great equalizer, the amoral force that shattered the walls and towers built by the living to draw fictitious distinctions between one another. To allow the memory of those lives to rob death of its leveling power was a betrayal of the guild's ideals.

Still, Calandra wondered. What had this woman left unfinished? Did her regrets follow her across the threshold? Who had she left behind and how would their lives change without her?

She thought about Beyland, about how long he would last if she were gone.

What would he do when Arden came to his door looking to collect on that foolhardy loan?

The dead face seemed to glare at her, its vacant eyes digging into her flesh like rusty hooks.

How much longer can you keep doing this?

Calandra wheeled the cart around and pushed it back up the long passageway.

After emerging from the crypts, she bolted the doors shut and made her way back to the mortuary's main preparation chamber. The night shift workers there moved from table to table with candles in hand, carefully inspecting the corpses laid out upon each slab. Unidentified bodies occupied a special section near the front of the room. Calandra counted nearly a dozen of them, more than enough to begin the tedious identification process.

Had she not snuck several bodies into the crypts over the last few nights, they would have been able to begin identifying them even sooner.

"Miss Calandra?"

Tarl's voice startled her enough to make her jump. She spun around to find the large worker standing just a few feet behind her. For a moment, she wondered if he had been following her, watching her slip away when she thought no one was looking to smuggle a corpse into the crypts below.

But she saw no suspicion on his face, no hints of accusation. Only the same adoring expression he reserved for whenever he spoke to her.

No matter the circumstances, Tarl always seemed happy to see her.

What would you do if you caught me? Would you turn me in or offer to help?

"Yes, Tarl," she said. "What is it?"

"Where've you been?" he asked. "I looked all over for you."

"Just having a look down below. Wanted to make sure that problem from last week got sorted out."

Tarl furrowed his brow. "Problem?"

"The old bodies, remember?"

He nodded slowly. Calandra had a hard time telling if he actually recalled the situation or if he was afraid to admit he had forgotten.

"Everything okay now?"

Calandra nodded. "Seems to be in order, yes. Now what was it you needed?"

"Keldun's been asking for you," Tarl said. "He's waiting out by the gate."

"Someone dropping off a freshie?"

"Don't know, Miss Calandra. He just said to come get you."

Damn. Must be another messy one.

"Get a table cleared off," she said. "I'll send for a cart if we need it."

Tarl grunted and hurried off to prepare one of the chamber's many tables to receive a new arrival. He snapped at a few apprentice workers to scrub the slab's surface with scouring powder while he fetched a bundle of clean dissection instruments.

Calandra gathered up the registry book from her desk, and then stepped out of the chamber to join Keldun near the Mortuary's main gate. She found him standing watch over a thin man dressed in a brown cloak and leaning against a rickety cart that was hitched up to a skinny mule.

The sight made her sneer.

Collector.

While the Undertakers Guild relied upon collectors to haul corpses to the city's various mortuaries, most guild members regarded such body scavengers with disdain. In more upstanding districts, the guild usually sent out its own agents to collect the dead with a degree of dignity. In Lowtown, however, paying a bounty of a few marks to anyone willing to haul a corpse over to the Deadhouse proved cheaper and easier. Obvious murder victims, of course, had to be reported to the local watch, but the collectors had the pick of everything else.

As far as Calandra was concerned, all of them were parasites profiting off death and the guild's parsimonious refusal to gather Lowtown's dead itself.

Keldun waved to her when she entered the courtyard. "You should have a look at this."

The collector stepped forward as they approached his wagon.

"Never seen one like it," he said. "Found him face down in an alleyway, buried under a pile of trash."

Calandra ignored the comment, instead skirting around the collector to inspect his grisly cargo. The little cart had enough space to haul half a dozen bodies, but it held only one at the moment. A heavy blanket covered the corpse, stained black with mildew and old blood.

"Let's have a look," she said.

The collector grabbed the blanket and pulled it back to reveal a body covered with bulging black sores. At a glance, they looked like plague boils, but closer examination revealed that they were solid, almost like petrified flesh, rather than soft, puss filled blisters.

"Any idea what could do something like this?" Keldun asked.

Calandra shook her head, unable to muster the words to answer. She was too busy staring at the dead man's face.

His familiar face.

Kardi.

She stared at that face for several seconds before finally tearing her gaze away.

"Where did you find him?" she asked the collector.

"Over round Caterwaul way. Just shy of Coldwater."

Calandra knew Caterwaul, a broken cobblestone street that meandered into a large cul-de-sac on the outskirts of Sinkhole.

Not too close to the theater, but still...

"You find anything around him?" she asked. "Drugs, drink, anything like that?"

The collector shook his head. "Nothing, but I don't think he got there on his own."

"How's that?" Keldun asked.

"Well, he was under a fair piece of muck and junk but weren't none of it been there for long. You can tell by the way the mud settles, see? I guess he weren't there but for more than a day."

Keldun scowled. "And what made you go digging there to start with?"

"I got my places that's always worth a look," the collector said. "And I got a sharp eye for things that's amiss, I do."

Calandra opened her ledger and hastily scribbled down a description of the body.

She avoided listing his name.

"Well, you want him or not?" the collector asked.

Calandra looked at Keldun. "Go tell Tarl to bring out a cart. Make sure he brings a mask. And fetch twenty marks for our friend here."

"Twenty marks!" Keldun said. "Are you—?"

"I said twenty. As the ranking guild member on duty, payment for corpses is solely at my discretion. Do you have a problem with that?"

Keldun lowered his head, perhaps realizing he had overstepped his bounds.

"No," he said. "No, I don't."

"Good. Then get moving."

Calandra turned back to the collector.

"Twenty marks is a high price. I expect to get more out of it than just another corpse."

"I'm listening."

"You don't mention a word of this to anyone. Not to the watch, not to another undertaker, not to your scavenger friends."

The collector nodded. "I get you."

Calandra glanced over at the body again. Seeing Kardi's face distorted by those ghastly black welts made her shiver.

Keep it together, now. You've seen worse.

As much as she tried to convince herself of that, she doubted it was true.

"One more thing," she said. "You find any more like this one, I want you to bring it straight to me, understand? Don't try to leave it with somebody else here. You ask for me by name, got that?"

"Yeah," he said. "I got it."

She stayed by the wagon until Tarl wheeled a cart outside to collect the body. One of the old spader masks they kept on hand was strapped around his face.

"Where you want him, Miss Calandra?"

"Not in the main chamber," she said. "Put him in the plague room. Whatever killed him might still be contagious."

The lie came more easily than she expected, though Tarl was hardly a difficult audience. She saw the collector raise an eyebrow, but he kept his mouth shut. Probably for fear of losing out on the marks she promised him.

So long as nobody examined the body closely, it could pass for a plague victim. Only closer inspection would reveal that the boils were hard as stone, or that the corpse lacked the other tell-tale symptoms of the plague.

And no one was likely to know what Calandra knew. Not unless they examined the body of the man Nicalene claimed to have killed in much the same fashion about a week earlier. Everything matched the description she relayed with Calandra during their previous conversation: the hardened black boils, the vacant eyes, the contorted expression.

What have you brought into our midst, Beyland?

She barely noticed Keldun bring the collector his marks while Tarl transferred the body onto the cart. Despite the boils covering most of his face, Kardi remained mostly recognizable. Calandra had a good sense of what she was looking at, but she imagined that anyone possessing even a casual familiarity with Kardi would be able to identify the body. Should an inquisitive watch member start an investigation into his death, the path would quickly lead to Beyland.

All it would take was one report of an unexplained death in the mortuary.

"Tarl, wait," she said. "I've changed my mind. Take him straight to the furnace."

Tarl's face scrunched up, betraying his confusion. "But, Miss Calandra, shouldn't—?"

"Are you questioning my judgment, laborer?"

The reprimand struck him hard. For a moment, he simply stared at her in bewilderment. Finally, though, he nodded.

"No, ma'am. Sorry, ma'am. Straight to the furnace, just like you said."

He went back to pushing the cart toward the Mortuary. Calandra fell in alongside him, trying her best to avoid looking at Kardi's dead face.

"It looks like a bad case," she said. "I don't want the body festering in the plague room, even if it is sealed off from everything else. Besides, you know how skittish your mates get whenever we put someone in there. No sense in causing a panic over one body."

Tarl shrugged. "Whatever you say, ma'am."

He did not sound very convinced.

Calandra wrapped the stained blanket tightly around the corpse and tied off each end before Tarl wheeled the cart into the Deadhouse. Although a few laborers glanced at them as they passed, no one spoke or tried to get a better view of the body. When they reached the back of the preparation chamber, she opened the iron-plated door leading into the furnace room.

The immense cremation oven took up most of the space inside, standing a full fifteen feet tall and stretching almost twice as wide. Constructed from meticulously carved stone and expertly cast iron, the furnace resembled a great, black toad, fattened on centuries of regular meals. Two hatch doors on its face opened to reveal small chambers where bodies could be loaded for cremation when ashes were requested by the deceased's relations. Several vents ringed the uppermost section, each one opened or closed by a long metal rod to stoke the fire smoldering inside the great oven.

Every day, the undertakers appeased the furnace's ravenous appetite with unidentified and unwanted bodies. During the day shift, half a dozen men kept the ghastly furnace stoked, preserving a fire that had been burning in its blackened heart for centuries. Only two workers manned the chamber during the night shift, the bare minimum required to operate the winches located atop the scaffolding on either side of the furnace. The winch on the left side opened the main door on the furnace's roof. On the right side, a crane stood ready to lift cartloads of bodies into a metal bin, which another winch could then tip over to dump several corpses into the furnace all at once.

Although a series of vents in the ceiling channeled heat and smoke out through the mortuary's roof, the chamber still felt unbearably hot and dry. The night shift operators kept themselves busy scrubbing the furnace's exterior with wire brushes, scrapping through layer upon layer of ash and soot. Their diligent work only cast more dust into the already smoky air.

Calandra limited herself to short, shallow breaths when she entered the chamber, mindful that drawing too deep a breath could scorch her throat and lungs. After a few weeks of exposure to the superheated air, most furnace operators developed coarse, raspy voices thanks to their newly calloused windpipes. Rather than calling out to announce her arrival, Calandra stepped over to the bell mounted on a post just inside the door.

The furnace workers looked up when the bell's clanging echoed throughout the chamber. One of the men quickly went back to scrubbing, while the other one strode over to greet Calandra.

"Help you?"

Calandra nodded and turned to gesture at Tarl, who was only now pushing his cart through the door.

"Plague victim," she said. "Need him gone. No remains."

The worker sighed but gave her a curt nod. "Bring him over."

Tarl lifted the body out of the cart and placed it in a large bin that the furnace workers then hauled up to the platform atop the scaffolding. Once the corpse was in position, they opened the main furnace door and cast it into the fire.

The entire process took only a few moments.

Calandra imagined Kardi's face melting away to reveal the bones beneath. Then the bones caught fire, burning away to little more than powdery, black dust. Bits of dust popped and crackled in the intense flame before vanishing completely, scorched out of physical existence and memory.

Goodbye, Kardi.

Nicalene. Kardi's death was on her hands, Calandra was sure of it. The woman had killed before, but not out of intent. Had this been an accident too? Even if it had been, who was to say it would not happen again?

Beyland spent almost every waking hour of his days with Nicalene now. If she remained incapable of controlling whatever power she seemed to possess, Beyland might be in terrible danger.

Calandra left the furnace chamber and returned to her desk. She looked at the entry she made for Kardi. It marked him as an "unidentified male" and nothing more. After staring at the page for several minutes, she made an addendum to the report.

Cause of death: plague (high contamination risk)
Body incinerated to preserve integrity of public health.

She closed the book and sighed.

What's one more lie at this point?

THE REST OF the shift proved uneventful. A steady trickle of bodies rolled in from the city streets, most of them vagrants and squatters already a few days dead. They went to the slabs for cleaning and identification. Calandra inspected every one, marking the time of arrival, the place of origin, and the probable cause of death. Some causes were obvious enough, maybe a broken bone given over to rot or other physical trauma. For others she had to perform an autopsy, cutting into their flesh in search of ruptured organs, waterlogged lungs, or malformed tumors.

She welcomed the grisly work. It helped keep her mind off Nicalene.

Lerris did not show up for her shift the next morning. The first of the day workers arrived shortly after sunrise and the rest streamed in as the hazy light filtered through the Deadhouse windows. Calandra oversaw the shift change, making sure the night crew cleaned and stowed their tools before logging their departure in one of her many record books. On most mornings, she hated the tedium of the process, but today it gave her a good excuse to put off going home to face Beyland and Nicalene.

She still had no idea what she would say to them. Between what she now knew about Nicalene's strange powers and Beyland's violent outburst during their last argument, Calandra was hesitant to confront either of them about Kardi's death. She kept thinking back to the stranger she glimpsed in Beyland's eyes when he turned on her. Since Nicalene's arrival, Beyland seemed less and less like the brother she had known her whole life. On the surface, the change was for the better. She never saw him more focused on his work or more committed to seeing his lofty ambitious through to completion. But in that one moment, he showed a side that was dangerous, murderous even.

Kardi and Beyland had known each other for years. As far as Calandra could tell, he was her brother's closest friend. If Nicalene was indeed responsible for Kardi's death, would Beyland be able to put all that history aside to help cover up the murder? Did protecting Nicalene mean that much to him? The question made Calandra even more uncomfortable.

Would you dump me in some trash pit if Nicalene lost control again, Beyland? A whole lifetime of looking out for each other thrown away just like that?

She was still trying to sort out what she would say to her brother when she noticed an unfamiliar woman step inside the preparation chamber. Her clothing marked her as a journeyman undertaker, but one of slightly higher rank than Calandra and Lerris. She wore her brown hair tied up in a knot, which combined with her stony expression to make her appear older than she probably was.

A few moments after the woman entered the chamber, a laborer wheeled a body in behind her on a small cart. She gestured to the nearest empty table.

"Put it over there," she said. "Have it cleaned and readied for incineration within the hour."

Calandra closed the logbook and strode over to the newcomer, who continued to oversee the workers as they moved the body.

"Excuse me," Calandra said. "What's going on here?"

The blonde woman turned to meet her.

"Ah, yes," she said. "You must be Calandra, the night shift overseer?"

"You have me at a disadvantage, I'm afraid. Who are you and what are you doing here?"

The woman bowed her head slightly with a hardened expression. "Forgive me, I should have introduced myself from the start. My name is Moriel, Undertaker, Second Grade."

Second grade? What the hells is she doing down here rubbing elbows with the Lowtown rabble?

Calandra swallowed the rest of her anger. While guild bylaws did not require her to make any formal show of deference to a higher-ranking member, she was expected to be as cooperative and forthcoming as possible.

"Are you here for an inspection?" she asked. "I wasn't informed of any—"

"Calm yourself, sister. I'm not here to conduct an inspection."

Then what...?

Her gaze drifted to the body, which by that point rested on the slab. A shroud still covered the face, but one of the arms had fallen off the table and now dangled limply beside it. The yellowish fingernails were in wretched condition, and the leathery skin looked dry and cracked. Dried blood seeped through the flesh in a few places.

Calandra would have recognized that hand anywhere.

She stepped over to the slab and lifted the shroud from the corpse.

Impossible...

The dead woman's face stared ahead blankly, but even in death, there were traces of anger, resentment, regret, and fear in every dried-out wrinkle.

Calandra had no trouble identifying that face.

Lerris.

"What happened?" she asked.

"Suicide," Moriel said. "Slipped a noose around her neck and flung herself out the second story window of her tenement flat. By the time the neighbors hauled her back up, it was too late. The watch sent word of her death to the guildhall a little while after midnight."

Moriel mentioned a few more details about the suicide, but Calandra stopped listening. All she could think of was the way Lerris had cowered before her after their confrontation in the crypts. Lerris had scarcely spoken a word since then, to Calandra or anyone else. Some of the workers, the very same ones she once delighted in terrorizing, had taken to whispering that the only thing setting her apart from the corpses was the fact that she could still walk.

The truth of the matter seemed obvious to Calandra now. Some part of Lerris had died that morning in the crypt. The rest of her just needed a few more days to realize it.

Oh gods, what have I done?

A chill swept over her body, causing her hands to tremble.

"Calandra?"

Moriel's voice shook her free of her stupor. She stepped back from the slab and took a deep breath.

Don't you cry for her, damn you. She doesn't deserve your tears. Don't you cry...

"I'm fine," she said. "Just a little shocked. I knew she was unhappy, but I never expected something like this."

Moriel grunted. "Yes, well, it's an unfortunate loss for the guild. A service will be held for her this morning. Lerris had no family, so her body will be incinerated. Unless, of course, you wish to claim her remains?"

Calandra shook her head. The thought of Lerris's ashes in her home made her stomach turn.

"Very well, then," Moriel said. "Until such a time when an official replacement can be appointed in place of Lerris, I will be overseeing the operations of this mortuary's day shift."

Calandra expected as much. The guild rarely filled openings quickly, always reviewing service records carefully before appointing someone to a new position. As the Lowtown Mortuary's night shift overseer, she stood a good chance of being selected to replace Lerris.

"I'll need to conduct a review of your operations here," Moriel said. "Is there anything out of the ordinary I should know about ahead of time?"

The question caught Calandra off guard.

She suddenly remembered her bargain with Lerris to feed the demands of the bodysnatchers operating in the crypts below. Over the course of the last week, they caused several bodies to simply vanish from the Mortuary's records. Calandra covered their indiscretions far better than Lerris ever managed, but no amount of creative bookkeeping could hide the body she deposited for "collection" last night.

"No," Calandra said, hoping she sounded less nervous than she felt. "Nothing I know of, at least. Lerris was known to make an error every now and then, but nothing more than honest mistakes."

Moriel scowled. "A mistake is a mistake, honest or no. You'll be sure to recognize no such distinctions in the future. Do I make myself clear?"

"Of course," Calandra said, nodding.

Moriel gestured toward the desk.

"I'll have a look at your logs now, if you don't mind?"

Calandra accompanied her over to the desk, where she opened the logbooks for Moriel to review. The undertaker examined them scrupulously, asking for clarification on several entries and shaking her head at the "poor quality" of others. When she reached the last page, she pointed to an entry and glared at Calandra.

"What's this about an incinerated plague victim? A 'high contamination risk' and you didn't think to file a report for further investigation?"

Calandra shrugged. "It seemed to be an isolated case," she said, trying to keep her voice steady. "If I filed a report on every unusual death, the guild wouldn't have time to review them all, much less take action."

Moriel grunted, but she seemed unconvinced.

Calandra went on. "Lerris insisted that we needn't waste the guild's time unless absolutely necessary. She told me not to report on something until I'd seen it more than once."

The statement contained an element of truth. Lerris had been incredibly lax about reporting unusual deaths. The problem was that Calandra never followed her example. If Moriel dug through the records, she would find that she reported such cases without fail, making last night's omission all the more strange.

Moriel went on staring at her with the same unmoving expression. "Highly irregular. See that you follow proper procedure from now on."

Calandra nodded. "Yes, ma'am. Of course."

Moriel closed the logbooks and glanced around the chamber. "Which way to the crypts? I'll need to inspect them as well."

Calandra's heart beat increased until she thought it would crack a rib.

"Is…is that really necessary?" she asked

"After the lax bookkeeping I've seen here? Yes, absolutely. Henceforth, the crypts are to undergo visual inspection upon every shift change. No exceptions."

Calandra nodded and said something about understanding Moriel's concerns, but she was only partially conscious of her response. Most of her attention focused on the body she left down in the catacombs. If Moriel went deep enough to find that corpse, no amount of lying would be able to obscure what was going on.

Damn you, Lerris. You knew this would happen, didn't you, you miserable bitch?

"Calandra," Morel said, "the crypts?"

Calandra swallowed, but her throat still felt dry.

"Right," she said. "This way."

CALANDRA MADE HER way back home to the Moonvale Theater in a staggered daze. Every time she closed her eyes, she saw the catacomb tunnel ahead of her, leading ever downward into the deepest bowels of the Deadhouse's crypt. Each step made her blood pump faster, and she feared that her heart would burst before they reached the intersection where she deposited the Karthean woman's corpse for the sorceress's misshapen bodysnatchers to collect. Twice she thought she spotted the vague outlines of a body sprawled across the tunnel floor. Deeper and deeper they went, pushing far beyond the crypt chambers still in regular use. Not a word passed between them, though Moriel occasionally uttered a dissatisfied grunt at the sight of crumbling doorways and rat holes burrowed into the walls.

But when they finally reached the intersection, there was no sign of the corpse. For a moment, she worried that Moriel would want to descend even deeper. After taking a long look down the steep tunnel plunging into the crypt's oldest depths, Moriel turned around.

Calandra never had an opportunity to check for her payment, which should have been waiting for her under a partially exposed stone.

After returning to the surface, Moriel laid out several new procedures for the mortuary staff. Key among them was the stipulation that no one, not even a highgrade undertaker, was permitted to enter the crypts alone. She claimed it was too great a risk for accidents.

Or fraud.

The rain started when she was about halfway home. Warm and oily, a typical Blackspire summer shower. Raindrops sizzled when they hit the cobblestones, causing the whole street to sound like it swarmed with ravenous insects. Calandra pulled her shawl over her head, but it was soaked through before she reached the next intersection. The water reeked of sulfur and made her itch wherever it touched her skin.

No telling what noxious fumes the stormclouds picked up while they hung over the city for weeks at a time.

Caught out in the weather and drenched to the bone. Might as well be drowning in a puddle while I'm at it.

Without the money made shuffling corpses along to the bodysnatchers, Calandra knew she had little hope of repaying Beyland's debts.

Arden would come looking for her soon.

She knew his sort well enough to guess how that meeting would turn out.

Damn you, Beyland. You had to go and dream big, didn't you?

The Moonvale Theater looked especially grim beneath the black clouds. Older and larger than its neighbors, the theater's rooftop sluices cast great streams of water onto nearby roofs or through open windows. A few vagrants huddled close to its walls to keep out of the rain. Under normal circumstances, Calandra would have shouted at them to be on their way, but today she lacked the strength to confront them. A few of them watched her circle around to the rear entrance. When she closed the back gate behind her, she locked it.

Not that it matters. What do they think's here to take, anyway?

She heard voices before she stepped inside the theater's backstage area.

Two women, neither of whose voice Calandra recognized and a man talked over each other as she closed the theater's door.

Now what?

She stripped off her drenched shawl and let it drop to the floor. If she neglected to scrub it with clean water before the rain dried, the fabric would begin to fray and lose its color within a few days.

Slowly, Calandra stepped around the curtains to find a small group of strangers gathered upon the stage. Each of them referred to a small stack of papers as they spoke.

Beyland presided over the assemblage, furiously scribbling notes onto parchment from his seat some distance beyond the stage. His face was drawn and haggard, but his demeanor nevertheless suggested that some unseen, manic energy coursed through him.

"Beyland?" she asked. "What's going on here?"

A few of the strangers on the stage glanced up at her, but most of them went on reciting dialogue.

"Cal!" Beyland said, waving to her. "Come here. I have to show you something."

Calandra walked around the edge of the stage and made her way through the seating area to join her brother. Sheaves of paper lay strewn all around him, most of them covered with crossed out passages and crude sketches.

"Look here," he said. "I'm almost finished! Can you believe that? Finally figured out the conclusion. Well, I had a little help, to be honest, but I still had to flesh out the basic idea."

Back on the stage, a few of the strangers split off from the rest to read amongst themselves, but most of them remained completely oblivious to the others.

"Who are these people, Beyland?"

"Oh, them? Nicalene and I are bringing people in for auditions. We're hoping to get production underway in a few weeks."

Nicalene…

"Where is Nicalene right now?"

Beyland nodded toward the ceiling and went back to writing. "Still asleep. She's been really tired the last day or two."

Calandra watched her brother closely, but he was too absorbed in his work to reveal much of anything.

"Beyland," she said, "I need to ask you something."

"Sure, Cal."

Despite his answer, he carried on writing, his attention completely focused upon that tiny point where his stylus made contact with the paper.

Look me in the eye, you little scamp.

Calandra reached out to grab her brother by the wrist. Beyland jumped at her touch and nearly dropped his stack of papers. He looked at her, his expression caught somewhere between confusion and annoyance.

"Hey," he said, "what's—?"

"When was the last time you saw Kardi?"

Beyland stared at her for a moment without saying a word. "A few days back, I guess," he said.

Calandra watched for something, anything in his demeanor that might betray him, might tell her how much he really knew about Kardi's death. "I thought he'd be here working on the play," she said. "Wasn't he excited to help out?"

Beyland shrugged. "Guess he changed his mind."

"Doesn't sound like him."

Another shrug. "You know how he is, Cal. Unreliable. Not sure we'd want to trust him with something this important anyway."

Calandra was unsure if it was an imperceptible shift in tone or the way a few stray strands of hair seemed to tremble over his forehead.

Whatever it was, though, it told her everything she needed to know.

It told her that Beyland was lying about Kardi.

She drew away from him, struggling to keep her hands from shaking.

"Cal? What's wrong?"

She wanted to scream at him, to knock him off the bench and make him eat that stack of papers. She wanted to know why he dragged his best friend off to rot in the mud and trash of some back alley.

But the words would not come. Some force paralyzed her, held her rooted in place with fear and uncertainty.

She had felt the sensation before, back when Lerris used to lord over her every movement like some tormenting demon.

Beyland...what have you done?

Calandra backed away, then turned and ran up the stairs. She went straight to her room and locked the door behind her.

The room felt smaller than she remembered.

Small, empty, and cold.

26
THE RECKONING

Grisel's roof proved easy enough to find.

A well-placed bribe at the Spaders Guild gave him the address, but Arden worried that tracking it down might take a bit of legwork. Pigshire's streets were notorious for their numbering patterns, sometimes following irregular intervals, skipping dozens of numbers at a time, or even running in reverse. Luckily for him, the buildings along Crowsneck Street proved more or less predictable, and he located the crumbling, three-story tenement within an hour of entering the borough.

The rain poured all day. Most of Lowtown's earthen streets were already soaked to capacity before the stormclouds opened up on them. By noon, the alleyways transformed into muddy bogs. The few unfortunate sods trudging through the weather kept to the gutters, careful to avoid the deeper waters in the center of the street. Sometimes the water actually flowed, usually in places where the ground sloped downhill, ever so slightly. More often, however, it gathered in thick, fetid puddles, mixing with refuse, muck, and waste. Dead animals floated in some of the larger pools, and children occasionally tossed something into the puddles from high windows in a vilehearted effort to splash passersby.

Under most circumstances, Arden would have watched over the place for the better part of the day, taking note of comers and goers. It never failed to amaze him how many people stupidly returned home even when they knew they were being hunted. Unfortunately, Arden had no time to find out if Grisel was smarter than he looked.

Dhrath wanted results. If Arden failed to deliver them soon, he might well lose what little favor he had remaining with the broker. With Halvid's fever in full bloom, Arden could not allow that to happen.

The tenement's main door hung loosely from its hinges, held in place by a tightly wrapped length of wire. Arden opened the door carefully, worried the shoddy workmanship might give way at the slightest tremor.

A big man sat at the bottom of the staircase opposite the doorway. Broad shouldered and thick chested, he had the lumpy build of a man blessed with great strength but not the discipline to make the most of that gift. His clothing, while hardly luxurious, looked too expensive for him to be a vagrant. A thin trail of black spittle had dried upon his chin.

Nightroot chewer.

Arden kicked the man's foot. The reaction took a few seconds in coming, but when it hit, the man's eyelids fluttered open and he looked up at Arden with an unfocused stare.

"Hey," he mumbled, a clump of black chew tumbling from his mouth and splattering into his lap.

"Nasty habit you've got there, friend."

Eyes still unfocused, the man sneered, revealing the stained teeth and split gums beneath his chapped lips. "The fuck're you?"

He tried to get up, but Arden hooked his foot behind the man's leg and swept it out from under him with a gentle tug. The sudden loss of balance left him flat on his back. Arden pressed his boot heel on the man's crotch.

"Don't bother. You can tell me everything I need to know from right there."

The man winced as Arden pushed his foot down a little harder.

"What's your name, friend?" Arden asked.

"Wurgim."

"You live here?"

The big man nodded and tried to wriggle out from under the boot. Arden only pressed down harder.

"Oh, I'd keep real still if I were you," Arden said.

Wurgim clenched his teeth and stopped struggling.

"I'm looking for somebody, Wurgim. A spader by the name of Grisel, keeps a roof here. You know him?"

Wurgim's eyes focused a bit more now. "Grisel? Yeah, second floor. Not seen 'im awhile."

"He got a lady friend? Black hair, light skin?"

Another nod. "Nicalene. Smelled good."

Finally, Arden had a name to go on.

Nicalene, is it?

"Know her well, do you?"

"Liked root. Bought from Felski once."

Arden knew the name of every dealer in Lowtown worth knowing about, but he did not know anyone named Felski. Probably some small-time corner dealer with ties to one of Pigshire's gangs.

"You seen her around lately?"

"Don't...don't think so."

Arden applied a bit more pressure with his boot. "Don't get cute with me now, Wurgim. You seen her or not?"

Wurgim's breathing quickened and his eyes lost focus again.

"Don't 'member," he said, muttering through slackened lips.

Bloody root chewers.

"You don't remember, do you? Maybe you just need a little incentive."

He ground his boot heel deeper against Wurgim's crotch, sending shudders through the big man's body.

"How about now? This stirring up any memories?"

Wurgim cried out, a hoarse, choked sound that reminded Arden of a wounded dog's yelping.

"You mentioned somebody named Felski. How about we start there?"

The big man muttered something unintelligible.

"We're getting off to a bad start, Wurgim. Now let's try again: Who is Felski?"

Before Arden could ask another question, a hand grabbed his face from behind and cold steel pressed against his neck.

He never heard anyone approaching.

Too worn out to spot a hog in a privy.

A thin, almost shrill voice whispered into his ear. "I don't much care for strange folks squawking my name when we ain't been properly introduced."

Arden almost laughed. "Felski, is it?"

"Shut up! You want to go on breathing, I'd advise you to stop humping my brother's dick with your foot."

Arden complied, lifting his boot to allow Wurgim to roll over and groan loudly.

"Now you're going to tell me who you are and which gutterscum sent you," Felski said. "I don't like what I hear, I bleed you right here and now, got that?"

Must not have heard me asking about Grisel. Maybe he heard the scuffle upstairs and came down for a look.

The knife blade trembled slightly, which led Arden to believe that Felski lacked a strong grip.

Probably smaller than me. Smaller and weaker.

"Yeah, I got it," he said, playing for time. "Name's Arden. Nobody sent me."

Felski scoffed. "I ain't buying that. Ain't nobody come round here looking for us that wasn't sent by somebody. Who you work for, eh? Vanick? Olgeldor?"

Arden recognized the names; two-bit gutterscum gangers with delusions of one day making a play at lording over a quarter of their own. Olgeldor was the smarter of the two, but Vanick was nastier. If they shared a brain, they might stand a chance of reaching broker status. Things being as they were, though, they were more likely to tear each other apart before their operations could amount to anything.

"You think I'm here for you, is that it?" Arden asked. "What makes you think I give a damn about you and your root addled brother here?"

"Don't think you can talk your way outta this shit! Answer the bloody question! Who sent you?"

The knife wavered, moving ever so slightly away from his skin. Arden sprang into motion and seized Felski's wrist before the blade could swipe across his throat. He shot an elbow backward to smash against the rogue's ribcage, which knocked the wind from his lungs and caused him to drop the knife. Spinning around, Arden grabbed Felski by the throat and forced him back against the opposite wall. The squirming scamp looked a lot like a shorter, skinnier Wurgim, but he was missing the telltale stained teeth and gums of a nightroot addict.

Arden smashed his knee against Felski's crotch and let him fall to the ground in a heap. By the time he turned around, Wurgim was getting to his feet and reaching for his brother's knife.

"I think I told you something about keeping still, friend."

He swung his boot upward to catch Wurgim full in the face. A few of his teeth clattered to the ground as he flopped back against the wall with a yelp.

Piss ants.

Arden picked up the knife and knelt beside the smaller brother.

"Why don't you and I have a little chat while your brother's gathering up his teeth. You tell me what I want to know, and I promise you'll be back to selling your street junk to whatever degenerate leeches you like to cater to. You lie to me or I think you're lying to me, well…"

He pressed the flat of the blade against Felski's ear and slowly pulled it across.

"Let's just say it would be a poor business decision for you. Understand?"

Still wincing, Felski managed a nod.

"Good. Let's start with what you know about your old neighbor Grisel and his friend Nicalene."

GRISEL'S FLAT WAS not much to look at. Arden thought a spader would have pulled in enough coin to at least afford a place with a door.

The single room proved unremarkable. A bed wide enough for two took up most of the floor space, and a large wardrobe stood against the far wall. Arden pulled the door open to find a full set of spader gear: boots, overalls, mask, the works. An old travelling chest sat next to the wardrobe, overflowing with threadbare dresses and undergarments. One of the floorboards rested slightly ajar, revealing a small cubby hole, probably where Grisel stashed his coin. The window was shut tight, and a splatter of grayish muck clung stubbornly to the glass despite the rain.

No one had bothered to make the bed. Little clusters of mouse pellets lay scattered across the sheets. If Grisel or Nicalene had returned to the flat recently, they certainly had not slept there.

Arden sat down on the edge of the bed and rubbed his eyes.

Having hardly slept over the last two days, he figured that was bound to catch up with him.

The only detail Felski coughed up was the fact that Grisel and Nicalene did not get along so well. The way the dealer told it, she used to look him up after a fight with Grisel. But that was back when she first moved into the place, before she kicked all her old habits about a year ago. Felski had not sold her anything since then.

Considering what he saw at the *Goat*, Arden wondered if she had picked up some newer, nastier habits instead.

Someone opened the door to the first room on the floor. Arden reached for his axe as he listened to the footsteps approaching Grisel's flat.

He almost leapt at the doorway when he saw a slender woman peek inside the room, but she did not match Nicalene's description. She was too skinny, and her hair was the wrong color.

Arden had a hard time looking away from her all the same. She wore a low-cut crimson dress with a black shawl wrapped around her neck and shoulders. The hemline scarcely reached past her knees, and the wet fabric clung to her thighs. Her reddish hair tumbled over her shoulders, ending in soft curls that writhed whenever she drew breath.

Between the woman's appearance and bearing, Arden could guess how she paid her way. While she would draw little more than mocking scorn from the painted prostitutes of neighboring Spiresreach, she might as well have been a goddess among Lowtown's typical fare.

"The fuck are you?" she asked.

Direct.

"Name's Arden. You live here?"

She crossed her arms and leaned against the doorway. "Arden, is it? Arden Belarius?"

That was a surprise.

Arden disliked surprises.

He rose from the bed, his hand still resting on the axe strapped to the back of his hip.

"Afraid you've got me at a disadvantage," he said. "Miss…?"

"Sedina. You're one of Dhrath's, aren't you?"

"You seem to know an awful lot just from a name and a glance."

She smiled. "Don't be so touchy. Woman like me has plenty good reason to be in the know about your lot."

Arden supposed that was true. Solitary prostitutes like Sedina were rare. Lowtown's brokers ran most of the district's brothels, and the girls who failed to meet their standards were left sharing a cut of their takes with whichever street gang managed to muscle in on them. Sedina probably had a well-placed benefactor somewhere, somebody who could keep shitheels like Felski from extorting her.

"What do you hear about me?" he asked.

Sedina glanced at his waist, right about where his hand reached behind his back. "I heard you've got a way of making people talk."

"People tend to exaggerate that sort of thing."

Sedina shook her head. "I've got it on good authority. First-hand, you might say. Or what's left of it."

Arden released his axe and brought both hands into view. "I didn't come here for you, if that's what you're worried about."

She smiled, cocking her hips slightly and tossing her hair to one side of her face. Only then did Arden realize he was staring at her lithe figure.

Stupid old man. Playing right into her hands.

"That what you tell the Tammercums too?" she asked. "Felski and Wurgim are still sobbing downstairs. Not that they didn't have it coming, mind you."

Arden scowled.

He had wasted enough time on the conversation.

"Grisel. Nicalene," he said. "Tell me what you know."

"Not much to tell. Nicalene walked out on him about a week back. Took him for what little he had, the bitch. He went out looking for her after he found out. Not seen him since."

"And her?"

Sedina bristled. "Not a sign. Doubt she'd see fit to call on me anyway. We didn't much care for each other."

"Why's that?"

"Grisel and me go back a long while before she came along. She didn't like being reminded of it. Never quite trusted him to keep away, I guess."

Arden's gaze drifted to Sedina's breasts, then down to her curved waist.

He understood Nicalene's concern.

When was the last time he had been with a woman? A year? Maybe more?

Too long.

"Did he say anything unusual before he disappeared? Like maybe something strange happened to him right before then?"

Sedina shook her head. "Only that Nicalene robbed him blind and ran off. Last I saw him, he was going out to look for her. After he didn't come back for a few nights, I figured he asked somebody the wrong sort of question or Nicalene got some gutterscum ganger to put him to pavement."

"She the type to do that?"

"Used to be, maybe," she said. "Way Grisel told it, she's run with some rough crowds in her day. Moving under his roof seemed to settle her down, but who knows. Hard to leave that life behind, even when you want to."

Something about that last sentence rang true for Arden. He could see from Sedina's expression that she shared the sentiment.

"She's a survivor," she said. "She doesn't much look like it, but she's got plenty of fight in her. Grisel too. He's a stubborn bastard, the sort that'd cut off a hand to make a point about his little finger."

After Arden said nothing, Sedina smiled and let out a little chuckle.

"But then, I guess you already knew that didn't you?"

Arden glared at her, wondering what clues she possibly could have drawn from his stony expression.

"You got any idea where I could find either of them now?"

"None."

He could have threatened her, hurt her even, but there seemed no sense in it. She knew full well what he could do to her. If she chose to withhold something, it was because that did not frighten her.

"He got any friends? Relations?"

"No family, least none he ever mentioned. Has a few spader mates, naturally. Not sure what more they could tell you."

"Got names, these mates?"

"Long time ago," she said. "Never had much cause to learn."

Right...

"Told your friends downstairs to keep a sharp eye," he said. "Might be I'll drop in sometime to see if either of them turn up. Might be I'll have a thing or two to ask you."

Sedina smiled and shifted her hips. "I don't usually make time for questions. But if you're looking for a little company, I might be inclined to whisper a thing or two."

Arden forced himself to look her in the eyes. "Not interested."

She laughed. "Don't lie to yourself, Arden. You don't think I've seen that same look on a hundred faces before? The sort that's wound up so tight they're ready to snap in two? You can't walk around like that forever, no matter what you keep telling yourself. What's your story, anyway? Crack one skull too many and started to feel the guilt? Scared off too many women? Dead wife you can't get off your mind? Got some motherless whelp wondering if this is the night you don't come home?"

Arden lunged forward. Grabbing her by her shawl, he yanked her clear of the doorway and forced her against the wall alongside it.

"I said I'm not interested. You don't know a thing about me."

Another smile. She met his baleful glare without a trace of fear in her eyes.

"That's where you're wrong," she said. "You think you're a hard man to figure out? I knew everything I needed to know about you the moment you looked at me. Desperate. Lonely. Scared. Terrified somebody might realize it. You're all the same. All of you strutting around like you're made of iron, but the truth is you're rusting away on the inside. Just another hollow golem waiting to split open when you fall. That sound about right? Or do you need to cut off a few of my fingers before you'll believe I'm telling it true?"

Arden stared at her for a moment, torn between seething anger and impotent frustration. When he finally let her go, he stepped back and watched her casually adjust her shawl.

"Two days," he said. "I'll be back here in two days to check in."

"Check in all you like," Sedina said. "Just don't expect me to give a damn about it."

SEDINA'S WORDS STAYED with him long after he left Grisel's crumbling tenement.

He managed to block out her face and to forget those cutting eyes, but he could not shake her voice. It clawed at him, trailing just a step behind no matter how quickly he walked.

Maybe she was right. Maybe he was stumbling around in the dark, directionless. He certainly felt like he could never get anywhere worthwhile. What little coin he had stashed away was long since spent, he still owed Dhrath several more years of service, and Halvid's fever had returned worse than ever.

Halvid...

Arden pictured the boy as he last saw him, covered in sweat and groaning in pain, unable to eat or drink thanks to his swollen tongue.

The gods are wicked and cruel.

He wanted to go back and tell Sedina that she was wrong. He was not like the other men she knew, not like the backstabbing Tammercums or any of the soulless killers that brokers like Dhrath paid to deliver messages at knifepoint.

They might be dead inside, but he had plenty to live for, a future worth seeing.

And if the boy dies? What then?

The question came in her voice, but deep down he knew the doubt was his own.

He shoved the thought aside, instead channeling his anger toward Sedina's cavalier assessment of his character. She could not know what he had gone through, what he sacrificed to even get inside that blighted city's walls.

How could she possibly understand a thing about him, anyway?

No matter how hard he tried, her voice stayed in his thoughts.

After leaving Pigshire, Arden made his way down Caraval Street until it met up with Dustwalk in the Coldwater borough. The Moonvale Theater loomed on the corner, the rain spilling over its angled roof in a steady gush. As bad as the weather was, it could not keep the city's denizens indoors. Coldwater's mostly paved streets could withstand a heavy downpour for at least a day or two before flooding, so the local traders, laborers, and vagrants still went about their daily routines.

Arden situated himself amongst a small pack of beggars huddled beneath the second story overhang of a woodcarver's shop. One of the wretches spoke to him when he joined them, but a stern glare was enough to cut off any chance of conversation. Sheltered from the rain, he leaned against the wall and watched the theater.

The rain seemed to suck out a portion of everyone's breath. No one tried to shout over the downpour's steady drone. Watch patrols occasionally shuffled by, but they seemed uninterested in doing much more than trudging from point to point along their route. Except for the occasional messenger hurrying by, most everyone caught out in the rain moved at about half their usual speed. When dusk arrived, it settled quickly and heavily behind the dark clouds.

Arden remained among the vagrants until he spotted Calandra step out from behind the theater to make her way down Dustwalk. A hooded cloak obscured her face entirely and covered much of her body, but Arden knew her walk so well by now that he could have picked her out from a crowd no matter what she wore.

The rain did not slow her pace. If anything, she moved with more urgency than he was used to seeing.

Something's wrong. She's worried. Or scared.

Arden stepped into the street and followed her.

He caught up to her about halfway to the mortuary, seizing her by the arm and pulling her toward a nearby alley.

"Hell of a day to be caught in the weather," he said.

Her tension faded slightly when he spoke, and she let him guide her beneath a ledge that shielded them from much of the rain. She turned around to face him, her eyes duller than usual and her expression dour.

The sight caught Arden by surprise. There was more behind the expression than simple fatigue. He saw a weariness, perhaps even resignation. The stern sense of determination seemed to have vanished.

Sedina's damnable voice still whispered in his ears as he looked at her. Whether the words mocked him or Calandra was hard to tell, but he did recognize the sharp sensation that briefly spiked through his chest.

Sympathy.

For a moment, Arden forgot himself, forgot who he was and why he was there. All he knew was that the woman before him was suffering and he wanted nothing more in the world than to be able to help her.

Then Sedina's voice turned sharper, cutting through his rush of magnanimity.

"She's suffering because of you."

Arden scowled, hoping the expression might conceal his bitter disappointment.

The gods are wicked and cruel.

"What's the matter with you?" he asked, his stomach knotting up at the harshness of his voice.

He waited for her to answer, but she said nothing. She lowered her gaze to stare at the puddles of water collecting in the alley.

Arden let go of her arm and took a step back. "You got something for me?"

She muttered something, her face still pointing downward.

"What was that?" He reached out to grasp her chin and gently lifted her head to make her look at him. Her dim eyes finally met his and he felt a chill run along his spine. She stared at him as though he was somewhere else entirely, her gaze vacant and hopeless.

"I'm a little short," she said.

More bad news.

"By how much?"

She reached into her satchel and withdrew a small handful of coins. Five, maybe six, marks worth at the most.

Far short of her usual payment.

"What's this?" he asked, glancing down at the money.

"It's all I have."

"What happened to the rest?"

"There isn't any," she said. "This is all the coin I've got left to my name."

Arden felt a tinge of panic. Calandra's steady payments had kept him stocked with the salves and herbs he needed to keep Halvid's fever under control. Sooner or later, though, he would have to pass some of that coin on to Dhrath before the cephalin realized he was skimming off the top. He knew Calandra's payments would fall off sooner or later, but he thought he could find Nicalene before then and use the bounty to pay back whatever coin he took out of them.

If the money dried up now, Dhrath would undoubtedly get suspicious.

"Seems to me like you had plenty to spare last we met."

She glared at him, her eyes regaining just enough life to turn venomous. "Yeah, well, I guess things change, don't they?"

Arden sighed. "That's going to be a problem. You remember our arrangement, don't you?"

Calandra nodded.

"Then you know what I have to do if you don't deliver?" he asked.

She closed her eyes and nodded again.

Arden pulled her cloak's hood back to reveal her disheveled hair. He rubbed a few strands between his fingers.

Soft...

"What are you doing?" she asked, her lips trembling.

He ignored the question, instead brushing his fingertips against her cheek and letting his gaze drift down to her narrow shoulders. Her dark skin was warm to the touch, and he could almost feel her naked body pressed against him.

It's been a long time.

"I'm thinking we might work something out," he said, placing a hand against her hip. "For an extension."

Calandra took a deep breath, her eyes still closed. Although it might have just been a random bit of rain splashed in her eye, Arden thought he saw a tear taking shape.

He heard Sedina's voice again, distant this time.

What was the look she recognized in his face? At first, Arden thought she just meant men who went too long without a woman's touch, but she gave the impression that it was something more than that, something that even she could never satisfy.

Looking at Calandra now, vulnerable and alone, Arden wondered if he was a little closer to understanding Sedina's remark.

What are you doing? Stop this.

He withdrew from her.

Calandra opened her eyes, revealing a mixture of confusion and relief.

"One week," Arden said, his voice regaining its coarse edge. "Sort something out by then, or I'll have to take the coin out of your brother's hide. Understand?"

She nodded, her expression blank.

Arden turned away from her and strode out of the alley without another word.

His heart went on pounding for several blocks.

THE RAIN REFUSED to let up on the walk back to his flat. If anything, it seemed to come down even harder, hammering down on the city in a futile effort to rinse away its filth.

Arden certainly did not feel any cleaner.

Carbuncle's streets were darker than usual. Few of the lightboys had braved the weather to light the lamps, leaving nothing but the dull glow from the occasional window to illuminate the district's waterlogged roadways.

Arden found himself troubled by the darkness. Walking in the center of the street, he felt like a bit of cork bobbing aimlessly in the middle of a vast, shadowy ocean. He half expected a black wave to rise out of the darkness and drag him beneath the surface, slowly crushing the air from his lungs.

The gods are wicked and cruel.

Memory guided him home more than sight. When he finally climbed the staircase leading up to the flat, he wondered if he would manage to get more than a few hours of sleep. If Halvid fell under the sway of another coughing fit, sleep would be impossible. Arden hoped the boy had not suffered too greatly while he was gone. As much as he hated leaving Halvid to face his illness alone, he lacked any alternative. He was never going to make any coin sitting next to the bed all day.

When he reached the top of the stairs, he found the door slightly ajar. Candlelight peeked through the opening, flickering like some distant, dying star.

Oh no...

Arden reached around to his back and grasped his axe before he slowly pushed the door open.

A single candle burned on Halvid's bedside table, giving off just enough light to illuminate most of the room dimly. Four men stood near the bed. Despite the darkness, Arden could make out their clothing well enough to identify them.

Men of the watch. Not a good sign.

"About time you showed up. Thought we was going to have to hunt you down and drag you back here."

The voice came not from the watchmen, but rather from Halvid's bed. Arden realized then that the figure lying there was much too large to be his son.

He recognized the voice, despite having heard it only once before.

You bastard.

"Raugov," he said. "Where's my son?"

The wild-eyed thug rolled over and sat up, his arms spread wide. "Afraid I can't tell you that. Not yet, leastways."

Arden scowled. "If you've hurt him—"

"Oh, be still," Raugov said, waving his hand. "The whelp's fine, except of course for that fever of his. Nasty stuff. The boys here were afraid to even touch him."

Arden glanced at the men of the watch. They were all older, longtime veterans of the streets. The embittered, cynical sort that was almost guaranteed to be on the take from someone worse than them.

"What have you done with him?"

Raugov stood up. In the dim light, he seemed even bigger now than when they were at Dhrath's Keep.

"I told you he's fine. Whether or not he stays that way, depends on you. And unless you want him to start losing fingers, I suggest you bring your hands up where we can see them right now."

Arden thought about pulling his axe free and throwing it at Raugov, but his aim was lousy enough that he was as likely to hit him with the handle as with the blade. Even if he got lucky and buried the axe in Raugov's forehead, the men of the watch were unlikely to run for their lives. There was also the small matter of Halvid's whereabouts. Without Raugov, it would take Arden several days, maybe even weeks, to find him.

If Halvid's fever worsened before then, he would certainly die.

Not much choice, is there?

He held his empty hands out to his sides. "I'm listening."

Raugov chuckled and crossed his thick arms. "Been doing a bit of listening myself lately. Turns out people got a lot to say when you cut a few bits of them away. Course I don't need to tell you about that, do I?"

Arden scowled, but he was not about to take the bait. "Get to the point. What do you want from me?"

Raugov shrugged. "Had a word with some piss ant dealers over in Pigshire yesterday. Told me the damnedest story about one of their men turning up dead about a week or so back."

Arden's stomach knotted. Raugov did not need to provide any more details for him to know his time had run out.

"Some strung out cunt burned him to ash, they said. Not sure how she did it, but they said a friend of hers came looking for her. Guy by the name of Grisel."

Shit.

"Dhrath put you up to this, then?" Arden asked.

Raugov smiled. "If Dhrath knew that you had your hands on the guy he's looking for a week back without letting him know about it, you'd be dead already."

Arden glanced at the men of the watch. "What's your play, then?"

"Grisel. I want to know where you got him stashed. You're going to take me to him, and then I'm going to hand him over to Dhrath while you explain why you're holding out on him."

Arden knew perfectly well how that conversation would turn out. "And what about my son?"

"Once Dhrath's done with you, I'll send your boy to the orphanage over in Coldwater."

Arden knew the place. The overseer paid decent money for unwanted children, most of whom wound up working the looms he kept running in the basement. While the children received food and lodging, few of them survived the wretched working conditions long enough to adulthood.

"He's sick," Arden said. "They'll throw him on the street when his fever flares up again."

"Maybe. But at least he'll have a chance. You don't give me what I want, I guarantee he won't live another day."

"He's just a boy, damn you. He doesn't have anything to do with this."

Raugov let out a short, humorless laugh. "He's your son, ain't he? That means he's involved, whether you like it or not."

The gods are wicked and cruel.

And so are you, Arden Belarius. Don't let this bastard be the one to bring you down.

Arden glared at Raugov. "There's a bit of a problem with your plan."

Raugov raised an eyebrow. "What's that?"

"I don't have Grisel anymore."

The two men stared at each other for several seconds. Raugov finally blinked and took a step toward him.

"Say again, now?" he asked.

"I don't have him. Bastard got away shortly after I took him. Been looking for him ever since. Didn't even know Dhrath wanted him until he was gone."

Raugov glanced at one of his companions, who gave him nothing more than a shrug.

"Then I guess Dhrath will have to make do with you," he said.

"Wait," Arden said, holding his hands up before the men of the watch could move toward him. "You're forgetting something important, Raugov. The woman. The one who killed the dealer at *The Bleating Goat*."

"What about her?"

"I saw that body up close. Nothing could have caused wounds like that except for sorcery of some kind. You have any idea the kind of bounty Dhrath pays for a sorcerer walking around Lowtown without his say so?"

Raugov stared at him for a moment before nodding slowly. "Go on."

"Grisel and this woman got a history. We track him down, might be he can lead us right to her. Once we find her, we hand her over to Dhrath and split the bounty."

"Or I take the whole bounty and you get your boy back."

Arden doubted Raugov would make good on that bargain. He was just as likely to keep Halvid and hand Arden over to Dhrath after they got their hands on Nicalene. Of course, they had to find her first. Based on what he learned from Grisel's neighbors, the spader probably had nothing worthwhile to tell them anyway.

But Raugov did not know that. By the time he figured it out, Arden hoped he could find some way of dealing with him without further endangering Halvid.

"Fine," Arden said. "The bounty's yours on the condition that you let Halvid go."

Raugov strode over to Arden and extended his hand. "You got my word."

Arden did not care if the man's word was worthless. He just needed to get out of that flat alive.

He took Raugov's hand. "Done."

DESPITE TAKING AN immediate disliking to Raugov, Arden had to admit that the man possessed an admirable determination. Rather than waiting to hunt for Grisel until the morning, Raugov demanded that they begin immediately, which suited Arden perfectly well. Every moment they delayed potentially pushed Halvid closer to death.

Without any solid leads, Arden convinced Raugov to question the spader crews working in the area. It took more than a little rain to keep the spaders off the streets for the night, so they found a crew without too much trouble. While the first group did not know Grisel's name, a few men on the second crew Arden questioned had worked with him a few months back. Several weeks had gone by since they last spoke to him, but they knew the last crew he worked with.

Even better, they knew where that crew was assigned for the next few nights.

The rain had let up slightly by the time they found Grisel's old crew shoveling the muck out from Eelsbrook Street, but not enough to improve anyone's mood. Raugov and his hired watchmen kept close to Arden as he approached the crew, perhaps worrying that he might try to escape or whisper some secret betrayal to the spaders. Arden doubted they would care enough to help him anyway, even if Raugov threw him to the ground and bludgeoned him to death.

While the downpour washed away a good portion of the street's muck, tightly packed islets of dirt, trash, and waste held together in several places. Tangled clumps of street debris floated directly into them, building up sporadic dikes that caught even more flotsam and jetsam carried downstream. The spaders busied themselves clearing the trash piles and then breaking up the islands of gunk and mud with their shovels. Debris and muck went into the wagon, slowly forming a slimy mound of blackish waste.

Although the rain diluted some of the street's more offensive odors, the oily water hardly cleansed the air, leaving a burning, acrid taste upon the tongue after every breath.

One of the spaders glanced at Arden as he approached.

He did not seem to notice the men of the watch trailing behind Raugov.

"Piss off, fella," he said. "Don't go getting in our way."

Arden ignored his warning and kept walking toward the wagon.

"Who's in charge of this crew?" he asked. "I need to have a word with him."

The spader turned his full attention to Arden but stopped short when he spotted Raugov and his entourage of corrupt watchmen. After staring at them for a few moments, he turned back to the wagon.

"Jaspen! Watch come calling!"

At his call, the rest of the crew stopped working and looked up. Two spaders stepped out from the front end of the wagon and made their way back to join the rest of the crew.

"What's going on back here?" the smaller of the two asked.

His companion, a mountain of a man bigger than Raugov, said nothing.

"Jaspen, is it?" Arden asked. "You got say over this lot?"

"Yeah, that's right." Jaspen looked past Arden as he approached, noting the armed watchmen standing just behind Raugov. "Who the fuck are you? You ain't no man of the watch, that's for sure."

Raugov stepped forward, moving alongside Arden.

"You best watch that tongue of yours," he said. "Unless you want your shit shoveling lads here to be scooping it out of the street."

Idiot.

Jaspen stopped and glared at them. He pointed the spade end of his shovel at Raugov.

"Oi," he said to Arden. "Me and mine'll leave little bits of your lady friend here in every privy on this street if she keeps rattling her jaw like that."

The men of the watch stepped closer, their hands drifting to their weapons. Arden grabbed Raugov's arm before he could move toward the spaders.

"What do you think you're doing?" he said, growling into Raugov's ear. "Stay behind me and put your teeth together. I'll handle this."

"The hells you will. You're wasting our time. I can make any of this lot sing if—"

"Just keep your bloody mouth shut, will you?"

Jaspen laughed.

"Oh, look here," he said. "It's a lovers' spat. Ain't that sweet, Meaty?"

"Sweet," the big spader said through a lopsided grin.

The rest of the spaders moved into a small group behind Jaspen and Meaty, gripping their shovels like halberds.

This could get out of hand any second.

Arden extended his arm to gently push past Raugov.

"Listen, now," he said. "We ain't here to cause trouble. I'm just looking for somebody you might know. A spader who used to be a part of your crew."

Jaspen stole a glance at Meaty, almost too fast to catch anyone's attention.

But Arden noticed.

You know something.

"Guy by the name of Grisel," Arden said. "Sound familiar?"

Jaspen shrugged. "Sure. Worked with him a bit, a while back. Course that don't mean much. I got lots of spaders coming through my crew these days."

Right...

Arden scanned the faces gathered behind Jaspen. A few flashes of recognition, enough to tell him that the others were hiding it well.

"You seen him lately?"

Jaspen shook his head. "Afraid the memory of him's a bit fuzzy. Don't much recall what he was up to last we spoke. You, Meaty?"

"Fuzzy," the big man said, his head shaking slowly.

Both of them. What do they know? Could they be hiding him somewhere?

"You got any idea where I might find him?" Arden asked.

"Afraid not. Especially when I don't know who's asking."

Let's see about that, then.

"Name's Arden. You might call me an old acquaintance."

Jaspen's eye twitched at the name. A subtle reaction, but an unmistakable one.

Told you all about me, didn't he?

"Well, he ain't around now in any case," Jaspen said. "Which means you got no cause to be around here neither."

Meaty grunted. "No cause."

Arden doubted he could get anything more out of them, at least not under the circumstances. Whether they realized it or not, they had just provided him with plenty of information. Even if they did not know exactly where Grisel was hiding out, they had obviously spoken to him, which meant they knew how to contact him.

That left him with two options: follow Jaspen and Meaty after their shift ended or find where they lived and turn the places over. With Raugov and the men of the watch to help him, Arden had a mind to do both.

And if those efforts failed, he could always resort to more direct interrogation methods. He preferred to avoid drawing the ire of the Spaders Guild. Apprehending Grisel from the back rooms of a disreputable winesink was one thing, but this Jaspen was a shift foreman. There would be questions if he disappeared, not to mention an entire crew full of witnesses who knew Arden and Raugov's faces.

"Well, then," Arden said, "I suppose we'll just move along. I'm sure Grisel will turn up eventually. He can't stay in the gutter forever."

He wanted to let the last comment sink in for a moment, but then Raugov pushed by him, moving too quickly for Arden to stop him.

"You're a liar," he said. "Both of you know exactly where your little friend is and you're bloody well going to tell us."

Raugov jabbed his finger against Jaspen's chest.

Oh, no—

"Don't you touch me!" Jaspen said, swatting Raugov's hand away.

Raugov lunged forward to shove the spader, sending him stumbling back.

"Stop it!" Arden said. He reached out to restrain Raugov, but Meaty, who moved fast for a man his size, beat him there. The spader half

pushed, half tackled Raugov, driving him back several steps before finally forcing him to the ground. Meaty landed a few punches to Raugov's
face before the men of the watch moved in to separate them.

The first one to reach them drew his sword.

"No!"

Arden's cry came too late. The watchman drove the blade into
Meaty's side before his companions pulled him free of Raugov. Blood
streamed from the spader's wound, and he let out a hoarse groan as he fell
to the street. Raugov drew a dagger from his belt as he got up and stabbed
it into Meaty's chest.

The next few seconds flew by in a chaotic wave of blood and steel.
Arden heard the spaders shouting behind him before he turned around just
in time to avoid having his skull cracked by a shovel. Raugov and the rest
of the watchmen stood their ground, drawing their swords to swipe and
stab at the charging spaders. Arden managed to duck under an attack and
then sent his assailant sprawling to the ground with a simple shove.
Raugov turned stabbing shovels aside with his blade and sidestepped wild
swings aimed at his head.

Enraged as they were, the spaders were still laborers, not fighters. But
the men of the watch were not very good fighters either. They had gone
soft after years of roughing up starving vagrants and weak-kneed cutpurses. Outnumbered and overwhelmed, they gave ground before most of the
spaders even joined the fray. They landed a few lucky blows to draw
blood, but not nearly enough to convince their assailants to turn back.

Arden knew the watchmen could break ranks and run for their lives at
any moment. If he and Raugov failed to get clear of the battle before then,
the spaders would overwhelm them.

Ducking and dodging through the melee, he grabbed Raugov by the
arm and pulled him away from his attackers.

"Move, damn you! Move!"

Two of the watchmen turned and fled as the rest of the spaders joined
the battle. While the remaining men disappeared under a swirling cloud
of spades, their cries quickly joined by the sound of crunching bone.

Raugov did not need much convincing after that. He joined Arden in a
headlong run down the street. They plunged into darkness as soon as they
moved beyond the light cast by the spaders' work lanterns. A few spaders
chased after them. Arden could not see more than a few yards a head in
the darkness, but he heard their pursuers shouting insults and threats close
behind them. After running a short distance, Arden noticed Raugov was
limping and falling back.

"You hurt?"

Raugov snarled. "Don't you worry about me, damn you!"

Arden slowed his pace to let Raugov catch up, but he heard the spaders gaining on them.

Got to get off this street.

He grabbed Raugov and steered him toward a narrow alley that he knew branched off just a short distance ahead.

"This way."

After turning down the alley, Arden pushed Raugov inside a tight crevice between two buildings. The space was just wide enough for the two of them, and Arden clamped his hand over Raugov's mouth.

"Quiet now," he said.

Moments later, the spaders rushed by the alleyway's entrance. One of them slowed his pace enough to peek into the alley, but then quickly rejoined his companions. Arden held his breath until the spaders' voices faded into the distance.

They emerged from their hiding place, and Raugov fell to his knees when Arden released him.

"Where are you hurt?"

"Left side. Might have bruised the bone. Bastard could have sliced me open with that spade, though. Guess I got lucky."

Arden reached for his axe.

Not lucky enough.

He pulled the axe free and smashed the blunt end against the back of Raugov's skull. As he keeled forward, Arden drove a knee into his back and pressed the axe blade against his neck.

"What were you thinking back there? Do you have any idea what you just did?"

Raugov coughed, struggling to force the words through his lips. "Bastard was lying to us!"

"You think I didn't know that? If you had kept your mouth shut, we could be kicking in the door to their roof right now and finding where they're hiding Grisel. Now we'll be lucky if the spaders and the watch aren't having a war in the streets come dawn.

"You see, Raugov. This is why I don't work with piss ant cutters like you. Only reason I didn't let those spaders chop you up and dump you in their wagon with the rest of Lowtown's waste is because you got something I want. But I've only got so much patience and my trust is a little shaken right now. Way I see it, it's time to renegotiate this relationship of ours. So here's how it's going to be: you tell me where you've got my son holed up or else those spaders are going to have themselves a nice surprise when they're walking back to their mates in a few minutes."

Raugov cursed under his breath. "Graywight," he said. "My old gang had a safehouse there near the corner of Nockwall. Only place there with a third floor."

"Your mates keeping him company, are they?"

"That's right. They don't hear back from me by tomorrow, they start taking pieces out of him."

Arden leaned down to whisper into Raugov's ear. "You let me worry about that. You'd better busy that little brain of yours with questions of a more eternal nature."

Before Raugov could reply, Arden pushed his head against the ground and brought the axe blade down against the back of his neck. The blow severed Raugov's spine, and his body went completely limp.

"My legs...I can't...my arms! I can't...can't feel anything!"

Arden stood up and returned his axe to the sheath on his back.

He grabbed Raugov's limp arm and pulled him toward the crevice between the buildings.

"You know, there's nothing quite so helpless as a child. They count on us for everything. Left on their own, they're at the mercy of a world that can grind the strongest men down to nothing. There's something unfair about that, don't you think? That they have to depend on the people around them to keep them safe, no matter how terrible those people might be? It's the greatest injustice in the universe, cruel even."

The gods are wicked and cruel.

"Do you remember what it's like to be helpless, Raugov? What it's like to be an innocent child under the knife of a harsh, careless world?"

He tucked Raugov's limbs inside the crevice so that no one would be able to see them from the street.

"Arden...please...don't leave me...don't leave me like this..."

Arden cut a strip of cloth from Raugov's clothing.

"Do you know what the real tragedy is? When a child cries out for help, no one ever seems to hear them."

He wadded up the cloth and shoved it into Raugov's mouth.

"Now you just sit here and think about that for a while. Think about what it must be like to be an innocent, defenseless child in a world full of men like you and me."

With that, Arden turned his back on Raugov and walked away, moving deeper into the alleyway.

He never looked back or thought about what he had done. One word dominated his thoughts.

Graywight.

Grisel did not matter anymore.

Nicalene did not matter anymore.

Sooner or later, Dhrath would learn Arden had lied to him.

Sooner or later, he wouldd find out about Raugov.

When that happened, Arden would be a dead man.

The alleyway intersected with another street, and Arden turned left to follow its course northward. Even in the moonless night, he could make out the black form of the spire projecting up from the heart of the city, a darkness deeper than the cold void between the stars and every bit as uncaring.

He had to get away from Blackspire before the city consumed him entirely. Before it stole his only son away into the deep, uncaring darkness that hung over the city like a funeral shroud.

Before it smothered the last bit of humanity Arden had left.

27
THE CHOICE

The Moonvale Theater's stage seemed so far away when viewed from the back row, especially with only a few candles to provide light. Nicalene tried to imagine what the actors might look like down there.

Distant.

Small.

Insignificant.

Alone.

You know all about that, don't you?

Nicalene closed her eyes and took a deep breath.

Beyland had not mentioned Kardi's name since he dragged the corpse outside. She tried to talk to him about what happened, about the power she felt coursing through her body and way her whole world had twisted to take on the aspect of some dreadful nightmare that belonged to someone else. Each time, though, he brushed the matter aside. He told her not to worry about it, that he had taken care of everything and she had nothing left to fear.

Then he went on pretending like his friend had never existed.

Calandra knew better. She suspected something. Nicalene could see that much in her eyes. The way she stared at her brother when he his back was turned and the way she chose her words so carefully.

Maybe she thought it strange the way Kardi apparently disappeared.

Or maybe she saw his blackened, blistered body pass through the Deadhouse.

Whatever Calandra knew, she seemed determined to keep it to herself. Perhaps it was more of a willful act of ignorance rather than a conscious decision. If she smothered her suspicions long enough, she might find a way of forgetting they ever existed.

Nicalene doubted she could manage the same feat.

Her hand drifted back to her chest. The black stone felt warm, alive even.

She opened her eyes and froze when she saw a figure standing on the stage below.

Who the hell...?

Tall and slender, the figure's short hair and gray skin betrayed her identity even before her yellow eyes stared up at Nicalene.

The ashen woman.

Unmoving and silent, she stood apart from the confines of time and space while the glass beads of her exquisite gown reflected the flickered candlelight in a thousand directions. The gown trailed several yards behind her like shimmering water cascading down a mountainside. Even from a distance, her features remained frighteningly sharp, as if every contour of her body had been carved to absolute perfection by a most meticulous sculptor.

Nicalene slowly stood up, never taking her gaze off the bizarre figure. She kept her hand over her chest. The stone throbbed, pulsing in time with her heartbeat.

"Who are you?" she asked.

The ashen woman ignored her, staring blankly ahead with yellow eyes.

"What do you want from me, damn you?" She raised her voice, but the figure still refused to respond.

Nicalene moved toward the stage.

Are you really here this time?

Aside from her dreams, every previous glimpse Nicalene caught of the ashen woman came in the mirror upstairs. Something about this appearance felt more real. Every few steps, she blinked, hoping that the strange figure would disappear by the time she opened her eyelids again. It made no difference. If anything, the ashen woman's features seemed sharper and more distinct than her surroundings, almost as if she possessed more substance than the physical objects around her.

Nicalene stepped onto the stage. Trembling, she reached out to touch the ashen woman's arm. Her fingertips came within a hair's width of brushing against the skin when the woman's hand snapped upward to seize Nicalene's wrist. Intense heat scorched her flesh and she tried to scream, but the air fled from her lungs and throat in a rush of dry air when she opened her mouth.

The ashen woman glared at her, her yellow eyes glistening like polished gold. For the first time, Nicalene noticed the inhuman qualities of the ashen woman's face: her aquiline nose, her narrow jaw, her sculpted cheekbones. A sorcerous fire smoldered beneath her skin, the flames occasionally glinting deep within her pores. When the woman parted her thin lips to speak, she revealed a set of white, pointed teeth.

"She knows about us. She knows everything."

"What?" Nicalene said. "Who are you talking about?"

"She must pay for what she's done. For what she's going to do. We can't let her go unchecked any longer, even if it means all our deaths."

Nicalene tried to pull her wrist free from the ashen woman's burning grip. She felt like her flesh was melting away to expose the bone beneath.

"Let go!" Her voice was almost a scream. "You're hurting me!"

The ashen woman sneered, her yellow eyes gleaming. "She's coming for you. She's coming for both of us."

"Stop it! I don't know what you're talking about!"

A smile this time, cold and hateful. "Don't you? Stop lying to yourself and blundering through the dark without care. She has a thousand blades hidden in the night. Open your eyes before one of them finds you."

The ashen woman's face burst into a cloud of smoke that swirled around Nicalene's body, its writhing tendrils stabbing down her throat and scalding her eyes. She lost all sense of balance and space, drifting like a brittle, dried out leaf upon the back of a tumultuous thunderstorm. Through the briefest gaps in the thick smoke, she glimpsed more unfamiliar faces, some ashen, some human. All of them stared back at her, their eyes filled with hatred and fear. She felt hidden daggers slip between her ribs, stab into the small of her back. Another hundred score deaths coursed through her consciousness, each one trying to smother her out of existence, each one failing to extinguish the tiniest of sparks.

"Nicalene?"

The voice cut through the smoke, ringing clearly over the din of half-shaped memories. Nicalene opened her eyes to find Beyland at her side, steadying her.

Of the ashen woman, she saw no sign.

"Are you okay?" Beyland asked. "I heard you shouting at someone."

Nicalene glanced down at her hands. A thick smear of ash encircled one of her wrists.

Oh, gods. She was *here.*

"I…I had a nightmare, I think," she said, hoping her tone proved convincing. "Must have fallen asleep after I came down here."

Beyland slid his hand up her arm to rub her shoulder. "You really should be more careful. If you're walking around in your sleep, you could get yourself hurt."

Nicalene pulled away from him. "Please, don't."

"What's wrong? I'm not going to—"

"I just don't want to take any more chances, Beyland. If something…happened to you because…because of me, I—"

"I'm not afraid of you, Nicalene. I'll never be afraid of you. I promise."

Nicalene wanted to believe that. Beyland had been nothing but kind to her, had accepted her without question from the moment he saw her. After Kardi's death, she also knew what he was willing to do to protect her.

And yet something about his devotion left her disquieted. Maybe it was the way he looked at her or the tinge of fanaticism in his voice. She had known enough men to recognize the symptoms of obsession.

The stone in her chest felt warm again, flickering like a candle pushing back against the dark. She gave up trying to connect its behavior to her emotions or mood. The thing seemed to have a life all its own, one she still could not quite understand.

"I need to sit down," she said, making her way over to the first row of benches. "Feeling a bit lightheaded."

Beyland helped her to her seat, but instead of joining her, he stepped back onto the stage.

"The sun will be coming up in a few hours," Beyland said, glancing up at the windows near the ceiling. "You feeling up to more auditions today?"

Nicalene groaned. She was fairly certain every failed actor in Blackspire had made his way through the Moonvale Theater over the last few days. A few of them managed to stand out from the crowd, though given the competition that was hardly an accomplishment.

"That depends," she said. "How much longer until it's finished?"

Beyland had been working on the play's ending for over a week now. Even with Nicalene's guidance, the final scene continued to prove elusive. She was starting to think that it would never be completed.

"Not long," he said. "I'm really close. A few more lines of dialogue and it will be perfect."

"And when will I get to read it?"

Beyland looked down at her, his eyes still and bright.

Nicalene recognized that hint of obsession again. Was it directed at his work or at her?

"Soon," he said.

You mean it this time, don't you?

"I suppose I might as well sit in on this latest batch. I'm not likely to get any rest with all the caterwauling down here."

Beyland laughed. "They've been pretty bad, haven't they?"

"The worst."

"We'll have to make the most of what we have, I'm afraid. That's what the director is for, right?"

Nicalene understood that, of course, but she wondered if Beyland was up to the task. As far as she knew, he never actually organized a production before.

"What parts are you reading for today?" she asked.

"Most of the big ones. I've got a few people lined up who might be a good fit for the writer. Maybe one or two who could be the queen? Not sure about the others, but hopefully we'll be able to fill a few supporting parts."

Nicalene glanced down at her wrist.

The ash still clung to her skin.

"What about...her?" she asked. "The ashen woman?"

"What are you talking about? We don't need to cast that part."

Don't need to cast her?

"Beyland, she's the most important character in the whole damn play! If that part doesn't work, the whole production will fall apart."

"I know," he said, smiling. "That's why I already have the perfect actress to play her."

The implication did not sink in right away, but when it did, Nicalene had to force herself to remain seated.

No...

"Wait," she said, "you can't mean—"

"Of course, I do," Beyland said. "It has to be you, Nicalene. It's always been you. You're the one I've had in mind for this part from the very beginning. How could you not see that?"

Nicalene thought back to all their discussions about the character, about the world she inhabited, and the forces arrayed against her. Although she had to admit that she felt a close connection to the role, she never seriously considered portraying her. After her all too frequent waking dreams and visions, she feared that stepping into the character might bring her too close to something better left undisturbed.

"I...I don't know," she said. "I'm not an actress. You know that."

Beyland shook his head.

"That's not true, Nicalene. You said so yourself: performing on stage was your first dream and the thing you wanted to do more than anything else. Maybe life pulled you in another direction, but it's never too late to go back. Forget about whatever happened to you before you came here. I know you can do this. You have to do this. Nobody else can."

She wanted to be angry with him. What right did he have to make that decision for her? To simply presume that she would even want to take on that responsibility?

But the anger refused to take hold, no matter how much she tried to muster it. Beyland's appeal reached deep into her soul and touched a part of her youthful idealism. The feeling only seemed to deepen once exposed.

Nicalene spent most of her life forgetting her dreams ever existed, burying them beneath many layers of fear and doubt. Both crept into her mind now, reminding her of the many failures and betrayals that turned her youthful dreams into nightmares. Frantic, she imagined all the ways Beyland's scheme could go wrong, how she could singlehandedly ruin everything he worked to build. The weight of that responsibility crushed her, grinding away at her already wavering resolve.

I can't do this. You don't know what you're asking. Don't know who you're asking.

"Beyland," she said, "I'm not who you think I am. I can't be what you need me to be. Don't you see that?"

He sat down beside her and took her hand. "I believe in you, Nicalene. Even if you don't."

LIKE MOST OF the decrepit winesinks scattered throughout Pigshire, *The Defenestrated Despot* kept its doors open and the drink flowing until well after sunrise. An hour before dawn, local workers stumbled in after their night shifts to mingle in the common room with men stopping by for a fix before the start of their tedious workday. They huddled around tables to bitch about their pay even as they wasted it on sour wine and stale bread. A cadre of thick-necked thugs kept the patrons in line, occasionally reminding everyone of the winesink's namesake by heaving the odd malcontent into the muddy street.

Nicalene had not been inside the place in years, but not much had changed since her last visit. The same mangled, dented suit of armor still hung on the wall behind the bar. Gullible drunks sometimes paid as much as a halfmark to touch it, believing the rumors that it once belonged to the infamous Nahoris Sendrak, captain of the traitorous 9th Legion and self-proclaimed "Tyrant of Blackspire." Most of them knew the story well enough to remember how Sendrak was thrown out the highest window of the Margrave's palace after his defeat, but they were usually too intoxicated to notice that the armor was a cheap facsimile made of second hand tin.

The crusty eyed old woman pouring drinks behind the counter looked familiar, but Nicalene forgot her name. After paying for her drink, she found a seat at a small, empty table near the back. A sharp glare proved sufficient to keep passersby at a distance. Aside from a few leering glances, no one paid much attention to her.

That suited her well enough. She had not gone to the *Despot* for conversation, after all.

The wine tasted awful. Somebody had sprinkled charcoal into the barrel to mask the sourness, but they added too much. Each sip left her mouth dry and tasting of ash.

Serves you right.

She watched Pigshire's workers come and go through the doorway, some of them eager, or at least relieved, to be going home. Others looked like they were walking to the gallows. She could not always tell whether their day was ending or beginning.

Grisel used to get the same look. Sometimes he left with it, other times it followed him back to their flat.

Grisel. Stupid bastard.

Nicalene took another gulp of her drink and choked the vile stuff down.

Not as stupid as me, though, are you?

She had waited for Beyland to go back to bed before slipping out the theater's back door. Finding her way back to Pigshire was easy enough, even in the rain. The *Despot* was hardly her first choice, but it was closer to Coldwater Borough than any of her other old haunts.

What she had not worked out yet was where to go next.

Nicalene had lived under more than a dozen roofs and with at least as many people, most of them men she would rather forget. Even if some of those places might take her back for a few nights, all of them had too many bad memories nestled in dark corners. She still had some of the coin she nicked from Grisel, of course, but it would not get her very far for very long. Every plan she formulated left her right back in Lowtown, right back where she started.

Right back where she always ended up.

Alone. Desperate. Afraid.

I believe in you, Nicalene. Even if you don't.

Beyland's words kept coming back to her, taunting her, tormenting her. They were the words she had been waiting to hear, the words she needed to hear her entire life.

And now that she finally heard them, they terrified her.

Oh, Beyland, why did you have to be such a fool?

In all their time together, Grisel never once uttered those words. She always resented him for that, right up to the day she walked out of his life. But now she understood why he never said them. Unlike Beyland, Grisel knew her, knew her better than she knew herself. He never allowed himself to believe in her because he knew she would find a way to let him down. Nicalene hated him for that. She hated him for never giving her that chance, for never helping her to prove to him, to prove to everyone, that they were wrong about her.

But she hated herself even more because, deep down, she knew he was right. Never had she done anything worthwhile in her entire life. In fact, the only thing she seemed to have any talent for at all was letting people down, herself most of all.

It's better this way, Beyland. Better that you know now before you really *get yourself hurt.*

She took another drink. The wine tasted dry, scorching her throat as it trickled down her throat.

A trio of whores entertained overeager patrons a few tables away. One of the men, older than his companions, looked like an officer of the watch, though he lacked the telltale strip of blue fabric on his arm. He leaned back in his chair and laughed while the younger men groped clumsily at the women.

New recruits, most likely. The watch strongly disapproved of prostitution, at least officially. What the men did on their own time, though, was another matter. The threat of spending the night naked in a cold cell had a way of ensuring that the men of the watch enjoyed rather favorable rates, as well.

Hypocrites.

Nicalene watched the bawdry exchange closely, trying to picture herself in place of one of the women. They were younger than her, little more than girls. She wondered how much more coin that would bring them.

What would they say if she tried to ply their trade? Would they even consider her a threat? Or would they simply laugh at her and have her thrown out in the streets, leaving her to offer herself up to any shiftless bastard with nothing but a few quartermarks and a stiff cock to his name?

That's where the old ones always end up, isn't it?

She looked away from the scene and drained the rest of her cup.

There was enough coin left over from Grisel's stash to keep her off the streets for a few weeks, maybe a month or two. After that, she needed to pay her own way somehow. If she failed to do that, there was a good chance she would wind up following some sticker down a dark alley and never come out.

What would you think of me then, Beyland?

Tiny bits of black charcoal clung to the bottom of her cup. She considered going to fetch a second drink, but the thought of forcing down more of that vile swill made her stomach churn. An empty cup would soon draw attention, however. If she left it unfilled, one of the thugs watching the door would be along to escort her out, forcefully if she protested.

There were a dozen other places she could go from there, but they were all the same. Winesinks, flophouses, nightroot cellars. All of them waiting to suck her dry, bit by bit.

Never a moment's peace in this wretched city.

The stone in her chest sent a faint swell of heat through her body. She closed her eyes and rubbed her hand over its hard surface, thankful that her loose-fitting dress covered it completely.

Then there's you...

When she opened her eyes, Nicalene half expected to find the ashen woman sitting across from her.

But the seat was still empty.

She sighed.

I must be going mad.

She needed to talk to the ghulans again. They had to have learned something about her condition by now. If they could extract the stone, maybe they could find a buyer for it. Surely some fool aristocrat from High Ridge or Crown Gate would pay a small fortune trying to harness whatever power it possessed.

Then again, the sort of people who could afford to offer such a high price probably would not care if the ghulans cut the damn thing out of her chest and dumped her in the river to bleed out.

How much did she trust the ghulans, anyway? They had a good reputation, certainly, but they wer also inhuman. Did human life mean anything to them? Nicalene knew little about their kind, only that they always travelled in pairs. The precise nature of that relationship was unclear. Siblings? Lovers? Whatever the truth, it seemed unnatural, or at least not a practice that humans could understand.

A serving woman approached her table with a jug of wine.

"Another drink for a tenthmark, dear?"

Nicalene glanced up at her. The woman was older than her, but her worn features made it difficult to tell by how much. There was a weariness in her eyes that made Nicalene's skin shiver. She looked down at the back of her hands, scrutinizing every wrinkle.

An old hag's hands, that's what they are. The rest of me will be along soon...

She reached into her satchel, fished out a halfmark, and slapped the coin down on the table.

"Fill it. And leave the jug."

The woman let out a nervous laugh and said something she probably thought sounded clever. Nicalene ignored her.

A whore at the nearby table yelped when one of the young watchmen squeezed her breast. His friends shouted out encouragements and dares while the other women squirmed in their laps.

Stupid pigs.

The older watchman appeared to share her sentiment. He grunted and pushed his chair back from the table.

"Don't be out too long, lads," he said. "You've got a long shift ahead of you tonight."

As he stood up to leave, his gaze lingered for a moment on Nicalene. She stared at him unflinchingly, her contempt for the scene still etched plainly upon her face.

The watchman grabbed his cup, walked over to her table, and picked up the wine jug to slosh its contents around.

"Plan on spending the whole day here, are you?"

Nicalene pulled the jug out of his hand and refilled her cup. "Piss off."

The man laughed.

It was the first genuine emotion Nicalene had observed since she walked through the door.

"Haven't seen you in here before. Pretty plain you're not here to whore around, either."

"That so?"

"Course not. You wouldn't be paying your way otherwise."

"Real observant, aren't you?"

"I notice a thing or two about folks. Take you, for instance. Good skin, decent clothes, soft hands. You ain't the working sort, but you ain't highborn neither. Not with that mouth of yours. That don't leave many options in these parts. Entertainer, if I had to wager. Actress, maybe, or a dancer?"

Nicalene took a drink and tried to ignore the tiny flutter of pride in her stomach.

"Actress," she said.

The man smiled. "See? What'd I tell you?" He eased into the chair across from her and refilled both their cups.

More squeals from the nearby table. Nicalene barely noticed.

"Sounds like your lads are getting out of hand over there."

The man grunted. "Overeager boys. Half of them will cum before they get their belts off."

"Seems like a waste of coin."

"They need to learn sooner or later. Better they figure it out now with a woman than with one of the goats in the guardhouse yard. Or with each other."

Men...

"What about you?" Nicalene asked. "I thought a man of the watch was supposed to lead by example."

He took a long drink from his cup. "Not as young as I used to be. Don't see much point in paying for company anymore, I guess."

Nicalene laughed. "Tired of having them slip off with your coin after you pass out, you mean."

"Oh, that never much stopped me before. But sooner or later a man reaches a point where he can't pretend she's there for something more than his coin."

She sipped at her wine. "Maybe you never found the right sort of liar."

"You're the actress, darling. I expect you'd know all about performing for a crowd wanting to believe in something that ain't so."

The wine turned bitter in her stomach. She looked down at her cup and swished the bits of charcoal around a few times.

"I know you can't keep doing it forever," she said. "Not without losing the parts of you that matter."

The watchman sighed. "Well, I'd say that's probably true of all of us eventually. Suppose we're all stumbling through the dark hoping that knife doesn't find us just yet."

A knife in the dark...

Nicalene looked up, the movement abrupt enough to make the watchman flinch. "What did you say?"

"Eh?"

"About a knife."

He smiled. "Sorry, I didn't mean nothing by it. An old watch saying about how every night could be your last out there."

The stone felt warmer now, pulsing in time with her heartbeat. She glanced around the common room, fearful that she might spot the ashen women emerging from the shadows.

But she saw nothing. Just the same collection of dregs and drunkards as before.

"Hey," the watchman said, "what's wrong? There someone looking for you or something?" He placed his hand on her wrist.

"It's...it's nothing." She turned to meet his concerned gaze. "Noth—"

Every muscle in her body tightened, and the stone felt hot enough to melt her skin.

Oh, no. Not here! Not now!

The ashen woman sat beside the watchman, her yellow eyes staring straight ahead with inhuman intensity. It was her hand, not his, wrapped around Nicalene's wrist.

"It's not safe here," the woman said. "They're coming for you. She's coming for you."

Nicalene jerked her arm free and scrambled out of her seat. "Stop it, damn you! Leave me alone!"

The watchman raised his hands, perplexed. "I'm sorry," he said. "I didn't mean to—"

A firm hand clamped down on her shoulder.

"They're coming!"

The fire in her chest shot down her arm as she reached up to grasp the forearm of the young watchman standing behind her.

"No!"

His flesh bubbled up like boiling fat when Nicalene found her grip. Stools fell over as the winesink patrons leapt to their feet. Some of them screamed, though none cried out so loudly as the man writhing in her grasp. But even his voice seemed distant, almost muffled as the swirling air thudded against her ears. Her vision flickered and faded, the faces around her melding together in a blurred soup of indistinct, and often in-human, shapes.

Then a nearby voice managed to push above the din. "What are you doing? Let him go!"

Something grabbed her arm and pulled her backward. Nicalene lost her hold on the watchman's forearm as she stumbled. Her vision cleared slightly, but now she felt drunk, like her head might explode if she tried to focus her attention on anything. She pulled away from the hands holding her steady and staggered across the common room. People scrambled to get out of her way, and she heard a pitiful voice sobbing behind her. Glancing back, she made out the faint impression of a man cradling his arm.

The ashen woman stood behind him, her every feature so sharp and clear that merely looking at her made Nicalene's eyes sting.

"She's coming for you. For him."

Him?

Faint impressions of movement flashed by, some of them fuzzy and indistinct, but others more like shadows. Several figures coalesced around the man with the wounded arm, their faces distant and distorted. Else-where, the dead loomed like withered trees to bare their blackened and scarred flesh for her to see. She backed away, unable to bring herself to view them in full.

A silver shadow brushed past her, sending a warm tremor up her spine.

Beyland?

The shadow washed over her, caressing her skin even as it held her firmly in place.

Not Beyland...

Cold air closed in around her chest, driving the heat from her body and leaving her adrift in an icy void.

Grisel? Is that you?

Nicalene spun around, waving her arms in a vain attempt to clear the way around her. The spectral images wilted at her touch, only to resume form elsewhere. Occasionally, she bumped against something tangible, something real, though it quickly gave way before her. Voices murmured all around her, though only a few words rang out clearly through the din.

"…witch…"

"…murderer…"

"…demon…"

"…freak…"

Shut up, damn you! Shut up!

The heat swelled from deep within her chest once more, and she felt lightheaded. Streaks of black fire shot from her fingertips, shattering tables and punching holes in the walls. Occasionally, she heard someone scream, followed by the reek of scorched leather and flesh.

No! Stop!

Nicalene squeezed her hands into fists, clenching them so tightly that her nails cut through the skin. The pain cleared her vision for the briefest of moments, permitting her a view of the smoldering interior of the winesink while most of its patrons cowered in terror. She felt the delirium seeping back into her mind, gnawing at her sense of what was real. The black stone in her chest pulsated, sending jolts of heightened awareness through her bones with every breath.

Frantic, she staggered out the door and into the rain.

Somewhere behind her, she heard the ashen woman laughing.

28
THE HOUND

"Gods damn it, Grisel, you look at me when I'm talking to you!"

Grisel choked down a curse of his own and glared at Jaspen instead.

There was no point arguing about it anyway.

Not when Jaspen clearly had the right of things.

Meaty held on long enough for them to get him back to the guild-house. The guild physician tried to sew him up, but by that point he had simply lost too much blood. He died before sunrise. Jaspen stayed with him all the way to the end, just like in life.

Then he went looking for Grisel.

"If you'd have just gone to the guild with this like I told you, none of this would have happened," Jaspen said. "But no, you had to run off on your own just like you always do, never stopping to think about anybody but yourself."

Grisel bit his lip and nodded. He had only returned from his meeting with Tameris for a short while before Jaspen stormed into the flat to tell him Meaty was dead.

Dead because of me.

The news hit him hard; he and Meaty had been mates for years, ever since coming up through the guild together with Jaspen. Among all the scrapes and gutterscums he ever met in Lowtown, Meaty was the last one who deserved to die.

Grisel sat down on the stool next to Meaty's cot. The blanket was still thrown to one side, half of it on the floor. He could not bring himself to look at it.

"How the hells was I supposed to know, Jaspen? Arden didn't seem like the type to—"

"Stop! Stop it!" Jaspen went on pacing and scowling. Whenever he spoke, he glared at Grisel and stepped closer to him. This time, he leaned in so close that he hovered almost directly above him. "You still ain't listening, mate. It wasn't him that started the fight, but that don't much matter. If you'd just done what I said to do, the guild could've put out word to the crews and been ready for something like this."

Grisel stood up, forcing Jaspen to back off to avoid butting heads. "Hey, you think I wanted this to happen? That I don't give a toss what goes down with my friends so long as I get mine? Fuck you! How do you think I feel knowing that one of my best mates got knifed by some broker's cutter because they were trying to find me? Gods, Jaspen, if I'd have known this was going to happen, I would have stayed where Arden had me locked up. So yeah, I know he's dead because of me and I'm sorry. Okay? I'm fucking sorry! I'm sorry all of this happened, that the both of you got dragged into this. But don't you stand there and act like I don't give a toss that he's gone now because you know damn well I'd have traded places with him, same as you would."

Jaspen stared at him, nostrils flaring as he clenched his fists. For a moment, Grisel thought his friend might try to knock out his teeth. Then the anger drained from his face, followed by a long sigh. Jaspen's shoulders slumped and his gaze drifted to Meaty's cot.

"Look, Grisel…I'm…I'm sorry… I know you didn't want any of this to happen, mate. I do. I just…I just can't believe…"

Tears clouded his eyes, and his lips trembled as he tried to finish his sentence. Grisel stood up and hugged him.

"It ain't fair, mate," Jaspen said, his voice cracking. "What'd he ever do to deserve this?"

"Nothing. He didn't do nothing to deserve it. Just like I didn't deserve to lose my fingers and Nicalene didn't deserve what happened to her. All of us just in the wrong place at the wrong time to get pushed around by these bastards who think our kind don't amount to nothing."

Jaspen embraced him and sobbed against his shoulder. "It ain't right…"

"No. No, it ain't."

"Feels like everything's darker without him here. We been together for so long, I can't hardly remember him not being around, you know?"

Grisel did not doubt that. When he first met Jaspen and Meaty, they had already been mates for years. Their hard years as guild apprentices brought them closer together, but Grisel was always the third member of the trio. The other two had too much history, too much experience together for Grisel to get that close to either of them.

"I'm going to make that bastard Dhrath pay for this," Grisel said. "We've got a plan to—"

Jaspen pulled away from him, his eyes still wet with tears. "No. This has to stop. No more plans, no more running around on your own. You've got to come clean to the guild now."

"I can't do that, not after what I found out from Twiceborn. Nicalene's connected to all of this, mate. If Dhrath gets his slimy arms on that stone, he could put the whole guild to pavement along with the rest of Lowtown."

Jaspen shook his head. "No bloody way, Grisel. We're doing this my way from now on. You're going to tell the guildmasters everything you know before we take this to the Assembly."

"The Assembly? Are you out of your stupid skull? Dhrath's got most of it in his pocket, especially now that Trinn Harmyndri's turned up dead."

"Not the ones we're talking to. While you were out dicking around yesterday, Trinn's girlfriend got voted to replace her. Name's Olynia. Do you remember her?"

Grisel never much cared for politics, either with the Assembly or among Lowtown's various guilds, but he overheard quite a lot from Jaspen and Meaty's conversations. Near as he could tell, the two of them were only a few steps away from becoming active revolutionaries. Olynia's name came up on several occasions, usually whenever talk of a guild strike was in the air.

"Yeah," he said. "She's that brickthrower with the Carvers Guild, right?"

Jaspen nodded. "She's setting up a meeting tonight with some of the guilds to talk about ending the brokers' grip on the Assembly and the watch. Word is that she's got an ally with enough pull to do some damage."

"Who?"

"Ember Morangine."

Grisel laughed. "You're joking, right? Lord Morangine himself wants to lend a hand to the guilds all of a sudden? He's the one that's been trying to bury us for years! You honestly think you can trust him?"

"I trust Olynia. She says he's on the level, at least as far as this goes. Something about him being upset about another Assembly member's death."

"Even if she's right, nothing's going to matter if Dhrath or Arden manage to get to Nicalene before we do. I know you think this is crazy, but—"

"Dammit, Grisel, will you forget about that stupid bitch? She ain't brought you nothing but bad luck anyway. I know you're bitter she made off with your payday, but you can't let yourself get swept up in this fool's talk about magic rocks and spirits."

Stupid bitch?

Grisel grabbed Jaspen by his overall straps and shoved him against the wall. "You watch your guttersucking mouth about her! What do you know about trying to save somebody you love?"

His friend just stared at him with eyes devoid of any emotion.

Oh, hells...

Grisel let him go and stepped away back slowly. "Jaspen, I'm sorry. I didn't think..."

They stared at each other for a moment before Jaspen shook his head. "No, it's... I was out of line, mate. I just...I didn't realize she meant that much to you is all."

Neither did I.

Jaspen sighed. "I reckon if it was Meaty in trouble, I'd be saying the same thing. You ought to get going, then."

"Listen, about Meaty. I know you were close, maybe more than that. Look, if I ever said anything that...well, that..."

"Forget it, mate. Just...just get out of here. Don't tell me where you're going or what you're planning to do. It's better for both of us if I don't know. You go do what you think you have to do and let me worry about the guild, okay?"

Grisel nodded. He wanted to say something else, something that might convey sympathy, reassurance, and gratitude all at once, but his vocabulary and sense of the moment fell far short of the task.

"Thanks, Jaspen. I owe you one."

It was the best he could muster.

Jaspen nodded. "Yeah..."

THE RAIN LET up a few times during the day, but it never quite stopped, always coming down hard enough to keep the streets clear of their usual travelers. With no crowds to blend in with, Grisel had to avoid the main streets. He simply could not take the chance that Arden or one of his thugs would be waiting on some street corner to throw a sack over his head and beat him senseless. Although the trip took him twice as much time as usual, he meandered down alleyways and narrow, unmarked walkways to traverse Pigshire.

His crumbling tenement was precisely where he had left it. Taller than its neighbors, the building had entered the early stages of a long decay that would end with it collapsing under its own weight. Grisel had lived there for the last five years. He never imagined he would be there for so long. The place might not have been much to look at, even by Pigshire standards, but the price was good and the neighbors tolerable. Had things not gone sideways, he imagined he might have spent another five years there.

Nicalene always hated it, though. Deep down, she just was not meant to live in a shithole like Pigshire, or Lowtown for that matter. Grisel knew that, but after all their time together he never bothered to do anything about it. Whenever she bitched about the place, he reminded her how lucky she was to have a roof at all. After all, if he never took her in, she would have ended up on a lonely slab in the Deadhouse sooner or later.

Maybe he could have been nicer about pointing that out. She could be hard as a nail, but she had her softer moments. Those moments became less and less frequent as time went by and attitudes hardened. In their last month together, they hardly even spoke. Even the sex, long sustained by mutual anger and frustration, became an empty gesture, devoid of purpose or feeling.

How'd we let it get so bad?

Grisel found the front gate only partially repaired, connected to the doorframe by a loose length of wire. Wurgim had been working on it the night he found the stone, but it was hard to tell if the big man considered the door "repaired" at this point.

One of the Tamercums usually sat outside the gate or near the bottom of the steps inside, but Grisel saw no sign of them today. He was glad for their absence since his return after being gone for a whole week would prompt plenty of questions, maybe even suspicion. The damned brothers were always picking at other people's affairs, especially among their neighbors. For all he knew, they already had ties to Dhrath and were actively looking for him.

Don't worry about them now. Just get in and get back out.

He went up the stairs and carefully opened the door leading to his flat. Three rooms stood between the stairwell and his, each of them separated by nothing more than a curtain. Sedina's room was first, but Grisel found no sign of her inside. She rarely kept a steady schedule, always coming and going as her work demanded. Her sparsely decorated room was well ordered, with the bed's sheets tucked tightly under the mattress and the half-melted candle on the wardrobe covered with a tin cap.

The last time he saw her, she was sprawled out naked upon her soft bed, her skin sheathed in sweat. He could still taste her when he closed his eyes.

Moving into the next room, he breathed a sigh when he found it empty. The Tamercums were nowhere to be seen. He imagined they were out peddling nightroot to despondent workers in some Pigshire winesink. The room beside his proved empty as well, but that was no great surprise since Tupin worked during the day. While the little bastard probably could not cause any trouble even if he wanted to, Grisel was glad he to avoid listening to his stupid attempts at insulting humor.

His flat looked much the same way the way he left it. Mice nested in the bed now, leaving tiny pellets and dark stains all over the sheets. The little bastards had moved in quickly, but nobody turned the place over yet to flush them out since Grisel was paid through to the end of the month.

From the wardrobe, Grisel pulled out his spader overalls and a mask, along with a fresh set of underclothes. After donning his own garments, he went to Nicalene's chest and grabbed an armload of dresses and shirts. Tameris shared no specifics about what type of personal items she needed for her sorcery, but Grisel doubted he could find anything better than her clothing. He wrapped the garments in Jaspen's shirt and tied the bundle using his spare pants. After hoisting the makeshift sack over his shoulder, he grabbed the spade leaning against the wall next to the wardrobe and turned to leave.

He stopped dead still when he found someone standing in the doorway watching him.

That's not good.

Felski Tamercum picked at his fingernails with a dagger, casually flicking bits of dirt onto the floor. "Good to see you, Grisel. Been a while, ain't it?"

"The hells you doing in my flat, Felski?"

"Me and Wurgim been worried about you. I like to drop by and have a look see whenever I get home. Thought maybe you and that woman of yours ran off to some dreamleech den and lost track of the days. I know she had a taste for it, anyway."

Grisel glared at him. "Yeah, well good for her. Maybe that's where she ended up, but I don't much give a toss anymore. Meantime, I'm just back to clean out a few things."

"So, you ain't been out with her, eh? Where you been, then, huh?"

"Don't see how it's any of your business."

Felski shrugged. He twirled the dagger round and round in his hand. "Neighbors got a right to know who they're living next to, don't they? Especially when people come around asking questions."

"What kind of questions?"

"Why don't we take a little walk and I'll show you? Got a concerned friend who wants to have a word with you. The girl, too, wherever she is."

Arden. He's been here already.

"Piss off," Grisel said.

Felski took a step into the flat, leaving enough space in the door for his big brother, Wurgim, to step through behind him with a smith's hammer in hand. "That ain't no way to accept a neighbor's hospitality. You're going to offend my brother talking like that."

Wurgim grunted as he tried to sneer. Grisel seemed to recall the bigger Tamercum having more teeth before.

Got a way with people, don't you, Arden?

He dropped the bundle of clothing. "I'm not in much of a talking mood today."

Felski smiled. "Hoped you might feel that way. Wurgim?"

The big Tamercum lunged forward, hopping onto the bed as he raised his hammer. Grisel spun the spade around to grip it with both hands and stabbed the blunt end forward like a spear. The tip caught Wurgim just below the rib cage and forced air back up his throat. He coughed wetly and doubled over, dropping his hammer. Grisel adjusted his grip on the spade to smash the shovel's face against the side of Wurgim's head. The blow knocked several more teeth loose and sent him reeling onto the bed.

Felski moved quickly, slipping around the bed to strike with his dagger, but Grisel swung the blunt end of the spade around to fend him off. Felski avoided the blow, losing his balance in the process. Grisel pressed him, this time slamming the shovel end squarely against his chest. Felski screamed in pain as he fell back, clutching his ribs.

Grisel raised the spade with the intention of breaking one of Felski's arms, but Wurgim intervened before he could strike. The big man grabbed him with one hand and wrapped his other arm around Grisel in a bear hug. Wurgim hoisted him off the ground and squeezed him so hard he felt like his lungs would collapse.

"Got him, Felski! Got him!"

Despite Wurgim's enthusiasm, Felski was slow to get up, giving Grisel precious seconds to react. Clumsily maneuvering the spade with his pinned arms, he managed to jab the blunt end directly over his shoulder to poke the brute in the eye. Wurgim cried out and released his foe to clutch at his bleeding eye socket.

Grisel took a few frantic gasps to fill his lungs, then whirled around to hammer at the big man with the spade's shovel end. Still grasping at his eye, the blow caught him off guard and sent him tumbling to the ground. Adjusting his grip, Grisel stabbed the shovel directly against Wurgim's chest. The impact snapped the sternum and several ribs like wet twigs and sent the big man's body into convulsions.

A thick, gurgling sound bubbled through his toothless mouth as his eyes opened wide with panicked terror. Grisel staggered back, his head spinning. He felt his stomach churning in time with Wurgim's dying gasps.

Have to get out...

He turned around to find Felski lunging at him with his dagger.

Stupid, stupid, stupid!

Felski got inside the spade's reach before Grisel could raise it in defense. Stumbling backward to avoid the dagger, Grisel dropped the spade and threw up his hands to catch Felski's arms. They fell to the floor together, wrestling for position, but Felski had the momentum and managed to stay on top of Grisel. He leaned all of his weight behind the dagger, slowly forcing the blade closer to Grisel's chest.

"You're a dead man, spader! After what you just done to my brother, you're a fucking dead man!"

The dagger's tip pressed against Grisel's leather overalls. His arms felt like they were on fire as every muscle in his body strained to keep that blade from plunging into his heart.

Can't stop him...

Felski laughed, his face twisting with murderous rage.

Grisel closed his eyes.

"Dead, dead, dead, dead, dead!"

Something warm and wet splashed against his mouth and the pressure weighing down on him relented.

What the...?

He opened his eyes to find blood gushing from a wide gash in Felski's throat. The blade tumbled harmlessly to the floor as the would-be killer's body went limp. Grisel pushed the corpse to the side and frantically wiped at the blood covering his mouth and neck.

Sedina, dressed in a black dress adorned with a red shawl draped over one shoulder, stood over him holding a bloody dagger.

"Grisel? Are you okay?"

He grabbed the corner of a bed sheet to wipe the blood from his face. "Yeah, I think so. Where the hells did you come from?"

"I just returned to my flat and heard the scuffle. Sounded serious, so I came to have a look."

"Glad you did." He kicked at Felski's corpse. "This shitheel would have run me through if you hadn't come along. Thanks."

"The both of them have been watching for you to come back ever since Arden was here looking for you."

"Arden, eh? I figured. You talk to him?"

"Yeah, I did." She glanced down at his bandaged hand. "The better question is what does he want with you?"

Grisel shook his head as he stood up. "It's got to do with Nicalene. He's after her for something she took. Something she took from me, really. Thinks I can help him find her."

"You know where she is now?" Sedina wiped her dagger clean on Felski's trouser leg.

He picked up the bundle of clothes. "I will soon."

Sedina looked over the bodies. Wurgim's limbs still twitched slightly in time with his labored breathing. "The big one's still alive."

"He won't be for much longer," he said. "Should we...you know...?"

"What? Put him out of his misery?"

Grisel nodded.

"Leave him," she said. "He had it coming. Both of them did."

"What do we do with the bodies? We can't just leave them here like this."

Sedina shrugged. "You planning on coming back here?"

"I don't know. Guess I hadn't thought about it."

"Well, I've got enough coin stashed to move on. Maybe enough to get a place in Spiresreach, or West Gate, even. I figure it's past time to get a new start, don't you?"

Grisel looked around the disheveled flat.

Five years is a long time in a place like this...

"I don't know if I can," he said. "Not just yet. Not till I get this thing with Nicalene sorted."

Sedina sighed. She walked over and kissed him on the cheek.

"Goodbye, Grisel. I hope you find what you think you're looking for."

TAMERIS INSPECTED EVERY article of clothing carefully. For each garment, she squinted to examine the weave, rubbed her fingers over the seams, and sniffed at the fabric before tossing it into one of two piles. When she finally finished, one pile proved much larger than the other, which consisted of only four pieces.

"Better than nothing," she said.

Grisel picked up a shirt from the larger pile. "What's wrong with this lot?"

"Weak connection to her. Would have been better if they hadn't been washed; at least they'd have the scent."

"Are you sending a hound after her?"

Tameris shrugged, smiling just enough to reveal a sliver of her yellowish teeth. "In a manner of speaking, yes."

Grisel tossed the shirt onto the pile.

Got a way of making people uncomfortable, don't you?

She gathered the clothes she wanted and handed them to the servant who escorted Grisel through the interconnected network of earthen basements beneath Sinkhole's streets earlier. He was an odd-looking man, with sloped shoulders and a hunched back. Patches of his dry skin bore plague scars, probably suffered when he was much younger. Whenever he looked at Grisel with his mismatched eyes, he seemed to be staring somewhere far beyond him. On the few occasions when the servant actually spoke, the words came out slow and deliberate, without a hint of inflection or emotion.

"Come with me." Tameris took a burning candle in hand and walked to the narrow door on the opposite end of the room. The servant waited for Grisel to move before falling behind him. "Everything we touch, everything we possess, all of it carries a faint impression of our spirit. The longer we hold onto an object, the stronger that connection becomes."

Once opened, the door revealed a cramped tunnel propped up by wooden beams. Sloped slightly downward, the passage descended for about fifty feet before turning sharply to the left and continuing into the earth.

What the hells is she up to down here?

"Near as anyone can tell, no two people's spirits look the same. Similar, maybe, but not identical."

"Kind of like looking at somebody's face, right?"

"Yes." She rounded another corner to continue their descent. "Only even more distinctive. Some scholars think there's a finite number of human spirits in the world, that they get passed on from the dead to the living. There's another theory that they're derived from your parents, same as your flesh."

"What do you think?"

"Me?" She laughed. "I like to think they're all drawn from somewhere. Somewhere close to here."

Grisel thought about what she could mean by that.

"The spire," he said, recalling her fascination with the ominous landmark. "You're talking about the spire, aren't you?"

Before Tameris could answer, she made another hard-left turn and came to a stop before a reinforced wooden door banded by iron strips. The door sat inside a heavy, wooden frame embedded into the tunnel walls. It looked sturdy; a dozen men with a small battering ram probably could not force their way through.

"Here we are." She placed her hand over the locking mechanism and whispered something Grisel missed. Gears and pulleys groaned on the other side. The door slowly unlatched and creaked open.

The room beyond was pitch dark, but Grisel knew it was big by the way their footsteps echoed back to him when they stepped inside. Although the air felt cooler and damper than the stuffy, dry air of the chambers above them, it retained the same distinctive chemical-laden odor. Tameris knelt next to an oil lantern just inside the door and used her candle to light it. When the wick caught fire, it pushed the darkness back enough to reveal the wet stone floor beneath them. Several tables stood near the door, all of them covered with a bizarre array of instruments and containers. For every tool Grisel recognized, he saw at least two more that were completely unfamiliar. Several glass bottles reflected the lantern's light, some of them filled with oddly colored liquids. The air inside the chamber felt cool and damp.

Tameris blew out the candle and lifted the lantern. "Stay close. And don't touch anything."

She moved deeper into the chamber, passing several more tables and a few stone slabs, not unlike those found in the Lowtown mortuary. A few dozen yards more and they came across the first of several wooden shacks spreading around them. Slightly larger than two spader wagons shoved together, the structures rose only a foot or two above their heads. None of the makeshift buildings featured windows, only a single door locked shut with a heavy chain.

"What's inside all these shacks?"

"Storage."

Right...

Tameris stopped next to one of the doors and grabbed the chain lashed around the handle. There was no lock of any kind, just a single, unbroken length of chain. She whispered something under her breath and one of the links turned to dust, allowing her to pull the chain free.

Before opening the door, she looked back at Grisel. "Try not to make any sudden movements."

What the hells does she have in there?

Reluctantly, he followed her into the dark shack.

The room inside was completely empty except for the body resting limply against the back wall, its head hanging down so far that the chin rested on its chest. Tameris knelt beside the figure and placed her hand on its forehead.

"Wake."

For a moment, nothing happened. Then a leg twitched, followed by an arm. The figure's head lifted, exposing his face to the light.

Grisel had seen its face before.

It can't be...

"Thought you might appreciate seeing a familiar face, but I don't think the two of you have been formally introduced," Tameris said. "Grisel, say hello to Kaurgen."

Kaurgen stared at him with dull, dead eyes. A ragged, red scar ran down the center of his face, tracing a line from his upper lip, over his chin, and finally ending where his neck met the lower jaw.

Grisel took a step back, bumping into Tameris's servant, who still carried Nicalene's clothes in his gnarled hands. He turned to look at the hunched wretch and wondered why he failed to notice that the misshapen thing never drew a breath.

"How…how did you…?"

"I could explain," she said, "but I doubt you'd understand any of it."

Grisel grabbed her arm. "Why don't you let me be the judge of what I understand? Tell me."

Tameris sighed and nodded. "I got his body from the Deadhouse. Corpse was well preserved. Probably a byproduct of prolonged contact with the stone. A good portion of his memories were still intact when I received him. When I got to digging, I found out that some of those memories formed after he died."

A "mutual acquaintance," was it?

"That's how you knew about how I found him."

"Yes, now you know. Can we get on with this now?"

Grisel nodded and released her arm.

"Good," she said. "Bring those clothes over here, will you?"

He took Nicalene's clothing from the hunched servant, who still watched them from the doorway.

How many of these poor bastards do you have running around doing your errands?

He handed the garments over to Tameris and stepped back, not wanting to get too close to the man he had fished out of a privy a week ago. Without moving an inch, Kaurgen's soulless gaze remained fixed on Grisel.

You remember me, shitsucker?

"How can you actually look into a dead man's memories?" he asked.

Tameris sighed, loudly enough that Grisel could not miss her annoyance.

Not that he gave a damn.

"In a manner of speaking, yes," she said, "but 'looking' isn't quite the best way to describe it. The memories deteriorate faster than the body. They're usually scattered and incoherent, not worth trying to make sense of."

Grisel stared back at Kaurgen. The dead man's vacant eyes made his skin shiver.

"Does he still remember being alive?"

Tameris shook her head as she unfolded and stacked Nicalene's clothes atop one another. "Not anymore. Whatever traces he had left wouldn't have survived the reanimation process."

"Does it always work like that?"

She paused, biting at her lower lip before answering. "Something always gets lost when you're brought back. Always. How much you lose depends on the way you return. For this one and the others? Nothing survives."

The answer surprised him. It was the first time he saw a crack in that hardened exterior. He wanted to press her, but before he could ask another question, she placed the stack of garments onto Kaurgen's lap.

What are you up to now?

"Hey, I thought you needed these for some kind of spell to find Nicalene."

"I wish it were that simple, but there's not a sorcerer in all of Blackspire who could pull that off. Fortunately, I know a few tricks that might work just as well, even if they take a bit longer."

"What kind of tricks?"

Kaurgen's hands closed around the fabric. He lifted the garments to his face and sniffed.

"Well, you asked about a hound earlier," she said. "Now you've got one."

As Tameris spoke, the entire lower portion of Kaurgen's face split open, separating along the long red scar line to splay out like the blooming pedals of a ghastly flower. Grisel watched in horror as an array of little tendrils, each one about the length of his thumbnail, protruded from the exposed flesh. Kaurgen lifted Nicalene's clothing to his maw to let the tentacles probe the fabric.

"What did you do to him?" Grisel barely got the words through his trembling lips as the fleshy appendages writhed over the clothing.

Tameris had no such reservations. "A simple work of fleshcraft. I sculpted his jaw and oral cavity to accommodate sensory glands that detect—"

Grisel's stomach heaved. He spun away from the grisly sight and staggered out of the little shack to throw up. When he finished retching, he looked at the barely visible door of the building directly opposite the one they entered a few minutes earlier.

How many of those buildings were down in that dark chamber? They had passed at least four or five that he could see. What other horrors slumbered behind chained doors, waiting for Tameris to stir them to unlife with nothing more than a word?

This is wrong.

"Grisel?"

He jumped at the sound of her voice. When he turned, he found Tameris waiting outside the doorway, lantern in hand. Kaurgen stood next to her, his face returned to normal, except for his dead eyes and the ugly scar that Grisel now understood was no scar at all.

"He's got her scent," Tameris said. "Take him to the last place you know she visited. He'll pick up the trail from there."

Grisel looked at the dead man. Except for the eyes, the scar, and the fact that he did not breathe, nothing betrayed his true, abominable nature.

On a busier street or in some of the rougher buroughs, he might not even draw a second glance from strangers.

"Will he need to...uh...?" Grisel rubbed at his chin.

Tameris shrugged. "Possibly, if the trail goes too cold. But he won't do it if anyone else is around."

Grisel looked at the dead man. His face remained still as stone. "Does he still understand us?"

"Of course. He wouldn't be able to follow your commands otherwise."

"My commands?"

"Yes. I've conditioned him to follow your lead. Once you've found Nicalene, bring her back here, or if you can't bring her here, send Kaurgen to get me."

"Wait, you're not coming with us?"

Tameris glanced at one of the nearby shacks. "Nicalene's only one part of a bigger picture, Grisel. An important part, no question, but not the only factor to consider. Changes are coming in Lowtown. Big changes, in all the boroughs. I need to make sure I'm ready for them."

He did not like the sound of that, but it rang true to him, especially after what Jaspen told him about the guild's dealings with a divided Assembly.

Better watch yourself out there, mate. I don't need to be losing the only two friends I got in as many days.

Grisel glared at Kaurgen. "All things considered, I reckon I'd have been better off leaving you in the cesspit."

The dead man just stared at him with the same blank expression.

Tameris laughed. "Don't expect much conversation. He can't talk after what I did to his jaw."

Figures.

"Just as well," she said. "He seems like a right bastard anyway."

Kaurgen grunted.

"Right..."

29
THE INSURRECTIONISTS

The slaughterhouse smelled of old blood and salted meat. Gutted hogs and cattle dangled from hooks, each one connected to a chain snarled in the barn's exposed rafters. Wheelbarrows and buckets, made mainly of wood and lined with cheap tin, filled most of the floor space near the big sliding doors along the back wall. When the butchers and the carvers arrived for the day, they opened the doors to carry away the loads of splintered bone, ruptured organs, and fatty skin and dumped them in the waste culverts of Pigshire's winding alleyways. A well in the courtyard behind the slaughterhouse provided the place with water, but not enough to waste on unnecessary cleaning. Years of dried blood caked on the seldom rinsed containers, with chunks of bone and sinew bonding to the tin-lined interiors.

Fresh meat went out a smaller side door, where it could be loaded onto a mule cart and hauled to street markets all across Lowtown. Skinned hides went into the long troughs along the opposite wall to be soaked in a mixture of water and stale piss to prepare them for sale to the borough's tanneries. A stack of crates stood next to the troughs, each one filled with salt imported from the coastal salt farms some fifty miles beyond the city walls.

The pungent stench was bad enough to make Ember doubt he could ever taste meat again without remembering the vile place.

Olynia, of course, took great pleasure at his discomfort.

Ember half suspected that she arranged for them to arrive early just to watch him squirm.

Yimina stayed close, taking him by the arm whenever a chance waft of some noxious odor caused him to gag.

"Are you okay?" she asked. "You look like you're going to be sick."

"Fine," he said, waving her away. "I'm fine."

Olynia snickered at the exchange. "What's wrong, Lord Morangine?" she said when he nearly vomited a short while later. "Is the livelihood of your people not to your liking?"

Ember glared at her but said nothing.

He resolved that if he was going to throw up, he would be sure to do it all over her.

"Where are they?" Yimina asked. "They should be here by now."

Olynia shrugged. "They'll be along. The rain probably flooded a few streets between here and the guildhouse."

"You shouldn't have told them I was coming with you," Ember said. "Wouldn't be surprised if some of them wanted to reconsider after they learned of my involvement."

"Better to avoid any surprises," Olynia said.

Maybe...

Ember had spent most of the past year making life difficult for the Spaders Guild. They were not likely to forget that fact just because Olynia had vouched for him.

"What if they ran into a watch patrol?" Yimina asked. "After what happened last night, they're bound to be out in force today."

"They have enough to worry about as it is," Olynia said. "The spaders are threatening to strike after what happened last night. They're already gathering outside a few of the watch guardhouses to demand justice for their man."

"What about the other guilds?" Ember asked. "Are they siding with the spaders?"

"Not officially. At least not yet. Some of them are still deciding what to do. Others are petitioning the Assembly or the watch itself. They're not striking yet, but they're getting a late start to the day to send a message to everyone what will happen if they do."

Yimina looked around the slaughterhouse. "That why this place is empty?"

Olynia nodded.

Someone knocked on the back wall's sliding door.

"That must be them," Olynia said. She unlocked the door and pulled it halfway open to reveal half a dozen men dressed in typical spader garb. The rain was still coming down hard, splashing against their bald heads and bare shoulders. Their overalls and boots were quite water resistant, so when they stepped out of the weather, the water sluiced off the treated material like it might run down a shingled roof.

Olynia greeted each of the men, though she only appeared to know half of them personally. Ember did not recognize any of the spaders. With their bald heads and drab work gear, they all looked the same to him. Only after Olynia directed them to close the door did she turn to wave Ember over.

"I think most of you are familiar with Assemblyman Ember Morangine, yes?"

Ember bowed his head slightly. "Gentlemen. Thank you for coming."

One of the spaders grunted.

"Gods," another said. "Can't believe we're standing in the same room with this shitboot."

Another spader, this one tall and dark skinned, grabbed his friend by his overall strap. "And I can't believe you're still not keeping your bloody mouth shut. Now get your ass over to that door and keep a sharp watch, you hear?"

Scowling, the scolded spader followed three others to stand guard over the slaughterhouse's entrances. The dark skinned spader remained where he stood alongside the group's eldest member.

"Sorry about that," the older man said. "Afraid some of the lads have formed a bad impression of you, Morangine. Guess I'm to blame for some of that."

That voice. I've heard that voice before.

Ember raised an eyebrow. "And why should that be?"

The man smiled. "That's the problem with noble cunts like you, Morangine. You don't even remember people like me when it would do you some good."

Ember studied the spader closely. The recognition gradually came into focus rather than hitting him all at once. "Ah, of course. You're the guild ambassador, aren't you?"

The spader smiled. "Maybe there's hope for you yet. I suppose we'll see about that soon enough, won't we?"

Olynia stepped over to Ember's side. "Ambassador Torrvik, we don't have much time. Can you tell us what you know about this business with the watch?"

Torrvik turned to the spader beside him. "Jaspen here knows better than anyone. He was shift leader on the crew the watch attacked."

Jaspen described the unfortunate encounter, explaining how a group of watchmen came upon his crew in the night and demanded information about a missing spader. The watchmen were not following the watch captain's orders, but did the bidding of two men known to be in the employ of a Carbuncle broker.

Ember did not need to hear the name to know Jaspen was referring to Dhrath. But something about that conclusion felt off. He wondered what the broker would want with a common spader.

A seemingly random detail fluttered through his mind, something Twiceborn said when they met at the Bower, something about the way Kaurgen died.

He had drowned in a privy. If that was true, then a spader probably fished him out.

He thinks this spader has whatever Kaurgen stole for him!

"This broker's men," Ember asked, "who were they?"

"One by the name of Arden," Jaspen said. "Arden Belarius. He seemed the more sensible of the two. Tried to stop his mate from starting the fight. No idea about the other one's name, but we found his body stuffed into an alley after they ran off. Guess Arden didn't much care for the way he screwed things up. Nasty piece of work. Karthean. Even had his teeth filed down to points."

Raugov.

He must have given a reaction of some kind, because Olynia and the spaders exchanged glances before turning to him.

"What is it?" Olynia asked.

"I think I know that one," Ember said. "His name's Raugov. He runs a lot of Dhrath's operations in Coldwater and Pigshire."

In all likelihood, he also had something to do with Lorvie and Trinn's deaths.

But Ember decided to withhold that information for the moment. He needed Olynia burning for revenge if they were going to wrest control of the Assembly back from Dhrath.

"Friend of yours, Morangine?" Torrvik asked.

Ember looked at Yimina. "No. Far from it."

"Look, we're all fighting for the same thing here," Olynia said. "Unless we can stop brokers like Dhrath from tightening their grip on the watch and the Assembly, good people like Trinn and your friend Meaty are going to keep dying."

Torrvik glared at Ember. "Is it true what Olynia tells us about the Assembly? That this cephalin broker's got leverage over everyone?"

Ember nodded. "It's only a matter of time before he gets the Assembly to break the guilds. The watch lacks the strength to do it quite yet, but with the Assembly under his power, he can increase its recruiting and equipment allowances until it's the size of a small army."

"Sounds like a stretch," Torrvik said. "How do you know all of this anyway? Why should we take your word for it?"

"Because it was my plan. Part of it anyway."

Torrvik scowled. "Go on."

"I wanted to break the Assembly's contract with the spaders and hand over the work to a cheaper labor force. They might not do the job nearly as well, but that didn't much matter. What mattered was that the new workers wouldn't cost so damned much. We could have apportioned half of what we paid to you lot and still pocketed a good portion of that without anybody noticing."

"Money," Torrvik said. "That's why you were always out to break us."

"Why?" Jaspen asked. "You're a supposed to be a lord, ain't you? Why do you need to take away our coin?"

"Because he's poor," Olynia said, laughing. "Take away his crumbling estate and Lord Morangine has nothing but a fancy name to set him apart from a common gutterscum. Isn't that right?"

Her words struck at his pride, but he could not refute them. Olynia was right. Everything his family once possessed was gone. He had nothing left of that illustrious legacy but a dilapidated manse, a lifelong servant, and his family name.

Ember clenched his teeth and nodded. "It's true. Aside from the paltry service fee owed to me for committing my time to Assembly business, I have nothing. The last of the family's assets went toward clearing away my father's debts. I probably have less coin to my name than you lot."

"How did you get mixed up with Dhrath?" Torrvik asked.

"He already had sway over most of the Assembly because he figured out ways to lean on anyone who purchased a seat. The only members he couldn't keep in line were the three legacy seats and the elected seats. Once we cut a deal with him, we had enough pull to get anything we needed passed. The plan was to cancel the guild's contract, then I'd provide the labor force to replace the spaders while he used the watch to keep you in line.

"But once the whole scheme got underway, he decided it would be easier to keep me in line the same way he controlled everyone else. If I didn't do as he said, he'd have me killed. Which is what happened to Trinn Harmyndri and Lorvie Tinderhov."

Olynia nodded. "That's why what happened to your man last night is bound to keep happening. As long as he has most of the Assembly and the watch in his grip, how are you supposed to seek justice? Dhrath must be stopped before he destroys all of us."

"And how do you plan to do that?" Jaspen asked.

Ember took a calming breath.

Here it comes.

"Simple," he said. "We're going to kill him."

Jaspen laughed. "Just like that?"

"That's the idea."

"And how do you intend to do that?" Torrvik asked. "He's a cephalin. Even if he doesn't know you're coming, he'll turn your brain to porridge before you get within ten feet of him."

"You let me worry about getting close to him," Ember said.

Olynia came to his defense. "Morangine has a plan, but we need your help to carry it off."

Torrvik and Jaspen looked at each other, then leaned closer to whisper back and forth.

Ember felt uneasy as he watched them. Although he told Olynia about Twiceborn and his plan to replace the spaders with a workforce of mindless, reanimated corpses, he thought it best not to share that point with the spaders. He was a bit surprised she agreed with him, but she clearly understood that this particular truth was not worth threatening their alliance with the spaders. The more he collaborated with Olynia, the more he realized she differed from her predecessor. Where Trinn was an unrestrained idealist, her still-mourning lover had a pragmatic streak to match that idealistic vision.

A rather ruthless pragmatic streak, in fact.

He was still unsure how he felt about that.

"What do you need from the guild, precisely?" Torrvik asked.

"Manpower," Ember said. "We need you gathered outside every watch guardhouse and banging on the walls of the Assembly Hall. We need enough unrest in Lowtown that Dhrath's too busy trying to put out fires to notice us coming for him."

"And what about after he's dead?" Jaspen asked. "How do we know you won't sell us out afterward? With all those spaders in the streets, it'd be easy for you to call it a riot and send the watch to kick our heads in."

"You'll be protected, Jaspen," Olynia said. "You have my word on that. Once Dhrath is out of the way, we have a few plans for dealing with the Assembly and the watch. Plans that we'll need support from the guilds to make happen. The Carvers Guild is already with us, and we're meeting with the tanners and the masons later today. I'm certain we'll be able to secure their support. The question for you is whether the spaders want to have a stake in the future or if they're content to take their chances with the past."

Torrvik thought for a moment, then nodded. "I'll relay what you've told us back to the guildmasters. The guild will have to put the matter to a vote, but after what happened last night, I believe you'll have our support before the day is out."

Olynia shook his hand. "I know we can count on you. The Spaders Guild has—"

One of the spaders watching the side door called out to them. "Oi! There's something going on outside!"

Ember glared at Torrvik. "Were you followed?"

The spader shook his head. "Impossible. We doubled back twice to make sure the watch wasn't behind us."

Something heavy banged against the side door. The spader bracing himself against the door fell back as the wood buckled. Another blow followed quickly, this time punching the iron capped head of a battering ram through the wood. The door came apart, pulling free from the hinges, and a pair of watchmen crashed into the room. They swung the ram forward once more to smash the prone spader's skull before they cast it aside and drew their short swords. More men of the watch, all clad in weathered mail hauberks and iron helmets, streamed through the door.

Jaspen and Torrvik ran for the back door, where two of their spader companions threw the latch to unlock it. Sliding the door open revealed several more armed watchmen standing outside in the rain. The spaders tried to rush by them, but they barely got more than a few steps before the men of the watch blocked their escape route. Jaspen took a blow to the head from a sword pommel and collapsed. The watchmen kicked him repeatedly until he curled into a ball and remained still. One of the spaders almost slipped through the gauntlet, but the last man tripped him and landed a swift kick to his face when he hit the ground. The other spader disappeared beneath a swarming mass of blades, boots, and mailed fists.

Torrvik was not so lucky. A blade caught him squarely in the gut, punching the tip all the way through to the back of his overalls. He fell to his knees, blood pumping into his throat before he could cry out. Then he keeled over, falling face first onto a floor stained with the blood of a thousand deaths.

Ember's mind spun in circles as chaos unfolded. He did not know whether he should surrender, fight, or run for his life. Olynia shouted something, but missed whatever she said. The last of the spaders forced the front door open only to be met with a bristling wall of swordpoints. The desperate man fell to the ground, begging for mercy. The first watchman through the door knocked out his teeth with a swift kick.

Someone grabbed his arm and jerked him into motion.

"Move!"

Yimina?

The world moved too fast for him to keep up. By the time he told his limbs to follow Yimina's lead, she was already changing direction, dragging him along like a witless child.

Everything crashed to a stop when she threw him against one of the carcasses dangling from the rafters.

"Climb!"

Yimina scrambled up the dead animal to grasp the chain above it, then quickly scurried toward the ceiling.

"Stop them!"

Whoever shouted at them was getting closer.

"Come on!" Yminia was halfway up the chain now, almost within reach of the rafters. Looking up, Ember spotted the narrow opening where the wall and roof met, probably to vent fumes out of the slaughterhouse. It was just large enough for a person to squeeze through.

Ember jumped up to grab the carcass and climbed after her.

He managed to get one hand on the chain before someone grabbed his leg and dragged him to the floor.

"Ember!" Yimina's voice came from somewhere far above him, but it was impossible to find her while he was manhandled by several watchmen.

I'm sorry, Yimina. You tried...

"Run!" he said, screaming as loud as he could. "Tell her!"

It was all he could get out before a blow to the head cast him into the cold, silent darkness.

EMBER DREAMED ABOUT his mother in the dark.

He could not say how he knew it was his mother, considering that she died giving birth to him, but he was convinced it was her.

She asked him about his dog, which seemed strange since he never had a dog. That did not stop him from talking about the animal at length, though the thing he described sounded more like a cat.

"That's lovely, dear." She said anything else, just repeated that same phrase whenever he spoke.

Someone knocked at the door to their little cottage.

"Visitors, Mother," he said.

"That's lovely, dear."

"I'll get the door."

"That's lovely, dear."

A torrent of water poured across the threshold when he opened the door. The briny liquid stung his eyes and scalded his mouth. A writhing, tentacled mass of flesh lunged at him, wrapping its suckered tendrils around his limbs.

The thing's gnashing beak snapped at his throat.

He cried out for help, somehow still able to speak despite the seawater filling his lungs.

"Help, Mother! He's got me! He's got me!"

"That's lovely, dear."

A BUCKET OF lukewarm water shocked him back to consciousness.

The shock wore off after a few moments, while his senses slowly reoriented themselves. Only then did his nose tell him that he had not been doused with water.

"Time to wake up, rich man."

Ember lay on the stone floor of a holding cell. A tall man dressed in a mail hauberk stood on the opposite side of the iron bars, bucket in hand.

"Where...where am I?"

The man laughed. "I wouldn't much worry about that now, rich man. I'd be more concerned about where you're going."

Ember glared at him, studying his armor carefully. The blue cloth wrapped around his arm marked him as a man of the watch, but the blue stone dangling from the cord around his neck marked him as an officer of higher rank.

"You in charge here?"

The man grunted, half smiling with smug satisfaction. "Captain Rheinmak, commander of the Pigshire Watch."

Wonderful.

"Where are the others?"

"The rest of the traitors? Oh, you'll be seeing them soon enough. You should be grateful. Most traitors suffer through the pain of a public execution. We quartered a man in this guardhouse's courtyard when I was a first-year recruit. I can't recall what he did, to be honest. Doesn't really matter. I'd rather hoped it would be a regular occurrence, but we haven't seen its like since then. Pity."

"Why no execution this time?"

Rheinmak smiled. "Oh, you've got a special appointment, rich man. Mister Dhrath wants a word with you, personally. And believe me, an audience with that squidfaced sod's not something a man easily forgets."

Ember had a hard time reading the watch captain's expression. The sadistic pleasure at Ember's predicament was easy enough to see, but there was a glimmer of pity in his eyes. He had a feeling Rheinmak knew all too well what Dhrath had in store for him.

"We'll be getting underway soon enough with you and all your traitor friends. Meantime, somebody'd like to have a word with you before your brain's running out your nose and ears."

The captain waved someone over to the cell. Footsteps sounded on the stone floor until a familiar face came into view.

"Hello, Ember."

Ithlene. Naturally...

"Had a feeling you might be the one behind this," he said.

"Why's that?" She raised an eyebrow and smirked.

"Because Armille's too stupid and Cambin's too cautious. You also know me well enough to guess that I wouldn't stay in line. How long have you had people following me?"

She laughed. "Since you made the case for Olynia. I figured you had some sort of play in mind, but I have to say I'm a little disappointed. Recruiting the guilds to face the watch *and* Dharth's gangs? A bit desperate, don't you think?"

Ember shrugged. "Bad options. Not like I could call in one of the legions, could I?"

"Well, I appreciated the irony, at least."

I'll be you do.

"What do you want from me now?" he asked. "Just hoping to get in a good gloat while you have the chance?"

Ithlene faked an exasperated gasp. "After all we've been through together, now you're going to accuse me of taking pleasure in—"

"Oh, spare me the indignation. You're the real traitor here. We had a deal in place, but you had to go twist it up because you didn't have the patience to see things done right."

She sneered. "You act like this was all my fault when you're the one who's been pissing Dhrath off for months. He got tired of you dragging your feet. Maybe you had a good plan at the beginning, but it wasn't doing him or us any good the way you kept sitting on it."

"That's not the way the Assembly works, and you know it," Ember said, all but snarling at her now. "You can't just snap your fingers and get rid of the most powerful guild in the district overnight. A goal like that takes time and planning. Besides, if I hadn't brought you in on the plan, you'd still be trying to figure out who holds which seat."

She smiled. "There you go again thinking you're some political mastermind. Admit it, you got sloppy. You're the one who went and got Lorvie killed, remember?"

Ember tried to muster his anger but found only guilt. Ithlene was right about that, after all.

"Yeah," he said, lowering his head. "I remember."

"You know, Ember, you could save us all a lot of trouble if you'd just tell us who you've been dealing with all this time. How about the supplier for this labor force you kept promising? If you tell me now, I might be able to convince Dhrath not to turn you into a drooling idiot."

Ember laughed. "Who's kidding themselves now? You expect me to believe Dhrath gives a toss about what you want?" He nodded to Rheinmak. "I'd be surprised if he doesn't have this bootlicker put you to pavement just for good measure after you hand me over."

Ithlene scowled and clenched her hands into fists. "We'll find out, you know. Dhrath will pull it out of that big head of yours and squeeze the rest of your mind until it's dry. He'll find out everything, even where that whore bodyguard of yours is hiding out."

Yimina. He had resisted asking about her, fearful of what he might learn. If she managed to escape the watch at the slaughterhouse, though, he doubted any of Rheinmak's men had the wherewithal to find her.

He smiled. "Guess it's a good thing I don't know where she's gone, then, isn't it?"

Rheinmak shifted nervously, though his face remained stern as ever. "Won't much matter, rich man. Once Dhrath gets in there, he'll find all your secrets. Every last, juicy one. Believe me, I seen it."

Ember tried to look him in the eye, but the watchman avoided his gaze.

You haven't just seen it have you?

Ithlene nodded. "We'll find her soon enough. I expect she'll come for you eventually, and when she does, we'll take her. What happens after that is up to you. I'd hate to see her spend her last days before a painful execution in the stocks beside her witless master."

He hoped Yimina could get word about his capture to Twiceborn before she did something as stupid as trying to rescue him alone. Of course, there was no guarantee Twiceborn would give a damn. She hardly struck him as the loyal or the sentimental type, but she did have a way of looking after her own interests. If Dhrath really could read his mind, the cephalin would discover how much of a threat Twiceborn posed to his ambitions. Once Ember was out of the picture, Dhrath would set his sights on the sorceress. Whether she decided to retaliate or simply cut her losses and flee the city was impossible to predict.

"Last chance, my friend," Ithlene said. "Much as I hate to admit it, I probably do owe you a small favor. Let me help you. Give me the name and I promise you I'll do what I can with Dhrath."

Her face had softened, her eyes friendly and inviting.

Ember smiled. "You've come a long way, girl."

Then he leaned forward and spat on her shoe.

"But you're still a terrible liar," he said.

Rheinmak tried to restrain a snicker, but mostly failed. Ithlene shot him a glare that could have melted the cell's iron bars.

"Throw his ass in the wagon with the others," she said. "And make sure you're rough about it."

The watch captain regained his composure quickly. "Yes, ma'am."

Ithlene stomped away from the cell without another word. She refused to even look at him again.

Backstabbing bitch.

Rheinmak stepped up to the bars, his lip curled in a sneer. "You got stones, rich man. But where you're going, they ain't going to be much help."

Ember worried that the watch captain might be right.

30

THE PROTECTOR

Between the rain pouring down and several streets flooding during the night, Calandra got back to the theater later than usual after her shift ended. The long, dreary walk felt like a march to the gallows, and her mood was darker than the rainclouds overhead by the time she returned.

She made it through another day without raising Moriel's suspicions. Avoiding her overseer's scrutiny felt like the least of her problems. Sooner or later, the bodysnatching sorceress below the mortuary would begin to wonder why her supply of corpses had dried up. Calandra hated to imagine what that frightful woman would do when that happened. Would she slither out of the shadows one night to demand an explanation? Would she just take to stealing bodies from the crypts? As frightful as the first possibility was, the second seemed even worse. Calandra could handle another threat, even from a sorceress who could turn her skin inside out with foul spellcraft. But if bodies turned up missing during Moriel's morning inspection, she would be in grave trouble with the guild.

Compared to what the guild might have in store for her, the bodysnatcher's magics sounded downright merciful.

Then there was the matter of Beyland's debt to Dhrath. Arden was unlikely to grant her another extension the next time he waylaid her. She had less than a dozen marks in her pocket, far short of what she would need to satisfy him. Her next guild payment came in three days, but even that would not give her enough coin.

She considered trying to barter some of the old props and stage equipment from the theater to raise money, but she doubted there was much of a market for such items in Lowtown. Much of the stuff was in terrible condition anyway, and unlikely to bring a reasonable price. Still, it was worth a try. Beyland may not like the idea very much, but Calandra was becoming less and less interested in what her brother wanted.

Thinking about Beyland only reminded her of another, far more complicated problem.

Nicalene. What am supposed to do about you?

After entering the theater through the back gate, Calandra draped her cloak over an old piece of wooden scenery and inspected everything stored in the backstage area. The search left her discouraged. Most of the curtains and backdrops were too moth eaten or mildewed to sell, and the various scenery setpieces would probably fetch a better price as firewood.

Maybe the costumes in the wardrobe upstairs. At least the fabric might be worth selling.

She would have to fight Beyland over that. He never let her sell so much as a prop candleholder without throwing a fit about it. Now that he was so absorbed in this new play, he was sure to be even more intractable.

He was still unaware of how much she knew about his debt, their debt, to Dhrath. If she confronted him about it, maybe he would be more likely to listen to suggestions for dealing with the problem.

Calandra was still considering her options when she proceeded into the main section of the theater and found Beyland sitting in the middle of the stage staring blankly at the floor. He did not look up when she approached him.

"Beyland?"

The flesh around his bloodshot eyes was red and puffy. He seemed to stare at nothing in particular. Loose pages covered with scribbled out text lay strewn all around him.

"Beyland? Are you okay?"

She placed her hand on his shoulder.

No reaction.

"Beyland?" She shook him gently. "Can you hear me?"

He took a deep breath, his entire body shuddering. "She's gone."

"What? What are you talking about?"

"Nicalene. She's gone."

Calandra glanced around the theater. "Gone? Are you sure? Maybe she's upstairs, sleeping. You know she's been tired lately."

"No, Cal. I looked everywhere."

Where could she have gone? She couldn't just leave in this rain.

Beyland shivered and rubbed his arms. "I felt it when I woke up. I felt...it was so cold."

"Did she say anything last night? Anything strange or out of the ordinary?"

As if anything about her was ordinary.

He shook his head. "I...I told her I wanted her to be the star of the play...that I wrote it for her. I don't understand, Cal. Why would she...?"

The words trailed off into incoherent sobbing. She watched him cry, shuddering and choking like he could scarcely draw breath. The more emotional he became, the angrier Calandra felt. Her world had been coming apart ever since Nicalene came into their lives. Not all of it was her fault, but Calandra found it easy to associate the woman with every new-found misfortune.

A day ago, she would have rejoiced at the thought of Nicalene leaving of her own accord, clinging to the naïve hope that her departure might bring her brother back from the edge of whatever madness seemed to be creeping into his soul since that star-crossed woman arrived.

Damn you, Nicalene. Of all the days you finally work yourself up to stepping out.

Calandra knelt down and grabbed him by the shoulders.

"Listen to me, Beyland, I know you're upset, but you have to pull yourself together. I need your help. And I need you to start being honest with me."

He tried to draw back from her, but she held him firmly. "What are you talking about, Cal? I'm always honest with—"

"Stop. Just...stop it. I know about Kardi. I know what Nicalene did to him."

The words tumbled from her lips before she could think to stop them. She was not ready to confront him about Kardi's murder, not yet and certainly not while he was in this state.

Beyland shook his head. "No. No, you don't underst—"

"I do understand, damn it! I saw his body come through the mortuary! I saw what happened to it! Nicalene told me everything about the night you found her, how she killed some poor wretch the same way."

He seemed so much stronger when she last pressed him about Kardi, threatening even. The pitiful creature before her looked nothing like that. Whatever power he drew from Nicalene had clearly vanished along with her.

He stared at her slack-jawed, his eyes losing focus. "I...I didn't...I thought..."

"No, you didn't," Calandra's fingernails bit into his shoulders. "You didn't think. Just like you didn't think when you made a deal with a broker to buy this place and never told me about it."

Beyland half snapped out of his stupor, just enough to meet his sister's accusing glare. The color drained from his face as he grasped for words.

"How...how did you find out about that?"

"Because one of the broker's thugs came to me to get the money you haven't paid back. What did you think was going to happen when you didn't repay him? That he would just let it go because your dream of running a theater didn't work out?"

"I'm sorry," he said, trying to pull away from her. "I thought I'd have more time until I needed to have the money."

Calandra shoved him to the floor. She wanted to batter him with her fists, but instead she stood up and walked to the edge of the stage.

"Gods, you're stupid. Do you have any idea how badly you've screwed us?"

"We can get the money! There's got to be some—"

She spun around and threw her hands up. "No! There's not! I've been through everything I can think of. We don't have any coin left stashed away, and my pay from the guild isn't nearly enough. Do you know what I tried to do to make the payments? I sold corpses to bodysnatchers down in the catacombs. Do you have any idea what the guild will do to me if they find out about that?"

Beyland stared at her, bewildered. "I…I don't know what to say, Cal."

She shook her head. "Then don't say anything. Don't say a bloody word. Just…just go upstairs and leave me in peace for a few minutes, will you? I've got to think about what we're going to do, and I can't focus with you sobbing like that."

He opened his mouth to respond but seemed to think better of it when Calandra glared at him.

"Right," he said, fighting back tears. "Okay."

Calandra waited until he went up the steps to bury her head in her hands and sob.

What are you doing?

Why had she screamed at him like that? Had she been storing up all her anger over the situation with Nicalene or was it simply a frustration over his complete inability to take responsibility for anything?

Not that the real reason mattered, since the damage was already done. Beyland would withdraw into his shell like he always did after one of their fights. She would be lucky to get a word out of him for a week, not unless she brought him some news about Nicalene.

Maybe I should go look for her. She couldn't have gone far in this weather.

Someone banged on the back door, hard enough to send echoes through the seating area.

Nicalene?

Confused, Calandra made her way across the stage and through the backstage storage area. She unlatched the small slide piece that covered a viewing hole to peek outside.

When she saw the familiar man standing there with a frail child in his arms, she gasped.

Arden?

They stared at each other through that tiny hole for a moment before Arden broke the silence.

"I'm sorry," he said. "I didn't know where else—"

"Who is that?"

Arden glanced down at the boy, then looked back at Calandra. "This is my son. He's sick. Fever."

He looked different than the times when he came upon her in the night. Maybe it was the light that made his face seem less threatening, or perhaps it was simply the sight of him cradling that pitiful little boy against his broad chest. When he looked at her, there was a warmth in his eyes that she certainly had not noticed before.

"I don't understand," she said. "Why come to me? I'm an undertaker, not an apothecary."

"Please," Arden said. "We don't have anywhere else to go."

Calandra froze, her mind unable to process what was unfolding just outside her door. How could she let the man who threatened to hurt her and Beyland over an unpaid debt into their home?

The boy groaned. Arden looked down at him and whispered something. Calandra could not hear his reassuring words over the rain.

"If I don't get him out of this weather, he may die."

This can't be happening.

Calandra closed the viewing slide, then unlatched the door and pulled it open.

"Bring him in," she said. "I'll get a blanket."

THE BOY'S FEVER was worse than anything Calandra had seen before. His skin was more than just hot to the touch; it felt like it might actually burn her. Little clusters of blisters sprouted all over his body. Some of them ruptured when the boy moved too much, releasing a foul-smelling, whitish fluid that left milky stains on his clothing.

Arden assured her that whatever caused the condition was not contagious, although she had little reason to trust anything he said at this point.

They moved the boy upstairs and placed him on Calandra's bed. Arden opened a small satchel containing a few vials of medicinal oils while Calandra went to fetch a bowl of rainwater. By the time she returned, Arden had applied what little oil he had left to the most irritated patches of skin. He soaked a rag in the water and pressed it against the boy's forehead.

Calandra watched him tend to his son with a measure of disbelief. She would never have imagined that he was capable of such tender care.

When he had done all he could, Arden slumped to his knees beside the bed and let out a long, weary sigh.

That was when Calandra noticed the wet patch of blood on his hip.

"You're bleeding," she said.

He glanced down at the wound and grunted. "Took a knife to the side. I don't think it's bad."

"Looks like it's still bleeding. Must be deeper than you think. Come downstairs and I'll take a look at it."

Arden shook his head. "I shouldn't leave him."

"He'll be fine. There's nothing else you can do for him right now, especially if you pass out beside him because you were too damn stubborn to tend to yourself."

He placed his hand on the boy's arm. "I'll be back soon."

Calandra led him down to the kitchen area, off to the side of the main theater room. She cleared a pile of unwashed dishes from the table and helped Arden climb onto it. Once she had him situated, she fetched her satchel, which contained her personal undertaker's tools.

Arden chuckled when she laid the blades, tweezers, and hooks out beside him. "I'm not dead yet, you know."

She selected a pair of wide-bladed scissors. "Shut up and lie down."

He grunted, but ultimately complied, unlatching his belt so Calandra could get a better look at the wound. Her gaze kept drifting to the hand axe he kept tucked away in a special belt loop. The blade looked clean, but portions of the handle were stained with blood.

Tools of the trade...

The wound on his hip looked worse from this angle. She cut away the bloody fabric to expose the deep gash underneath. Blood still seeped out, slow and thick. Based on the wound's size and location, she could have pushed her finger inside it and rubbed the bone underneath.

"You do this much?" Arden asked.

"Not when they can talk back, no. I need to clean this before I can sew it up. Probably going to hurt pretty bad when I do it."

He grunted again. "Don't suppose you could at least offer me a drink?"

Calandra laughed before she caught herself.

Stop it. He's not your friend, remember?

"Don't have anything strong enough to help," she said.

Arden sighed. "Well, it won't be the first time. Might as well get on with it."

Calandra grabbed a wet rag and scrubbed at the ragged flesh around the wound. "You said you took a knife. What happened? Somebody take exception to you shaking them down."

"Not quite. Let's just say the guy took exception to me throwing his friend out a window."

Charming. You certainly have a way with people, don't you?

"Well, all things considered, you got pretty lucky. A few inches to the left and the blade might have punctured an organ or an artery."

"Guess I've always been lucky when it comes to hurting people."

Calandra stopped scrubbing and looked up at Arden's face. He was staring directly at her, the same way he looked at her in the alley the last time they met.

She returned to cleaning the wound. "Can you look somewhere else, please?"

"Sorry," he said. "I didn't mean anything by it."

Sure, you didn't...

After brushing most of the bits of clotted blood away, she grabbed a needle and the spool of horsehair from her kit. "I'm not used to doing this when they're still breathing. I'll try to make it as clean as I can."

Arden nodded, but said nothing. He winced when she jabbed the needle into his flesh.

"What's the boy's name?" Calandra asked.

"Halvid."

"You plan on telling me what you're doing carrying a fever wracked boy through the rain this early in the morning?"

She looped the first stitch through, pulling it tight to suture one corner of the wound.

"It's a long story," he said through clenched teeth.

We've all got long stories. What makes you think yours is so special?

"Don't suppose it has something to do with this wound, does it?"

He did not answer right away, and Calandra thought he might avoid the question entirely. After she tugged the second stitch tight, he spoke again.

"I messed up. Thought I found a way to get out from under a lot of bad choices. Turned out all I did was put the only thing I have left to care about in danger. Another one of Dhrath's men got to Halvid, tried to use him to get me to dance on a string."

Calandra shook her head. "Guess you know a thing or two about threatening to take away the things people love, don't you?"

Another long silence.

"Yeah," he said. "Suppose you'd find that fitting, wouldn't you? Can't say I blame you. The gods are wicked and cruel."

Yes, they are.

"Did they get you to dance, then?"

"Just long enough for me to find out where they were keeping him. Then I cut the strings. Broke into the place and killed all of them. Course,

I didn't think about where we were going to go once I had him back. Dhrath will be coming for me once word gets back to him. He doesn't much like deserters."

Calandra looped the final stitch through the wound. She managed to close the gash up tightly, but Arden would have a nasty scar once it healed.

"So where does he find people like you, anyway?" she asked. "Just look for the nastiest drunks at the local winesink?"

Arden let out a short laugh. "Some of them, sure. People like me are a little harder to find. Not many cutters in Lowtown spent most of their lives fighting in mercenary companies around the world."

"You're not from the city, then?"

"Far from it. Lived in just about every corner of the continent, though. Not a bad life, to tell it true, but dangerous. And uncertain. After Halvid's mother died, that was the first time he came down with the fever. It got worse after that. I couldn't bring him with me on campaign and I didn't trust anyone to care for him. Figured if I settled down, it'd be easier to watch over him, get him the medicines he needed.

"Course, they don't just let anybody come through the gates to stay here. I could have hired on with plenty of people to become a resident, but the gatekeepers were never going to let Halvid come in being as sick as he is. Dhrath got us both admitted, on the condition that I work for him to pay off the bribes and favors it took to get us inside."

Calandra snipped the string away from the needle and tied it off. "How long ago was that?"

"Four years."

"And you still haven't paid off the debt?"

Arden grunted. "I'd be surprised if he even keeps track anymore. If I threaten to leave or step out of line, he can still report Halvid to the gate-keepers. They'll cast him out of the city without another thought. I can't let that happen. He wouldn't last a month out there, not without good, steady rest and decent medicine."

Calandra stepped back to inspect her handiwork. The stitching was not half bad. Good enough that the wound would stop bleeding, at least.

"That should hold," she said. "Just don't go getting yourself into an-other knife fight anytime soon, okay? We still need to cover it up with bandaging."

He sat up and poked at the wound. "Stitches feel strong. Good work. You'd have made a good field surgeon."

"What are you going to do now? Won't Dhrath be looking for you when he finds out what you've done?"

"Might already know, the bastard. I can't afford to stay in Lowtown; he's got enough connections in every borough to find me no matter where I hide out. It probably won't be safe anywhere in the city, for that matter."

That was hardly reassuring. Everything he said about avoiding Dhrath applied just as much to her and Beyland if their attempts to scrounge up the money to pay off their debt were futile.

"How about some other city?" she asked. "Surely you could find the medicines your son needs in one of them. Rickenwick, maybe? Or what about Selarna? It's a seaport, at least."

Arden shook his head. "There's a price on my head in both of them. Marlorg, too. Nasty byproduct of the sellsword business. When you hire on with the losing side in a civil war, you end up getting branded a traitor along with your employer. Even when you back the winners, things can still turn out bad. When your employer breaches a contract, it's just business, but when you break terms or don't keep up your end, they tend to call it treason."

"What about Karthea?" Calandra asked. "You could go book passage with a Mireshore captain bound for Kormur or Guhln."

"Maybe. There aren't many ships heading to Karthea on this side of the river. Even if I could find someone willing to take on passengers, it would cost more than I've got, especially if I have to convince them to let a sick child aboard."

Calandra found a clean rag and tied it against Arden's wound with a strip of cloth.

"You'll need to keep a close eye on this for the next few days," she said. "Should be fine once it scabs over."

Arden nodded. "I've had a few of these in my time. I know what to look for."

She wiped her tools clean and returned them to her satchel. Arden watched her, never saying a word. When Calandra finished, she crossed her arms and glared at him.

"Where does this leave me and Beyland? Is there going to be someone worse than *you* trailing me to the mortuary every day until I cough up enough coin to satisfy your old boss?"

Arden looked away, staring down at the floor. "Yeah. Probably. He's got bigger problems at the moment, but Dhrath never forgets anything. When he can spare the manpower, he'll assign somebody to collect from your brother. Probably somebody with a lot less scruples than me."

Calandra sighed. "What should I do? We might be able to make another payment or two by selling some things here in the theater, but there's no way I can pay off the full amount."

Arden scratched at his stubbled chin. He looked tired, not simply fatigued, but worn down like a stone monument that could feel its features being ground to dust by the wind.

"Why don't you come with me?" he asked.

She gawked at him. "What, you mean leave the city? Sail for Karthea?"

"Why not? We both need to get away from Dhrath. Why not get as far away from him as possible? Maybe between the two of us, we could scrounge up enough coin to buy our way onto a ship bound for the southlands."

Calandra tried to sort out how she felt about the suggestion. Fleeing across the southern sea might solve the immediate problem of being at the mercy of a ruthless broker, but she disliked the thought of leaving Blackspire, especially for some foreign land a thousand miles away. She had lived in the city her entire life. All the things she accomplished and been a part of resided within its towering walls. Leaving the city would mean throwing that all away. The Undertakers Guild would brand her a deserter, which was only a step above a death sentence in the eyes of her peers. If her former guild brothers and sisters happened upon her, they were within their rights, and actually encouraged, to beat her to a bloody pulp.

Even after her recent stint as a bodysnatcher, Calandra still held out hope that she could maintain her good standing in the guild and resume the arduous process of climbing her way up the ranks.

Then there was her brother to consider.

"What about Beyland?" she said. "I don't think anything could convince him to leave, not when he's so close to getting his production underway."

He looked at her in that strange way again. "Then leave him. If he doesn't have the sense to get out, then why should you risk your life by staying?"

You didn't want him to come with us in the first place, did you?

"I can't," she said. "He's my brother. I couldn't leave him behind any more than you could leave your son."

Arden's shoulders slumped. He closed his eyes and sighed. "I know. I just…I'm sorry. You're right. We can't just abandon the people we love so easily, can we?"

She thought about Beyland mourning Nicalene's departure in his room upstairs.

"It's like you said earlier," she said. "The gods are wicked and cruel."

Beyland would certainly agree with the observation. Nicalene too, probably.

She wondered if Lerris had the same thought before she ended her miserable life.

Arden sat up straight, his attention snapping to the doorway that led to the main part of the theater. "Did you hear that? Sounded like the back gate."

Calandra had not heard anything. She took a step towards the door before Arden grabbed her by the arm.

"Wait," he said. "It could be somebody from Dhrath."

He picked up his axe as he climbed off the table. Calandra pulled away from his grasp and went to the door. Arden limped along behind her.

"Carefully," he said.

Calandra pushed the door open and peeked into the theater.

Her heart all but lept into her throat when she saw the black-haired woman lying unconscious in the middle of the stage.

"Nicalene!" She flung the door open and ran across the stage. "Beyland! Get down here! Nicalene's here! She came back!"

The poor woman was so wet that she looked like she had been dumped into the river. Her breathing was shallow and her skin warm to the touch. Calandra rolled her onto her back and gasped. The black stone embedded in Nicalene's chest burned a hole in her clothing, and thin wisps of steam rose from the stone whenever it came into contact with water.

Calandra did not dare touch it.

Beyland came quickly, calling out Nicalene's name as he hurried down the stairs. For a moment, Calandra wondered how she would explain Arden's presence to her brother, but when she glanced back at the kitchen door, she saw no sign of the man.

All things considered, she was glad he elected to keep out of sight. They could deal with that unpleasantness later.

"Nicalene!" Beyland said when he emerged from the stairwell. "What happened?"

Calandra stopped him a few paces short of the unconscious woman. "I don't know. She just stumbled inside and collapsed. Must have gotten caught in the rain, but it feels like she has a fever of some kind."

"Where could she have gone? Do you think it was something I said? Something that scared her or—"

Calandra gave him a gentle shake. "Stop it, Beyland! That doesn't matter right now. We have to get her upstairs and out of these wet clothes, understand?"

Beyland nodded. "Right. Right. Just tell me what to do... Anything..."

She tried to ignore her brother's troubling obsession as he helped to hoist the delirious woman off the ground and carry her up the stairs. After they got her onto the bed, they stripped away her wet clothing and dried her off as best they could manage. Once or twice, their fingers brushed against the black stone, which was hot enough to sear skin as surely as a kettle heated over an open flame. When they could do nothing more, Calandra left Beyland sitting on a stool next to the bed, watching over her with his undivided attention. She went back downstairs to find Arden.

She found him waiting for her in the kitchen, axe still in hand. His face had the same cold expression as when he cornered her in that dark alley for the first time. All the vulnerability, the tenderness she saw earlier in the morning had vanished.

"She still out?" he asked.

Calandra nodded.

"How long have you known this woman?"

"Beyland brought her home about a week ago," she said. "Said she was in some kind of trouble and needed his help. I didn't like it, but I couldn't just put her out on the street in the condition she was in."

Arden grunted. "She hurt anybody?"

How could you know that?

"There was...an accident. One of Beyland's friends. I wasn't here when it happened, but I saw the body afterward. She..."

She struggled to find some way of describing what Nicalene had done to Kardi, but nothing seemed to fully convey the awful truth.

Arden finished her sentence for her. "Left him covered in black welts, all of them hard as rock, like she'd boiled his blood then turned it to stone."

Calandra stared at him for a moment, then nodded. The description, while crude, fit what had happened.

"You know something about her, don't you?" she asked.

Arden put the axe down. With the weapon set aside, some small measure of humanity crept back into his face.

But only a little.

"What would you say if there was a way to wipe both of our debts with Dhrath clean?"

Calandra felt sick. She had a good idea of what Arden was going to say next. After everything she survived over the last week, the fact that Arden might be involved with whatever trouble Nicalene had stirred up hardly surprised her.

If anything, she would have been more surprised to learn that her troubles were unrelated at this point.

The gods are wicked and cruel.

She folded her arms over her chest and glared at Arden, trying to match his stoic expression.

"I'm listening."

31
THE PRICE

Arden laid out everything he knew about Nicalene, beginning with his investigation at *The Bleating Goat* and his disastrous confrontation with Grisel's spader crew. He also explained Dhrath's enduring paranoia over anyone skilled in the magical arts, that the broker had a standing bounty on any sorcerer in Lowtown. After he finished, Calandra filled in the gaps in his knowledge. She told him how Nicalene happened upon that strange black stone and how it became embedded in her chest.

Now he understood why Dhrath wanted Grisel so badly, why he was so hells bent on recovering that strange stone.

The conversation also left him convinced of one thing: Dhrath would almost certainly wipe their debts clean in exchange for Nicalene.

Calandra fell silent for a long while after hearing his proposal.

"You're worried about your brother," Arden said, finally.

She nodded.

"Look, if half of what you've told me about his obsession with her is true, then getting her out of the picture is the best thing you can do for him. Besides, how long before there's another accident? For all we know, she might have killed someone this morning."

"Do you think I haven't thought of that? Even if we could get her out of here without him knowing, I don't know if I could live with the guilt of that secret. And if he did find out, he'd never forgive me. I...I don't know what he'd do. He might hurt himself, or me, for that matter."

Arden sighed. "Do you want to know what will happen to you and your brother if you can't pay off your debt to Dhrath?"

Calandra shuddered and looked at the floor. "Don't. Don't do this."

"I've seen what he does to people, Calandra. He's not like you and me. Don't ever forget that. He's not human. What does a human life matter to a cephalin? Dhrath's got maybe five years, ten if he's lucky. He doesn't have time for second chances or forgiveness. When someone wastes his time, he wants to punish them for every single moment he lost because of them. You think I know a thing or two about hurting people? I'm a clumsy oaf compared to Dhrath. Once he gets inside your mind, he can rip it apart piece by piece. I've seen him take days, even weeks, to kill people. If you're thinking death at his hands is a fair trade for having a clear conscience, I can promise that you're badly mistaken."

She closed her eyes and cursed under her breath.

"Is she still unconscious?" Arden asked.

"Yes. Fever, from the looks of it. Whether it's natural or not, I can't tell."

They had to move quickly. As long as Nicalene slept, she could be restrained and hauled over to Carbuncle without anyone getting their blood boiled.

"Calandra, you'll never get another chance at a clean break like this. If you really want to keep you and your brother safe and live out the rest of your lives together, then you don't have any other options. Dhrath will come for both of you sooner or later. And that's if Nicalene doesn't lose her head again and burn this place to the ground first."

She glared at him. "What if I refused? What would you do then? Would you kill us both and take her anyway? You're talking like you've earned a lot of my trust somehow, but I'm having a hard time seeing where it's coming from."

Arden sighed. He *had* thought about taking such drastic action. A little extra blood on his hands was not likely to push his soul any closer to damnation. He had done more than enough to ensure a harsh judgment from whatever gods he ended up facing when he died.

More than anything else, he feared Calandra's expression twisting to convey a single, unspoken word every time he closed his eyes.

Why?

Arden did not care about Beyland. He could easily sneak upstairs and bludgeon the unsuspecting artist. In fact, it would be easier to take Nicalene if he did just that. Beyland was nobody to him, just one more clueless shitheel who thought Lowtown operated according to his convenience. Arden would trample over all of them if it meant helping his son.

Calandra was different. He hated the way she looked at him, the way she spoke to him, her voice dripping with judgment. But being around her also energized him, made him remember what it was like to want to be close to someone. What it felt like to to smell their skin and touch their hair.

"You're right," he said. "I can't give you a good reason to trust me. But both of us have the same problem. A problem with only one solution, which is staring us in the face right now. I'm going to ask you one last time to help me, but you're not only helping me. You're helping your brother. And yourself. And you're helping my son, who doesn't deserve any of this just because his father's a bad man."

"And what if I say no?"

"Then I'll leave. I'll take Halvid and go. You'll never have to see me again."

"And Nicalene? What about her?"

"She goes back to being your problem. I won't touch her."

Calandra rubbed her face and groaned. Arden let her sort her feelings out, though every moment lost made his heart pound faster.

When she nodded, the tension in his muscles bled away.

"Okay. What do you need me to do?"

ARDEN PRESSED HIS back against the wall next to Calandra's door. Halvid lay asleep on the bed nearby, his uneven rasps occasionally growing loud enough to break the still air.

Hang on, boy. We'll get through this. Together.

He coiled the ends of the rope around his hands. Thick as two fingers, the rope was strong enough to hoist the heavy, canvas backdrops above the theater's main stage.

More than suitable for the duty Arden had in mind.

Voices carried down the hall. Calandra's first, then Beyland's.

He took the bait.

Arden pulled the rope taut.

"—know what else to do," she said. "He said something about Nicalene before he passed out."

"How did he know she was here?" Beyland asked. "Maybe he followed her?"

"I don't know, but he's in bad shape. I think she might have done something to him."

The door swung open, nearly striking Arden. Calandra stepped into the room.

"He's over here on the bed," she said, positioning herself to leave a clear path between the door and the bed. "You've seen what that stone of hers does to people. Tell me if this looks the same to you."

Beyland lingered in the hallway. "I can't believe she would hurt a kid, Cal."

You'd be surprised what people will do to a child.

Men and gods alike. Women too.

"Just come have a look, will you?" Calandra asked.

Come on, damn you...

"Fine, fine." Beyland entered the room. "But I don't know—"

He made it three steps beyond the door before Arden looped the rope around his neck and forced him to the ground.

Calandra gasped and jumped back as her brother struggled to escape.

Arden torqued the rope to close off his windpipe. His knee drove down on Beyland's back to pin him against the floor.

Easy, now. Don't fight it.

"I'm sorry, Beyland," Calandra said, her voice no more than a whisper. "I'm so sorry."

The fight went out of him quickly. By the time Arden counted to twenty, his limbs barely twitched any longer. When he reached thirty, Beyland lost consciousness.

Arden dropped the rope and stood up. Calandra knelt beside her brother's limp form.

"Is he...?"

"He'll be fine. But there's no telling how long he'll be out. Get his legs. We'll need to tie him up good."

They carried Beyland to his room and bound his arms and legs with a thinner length of rope found downstairs. Arden pulled a canvas sack over his head before they left him lying on the floor.

Then they went back to Nicalene's room.

"How are we going to do this?" Calandra asked.

"Simple. We get her dressed and I carry her out of here."

"What? Just like that? You're not even going to tie her up?"

Arden chuckled. "And have every watch patrol in Coldwater asking why I'm dragging a bound and gagged woman down the street? Even with the rain, we wouldn't make it halfway to Carbuncle before someone called us out. Now if I'm carrying my drunk sister home to her husband, who's going to have a problem with that?"

"And if she wakes up? What then?"

"Then I tell her she's lucky I found her passed out in an alley before some gutterscum climbed on her for a cheap thrill. But we need to hurry; we can't have her waking up here."

He pulled the bedsheets back to reveal Nicalene's naked body. The black stone embedded in her chest glistened with sweat.

Arden could not help but stare.

Gods...is that really what Dhrath's after?

Calandra nudged him. "Hey, you said to hurry, remember?"

"Right..."

They pulled a loose-fitting dress over her body, then hoisted her out of the bed to carry her down the stairs. When they reached the stage, Arden donned his coat and slung Nicalene over his shoulder.

"Okay, I've got her. Grab your coat and boots. It'll take about an hour to get over to Dhrath's in this weather."

Calandra dressed quickly while Arden made his way over to the back door. "What do we do when we get there?" she asked.

That's the tricky part...

He pulled a small pouch from one of his pockets and tossed it to her.

"What's this?"

"A pinch of nightroot. I've been holding onto it for a time like this."

Calandra's face darkened. "You've got to be joking."

"Don't worry. It's not what you think. I'll explain on the way."

She raised an eyebrow and scowled at him.

Arden smiled. "Trust me."

ALTHOUGH ARDEN DREW a few prolonged stares as he trudged through the wet streets with Nicalene draped over his shoulder, no one stopped him to ask where he was going or what was wrong with her. Even when they marched past a watch guardhouse, the armed men outside barely noticed them.

After last night's scuffle with the spaders, they had bigger problems to worry about.

The city had grown restless. Heavy rainfall usually kept the streets cleared, but today laborers, merchants, and impoverished common folk gathered beneath roof overhangs and ledges, many of them engaged in animated discussions. The few watch detachments that ventured beyond their walls went in force, often baring naked steel despite the rain.

Trust was a hard thing to come by. Guild workers glowered at the watchmen, insulting them in hushed tones whenever the armed patrols passed workshops and common rooms. The men of the watch turned on anyone who stared at them for too long, barking orders at loitering groups to move along, though they rarely indicated where those men should go in such weather.

If the rain held steady for a few more days, the tensions and anxieties would likely fade, forgotten and smothered by the bloated clouds. But if the weather broke soon, the seething factions would collide in the streets, causing riots to break out.

When they reached the crumbled foundation of the wall marking the Carbuncle's boundary, Arden glimpsed the spire through a brief gap in the clouds. The ominous landmark's black surface reminded him of the stone in Nicalene's chest.

Probably better for everyone if we dumped her off in the Break.

He glanced at Calandra. She had matched his pace since leaving the theater, her expression stoic and cold.

Maybe not everyone…

Halfway up the borough's central hill, he directed her down an alley that ran by a tottering old house missing most of its roof. The door hung partly off the hinges, but it held firm when Arden pushed it open.

A dog scurried into the rain when the stepped inside.

Nobody here. Good.

"What's wrong?" Calandra asked, pulling her hood back after she moved beneath the roof.

Arden set Nicalene down on a flat section of the old wooden floor, careful not to jar her too much. She had been still since they left the theater, but he was not taking any chances. He produced a thin length of cord from his pocket and set about binding Nicalene's arms and legs.

"You're going to wait here with her while I go have a word with Dhrath."

"Wait here? No, I'm going with you. We agreed on that, remember?"

Arden shook his head. "If we walk in there with Nicalene in tow, we're as good as dead. Once Dhrath knows we have her, he won't think twice about killing us."

"Then how are we supposed to make this deal?"

"We negotiate. If he knows we have her, but needs us to actually find her, then we have bargaining power. Otherwise, we're fucked."

"You mean dead."

"Same thing." After he tied Nicalene up, Arden took out his pouch of nightroot and dabbled a bit of the stuff into his palm.

He offered it to Calandra, who rolled her eyes. "No. I'm not touching that stuff."

"You don't have a choice," Arden said. "You want to make this deal with Dhrath? Then chew."

Her lip curled into a snarl, but Calandra took the nightroot and put it in her mouth. Arden scooped out a handful and did the same.

Gods, how did Beyland ever stand this? It tastes awful.

Calandra choked and nearly spat her dose out before clamping her hand over her mouth. She chewed slowly, her face contorting like churned butter. "How is this supposed to help us?"

"Dhrath's a cephalin, remember? He can read your thoughts, but it's not like reading a book. More like trying to listen to people talking in a crowded winesink, only every person there is either some version of you or somebody you know. He picks up bits and pieces of what you're thinking at the moment or what you remember from the past. Now, you can train yourself to only focus on one thought at a time, keep him from grabbing anything off the surface. But that takes years and plenty of discipline. Fortunately, there's a much simpler option."

Calandra licked the last few flecks of root from her palm. "You get high?"

Arden nodded. "The other option is to scatter your thoughts and senses even more. Firedust would work better, except you'd be too cranked up to do much of anything. Nightroot isn't as good, but it clouds your mind just enough to keep him from turning it against you."

Calandra swayed, her eyes widening.

Must be kicking in already. Potent stuff.

"I've…I mean, I never…"

"Try to keep your breathing steady," Arden said. "If your head starts spinning, focus on one spot and concentrate on it."

His lips tingled as he chewed. The sensation spread to his cheeks and inched down his neck. Calandra wobbled, almost falling before she steadied herself against Arden. Her fingers sent a jolt down his arm.

She caught him staring at her when she glanced up to apologize. "Why are you looking at me like that?"

You know why.

Arden rubbed at his numb face. "Nothing."

Calandra groaned and knelt beside Nicalene. "I think I'm going to be sick."

"Some people get nausea the first few times. It'll pass. Just make sure you don't pass out or go wandering off before I get back."

"Get back? Where are you going?"

"I'm going to meet with Dhrath, let him know we've got what he wants. We hand her over on our terms, not his. If he agrees to that, I'll come back, and we go from there."

"What if he doesn't agree?"

No point in answering that question.

"Just stay here and keep out of sight. I shouldn't be long."

Arden stepped outside. The rain danced when it splashed against him, pulsating to an intricate rhythm intertwined with his heartbeat.

The nightroot was taking hold.

"Be careful, Arden."

He glanced back at Calandra. She had not moved from her spot beside Nicalene.

Had she really spoken or was it the nightroot talking?

Get moving, old man. Time's against you.

He made his way down the alley and back into the main street.

"Arden?"

This time, he was sure it someone other than Calandra calling his name.

Not now…

Captain Rheinmak stood at the head of a watch patrol ten yards down the hill. A mangy ox pulled a prisoner wagon behind them.

"Well, well, well. Imagine meeting you here!"

Arden grunted. "Yeah. Imagine."

Rheinmak's hand went to his sword's pommel as he moved closer. His men followed his lead.

"I don't want any trouble, Rheinmak. Just going to have a word with Mister Dhrath is all."

The officer laughed. "Yes, I'm sure the two of you have a lot to talk about. Sorry to hear about Raugov, by the way. Terrible way to go. Must have taken a right heartless bastard to leave him crippled like that for the spaders to find."

"Don't know anything about it. We got separated."

"Course you did." Rheinmak nodded to his men and they fanned across the street as they advanced. "Tell you what, Arden, we're heading that way ourselves. Why don't you step over here and join us?"

Arden reached for his axe.

"Oh, I wouldn't do that if I were you. My men are edgy enough after last night. Don't want to give them a reason to take it out on you, would you?"

The men nearest the sides of the street took longer steps than the others, first moving abreast of Arden, then flanking him. One watchman stopped in front of the alley leading to Calandra and Nicalene.

Arden's knees buckled slightly, and his arms grew heavy.

Damn nightroot…

"Put that axe of yours down nice and slow," Rheinmak said. "I'd hate for there to be a misunderstanding of any kind."

I bet you would.

If he let Rheinmak take him, his plan to cut a deal with Dhrath would be ruined. Even if Dhrath agreed to his terms, the watch would pin last night's disastrous encounter with the spaders on him. Absolving his debt would mean little if the watch hanged him to appease the guilds.

He tried to find some way out, but the nightroot clouded his mind, making it hard to string multiple thoughts together.

Calandra. Have to get back to warn Calandra.

If she and Nicalene fell into Rheinmak's hands, they were both finished. Dhrath would kill Calandra just for knowing about Nicalene.

Gods only knew what the cephalin had in store for Nicalene herself.

The watchman by the alley was barely old enough to grow whiskers. His fingers twitched around his sword's handle.

Two strides would put him in arm's reach.

Arden glared at Rheinmak, his hand still on his axe.

The watch captain shook his head. "Don't be a fool, Arden."

Too late for that, I think.

He moved, every muscle exploding with violence as he lunged at the young watchman blocking his escape. Before his first step landed, he anticipated his opponent's reaction and identified precisely where to position his body to strike with maximum force. He knew the steps of that deadly dance by instinct now, having spent his entire adult life practicing with every partner imaginable.

But this time, something went wrong.

His hand caught on his wet coat and he dropped his axe. When his lead foot planted to bear his weight, his knee gave out, pitching him forward in a tangle of sluggish limbs.

Bloody nightroot!

The watchman jumped back as Arden crashed onto street, flailing to grab his axe as it skittered across the wet stones.

"Calandra! Run! Get—"

A boot smashed against the side of his head, followed by a series of blows to the rest of his body.

"That's enough, dammit!" Rheinmak pulled a few of his men away from Arden and directed them toward the alley. "He was calling out to somebody! Go find them!"

His head throbbed, and he could not tell whether from the nightroot or the kick to the skull.

Stupid, stupid, stupid...

"Get him bound up and in the wagon with the others. Squidface will be in for a nice surprise when we drag him in."

Two men rolled him on his side and tied his wrists together.

Rheinmak knelt down and ran his finger across Arden's lips. "Didn't figure you for a chewer. Not so proud of yourself now, are you?"

Somewhere amidst the roaring rainfall, Calandra cried out.

No...

"Found this one trying to hide from us, sir."

Rheinmak stood up. "The surprises keep coming. You're a long way from the Deadhouse, aren't you, dearie?"

Calandra spat at him, though it was a futile gesture in the rain. Rheinmak simply laughed at the futile gesture.

"Throw her in too."

They dragged Arden to his feet and pulled a wet gag over his mouth before directing him toward the wagon.

One of the watchmen returned from the alley waving to Rheinmak. "Sir, there's another woman back there where this one was hiding. She's already tied up and out cold. Do we bring her too?"

Rheinmak glanced at Arden. "You're up to something, aren't you? Tell me what's going on here and maybe I can put in a good word with Mister Dhrath. He might even let your friend from the mortuary live. Who's this girl you've got all tied up, eh? We'll find out who she is sooner or later, you know. Might as well save everyone the trouble and tell me know, don't you think?"

Arden shook his head. "Don't...know her..."

The watch captain smiled. "And I don't believe you." He gestured to the wagon. "Bring her. And be quick about it. I've spent enough time in this sodding rain for one day."

Two men shoved Arden to the back of the wagon and unlocked the door. Three gagged prisoners rode inside, their arms tied to a metal rod running along the wagon's ceiling, which forced them to stand up. The first prisoner, a woman, Arden did not recognize. He found the second man, dressed in expensive, if well worn, clothing, slightly familiar. Maybe someone he met in passing once or twice?

The third prisoner's eyes widened when he saw Arden climb into the wagon.

Jaspen, wasn't it? What the hells are you doing here?

The watchmen pushed the other prisoners to the front of the wagon to make room for Arden and Calandra. They dragged Nicalene over after they secured everyone. Jaspen muttered something through his gag when the men lifted her into the wagon.

"Shut up, you!" one of the watchmen said, kicking the spader's shin.

So, you do know her, don't you?

He thought about Grisel. Had Dhrath managed to track him down too?

The door slammed shut, plunging the rolling prison cell into darkness. Outside, the watchmen took up position once more and the wagon lurched forward, rocking unsteadily as it rolled across the uneven street.

Dhrath was waiting for them.

Arden dangled limply from the rod, his shoulders aching from the weight of his body and his drenched clothing.

He had run out of ideas.

Closing his eyes, he hoped Dhrath would decide to execute him before the nightroot high ran its course.

32

THE KEEP

Kaurgen moved quickly, almost too fast for Grisel to keep up with at times. He traversed narrow alleyways, waded through flooded streets, and climbed over fences and barricades. Twice he tried to scale a building before Grisel stopped him and demanded that they find a way around instead. He never grew tired, always moving forward at a relentless pace. Grisel was no stranger to hard work, but he still lagged a good distance behind Kaurgen most of the time, occasionally stopping to lean on his shovel and catch his breath.

Shouldn't be so hard to chase after a dead man.

The rain had not interfered with Kaurgen's tracking abilities. After leaving Tameris's hideout in Sinkhole, the reanimated oddity headed directly for Coldwater. He veered off his path every few blocks, sometimes following the unseen trail for a long way before reverting to his original course. One such divergence took them past Uthan and Carta's little shop. Grisel knew Nicalene had been there, but he doubted she would return. If she did, the ghulans would let him know. Kaurgen also skirted by *The Defenestrated Despot*, an old winesink Nicalene used to frequent.

Picking up those old habits again, are you?

The whole of Lowtown was on edge after last night's scrum between the spaders and the watch. If the rain had not driven everyone indoors, there might have been trouble in the streets. Grisel kept his head down and his mouth shut when Kaurgen led him by watch patrols or angry laborers huddled in shop doorways. If he had time, he would have changed out of his spader gear to avoid notice completely. As it was, men of the watch eyed him closely, and he exchanged the briefest of greetings with any guildsmen he passed. Workers occasionally waved for him to join them, but he either ignored them or shook his head and pointed down the street to indicate he had to be somewhere else.

After winding through Coldwater's streets for most of the morning, sometimes doubling back or crossing over previous paths, Kaurgen finally came to a stop outside an aging theater. Grisel joined him on the opposite side of the street, struggling to catch his breath.

A theater. Of course, you'd find your way to a theater.

"She in there?"

Kaurgen shrugged.

"The hells does that mean? You don't know?"

Another shrug.

"Thanks for clearing that up."

The hound pointed to the theater and took a long, deep sniff.

"Scent's stronger here, is that it?"

A nod.

"Okay, now we're getting somewhere. But you're not sure if she's actually there right now?"

Kaurgen pointed to the southwest. If they followed those winding streets long enough, they would end up in Carbuncle.

"She's been that way too, has she? Recently?"

He shrugged.

Grisel rolled his eyes. "Glad we've got our communication sorted."

Should have left you floating in the cesspit where I found you.

Kaurgen pointed at the theater.

"Alright, alright. Let's go have a look, then."

Grisel crossed the street and walked behind the theater. The back entrance was closed and locked. He thought about climbing to one of the high windows but scaling the wall in the rain seemed unwise.

While he scanned the building for another way inside, Kaurgen grabbed the handle and threw his weight against the door. Something cracked inside. Another slam and the door gave way, the lock tearing free from the frame and clattering to the ground.

Kaurgen stepped back and gestured for Grisel to enter.

Stronger than he looks.

"Careful," Grisel said. "Someone might have heard that."

The rear entrance must have been used for performers and stagehands since it led into a backstage area filled with old props and scenery backdrops. A thick layer of dust covered much of the equipment. Beyond the storage area was the main theater stage, which took up the entire ground floor. Light filtered through the glass windows high above, illuminating the whole stage while leaving the seating area in shadow.

Damn. Quite a place...

When they first met, Nicalene talked about wanting to be an actress. She had been serious enough about it at some point that she learned to read. Whenever she got drunk, she broke into long monologues learned from some play or another. Other times, she just cried. Although she was not too old for the stage, there were precious few opportunities for a woman her age to join a troupe. Grisel used to listen, but he heard the same story too many times to keep taking it seriously.

Maybe if I had, none of this would have happened.

He found a scattered pile of papers near the edge of the stage. The handwriting was not Nicalene's, and no familiar words jumped out from the scrawl.

Kaurgen sniffed at the steps leading up to the second floor.

"She's been up there?"

A nod.

Grisel crept up the staircase, each step reminding him of his tumble down the steps at *The Bleating Goat*. He was lucky he avoided breaking his neck that night.

Hopefully Arden's not waiting for me upstairs again.

The stairs led to a long hallway with rooms along the east wall. Most of the doors stood open, but the one closest to him was closed. Behind it, he heard someone mumbling incoherently.

Somebody's here, at least.

Kaurgen slid by him and took up position against the wall.

Grisel opened the door.

A young man sat on the floor with his back against a bed. His arms and legs were bound with thin rope and his mouth gagged with a strip of fabric. He stared wide-eyed at the visitors.

Grisel glanced at Kaurgen, but the hound's expression remained as vacant as before.

"Check the other rooms," he said.

Kaurgen nodded and disappeared down the hallway. Grisel leaned his shovel against the wall and knelt beside the bound man.

"Easy. I'm not going to hurt you."

Well, not unless you've got it coming.

"Listen, now. I'm going to take this gag off and you're going to answer some questions, understand? You play along, then we'll talk about untying you. I don't like what I hear, the gag goes back in and I leave you how I found you. Got it?"

He nodded.

Grisel untied the strip of cloth and pulled it away from the man's mouth.

"What's your name?" Grisel asked.

"B...Beyland."

"This your place, Beyland?"

Another nod. "Mine and my sister's."

"Where's she now?"

"I…I don't know. I think she left with whoever choked me out. They took Nicalene…"

Grisel grabbed his shirt and pulled him closer. "Nicalene? She was here?"

He nodded, slower this time.

"How'd she get here?"

Beyland opened his mouth, but then closed it.

"Don't get cute with me, Beyland. How'd she get here?"

"She was in trouble after she hurt somebody. She didn't mean to, but—"

"Where? *The Bleating Goat*? Was that where you found her?"

He nodded.

No wonder Kaurgen tracked her here. She was hiding out here all this time.

Kaurgen reappeared at the door.

"Anybody else?" Grisel asked.

The hound gestured for him to follow.

"Wait here. I'll be right back."

He hoped Beyland was wrong, that he would find Nicalene asleep in the next room. Instead, Kaurgen led him to the room at the end of the hall where a small boy lay asleep in the bed. Blisters and little scabs covered portions of his exposed skin, and he breathed with short, rasping gasps.

Who is this? Beyland didn't say anything about a kid.

"He the only other one here?"

Kaurgen nodded.

"Okay. Keep an eye on him. I'm going to see if I can get more out of Beyland."

He returned to the first room. Beyland remained right where he'd left him beside the bed.

"Who's the kid?"

"I don't know. My sister called me in to look at him when somebody jumped me from behind."

"This guy that jumped you, did you see him?"

"No, but he was big."

"You catch a name? Anything?"

Beyland shook his head. "No. My sister found out that I owed a lot of money to somebody, more than we could pay. Maybe she was trying to cut a deal. Nicalene was scared of something, maybe they were after her too?"

Grisel could have guessed the answer to his next question, but he asked it anyway. "Who do you owe money to, Beyland?"

"Dhrath."

Arden. Has to be.

He pulled a small knife from his belt and grabbed the cord holding Beyland's legs together. "Start at the beginning. Tell me everything that happened since you met Nicalene."

BY THE TIME Beyland finished, Grisel wanted to punch him.

The dumb bastard obviously loved her.

Did Nicalene feel the same way? That was more difficult to know.

Grisel's head hurt.

"Do you love her?" He still did not have an answer to Tameris's question.

After cutting Beyland free, they went back downstairs. Grisel directed Kaurgen to bring the boy along with them.

"Do you think this Arden character will take Nicalene back to Dhrath?" Beyland asked.

"It's the only thing that makes sense," Grisel said. "Near as Kaurgen can tell, she was headed toward Carbuncle. That's where Dhrath keeps his roof."

Beyland glanced at Kaurgen, blinking rapidly. "How does he know that? How did he track her here in the first place?"

"Trust me, you're better off not knowing." He turned to the hound. "Take the kid and get back to Tameris. You know which trail to follow to find us, right?"

Kaurgen nodded.

"Get your ass moving, then. We're going to need all the help she can give us once we get there."

"Are you sure it's a good idea to send the boy with...him?" Beyland asked.

Grisel shrugged. "Better than leaving him here alone."

Especially if none of us come back.

Kaurgen scooped the boy up and carried him out the back door into the rain.

After the hound left, Grisel picked up his shovel and turned to Beyland. "Don't suppose you've got a blade or anythingt handy, do you?"

Beyland shook his head. "Never really had a need for a weapon."

Of course not.

"Right," he said. "Come on, we best get moving."

Beyland donned a cloak and followed him outside. He moved along-side Grisel before they reached the first cross street. "You never told me how you know Nicalene."

"What," Grisel said, "she never mentioned me?"

"She didn't like to talk about the past."

The past. That all I am to her now?

"That so? Well, she lived under my roof for the last two years. Maybe I was too giving for my own good."

"Were the two of you…you know…?"

Grisel scowled at him. "Yeah. Yeah, we were. Till she stepped out on me and robbed me blind."

"That…that doesn't sound like Nicalene. I can't imagine her hurting anyone."

"Possible you ain't known her long enough."

Grisel pulled ahead of him before he could ask another question. The thought of Nicalene spending the last week helping Beyland write his silly play while he suffered at Arden's hands on her account made his stomach turn.

Did she have any idea what he had gone through, what he suffered because of her?

He could have told Arden everything he knew about her that first night at the *Goat*. If all he cared about was what she stole from him, maybe he would have. But something stopped him, some part of him that would rather die than see her suffer.

"Do you love her?"

He felt like he was getting closer to an answer, but he still needed to see her again, to look into her eyes.

Maybe then, he would know for sure.

Beyland took the hint and stayed quiet for the rest of the way to Carbuncle. Only when they spotted the charred stone of Dhrath's Keep atop the borough's central hill did he speak again.

"I forgot how big it is."

Grisel had seen the tower up close only a few times. His work assignments mostly kept him in Pigshire and Coldwater, rarely venturing past Carbuncle's outskirts. When he did get called to work there, it was underground work on the borough's elaborate drainage system.

"Yeah," he said. "It ain't the spire, but it leaves an impression."

Beyland shuddered, though the rain was not cold enough to give him a chill.

Bad memories, no doubt.

"How'd somebody like you get mixed up with Dhrath, anyway?" Grisel asked.

"I needed more money to buy the Moonvale Theater. Thought it would be successful enough to pay him back."

"I'm sure that's what everybody says when they get in his pocket."

Beyland stopped and stared at the tower. "How are we going to get in that place? We can't just walk up to the door and knock."

"Don't worry. That's the one thing about this plan I've got sorted. Follow me."

Grisel led him around the hill until they came to a wide ditch about the size of a small house. Water filled it two thirds of the way to the top.

"What is this?" Beyland asked.

"It's one of the borough's four drainage basins. Keeps the water from washing out the foundations of the buildings at the top of the hill. There are drains in the streets that connect to a central channel running under-ground. This is where it empties out."

"How does that help us?"

Grisel smiled. "Because if you crawl up that tunnel, it ties in with the street drainage system, with lines leading to every street drain. Including the ones inside the keep's outer wall."

Beyland blinked, then glanced at the hilltop. "How...how do you crawl up, exactly?"

"One foot at a time. Real careful-like."

"It's a long way to the top."

"You'd better lose the cloak," Grisel said, wading into the basin. "Trust me, you don't want it catching on anything in there."

THE CLIMB UP the drainage channel proved far less perilous than Grisel's earlier climb out of the cesspit. Since the channel followed the gently sloping hillside, it never angled vertically. Although the wet stone was slippery, especially with a steady stream of water flowing downhill, the rougher stone along the sides provided decent enough grip for them to ascend.

Beyland managed better than Grisel expected, only slipping a few times. His progress was slower, so Grisel had to wait for him once he reached the central drainage cistern where all the street drains funneled rainwater. The cistern was circular, roughly fifty feet wide at its broadest point. A series of narrow tunnels lined the uppermost portion of the wall, each one dumping many gallons of water down stone chutes that emptied into the pool at the center, which then drained into the four channels lead-ing to the basins halfway down the hill. A circular pattern of iron grates lined the ceiling far above, scarcely allowing any light in, especially with all the water pouring through.

Grisel reached into his spader belt and withdrew his amber daystones. The stones gave off their familiar, dull light when he clicked them together, just enough enough to dimly illuminate an area about twenty feet wide.

When Beyland joined him, he pointed to the contraption, which Grisel had wrapped around his wrist. "What's that?"

"Daystones. Amber treated with an alchemical fire. Every spader carries a set. Can't use open flames with all the fumes we come across."

Grisel raised his arm to inspect the drainage tunnels lining the walls. "The street drains all feed into those lines. We'll have to climb up these chutes and crawl down the tunnel to get to the keep."

"Do you know which one? How far is it?"

He pointed at the ceiling. "You see those grates up there? That's the dead center of the hilltop. Dhrath's Keep is just one street over, about thirty yards east."

"How do you know all this?"

"This system needs cleaning out every few years. The guild sent a crew of a dozen men down here just a few months back. My name got drawn from a lot to join it."

"Bad luck, eh?"

Grisel laughed. "You kidding me? We got double pay for this detail. Why do you think they awarded the job by lot? Otherwise every spader in Lowtown would volunteer."

"Oh," Beyland said, embarrassed.

"Forget it." He pointed out one of the drains. "That's the one we need. Come on."

They climbed up the stone chute funneling water into the cistern and crawled through the drain tunnel, which was about two feet wide. Water filled the bottom six inches, leaving just enough room for them to fit inside and keep their faces out of the water. Every few yards, they passed under a drain line leading to the street, which dumped more water down on them. Grisel crawled past the first five drains before twisting his body around to stand up in the sixth drain. A series of footholds had been cut into the stone leading up to the grate, some ten feet above them.

"This is it." He blew on the daystones to extinguish them and returned them to their pouch before climbing up the footholds. Beyland grunted below him as he wriggled into the vertical drain to follow.

When Grisel reached the top, he peeked through the grate to see if anyone was around. The small courtyard area above the drain separated the keep's outer gate and its inner stronghold. He did not see any guards, so he braced his shoulder against the grate and pushed it open. The steady drumming of rainfall covered most of the noise he made removing the grate. He climbed up, then reached down to help Beyland out. Once they were both clear, he returned the grate to its place and hurried over to the stronghold's inner wall. When he peeked around the corner, Grisel saw the main gate. Four men stood guard there, huddled beneath the archway around the gate. There was just enough shelter there to keep them dry.

Can't go that way.

"Now what?" Beyland asked.

Grisel pointed to the opposite end of the keep's pitted wall. "Around back. Maybe there's another way in."

The stronghold lacked a rear entrance, but they located a separate building there. Little more than a shack, the structure resembled a stable, but it was far too small to keep livestock. The door had no lock, but a series of sliding bolts ensured it could not be opened from the inside.

Prisoners?

Nicalene...

"Come on," Grisel said. "Let's have a look inside."

They crept to the building and slid the bolts from their brackets. Grisel pulled the door open to find a series of stalls running down each side of a central walkway. Iron bars covered each stall. The place reeked of waste and rotting meat. Beyland reeled back from the door, choking, but the stench did little to phase Grisel's hardened senses.

He stepped inside.

The pitiful, shriveled things in the first few stalls had been people at one point in time, but captivity had reduced them to subhuman, starving wretches. Chains bound them to the back wall of their tiny cells. Few of them had the strength to look at him as he walked by.

Poor bastards.

Most of the middle stalls held healthier prisoners, common folk similarly chained to the wall. This group was gagged as well as bound, but they averted their gazes when Grisel approached. Every one of them bore scars from repeated lashings.

What had they done to deserve this fate? None of them looked particularly threatening. Was this how Dhrath punished the people who crossed him? Did he have a cell set aside for Beyland when he failed to make good on his debt?

He gasped when he peeked into the next cell and saw a familiar face.

"Jaspen!"

His friend's eyes snapped open and he pulled at his bonds while mumbling through the leather gag pulled over his mouth.

"Quiet down," he said. "I'm going to get you out of here."

He tugged on the cell door, but the lock refused to budge.

Dammit. Has to be a key somewhere around here.

He looked back to the entrance and saw a keyring dangling from a hook next to the door. Beyland stood nearby, still swaying unsteadily.

"Beyland, bring me those keys, will you? And breathe through your mouth."

Following that advice, Beyland grabbed the keys and made his way to Grisel. As he handed them over, he looked into the cell next to Jaspen's and cried out when he saw the woman locked inside.

"Cal!"

"You know her?" Grisel asked, sliding the key into the lock to open Jaspen's cell door.

"She's my sister!" He moved on to peer into the other cells. "Where's Nicalene? Is she here too?"

"Keep your voice down, damn it," Grisel said as he unlocked the manacles around Jaspen's wrists. Once his arms were free, the spader ripped away his gag and coughed.

"Grisel! What are you doing here?"

"I don't have time to explain, mate."

Beyland returned to his sister's cell. "She's not here, Grisel."

Dammit.

"Nicalene?" Jaspen said. "She's here. Rheinmak found her when he locked up this shitsucker."

Jaspen pointed to the cell directly across from his. Grisel turned and laughed when he saw Arden bound and gagged.

"Rheinmak, eh? Guess somebody's not in favor these days. Where's Nicalene now?"

"Inside," Jaspen said. "One of the guards came for her not long ago. Let me have those keys. Olynia and Morangine are over there. We've got to get them out of this place."

"What happened?" Grisel handed the keys over. "You were supposed to be meeting with them this morning."

"We did, but that bastard Rheinmak was there. They ambushed us; killed almost everybody else. Locked the rest of us up in a guardhouse cell before they hauled us over here."

Jaspen unlocked Olynia first. She rubbed her wrists and nodded at Grisel. "My thanks, friend."

Grisel glanced back at the door.

He half expected to find one of Dhrath's men standing there, but the doorway remained clear.

Jaspen finished unlocking the man next to Olynia. He stumbled out of his cell and stared disbelievingly at Grisel. "We need to hurry," he said. "Dhrath will know we've escaped soon if he doesn't already."

"The keys," Beyland said. "Give me the damn keys!"

Jaspen tossed the keys to him. "Morangine's right, Grisel. You got a plan to get out of here?"

"I ain't leaving without Nicalene," Grisel said.

"Come on, Grisel. Do you have any idea what's at stake here? We've got to get the Assembly members out of here. There's a revolution brewing out there, mate! It'll all be for nothing if these two get caught again."

Beyland unlocked his sister and embraced her. When he let her go, she snatched the keys from him and went to Arden's cell. Grisel grabbed her wrist.

"Oh, no, you don't. We're leaving that shitheel here to rot."

She glared at him. "Let go of me."

"Or what?"

Morangine pushed through the group to reach Grisel. "In case you hadn't noticed, spader, we're a bit short of allies at the moment. If you have a problem with this one, then I suggest you get it sorted after we get out of here. Right now, we need as much help as we can get."

Grisel sneered. "That the way you see it, Lord Morangine? What makes you think I give a toss what you want, anyway?"

"Because right now we all share a common enemy, and every moment we spend squabbling with each other in here makes our escape less likely."

Grisel glared at Jaspen.

"He's right, mate," his friend said, scowling. "Let her go."

Fine. But this isn't over between us.

He questioned Arden as soon as Beyland's sister freed him. "Tell me about Nicalene. Where does Dhrath have her?"

"Probably in the main audience chamber," Arden said. "It's where he meets everyone. But if you just barge in there, nothing's going to stop him from killing you with a thought."

Grisel scoffed. "I'll take my chances."

"What's the best way out of here?" Morangine asked.

Arden shrugged. "The front gate, probably. If it's open, we could probably rush by the guards before they could react."

Beyland shook his head. "The gate's closed. We already checked."

"How'd you get in here, Grisel?" Jaspen asked.

"We climbed up the cistern drain. You could go out the same way, probably even easier."

Jaspen nodded. "Okay, then. Let's get everyone there, and then you can do whatever you want about Nicalene."

They filed out of the makeshift prison, leaving behind the rest of the poor, locked up sods. Grisel directed them toward the drain, but when they were halfway across the yard, the earth shook violently, throwing them all to the ground. Bits of stone broke free from the stronghold and tumbled around them.

"What was that?" Jaspen asked.

Grisel's heart fluttered. Something in the air had shifted, changed the texture of the water streaking down his skin.

Nicalene. Dhrath's got her!

By sheer chance, he met Beyland's gaze.

You feel it too, don't you?

The ground shook again.

"The front gate," Arden said. "We'll have to chance it."

Jaspen nodded. "Lead the way."

As soon as the group rounded the corner, they came face to face with an armed guard. He cried out to the others and hoisted his axe to strike.

So much for that idea.

The four guards from the front gate came running, backed up by a group of watchmen Grisel had not seen earlier, bringing their number to ten in all, each of them armed. They spread out to block any avenue of escape. Captain Rheinmak stepped into view, emerging from somewhere around the front of the keep.

"How did this lot get free? Get them back in their cages, and don't be afraid to run them through if they fight back."

Before the armed men could advance, a loud crash thundered across the yard. At first, Grisel thought it came from within the keep again, but it did not shake the earth beneath their feet. Another crash followed, this time clearly originating somewhere behind Rheinmak.

The gate! Someone's pounding on the gate!

Some of the guards turned their backs on the group and hurried to defend the front gate.

"Get everyone out here!" Rheinmak said, shoving one of the guards toward the keep.

Another dozen armed men rushed outside within moments, all of them lining up in formation before the gate.

The ground shook again and the air trembled to match it. Some of the guards fell down.

Another crash rang out at the outer gate, and this time it buckled.

"Hold fast," Rheinmak said. "Stand your ground!"

The outer gate ripped free from its hinges and splintered into pieces.

A woman stood on the other side, clad in spader gear and a mask with a black coat trailing behind her. Black and crimson smoke swirled around her outstretched hands.

Tameris!

Behind the sorceress stood a gang of ghastly, pale figures clad in a motley of improvised armor. Rheinmak hesitated, glancing back at his bewildered men, and taking his eyes off Tameris's makeshift army.

When he raised his sword to give an order, the horde charged through the gate.

They attacked with a savagery that made Grisel's stomach turn. Some of them lumbered forward, driven by misshapen lumps of muscle sewn under their skin to smash armored men with bare fists. Others flailed at their foes with barbed whips snaking out from their forearms or stabbed and slashed with knives embedded between their fingers. A few were truly monstrous, their mouths opening to reveal rows of grinding teeth that stripped flesh away from bone when closed around arms, shoulders, and skulls.

But most unsettling of all was the way they tore through the defenders without making a sound. Even when one of them fell under a rain of blows, it simply collapsed in silence, as if its death had gone unnoticed by men and gods alike.

Meanwhile, Tameris stood well behind the melee. Behind her mask, she laughed. It was a thin, hollow noise, like a dry wind blowing through shriveled river reeds.

When the outcome of the battle became obvious, many of the watchmen and Dhrath's guards tried to surrender. But Tameris's creatures gave no quarter. They struck unarmed men down where they stood, fighting with no less ferocity than upon their initial assault.

Rheinmak turned to flee, but a slender woman with hooks in her fingertips ran him down. She sank the hooks into his neck and tore out his throat in a single, careless motion. He fell to the ground, desperately trying to stanch the blood flow. The woman fell upon him as he went down, rending and tearing at his flesh, each swipe ripping away another bloody chunk.

Grisel went numb as the carnage finally ebbed to a halt. Tameris waded through the blood strewn yard, directing several of her minions to the keep's entrance.

"Where's Nicalene?" she asked.

Remarkably, Grisel had forgotten about her.

"Inside," he said. "With Dhrath."

Tameris nodded. "All of you better get out of here while you can."

No one needed further encouragement. Morangine exchanged a long glance with Tameris, enough to make Grisel wonder if there was some connection there, but he eventually fell in with the others as they hurried out the gate.

Beyland lingered as well, pulling away from his sister's grasp to stare at Dhrath's Keep.

She begged him to follow, but he was not listening to her any longer. When she tried to drag him away, he pushed her to the ground.

Tameris glanced at him, then turned to Arden, who lingered nearby Beyland's sister.

"Get him out of here before he gets himself killed," she said.

Arden rushed forward and grabbed a kicking and screaming Beyland around the waist to drag him through the gate.

When everyone had gone, Tameris turned back to Grisel.

The earth shook again, more violently this time. A huge chunk of stone broke free from the top of the keep and crashed in the yard behind him.

What's happening in there?

"It's time to do your part, Grisel," Tameris said.

She gestured to her monstrous creations gathered near the keep's entrance.

"Dhrath's using his power to try to take the stone from her, but he won't be able to control what he's unleashing. If you can't help her remember who she is, she might destroy the whole city. You're the only person with enough of a connection to her to reach her."

Grisel stared at the keep as another tremor shook fragments of mortar loose from the walls.

"What if I can't? I don't even know what I'm supposed to do!"

"Do you love her?"

He met Tameris's black-eyed gaze.

"Yes."

"Then help her."

Grisel closed his eyes and cursed at himself.

Then he ran into the keep.

Somewhere behind him, Tameris laughed again.

33
THE ASHEN

Silence fell over the theater after the last syllable passed between her thin lips.

No whispers from the audience. No movement in the seats.

Nothing. Just infinite, unbroken emptiness.

Turning her back to the crowd, her glistening dress swirled around her like a spectral aura. An enchantment in the fabric kept it a hair's breadth from her skin, preventing it from brushing against her sensitive flesh. When the dress stilled, she lowered her head.

Someone clapped.

Like a trickle of water giving way to a torrential flood, that first reaction became a crescendo, giving birth to a roar of applause.

Somewhere, in one of the balconies overlooking the stage, the Empress glared at her.

She could feel her envy, her hatred.

The Empress would be coming for her now.

She strode off the stage. Her loyal supporters waited for her behind the curtain, weapons at the ready.

A familiar face was missing. It was the face she drew courage from when she felt the darkness closing in on her.

Where is he?

She brushed the question aside. She could not afford any distractions. Not now.

"It's time," she said.

They escorted her into the bowels of the theater, winding through the tangled, labyrinthine passages leading to storerooms, dormitories, and smaller amphitheaters. When they reached her personal chamber, she waved her hand over the door to dispel the protective wards.

"Wait here. Let no one pass."

She slipped inside and closed the door behind her. A stillness hung over the room, and not even her footfalls on the stone floor made a sound. She pulled the jewelry chest from its hiding place beneath the bed. Another wave of her hand caused the locks to spring open. She lifted the lid.

The black stone nestled inside sucked the light toward it, bending the room's shadows like trees in a steady wind.

She took the stone in her hand. Heat coursed up her arm, stoking the fire already burning in her sorcerous blood. The veins beneath her ashen skin glowed.

The Empress could not stop her now.

She would still try.

And then she would die.

Like everyone who suffered at her hand.

Like everyone she was supposed to love.

She donned the necklace, the black stone resting heavily against her chest.

The relic had travelled halfway around the world to reach her. With it, she forged a personal connection to a power more ancient than the primordial city crumbling around her.

Now it would help her reshape that city by scouring away the cancer that had gnawed upon its soul for far too long.

She rose and went to the door.

The hall outside was empty, her loyal fighters nowhere to be found.

Somewhere in the distance, water sloshed against stone.

And where do you think you're going with that treasure of yours?

She froze.

That voice...

Which one are you, I wonder? Do you even know yourself?

She could not identify the voice, but she recognized it from somewhere before. The scolding tone was like ice trickling down her spine.

Splashing water echoed down the hallway, moving closer and closer.

"Who's there? Show yourself!"

Oh, I think not. Why don't you be a dear and leave the stone where you found it? I bet it's brought you nothing but misfortune.

A different voice this time, brash and belligerent. She pictured a human face, fat and bearded with hateful little eyes.

Who are you?

I might ask the same of you.

She had not spoken aloud. Someone, or something, was reading her thoughts, violating her mind.

A torrent of water gushed down both ends of the hallway, swallowing everything in its path. Something writhed just beneath the water's black surface as it rushed toward her. She turned around to open the door, but it would not budge.

Be still, now. There's no need to fight. You'll only bring more pain upon yourself.

A woman's voice. Cold and cruel.

The Empress?

No, a cruder kind of hatred…something petty, more human.

She dispelled the door's wards again, but it made no difference.

The water roared through the hall, racing toward her with monstrous speed.

Be still, now.

She grasped the black stone and drew forth the power burning inside it. Fire surged through her and unleashed a shockwave of intense heat. The water crashed against an invisible wall, swirling and churning as it tried to punch through to wash over her.

Interesting.

Gripping the stone so tightly that her knuckles burned, she tried the door again. This time the handle moved, groaning under the pressure before yielding. The water breached the invisible barrier and flooded the rest of the hallway as she pushed into the room and slammed the door shut.

She backed away from the door until she bumped into the mirror hanging from the back wall. The reflection staring back at her was not her own, but rather a human woman with long, dark hair and pale skin. A black stone, identical to the one dangling from her neck, was embedded in her chest, fused directly to the skin.

Confusing, isn't it? Your minds are so weak, so easily misled, so eager to be deceived. I pity you all, truly I do.

Another familiar voice, this one a mixture of several distinct speakers, all of them dripping with scorn.

She looked down at her ashen hands, fearful that some change might have come over her. In the mirror, a long tentacle covered with suckers slid over the dark-haired woman's shoulder, coiling around her neck and slithering between her breasts to caress the black stone nestled there.

"No!"

The mirror cracked, fragmenting the reflection into hundreds of smaller images, some of them still portraying the human woman while others showed her true self.

Is there still some fight left in you?

That voice she recognized clearly.

It belonged to someone she trusted. Someone who abandoned her when she needed him most.

Snarling, she flung the door open and summoned the stone's power again, reducing the water outside to vapor in an instant. The earth trembled, shattering the mirror behind her.

Impressive...

She stepped into the mist-shrouded hallway.

Something wet slithered in the distance.

This has gone on long enough, don't you think? Time to hand over what's mine.

Her stomach quivered at the faint memory of greasy hands sliding over her hips.

Was that her memory or another's?

She looked down at her hands. Their appearance shifted with the writhing mist, sometimes slender, elegant and ashen colored, sometimes clumsy things, fleshy and pale.

The slithering drew closer.

Just another moment. It will all be over soon.

She tried to run, but the mist disoriented her. The sound of soft, slimy flesh sliding over rock came from all around her now.

A figure emerged before her, ashen skinned and clad in shimmering fabric.

You've come! You're here!

Courage swelled within her when she met his gaze. She stepped forward to touch his face.

There was a sadness in his eyes, a glimmer of guilt that made her pause.

Something's wrong.

"I'm sorry," he said.

Then he plunged a dagger into her stomach.

No...why...?

A tear ran down his face as he whispered, "For the Empress..."

She fell to the stone floor, warmth draining away from her. Her body felt heavy now, all its former elegance fading as the mist cleared.

You humans are all the same. So quick to love, so foolish to trust. And where does it leave you in the end? What does it get you?

The voice gave way to something wet and heavy lurching toward her. She gasped for breath, but the air scorched her throat, tasting of brine and ice.

She let the stone drop from her hand. It cracked the floor when it landed, sending out another wave of tremors.

"Nothing," she said, whispering through ragged lips.

That's right. Nothing. That's what all of you are, what your kind amounts to. Nothing.

A slimy tentacle wrapped around her arm, followed by another around her waist.

Nothing...

"Nicalene!"

The name echoed down the hall, reverberating against the walls before it reached her ears.

"Nicalene!"

The voice rang out clearly, from a single source.

What have we here?

"Don't listen to him! Don't give in!"

Nicalene. I know that name...

That's quite enough out of you.

A scream rang out, loud enough to blast the walls to dust and blow away the swirling mist. She closed her eyes and screamed, desperate to keep the unbearable noise at bay.

The cry tore at her soul, breaking her heart to pieces and stabbing into her bones with a thousand, icy needles.

It was a sound of unfathomable pain.

I know that voice...

The name came to her slowly, driven forth by memories of joy, anger, and sadness. It took shape at the forefront of her mind, burning away the thoughts and impressions that did not belong to her. Her flesh no longer felt heavy and misshapen, but rather her own once more.

I know you.

What was that?

Grisel.

She opened her eyes.

They stood suspended in an infinite blackness, a void bereft of any physical surroundings. A huge, slime coated mass of tentacles and suckers writhed before her. The creature's beady, black eyes held her in place as surely as the slithering tendrils wrapped around her arms.

Grisel floated nearby, screaming as the suckered arms struck at his broken skull like lashes, sheering away bits of his brain with every strike.

"Don't listen to him," he had said. *"Don't give in."*

You came for me...

What are you doing?

For me.

Nicalene.

No! Stop that!

She felt the stone buried in her chest. Somewhere, she heard the ashen woman crying out, but she ignored her. Whoever she was, she was dead and buried now, a ghost from another time, another place.

My name is Nicalene!

SHUT UP!

She opened herself to the power building inside, let it filter through her blood, her bones, her soul. A thousand lifetimes flashed through her mind, but she shoved them all aside, focusing on the only one that mattered.

Her life.

NO! DON'T—

The bodiless voice broke off, interrupted by a thousand distinct screams. Nicalene could identify every one of them, knew them all from the depths of her memory. They pleaded with her, begging for the agony to end.

But she could not stop now even if she wanted to. The stone's power raged through her unchecked, ripping through the unseen bonds of time and space and bending what poured through the cracks to its inchoate, unthinking will.

Caught in the storm, she reached out to Grisel.

His hand closed around hers, weak and trembling.

Stay with me...please...

A flash of light blasted the void away, breaking their bodies into a swirling maelstrom of fragments and flinging them across the infinite gulf of space.

Amidst the seething turmoil, she heard Grisel's voice.

"I'm here."

34
THE ASCENSION

Ember poured the rest of the wine into his cup. A good vintage, old enough that he did not recognize the vintner's mark. He massaged his wrists and sighed.

Yimina sat across from him, twirling a fork between her fingers.

"Still sore?" she asked.

He nodded. "My skin's a little raw."

She smiled. "Good thing your captivity was so short. It might have left a scar."

"I'm touched by your concern."

"You should be. I could have left you to fend for yourself, you know. Could have walked right by Twiceborn's place and moved on to Spiresreach. I'm sure there's some paranoid merchant up there looking a good dagger."

Ember took a drink. "No doubt. Especially one with all her eyes and teeth."

She leaned back in her chair and put her feet on the table. "Probably would have paid better, at least."

"Certainly." He glanced around the deteriorated room. "Though I doubt you would enjoy such luxurious accommodations."

Yimina chuckled and sipped at her wine. "Oh, I'm sure I could adjust to life among the common class eventually."

Why didn't you, I wonder?

"Why stop at Spiresreach?" he asked. "You could have crossed the Saven, made your way back to High Ridge. No less work for you there, I'd wager."

She bristled at the suggestion, her previous humor fading. "No. Memories there have a way of festering, not fading."

"Do they? It's been a long time. Don't you ever think about—?"

"No," she said, her voice cold and flat. "There are some places you don't go back to, not if you can help it." She drained the rest of her cup and set it down on the table with a loud clank. "Spiresreach, High Ridge, it doesn't matter. My place is here. You know that."

"My father's been dead a long time, Yimina. Whatever obligation you think—"

She stabbed the fork into the table. "Don't bring your father into this. The debt I owed him was paid in full long ago. Him and your grandmother both."

Ember took a deep breath and nodded. "I'm sorry. I should know better than to say things like that." He reached across the table to grasp her hand. "Sometimes I just…well, I wonder if I would be as loyal if our positions were reversed."

"You think too much." She smiled. "You always have."

Who would know better?

Someone knocked at the manse's front door.

It's time.

"That's her," he said. "We'd best not keep her waiting."

Yimina strapped her spring-loaded dagger harnesses to her forearms. Ember pulled on his cloak as he went to the door.

Twiceborn waited outside, accompanied by four of her undead minions. The rain had finally let up, but the summer heat swept in after it, turning the city into a steaming pit. A thick fog hung over the streets, faintly illuminated by the diffused light from the street lamps.

Ember was relieved that the sorceress had brought the least remarkable examples of her fell fleshcraft. He had yet to shake the image of her more inhuman handiwork ripping through the fighting men at Dhrath's Keep earlier in the day.

"Did you find them?" he asked.

Twiceborn smiled. "All of them. Right where you expected: huddled in a winesink trying to drink themselves into oblivion."

Predictable. Predictable and stupid.

"Let's get this over with, then."

"Follow me." Twiceborn snapped her fingers and her minions started down the street. There was a smoothness to their movements that Ember found disturbing. Nothing graceful, but rather a precision that avoided any unnecessary motion.

"Have you been back to Dhrath's Keep since…?"

"Yes," she said. "Not much to see, really. The whole place came straight down, fortunately. Could have flattened half the hilltop had it fallen the wrong way."

"Dhrath?"

Twiceborn shook her head.

"Did you find what he was after, at least? The stone from the woman?"

Twiceborn did not answer.

Could be a yes or a no. Hard to get a read on her.

"What's happening with the watch?" he asked. "Were you able to use Arden?"

She nodded. "He proved remarkably cooperative once he learned I had his son. Gave up the names of every watch officer on the take from Dhrath."

"And?"

"Let's just say the watch will have fewer corruption problems tomorrow than it did this morning."

"What about the rest of Dhrath's associates? The gangs, the enforcers, the dealers; what'll become of them?"

Twiceborn smiled. "For the moment, nothing. I'm going to let them sort things out for a few days, see which ones are worth salvaging and which ones are dead weight. Then I'll find out if they're smart enough to see things my way."

Something about the comment chilled him. Twiceborn might not have been able to read minds but trading a cephalin for a sorceress was hardly a reassuring change in Lowtown's criminal underworld.

Gods... Did I help create a monster even worse than Dhrath?

They followed Twiceborn down Blackhoof Street to a crumbling heap of a stone building that once served as a poorhouse. The watch put the place to the torch before Ember was born, officially to eradicate all traces of a disease outbreak, but also to deter the wretches from neighboring boroughs to cross into Coldwater in search of relief. Legend had it that the watch did not bother to empty the poorhouse before setting it alight, perhaps even barricading the door to prevent the miserable souls inside from escaping.

Whatever of the truth, local residents insisted the place was haunted by vengeful spirits. No one dared to venture there, even the destitute and the desperate.

They entered the building through a wide crack in the western wall. A single candle burned in the center of the old sickbed room. Gnarled, rusty remnants of furniture littered the area, and the whole place smelled of wet ash. Three more of Twiceborn's minions waited for them inside. They were larger and bulkier than the others, with hunched backs and knotted shoulders.

Three bound figures sat on their knees next to the candle, canvas sacks pulled over their heads.

Ember nodded to Twiceborn. She snapped her fingers and the three brutes pulled the sacks away to reveal the prisoners.

Cambin Domoch.

Armille Trendar.

Ithlene Beniquorra.

They stared at him, dumbstruck.

"Well, well, well," Ember said, "what a surprise meeting you here."

Cambin found his courage first, or at least his bluster. "Ember! What's the meaning of this?"

"I think you know exactly what's going on, you backstabbing bastard. The three of you thought you could cut your own deal with Dhrath and squeeze me out of the picture."

"Don't play the victim, Ember," Armille said. "You're the one who went and made a mess of everything with the vote, told us that you had Lorvie locked down when the truth was you didn't have control over anything."

Ember's teeth clenched when he heard her name. He stepped forward and planted his boot in Armille's midsection. The assemblyman doubled over, half coughing, half wailing.

"Don't you dare use her name again, you shitsucker. She was the one person on that crooked council with a shred of innocence. She didn't deserve what you bastards did to her."

"Do you think we wanted her dead?" Cambin said. "We didn't tell anyone to—"

Ember grabbed the old man's hair and jerked his neck back as far as it would bend.

"What did you think would happen? Did you think you could promise someone like Dhrath results, and he'd just let it slide when you didn't deliver?"

He shoved Cambin to the ground and gave him a swift kick to the ribcage.

"Stop it, Ember!" Ithlene said, finally breaking her silence. Ember glared at her, remembering the look on her face when she gave Rheinmak the order to hand him over to Dhrath.

"Oh, I'm going to stop it," he said. "I'm going to stop all of this. All of this bickering, all of this backstabbing and sniveling, underhanded politicking. No more brokers like Dhrath lording themselves over the Assembly, no more watch captains on the take from the people they're supposed to be fighting, and no more mobs calling for blood and vengeance in the streets."

Ithlene stared at him. "And what's going to stop people like you?"

"That's where you've got it wrong, Ithlene. Lowtown needs people like me. It's always needed people like me, people who know how to bend it just enough to steer it in the right direction. But you three, you only know how to latch onto whoever promises to keep a seat under your asses. What do you care if the city burns so long as you get a good view of the fire?"

She spat at his feet. "Talk yourself up all you want. In the end, you're no different from Dhrath, or from any of us. You were out for yourself when this all started and you're out for yourself now, so spare us the righteousness."

We'll see about that...

He turned to Yimina. "I think we're finished here."

"Finished?" Ithlene asked. "Finished with what?"

Ember nodded at Twiceborn. She snapped her fingers again and her brutish minions jerked the prisoners to their feet.

Ithlene called out again, her former bravado giving way to panic. "Ember! Stop! Come back! Please! Ember!"

Yimina followed behind Ember as he left the poorhouse and walked down Blackhoof Street.

"You're sure you want to do this?" she asked. "Once you start down this road, there won't be any turning back."

He recalled something his grandmother told him about taking risks: *"Lots of people look before they leap, boy. They're the same ones who keep stepping in shit all the time."*

Would she have approved of what he set in motion tonight?

Not that it mattered anymore.

One way or another, he had to see it through to the end now.

"It's already too late," he said.

EMBER MET OLYNIA outside the Assembly Hall just after dawn. A pathway opened in the crowd, allowing him to make his way to the steps leading up to the main entrance. People stared at him as he strode through the gathering, but where he once might have ignored them, he instead shook hands, clapped shoulders, and exchanged brief pleasantries.

He put on his best face, though he imagined it was not terribly convincing for those who knew anything about him. Had Olynia not used her extensive connections with the guilds and the common folk, he never would have agreed to mingle with them.

Only days earlier, the same crowd had been baying for his blood, after all.

Olynia was halfway through her speech by the time he reached her on the steps. It was a rousing call to arms, a demand for retribution and change. The crowd liked it well enough, although it was hard to tell how many of them understood the finer points of her argument.

Not that it mattered, really.

The people gathered outside the hall did not need to understand every detail so long as they were ready to do what men like Ember always feared they would do.

When Olyina finished, she waved for Ember to join her. He stepped up alongside her and faced the crowd.

"They're ready, now," she said. "All they need is a little push."

Ember raised his hand to call for silence. "Citizens! Some of you know my face, but others only my name. I am Ember Morangine, grandson of Desidori Morangine. Though I stand here before you today, I don't pretend to be one of you. My family has held a seat on the Assembly of Notables since its beginning and has long benefited from the privileges that go with it. I confess that until recently, I didn't understand what that meant. But in these last few weeks I've learned of a sickness growing within the Assembly, a sickness that's long been festering in all of Lowtown. For too long I ignored the signs, missed the corrupt influence of the brokers undermining the Assembly's efforts at every turn, failed to see them bend an instrument of justice into another whore to be bought and sold however they please."

A few angry shouts went up from the crowd in agreement. The reaction gave him some confidence. He worried that they would never give him a chance to get through his speech, instead dismissing him as a detached aristocrat playing at being a man of the people.

Which was, after all, precisely what he was doing.

"Trinn Harmyndri saw what I couldn't. She knew the Assembly no longer served the very people it was charged to protect. She saw the way it allowed the guilds to be undermined, the way the watch grew fat and vile on a steady diet of bribes, and the way it ignored your cries for justice at every turn. Many times, she tried to tell me, to make me understand, but I was blind to the threat, dismissed it as the petty concerns of a political novice. But she went on believing, went on fighting for what was right. And the brokers made her pay for it with her life."

Another wave of anger swept over the crowd. Trinn's death was still a raw wound for most of them.

"And she wasn't the only victim! Lorvie Tinderhov, whose family served the people of Lowtown for generations, whose innocence and kindness outshone that of all her peers combined, met a vicious and undeserved fate for refusing to fall in line with the whims of the brokers."

Invoking Lorvie did not draw as much enthusiasm from the crowd, but Ember had not expected it to. What he wanted them to remember was the way his voice trembled when he spoke her name, the way his eyes teared up at the mention of her murder. They needed to see him care about someone, had to see him suffer like they had suffered.

"After their deaths became known, I advocated for Olynia to take Trinn's place. I saw in her something of Trinn's strength, her dignity, and her commitment to justice. Together, we hoped to cleanse the Assembly of the cancer eating away at its soul, but we didn't know just how deep the sickness ran. When our efforts became a threat, our fellow Assembly members had us wrongfully arrested, thrown into a cell like common criminals, and charged with treason. Treason! Can you imagine a greater height of injustice?"

Pockets of outrage flared up throughout the crowd. Ember raised his voice to project over the noise.

"Had brave citizens not come to our aid, we might well be lying dead alongside Trinn and Lorvie, two more victims sacrificed to preserve the wicked ambitions of ruthless brokers and corrupt officials. What further evils might those same brokers visit upon you through the Assembly? How would it help you when its self-serving laws are enforced by complicit men of the watch? What assurance do we have that there won't be more deaths to follow? That Olynia and myself won't be found dead within the week?"

The crowd churned with rage now, either angered by Ember's words or the implications left unsaid.

Now for the big push...

"But there is a way out, my friends! There is a way to restore integrity to the law, to cleanse our ancient institutions of the sickness in their souls. Today, Olynia and I have summoned you, the citizens of Lowtown, before the Assembly Hall to call for a vote of no confidence in the Assembly of Notables, to call for its immediate dissolution."

The crowd roared with approval, although Ember doubted that a third of them understood what he just told them. No one had engineered a "no confidence" vote in their lifetimes, or their great-grandparents' lifetimes, for that matter. In fact, the mechanics, not to mention the legality, of such a measure were not exactly clear to begin with, even in the Assembly's historical records.

But Ember knew none of that mattered to his audience. Not after he included the phrase "immediate dissolution."

Olynia leaned over to speak into his ear. "You're better at this than I thought. Almost good enough to give me second thoughts about this deal of ours."

Ember smiled. "Don't spoil the moment. There'll be time enough for knives later."

She laughed, but her reaction lacked any genuine humor.

What would Trinn think of you now, I wonder?

THE ASSEMBLY MEMBERS exchanged troubled glances.

"A 'no confidence' petition?" Mendin asked. "In all my years of service to this august body, I've never heard of such a thing."

Ember fought the urge to roll his eyes. "There's precedent. According to the records in the archives, the Assembly has been dissolved at least four times. Maybe more. There are several decades without any records at all."

Olynia nodded. "Each time involved accusations of corruption or abuse of power and brought about changes to the Assembly. Why do you think it's not filled with hereditary seats anymore?"

"The last petition came three hundred years ago," Ember said. "It dissolved the Assembly and designated three seats to be filled by a citizen plebiscite."

Selinis, who currently held one of those three seats, stood up. "Then are we to understand that you intend to add more such seats? To make the Assembly even more representative of the people?"

"Ideally, yes," Olynia said. "But there are concerns that the problems with the Assembly go far beyond the allocation of seats."

Murga leaned forward, his beady eyes narrowing. "What are you suggesting, exactly?"

Ember glared at him. "I believe she's referring to the fact that three members of this Assembly orchestrated the murder of two fellow members and arranged for the capture of two more, all at the behest of the broker who controlled their seats. Clearly we have to address such wanton corruption before reconstituting the Assembly."

Murga slumped back in his chair, scowling. Ember did not have to remind anyone that his hefty colleague was heavily indebted to an alliance of brokers in Pigshire.

Harik grumbled, puffing out his chest like he always did when he thought he was about to make an important point. "And how do you intend to accomplish that without the Assembly's guidance?"

"Again, there's precedent," Ember said. "In previous cases of dissolution, legal power devolves to either a viscount appointed by the Crown or to consuls selected by citizen plebiscite. As this petition originated with Lowtown's citizens, a coalition of guildmasters and other leading citizens have already appointed two consuls to assume power from the Assembly and oversee the transition."

Murga scowled. "And who are these consuls?"

Ember glanced at Olynia.

She took a step forward and bowed slightly. "The people of Lowtown have seen fit to bestow this honor upon myself and Ember Morangine. As of this afternoon, we will assume—"

"This is ridiculous!" Mendin said, slamming his fist on his desk. "I'll not simply stand by while the mob out there tries to rob the Assembly of its rightful power! There must be some means of refuting this petition, no?"

"Of course, there is," Ember said. "The Assembly can halt the dissolution with a simple majority vote, provided it then makes efforts to address the grievances that led to the petition in the first place."

Murga laughed. "Well, then, let's put this matter to rest! I call for a vote to reject this petition. All in favor?"

"I'm afraid you can't call for a vote right now, Assemblyman," Olynia said.

Mendin looked at his colleagues, confused. "What do you mean?"

Olynia gave him a wry smile.

A cruel touch.

"Apparently you haven't noticed," she said, "but you're one member short of a voting quorum."

Without Ember and Olynia seated, only seven members of the Assembly were present. While a seven member quorum could hear petitions, the Assembly needed at least nine members to introduce or vote on any measure.

Mendin stammered, knocking items off his desk as he looked over the empty seats. "Where...where are the others? Ithlene? Cambin? Armille? They should be here!"

Ember shrugged. "I suppose they've taken the death of their broker benefactor harder than expected."

"You've done something to them, haven't you?" Murga asked.

"The watch will never stand for this," Harik said. "When they hear what you've done, they'll throw you back in a cell for treason."

Ember smiled. "I'm touched by your concern, Assemblyman, but if you inspect the petition we've presented thoroughly, you'll see that both the Coldwater and Pigshire Watches are among the signatories. The other boroughs will follow their example, I think."

The rest of the Assembly went on staring at them, plainly stunned by the turn of events.

Olynia bowed again. "If there's nothing more you'd care to discuss, then I'm sure you understand that Lord Morangine and myself have a great deal of work to attend to and we'll require the use of the Assembly Hall to do it. We ask that you vacate the building by midday. The citizens gathered outside will not prevent you from leaving or harass you in any way, but if you wish to have a watch escort, we will be happy to arrange one."

She turned to depart the hall, leaving Ember to stare down the few Assembly members who had yet to slump down in their seats, dejected. One by one, the rest gave in, some shaking their heads in disbelief while others stood up and left the hall for the last time.

Mendin was the last to admit defeat. The old man scowled at Ember, gnawing at his lip while his face twitched.

"Five decades I've sat on this Assembly, you miserable whelp. Five decades of keeping the degenerate wretches of this borough from each other's throats. And now, here you are, taking it all for yourself and burning down everything I've ever worked for."

Finally, he sank into his seat, his shoulders drooping so low that they all but vanished from sight.

Only then did Ember turn to leave.

"Morangine…"

He stopped, but he refused to look back at the old man.

"Your grandmother. She was the nastiest, most cutthroat bitch of a woman I ever knew. I never hated anyone more than I hated her, and she deserved every bit of that hatred. But what you did here today…well, I think that'd impress even her."

Ember left Mendin glowering behind him in the Assembly Hall.

He waited until he got outside to smile.

Consul Morangine. There's a title she never had.

With the Assembly of Notables formally disbanded, he and Olynia held complete political authority over Lowtown. They could issue laws, organize militia forces, set trade terms, and even collect taxes. Eventually, of course, there would be pressure to reform the Assembly, but if they kept the guilds on their side and the common folk happy, that day could be long in the coming indeed. He neglected to mention to the Assembly that the last time two consuls were appointed, they governed Lowtown for almost twenty years before their rivalry nearly sparked a civil war, forcing the Margrave to send in one of the legions to stop the fighting and reestablish the Assembly.

Twenty years sounds like a fine goal to start with.

But he was getting ahead of himself. There were still quite a few problems to resolve before he could think about the long-term future of his consular authority, among them cracking down on many of the brokers and consolidating the watches from each borough into a single, cohesive force.

Olynia would have a number of ambitions as well, most likely using her newfound power to pursue the social and economic goals Trinn cared so much about. She would push for more poorhouses, more physicians, more protections for laborers, and the like.

Sooner or later, their ambitions would come into conflict.

Ten years. Maybe that's more realistic.

The crowd was already cheering for Olynia by the time Ember joined her on the steps. He acknowledged the applause but kept his distance from his new political partner.

Enjoy your moment. We'll see how long you can keep them loving you.

Yimina found him quickly, gliding through the crowd to stand alongside him. She took his hand and leaned in close to him. "How did they take the news?"

He laughed. "Badly. We'll need to keep an eye on Murga and Harik. They might try something stupid."

She nodded at Olynia. "She seems to be pleased with herself."

"For now. She'll be coming for me soon. We'll need to know who her people are, make sure she doesn't get any cozier with the guilds."

"Already working on it."

Ember ran his fingers through Yimina's blonde hair and kissed her. "What would I do without you?"

"You'll never have to find out. I've always been here for you, and I always will be."

He smiled and turned back to Olynia. She called for silence and launched into another stirring oration, this time announcing the formal dissolution of the Assembly of Notables and the establishment of consular authority over Lowtown's six boroughs.

"We'll need to keep a tight grip on the watch," Ember said. "She's too close to the guilds and the commoners for them to trust her right away. If we can secure their support now, she'll never have the chance to turn them against us."

"Pigshire's watch is going to be a mess after Twiceborn gets through with them. If you want to rebuild it with loyalists, you'll need to find someone you can trust with experience commanding men."

Ember nodded. "Don't worry, I've already got the ideal candidate in mind."

35
THE DEPARTED

The spaders arrived at the Deadhouse around midnight. There were six of them, all carrying their distinctive shovels and keeping a lookout for any potential trouble. Tensions were still high after the incident in Carbuncle and the dissolution of the Assembly. Although the newly elected consuls promised to purge the watch of any corrupt officers responsible for provoking conflict, the guild was not taking any chances. They travelled everywhere in force now, always ready for trouble.

Calandra met the group at the front gate. She recognized Jaspen immediately, but not the others.

"Thanks for coming," she said.

He stepped forward to greet her. "Calandra, wasn't it?" He extended his hand, but she hesitated to take it. "Don't worry, I didn't come from a detail."

"But I have," she said. "Sorry. We try to minimize contact while we're working. I'm sure you understand."

Jaspen grunted. "Yeah, sure."

They stared at each other for a moment. Jaspen's companions shuffled their feet and tapped their shovels against the cobblestones.

The bruises on his face had healed a bit since she last saw him.

"You look well," she said. "Considering the circumstances, of course."

"Look, I'd like to get this over with if you don't mind?"

Calandra nodded, feeling a little foolish for trying to make small talk. She barely knew the man, of course, but their brief experience together as prisoners had established an inkling of a bond between them.

Another time, maybe.

"This way," she said, guiding him inside and across the yard to the mortuary's main entrance.

"When did they bring him in?"

Calandra shook her head. "Some time this morning, I'd guess. We usually keep good records of arrivals, but we've had so many these last few days we've fallen a bit behind on the entries."

Bodies started streaming in from the ruins of Dhrath's Keep the day after it collapsed. The walls had caved in on themselves, reducing the place to a pile of charred brick and burying everyone left inside. While local laborers scavenged through the rubble for salvageable stone, the collectors circled like vultures, snatching up any bodies they uncovered and delivering them to the mortuary.

Around the same time, dead watch officers started turning up outside the gate. No one tried to claim a fee for dropping them off, which was probably wise considering the obviously violent causes of death. A tag identified each of them by name and accused them of both corruption and treason.

Calandra recognized a few of the officers.

The accusations came as no surprise.

She led Jaspen into the preparation chamber. If they continued to receive bodies at the same rate for another day, they would run out of tables. Calandra had not seen the place so full since the last plague outbreak in Sinkhole several years ago. That had been much worse in terms of sheer numbers, but not quite so messy. Most of the bodies coming from Carbuncle were smashed beyond recognition. The watch officers were hardly better off. Were it not for their tags, identifying some of them would be impossible.

"Here he is," she said, stopping beside a table covered by a roughspun blanket. "It's...not pretty, I'm afraid. Are you sure you're ready to—"

"Do it," Jaspen said. "I have to see if it's him."

Calandra pulled the blanket down to reveal the smashed remains of a man in spader overalls. His upper body was mangled from the middle of his chest to what was left of the shattered skull.

"Looks like his head was crushed by a falling block. The collector who brought him in couldn't find his spader tags. I don't know if there was another spader in the keep when it collapsed, so I thought you could—"

"The hands."

"What?"

"Show me his hands."

Calandra pulled the blanket off the body. Jaspen lifted the corpse's left hand, which was wrapped with a bandage to cover the stumps of two severed fingers.

"Yeah," he said, "that's him. Grisel."

The spader's voice wavered a bit. He grasped his dead friend's intact hand and squeezed it.

"You crazy bastard. Just had to go and do something stupid, didn't you?"

"Do you need a moment alone with him?" Calandra asked. "I can—"

"No," he said, struggling to hold back tears. "I'm fine. It's just...we'd been mates for a long while, you know? Came up together as apprentices. He could be a stubborn ass sometimes, most of the time, really. But he was a good mate, him and Meaty both. Now they're gone and it's just me. Don't know what makes me so lucky."

Calandra shrugged. "I think most everyone who comes here wonders the same thing. They look at their friends, their kin, the people they loved. They want to believe there's a reason behind it all, why some of us die and others go on living. I imagine the dead have the same question."

"What do you tell them? The living ones, I mean."

"I don't have a good answer. Maybe Grisel died because the gods decided it was his time. Or maybe they don't give a toss. Maybe it was just dumb luck. I don't know that it's really important one way or another. All you can do is ask whether he died doing something he believed in. If he did, then not much else matters, does it?"

Jaspen stared at what was left of Grisel's mangled skull. He let out a long sigh. "Yeah. I guess you're right. Like I said, he could be a stubborn bastard. Guess if he hadn't done what he did, he'd spend the rest of his life beating himself up over it."

"All the same," she said, "I'm sorry for your loss, truly I am. He saved my life as well as yours, remember? I never even got the chance to thank him."

He nodded, still staring at the corpse. "What'll you do with him now?"

"That depends. Does he have any kin?"

"No. His family died in a plague outbreak with he was a kid. Grew up fostered in the guild. Guess I'm the closest thing to family he's got."

"Then the decision's yours. I can release the body to you for burial or I can burn it here.

He returned Grisel's limp hand to his side. "Burn him. He never much liked being fenced in, so I doubt he'd care to be buried in a box."

"I'll make the arrangements, then." Calandra pulled the blanket over the corpse again, but Jaspen kept staring at it.

"What about Nicalene?" he asked.

The name made her jump. "Yes? What about her?"

"Has she come through here?"

Calandra shook her head. "Not that I've seen."

"You think she's still out there somewhere? That maybe she got out?"

"If she was with Grisel in the keep, then the odds of her surviving aren't very good. There might not have been enough of her body to be worth bringing back."

"Too bad. Seems like they ought to be laid to rest together."

Beyland might disagree with that.

"He loved her, didn't he?" she asked.

Jaspen pursed his lips before finally nodding. "Yeah. I guess he did. We gave him a hard time, but he never let us get away with saying something mean about her."

"What about her? How did she feel?"

"Can't rightly say. I didn't know her all that well. They had their problems, I guess, especially at the end. Grisel tried to make her happy, but he wasn't the best at sharing how he felt."

"Well," she said, "maybe they got to be together for one last moment before he died."

Japsen sighed. "I hope so. You need me to do anything else?"

"No. I'll mark his name in the records and schedule him for cremation."

"Right. Suppose I should thank you for sending for me. I assumed he didn't make it out, but the not knowing was eating at me."

The spader stepped back from the body and rubbed his face. He took several deep breaths, still staring at his friend's corpse.

Something tells me the knowing will go right on eating at you.

She tried to change the subject. "I heard the consuls renewed the Spaders Guild's contract along with ours. You must all be a bit relieved after everything that's happened."

Jaspen shrugged. "I suppose. We don't much trust Morangine to keep dealing with us straight, but Olynia's been a good friend of the spaders for a while."

"You hear anything about what they've done with the watch? We've had a lot of watch officers showing up dead."

He scowled. "Morangine's up to something with them. Word is he's appointed a new commander over all the boroughs to bring them under consular authority."

"You know who it is?"

"Not for certain. But I don't like the rumors we're hearing."

Calandra nodded. "I've kept you here long enough with this chatter. Can I show you out?"

Jaspen shook his head. "No, it's fine. I can find my own way. Ain't exactly a maze, this place."

Neither of them laughed.

BEYLAND WAS STILL upstairs when she reached the theater the next morning.

He had not spoken to her since their escape from Carbuncle. She knew he blamed her for Nicalene, for conspiring with Arden to sell her off to Dhrath.

After three days of complete silence, she wondered if he genuinely hated her and would never forgive her.

Maybe he's right.

It still did not sit well with her, what she did to Nicalene. She could justify it all as a way of making the best of a bad situation, of trying to do what was best for her and her brother in the long run, but the guilt was stubbornly persistent.

Although she no longer had to worry about her brother's debt to Dhrath, she was scarcely resting any easier. Every morning she returned from her shift, she half-expected to find Beyland dead by his own hand. If he did not attempt suicide, there was always the chance of him returning to his old habits, sneaking down to some teetering winesink for a pinch of firedust. She wondered if she could handle another bout of addiction, especially after all they had just been through. Sooner or later, she would wear down, unable to protect her brother from himself any longer.

She wished he could go back to working on his play. He had been so close to finishing the work, and Nicalene probably would have wanted him to complete it. At least it would occupy him, maybe even give him some way of channeling his sense of anger and loss.

When Calandra walked across the stage, she noticed the strewn papers from when she left sat in a neat pile now, with only a few crumpled pages discarded nearby. Beyland must have put them in order while she was gone, which meant he was finally leaving his room.

Is he writing again? That has to be a good sign.

Two envelopes sat atop the stacked papers. Calandra did not remember seeing them among the scattered pages earlier.

She picked them up. One was marked with the letter "C" and the other with a "B."

Calandra and Beyland, is that it?

She glanced around the theater, wondering if whoever left the letters was still inside. The place looked and sounded empty.

Curious, she returned the "B" envelop to the pile and opened the other one. A small piece of thin paper was nestled inside. She pulled it out and unfolded it.

The handwriting was crude and uneven, obviously scrawled by an unpracticed hand. Even so, she had little trouble discerning the two words written there:

"Thank you."

Just below the message, a single letter served as the signature.

"-N."

Calandra's knees buckled and she dropped to the floor. She reread the message and the letter over and over and over.

It can't be...

She glanced over at the other envelope, the one marked with a *"B."*

When her strength returned, she snatched up the envelope and ran for the stairs.

"Beyland! You'd better look at this!"

36
THE FORSAKEN

The *Ashen Woman* had been playing at the Moonvale Theater for two weeks before Arden mustered the courage to attend.

He arrived as late as possible, slipping inside just before the doors closed and taking a seat in the back benches of the packed gallery. The play opened with a rousing argument between two lovers while they plotted some conspiracy to bring down a wicked ruler. In the scenes that followed, the titular Ashen Woman struggled with her decision to turn traitor, having spent many years helping the ruler obtain power in the first place. But even as her commitment to the cause strengthened, her lover's misgivings gradually sowed the seeds of their failure. In a thrilling climax, the Ashen Woman delivered a performance before the ruler's court, only to be betrayed by her lover in the moment of her apparent triumph. The curtain closed after she delivered a stirring soliloquy about love falling victim to fear.

Arden found the story a bit morose and self-defeating, but the audience seemed to like it well enough. They applauded the actors during the curtain call and debated with one another over who delivered the most standout performance. The general agreement seemed to be that the actress who played the Ashen Woman was worthy of a place in the prestigious theaters of High Ridge.

While the young woman certainly had talent, Arden wondered if Nicalene would have given a more moving portrayal of the doomed character. The part was so well suited to her that he was convinced Beyland wrote it with her in mind.

After the curtain call, the actors called Beyland from backstage to take a bow. He clearly relished the acclaim, smiling and waving enthusiastically. When the cheers died down, he said a few words of thanks and complimented the cast.

He dedicated the play to a woman he neglected to name, a woman who inspired him and changed his life.

Made a mark on all of us one way or another.

Arden took the opportunity to head for the exit before anyone else rose to leave. The last thing he wanted was for Beyland to spot him in the crowd.

Calandra stood by the exit waiting for him, her arms crossed and a scowl upon her face.

Although a part of him had hoped he would run into her at the theater, he now wished their paths had not crossed.

"I'm a little surprised to see you here," she said.

He glanced back at the stage. Beyland was still talking, but he seemed to be winding toward the end.

"Can we take this outside?" he asked.

Calandra nodded and stepped aside to let him open the door. Dark clouds floated above the city, ready to dump their contents upon anyone unfortunate enough to be caught in the streets. Just over the rooftops to the northwest, the spire rose from the city center and punctured the cloud cover, almost as if it bore the weight of the sky upon its peak. Of course, the actual peak was somewhere far above the clouds, if it existed at all. Perhaps, somewhere hundreds of miles above the city, the spire held the heavens themselves aloft.

Arden gestured down the street. "Walk with me, will you?"

Calandra shrugged and started walking. He fell in alongside her. They kept away from the middle of the street as a steady stream of mule-drawn wagons rolled by. Laborers shuffling to and from their homes pushed by street merchants and criers seeking to draw customers to nearby shops.

He still was not used to walking the streets during the day. Blackspire felt like a completely different place after sunrise, livelier, younger. He did not miss the oppressive darkness of the nights.

"Thought you'd be asleep at this hour," he said.

"The guild's moving me over to the daytime shift next week. They gave me a few days to adjust to the hours."

"You must be glad for that."

She shrugged. "Maybe I'll finally get some decent rest. It's been hard to sleep while Beyland's putting on shows during the day."

"He seems to be doing well. The play's been quite a success from what I've heard."

"How'd you like it?"

Arden chuckled. "Oh, I'm not much of an artist. Not sure I quite understood everything, but it does leave an impression."

"Yeah. It does. I think it was good for him to finish it. Helped him to move on after…well, after what happened."

He glanced at her. She kept her gaze straight ahead.

"He still angry about what happened?" he asked. "With Nicalene, I mean, the way we took her."

Calandra pursed her lips before answering. "I don't know that he'll ever forgive me completely, to be honest. But we've put it behind us, or at least we pretend not to think about it anymore."

Arden nodded. "I know it was a tough choice for you. Maybe he'll understand one day, after the pain's not so close."

"I hear you've done well for yourself," she said, changing the subject almost as soon as he finished his sentence.

Arden wanted to keep a low profile when he came to the theater, so he left his armor and insignia at the local watch guardhouse. He even left his sword behind. Unless someone recognized his face, there was nothing to indicate that he held an officer's rank in the watch.

"Suppose most everyone's heard that news by now, haven't they?" he asked.

"I guess you decided not to leave the city after all, then."

"Well, Dhrath dying changed a lot of things. Didn't see much need to go on the run, especially with Halvid being sick. Turns out doing Dhrath's dirty work for so many years made me valuable to the consuls. After I helped root out the worst officers among the watch, they asked me to stay on and put it back together in every borough, starting with Coldwater. Pay's decent, good enough to get the medicine I need for Halvid."

"How is he?"

Arden sighed. "The fever backed down, but he's still in a lot of pain. Looks like he might be through the worst of it."

Thunder boomed overhead. Some pedestrians looked skyward while others pulled their cloaks' hoods over their heads.

"I hear they've finished clearing out the rubble in Carbuncle," she said.

"Finally, yes. The stonemasons salvaged all the stone they could use, I think."

The work had been quite an undertaking. After the borough's laborers picked over some of the remains for intact blocks, the Stonemasons Guild turned up with heavy wagons to haul the rest away. In keeping with the city's scavenger tradition, pieces of Dhrath's Keep would find their way into walls, streets, and foundations all across Lowtown over the next few years.

"The collectors gathered quite a few bodies there," Arden said. "I guess you saw most of them."

She nodded but said nothing.

"Morangine told me Grisel came through the Deadhouse a few days after the place came down."

Calandra shrugged. "What was left of him, anyway. Poor bastard got his skull smashed to a pulp."

The gods are wicked and cruel.

Sorry, Grisel.

"And Nicalene?"

Calandra shook her head. "Never saw her. Body was probably too mangled for the collectors to bother bringing in. I was surprised we had enough of Grisel left to identify, really."

Twice now, she moved on after quickly answering his question about Nicalene.

Did she know more than she let on?

Arden doubted she had much to gain by keeping anything from him.

Unless she's still alive.

They reached a circular intersection where several streets joined together. Arden stopped outside a walled estate wedged between two streets as they drew closer to the intersection. Calandra took a few more steps before she paused and looked back at him. Her eyes held him in place, and he forgot whatever he was going to ask her about Nicalene.

They stared at each other for a long while, neither one able to turn away.

"What is it?" she asked, finally.

No way around it now.

"Listen, Calandra, there's something I need to tell you."

She folded her arms over her chest again. "Go on."

"I'm sorry for what I put you through. For…threatening you like I did. There's a lot of things I've done since I came here, things I'm not proud of. Maybe I had a good reason, maybe I didn't, but I know a lot of people suffered on my account. People talk about the gods making decent people suffer for no good reason, but the truth is that they're no worse than people like me. I know there's no way to change the things I've done, but I'm trying to set a lot of things right now. Trying to find a way to start over and find that sense of honor I used to have before I came to this city."

Calandra's expression remained the same as she stared at him at him.

Go on, you old fool. Tell her everything.

"I don't think I realized just how far I'd gone before I met you. There was something about you, something that made me remember there's another way of living, some way that doesn't leave you feeling like you've hollowed yourself out just to survive. I've got a long way to go to figure out how to do that again, but…but I keep hoping that maybe there's some chance that when I do, you'll still be here. That maybe we can put the awful way we met behind us and start off differently."

Calandra bit her lower lip and took a deep breath through her nose. Thunder rang out again, louder this time. The first few raindrops fell from the ashen clouds.

"I...I'm sorry," she said, her lip trembling. "I need to get back before the rain comes."

No, don't go...

"Goodbye, Arden."

She spun away and set off toward the theater, falling in with the street's foot traffic. Arden watched her blend in with the crowd and disappear. The rain came down heavier now, driving people into alleys and under ledges for cover.

Arden stood alone in the rain for a long time.

For a moment, he thought he caught the smell of brine.

The gods are wicked and cruel...

37

THE REVENANTS

The Saven River sliced through the heart of Blackspire like a poorly healed scar, completely separating the city's wealthy northern districts from their grimy, industrialized neighbors. During the day, river galleys from the settlements upriver and sail-driven cogs from the southern sea competed for anchorage space in the deepest waters while an armada of lighters ferried goods to and from the shore. Well-connected trade ships offered up substantial fees for a loading place somewhere along the northern shore's labyrinthine network of docks. Laborers stood ready to swarm aboard newly arrived vessels to relieve them of their cargo and load it onto wagons for distribution throughout the city. Once emptied, the ships took on the varied shipments gathered up by prosperous West Gate merchants. The heavy traffic persisted throughout the daylight hours, making the aptly named Dockside one of the most vibrant districts in the city.

Ship captains looking to avoid the northern shore's excessive dockage rates found more favorable terms on the south side of the river, provided their ships had shallow enough drafts to avoid running aground in Mire Shore's swampy waters. A sprawl of moldering docks covered the district's mosquito-infested marsh, most of it looking more likely to fall into the water than accommodate commercial shipping. In addition to lower fees, Mire Shore provided easy access to the manufactured goods churned out by Spiresreach's factory houses and guild halls. Dozens of local riverboats ferried shipments from Mire Shore to Dockside, feeding the bustling export business that kept foreign coin flowing into Blackspire's coffers. Smugglers also took advantage of the poorly regulated southern docks to operate a thriving black market, much to the dismay of authorities in the city's northern districts.

After nightfall, the gatehouses hoisted massive chains up from the riverbed to block all traffic. A thin cloud of fog settled over the water on all but the hottest summer nights, making navigating the river in the dark quite dangerous. Only the most daring, or foolish, captains attempted to cross the Saven's wide expanse during the night. Larger ships rarely strayed from the shoreline after dusk, and city law prohibited them from dropping anchor for the night. Without larger ships churning up wake, the sluggish river became so calm that it resembled a vast sheet of black ice.

Moored to one of Mire Shore's tottering docks, the *Tuckerspur* floated gently upon the water's still surface. Although small for a seaworthy cog, her draft was almost too deep for the southern shore's shallow waters. When the dry season arrived in a few months, ships like the *Tuckerspur* would run aground in the mud trying to reach all but the largest docks. For the time being, she fit neatly into a mooring tucked behind a winding corridor of walkways and pilings. Difficult to access without assistance from dock workers, such spots were highly prized by smugglers and privateers.

The air was still warm after the humid rains, but Nicalene shivered all the same.

She was always cold now. Tameris said the feeling would pass eventually, but it might take weeks or months.

Maybe even years.

"Friend Nicalene, are you well?" Carta stood near the *Tuckerspur*'s bow, clad from head to toe in her heavy, brownish-gray coat with blue trim despite the heat. Her partner, Uthan, waited beside her in his green trimmed coat. Dark goggles covered most of their faces, and they wore a scarf over their mouths, which muffled their chiming, sing-song voices slightly.

Uthan cocked his head to one side. "Not too late to turn back."

"No," Nicalene said. "I'm fine. Just had a chill is all."

The ghulans exchanged a glance.

"As you wish, friend Nicalene," Uthan said.

"Come along then," Carta said. "She'll be waiting."

"Yes, we needn't test her patience."

The ghulans pressed ahead, scampering toward the *Tuckerspur*'s gangplank. A woman waited for them there, picking at her fingernails with a needle. Two broad shouldered men with glazed over eyes stood behind her, each with a hatchet dangling from his belt.

Tameris.

She had seen little of the sorceress over the last two weeks, after she was left in the tender care of the ghulans. Everything before that was a jumble of blurred images. Some of them, the more recent ones, were stronger than the others.

The theater. That she remembered pretty clearly. The way Beyland and Calandra protected and cared for her, put themselves in danger to help her. She remembered Beyland's play, the way it defined so much of their brief relationship, but so much about him remained beyond her mind's reach.

And Grisel. She remembered Grisel, though only in glimpses and emotional impressions. Tameris and the ghulans tried to fill in the blanks in her memory, telling her about her connection and history with Grisel. They need not have bothered. She could still feel him beside her, his hand wrapped around hers.

The feeling helped drive back the cold, but there was a dark edge to it, one that she might tumble over if she became too lost in it.

A pair of yellow eyes stared back at her from that darkness. Sometimes she saw a face, a woman's face, sharp cheekbones and a long, narrow jaw. Her skin was the color of ash, her breath like sulfur.

She held a black stone close to her chest.

The sight of it always left Nicalene cold.

Cold, alone, and afraid.

Tameris greeted them with a curt nod as she slipped the needle into one of her coat's many pockets. The ghulans offered a more enthusiastic greeting, but the sorceress ignored it.

She was not much for pleasantries. "Wasn't sure if you'd come."

Nicalene shrugged. "Thought being here might stir something up."

Tameris pointed to Nicalene's chest. "Let me have a look."

She untied the cord holding her shirt closed and pulled the fabric down to reveal the ugly, scarred patch of scabs marring her chest. Tiny slivers of black stone stood out in the wound, portions of them peeking through the flesh.

The sorceress nodded. "Healing looks good. Are you still getting the chills?"

"Yes. Not as much as before, though."

"Well, that should pass soon." She closed the shirt and glanced at the ship's gangplank. "Are you ready?"

Nicalene took a deep breath. "I guess so."

Carta took her hand and patted it. "We'll wait here."

"If you should need us," Uthan said.

"Thank you," Nicalene said. "For everything. I'm sorry I didn't…that I can't…"

"There's nothing to forgive," Uthan said, taking her other hand.

"No cause to forget, friend Nicalene."

While the ghulans fawned over her, Tameris started up the gangplank while her bodyguards simply watched her ascend. Nicalene followed her until she stepped onto the *Tuckerspur*'s deck. The ship was deserted, the hull below creaking as the tide pulled at its joints.

"Where's the crew?" she asked.

"Ashore. They'll spend tonight passed out in some local winesink before the ship pushes off in the morning."

Nicalene had seen sailors or armed men keeping watch over other ships moored at the docks, most likely to deter thieves or gangs of drunken youths looking to stir up trouble.

"No guards," she said. "Aren't they worried someone will rob them in the night?"

Tameris shook her head. "They're here. You just don't see them."

Still looks empty to me.

"Up there," Tameris said, pointing to the stairs that led up to the aftcastle. Nicalene followed her, but found the upper deck as deserted as the rest of the ship.

"I don't understand. Where—?"

Tameris slapped her arm. "Quiet!"

The shadows at the back of the ship fluttered, then swirled erratically. Nicalene gawked as a figure slowly materialized there to step out from the darkness.

Oh, gods...it's true.

The Nosgarrian stood a head taller than either of them and he was slender, almost delicate. His clothing looked more like strips of fabric draped over his body than fitted garments, leaving his dark gray skin exposed to the wet air. An ornate sword, thin and curved like a scythe blade, dangled at his side. His bare feet left sooty prints when he walked, and his yellow eyes glowed faintly in the dim light.

Nicalene had seen eyes like that before, seen the sharp, angled face too narrow and perfect to pass for human.

The ashen woman.

The dark face kept taunting her every time she dreamed too deeply.

When the Nosgarrian moved, he expended no more effort than was absolutely necessary, which gave an impression of grace and rigidity all at once. He made no gesture to greet or acknowledge them, though he clearly looked at Tameris.

"Twiceborn, I presume?" His voice was like a basket of writhing snakes.

Tameris bowed her head. "My lord. It is a great honor to meet you at last."

If the greeting pleased him, he gave no indication of it.

"You've brought what I'm here for?"

"Of course." She reached into one of her many pockets to produce a large leather pouch that she offered to him. "Here it is."

When he reached for the pouch, she withdrew it.

"My payment?"

His yellow eyes narrowed, and he stared at Tameris. She did not flinch or look away.

You've got guts, woman.

Finally, the Nosgarrian waved his hand and nodded. "Yes, of course."

Something moved down on the lower deck. Nicalene glanced over in time to see two more Nosgarrians carry a small chest to the top of the gangplank before each one disappeared into a pocket of darkness.

Had they been there before? Nicalene could not say for sure, but they had certainly escaped her notice.

The Nosgarrian held his hand out. "I'll have what's mine now, yes?"

Tameris extended the stone to him. "As we agreed."

He let out a faint gasp when his slender fingers closed around the stone.

"Who is she?"

The question tumbled from her mouth before Nicalene could stop it. Both Tameris and the Nosgarrian stared at her, as if they only just realized she was there. The Nosgarrian's gaze hardened, his face sharpening to a fine edge to glare at her.

"You've seen her, haven't you?" he said.

Nicalene nodded.

"She's the one who bonded with the stone," Tameris said.

"Impossible," he said. "No human could possibly survive that."

Tameris grinned slightly. "She didn't."

He glared at the sorceress, then turned back to Nicalene.

"Show him," Tameris said.

Nicalene opened her shirt to expose the fist-sized scar between her breasts. The Nosgarrian reached out and brushed his fingertips against the rough flesh, flinching when he touched the slivers of black stone embedded there.

"Impressive," he said. "These splinters... From the spire as well, are they?"

"Yes," Tameris said. "Fragments recovered from the earth around it. Not nearly as potent as the shard you have there, but strong enough to reanimate flesh and spirit alike."

The Nosgarrian continued staring at Nicalene. "What about memories? Do you remember anything from when you were bonded?"

"I remember pieces, mostly," she said. "Images here and there. A woman's face, a stage of some kind."

"You remember her face?" he asked.

Nicalene nodded. "Who is she?"

He looked down at the stone. "Illurasine. My ancestor. The great shame of a proud lineage. She fought alongside the Empress in the Great War, but pride poisoned her heart and turned it toward treason. With this shard, she thought to destroy the Empress, but…"

An image flashed through Nicalene's mind as he trailed off, a trusted confidant driving a dagger into her gut.

"But she was betrayed, wasn't she? Murdered by her own lover."

The Nosgarrian's eyes widened. "Yes. In the end, he could not bring himself to betray his Empress, but he kept this shard to remember her, to remember what he almost did to win her undying love. We've always believed that some portion of her spirit found its way into the shard before she died, but no one dared to meddle with its power."

Nicalene's gaze fell to the stone. She could almost feel it sending ripples of heat through her body once again.

"It's true," she said. "She was so close. I could feel her heart pumping blood through my veins, feel her breath in my lungs…"

He touched her cheek, gently running his fingertips across her smooth, pale skin.

"When this relic was taken from my home by a common thief, I feared it would be lost for all time. I never dared hope that Illurasine would reach across the vastness of time to touch a kindred soul. Tell me, what is your name?"

"Nicalene. My name's Nicalene."

"Come with me, Nicalene. Leave this wretched city behind and return with me to Nosgarr. Help me to know the mind of the ancestor I thought forever lost to me, and I will help you forge a new set of memories unlike anything you ever dreamed possible."

Nicalene stepped back, her heart racing. The offer tempted her greatly, but her hazy, muddled memories of Blackspire grasped at her, holding her back.

What if there's some reason for me to be here, something I've forgotten?

She turned to Tameris, but the sorceress's expression was inscrutable as ever.

"My memories," she said, "do you think they'll return?"

"Some, perhaps. But there's no certainty. What I can tell you for certain is that there are some things in all our pasts better off forgotten. Not many people get a chance to start anew, unburdened by the failures and guilt of an old life."

Tameris pulled her collar down to reveal a patch of scar tissue above her left breast. Tiny, black slivers stood out just beneath the skin.

Twiceborn…

"I've remembered all I care to," she said. "All that I need. The rest I don't think about anymore. It belonged to someone else. Someone who died a long time ago."

Someone else…

The phrase resonated with her. When she tried to delve into her memories, she might as well have been looking at another person's past. A dark cloud hung over those distorted images. Occasionally, something good took shape there, something worth remembering.

She saw Grisel's face, felt his hand in hers.

Grisel, who came for her when she was lost.

Grisel, who dragged her out of a monster's trap.

Grisel, who gave his life to be with her one last time.

Now he was gone, but the memory of those final moments endured, bleeding into the city streets until the two became inseparable.

Whether or not she ever remembered the past, she would certainly never be able to escape it so long as she stayed in Blackspire.

"Our ship departs after dawn," the Nosgarrian said. "I can give you until then to make—"

Nicalene shook her head. "I don't need more time. I want to come with you. There's nothing left for me in this city."

He bowed his head. "As you wish."

She turned to Tameris again, who only nodded. "Our time together wasn't meant to last."

"I'm sorry," Nicalene said. "I didn't—"

"No, don't apologize. I understand."

Tameris bowed to the Nosgarrian. "My lord, I now take leave of you."

He nodded, holding the stone against his chest. "You've helped to restore my family's sacred honor, Twiceborn. So long as I reside in the land of Nosgarr, you shall always have a friend there."

The sorceress turned to climb down the steps, but she paused before striding by Nicalene.

"Goodbye, Nicalene. I hope you find what you're looking for, whatever it may be."

And then she left.

Nicalene walked to the aftcastle's railing to gaze at the city's black horizon. She knew the spire stood somewhere in that direction, vaulting thousands of feet above them and lending the city an almost mythic appearance.

Farewell, Blackspire.

I should have left you long ago.

BENJAMIN SPERDUTO is a copywriter and former history teacher who has also worked as a freelance editor and writer. As an only child growing up in rural Ohio, he developed an overactive imagination from an early age. When it was no longer socially acceptable to fight orcs and cave trolls with his homemade wooden sword, he turned that imagination toward writing fiction and creating fantasy worlds for roleplaying games.

His first two novels, *The Walls of Dalgorod* (2015) and *Mirona's Law* (2017), draw heavily upon his graduate studies in Russian history. When not writing or developing his latest roleplaying game idea, he also records electronic music under the name Morana's Breath. A graduate of the University of South Florida, Benjamin lives and works in Tampa, Florida, where due to his casual relationship with a razor and comb, he is sometimes mistaken for a person of interest.

Find Benjamin online at https://benjaminsperduto.com/

#BLACKSPIRE

CPSIA information can be obtained
at www.ICGtesting.com
Printed in the USA
LVHW041317081220
673632LV00001B/29